Praise fo[r]

Forge Books by Win Blevins

Beauty
for Ashes

Heaven Is a
Long Way
Off

WIN BLEVINS

A TOM DOHERTY ASSOCIATES BOOK | NEW YORK

This is a work of fiction. All of the characters, organizations, and events portrayed in these novels are either products of the author's imagination or are used fictitiously.

BEAUTY FOR ASHES AND HEAVEN IS A LONG WAY OFF

Beauty for Ashes copyright © 2004 by Win Blevins

Heaven Is a Long Way Off copyright © 2006 by Win Blevins

All rights reserved.

A Forge Book
Published by Tom Doherty Associates, LLC
175 Fifth Avenue
New York, NY 10010

www.tor-forge.com

Forge® is a registered trademark of Tom Doherty Associates, LLC.

ISBN 978-0-7653-8240-5

Our books may be purchased in bulk for promotional, educational, or business use. Please contact your local bookseller or the Macmillan Corporate and Premium Sales Department at (800) 221-7945, extension 5442, or by e-mail at MacmillanSpecialMarkets@macmillan.com.

First Edition: December 2015

Printed in the United States of America

0 9 8 7 6 5 4 3 2 1

CONTENTS

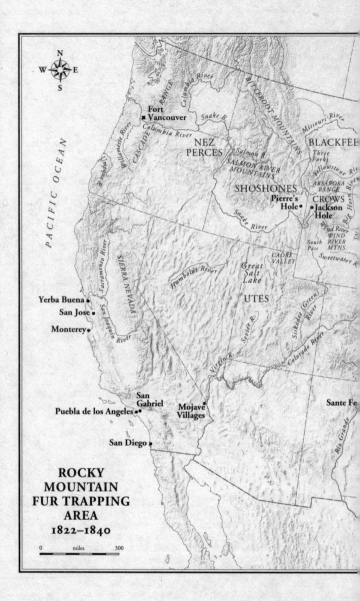

ROCKY
MOUNTAIN
FUR TRAPPING
AREA
1822–1840

0   miles   300

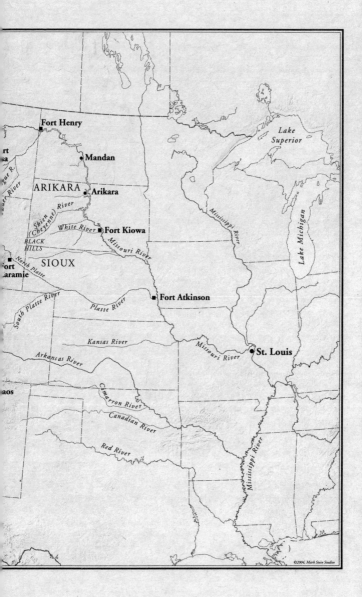

Fort Henry

Mandan

ARIKARA   Arikara

Shien
(Cheyenne) River

White River   Fort Kiowa

BLACK
HILLS

North Platte

SIOUX

Fort
Laramie

South Platte River

Platte River   Fort Atkinson

Kansas River

Arkansas River

aos

Cimarron River

Canadian River

Red River

Missouri River

Mississippi River

Lake
Superior

Lake Michigan

Missouri River

St. Louis

Mississippi River

©2004, Mark Stein Studios

Beauty
for Ashes

This book is for Meredith—
wife, partner, friend, all.

The spirit of the Lord . . . hath sent me to bind up the brokenhearted . . . to comfort all that mourn . . . to give unto them beauty for ashes, the oil of joy for mourning, the garment of praise for the spirit of heaviness.

—ISAIAH 61:1–3

PART ONE

Stalking
Love

Chapter One

Sam pictured himself as a hollow bone, stripped of the marrow that made him alive.

A hollow man notices little. He barely registered his fellow passengers, the captain, and crew. He barely knew the name of the steamboat, or the ports they stopped in, Cincinnati, Louisville, Evansville . . .

He did feel the force of the current, the urge of the river, westward, westward, down the Ohio River. As much as he could experience any emotion, he was glad.

At night he dreamt of emptiness. He slept outside on the bow of the steamer, wrapped in the moon's misty light and curled up with his pet coyote. Sometimes he dreamt that he was a feather, drifting on the wind alone. He had heard Crow men, his friends, make a piping music with the hollow bone from the wing of an eagle. But Sam's flight made no music. The air passed through him, sterile, and no song filled his emptiness.

For the past two years he had wandered as a beaver hunter through the Rocky Mountains and the huge plains that stretched from them to the Missouri River. Two weeks ago he had started home, drawn by a force he could not name. After traveling a thousand miles he found a world and a family he no longer knew. He felled his older brother with a fist. He said a hurried goodbye to his mother and his sisters, a last goodbye. In effect, he had tipped his life upside down and poured out his past, his family, his home.

Now he was empty.

It was Sam's nature to be curious, especially curious about

people. Yet these days he wanted to talk only to his coyote, Coy. Why? He didn't know. He didn't always know himself.

He paid attention mostly to the motion of the currents, downriver. He didn't see the passing woodlands of Ohio, Kentucky, Indiana, Illinois, though he knew they were beautiful. He used mostly his mind's eye. He saw stretches of plain so vast they must embrace the whole world. He saw mountains rolling sensuously against a lilac sky. He tasted the water in clear mountain creeks, so cold it hurt the gullet. He saw huge herds of buffalo running across the grasslands, so thick a man could dance across an entire herd and never touch the ground. He saw friends, both trappers and Indians. He saw his best friend, Blue Medicine Horse, and the woman he loved, Meadowlark.

When he looked at his fellow passengers, and only then, he thought of what was behind him. Home, yes, maybe that was the word for it, which was closed to him now. He said the word in his mind only—homeless.

He set his feet on the bow of the steamboat, which now rode the turbulent waters of the Ohio and would soon churn up the great Mississippi to St. Louis, the river town. There he would set off for the Rocky Mountains, alone. Home? He didn't know. He only wanted to be there, now.

Sometimes, wrapped in his blankets on the bow, he had another dream. In this dream he was not a hollow feather floating on the wind. He was a buffalo, a buffalo not of the earthly world, but of another dimension, maybe the spirit world. There something happened to him and the buffalo, something that could not happen in the ordinary world.

This realm seemed to him more real than the ordinary world, and more alive. In his dream he held his arms out toward the Spirit Buffalo, but it was always too far away, elusive, and mysterious. In the West, when he got there, he would feel the buffalo close again, and vital.

He was aware that his companions on the boat had no thought of buffalo, and certainly not Spirit Buffalo. They

cared nothing about the tow-headed youth who was obviously
the expedition's poorest, least-educated, least-decorous passenger. They showed distaste for the dog that hung near him.
(Sam had been obliged to lie to the captain that his coyote
was a common dog.) Sam overheard the captain dismissing
him curtly to Mrs. Goodwill as "a backwoodsman of the
roughest sort." He noticed how they avoided him.

They felt equally alien to him. He rolled into the rhythm
of the waters.

AFTER THE BOAT turned up the Mississippi, closer to buffalo country, Sam saw the Spirit Buffalo more often, saw it
with his inner eyes.

The Spirit Buffalo taunted him every night. Sometimes he
pictured it exactly as it first came to him. On these nights he
once again performed the miracle. He entered into the body
of the Spirit Buffalo, knitted himself into it, mingled his
blood with its blood, its heart with his own, and they breathed
with one breath. Then he and the Buffalo rose as one man-
beast, surveyed all, and set forth.

"Samalo." That one word sounded, though he didn't know
who spoke it. It was his own name and the name Buffalo
joined. One creature—Samalo.

Some nights he got just pieces of the dream, and some
nights the pieces were mad, like a painting on glass—but the
glass had been dropped, the paintings turned to shards, glinting hints of a beauty that once had been, and might or might
not be again.

Sam would put the painting back together—once he was
in the West, once he got up the Missouri River to the country where the buffalo lived, the buffalo that were physical and
fed the belly, and the Buffalo that fed the spirit.

And once he was in the West, he would make his way to
the Wind River Mountains, where her village lived, and seek
out Meadowlark.

Passengers embarked, passengers disembarked, and Sam spoke to few. Port after port passed. Sam learned the rhythm of his travel.

In St. Louis the clerk asked his name. Sam nearly said "Samalo," but managed to announce clearly, "Sam Morgan." The clerk informed him that General Ashley expected him to join the outfit at Fort Atkinson. Four hundred miles of country to ride alone, but that didn't bother Sam—it was to the west.

He went about his business, tied up loose ends. He visited with dear friends from his first trip to St. Louis, Abby and Grumble, and said goodbye to them with indecent haste. "When I get to the West," he kept saying to himself, "I will come alive."

Chapter Two

Fort Atkinson was a damned funny place to feel like home. It was home to the U.S. Army, an organization no mountain man wanted much to do with. On the other hand, right now it was full of Sam's mountain man friends. And this spot, not far upstream from where the Platte River flowed into the Missouri, was the beginning of the West. Here was the demarcation between the upper and lower Missouri Rivers, and between the prairies to the east and the arid plains of the West. It was also, effectively, the last bit of the U.S. The wilds beyond were marked *unknown* on the maps. Sam couldn't wait to get there.

He clucked his problematic mare up to the fort. She'd been problematic, and he was tired of her, tired of pushing hard, ready to rest, and ready for some company. This wasn't a bit like when he got to Fort Atkinson a couple of months ago. Then he'd walked, come all the way from the Rocky Mountains on foot and alone, half-starved to death. Then Fort Atkinson felt like survival. Now it felt like a beginning.

Out of a sense of propriety, he checked in first with the man who owned and ran the company, General William Ashley. But Ashley gave Coy a wary look. "I have to talk to this man about horses," he said. "I'll see you later."

A cold greeting, it seemed to Sam, when you've ridden more than four hundred miles alone through dangerous country to catch up with a man at his request.

Later, though, turned out to be a very good time. Supper. Sam was chewing and jawing around a fire with his old partner Gideon Poor Boy, a French-Canadian whose father was a French Jew and mother a Cree. Chesty as a bear and friendly as a St. Bernard, Gideon was relating his adventures. He'd gone back up the Platte to raise a cache of peltries and brought them to Fort Atkinson, all to earn a few dollars for their employer the general.

"Hey, Sam."

Sam was so glad to hear this voice he jumped up and clapped Tom Fitzpatrick on the shoulder. He shook hands with another old friend behind Fitzpatrick, James Clyman.

"See your brother didn't take your scalp," said Clyman.

Sam smiled wryly. Most of the fur men probably thought it was funny to take some weeks off to go home. Probably most of them didn't have homes, or weren't welcome there. *Now I don't have a home either.* That picture jumped into his mind—his older brother Owen, head of the Morgan clan, on the end of Sam's fist.

"How you doing, Towhead?"

"Don't call me Towhead." Fitz was always joshing Sam about his white hair. "Sit down and have some coffee."

They did, and traded news of the day. New men sidled by too, green hands, some even younger than Sam. They wanted to become mountain men—Sam wondered if he looked as green a year and a half ago.

One new man sat, Jim Beckwourth he called himself. He was black. "I'm a mulatto," Beckwourth explained. "You might say I'm a confusion of black and white." He grinned ironically. "What else could I be, mother a slave, father *Sir* Jennings Beckwourth?"

That grin was fine, but Sam knew a brag when he heard one.

"Who's your friend?" asked Jim, nodding his head at Coy.

"Coyote pup. Found him when I walked down the Platte last summer. That's a big story, I'll tell you some time."

"Sam is greatly attached to his canine companion," said Clyman.

"Oh, *mi coyote.*" This was Fitz. He pronounced it the Spanish way, *koy-oh-tay.*

Ashley stepped up, and the men fell quiet. The general stayed a few minutes but stood the whole time and spoke of nothing but business. "Can't get enough horses," he said. "We're leaving in a few days, with or without them."

The old hands—Sam was an old hand, though not quite twenty—eyed each other. They knew how bad it was, traveling and trapping without enough mounts. Ashley had been told, but he didn't *know.*

Later, in the full dark, when the group was down to Sam, Gideon, Beckwourth, Clyman, and Fitzpatrick, the Irishman said, "Sam, you went off quick in September. Did you hear the big story about Glass?"

Sam gave him a quizzical look. "I remember Hugh Glass from the fight at the Arickaree villages, but . . ."

"Didn't think so."

"You know you're a story yourself," said Gideon. "Walking down the Platte maybe seven hundred miles alone, coming in half-starved."

"Gideon and I are stories too," said Fitzpatrick. They'd done almost the same thing, arriving a little later. "But Glass is a story unto himself."

Several men reached for their white clay pipes, looking forward to the tale.

Stories were getting to be a big part of this Rocky Mountain fur trade, new as it was. John Colter, for example—men still told about how he ran from the Blackfeet naked, escaped from them, and made his way back to the fort. Of the men now in the mountains, Sam's captain of last year, Jedediah

Smith, was a story: Diah traveled alone down the Missouri River from Henry's Fort to below the Arickaree villages, where he delivered an urgent message to General Ashley, who was coming up the river—"Bring horses, lots of them. Trapping doesn't work without horses." Then, more daringly, Diah found a land route back to Henry with an express pleading for help. This was not to mention the time he got mauled by a grizzly, was sewn up by Clyman, yet stayed cool enough to give instructions about his care.

"You remember, Glass went with Major Henry after the Arickaree fight."

"And that was fine wit' us," put in Gideon. Everyone chuckled. Glass was an ornery fellow.

"Undisciplined as always, he was going through a thicket along a creek by himself, out in front, when he ran into a grizzly. The brigade came fast when they heard Glass screaming, and a dozen rifles did away with Old Ephraim. Well, anyone could see, Glass, he was a goner. The brigade waited to give him a decent burial.

"A few minutes, then a few hours—amazing, Glass was still holding on. Every man admired his grit."

"Wagh!" exclaimed Gideon.

"Henry, though, was worried. The Arickarees were still around somewhere. The major had an obligation to keep the whole brigade safe. So he asked for volunteers to stay with Glass until he died and then bury him. Henry offered a reward for taking this risk.

"Do you remember Jim Bridger?"

"No."

"New to the mountains, young, practically a boy, like you."

"I'm not any newer than you," Sam reminded Fitz. Though Fitz was five years older, they'd come to the mountains the same year.

"True enough. Bridger, anyway, he volunteered. So did an older man named John Fitzgerald. They stayed while Henry took the trail.

"That cursed Glass, though, he just kept breathing. Bridger

and Fitzgerald watched and fidgeted. One day, two, three. Why didn't Glass get down to business and die?

"Now Fitzgerald began to work on Bridger's mind, how the money wasn't enough, the risk bigger than the major figured, how they were going to die out here.

"On the fifth day Bridger caved in.

"Fitzgerald made Bridger take Glass's possibles—his rifle, his knife, his shot pouch, his flint and steel for making fire—everything needed to survive out here in this blasted wilderness. Otherwise, argued Fitzgerald, everyone would know. Know, that is, what Bridger was so ashamed to do, abandon Glass while he lived.

"Bridger hated it, but he was rattled. They took all, and away they went."

"Bastards," murmured Sam.

"But boyo, when Glass came to, he remembered. 'Henry paid Bridger and Fitzgerald to stay with me. They abandoned me. And robbed me.'

"This lit the fire in Glass's belly. Soon he was inching over to the little creek to drink, and nibbling on the chokecherries hanging nearby.

"When he felt strong enough to go after his betrayers, he headed back to Fort Kiowa, where they'd started out. But Hugh Glass couldn't walk." Fitz made a dramatic pause. "So he crawled."

"That child is some!" said Gideon.

Fitz plunged on. "He crawled down White River, his wounds bleeding every time he moved. He ate roots, berries, and the like. Once, it's told, he came on a buffalo felled by wolves, chased them off and fed on the raw meat."

"Wagh!" grunted Gideon.

"At Kiowa, instead of recuperating, he insisted on going after Fitzgerald and Bridger. He started upriver with a boat of a half-dozen men. The trip went bad. His companions got killed by Arickarees, but Hugh survived. Lads, he had grit, but he also had luck, mountain luck. And he must have been hell bent on revenge. On upriver he went, alone.

"On the last day of 1823, Hugh found the new fort on the Yellowstone. Right while the crew was celebrating drunkenly, a ghost appeared. A battered, scarred, emaciated figure. No one could believe it was Hugh Glass, believed dead for three months."

"Wagh!"

"The man most shocked by the appearance of this ghost was Jim Bridger.

"Glass went straight at his betrayer. But the fire in his belly, maybe after several months the coals had begun to cool.

"Anyhow, face to face with Bridger at last, Glass says, 'Yes, it is Glass that is before you, the man who gives you nightmares. The man you left to a cruel death on the prairie. And worse, you robbed me when I was helpless. You took my rifle, my knife, everything I might use to save myself. I swore I'd take revenge on you, and that other ass, Fitzgerald. I crawled back to the Missouri, and came this long way upriver, aiming to drink your blood.'"

Fitz's listeners held their breath.

"Glass glared at Bridger now, but his eyes lost their flame. 'I can't do it. You have nothing to fear from me. You're free. On account of your youth, I forgive you.'"

Whew! Sam felt damn glad he wasn't Jim Bridger. Bridger was trapping with Captain Weber now, somewhere in the Siskadee country. And every man he traveled with, or ever would, knew he was a fellow who'd walk out on you when things got rough.

"Still, there was that damned Fitzgerald, plenty old enough to know better. Fitzgerald had quit and had gone down to Fort Atkinson, and took Glass's rifle with him. Quick as it began to thaw, Glass headed out. When he got to the fort, he found Fitzgerald had become a soldier, and the commander told him shooting up U.S. soldiers wasn't permitted. Glass got his rifle back, turned Fitzgerald over to God and his own conscience, and headed for Santa Fe.

"Now, lads, what do you think of that?"

"Grit," said Gideon.

"Will to survive," said Sam.

"Mountain luck," said Clyman.

They regarded each other. The Irishman who left County Cavan to get away from the priests. The Virginian, the group's elder. The French-Canadian, who knew death companionably. The mulatto, young and vigorously alive.

The white-haired young man from Pennsylvania, far from home, was constantly learning, and it wasn't comfortable.

Chapter Three

Sam felt edgy. A cold, restless wind flicked at his face. The mare fidgeted, pawed around like she wanted to get down off this sandstone outcropping, out of the wind. Coy mewled. Sam couldn't tell what the coyote pup wanted.

Sam looked around, west, north to the hills, east. Nothing. He'd come up from the south and seen nothing. His cheeks were getting leathery from the cold. The wind brought dust to his nose, plus alkali, sage, and the musky smell of buffalo.

The alkali and sage reminded him, and he thought how glad he was to be back in the real West, where the plains began to break and jumble and lift toward the mountains, and where the buffalo lived. He decided to look a little harder for buffalo, and maybe ride a little further, on that faint hope.

The brigade was hungry. They'd left Fort Atkinson on the Missouri River on the first day of November, headed for the Rocky Mountains on faith—had to be faith, because they didn't have enough food or horses. General Ashley hoped to trade with the Pawnee Loups. Word at the fort was, these Pawnees were in an uproar. The general issued his orders anyway.

Sam did his duty—went to Ashley and told about his run-in with the Loup Pawnees three months ago, how they caught him and intended to torture him, but a good fellow named Third Wing sneaked him out of camp. Sam had to add that, in stealing his rifle back, he killed a Pawnee guard. He didn't say that the guard was the first man he ever killed. He told how the Pawnees searched the whole country for him, but he got away. How they probably still hated him.

Ashley brushed the information aside. He was a man of firm purpose. He led the way west into the plains winter, counting on the Pawnee Loups.

Now, nine days out, they were on starving times. On the second day a blizzard staggered them. On the fifth day another one blitzed them, a foot of Rocky Mountain snow.

The Pawnees were not where Ashley expected, at the Loup River. A day went by while two of the leaders, Fitzpatrick and Clyman, searched for sign of them up the tributary. They saw nothing, no Indians and no buffalo.

So some flour stirred into water was the daily ration of each of the twenty-five men. Half rations of food, or quarter, and double rations of cold and snow. In bitter weather a man needed more meat, and they had none. Which was why Sam was out here a couple of miles north of the river toward some hills, hunting.

From the breakfast fire this morning, he thought he'd seen a lone beast. The brigade had no breakfast, just the warmth of some flames and coffee. No one else could see the buffalo. Odd, how men get down at the mouth and mutter in their beards when they're cold and hungry, and say or do as little as possible.

"Hunt it if you want to," Fitzpatrick said, "and catch up tonight."

An hour later Sam couldn't tell whether he'd seen a buffalo or mistaken these two scrubby trees for one. They stood behind each other on the rim of the sandstone in the right shape, if you stood at a certain angle. Maybe his hope shaped his eyesight. At night he was dreaming about food, sumptuous banquets of beef, chicken, ham, turkey, potatoes, garden vegetables, cheeses, bread, and butter, all spread out on a table before him. Not even buffalo and elk, which he preferred.

From above Sam studied the earth of the plain. There were lots of buffalo pies and would be lots of hoofprints—this was buffalo country. But he feared he wouldn't find any that looked fresh. He spoke to Coy. "Want to go a little further? Or turn around and catch up? A little further, and maybe . . ."

A shot roared. The mare crow-hopped sideways, and Sam nearly lost his seat. Coy arched his back and bristled. *Godamighty.* Shots—Indians!

Time to cache.

The mare crow-hopped again, and this time came to a stop teetering on the rim. "Idjit," he spat at her. She gave a whicker of protest.

Damned animal. Sam wheeled her and let the critter pussyfoot down the outcropping, muttering curses at her slowness. This mare was no favorite of Sam's. He wanted a horse that felt like a partner, the way Coy did. Gideon told him, though, "Don't ever get attached to any horse, because that's ze one ze Indians will run off."

Sam kicked her to a gallop and scurried down into a brushy draw. Whew. Now he was cached. Unless they saw him, he could sit this one out right here.

An hour later Sam rode out of the draw on the south and started a wide circle to the west. *Damn, I can never believe trouble is really trouble.* "Coy, it has to be a buffalo—what else would anyone shoot at out here?"

He put some words into the coyote pup's mouth. "What if it's a brigade member who's followed to help us hunt?"

Sam answered, "What if it's a lone Indian I could take? Buffalo meat's worth a risk, isn't it?"

He wanted to get a look into the next valley to the west, where the shot sounded like it came from. He made his way up another draw. At the last of the scrawny cedars, a hundred yards short of the lip of the hill, he tied his mount and walked on with Coy. The little coyote walked quieter than Sam anyway. He crawled to the summit and looked out from behind a rock.

A fine sight! A cow lay crumpled in the middle of the little valley—

Sam's hair crinkled and his toenails curled backward.

No one was gutting her out. Which meant . . .

He jumped up and sprinted for his mare.

Just before he got to the cedars—

"Hi-ya-ya, hi-ya-ya!" Out of the draw came the cry and the Indian.

Sam cursed out loud. The bastard was on Sam's mare.

I'm gonna be stuck on foot a long way out.

Stuck, hell, once I'm on foot, these Indians will kill me.

He dropped to sitting, propped his father's rifle on one knee, and steadied. The riding figure bobbed up and down in front of Sam's sight. *I'll shoot the damn mare,* he thought with satisfaction. He held on the mare's big hindquarters and fired.

The Indian pitched to the ground roaring. The mare skittered off. *Why doesn't she act hurt?*

Sam drew his pistol and ran forward.

The man scurried on hands and knees for his bow.

Sam caught up and held his pistol two-handed, straight at the bastard's face. The fellow was young, younger even than Sam's nineteen.

From hands and knees the Indian threw a sneer of hatred at him and lunged forward with a knife.

Coy skittered away, barking.

Sam shot the Indian in the thigh.

First he reloaded the rifle, which he called The Celt, as fast as he could. This Indian had no rifle. Which meant he had a partner close by, the shooter. Sam looked around carefully.

Coy snapped and snapped, keeping the Indian busy. The Indian swiped at Coy with the knife. Sam jumped forward and clubbed the man with the butt of his pistol. He sagged to the ground.

Sam breathed relief, and dragged him into the cedars. *Where's your damn partner?*

As the Indian regained consciousness, Sam checked him over. Pawnee, from the moccasins. Then he saw the blood on back of one leg. *Hell, I shot you in the butt.* He grinned.

Sound of hoofs. Along the ridge of the hill, in the distance, a rider.

Sam's mare was standing in the open twenty yards away, grazing.

Coy ran at the mare and herded her back to the cedars. Sam reloaded the pistol.

The wounded man looked daggers at Sam again.

Sam signed to him, 'I come in friendship. I do not want to hurt you or your friend. I do not want your buffalo.' Not that Sam had a chance at the meat with Pawnees around. 'Signal your friend to get off his horse and I won't shoot you or him.'

The rider had stopped on top of the hill. Certainly he had seen the saddled mare. The rider had the high ground, but Sam had the cover.

'Signal him to come closer,' Sam signed.

The Indian spat at Sam.

Sam leapt on him and pricked the bastard's throat with the tip of his butcher knife. "Now," he shouted in English, though the Pawnee couldn't understand him.

Sam backed away, knife held forward, and signed awkwardly, 'Tell him what I said now!'

The Indian spat at him. Coy bit the Indian on the forearm, and the man howled. He tried to get to his knees.

From six feet Sam lifted his pistol and shot the man's ear off.

The Indian screamed.

The rider galloped down the hill.

Sam jumped behind his hostage, lifted him, and catapulted him into a low cedar branch. The man crumpled across the branch.

The rider charged.

Sam lifted The Celt and shot the pony out from under him.

The rider hurtled across the bunch grass, tumbling over and over.

Sam reloaded The Celt.

The rider didn't move.

Sam reloaded the pistol.

The rider got to his feet woozily.

Sam walked into the clear. Coy growled and kept the wounded Indian in the tree.

The rider sank to one knee.

Sam yelled, *"Hau!"* Most Indians would understand the greeting.

The rider looked at him dizzily.

Sam signed, 'I do not want to kill you or your friend. Come closer.'

The rider sank into the grass.

Sam wondered how many Pawnees were around. If the young men had come out hunting, there could be two or a dozen.

He didn't intend to wait around to find out. He stepped into the cedars and took the mare's reins. "At least you don't run off," he said to her. He was half tempted to take an Indian pony instead.

Leading the mare, he walked toward the rider. Behind, he could hear Coy growling at the draped man. Sam picked up the dizzy one's rifle, an old fusil. "Spoils of war," he said with a grin.

He swung up on the mare and clucked at Coy. "Let's go. It's a hell of a ride to camp."

Chapter Four

B reakfast," said Gideon in Frenchy style, "ze best idea ze general has yet."

Sam and Beckwourth grinned around hump ribs. Sam was enjoying two of his favorite smells, broiled buffalo and burning sagebrush. It was enough to make him forget the campfire smoke that sometimes blew into his eyes.

"I thought white folks never went hungry," said Beckwourth.

"Even I look like a cub," said Gideon, who definitely was bear-sized.

Sam looked at Beckwourth with a half smile. Compared with Gideon and Sam, who'd marched down this same river last summer, eating only occasionally, the mulatto didn't know anything about hunger. And Gideon had a lot more dramatic hunger stories to tell, like the time he ate grasshoppers for a week.

Sam threw his half-gnawed rib to Coy. The coyote had learned to wait patiently during meals, knowing Sam would feed him.

"If your pup stay wit' us, Towhead," said Gideon mildly, "he maybe starve to death."

Sam frowned at the word "towhead."

"Hell," put in Beckwourth, "when we was starvin', he was feeding on deer mice and other little critters. He'll live long enough to chew our bones."

They might have chuckled if they weren't busy feeding.

After a minute Sam said, "I told you to stop that Towhead bull."

"Oh, I forget," said Gideon with a big smile.

The brigade was done missing breakfasts, at least for a while. Maybe they were done with dying horses, too, and eating horseflesh.

Three weeks out from Fort Atkinson the weather turned mild. One day they stumbled into a place on the river that was full of buffalo to hunt. Rushes lined the river, good feed for the gaunt horses. Paradise, Sam learned, depended on how painful your hell had been. The men spent several days gorging themselves.

Further up river they came upon the Grand Pawnees, who were headed south to warmer climates. At least these Pawnees weren't Sam's personal enemies. He wondered whether the two young men he'd wounded back yonder were Grand or Loup Pawnees. The Grands didn't say anything about the incident.

'Stop here,' the Indians signed, 'or you will all die. On toward the mountains there's not enough wood for fires ahead, and not enough feed for the horses.'

Ashley ignored them and followed the westward compass in his mind.

Finally, yesterday they came on the Pawnee Loups. That's why Sam was nervous at breakfast this morning.

Right then Ashley strode up, with Fitzpatrick and Clyman in file behind him. "Let's go, Sam. We need to palaver with the Loups."

Sam looked wildly at Ashley. "These are the ones . . ."

"Who are out for your hair, I know. Let's go."

Since Sam had learned a good deal of Crow tongue last winter, and was quick and accurate with sign talk, the general had decided he had an aptitude for languages and appointed him interpreter.

The argument was short, its conclusion predetermined.

Beckwourth and Gideon asked to go along, and Ashley agreed. As they rode out, he called to Zacharias Ham, "No Indians in camp, for any reason."

They rode. Frosty horse breath swirled around Sam's head. He began to think of what these Pawnees had once planned for him. The slowest possible torture until he died.

"Sam, stop maundering."

Sam threw Ashley a look. *You and your big words. You and your fancy ideas. You and your fixed notions.*

"You don't hesitate with Indians, you don't mollycoddle, you put everything right in front and show you're not afraid."

But what if I am?

Six horses jingle-jangled. Sam was taking the fusil, just in case.

"Get your head clear for your job," said Ashley. "Responsibility for the outcome is mine."

Sam bit his tongue and turned his head away. *Yeah, if I lose my scalp, you'll admit it was your fault.*

* * *

THERE WAS RAVEN, who still gave Sam nightmares. The chief had come to the edge of the village to greet the beaver men with the traditional sign for welcome. He was surrounded by Big Bellies. Third Wing wasn't there.

Raven was a short, chunky man with very dark skin, huge shoulders, and a beak nose. His head even seemed to have wings, for the hair pulled back above his ears flashed silver, like a raven's wings struck by light. His eyes glittered with a blackness that brought up the word "evil."

Sam gave Raven the sign of friendship.

The trappers dismounted and left Beckwourth with the mounts.

Ashley treats Jim like a servant, thought Sam.

"Holler if there's trouble," Ashley told Beckwourth.

And Jim pretends not to notice.

"I'll stay wit' him," said Gideon.

The big mulatto nodded. The whites had quickly learned that the Indians interpreted his black skin as a sign of being warlike all the time. Which was handy.

"Not that there'll be anything you can do except holler," muttered Sam.

Ashley scalded him with a look, and Sam shut his mouth.

The other four beaver men walked toward the council lodge with Raven, Sam and Ashley in front, Fitzpatrick and Clyman behind. No one needed to tell these old hands to keep their wits about them. The council lodge, at least, would be safe.

The ceremonial pipe seemed to last forever, but there was no rushing it. The smoke wafting toward the top hole in the tipi, Sam understood, declared everyone's friendly intentions. Sam would have felt more friendly had he not noticed a nasty glint of recognition in Raven's eyes.

When it was over, Sam made his way impatiently through the necessaries, translating into English as he signed. He greeted the respected Raven once more. The beaver men were passing through the country on the way to the mountains, and would like to make a gesture of thanks to the Pawnee people.

Clyman stuck out the beautiful blanket in chief's blue he carried and opened it to reveal half a dozen big twists of tobacco.

Raven nodded his approval. Several of the Big Bellies smiled.

Sam put the fusil next to the blanket. He signed, 'I took this rifle from a young Pawnee who attacked me. I hope he and his friend got back to the village safely. I want him to have his rifle.'

Raven looked at the Big Bellies. One of them nodded yes, said one word, and took the fusil.

'Badger's rifle,' signed Raven. Then he added with an enigmatic smile, 'You again.'

Ashley gave Sam a nod of approval. Sam knew his policy, Be straight up front with Indians.

'The beaver hunters would also like to trade with their friends the Pawnees,' Sam signed. 'We want horses and dried meat, and offer blankets, hatchets, knives, and cooking utensils in return.'

'Whiskey?' asked Raven with his fingers.

'And whiskey as a gift of friendship,' confirmed Sam. Last night they'd cached all the kegs of whiskey but two, which they would share with the Pawnees. It would lubricate the trading.

Raven talked with the Big Bellies in Pawnee. After a while he said, 'Tomorrow we move camp to the forks of the river, where we stay for the winter. Come there and we will trade with you.'

Ashley looked at Fitzpatrick. "Forks of the Platte are a couple of days upstream. Fine camping place, plenty of feed."

"Tell him," Ashley said to Sam, "we will be glad to join him at the forks." Sam did.

Raven nodded his acceptance, and Sam could see he was ready to rise and close the meeting.

Impetuously, Sam signed, 'Where is Third Wing?'

It was a risk. Changes that Sam didn't like registered in Raven's eyes. He glared at Sam.

'A foolish young white man with white hair,' Raven signed, staring blackly at Sam, 'was captured by my young men at the time when berries get ripe. Third Wing, even more foolishly, helped him escape. Since then he has not been well.'

'I want to see him.'

Lightning flashed in Raven's eyes.

Ashley butted in. "Tell him you regret what happened last summer. You regret killing that sentry. It was all a misunderstanding. You had to get your rifle back or die."

Sam signed that much. Raven paid close attention, but did not look mollified.

Ashley said, "Remind him you let his young warriors live when most men would have killed them."

Sam signed it. Letting those Indians live, in fact, had been controversial among his own friends.

Now Fitzpatrick jumped in with words to Ashley. "Have Sam tell Raven that Sam is important to you. You will give tobacco to the family of the sentry killed, and blankets, and a horse to express your sorrow at their loss."

Ashley nodded to Sam, and Sam signed it.

Raven said with his fingers, 'I cannot speak for the family. You must talk to them.'

Sam knew that meant it would be all right. He ventured again, 'May I see Third Wing?'

Raven stared at Sam, then signed, 'When you have spoken to the family of the fine young man Two Stones, Third Wing maybe will come to your camp.'

Sam and Fitz glanced at each other. "The line we're walking with these Pawnees is narrow," said Fitz, "and would be easy to fall off."

TWO STONES' FATHER and mother, waiting in front of their lodge, wore their mourning on the outside. The father had chopped off his hair crudely, and the mother bore scars on her forearms where she had hacked herself in her grief. They said nothing but seemed pleased by the gifts. Sam guessed that the kind and amount of the gifts meant nothing to them, but the fact of Ashley making this gesture did. They seemed willing enough for Sam to stay on the planet.

But the teenage brother half-hid inside the tipi, his face bristling with hatred. Sam knew he better check his back trail against that one.

The parents never did speak, which gave Sam the willies. Ashley handed over the gifts and ended things.

On the way out of the village Ashley said unnecessarily, "Don't get to feeling complacent, not for an instant."

No chance, thought Sam.

BACK AT CAMP the men were gathered around fires for a noon meal. Food and company were Sam's great yearnings. On his long walk from the Sweetwater River to Fort Atkinson, nearly three months alone, he'd missed people as much as food.

Ashley's twenty-five beaver hunters grouped themselves loosely into units of six or seven around the four leaders, the general, Fitzpatrick, Clyman, and Ham. And they ate heartily when the eating was good—next week might be starving times. Sam had lost thirty pounds on his long walk alone, regained it, and lost fifteen more on the way up the river this month. Feast or famine, for sure. Men wandered from fire to fire as the spirit moved them. Some didn't like Coy, claiming a coyote would sooner or later turn vicious, and they stayed away from the fire where Sam and Coy usually sat, Fitzpatrick's.

Through this meal Sam barely noticed the buffalo meat. He was thinking about Two Stones and his parents. Odd how knowing a name made the killing feel different. Back then Two Stones was just an obstacle between Sam and his rifle, The Celt, his only hope for survival on the plains. The creeping approach and swift knife to the throat had been a primitive exultation.

Now Sam's head jumped with pictures of blood spurting

between his own hands, vital life bursting out, ended forever. Sometimes his mind's eye rotated the faces of Two Stones' father and mother, bleak and forlorn. The holes in their hearts had been ripped by Sam's hands.

"Black life we live, no?" Gideon usually saw Sam's moods, in the way of friends.

"Yeah. Black."

They were still eating, Beckwourth too, after the other men had finished. "You people use 'black' like it means evil, forces of darkness," said Jim. "I don't care for that."

Sam cocked an eyebrow at his friend. Beckwourth concentrated on the buffalo meat on the tip of his knife. All three were quiet for a moment, preoccupied.

"What you think it means," Beckwourth asked, "when Raven says he's friendly and wants to trade?"

"Nothing," said a voice behind them. It was Tom Fitzpatrick. He squatted and sliced a hunk off the spitted buffalo roast above the fire.

"Nothing?" This was Beckwourth.

"The Arickarees traded with us and then attacked us," Fitz said. Sam and Gideon had been there.

Beckwourth looked at Sam.

"Nothing," Sam agreed.

"Treacherous bastard." Beckwourth pushed the words out over the meat in his mouth.

"I don't think so," said Sam.

Everyone looked at Sam. Raven had tried to torture and kill him.

"I agree," said Gideon.

Sam threw Coy a rib with some meat on it. "Looks to me like every tribe has pretty much the same name for themselves—the people, the true people, something like that. And pretty much the same name for everybody else—others, outsiders, enemies. That's how the tribes see the whole world. To Raven there are Pawnees, who are like him, and there's everybody else. His job is to protect the good people, his, against everything and everybody who's not Pawnee."

"So he don't hate us while he kills us?" Beckwourth gave an ironic grin.

"No," said Sam. "He doesn't hate us, period. Maybe he hates the Sioux and the Cheyennes—hostility there goes back generations. But he doesn't hate anybody else. We're just the others. To him we don't count."

"All Indians be like zis," put in Gideon.

Sam looked at his friends. Funny conversation this was, between a Pennsylvania backwoodsman like himself, an Irishman, a colored man, and a French-Canadian whose father was a Jew and mother an Indian.

Fitz pitched in. "Everybody's like this. Your father's people do it too. They're Jews and everyone else is a gentile."

Gideon shrugged. "My mother's people, the Crees, ze same."

"You white people are that way to us colored," said Beckwourth.

Sam looked into his friend's face. Sometimes he couldn't tell Jim's moods.

Sam said, "It's crazy. Look here. I like Hannibal." They'd all heard about the combination Delaware Indian and classical scholar more than once. "I like the Shawnees I've known, and despise General Harrison, who destroyed them for no reason. I love Meadowlark, a Crow, and like her brother. I didn't hate Two Stones, the Pawnee I killed, nor the ones I let go. But I'm damn mad at the Arickarees—they killed my friends." He looked Beckwourth candidly in the face. "I would fight for you against any white man, or red man, or black man." He turned his eyes to Gideon. "You too."

Said Fitz, "Next you'll be wanting us to love prairie wolves." He grinned and threw Coy his bone, too.

"Mine's different."

"He probably thinks you're not bad either, *mi coyote*," teased Fitz. "For a two-legged."

"Sometimes we have to kill," said Sam, "sometimes we choose to kill." His head still hurt with the memory of Two Stones.

"Hmpf," grunted Beckwourth loudly. "My pappy taught me something about that. Everything that lives, it kills and is killed."

"I rode to St. Louis on the steamboat with a scientific Frenchman," said Fitz. "He studies plants that grow in water. He had a microscope, showed me some Mississippi River water in it. Water's full of living creatures, little fellas, way too small to see with the naked eye. Every time you take a drink you kill a hundred or a thousand of them."

"Every time I take a drink," Sam pondered that.

"Every time, *mi coyote*," repeated Fitz.

Sam broke the silence. "When I kill, I don't like me much."

"Do it anyhow," said Beckwourth.

"If you want to partner me," said Gideon.

"But don't get to liking it," added Fitz.

THIRD WING DIDN'T show up that afternoon, or the evening either. Sam looked for him the next day as the Crows formed a long line of horse-drawn travois and rode upriver. The young men policed the line and kept lookout, but Third Wing wasn't among them. The mountain men, riding behind, said they'd seen no sign of any straggler. It was the same story the next day, and the third day, when they reached the forks and made camp. Sam walked over and over from the beaver men's camp above the north fork and the tipis of Raven's people. No Third Wing.

For a week they rested and fed their horses and themselves. Every day they traded with the Indians. Each Pawnee who came to camp kept his eyes open, but none acted hostile. The trading went well. Ashley got fifteen horses and a lot of pemmican. Some of the men even got squaws for the night. But no sign of Third Wing, and Sam did not dare to ask Raven.

Still Raven managed, talking to Ashley, to roll a stone into the garden of Sam's hopes. The chief and two Big Bellies said the route up the south fork toward the mountains had plenty of feed for the horses and plenty of wood for fires. But the north fork, they claimed, did not.

Ashley sent Sam for Clyman and Fitzpatrick. None of them had been up the south fork. On his long walk Sam came down the north fork, never saw the south fork until he got right here.

The whites squatted and scratched rivers and mountains in the dirt until it looked like what they'd seen. The Pawnees added the south fork and showed how it ran straight at some other mountains to the south. The north fork looped around the end of the same range.

Coy whined to come forward and show the two-leggeds how to dig in the earth, but Sam staked him several steps away.

They looked hopefully at Raven and the Big Bellies. 'On the north fork,' signed the Indians, 'little for the horses to eat, little wood for the men to burn.'

'Seemed like enough to me,' signed Sam.

'No. Too many men, too many horses for winter on the north fork. Must use south fork.'

Then the Big Bellies showed them where to cross the mountains when the snow melted, a line from the south fork to the northwest.

"It's the long way around to the Siskadee," Sam told Ashley.

The general looked at Clyman and Fitz.

"True enough," said Clyman.

"But it's only way now," said Fitz.

Sam made a face.

"What's wrong?" asked Ashley.

Sam just shook his head.

"Sam's counting on seeing Meadowlark this winter," said Fitz in a kindly tone. To Ashley's questioning face he added, "Look at his *gage d'amour*." Which meant the beautiful beaded pouch that hung inside his shirt. "Our coyote keeper has a Crow woman."

Ashley gave the briefest glance at the pouch, normally a gift an Indian woman used to signal her affection. He said, "I'm sure these Indians are telling us the truth. It's the south fork for us." He turned back to Raven and the Big Bellies. "Thank you."

Sam hung his head while he made the signs.

Then he flashed his eyes into Raven's face. He signed, 'Where's Third Wing?'

'He has not been well,' Raven signed back. His smile was superior, his eyes amused. 'Maybe he does not want to see you.'

SAM KICKED A snow-covered stone into the stream, the main river below the forks. Since it hurt, he kicked another one. "Very satisfying," he told Coy, "but I'm damned if I know why."

He looked through the graying evening at the western sky. It was the color of the mustard Katherine's mother made back home, and the lavender his mother grew to keep under your pillow for a calm mind and good sleep. Which seemed far away to Sam. His spirits felt the way the sky looked, battered and bruised.

He was well rid of Katherine—his brother Owen was welcome to her. And he didn't think he'd see his mother again. Pennsylvania was a long ways off, and he wanted to be in the mountains. Among the peaks and valleys that still lay to the west of these flat plains. He wished he could see the mountains from here.

Coy splashed into the river and lapped up the cold water. The sunset colors rippled with the colors of Sam's pain. He gazed at the western horizon. The lavender was a thin line of clouds hiding the last of the sun, not her mountains.

He seldom said the name Meadowlark, even in his thoughts. The picture of her, the touch of her, these came to his mind familiar as campfire smells, but he didn't let himself think her name.

"No Crow camp this winter," he said to the pup bitterly.

"Let her down again. 'The white man can't be trusted,' her parents will tell her. She'll make a tipi for another man."

That one hurt him sharply, right in the groin.

He stared at the horizon blankly. The sun was down, the light fading, like his chance with . . . her.

"Hnnn."

He spun around. A voice. Whose? Where?

His hair prickled. If it wasn't a friendly voice, he would already be dead. Still . . .

"Hnnn."

Then he saw. A man figure moved out of the grove of cottonwoods into the open. A scrawny, haggard Pawnee.

He gaped. He could hardly believe this was Third Wing.

Chapter Five

S am built the fire for the two of them on the riverbank, well away from camp. His companions might get grumpy about having both a coyote and Pawnee as dinner companions. He made the fire roar. Normally, he'd have built a smaller one, but he kept looking at Third Wing and wondering what had happened to . . . his friend?

Was "friend" the word for a man you'd only been around a few hours? But if he saved your life, what else could you call him?

Coy thought he was a friend too. Though the pup stayed clear of most people, he went to Third Wing right away and lay down against his foot like it was a corner of blanket, or a warm rock.

Third Wing flaunted Sam's hair at the world, two big hanks of white draping down his gleaming sheet of black onto his shoulders. That had been the price of Sam's life. Sam had never understood what Third Wing wanted with the hair. But there was a lot he didn't understand about Third Wing, or any Pawnee, or any Indian. Maybe any person.

Coy licked Third Wing's hand and accepted a few pats.

Mountain life was strange, and Third Wing was Sam's strangest experience. Last summer he'd been walking down the Platte alone, the river the Indians called Shell River. A hard time—Sam had gotten separated from his brigade, and very lost. Then Arapahos took his horse. He had only eleven rifle balls left, so couldn't get much food. And he guessed— only *guessed*—that the settlements were a seven-hundred-mile walk down river.

After maybe six weeks of walking, he was training Coy one afternoon, teaching him to jump up and take a stick from the hand. Some young men of the Loup Pawnees sneaked up on him, captured him, and took him back to camp.

The people were very curious about Coy and his tricks, so they wanted to keep the pup. The council of Big Bellies decided, though, that Sam would be given a choice for tomorrow—die quickly, or show brave as you die. Showing brave meant demonstrating how much pain you could stand without complaint. Never moan, never ask for water, never beg for death. The women did the torturing, because they gave a man a chance to be very, very brave.

Third Wing rescued him. Third Wing spoke English, so he promised to watch the captive overnight. At his tipi Third Wing fed Sam and offered him a deal—give me your beautiful white hair and I'll help you escape. Sam wondered if the Indian was out of his mind. But that didn't matter. Sam let the Pawnee cut his hair off right down to the nubs. He also held out for taking Coy with him. In the darkest hours, a shorn Sam followed Third Wing out of camp and to the river.

But he couldn't keep going. Without his rifle he would starve. One of his young captors had stolen it. So the next night Sam crept back into camp, killed a sentry—dammit, Two Stones, not just a sentry—and stole his rifle back.

Then he had to spend several days running and hiding from the angry Pawnees.

At that time Third Wing was a stocky man in his

mid-twenties. Four months later he looked like a half-starved, half-frozen relic.

They sliced meat off a spitted roast and ate in silence. Third Wing attacked food the way Coy did, like this was the last bite he'd ever get. Sam waited for him to say something. Maybe the fellow had gone the rest of the way crazy.

After a while, observing Sam feeding Coy fatty or gristly pieces, Third Wing did the same. He tossed the scraps with an odd smile, like he savored the irony of a half-starved man feeding a well-fatted coyote.

He ate for a long time after Sam quit, which was a good sign, but still said nothing.

When Third Wing let Coy lick the grease off his fingers and wiped his hands thoroughly on his hide leggings, Sam said, "I'm glad to see you. I thank you again for saving my life."

Third Wing flashed that same crazy grin at him. "Dumbest goddam thing I ever did."

Sam swallowed hard. To cover his feelings, he reached for the small white clay pipe in his *gage d'amour,* filled it with tobacco, and used sticks to get an ember and drop it onto the tobacco. When Sam had the pipe going, he handed it to Third Wing. The Pawnee took it shakily, overeager.

"What do you mean?"

"I mean my wife put my goddam moccasins outside the tipi."

Sam supposed Third Wing used the English he heard, without a sense that some of it was profane. He raised an eyebrow quizzically at Third Wing.

The Pawnee gave him a friendly smile. "When your woman puts your moccasins outside, that means you're through. Take your weapons and go. Your kids aren't even yours anymore." There was an edge of bitterness in Third Wing's voice.

He drew deep on the pipe and let the smoke wander upward from his lips. "She went to live with her sister's husband." His eyes lit up wildly. "He likes having two women to jump on top of."

"Where have you been living?"

Third Wing pretended to shrug lightly. "In a brush hut with the other young, single men." The word *single* bristled with sarcasm.

"What have you been eating?"

Third Wing took a while to answer. "I've been feeling kind of off, haven't hunted much."

Sam could see that. Coy whined like he also knew what it was like to be hungry.

"Why haven't you come around until now?"

"I was off on a vision quest."

"Starving yourself?"

"Yes."

Godawmighty, starving a starved man. Sam wanted to ask what Third Wing saw, but he didn't dare.

"Your wife, she leave you because of me?"

"The whole tribe thinks I'm strange about whites. I like white people, and I've been waiting for you." He looked into the night sky. Sam wondered what he saw there, among the pulsing stars, where some people saw stories. Third Wing was giving him the willies.

"Maybe some day I'll tell you why. Why I like you."

The guy was sweet. It was hard to be suspicious about him. "Tell me how you got such good English, too."

"Yip-YIP!" cried Coy, as though seconding the motion.

Third Wing grunted, took his belt knife, and sliced at the roast again. "Maybe I better eat while I can."

When he had devoured another half pound of meat, Third Wing went on, "I speak English good because traders raised me."

So Sam poked at that conversationally. "What traders? How long were you among them?"

Third Wing just waited until he'd finished eating and then said, "The traders out of Fort Osage found me alone on the river trail, near where Atkinson is now, it wasn't then. I was maybe five years old. I didn't remember anything about my family or my tribe, but the words I spoke were Pawnee. One of the traders, Gannett, he raised me, maybe, ten years. Not that he was much of a father. I more or less hung around Fort Osage like a stray dog. Seems Gannett didn't think a whole lot of me, either. When I was about fifteen, I had some trouble getting a bridle on a horse, and Gannett said, 'That boy's as much use as a third wing.' I figured a third wing would mess a bird up completely. Anyway, the name stuck."

"Why aren't you working at one of the trading posts?"

"Oh, not long after I got my name, Gannett took an outfit out to trade with the Loup Pawnees. Raven was curious about me, a red-skinned boy. When Gannett told him I spoke Pawnee, Raven checked but couldn't find anyone who remembered me. Maybe I came from the other big Pawnee tribe. Anyhow, Raven got one of the families to trade a horse for me." He laughed. "Hell, once I was worth a horse."

Sam didn't know what to say to this outburst of information and feeling.

Third Wing said, "Let's make camp together here."

Sam looked at the sky. Swept clear by the winds, no rain or snow tonight. "I'll get my blankets," said Sam.

When he got back, Third Wing had cleared an area for sleeping—the pebbles and little sticks were tossed away. He was bringing willows, their finger-shaped yellow leaves still on, and fashioning a hut from them. Sam cut the willows while Third Wing made them into a house. Sam had the teasing thought. *Just like a good little woman.*

He ended up lending most of his blankets to Third Wing. The Pawnee slept like a baby. Coy spooned up close to him on the belly side. Sam sat up most of the night, feeling bad about Third Wing, and wondering.

OVER THE NEXT few days Sam sometimes felt like he had two dogs tagging around with him, except that neither Coy nor Third Wing was a dog. Sam's job was to help Ashley with the trading. The general set his trade goods out—beads, vermilion, kettles, knives, cotton cloth, wool strouding, tobacco, and lots of other items, including the blankets they sat on. The Indians surveyed all, trying to keep their faces impassive and prevent their eyes from lighting up. At length they made offers.

The process was long, sometimes tedious and sometimes fun. The Pawnees treated the trading as a form of play. Back-and-forth banter wasn't easy in signs.

"Why don't you let me do the translating?" asked Third Wing. He was lounging on the edge of a trade blanket in the noonday sun, which was weak, this near the solstice.

Sam looked at Ashley. "Yes," said the general to Sam, "but you stay and help too."

"Goddam," said Third Wing, "my own people don't trust me, and neither do you whites." But he chuckled when he said it.

Always the disciplinarian, Ashley frowned at the "goddam," and the trading got started again. It went a lot faster with Third Wing making English out of Pawnee and then telling the people what Sam's answer was. Sam was sure Third Wing spiced the answers up with humor, and sometimes a mocking edge. Now and then the women giggled like the banter was bawdy.

At first they got a lot of buffalo robes, which would help the men stay warm at night. Then came jerked meat, which was welcome, because the winter was looking longer and hungrier to everyone. Trading for horseflesh, though, was slow and difficult. Only one animal the first day, three the second, two the third. Ashley wanted a pack horse for every man, twenty-five altogether.

ON THE SECOND night Jim Beckwourth and Gideon made a change in everyone's living arrangements. They dropped their bedrolls on the far side of Sam and Third Wing's fire. "We want to be over here," said the French-Canadian.

"Where there's some skin that ain't white," added Jim. He threw a shiny, big-toothed smile at Third Wing.

"I'm kinda mixed up between white and red," said Third Wing.

"Me too," said Gideon. "Born that way."

"I figure that makes us blood brothers," said Jim. They all chortled at that.

Jim told his story about what a gentleman his father, Sir Jennings Beckwourth, had been, a kind of aristocrat to hear Jim tell it. He didn't know how Sir Jennings came to be with his mother, a slave, "But I can guess." Sir Jennings even brought the family to St. Louis to get away from color prejudice and give the half-and-half children a decent chance in life.

"How'd that work?"

"Not a bit."

"May be better in the mountains," put in Sam.

"He's an optimist," said Gideon with a smile.

"I think white people is white people wherever you go," Jim said.

Third Wing hopped back into the conversation. "What do you mean," he asked Gideon, "born that way?"

"My father was a French Jew, my mother a Cree," said Gideon.

"You aren't much dark," said Third Wing.

"One of my sisters be light as cream," said Jim, who was dark. One of the odd things about Jim, Sam had noticed, was that he could talk good English to the general, better English than Sam's, and rough English to his fellow trappers. He also noticed that Jim wore a mustard seed in a drop of glass around his neck, an old way of warding off illness. Sam approved. Black folks, Indians, and country whites, he thought, knew some things fancy white people didn't.

"Here's what my father told me," said Jim, "and this child thinks it speaks to red as well as black. My father pointed at the piano where we gathered round to sing church songs, you know, hymns, and my father he says, 'There are twelve tones on the piano. Some of them are white, and some of them are black. Each one strikes a pure and beautiful tone, and music is made equally of both.'"

Third Wing cackled like that was one truly funny-peculiar story.

Gideon said, "Except people don't see it that way, do they?"

TWO MORE DAYS work and they had nine horses. It was slow. Fortunately, the winter weather was fine, the hunting was good, and the men were happy here.

Third Wing asked for a robe from Ashley for all the translating he was doing. He got a robe and a blanket.

Sam wanted to sit around with Gideon and Jim and Fitz and Clyman and tell stories. He wanted to hunt. Mostly he wanted this boring work to be over. As long as they were trading, though, Ashley would pack up and ride the south fork toward that big range of mountains. Then they would be moving away from the camp of the girl whose name he wouldn't speak, even to himself.

That night across the fire—still plenty of buffalo meat to eat and all four friends were doing their best on it—Third Wing asked Sam, "Why do you act so glum?"

Sam didn't answer.

"It's that Crow woman," Jim said. "Look at him fingering that *gage d'amour,* don't even know he's doing it."

Third Wing laughed.

"If you don't tell him," said Gideon, "I will."

So Sam did, told Third Wing how he got to know her when the brigade lived at the Crow village led by Rides Twice last winter, how enchanting she was, how beautifully she moved.

"Her name, it's Meadowlark," put in Gideon.

"Yeah. She's a virgin," Sam went on, "because she wants to lead that ceremony reserved for virgins."

"You hope she hasn't led it yet," said Jim with a chuckle.

"I didn't know where I stood with her until she gave me

this *gage d'amour*. Then I promised to come back last summer."

"Which you didn't," said Gideon.

"Life got in the way," said Sam. To Third Wing he added, "That's when I got lost."

"And came wandering down the river, half-addled and half-starved, and I saved your silly ass," said Third Wing.

"Yeah."

"So now you're worried," Third Wing went on. "You didn't show up last summer. If you don't go back to her this winter, it will be no more kootchy-coo." Sometimes Third Wing acted like his friend, sometimes his mother, and sometimes like a little kid.

"Yeah."

"Where is her village?"

"Wind River," said Gideon. "Up the north fork here a long way, up the Sweetwater, over a divide, follow Wind River upstream."

"So why don't we just go see her? Leave straight from here. Right away. What are we waiting for?"

Sam gawked at Third Wing.

"Young love is supposed to be keen," said Jim.

Third Wing held out his arms in a what-are-you-waiting-for gesture.

"You want to go?" Sam asked Third Wing, half-believing.

"What would I sit around here for?"

"You?" Sam asked Gideon.

"I like Crow women."

Sam looked at Jim.

"I like all women."

"Let's go!" Sam shouted.

Chapter Six

They took a week to get ready. Ashley insisted that Sam and Third Wing help him finish trading for those horses, and the general ended up with twenty-three new ones. Beckwourth shot a buffalo cow and a deer. Third Wing kept a low fire going all day, every day to dry the meat. Figuring the journey would take three weeks, they were taking a month's worth of food. All four men knew that could be a recipe for starvation—anything could happen in the mountains.

Third Wing contributed two pack horses.

Fitzpatrick came to their fire by the river the night before they left. He settled on his haunches and looked one by one at the four of them. His mouth had an ironic set, but his Irish eyes were full of merriment. "You *compañeros* following *mi coyote's* yen for poontang, you are lucky fellows. The general will not fire your arses. He will not even change your financial arrangements. You may chase skirts wherever you want to this winter, and make the same money—that's *if* you turn up next spring for the hunt."

"Being generous, is he, the general?" Beckwourth said.

"Why certainly," said Fitz with mock melody.

Coy crawled over between Third Wing's feet and turned onto his back. The Pawnee rubbed the belly obligingly. He said, "Ashley wants you to bring your beaver to him. He don't want you selling it to nobody else."

"He doesn't mind if we shine up his relationship wit' ze Crows either," said Gideon.

To Sam, Fitz added, "Meet us the day of the spring equinox, he says, on the Siskadee."

Third Wing gave Coy's belly a playful pinch. The dog yipped and mouthed the fingers. The Pawnee made a loud flutter with his lips and tongue. The pup yipped.

"Too early," said Sam.

"We'll frostbite our tails in the Southern Pass in March," said Gideon.

"So will you," said Sam.

Sam, Gideon, and Fitzpatrick remembered well the howling winds and choking blizzards on the pass last March, right before they had mountain luck and stumbled on beaver paradise in the valley of the Siskadee. Along with Bill Sublette and James Clyman, Sam had nearly frozen to death one night on the pass because the wind kept scattering their pathetic attempts at a fire. Only the next morning's discovery of a single live coal the size of a kernel of corn had saved them.

Coy slithered to the fire and put his head on his paws like he remembered and was trying to get warm. "You weren't even born when that happened," Sam told him. The pup mewled a little and didn't move.

"Diah and Sublette be on the Siskadee?" asked Sam.

"Yeah," said Fitz. "And I already told the general March is a hell-freezer-till-your-short-hairs-get-stiff. Make it the middle of April."

"Good," said Sam. He was eager to show cooperation with the general. Having an employer seemed proper.

"Now the general has a surprise for you." He walked off into the dark and came back leading a horse bearing big panniers, sacks that hung heavy on each side. "*Mi coyote,* you aren't thinking of how you should treat the Crows." He opened a pannier to show them. "This is tobacco, blankets, beads, strouding, all kind of foofuraw. You tell them these presents are from General Ashley."

"Dammit," said Sam, "we didn't think of presents."

"Gideon did," said Fitz, "that's how come you get all these nice things."

Gideon managed a half bow. "I have a word with Ashley private," he said. "I also have two jugs. One is for us on New Year's Eve, the ozzer for the Crows."

"I'll pretend I didn't hear that," said Fitz. The government forbade the use of whiskey in the Indian trade, but most traders disregarded this ban.

"You can take the pack horse too," said Fitz, "but remember, it's the general's."

Third Wing got up, took the panniers off, led the pack horse a dozen steps, and staked it with their other horses.

"Now *mi coyote,* how are you going to know when the first week of April comes?" asked Fitz. "You can't go by the Indian way, the moon when the grass greens up."

Sam just looked at him, stuck.

Fitzpatrick took out a stick stripped of bark, painted blue on one end, red on the other, and bare wood in the middle, which had lots of knife cuts on it, in lines. "This is my counting stick." He held it out to Sam.

The moment Sam grasped it, Coy snatched the stick and scooted away. He sat with his back to the fire, looking straight at Sam, stick in his mouth. Though his tail didn't wag, his legs trembled.

Sam patted the ground.

Coy bounded forward and laid the stick on the ground. Then he leapt into Sam's lap. At six or seven months, he was getting big for the lap.

Fitz grabbed the stick and looked to see whether his cuts were spoiled by tooth marks. Apparently not. "I keep the time for the brigade in the ledger. But a man who doesn't read or write"—like Sam—"can do it like this. See here, make seven notches for each day in a week, then make one of these big rings all the way around the stick. Those are weeks, or quarters of the moon. Every four quarters, make a ring and paint it with vermilion—that's a month." Sam nodded—he saw what the system was. "Today is December 21, the shortest day and longest night of the year. Tomorrow night's camp, make your own counting stick. When the rings say it's April, put your minds on moving out. Be on the Siskadee four moon from now."

"Only white men count their days," Beckwourth said with broad mockery.

"This should be long enough for even you boys to dip your wicks a lot of places," answered Fitz.

Sam blushed.

"Middle of April we'll be looking for you. When you get to where the Sandy comes into the Siskadee, if you don't see lots of sign we've been there, wait. If we've come and gone, I'll leave a cairn. One rock on the side of the cairn, that points whether I went upriver or downriver."

He looked all four of them in the eyes.

"Zis is easy," said Gideon. "I find your outfit anywhere in the Rocky Mountains, maybe by the smell of your feet."

Fitz grinned. "Don't end up walking back to civilization, boys."

Sam, Gideon, and Fitzpatrick all grinned. That wasn't on the agenda again.

Suddenly, wraithlike, Fitz was gone.

Sam laid awake all night, thinking of Meadowlark. He was up before the sun the next morning making coffee. The party rode off earlier than his companions wanted to, and they were grumbling.

MOUNTAIN LUCK SWINGS big each way. Easy—alive— hard—dead. Gone under, as the trappers called it, in the lingo they were developing. One winter trip goes lickety-split, the next one is inch by inch, leading the horse through thigh-deep snow, pulling your leg out of one deep hole, pushing it across the snow in front of you, and shifting your weight awkwardly forward so you can plunge a foot down again. Naturally, if you have a dog with you, or in Sam's case, a coyote, the critter will trot blithely over the surface of the snow, look back at you, and give you a superior smile.

That December their luck was variable, but mostly good. Where the Sweetwater River flowed into the Platte, they spent a day and a half sitting out a snowstorm. A tent gets close when you're in it all day—Sam spent the evening outside, watching the big flakes sift silently through the branches of cottonwood trees. Where they left the Sweetwater to cross over to Wind River, they got into deep snow in spots, and they huddled one afternoon and night below a cut bank, trying to get out of the screaming wind. Holding Coy to his front, Sam was not as shivery as his companions.

The country was mostly open, though. Beckwourth said it was because the damn wind blew the snow all the way to the Missouri River.

When wood failed them, they made fires of sagebrush and buffalo pies. The flames kept them warm, more or less, through the long nights. Thoughts of Meadowlark kept Sam nearly hot.

When you ride day after day through Indian country, your mind should never wander. There are always ridges to be scoured with the eyes, brushy flats to be inspected. You watch for anything that's out of place, a silhouette moving on a hilltop or a duck quacking up off the river for no reason.

Sam was inexperienced, though, and young, and hot-blooded. His mind ran from Meadowlark walking to Meadowlark smiling to Meadowlark snuggled up . . . He had no promises from her, only this one gift, the *gage d'amour* he always wore around his neck. He thought again of the reason she'd given for declining his courting, that she wanted to be one of the girls who led the dancers in the goose egg dance. The leaders had to be virgins, others explained to Sam, completely above suspicion. Meadowlark spent time with no young man.

But Sam couldn't keep from wondering. *Was she sincere? Was she stalling him to let someone else into her arms? Did she have that ceremony last summer?* Some summers they visited the River Crows, and that's when they did the ceremony. *If she did, did she go berry-picking afterwards with some good-looking stranger and take the pleasures of the flesh? Is she being courted? Is she already married?*

These thoughts bounced off Elk Mountain and back into Sam's mind, off the waters of the Sweetwater River and back to him, from the snowy world of the Wind River Mountains on the southwest to the red hills and gray, stony peaks of the steep Absarokas on the northeast and back, always, into

Sam's mind. When he woke in the middle of the night, these thoughts haunted him.

On the day of Christmas Eve Sam rode with his mind in the past. It was his twentieth birthday, and the fourth anniversary of his father's death. He didn't call up many words about Lew Morgan, and none of the kinds of words people said at a burying. He just let pictures float into his mind. He and Lew playing cat's cradle. The father teaching the child to milk the cow, shooting the warm milk into his boy's face, and the sweet taste of that milk right out of the tit. Learning to measure his powder with care, both kinds of powder, for the pan and for the barrel. Easing through the Pennsylvania woods behind Lew, trying not to make a sound, and failing. Then finding a spot and spending the whole day watching to see what was there—what birds lived in these trees and when they sang and when they were silent; the deer, grazing quietly because they didn't know human beings were around; the fish, and how you could build a dam and catch them with your hands and scoop them onto the bank. He stroked the stock of his rifle, where he'd had a brass plate put on and CELC engraved in a fancy script, surrounded by a circle of Celtic love knots, like the ones in a belt Sam's mother had given his father. But the name and the circle had been scorched by the prairie fire, and were only half legible. Still, his memories of his father gleamed.

That night, as they sat around the fire in the early dark, Third Wing said, "I have a treat for you." The two great whacks of Sam's hair, tied into Third Wing's, glinted dramatically white in the firelight. "First this." He disappeared into the darkness and brought back a tin cup filled with grease. Sam had noticed him rendering buffalo fat the last couple of days. Out of the grease hung a piece of patch cloth like a wick. Third Wing put the whole affair on the cold ground and used an ember to get the wick burning. It burned nicely because it was soaked in oil.

"This is your birthday candle. We couldn't make twenty of them," said Third Wing. "Blow it out for good luck."

Sam made an immense gust and out went the candle. Gideon and Beckwourth applauded.

"Now your very special surprise," said Third Wing.

He stepped into the dark again and brought back a tin bowl of . . . It looked sort of like . . . "Cherry ice cream," said Third Wing proudly.

"Well, ice cream Athabascan style," said Gideon.

Third Wing thrust the bowl forward. "Everyone help yourself."

The four spooned the goop into their coffee cups.

Sam scooped some up with his tongue, then kept himself from making a face.

"*Pas mal* when you get used to it," said Gideon. "I learned way north, when I spent the winter at Slave Lake."

Beckwourth did make a face.

Sam tried again, and didn't exactly dislike it. It was sweet.

"I put lots of sugar in it," Third Wing said, "to improve the taste."

"What is it?" Beckwourth asked.

"Liquid buffalo fat," said Gideon, "mushed up with snow."

"With lots of sugar," repeated Third Wing, "and all the chokecherries we had left."

"Thanks," said Sam.

"Happy birthday," said Third Wing.

"Happy birthday," the others chorused.

"Oh to be twenty again," chanted Gideon like he was in church.

"Thanks, everyone!" said Sam. He meant it.

Sneakily, later, he would give his cherry ice cream to Coy.

"Now I'm going to give you a special birthday present," said Third Wing.

Everyone fell silent. Sam could tell Gideon and Beckwourth didn't know about this.

"I'm going to tell you why I like you so much."

This was strange.

"I saw you in a dream before you ever came."

Sam felt weird. "What do you mean?"

"I saw a white man with white hair in a dream. So I was expecting you. Some time."

"What happened in the dream?"

"You came walking in the shape of buffalo, a red buffalo. Then you stopped, turned all the way around, and came walking as a yellow buffalo. Then you stopped, turned around, and came walking in a sacred way as a black buffalo. Then you stopped, turned around, and came toward us as a white buffalo."

Third Wing looked at his listeners as though expecting some reaction they didn't give, maybe awe.

"Just a minute," said Sam. "If it was a buffalo, why do you think it was me?"

"Your medicine, is it buffalo?"

Sam thought of his own dream, and the cow he joined beings with. Still, he said, "I don't know what you mean."

"I think it is buffalo, but . . . it was you that stood on the hill above the village." Then he explained, as though to children, "You in your human shape and your beautiful white hair. You carried a deer skin tanned beautifully white, and in it was some gift for the people. You opened it, and it shone. You set it down on the crest of the hill and walked away in a sacred manner."

He stopped awkwardly. "But I never saw what it was. Others rushed up the hill to see the gift, but I woke up. I don't know what you brought us."

The four men looked at each other, uncertain.

"But I knew you had a gift. That's why I saved you. You bore a gift."

"Third Wing, I honestly don't have anything for the Pawnee."

The Pawnee shrugged. "Maybe you don't know what it is, but you have it. The gift, that's why I want to be with you."

Sam considered, and then knew what he wanted to do. He scooted over to Third Wing, made his eyes big as a demon's, gave him a big smooch on the cheek, and said in a honeyed voice, "I like you, too."

Everyone laughed.

Sam fell asleep thinking, *He's a strange friend, but I like him.*

SAM'S COUNTING STICK told him when New Year's Eve was, and they broke open one of the two whiskey jugs and got uproariously drunk. Only Third Wing stayed mostly sober, so he could take care of the fools who overindulged, he said.

That night Gideon and Beckwourth got into a storytelling contest Sam would never forget. His favorite was one Gideon told. "Me, ze first winter I am on Saskatchewan River, I walk sometimes from trading post to village, maybe one hour walk. I need, you know, a woman warm against ze long, long winter. Very cold, Saskatchewan, very much snow. I am lonesome on the walk, so I whistle along the way. This was my favorite song,

As I strolled by,
At the clear fountain,
noticed the water was exquisite,
And dipped myself in it.
I've loved you so long—
I will never forget you.

"A young man in on ze far plains, during the long winter, he *naturalement* t'ink of his lady love back home, no?

"Remember, I whistle this song as I walk, no did sing it, just whistle.

"One winter day it is so cold. I remember my breath frosted my beard. The hairs in my nose, they crust with ice. My lungs hurt from drawing in ze air. But I whistle, always I whistle.

"I mean I try. Zis time it is for nothing, it . . . Nothing comes out. My whistles, ze cold freezes ze sound. I keep whistling, I am superstitious. If I don't send my song to my love, maybe she is, you know, *infidel* with another man."

"*Infidel* like you are, huh?" asked Sam, taking pleasure in catching on to a new word.

"Yes, *naturalement,* I am a man. Two weeks later, maybe three, comes ze wind we call chinook. You know? Warm winter wind, melts ze snow, bares ze ground, makes you feel good. After three days of chinook I must walk to village, and now is much more pleasant, neh?

"Oh, you don't know how pleasant. Because my whistles, it is warm, now they thaw out. They sing to me from every wild rose bush, from every blue spruce tree. Even ze snow, dripping from the branches, serenades me. I pretend the thawing whistles, zey are ze voice of my lover.

"I've loved you so long—
I will never forget you."

"That's horse puckey," said Jim, with a big grin.

"Says the world's biggest maker of horse puckey," said Sam.

"Whoo-oop! Lookee here!" Jim mock-roared. "I am a grizzly b'ar crossed with a mountain lion. I can outrun, outshoot, and outride, and outfight any man what takes breath within a thousand miles of the Missouri River. And I am the world's biggest maker of horse puckey," he concluded triumphantly.

"All right," he went on with buttery charm, "now, I got a story. . . ."

IN THE FAR, wee middle of that night Third Wing asked to hear the tale of how Sam got Coy.

"His medicine coyote," said Gideon.

"His familiar spirit," said Beckwourth.

"He's just my friend," said Sam.

"You aren't friends," said Beckwourth. "You're the master, he does what you say."

"We're friends," insisted Sam quietly. He thought a moment. He didn't believe Coy was his medicine animal. If he had a medicine animal, or should claim one, it was that buffalo cow back on the Platte, the one he entered into and joined with. Though he wasn't sure what a medicine animal was.

He did think he could tell the story of how he got Coy. It was related to the buffalo story, but not the same story.

"I was camped in a cottonwood grove on a little creek several miles north of the Platte. Alone—that was when I was doing my walk down the river to Atkinson."

"Baptism of fire, plains style," said Gideon, a veteran of the same walk.

"I shot a buffalo just before dark and got her gutted out. Woke up just before dawn, it looked like the sun was rising in the northwest, so bright and red it was. Until I smelled the smoke I didn't figure out what was happening. Prairie fire coming my way.

"I put it together fast as I could. Huge, huge prairie fire, wind whipping it straight toward me. Too wide to outrun to either side, too far to the river. I tried to get in the little creek, but there wasn't enough water—left half of me sticking out. Did get good and wet, though. Pawing around with no place to go, I heard a mewling sound. It was this pup here, only smaller, and he was poking at the slit in the buffalo, like he wanted to get in.

"Seemed crazy. I looked up at that fire. It was going to hit the grove right quick, and when it did the trees would turn into torches—you wouldn't have to touch flame to get burnt, 'All right,' I said to myself, 'It's crazy but it's the only chance.' I crept right into the buffalo belly, took the pup with me. Hell, all of me didn't even fit. Knees stuck out. When they got too hot, I turned over and my tail stuck out. Got burned pretty good.

"When the sound eased away—you can't imagine how loud a prairie fire roars—I waited and waited some more and finally crawled out." He thought of telling them about the strange feeling he had, like being born, but decided against it. "Everything was turned black. *Every*thing. The stink was beyond belief, and it stung your nose. Most places you couldn't step, even in a moccasin—too hot.

"Later I butchered out the buffalo—meat was good, even if it was toasted around the edges. Kept the pup. Fed him. Figured the pup saved my life."

He picked Coy and hugged, dog back to human chest. "This pup is my friend."

No one spoke, maybe out of respect, Sam thought, or maybe because the story wasn't a stretcher like they wanted.

"Up at Slave Lake, hell of a way to ze northwest and gone," began Gideon, "I came across a sow grizzly, and sudden I wondered where her cubs were . . ."

Third Wing egged on Gideon and Beckwourth, and they never stopped telling stories until the sun rose over the hills to the southeast. Then the four men and coyote slept all New Year's day. Sam didn't figure this country often brought in the new year so sunny and mild and pleasantly lazy.

Chapter Seven

S am spat his freezing hair out of his mouth—the hair was crinkled with ice. The weather was so nasty he had Coy up in the saddle with him, curled against his belly and around the horn.

It was three weeks and two days since they'd left the Ashley men at the forks of the Platte, according to his counting stick. He knew the tipis of the Crow village were in the cottonwoods along the river ahead. But on this bitter evening he couldn't see even their silhouettes, or any hint of a fire. His left ear ached from the wind and sleet slashing that side of his face. The hand leading the pack horse was too stiff either to grip or let go—the rope was wound several times around the hand. And his white hair, now finally grown back to decent length, was whipping ice into his mouth and eyes.

He had made it to Meadowlark's village, but at the moment he didn't give a damn.

"Riders," said Beckwourth.

Sam held up a hand, and all four stopped. Odd, though the youngest, Sam was a sort of leader here. He and Gideon had lived in this village last winter, but Sam alone spoke the Crow language. (Gideon had a few words of *amour*.)

Five horsemen came out of the lacing sleet and stopped facing Sam's party. Sam thought he recognized one figure.

"Ohchikaape." It meant, "Greetings after a long absence." "We come from General Ashley in friendship."

"Sam?" cried a voice in English. "Welcome back, Sam. I'm glad to see you."

"I'm glad to see you Blue Horse!" chimed in Sam. He felt a twinge of guilt at always thinking of Meadowlark and seldom of her brother, his noble-looking friend. He wanted to say lots of things to this comrade, but he forced himself to stick with business. "We want to speak with Rides Twice."

The young men with Blue Horse held the horses of both groups. Sam stopped to put Coy on a leash, which got him strange looks from whites and Indians alike.

The trappers limped into the village on numb feet that made them weave like drunken sailors. Their march had not a shred of dignity, but Gideon was still strong enough to lug the panniers, full of presents. "You can make a tent with the other young men," offered Blue Horse in English. He was still keeping one wary eye on the coyote.

"Pitch a tent," said Sam. He was acknowledging their former pact to help each other, one with Crow, the other with English. "We will do that tonight. Thank you."

A tent, though, was not what he wanted. He longed for the coziness of a real tipi and a center fire, preferably with Meadowlark in the buffalo robes at the rear.

As they approached the council lodge, Sam made himself remember the details of the Crow way of handling the sacred pipe, the proper Crow words to use in offering the smoke to the four directions. The presents would make the trappers welcome. These trade items were great luxuries to the Crows, who had no other access to them. He assumed the Crows would accept Third Wing. Both Crows and Pawnees were long-time enemies of the Sioux, and that should do it.

The problem was Coy. When they got to the lodge, Sam regretfully tied him to a lodge stake outside. Then they waited until Rides Twice and several Big Bellies went in. Sam ducked through the flap behind them. The lodge was cold, but a good center fire was already started. He wanted to crawl into a corner, wrap up in a buffalo robe, and sleep. *Right now I don't even want Meadowlark there with me.* He gave a crookedy smile. *Well, maybe I do.*

Rides Twice sat in his accustomed place behind the center fire. He motioned for Sam to sit to his left, and the others in the trapping party to Sam's left, and the Big Bellies to their left. He said in the Crow language, "Welcome, Sam, we are glad to see you again."

Sam lowered himself beside the chief. It was going to be a good winter.

EARLY THE NEXT morning Sam was sitting quietly by the river, on a cottonwood felled by a beaver, rubbing Coy's ears. The early morning fog half hid the two of them. His breath swirled up to join the fog. *My breath, the earth's breath,* he thought. He took off his other glove and changed hands. Coy's fur warmed his fingers better than the gloves. He watched the figures moving ghostly through the fog, to the river bank and back. He wasn't interested, though, in any figure except one, Meadowlark, and she didn't appear.

Beyond him the river was easy to get to, and the water formed a pool. Every morning the mothers and grandmothers sent the young women here to get water. But no Meadowlark yet.

When the weak winter sun had burned the fog off, Meadowlark's mother, Needle, came down the trail carrying a bucket. *Another trade item they need from us.*

Sam was miffed. The other young women must have told Meadowlark, or Needle, that the white man was waiting for her. *I'm sure she wants to see me.* Maybe it was her parents . . . *Maybe she still hasn't done the ceremony . . .*

Needle was usually merry. This time she walked with her eyes straight ahead, apparently seeing nothing but the path and the pool. Sam couldn't even tell whether she knew he was there. When she was gone, he and Coy traipsed back to the village. There would be meat for breakfast at the tent, and coffee. Sam had gotten to where he loved black coffee with sugar in it.

By midday the trappers had traded for a lodge cover and lodgepoles. Now they struggled to erect the tipi and get the cover on nice and tight, without wrinkles. Third Wing laughed a lot, Sam kept saying he didn't know what to do, Beckwourth gave instructions despite knowing nothing about tipis, and Gideon kept saying, "This is women's work." Except for Third Wing, they'd never have gotten the lodge up.

Sam remembered grumpily what happened last winter when he and Gideon put up their first lodge. Needle and her daughters came to help out, full of giggles at the white men's ineptitude. *Now we're just as clumsy, so where are you? Why don't you help?*

The four men stood back and looked at the small tipi, erect beside the brush huts of the young men. Altogether they'd done a half-assed job, but they would get by. Sam looked longingly toward the main circle. Like these men without families, the trappers weren't part of the circle that made these people a village, where everyone was arranged according to their relationship with everyone else.

Sam thought of what family he had. A brother who'd stolen Sam's girl and married her, and now hated Sam. A mother who loved both her sons in an ineffectual way, and wouldn't live long. Two sisters who loved Sam but were probably glad he was gone from the country and not causing trouble. Altogether, no one who wanted to see him coming.

Sam didn't see Meadowlark all day long.

* * *

"LET'S GET GOING," said Blue Horse, happy and proud to speak English again.

"We'll do it right here in front of the lodge," said Gideon.

Though the sun was about to drop behind the Wind River Mountains, they had a good while before dark—those mountains were high. It was a clear, windless afternoon, pleasantly cool before the plunge of the January night.

The four trappers and Blue Horse spread the blankets in front of the lodge and laid the trade goods out for display. Coy curled on a corner of the blanket. Soon Crows were bumping shoulders to see.

Sam had asked Blue Horse to help. Sam wasn't quite that sure of his Crow language.

The most popular item was a free cup of whiskey, as lubrication for the trade. Having neither Crow nor sign language, Beckwourth was assigned to play bartender and instructed to pour everyone a fair two fingers. "That don't make sense," Jim said with a laugh. "The cups are all different sizes." These cups were occasionally tin (luxury items) but mostly made of horn.

"Just do it," said Sam. He and Gideon had prepared the whiskey as instructed by Ashley—one part raw alcohol to four parts creek water, seasoned with tobacco and pepper. The Crows were so avid for it, men and women alike, that Sam was glad it would soon run out. Gideon had told him tales about Indians when they were really drunk—daughters seducing their fathers, husbands raping their daughters-in-law, men fighting with knives or tomahawks until someone was hurt bad or dead—every sort of behavior that forgot they were one people, all related.

Sam, Gideon, and Third Wing traded all manner of things for Crow beaver. Since the fur men had spent last winter with them, some Crows had taken to hunting beaver, not with traps but spears and clubs. General Ashley liked Crow beaver. He said the plews (the men's common word for the hides) were thicker and heavier, so he got a better price for them. As the men put it, Crow beaver was *some*.

The favorite Crow purchase was a blanket. The trappers had the good thick ones manufactured by Witney in England. Each small black stripe woven into the rug indicated a cost of one plew. The smallest blanket was three plews, and a really big one six.

The prices of other items were not openly declared, and so depended on the bargaining skill of buyer and seller, and maybe the inebriation of the buyer. Gideon was fair and firm in his prices and didn't bargain much. Since he spoke only a few words of Crow, it was mostly point, gesture, and shake your head yes or no. Sam was cordial and less particular about price. Blue Horse checked with Sam before he made a trade—he seemed to take pride in helping the trappers by getting good prices. Sam reflected again that everything about this young man seemed noble. He was going to be a leader.

The Crows seemed uninterested in one item. At Atkinson Ashley had paid Indian women to sew the Witney blankets into coats with hoods—capotes, the men called them. Sam wore a beauty made of a blanket with narrow red stripes on a white background. But the Crows seemed to want the blankets as they were.

It was Third Wing, oddly, who turned the trading into entertainment. He'd take a piece of calico cloth, hold it up in front of himself like a shirt, and do an ain't-I-a-handsome-fellow strut. Then he showed them what the wool strouding, red with blue and yellow stripes down one edge, looked like when wrapped like leggings. He put vermilion on his cheeks as rosy makeup, modeled a string of sky-blue seed beads as a necklace, and did a sexy woman's walk. This drew hoots from the women. He conducted a mock fight, butcher knife against cottonwood trunk, and threw a tomahawk into the trunk with a force and accuracy that scared Sam.

Sam jumped up and added to the show. He got Coy to sit, roll over, and jump for a bite of meat held in Sam's hand.

Since the Crows hadn't seen the coyote pup before, and had never seen even a dog obey commands, they were delighted.

The women (most of the customers were women) soon ran out of beaver pelts to trade and started offering buffalo robes. Ashley wanted some of these, and the four trappers would use them as warm bedding against the rest of the cold winter. The Indians also brought forward river otter skins, a bear hide, and thick wolf hides, all worth something, but not as much as beaver plews. After a while they were mostly offering to trade jerked meat and pemmican, the sausage-like blend of fine-ground dried meat and buffalo fat, with berries or rose hips mixed in. It was a nourishing food and would last forever—the men were glad to trade for it.

When dark came, the trading dropped off but continued slowly by the light of the nearby cook fires. Now Needle and Gray Hawk came. Needle was mostly interested in beads, which seemed more special as decoration than porcupine quills to the Crows, and in cloth, which was a complete novelty.

Sam stared at the two with one thought: *I haven't seen Meadowlark at all.* Even Blue Horse hadn't mentioned her. For that matter, Sam hadn't seen Meadowlark's sister either, or her younger brothers. He felt a chill: *She did the goose egg ceremony, married a River Crow, and is living with her husband far down the Missouri. And they don't want to tell me.*

Carefully, he insisted to himself that this was irrational. He didn't know anything about Meadowlark yet. Still, most of the tribe's women and many of the men had stopped by to trade, but not her. She loved beads, vermilion, wool strouding for knee leggings, and other white-man aids to looking good. He peered at the top of Needle's head as she bent over, lifting strings of different-colored beads. He looked into the impassive face of Gray Hawk. *You aren't about to tell me. So what's going on?*

He decided to tie Coy in the lodge, slip away without Blue Horse, and find her. He took a string of Russian blue beads, the finest beads they had, as a gift. Something else General Ashley would take out of his pay.

THE MAN WAS tall and well formed. Sam backed carefully between the tipis, outside the lodge circle and around it to another angle. When he came back into the circle, he saw the man's face by firelight—it was Red Roan, the son of Chief Rides Twice. *Damn.* It was an unusually handsome face belonging to a splendidly built fellow in his mid-twenties. Sam remembered now, he was a widower—his wife and son were taken by the Blackfeet. Meadowlark stood next to him, although she didn't let him wrap her in his blanket. Clearly, she had performed the goose egg ceremony and was accepting suitors. Red Roan was good-looking and much respected—a great catch. *Damn.*

He still couldn't see Meadowlark's face. Though he felt sure, he had to make certain. But Red Roan's big body blocked her features from behind, and from this direction the back of her head was to Sam. *Maybe they aren't courting.* But Sam knew this was a silly hope.

He hesitated, screwed up his courage, and walked up close. *Yes, it's Meadowlark.* He studied her face past the big man's shoulder. She was lovely, far lovelier even than he remembered. Sam shivered inside his red-and-white striped capote. He knew the custom. A girl would flirt with one suitor for a while, and others would patiently wait their turn. Sam was next. She was looking up into Red Roan's face in a way that looked adoring. *Oh, dammit, dammit.*

He stomped his cold feet, he fidgeted, and he fussed. In a few minutes—it was rude to monopolize a young woman's attention unless you were promised to each other—Red Roan meandered away. He had the swagger of a man who expects to get what he wants in life.

Meadowlark turned to go into her lodge, but Sam stepped forward and lightly took her elbow through the blanket. She turned to him, and he saw she was blushing a furious scarlet.

"I love you," Sam blurted. Since she couldn't understand the English, he unwisely added, *"apxisshe."* Though it meant "snubby nose," in Crow it was a term of endearment used by a lover. He had declared himself.

She lowered her head into her hands. When she looked back into his face, she reached out with one hand and touched the *gage d'amour* she'd given him, as though affirming something. Then she said in the Crow language, "I'm glad to see you."

That was enough for Sam. He was sure they'd be sharing a lodge within a couple of weeks.

He fished the string of Russian blues out of his capote pocket. "For you," he said.

She gasped. She looked up at him, her eyes lighted in the way every man wants to see.

"I'm sorry I didn't come to the village last summer." In summer these Crows rode down the Wind River, through a canyon where for some reason it changed its name to the Big Horn River, and north to a river called the Gray Bull. This site they regarded as a summer paradise.

She said nothing. Her face seemed to say, 'A maiden knows she will be disappointed sometimes.' He hated that. He couldn't tell whether her face shone in the moonlight, or shone because she was looking up at him, or shone in his mind only.

"I got lost," Sam said. "My companions sent me ahead to scout and then didn't come up. Some Arapahos stole my horse." Arapahos were enemies of the Crows. "I walked all the way down the Shell River," the one whites called the Platte, "to where we have a . . ."—he wondered what word to use for "fort"—"big house on the Muddy Water River." The Missouri, if he was speaking English.

He saw the question in her face. "I walked about seventy sleeps," he told her, "alone." He didn't mention having only eleven balls for his rifle, not being able to hunt much, and damn near starving to death.

"Seventy sleeps! You're a hero," she said.

Now Sam blushed. Wanting to cover up with some words or other, he broke out with, "Did you lead the dancers in the goose egg ceremony?"

Seemed everything either one of them said was embarrassing. "Yes, our relatives on the Muddy Waters River came to visit us and we danced."

The River Crows, Sam translated in his head, who lived on the upper Missouri in a village he'd never been to. *Thank God, you didn't marry one of your cousins.* He blundered forward, "Do you ever go to visit your relatives on the Muddy Waters?"

Now her eyes grew merry. "Rides Twice would never go down the Muddy Waters. One of our dogs, he likes to say, would not drink such water."

The eyes enchanted Sam. He wanted to kiss her—he was dizzy with wanting it. He reached out to draw her to him.

Just then her father stuck his head out the flap. "Meadowlark, it's time to come inside," Gray Hawk said abruptly, almost harshly.

With his hands on her upper arms, Sam felt Meadowlark stiffen. She turned away from him, then looked back over her shoulder. "Goodnight," she said. "I'm glad you're here."

Chapter Eight

Sam fumbled his way across their lodge, around the slumbering forms of Gideon, Beckwourth, and Third Wing, and pushed open the flap to the outside world. In front of him stood a spirit horse—it reared and tossed its head. The rising sun shot off the white coat in dazzling beams, and turned the mane and tail into long, flowing strings of black silk.

Suddenly, a dark figure darted from underneath. Sam

flinched a little. Then he recognized the silhouette and, yes, the smile of Blue Horse. "Wake up, sleeping head," Sam's friend called loudly.

"Sleepyhead," corrected Beckwourth as he peered out over Sam's shoulder.

"Sleepyhead," echoed Blue Horse dutifully. "Sam Morgan, rise up. I have brought you a gift."

Sam crawled out of the lodge, shivering in the dawn air.

Blue Horse led the mount in a circle. Sam saw now that it was the finest-looking Indian pony he'd seen, white with extraordinary markings—a black cap around the ears, black blaze on the chest, and black mane and tail.

"She's what we call a medicine hat pony, from the black on her head." The hat was almost a perfect, dark oval around the ears. "This blaze," he indicated the blaze on her chest, "we call the shield. She has hat and shield."

"She's gorgeous."

Blue Horse put the reins in Sam's hand. To the Crows reins meant a rope tied so it held the head and formed a loop around the lower jaw.

"A gift?" murmured Sam.

"I give Sam Morgan this horse," Blue Horse said ceremoniously, "in thanks for saving my life." He cocked an eye teasingly. "Or have you forgotten?"

Last winter, hunting in a brushy draw, Sam came on Blue Horse and a gray-hair lounging half-exhausted in front of a sweat lodge. About ten steps away a coyote was slinking toward them, shaking and frothing at the mouth. Sam shot the rabid coyote. Scared the devil out of Blue Horse and the gray-hair until they understood why he did it.

"Bell Rock also has a gift." Now another man stepped forward smiling—the gray-hair. Sam hadn't remembered his name. He had to be a medicine man, since he conducted sweat lodges. A medicine man built like a frog.

Bell Rock spoke in Crow in a deep, commanding voice. "I give you teaching this horse, and its rider, how to run the buffalo."

After a hesitation, Blue Horse added, "That's just as big a gift."

Sam took the reins of his horse and admired it. The mare was beautifully conformed, and from her teeth only two years old.

Beside Sam, Gideon said softly, "*Belle,* zis horse, she is *belle.*"

"You understand," said Blue Horse in English, "Bell Rock is good rider and very good horse teacher. Our men, they give him robes so he teach horses run buffalo. You let him teach."

Sam ran his hands up and down the neck of the animal. Coy crept stiffly out of the tipi and nearly got under its hooves. Sam snatched up his pup. He fondled the horse's muzzle. He checked all four hooves. The horse was sound. He thought of how he'd seen the Crow men ride their mounts right into the midst of the buffalo herd, both hands occupied with bow and arrow, guiding the horse with the knees only. The mounts made incredible adjustments, constantly saved the lives of horse and rider. "Good," he said. "This mare and I will learn from you."

"You eat," said Bell Rock in rough English, "we go."

"THIS HORSE," BELL Rock said, "is all raw. No human ever touch her back. Yesterday I teach her to lead." He mixed Crow and English, with Blue Horse sometimes helping out. Just then Coy nipped underneath the mare's hooves, and the pony skittered sideways. Sam nudged Coy off to one side and stayed between the pup and the horse. He was carrying his saddle and apishemore, a saddle pad made of buffalo calf skin—why, he didn't know. No one was going to be riding this animal anytime soon.

They walked toward the river, and the mare now followed on the lead rope docilely.

"How'd you get her to lead so quick?" Back in Pennsylvania they taught horses to lead when they were still too small to pull you around.

Bell Rock smiled enigmatically. "You have to be smarter than the horse, and sometimes quicker. When a horse fights, you can't try to overpower it. But when it rears or crow-hops, you can use that moment. It's off-balance. And more tricks, many more."

Sam looked at Blue Horse. "You coming along?"

"I also learn to train a horse for buffalo," said Blue Horse. His English was always pronounced slowly but well. Sam could hear the concentration on imitating each part of each word just right.

They stopped at a deep pool in the river.

"Give me the saddle and apishemore," said Bell Rock. "Now lead her into the pool." Bell Rock gave a sidewise grin and handed Sam the lead rope. "It's cold for her too," Bell Rock said. "That's good."

The instant Sam pulled on the rope, the medicine hat reared. Blue Horse and Bell Rock shooed the upright, paw-ing animal, and the mare bounded into the pool.

Sam got jerked in head over heels.

The cold was a universe he'd never known. It felt not like liquid, but a weight, an immense, crushing weight. In one in-stant he knew he was going to die, and the next instant he burst out of the water for breath.

When the water reached only to his waist, it was merely agonizing.

"Lucky you hold on to the rope," said Bell Rock.

Coy looked for a long moment and then jumped into the pool. He skittered out just as fast.

The medicine hat stood in the pool up to her withers. Her eyes rolled and she trembled all over. Maybe it was from the cold, or maybe from being held on the lead by Sam—she was looking at Sam insanely.

She couldn't rear or crow-hop or buck, or act up any other way. The deep water put a stop to that. Now Sam began to get what Bell Rock was doing.

Bell Rock stuck the saddle pad out at Sam. "Put it on her."

Sam did.

The medicine hat shivered when the pad hit her back. But she stayed still.

Sam reached to touch her muzzle and the horse threw her head. "Won't let me touch her."

"Be glad she's not trampling you," said Bell Rock. "Lead her around in a circle."

Sam did. Unexplainably, his legs sort of worked.

"Put your hands on the apishemore."

Sam did. The medicine hat twitched, but no more than that.

"Take this rope, tie the apishemore on." He handed Sam about ten feet of line braided from rawhide.

Sam had to dip arms and shoulders down into the cold to bring the rope around. He wanted to screech. But he knew if the mare wasn't deep in water, she would have been kicking the hell out of him.

"Enough for now," said Bell Rock.

At the tipi they staked the mare with the saddle pad still tied on.

Sam got out of his wet clothes and into his capote. Then he straddled the low center fire for a long moment, feeling the warmth climb up his legs to the middle region. He sighed loudly. After a couple of minutes he rejoined his friends outside.

"Look," said Bell Rock.

The medicine hat had lost interest in what was on her back and was munching on some winter-brown grass.

"Let's give her bark of the sweet cottonwood." They did. Of the two kinds of cottonwood, horses liked the bark of this one. "You will always stake her by the lodge, always bring her food, never turn her out with the horse herds."

Sam nodded. He got it. Not that he had any horse herds to turn her out with.

When they went back to the pool later, they got the saddle on the medicine hat, and left it on. That evening Sam tried to uncinch the saddle, but the mare kicked at him and crow-hopped in every direction. Back to the pool, back into the cold, and off with the saddle.

The next day they left it on all the next day and scarcely worked with the horse, except to lead it around. When the sun was almost behind the mountain, Bell Rock said, "Soon comes the great moment."

THAT EVENING SAM stood fidgeting near Meadowlark's lodge. His feet were freezing, so he stomped them. "They'll never be warm again," he told Coy, and cursed the river.

Coy whimpered. Sam could never tell what that meant. He thought maybe it was, "I'm sorry I don't understand what you're saying, friend." Coy sat patiently, his butt on the chill earth. Snow seldom stuck in this high valley of the Wind River, but the ground was plenty cold. It didn't seem to bother Coy. "Lucky fellow, you grow your own coat." It was thick, too. First winter on Earth, but Coy knew what to do to stay warm, or accepted the cold as part of living.

Tonight Red Roan was taking his time, seemed like all the time he damn well wanted, with Meadowlark. Sam's practice now was to stand with his back to them and glance over a shoulder once in a while. He couldn't stand to see Meadowlark looking happily up into Red Roan's face, maybe even adoringly. Every night when Red Roan walked away, Coy yipped a little to let Sam know.

Sam looked around at the lodge circle. Every tipi had a fire inside, and they glowed like lanterns in the midwinter darkness. Children were playing games in those tipis. Stories were being told. Women were beading moccasins, or other clothing. People were sitting close to the fire, or cozying between buffalo and elk robes. Sam stomped his feet hard.

A tap on the shoulder.

He made himself turn slowly, unbelieving. Yes, Red Roan.

The chief's son said slowly in the Crow language, as though speaking to a child, "You are training the horse. Good. Soon I teach the young men to shoot bow and arrow well. You want learn?" A big smile accompanied the invitation.

Sam thought how desperate he had been when he had only

eleven balls left for his rifle, how near he had come to star-vation. Though making arrows was laborious, going to the settlements for ammunition was harder.

This invitation seemed generous. "Yes."

Fear bit at his breath. Was this some trick?

"At the half moon," the big man padded away, light on his feet.

Sam stepped close to Meadowlark, wrapped in her blanket. Now he could forget about his feet. "I love you," he said. This was the way he began the courting each evening.

"I am glad to see you," she answered with a smile. She looked at him adoringly. Every night he tried to figure out whether this was the same look she gave Red Roan, but he never could.

He reached out and took the hands that held her blankets clasped. She squeezed his fingers, reached down, and picked up Coy. At about eight months the pup was getting big to pick up, though it seemed he was going to be a small coyote. Still, Meadowlark picked him up every evening. Sam wondered if that was her way of preventing him from embracing her, kissing her. He watched her nuzzle Coy with her face. Yes, she liked him. Sam had seen the delight on her face when this little animal responded well to Sam's commands. Crows didn't train their dogs like this, or pet them. She buried her nose in Coy's fur and rocked him. *Maybe she is avoiding holding hands with me.*

He told her about his day, what his progress was with Bell Rock and Blue Horse to train the medicine hat as a buffalo runner. He laughed at himself about the awful cold of the river. After a look of surprise—did Crow men confess weaknesses like this?—she laughed too.

Then he took a risk. "Red Roan offered to teach me, along with the other young men, how to shoot the bow and arrow well. Is he trying to fool me?"

"He's a good man," she said.

But there was something she wasn't saying.

"And . . . ?"

"I trust him." She smiled like a pixie. "He and Blue Dog are rivals, maybe a little. Red Roan is a war leader. My brother wants to be." After a moment she added, "My brother is a natural leader. Everyone has high hopes for him."

She gave him the news of her day. She was sewing elk teeth onto a dress. Sam knew it took a long time to collect enough of these rear teeth to decorate an entire dress. When she was finished with that, she would trim the yoke, sleeves and neckline with red wool strouding her mother had traded for. She gave Sam a look like, You're special because you brought this cloth to our village. The dress, altogether, would be very beautiful. She would save it for an important occasion, he knew. He hoped she would save it for the day she came to him and they set up their own lodge, together.

Coy mewled. Gray Hawk was sticking his head out of the lodge. "Time to come in," he told Meadowlark.

She gave Sam's hand a squeeze, set Coy down, and darted into the tipi.

Sam stood and looked at the sides of the lodge, shaped into flat planes by the poles. The fire was lower than half an hour ago. The family would sleep soon, and sleep warm, the parents in the robes at the back, the two daughters on the north side near the door.

Sam wished he had a family.

He strode out of the lodge circle, toward the quarters of the young men and the lodge of the trappers. There a fire would be waiting, and meat, and stories. Gideon, Beckwourth, and Third Wing were such storytellers that Sam could only listen, amazed.

He turned and looked again at the circle of relatives, peoples who made their lives together. The fires were low, making the lodges ghostly pyramids against the black night.

Again Sam wished he had a family.

* * *

THE GREAT MOMENT Bell Rock promised . . .

All right. Sam took a deep breath, or as deep as he could get, standing waist deep in this river. The cold made him want to scream.

Blue Horse held the medicine hat's reins. The friends grinned at each other, comrades in being foolish enough to get into this river in midwinter.

Bell Rock handed Sam the saddle pad and the saddle. The use of this saddle was Bell Rock's concession to Sam's being white. He arranged and smoothed the pad, taking his time. He set the saddle loosely on the medicine hat's back. No sense in hurrying when your next job is to . . . He just did it, as quick as he could. Ducked down into the water, grabbed the cinch, slid it through the double ring, pulled down hard.

Stand up! Out of the crush of the cold! He looked at Bell Rock, glad his teacher didn't know how poor the cinching job was.

He thought, bit his lip, ducked down again, and pulled the cinch tighter. The worst thing he could do, the first time on this horse, was to step in the stirrup and pull the saddle underneath her belly.

He gripped the saddle horn, stirruped the foot, and swung onto her back.

The mare stood still.

Maybe she rolled her eyes at Blue Horse, standing in front of her muzzle holding the reins. But she didn't buck. Couldn't, actually. He felt her quiver. He grinned madly. She was overloaded. The cold pummeling her senses. A man invading her back. And the deep water keeping her from doing what every instinct screamed for—to buck this man off.

He sat there, triumphant. He looked at the Wind River Mountains on the southwest, their snowy summits remote against a crystalline sky. He looked at the crazy jumble of red hills on the northeast, footstools of the Absaroka Mountains, strange, barren mazes. He grinned at Blue Horse, then at Bell Rock.

He swung down. The cold made his bones holler at him.

He stepped around to the mare's muzzle, looked her in the eye. He put a hand on the muzzle.

For the first time she didn't throw her head.

"Trade breath with her," Bell Rock said.

Sam looked up at him.

"Bend down, nose to nose. Let your breath go into her nostrils. Let her breath come into yours."

He did. Warm breath, warm muzzle—it was almost like kissing. He forced himself not to laugh. He looked into the mare's eyes. *Do we understand each other better, the breath and spirit of you in me, the breath and spirit of me in you?*

A memory seared him. The first night he dreamed of melding with the buffalo, the buffalo melding with him. One creature. "Samalo," he murmured then.

He stood back. Once more, now confident, he stirruped the foot and swung up. She quivered less this time. Once more he surveyed the world from horseback. Then he swung down and waded fast out of the water.

His lungs quit squeezing against the cold. He breathed normally for the first time in long minutes. "Enough," he said to Blue Horse, and his friend brought the mare up.

Coy ran up and jumped on him until Sam petted the pup.

Getting on was achievement enough for Sam this morning. He would give her sweet cottonwood bark now, a thank-you.

"Let's go get warm, Coy. Let's stand by the fire." He wanted to fill both their bellies with meat and the hot liquid it floated in.

"YOU CONDUCT THE sweat lodge ceremony?" Sam asked Bell Rock. They sat behind the center fire of Sam's lodge, dipping meat from the pot. It was their custom, the three of them, to lunch together after the morning's training session.

"Yes."

"What does it do?"

Bell Rock looked away and slowly put out some words.

"The sweat lodge is the womb, our mother. We go inside and invite the powers to come, the four directions, Mother Earth, Father Sky. . . . Whoever is in the lodge with me, he maybe asks them for something. He asks for help for his family and his people, that they have good lives. If someone's sick, he asks for healing. He's uncertain, he asks what to do. He has a problem, he asks for guidance. If he's a young man, he asks for a vision, then he goes on the mountain and looks for it."

Bell Rock looked into the pot for a moment, like he saw something other than meat in its rich juices.

Sam blurted out, "I had a dream. Will you help me understand it?"

Bell Rock said gently, "You ask me? Why not ask other beaver men?"

Sam felt like his tongue was lashed to a post. He stammered three or four times before he got out any words. "Hannibal McKye. My friend. Six months ago on the banks of the Missouri River. I told Hannibal my dream of . . . this buffalo." He started to say something about the mystic buffalo, but some sense said *no—keep it for the sweat lodge.*

"Hannibal's the only person I ever told. Hannibal said, 'Do a sweat lodge, tell a medicine man.' "

Sam looked at Bell Rock and Blue Horse. He reached for Coy and slid the pup onto his lap.

"Tell me more."

Now Sam must descend into a morass, or was it ascending into realms of fantasy? The Missouri River was within Bell Rock's ken, but Dartmouth College, a school founded in New England to teach Indians? Latin and Greek?

He blundered forward. "Hannibal McKye is an important man in my life. He's the son—it's hard even for me to believe it—of a man who teaches languages at a school for Indians, that man and one of his students, a Delaware woman. Delawares are Indians who live a hundred sleeps away, near the water-everywhere to the east. Hannibal reads a lot of languages, but he hunts and tracks and wears hides like any Indian. He *is* an Indian. And a white man, all at once. I met him by accident, it was like he was an angel." On top of what must already mystify Bell Rock, "angel" wouldn't do. "A spirit messenger." Sam spread his hands in futility. "He said, 'Do a sweat lodge, tell a medicine man.' "

Bell Rock waited, looking into Sam's eyes, maybe hunting for something. "You ask me for a sweat lodge, I do it as a gift."

"Ordinarily," said Blue Horse, "you give a medicine man a horse in return for this ceremony." Blue Horse's way was always to be a little formal and do things entirely the right way.

"As a gift," Bell Rock repeated, "I help you with your dream."

BELL ROCK UNTIED the thong that held his breechcloth up, and it dropped. He stepped out of the last of his garments, his moccasins. He and Blue Horse looked expectantly at Sam.

"It's ready. Go in, crawl sunwise around the lodge, and sit by the door." Bell Rock made a clockwise circle with his hand to indicate the way Sam should go.

As Sam slipped out of his hide trousers, a flash of memory hit him. When he had first been naked with a woman, Katherine, now his brother's wife, he had flushed with embarrassment. She laughed at how his pink skin looked against his white hair.

He knew he was flushing now. Off with the shirt, off with the moccasins, stand naked in the February cold. He shivered in one big jerk. It wasn't just the cold, but what was coming—or maybe the fact that he had no idea what was coming. He studied the lodge, which looked a bowl turned upside down. The inside would be low and dark, room only to sit or crouch. And it would be very, very dark.

That feeling lightninged. Once in a while it came up—*I'm living among an alien people. One day will they . . . ?* It always gave him a flicker of panic.

What was really going to happen behind that lodge door?

Blackness, chanting, strangeness, maybe a kind of madness. From here he could see the lava rocks in the hole in the center. Some spots glowed faintly red, like a warning. He knew Bell Rock would pour water on them and make steam. He had heard it got really hot.

"Your dream is waiting for you," said Bell Rock.

Sam sucked in his breath, thought of the buffalo, dipped low, and went.

The lodge was pleasantly warm. He crawled to the spot instructed and sat. Close to the lava rocks, his shins felt half ready to blister.

Bell Rock slipped in and sat on the other side of the door.

Coy yipped, and Sam saw Blue Horse grab him and pull him back. "No dogs in the lodge," Blue Horse shouted in English. Bell Rock grinned and called out, "Might as well talk to him in Crow—he speaks both the same!" Sam laughed and felt better.

Blue Horse handed in a bucket and dipper.

Sam smiled wryly. The bucket—at least there was something white-man in this place.

"Wet your hair if you want," said Bell Rock. He dipped his hands in the bucket and slicked his own with the water. Sam followed suit.

"Close the door," called Bell Rock. Blue Horse did. Bell Rock told him where to tuck it at the bottom. In moments the sweat lodge was as dark a place as Sam could remember. He couldn't see his own knees. "Now I'm throwing cedar on the rocks," Bell Rock said.

A sharp smell hit Sam's nostrils, pungent but good.

"First I'm going to warm up the lodge." Sam heard a faint splash of water and then a big *h-i-s-s-s*. Steam ate at his nostrils.

"I'm going to pour four rounds," said Bell Rock. "Four pours the first round, seven the second, ten the third, and the fourth uncounted." Sam wasn't sure what he meant by "pours." Dipperfuls?

"This is your first time. You may get uncomfortable. If you do, put your head down on the ground. It will be cooler there. If you get really uncomfortable, put your nose in the corner, where the lodge cover meets the ground. Try it."

Sam did. Right there the air was almost cold.

"Now you know you can take care of yourself."

H-i-s-s-s! A roar came from the rocks. Steam erupted around Sam's face and chest, almost scalding. He forced himself to stay upright.

Bell Rock began to pray. Sam couldn't remember most of the prayer later. He knew Bell Rock called to each of the four directions and invited them into the lodge.

H-i-s-s-s! Sam thought, *I don't know if I can stand this.* He told himself he had to stand it. If he embarrassed himself, everyone would hear about it, Meadowlark included. The feeling of being closed in was oppressive, maybe worse than the heat.

Bell Rock asked blessings on various groups of people, the unborn, the young, the mothers, the old—Sam didn't remember all of the ones the medicine man made supplications for.

H-i-s-s-s! Sam flopped sideways and put his nose to the ground. *I'm not going to make it.*

Later he remembered nothing of what Bell Rock said after this third pour.

When the lodge felt a little less hot, Sam sat up again. He was glad Bell Rock couldn't see him in the darkness.

Finally Bell Rock called out to Blue Horse, "Take the covers off."

A blazing shaft of light shocked Sam's eyes. After a moment, as the buffalo robes slid off the willow framework and onto the ground, the steam rose to the sky. Cool, delicious air curled into the lodge.

Blue Horse brought water, and Bell Rock and Sam drank, murmuring thank-yous to the powers.

When they had drunk enough—actually, Sam could have sucked down gallons of water—Blue Rock put the robes back on. Little by little, Sam returned in body and mind to the darkness, and the fear.

H-i-s-s-s! This time Bell Rock spoke a long prayer. In the intense heat, and maybe his worry, Sam's mind failed him. The Crow language suddenly sounded alien to him, and he didn't understand what Bell Rock was saying. He tried to count the number of times the medicine man dipped into the bucket and poured. Somehow by his count there were not seven pours as promised but ten or eleven. By a fierce act of will he kept himself upright until Bell Rock cried out for Blue Horse to remove the covers.

When Sam and the medicine man had cooled off, Blue Horse ceremoniously brought Bell Rock his sacred pipe, filled with tobacco and a plug of sage on top. This pipe wasn't like the ones Sam had seen before. Instead of red, its bowl was of black stone, and carved into the shaggy shape of a buffalo. The stem did not have elaborate decorations, like feathers or brass studs, but was unadorned. Sam was glad it was a buffalo pipe.

Then Bell Rock stunned Sam. He reached into the fire, picked up a red-hot coal with his bare fingers, and without hurry dropped it onto the tobacco in the bowl. He sucked, let a cloud of thick smoke float out, and with one hand brushed it onto his head. Then he lifted the pipe skyward and began to pray:

"I offer this smoke to the east, where things begin." After each direction he drew on the pipe and blew the smoke out. By turn, going sunwise, he invoked the south, the west, the north.

Again he held the pipe high and touched it to the ground, to one of the lava rocks. "Sun, we make this sweat lodge for you. We seek your great power, to see many things. Great mountains, rivers great and small, I offer you this smoke. Beings above, beings in the ground, I offer you this smoke. Earth, I offer you this smoke, and I offer smoke to the willows. I ask you to let us see the next time when the leaves come out, when they are fully grown, when they turn yellow, and when they fall—may we see each of these seasons again and again for many snows. I ask that wherever we go we may find things to eat that are fat. Wherever we go, may we blacken our faces." Sam knew that the Crows rubbed charcoal onto their faces to declare victory in battle. "Wherever we go, may the winds blow toward us." Sam guessed this was so the game would not smell the hunter.

"Today a young man lays before you what he saw in a dream. He cries for your help in understanding it—he cries for your help."

Now Bell Rock turned the pipe in a full circle and handed it to Sam. "Hold the pipe up," he said, "then touch it to the earth. When you're ready, cry out for the help of Sun in understanding your dream."

Sam did exactly as he was told. He raised the pipe to the infinite sky. He touched it to Mother Earth. He didn't know whether he believed in what he was doing, and was even unsure what believing might mean. Then he pointed his arms and the pipe directly to the sky and declared loudly, "Sun, I cry out for your help!" Amazingly, his voice broke.

His mind leapt in and interfered. *At least you're praying to something real,* it said, *the sun is real.*

Be quiet, he told his mind, *and let me do my work.* He threw his head far back now, far enough that the low winter sun struck his face fully, and ran down his chest. He thrust the pipe back over his head. "Sun, I cry out for your help!" His voice broke, but that was no longer amazing.

"Offer the sun some smoke," Bell Rock said quietly.

Sam did, and watched in intent silence as the smoke rose through the branches of the lodge and evaporated into the blue, blue sky. Pictures from his dream rose into his mind, sharp and clear. He focused on them.

When Sam finished smoking, Bell Rock said, "Put the covers back on."

Blue Horse did, and Bell Rock began the third round, the round of ten pours. This time he sang a song, a song that sounded extravagantly emotional, plaintive. Sam held the pictures of his dream in his mind, his attention entirely on them. He did pick up one phrase of the prayer several times—"Take pity on us."

This time Sam felt no need to lie down and reduce the heat. He lived in his dream.

"Take the covers off!"

This time Blue ripped them off with a big whisk, and cool air rolled onto Sam like spring rain.

When they had drunk some water, Bell Rock said, "Now tell me what you saw of the spirit world."

At this Blue Horse considerately walked out of hearing.

For a moment Sam was taken aback by these words, and couldn't speak. Then he brought himself back to the task at hand. He told his dream, and what led up to it.

"Before the dream, I was caught in a prairie fire. No way out—I was going to die. The animals all around me were fleeing toward the river, deer, coyotes, rabbits, mice, buffalo, everything. But the fire was on us, and they were being eaten.

"A coyote pup, the one right outside this lodge, came scrabbling desperately for a place to hide. There was a buffalo cow I'd just shot and gutted out. The pup scratched at its slit belly, trying to get inside. Just as desperate, I took the lesson and crawled inside the cow, dragging the pup with me. That saved us. When I saw the scorched land afterwards, I knew that almost all the other four-leggeds died, and whatever two-leggeds were in the path.

"A few days later I dreamed. I saw a buffalo cow laying on her side, and somehow she looked like she was waiting for me. She wasn't the same cow, though. This cow was whole, healthy, waiting for me. What she wanted, I couldn't tell. There was something special about her but I didn't know what it was. I was simply drawn to her, powerfully drawn.

"So, without knowing why, I laid down next to her in the dream, my back to her belly. Then it happened. I passed through her flesh into the center of her. Not just her middle, the center of everything she was.

"I began to change, or we began to change. I became her or she became me, I didn't know which. My hair turned into her fur. My arms reached up, my legs stretched down. I moved into her forelegs and her hind legs—my bones knitted into hers."

Sam looked at Bell Rock to see if the medicine man was laughing at him. Bell Rock showed no expression but high and grave attentiveness.

"My muscles, they joined up with hers. My belly swallowed her food. Then the amazing part. My heart pumped in the same rhythm as hers, and then my heartbeat was her heartbeat, not two sounding as one, but one beat, just one. Her blood was my blood. When I breathed, I smelled buffalo breath in my own nostrils."

He gazed into Bell Rock's eyes, and he could not have said what passed between the two of them.

"Then I stood up from the buffalo cow, except I wasn't just me. I was us. I looked around the world and wanted to set forth into it, ramble around, and I was man and buffalo.

"I woke up. I hugged Coy close. And I said something. 'I am Samalo.'"

"Samalo?" It was the first question Bell Rock had asked.

"My name, Sam, combined with the word for buffalo in English. Samalo."

Bell Rock nodded. He sat, saying nothing, his eyes far off. After what seemed a long while, he said, "Blue Horse, bring us some more hot rocks and put the covers back on."

The fourth round, the round of uncounted pours, went on forever. Bell Rock lifted an impassioned plea to Sun, more chanted than spoken. Sam's mind drifted into a netherworld. It felt lost, like it was floating on the steam he couldn't see, swirling this way and that without knowable reason. Part of his mind was moved, maybe, by the Crow words and phrases—*"Take pity on this young man, grant him . . . Heed our cries. . . . Send us . . . Reveal to us. . . ."*

The heat came at him in waves, and he refused to lie down. A big part of mind was occupied with enduring. He told himself repeatedly that he was making this sacrifice of pain in exchange for a blessing to the spirit. And part of his mind was pleading, *Let it end, let it be over.*

"Take off the covers," yelled Bell Rock.

Blue Horse was quick about it, maybe knowing how it felt. The air felt as good as ice in the mouth on a hot day. Sam got a picture of himself cannonballing into the deep spot in the freezing river, and loved it.

They drank. Now Sam had lost his embarrassment, and poured four or five dipperfuls into his belly.

Once more Bell Rock called for the sacred pipe, and they smoked.

When they were finished, the medicine man asked, "What do you understand from this dream?"

"Nothing," Sam blurted out. Then he corrected himself. "I guess it means the buffalo are important to me. Maybe my connection to the buffalo, or animals in general, is important to me."

Bell Rock waited.

Sam had nothing more to say.

Finally Bell Rock spoke. "There's a lot for you to learn here. Maybe I can guide you a little. But mainly I can help you arrive at it yourself.

"You're right, the buffalo are important to you. The powers have sent you a messenger that took the form of the buffalo. Only you can really understand what the messenger is telling you. I can point out some directions, but really it's up to you.

"From now on you should watch the buffalo for what they might be able to teach you. Watch for spirit messengers in the form of buffalo cows, yes, but also observe all ordinary buffalo. Study them, see what they do. Observe the wisdom of their everyday ways.

"Since you're a man, watch the bulls and what they do. For example, when they fight, the bulls are not quick, they're big and heavy, but they never flee. A bull will fight until he wins, or he will fight until he is defeated. But one thing he won't do—run away. You should think, maybe, whether that's the way you ought to conduct yourself when you go into battle.

"Remember, always look for buffalo cows that might really be messengers. If they are, listen with your heart open.

"Also watch the eagles. Eagles often bring messages from Sun."

Though all this seemed overwhelming to Sam, he repeated the words in his mind and held on to them carefully.

"Understand, the buffalo cow was sent to guide you. Animals are often people's guides. Most Crow men, almost all of us, have seen an animal in a vision, and those are our guides, our medicine. Probably every man wears something in tribute to his guide, a claw, or tooth, or feather, maybe. Or he paints something on his body. Perhaps you should think of doing something like that. Some men who dream of buffalo make hats out of buffalo hide and horns.

"Sometimes picture in your mind the buffalo cow of your dream. Ask her questions—maybe she will answer. Ask her for help. Listen to her without asking questions. Invite her to come to you, and just watch the way she comes, how she walks—sometimes there's a message there. Pay attention to whatever feelings you get, and whatever words surround them. Lots of times these messages are little feathery things, made of almost nothing, like the seeds that float down from the cottonwood trees. But like these seeds, the wispy messages sometimes bear great fruit.

"Return to this dream again and again in your mind. Don't grill it, like an attack. Hold it gently. Feel it. Listen to it. See if, over the years, it has messages you haven't understood yet."

Bell Rock waited and thought. "Anything else you want to ask about right now?"

"I dream about snakes, too."

"What about them?"

"I'm bad afraid of them."

Bell Rock smiled. "We'll leave that for another sweat, another time."

Bell Rock waited a while and then went on. "I think your

connection to all animals is important. You should pay attention to that. I study you white men, and I see beliefs that are strange to me. For example, you seem to see yourselves as apart from the animals, made separate in some way. You even think you are supposed to dominate the animals. You treat them as things to use, like a hatchet or a knife.

"We Crows see it differently. We think the buffalo and all the four-leggeds have their ways, which we must honor. The two-leggeds, we have our ways, but we are not the owners of everything. Maybe you think about that some."

Bell Rock waited. "We also think each animal has something to teach us. Maybe you think about that. The buffalo has something to teach you. So does the snake."

"I don't know if I can remember all this," said Sam.

"You'll remember what you need to know now," said Bell Rock. "One thing you haven't mentioned. You are male, the buffalo female. Maybe in some way you joined with the female in that dream, or maybe you should look for ways to include the female in your life path. I don't know how this might work."

Sam nodded. The female part, it seemed like too much.

"I come back, though, to the two most important things. Whatever message this buffalo brought you, only you can know it. Maybe you won't know it in words, maybe just something you feel in your heart. That's good.

"Also, use the buffalo cow as your helper. Ask for her guidance. Listen to what she says.

"Anything else you want to ask me?"

Sam didn't dare.

"Now comes a good part. You need a new name. You are not the same fellow as before your dream.

"A Crow man gets a new name when he does something worthwhile. Maybe when he gets a war honor, or does something else big."

Sam was excited.

"Let's go to my tipi."

When they crawled out of the sweat lodge, Coy bounded

all over Sam. "How did Blue Horse make you behave so well?" Sam cooed, rubbing the pup's head vigorously. "How did he get you to act good?"

At the tipi Bell Rock painted Sam's face red on the right side, blue on the left, the colors split right down the nose. "This will give you power," he said. "You must wear this paint tonight as a sign to all that you intend to do something. That will be to kill a buffalo cow from horseback and give the meat and the robe to old people who are poor and need it. When you have done this, I will give you a new name."

"All right," said Sam. He wanted to get to the river and look at his new, painted visage in the water.

Then he had an impulse. He said eagerly, "I'll kill a buffalo from the back of the medicine hat." Almost the moment the words were out, he was sorry. *Ahead of myself as always,* he thought. *I can't even ride the medicine hat.*

Chapter Nine

Sam kept working with the medicine hat in the mornings and standing with Meadowlark by her lodge at night.

The mare progressed. After letting Sam sit on her in deep water, one morning she stepped gingerly out of the freezing river with him on her back—he just whacked her lightly with one hand on the rump and out she went. There she stood on the riverbank sand, looking around nervously, uncertain what to do when a human being sat astride her. Sam wanted to let out a war whoop, but didn't dare.

Coy darted up and nipped at the mare's heels.

Sam landed *ker-plop!* in the river. O-o-w! He wished he'd come down in deep water. He stood up rubbing his bottom.

Now Blue Horse had Coy tucked under one arm. Bell Rock held the mare by the lead rope. "Lucky she didn't get away," he said. "Get back on."

Sam made a wry face and led the mare back into the deep water.

"Calm, easy," said Bell Rock.

Holding the lead rope again the horn, Sam swung back into the saddle. He let the mare just stand for a long moment. Then he tapped her rump with a hand, and she walked gingerly out of the river.

Man and horse shivered in the down-canyon wind.

"Slip down off her," said Bell Rock, "and get right back up." Sam did. The mare stood still, bewildered.

"Slip down."

They stopped worked for the morning. Sam was excited.

He made a little progress with Meadowlark, too. Every evening Sam waited for Red Roan to finish romancing her. Even when Sam went early, cutting his own supper short, Meadowlark stayed in the tipi until Red Roan arrived and stepped quickly to him, barely flicking her eyes in Sam's direction. Sometimes Coy barked, like he was trying to get her attention. More likely, Sam thought, he was protesting standing out in the cold while two men flirted with Meadowlark. Coyotes didn't fool around with flirting, he was sure of that.

This evening the wait was even longer than usual. At last Sam took his turn. They stood wrapped in a single blanket, and Meadowlark let him hold her hand. They gave each other the news of the day. They smiled moonily. They looked at the snowy peaks to the west and watched the evening star rise above them. Meadowlark pointed out what she called the Seven Stars, which Sam knew by the name Seven Sisters. She told him how the Seven Stars gave her grandfather an arrow bundle, and now her father was the keeper of that sacred bundle.

Though Sam was puzzled at what a sacred arrow bundle might be, he gave her his mother's story about the same stars. They were seven sisters, all but one in love with gods. The one who loved a mortal was embarrassed, and because of her mortification was the dimmest of the seven. Meadowlark liked this story. Sam liked realizing that his culture had fanciful tales to explain things, just like hers.

"Coy," he said to the coyote pup near his feet, "talk." This was a trick he'd been working on for a week.

Coy sat up on his haunches and raised his head to the night sky. *"Ow-o-o-o-o-o!"* he howled. *"Ow-o-o-o-o-o!"*

Dogs all over camp set up a howl. Angry exclamations came out of tipis.

Sam and Meadowlark looked into each other's eyes, giggling.

"When the Seven Sisters rise at dawn," Sam added, "that's in the spring, they're telling us it's time to plant the crops."

Then he had to explain what crops were, more than a little tobacco planted along the river, and how white people grew their food instead of hunting it.

Meadowlark said, "White people are full of wonders."

Awkward pause. Sam knew she meant her words and was also trying to be nice.

"I couldn't live white ways myself. They're *too* strange."

The two lovers broke into giggles. Gray Hawk coughed loudly in the lodge, Meadowlark's signal to go inside for the night.

She squeezed his hands and disappeared.

He and Meadowlark were not lovers, of course. As Sam neared his lodge, he felt grumpy. Here came another night of listening to the amorous adventures of his buddies. Gideon, Beckwourth, and even the Pawnee Third Wing apparently had no trouble getting mates regularly for little trips to the willows, and they enjoyed torturing Sam with endless recountings while the center fire died down, night after night.

It was clear that the Crows saw no particular virtue in chastity. Men chased whatever woman they had a yearning for, and that was regarded as natural, what a male of any species does. Women were less obvious about their adventures, but the beaver men soon learned that various married women had boyfriends. Their husbands disdained to notice, as jealousy was supposed to be beneath their dignity. And even more women would take a lover for an hour, especially if enticed with a string of beads.

Sam ducked through the lodge door and discovered, to his relief, that his lodgemates were all asleep. He stripped and crawled beneath his own blankets and on top of two buffalo robes. Coy was already curled where Sam put his bare feet.

The next morning, though, Gideon, Beckwourth, and Third Wing made their stories ricochet around the lodge again. While Sam built the morning fire to take the chill off, they lay in their blankets and traded stories of adventures among the willows. The way Third Wing told it, he pleasured a young woman named Muskrat every evening. Sam pretended not to hear.

"Hand me the *charqui*," Gideon said. He made it sound like a mock order.

Ignoring his tone, Sam picked up the parfleche box of dried meat and handed it to Gideon.

"Me too," said Third Wing.

"Me too," said Beckwourth.

Sam gave all of them a look, but handed the box from bedroll to bedroll. When Coy mewled, Sam gave him some meat too.

Third Wing took out a dried stick and held it stuck out from his groin. "Oh, Muskrat, Muskrat," he cooed.

Beckwourth did the same, crying "Oh, Sweetheart, oh, Sweetheart."

Suddenly Gideon stopped the laughter with a loud, "Sam needs a woman."

"That's right," said Third Wing.

"Damn right," said Beckwourth.

"Enough!" Sam growled.

"No, I mean it," Gideon went on. "You need to take a woman to the willows. If you don't, the Crows are going to think you're a weakling."

Sam ducked out of the lodge and came back with an armload of aspen for the fire.

"You need to think on this," said Beckwourth.

"Think on getting jollied in the willows," said Gideon.

"You're afraid it would make Meadowlark mad," Third Wing said.

"Actually, it would make her respect you," Gideon said.

"When in Rome," said Beckwourth.

"Half of the men are married to two women," Third Wing said.

"Makes you more of a man."

"Shut up," said Sam. The truth was, he'd made a resolution not to touch any woman until he got Meadowlark. Why, he couldn't have said. But he wanted it that way.

Scratch-scra-a-a-tch!

The beaver men looked at each other. They couldn't remember when anyone had scratched at their lodge flap, which was the Crow way of knocking on the door.

Sam called, "Come in."

A shadow darkened the entrance. Then the big form of Red Roan loomed, and Sam saw he was smiling.

"You want to learn the bow and arrow?" These words in Crow were aimed at Sam.

"Sure."

"Come at midday, over by the big yellow boulders." He motioned to the southwest. Sam knew the place.

"Good."

SAM AND COY walked toward the big yellow boulders in good spirits. A week or two ago, when Red Roan first mentioned working on bow and arrow, Sam gave Blue Horse a butchering knife to make him a good bow. Though Blue Horse was only twenty-two winters, everyone agreed he had a knack for making bows. At the same time Sam made a dozen arrows in the slow, meticulous way Blue Horse taught him last winter. He had to throw away several, but the dozen left were good. When he showed Blue Horse the arrows, Sam asked why Red Roan would help him with his archery. "He's a good man," Blue Horse said, "and he must teach his sisters' sons to shoot the bow and arrow."

Sam was sorry Blue Horse, who'd gone hunting, wouldn't get to see this new bow shoot.

On a flat area in front of the big yellow boulders, Red Roan, Blue Horse's younger brother, Flat Dog, and five twelve- or fourteen-year-old boys were shooting arrows at a target of grasses tied together with rawhide. They stopped immediately. "Time for our game," said Red Roan.

"Who wants the white man?" teased the biggest kid. "He won't be able to hit anything."

Sam gave the kid a look and got nothing but impudence back.

"This one is called Stripe," said Red Roan. "He has no manners." Red Roan gave Sam the names of the others. Sam knew Little Bull, the youngest brother of Meadowlark and Blue Horse, but he felt frozen in his brain and couldn't remember the others' names.

"We're going to play a game, rolling the buffalo chip," said Red Roan. He picked up a chip off the ground, an ancient one, very dry. A hole about the size of a boy's fist had been punched in it and in a stack of others nearby. "It's a simple game. I roll the chip across in front, and you boys shoot at the hole."

"The hole," Sam muttered in English. He also found it odd, at twenty, to be included as one of the boys.

Red Roan rolled a chip as a demonstration. Stripe pantomimed taking a shot at it.

Coy pranced forward and grabbed the chip in his mouth.

"Coy, no," called Sam in English. The pup looked back, chip poking out of his mouth.

"Coy, come."

The pup did.

Sam took the chip and handed it to Red Roan.

"Sit," he said.

The pup did.

"Stay put," Sam said.

"What did you say to him?" asked Flat Dog in Crow.

"I said no, uh, come, sit, and stay there."

"In your language?"

"Sure."

"Would dogs do that?"

Flat Dog had a face that looked put together out of mismatched pieces and a half smile that said everything in life is funny.

"Yeah."

"If you told them in Crow?"

"Yeah."

"What if you told the coyote in Crow?"

"No, he learned in English."

"The game," Red Roan interrupted. "If you miss, you let your arrow lie. If you hit the chip, you get your arrow back, but you don't get anyone else's arrows. If you put an arrow through the hole, you get to pick up all the arrows on the ground."

Sam nodded that he understood. "I probably can't hit a moving chip," he said.

The boys all looked at each other and nodded, like "We know."

"First we divide into teams."

Uh-oh, Sam thought, *bad news.*

"The game's over when one team gets all the arrows."

"And they keep them?" asked Sam.

"Sure," said Stripe, like "What do you think?"

"So Stripe and Little Bull, you choose sides," said Red Roan.

"I don't play," said Flat Dog softly to Sam. "Too old."

"Stripe, go first," said Red Roan.

"Beaver," said Stripe. A youngster as wide as he was short went to stand by Stripe.

"Straight Arm," said Little Bull immediately. He was a skinny kid with an angry face.

Stripe looked lingeringly over the faces of the two players remaining. He had a superior smile. *I'm going to be the last one chosen,* Sam told himself, and it made his gut ache. "I choose Spotted Rabbit." This was the youngest-looking kid, with a big smile and baby fat still in his face.

"You belong to the other team," Stripe told Sam. He flashed a giant smile that made Sam sick. "White man."

"My name is Sam," he said.

Coy whimpered.

"Sam," Stripe repeated softly, almost laughing. He gestured for Sam to stand by Little Bull.

Sam looked at Flat Dog, hideously embarrassed. He was willing to bet any of these boys could outshoot him. And he was older even than Flat Dog.

The two teams faced each other.

"Sorry you were last," said Flat Dog quietly.

Sam tried to shrug nonchalantly.

"The truth is," Flat Dog said, "no one wants to lose his arrows."

Sam was beginning to catch on, and he didn't like the setup one bit.

Red Roan put a stop to their talking with, "Who wants to go first?"

Stripe said, "Go ahead, show us what you can do, white man."

Sam ignored the gibe and took a shooting stance. About twenty steps away, very carefully, Red Roan rolled the chip across his front, giving it a good thrust so it wouldn't curl off one way or the other.

Sam let the arrow go, and his heart jumped up.

No, a miss. The arrow slipped by just behind. He felt good at coming so close.

Beaver shot first for the other team and put the arrow right through the hole. The chip spun a little on the arrow and stood up, pinned. Beaver collected Sam's arrow, and his own, without even a glance at Sam.

"That's all right, white man," said Stripe, "you have plenty of arrows to lose."

Then Sam noticed that the other players had only six or eight arrows each. "My name's Sam," he said.

Stripe flipped him an indolent smile and walked off without a word.

"Nephew," said Red Roan, "treat our guest respectfully." But the two grinned at each other.

"Should we have everyone start with the same number of arrows?" Little Bull asked.

"No," said Stripe, "the white man will need all he's got."

Straight Arm shot and ticked the edge of the chip, knocking it over. Red Roan tossed his arrow back.

Spotted Rabbit shot, a clean miss.

Little Bull hit the chip and knocked it into fragments. He collected his arrow.

"Are you ready, Stripe?"

Stripe nodded his head yes. Red Roan hurled a chip fast across the flat ground. Stripe nailed it with a perfect shot. He strode forward in a silky way to get his arrow and Spotted Rabbit's, no swagger but lots of feline arrogance.

Stripe hurled the arrow of Sam's captured by Beaver into the ground point first. "First round finished, your side loses one arrow," he said. "Come on, fellows, we have to get their arrows quicker than that."

Red Roan said, "Get us started again, white man."

"My name is Sam."

But he got into position to shoot. This time his arrow sailed a little sideways, but it knocked the chip down. When Red Roan flipped him the arrow, Sam breathed a sigh of relief.

Altogether in the second round, no one lost any arrows, and no one gained any.

The third round, though, was a disaster. The first five players missed, and Stripe hit, winning all five arrows. "Lucky for you we're on the same side," he said to his teammates. "Go to it, white man."

"My name's Sam," said Sam.

"What is a 'sam' in your language?" said Flat Dog.

Red Roan looked at Sam curiously.

Sam saw his chance. "He was a hero. His name means 'chosen of. . . .' Sam had to hesitate. His mother had said "chosen of God." In the Crow way of seeing things, the Creator was Old Man Coyote; but the supreme deity seemed to be Sun. Sam let it go. "Chosen of Sun."

"What did Sam do?" Spotted Rabbit was really interested.

"Sun revealed to him who should be chief of the Israelites, a man named Saul, so Sam anointed Saul as chief. Later, even though Sam was dead, he came back and charged Saul with failing to follow holy law."

"After he was dead?"

Sam nodded yes.

Spotted Rabbit's eyes grew very round. Little Bull looked impressed, too.

Sam said, "My culture has traditional and fanciful hero stories, just like yours does."

"Very good," said Stripe, and then he deliberately added, "May we win some more of your arrows now? White man?"

Later, when the last arrow was painfully extracted, Stripe said casually, "Thanks for the game, No Arrows."

Sam understood how complete his humiliation was when, in front of Meadowlark's tipi that night, Red Roan left with the words, "Good night, No Arrows."

Sam took his place next to Meadowlark and started to tell her about the game.

"Everyone has heard your new name," she said stiffly.

That night she cut their conversation very short.

THE NEXT TWO weeks Sam simmered. A number of Crows—far too many—called him by the name No Arrows. All he could do was ignore them. He spent all his physical energy on training the medicine hat, and all his emotional energy yearning for the moment Bell Rock would give him a new name. Nothing less would end the humiliation.

Every night he stood outside Meadowlark's lodge while she and Red Roan courted. When the chief's son walked away, Sam turned his back and refused to notice him. It was a piddling gesture, but all he could do. Once he heard Red Roan chuckle as he walked away.

Meadowlark seemed to cut their evening talks shorter and shorter.

Sam waited as a burning, spewing fuse waits.

Every day, all day, he trained the mare. He taught her to accept the improvised rope bridle easily, hand-feeding her sweet cottonwood bark each time she cooperated. And slowly he taught her to neck rein.

This was the crucial step. Feel the left rein on your neck, turn right. Feel the right rein on your neck, turn left. Part of it was also leg pressure. He moved his right leg forward and let her feel the pressure when she turned left, the opposite when she turned right. Eventually, she would respond to the pressure of the knees alone, leaving both of his hands free. Then she would be a buffalo horse.

He got to know her. He learned the feel of her back. He got to know when she was about to shy, or crow-hop, or do anything unexpected. He learned when she was tense and when relaxed. He got to where he knew her moods through her flesh.

One afternoon when Sam was cooling the mare down, Blue Horse asked, "Why are you in such a hurry with this horse?"

"I'm going to hunt my buffalo from her."

"You could use your other mare," said Bell Rock.

Sam said stiffly, "I'm going to hunt buffalo on this mare. I'm going to get a cow and give the meat and the hide to old people who need them." He looked hard at Bell Rock. This was the task the medicine man had assigned him.

"Then you'll earn a new name," Bell Rock said.

After she was neck-reining reasonably well, Sam tried her at different gaits. A cluck and a heel boosted her up to a trot, another cluck and heel to a lope, and yet another to a gallop. Sam found the rocking balance for her lope, and the forward balance for the gallop.

She learned to respond quickly to the feel of the bridle bringing her head back, slowing down, stopping.

After two weeks Sam showed Gideon. The mare responded quickly to all instructions from Sam's hands and legs. "She's a nice saddle horse," said Gideon.

"Not finished out," said Sam.

"A long way from a buffalo horse," said Bell Rock.

Sam knew that.

"Let's see what speed she has," said Blue Horse.

Sam, Blue Horse, and Flat Dog rode upstream to a nice, big flat. There they raced the three mounts all out. Flat Dog edged out Blue Horse, and Sam was a horse length behind.

"Let me ride her," said Flat Dog. He showed the funny, half-smile his face always wore.

Sam hesitated. No rider but him had ever been on her back. Then he swung down and held the reins while Flat Dog mounted.

The three raced back the other way along the flat. The medicine hat won by a horse's length.

"You need a little better balance when she's running all out," said Flat Dog.

"It will come," said Blue Horse.

Sam reminded himself that they had ridden even as children, and he'd essentially started a year and a half ago.

That evening the scouts brought in a report. A small herd of buffalo was ten miles down the valley.

Chapter Ten

The next morning the Wind River valley was a swamp of fog, the cottonwoods along the river hazy, dark lines, the peaks on both sides lost in the gray swirl.

Sam woke up irritable. First he'd sat up listening to four medicine men sing for the success of the hunt. Then he had to watch while they chose Red Roan as the leader of the hunt.

One man of medicine had seen the herd in a dream and told the scouts where to look. That medicine man picked Red Roan as the leader—he'd been successful in the past.

After the singing, Sam lay sleepless in the lodge, or had wild, chaotic dreams when he did drift off. But he forced himself—got the medicine hat saddled, pulled her picket pin, and led her to where the hunters and their women were assembling. After the men killed, the women would butcher.

When he appeared, some hunters suppressed mocking smiles. Others threw worried glances at the medicine hat.

Sam knew a bad horse, one who stumbled in the middle of a rampaging herd, or got gored, could kill his rider, and maybe get riders behind him killed.

Sam reached up and rubbed the mare's black hat and ears—she always liked that. He looked down at Coy and said, "Good pup, good pup." The little coyote now had sense enough to stay out from under the horses' hooves.

Bell Rock and his wife rode up beside Sam. The medicine man just nodded at him. No words were necessary. Both knew what Sam was taking on was dangerous. And both knew there was no way Sam wouldn't ride her on this hunt.

Blue Medicine Horse and Flat Dog slipped their mounts in next to him. Sam understood that their smiles were meant to be encouraging, and he appreciated that.

Stripe edged up and gave Sam an ironic smile.

Sam had a strong sense of foreboding. A message thumped in his chest like his heartbeat: *This is not a day for good things to happen.*

Gideon, Beckwourth, and Third Wing eased their horses in behind Sam. "Good day to hunt," Gideon said.

Sam resisted shaking his head no. Maybe a bad day for a lot of things, but he didn't care. No telling when another chance to run buffalo would come. Maybe next week, or maybe not until summer, when he got back from the spring trapping season. He couldn't take a chance on being No Arrows that long. He was about to lose Meadowlark even now. So today he was going to run buffalo, shoot a buffalo, and do what was required to get a new name. If a medicine man told the people he had earned a new name, the Crows would honor it.

He did not let himself know how much he yearned for honor.

A COUPLE OF miles away from the herd, the scouts rode up and gave their report. Where the herd was grazing, the river wound along the northeast side of the valley. The buffalo were on the southwest side of the stream, above a high, steep bank. It was a small herd, maybe fifty head.

"Is the bank high enough to run them off of?" said Red Roan.

Three of the four scouts thought so. The fourth agreed, but didn't think the fall was enough to kill all the buffalo. "Some will be killed, some hurt, all of them confused," he said.

"That's what we'll do," said Red Roan.

Sam felt a pang. If they herded the buffalo off the cliff, he wouldn't get to run the mare among them today. Or maybe he was relieved.

Red Roan and the scouts drew with sticks in the dirt and came up with a plan. The wind was directly up the canyon, from southeast to northwest. So when anyone flanked the buffalo on the downstream side, they would break the other way.

The hunters had divided themselves into three warrior clubs. Red Roan called out the plan. The four scouts and the Muddy Hands would ride along the river on the southeast side, out of sight in the cottonwoods. They would go a couple of miles beyond the buffalo, spread out on a long flank, and ride hard to the herd. Red Roan made sure Jackrabbit, the Muddy Hand leader, understood what to do.

The Kit Foxes, Red Roan said, would go into the aspens on the southwest side and stay well hidden. Today, since Blue Medicine Horse and Flat Dog were Kit Foxes, the white men were invited to ride with these hunters. The chief's son himself would lead the Foxes, and he almost glared at Sam when he repeated, "Well hidden." When the buffalo smelled or heard the hard-riding hunters from the south, the Foxes would cut off any who broke toward the west and turn them toward the river. Otherwise they would move all the buffalo lickety-split toward the river. "We'll run them hard, straight at the drop-off," he said.

The Knobby Sticks, about a dozen hunters led by Bull-All-the-Time, would remain on the upstream side and push the animals toward the river from that direction.

The Foxes and Knobby Sticks would wait for the Muddy Hands to make the buffalo break. Then all hell would break loose.

SAM HAD TO hold the medicine hat firm. She felt the tension mounting—everybody did—she was ready to run. That was good, he hoped.

The fog had gone up to Sun. The day was crystalline, under a sky that was deeper and higher than any Sam had ever seen in Pennsylvania. *Today,* he told himself, *I'm going to earn a new name.*

Or get bad hurt. The memory of the leg broken by a ball at the Arikara villages was still painful. Being flat on his back, then on crutches, then hobbling, weeks of being a cripple . . .

Pictures flitted through his mind—him and the mare flying off the cliff, black shadows leaping into blackness. He tried to ignore the clutter. The mare turning in the air and landing on her back, Sam being speared by the saddle horn underneath her. He could already feel his chest being crushed.

The buffalo were still grazing placidly. The Muddy Hands needed a lot of time, evidently. Jackrabbit would take no chances. . . .

An old bull, one of the biggest, raised his head. He held his muzzle into the wind. As suddenly as a leaf drops off a branch, he galloped upstream.

"Hi-yi-yi-yay! Hi-yi-yi-yay!" The Knobby Sticks charged the herd from Sam's left.

Suddenly the horses around Sam ran like hell. He jumped the mare to a gallop to catch up. Excited, he slapped her rump with hand. Now the cry was all around him—*"Hi-yi-yi-yay! Hi-yi-yi-yay!"*

He was dodging aspen trees at incredible speed. The mare was doing the job herself, without guidance, gliding left, veering right, occasionally jumping a downed tree. All that was a damn good sign for running buffalo.

When they burst out of the grove, the closest buffalo were no more than twenty yards away. *"Hi-yi-yi-yay!"* everyone yelled, or something like that. Red Roan galloped in front, hollering the loudest.

When the big bull broke, all the buffalo did. They ran in all directions at once, like balls scattering on a billiards table. One bull ran straight at Red Roan. Then the monster turned and headed downstream, but had to veer off to avoid the Muddy Hands. *"Hi-yi-yi-yay!"* It was a war cry and a declaration of triumph to come.

Sam yelled *"Hi-yi-yi-yay!"* right in the mare's ears, and suddenly she put on an extra burst of speed and took him to the front. Sam hadn't imagined a horse could run this fast. *"Hi-yi-yi-yay!"* he cried.

Faster, harder, faster, harder!

Riders closed in from the right and the left. The buffalo dashed first in one direction, then another. They milled. They bleated. At last they set their muzzles on the only direction open to them, straight toward the river. *Faster,* thought Sam, *faster. Run them so hard they go right off that cliff! Faster!*

A great noise, like a thousand people stomping their feet on a wooden floor. Rumps and shaggy heads rose and fell in rhythm. Horses screamed, buffalo bellowed. Mud clods the size of huge fists flew. A giant one hit the medicine hat in the muzzle—she trumpeted a complaint. Sam kicked her flanks and she ran faster.

Dung squirted out of buffalo bottoms and flicked backward from hooves. A green gob hit Sam in the corner of his right eye. The sting made him shout in pain. He wiped at it with a sleeve and urged the mare to go faster.

He was giddy with the chase.

Screams—incredible guttural screams!

Buffalo were pitching off the cliffs!

Others, he could see, tumbled into a ravine on the right that opened onto the river. Muddy Hands from downstream reined in at the rim and shot arrows into the gully.

All the damn buffalo don't need to go off the cliff, Sam told himself. *I can shoot one on the run.*

He dropped the reins—the mare did better without them— and knee-nudged her toward a cow to his left. They couldn't catch the cow. Sam kicked the mare, and she went faster, but not close enough for a shot.

Sam reminded himself, *It needs to be in the brisket just behind the right shoulder.* He bellowed at the top of his lungs.

Somehow the mare drew almost even with the cow.

Sam sighted as sharp as you can sight bouncing up and down on a galloping horse. He saw the brisket in The Celt's sights.

The cow went over the cliff.

The medicine hat wheeled right, screamed out a whinny, and fell over the cliff sideways.

In midair Sam got his left leg out from under the mare and kicked away.

Whummpf!

Slanted ground cracked his back. He rolled head over heels into a melee. The mare clipped his right ear with a hoof, and his mind spun like a dust devil. Another kick smashed his left hand. Screams—horse screams, human screams, buffalo screams, his own screams—tore his brain.

He got up on one knee. A buffalo bull charged straight at him, horns lowered.

The mare ran at the bull and collided with it hard, shoulder to shoulder.

She went down hard. The bull veered off, shook itself, and slowly turned to face Sam again.

The mare clambered to her feet.

The bull charged.

The mare reared and flashed her hooves in his eyes.

The bull stopped. It glared. Just as it was making up its mind to gore the medicine hat, the air glimmered, and an arrow quivered in its brisket. A second arrow passed straight through the chest and vibrated in the cold ground beyond.

Sam touched his right ear, and his hand came away thick with blood.

The bull stood, fierce, aroused. Its rump lowered for a charge.

Two more arrows whumped into the brisket.

The bull huffed air out, like blowing pain away.

Sam looked up and saw Bell Rock, Blue Horse, and Flat Dog drawing back the bowstrings hard.

He felt the blood split into two streams on the divide of his shoulder and curl down his chest and his back.

Blasts of gunpowder hammered his ears. Gideon and Beckwourth were doing their part on the bull, too.

The mare ran at the bull and bit him on the snout.

The buffalo stood still, like nothing had happened, or he had turned into a tree stump.

Sam scrambled up the steep dirt cliff as high as he could get. He started reloading The Celt, but his left hand would barely hold the rifle. He managed to shake powder into the muzzle—too much powder, he knew, but he had to do something.

A young bull ran at the medicine hat, horns lowered. She skittered away easily, but tripped on a fallen cow. The mare flipped over the cow and sprawled headlong. Sam's heart leapt out of his chest. The young bull stood over the cow like he'd lost interest. The mare scrambled back to her feet.

Sam rammed a ball down the muzzle, eyes fixed on the bull, which was still glaring at him.

The old bull buckled to one knee.

Sam lifted The Celt and held the bull's head in his sights.

Then he remembered what Gideon said. "You can't kill one straight on in the head. The skull bone is too thick."

The bull struggled back to four feet and planted them wide. His eyes rolled in horror. Blood gouted out of his mouth and nose.

Sam gushed his breath out. He knew that story—bull on the ground, from all the shots.

He shook his head—he was a little light-headed. He looked around. Everywhere buffalo were dying or struggling to live. They staggered around on three legs. They bleated, each cry as loud as ten stuck pigs. Yearlings ran around lost. One cow waded deeper and deeper into the river, as though looking for a place to drown. Arrows whistled down from the clifftop.

Sam knew he had to stay clear of those arrows. He looked up. Bell Rock, Flat Dog, and Blue Medicine Horse, almost shoulder to shoulder, were still whanging arrows into buffalo flesh.

Twenty yards from Sam a cow stood still in the midst of the tumult, solid on three legs, the near foreleg raised neatly, like a little finger stuck out from a cup of coffee. Sam figured the leg was broken.

He leveled The Celt right at the spot behind the shoulder. Ignoring the bolt of pain in his left hand, and pretending not to notice the rivulets of blood on his chest and back, he let fly.

The blast knocked Sam down.

The cow toppled like she'd been clobbered by a steamboat.

I got my cow.

Bell Rock grinnned down at Sam.

His head swimming a little, Sam looked around for the medicine hat. To his surprise she was on the cliff slope, half a dozen steps away. He edged over and took the reins. Evidently, once her personal enemy was down, she withdrew from the fight.

Carefully, Sam picked his way along the loose dirt of the slope toward the ravine.

The sides of the ravine were too steep to walk on, but the hunters were finished here. Half a dozen buffalo lay dead.

Sam weaved his way up the middle of the gully, a drunk leading a horse. Soon the ravine sauntered up to level ground.

He half-stumbled out onto the plain, dizzy with whatever had happened. He collapsed onto the earth. *Oh, things happened.*

Chapter Eleven

He woke to a tongue slobbering on his face.

Coy. I forgot Coy. The whole time. Where was Coy?

He tried to jerk his head away, but something held it in a vise.

This realization was knocked to smithereens by a stabbing pain in his ear.

"O-o-o-w!"

"You t'ink to bleed to death, *ami*?" said a calm voice.

Another stab. "O-o-o-w!"

"Easy. Half done."

Sam opened his eyes. Coy licked his mouth, but when he tried to move, the grip tightened.

Gideon bent close over his face. Against the sky, Beckwourth, Blue Horse, and Flat Dog. On their knees next to him, Bell Rock and Third Wing. If he believed the looks on their faces, he was in trouble. The beaver men didn't speak Crow and the Crows didn't speak English, but they didn't need to.

The medicine hat stomped her feet and flabbered her lips, like asking for attention.

"That mare done saved your ass," said Beckwourth.

"She was your *paladin*," said Gideon, with the French pronunciation.

"O-o-o-w!"

Third Wing was holding Sam's head hard.

"Remember Diah, when ze bear got him? Ze ear?"

Diah meant Jedediah Smith, the Bible-reading brigade

leader, and that was one of the big days of Sam's life. The griz rushed out of the bushes, knocked Diah down, and got his head in its mouth. After everyone shot at the bear, they checked Diah's head. His scalp was cut to quilt pieces, and his ear was about to fall off. James Clyman sewed it back onto his head, more or less. That ear was nothing Diah would want anyone to see, ever again.

That was all before Sam got Coy, who now sat a step away and whimpered.

"Your ear is not so bad. I am your Clyman. I, how you say . . ."

"Stitch," said Beckwourth.

Sam saw now that Bell Rock was carefully studying what Gideon's hands did. Next the medicine man would want to trade for needle and thread.

"O-o-o-w!"

"Be still," snapped Gideon.

Sam wondered if he cared whether he messed up Gideon's sewing job or not.

"You about lost too much blood," said Third Wing.

"We won't say 'Hold on to your hair' to Sam," drawled Beckwourth, "we'll say, 'Hold on to your ear.'"

"Very funny. O-o-o-w!"

Gideon gave a big, exasperated sigh. Beckwourth knelt beside Third Wing and helped him clamp Sam's head. "Do it."

Sam hollered "O-o-o-w!" about half a dozen more times, and it was over.

"Let us see you stand up," said Gideon.

Sam rolled over, raised onto all fours, tented his bottom up, and slowly stood . . . until he buckled to one knee.

The knee got Coy's paw. The pup yelped and skittered away.

"I don't know if he is good in ze head."

"Nothing important there," said Beckwourth.

Sam gave a lopsided smile and stood up. He rocked like a sailor on a pitching deck, and then steadied. Coy rubbed against his leg.

"We get the buffalo?"

"We're finished butchering them out," said Beckwourth.

Blue Horse spoke in Crow. "We're going to pack some meat back to camp now. We'll walk and lead the horses. Some of us will stay here tonight, until we come for the rest."

"But you will ride back," said Bell Rock, just like a doctor.

"Tied on," said Third Wing, like a mother.

"I got a cow," said Sam. He looked woozily from one face to another. "I got a cow."

"Are you giving the cow to an old couple?" asked Bell Rock.

Sam nodded. "Whoever you choose."

"Pack the meat on a travois. Lead the pack horse to their lodge. Drop the travois on the ground."

"We'll pack the cow back for you," said Third Wing.

Sam nodded that he understood all. Coy looked at everyone brightly, like he understood too.

"You earned a new name," said Bell Rock.

"What name?" blurted Sam. He would have shown better manners, except that his head wasn't right.

Bell Rock smiled and shrugged. "You'll find out."

"Next time," said Beckwourth, "don't near get killed for a name."

Sam squatted—going down felt risky—and petted Coy. "What about the mare?" said Sam. "Can she get a name too?"

Bell Rock gave Sam a look, like "Medicine men don't name horses." Blue Horse had a similar look. *All right, I know, Crows don't name horses.*

"So I'll name her. Hey, white people do." He ruffled Coy's head fur and thought. "What's a good name?"

"Bull-killer," said Beckwourth.

Sam shook his head and found out it hurt to shake it.

"Paladin," said Gideon. "How you say in English? Paladin? Is ugly that way."

"What's it mean?" asked Sam.

"Knight, a champion for his leader."

Sam nodded his head slowly, so the ear wouldn't hurt. Paladin sounded pretty good.

"Protector," said Third Wing.

"Guardian," said Beckwourth.

"Savior," said Third Wing.

"Save your what?" asked Beckwourth. Third Wing had gotten a little Christianity during his trading post years, and Beckwourth always mocked it.

"Our Lord and Savior," replied Third Wing with dignity.

"More like 'Save Your Ass,'" said Beckwourth.

Sam gave them all a wide, nutty grin. "Save Your is not bad."

Bell Rock butted in. "I name her."

The others looked at each other. "All right," said Sam.

"She is special horse, champion for Sam. Her name is Paladin."

The others checked each other with their eyes. "That's good," said Sam.

"But Save Your Ass would have been more fun," said Beckwourth.

So in a March twilight, while the people were at their cook fires, Bell Rock sent Sam and the village crier around the circle of lodges. "This young man has a new name," called the crier. "His name is Joins with Buffalo, which in his language is 'Samalo.'" The crier boomed out the words "Joins with Buffalo" like a flourish of trumpets.

Sam walked behind the crier slowly, ceremoniously. Coy traipsed behind. He looked hangdog, but he went everywhere Sam went.

"This young man has a new name," boomed the crier over and over. "He killed a buffalo cow and gave it to the elderly, who have great need. He is given the name Samalo, which in his language means, Joins with Buffalo."

Meadowlark and Blue Medicine Horse came out of their family's tipi and stood at something like attention while Sam and the crier passed. Their parents, Little Bull, and Flat Dog all came out and stood next to Blue Horse and Meadowlark.

Sam kept his eyes front. He felt like a fool, and at the same time giddy with pride.

IT CAME TO him some time that very night, some time in the wee hours. It was not a cracked dream, nor was it a broth of lost blood and a thunked head. *I can ask Meadowlark to marry me now.* He was sure of it—a man who had won a name could.

He pulled Coy close to his chest and belly. They liked to sleep cuddled up.

And when Sam woke the next morning, in an empty tipi and under a gray sky, he was still sure he could.

His neighbors said the other beaver men had let him sleep while they went to bring the meat back. They were worried about his injuries.

I will do it today.

He ate. He rested. He shook his head to see if anything felt loose. He fed the mare some cottonwood bark by hand, rubbed her muzzle, and called her repeatedly by her new name. "Paladin, want some bark? Paladin, you're a good woman. You saved my ass." He also laid his plans.

That night he caught a break. Since Red Roan and the meat party weren't back, Sam was the only man courting Meadowlark.

After a gray day the sunset wiped the sky clear. The night was so crystalline it felt brittle. When Meadowlark came out, Sam opened his blanket and wrapped her into it with him snugly. She smiled at him like he was special. Coy rubbed against both their legs and lay down. Sam looked up into the dark sky and pretended to count a thousand of the million-million stars. On moonless nights in the high mountains many, many more stars glittered against the darkness, four or five times as many as you ever saw in Pennsylvania.

He had to do it right away. He sucked a great, cold breath in. "Meadowlark, will . . . ?"

It wasn't right. He took both her hands in his. Still wasn't right. He turned Meadowlark away from Coy and got down on one knee. She giggled at this, but he said it was the way of his people, and she put on a straight face. It struck him that she knew what he was about to do.

"Will you marry me, Meadowlark?" The actual Crow words were "share a lodge with me," but Sam knew what he wanted to say.

She pulled him up by the hands, raised him until she could look upwards into his eyes. "I want to share a lodge with you," she said. More stars shone in her eyes than in the spangled sky.

He heard a dreaded "but . . ." in her voice. He waited.

"You will have to ask my brothers for me."

Blue Medicine Horse and Flat Dog, maybe Little Bull too. *This will be a cinch.*

He stood up. He lifted her chin and kissed her. The kiss was so long, Sam was surprised the sky was still moonless when it ended. Then he told himself, well, maybe one whole moon passed during the kiss.

"Every day now, will you teach me English?"

They kissed a lot more, rehearsing the good times to come.

Much later, when she saw Red Roan coming, Meadowlark slipped out of Sam's blanket and back into her tipi. Then she stuck her head back out the door and gave him the shiniest smile he'd ever seen.

Sam's blood fizzed with happiness.

"EIGHT HORSES," SAID Blue Medicine Horse.

"Eight horses," echoed Flat Dog. Whatever Flat Dog said always sounded like a joke, somehow.

"Eight horses?" Sam said slowly. As a gift for the bride's family, it was out of line. A chief's daughter wouldn't bring such a price.

Sam ran his eyes from brother to brother. As though to answer his skepticism, Flat Dog repeated, "Eight horses." Blue Horse sounded uncertain, maybe embarrassed, but Flat Dog was definite. Sam eyed him and got nothing back.

The Crow custom was that a young man seeking a girl's

hand made a gift to her brothers, or sometimes to her father. Sam was expecting such a request, but . . .

I want to take Meadowlark with me on the spring hunt.

"There's no way I can get eight horses until summer."

The brothers nodded, as much as to say, "We know."

So maybe your parents are putting me off, he thought. *But why?*

Maybe Gray Hawk and Needle are pushing her into Red Roan's arms.

Maybe she got carried away in the moment and has changed. . . . He put a stop to that line of thought.

"I leave in a quarter moon."

They nodded.

Everyone could see and feel the weather changing. Ice was off the river now. South-facing hillsides were clear of snow. Nights were less bitter. For the Crows this meant the coming of the sign that marked the change: thunder would soon be heard in the mountains. That would put an end to the season of story-telling, winter, and bring on the season of hunting and fighting. The village would join with other Crow villages for the spring buffalo hunt. Young men would gather into warrior clubs and plan what raids they would make against their enemies, Shoshone in the west, Blackfeet in the north, and in the east their most bitter foes, the Sioux, the ones they called Head Cutters.

For the beaver men, it meant the spring trapping season was at hand. Sam, Gideon, Beckwourth, and Third Wing would leave in a quarter moon for the Siskadee, to join their brethren.

Sam looked at the brothers, stupefied.

"Tell him." This was Flat Dog.

"We want to go with you," said Blue Horse.

"What?"

"We want to go with you," repeated Flat Dog.

"Trapping," said Blue Horse.

"With the white men," said Flat Dog.

Sam felt more stupefied, or maybe stupid.

"On the way back to the village," said Blue Horse, "we will get your eight horses and a lot more."

"If you take us," said Flat Dog, "you get your eight horses. If not . . ."

Cornered.

Sam grinned.

THAT NIGHT HIS friends' attitude around the center fire of the lodge was clear enough.

"Why not?" said Gideon, in a Gallic, it-makes-no-difference to me tone.

"Six men are safer than four," said Third Wing, ever the protective one.

"Think they'll still call us the white men?" asked Beckwourth.

They looked at each other. Beckwourth, a mulatto. Gideon, a French-Canadian Jew. Third Wing, a Pawnee. Sam, the only white.

And they were thinking of adding two Crows to the party.

"I'm losing track of white," said Sam.

In his buffalo robes through the night, Sam pondered on all of it. He didn't know. But he had to get the eight horses for Meadowlark.

"FRIEND."

This was Blue Horse, with Bell Rock and Flat Dog right behind him, squatting at the open door of the tipi.

Sam drained his coffee. Gideon, Beckwourth, and Third Wing were already out and about. Sam was lingering over the last of the coffee—he'd grown fond of the sweetness.

"Welcome."

"We have an invitation for you."

They came in and sat.

Sam waited.

"Would you like to be a Kit Fox?"

Sam really didn't know what the Kit Fox club was all about, or the other two main men's clubs, Knobby Sticks and Muddy Hands. They acted as police for the village, and in warm weather made war parties. He did know that almost every Crow man was a member of one club or the other. *If you want Meadowlark . . .*

"Yes, thank you. I am honored."

"Then you must spend today in the lodge," said Bell Rock. Sam knew the club lodge well, an oversized one. "First we must teach you a song."

The words were simple, but the feeling behind them was big:

iaxuxkekatū'e, bacbi'awak, cē'wak

Bell Rock's voice was passion, with strains of melancholy.

"You dear Foxes, I want to die, so I say."

"It is the way of the Fox," said Blue Medicine Horse. "We are made to die."

"Old age is an evil, bedeviled by many ills," said Bell Rock, in the tone of a ritualistic statement. "A man is lucky to die in his youth."

Sam suppressed a smile. He suspected that this ideal was like chastity, honored more in word than deed.

"Sing with us," said Bell Rock.

All four men lifted the song to the smoke hole and up to the sky.

You dear Foxes, I want to die, so I say.

The three Crows sang the words as though they were sacred. Sam did his best to bring conviction to them. He was willing to risk his life for his family, but he damn well didn't

intend to die. The words "I want to live" rolled over and over
in his head, tumbling with "I want to die."

They sang the song, and sang it again, and again.

At last Bell Rock was satisfied. "When you're finished with
Paladin come to the Kit Foxes lodge."

Sam led Paladin to water first thing every morning.

"It's a big day," said Flat Dog. For once the joker seemed
excited.

Lots of men milled around outside the lodge. Blue Horse,
Flat Dog, and Bell Rock came to Sam immediately. "You
may come in," said Bell Rock.

And just like that, without ceremony, it was done. Sam's
mind teetered a little. Am I becoming a Crow?

He corrected himself. *When I marry Meadowlark, our
children will be Crow. And white. Both. So I must be Crow*
and *white*.

The inside of the lodge looked ordinary, but the men did
not. Red Roan and others wore the gray or yellow-brown hides
of kit foxes as capes. Younger men carried long staffs, either
straight or hooked, wrapped full length in otter skins, and otter
skins also hanging from the shafts as decorations. Some of
them had painted their faces, one side red and the other yellow.

"We'll explain everything," said Blue Horse. "For now just
go with Flat Dog."

Instead of the usual seating pattern, a main circle around
the fire pit with others seated behind, there were three clus-
ters of men in the big lodge. Bell Rock went to one, Blue
Horse to another, Flat Dog and Sam to the third.

They sat with the youngest group of men. Several looked
at Sam oddly. He was the one man in the lodge, he supposed, who hadn't been born Crow.

"Blue Horse sits with the Little Foxes. They're second oldest. Bell Rock is a regular Kit Fox." He wiggled his eyebrows.
"That either means they're too old, too lazy, or too smart to
do the fighting. They pick us young guys for that.

"We are the Naughty Ones," Flat Dog went on. "We're

younger, and we're not supposed to be able to think for ourselves." He smiled slyly. "They actually assign older men to us to do the thinking. To humor them, sometimes we act like kids and play games. It's fun. Until it turns serious."

Sam watched for a few minutes. Some of the older men were consulting. Aside from that, everyone just seemed to be gossiping. "No meetings all winter?"

"The clubs get going in the spring."

"What's the purpose of today's meeting?"

"To choose leaders. For the summer action."

As though Flat Dog's words were a cue, two of the oldest men got up, carrying tobacco-filled pipes in their left hands. Some younger men joined them. These groups went to two young men of the Little Foxes, particularly good-looking fellows, each of them. An older man presented each of them a pipe. Each chosen man took the pipe and smoked it ritually, first offering smoke to the four directions.

"Those two will be the leaders until cold weather comes again," Flat Dog, "or as long as they live. In war they go first." He sighed. "Luckily, neither of them refused the pipe."

Sam soon saw what this meant. Next two old men approached other young men with pipes. "They are asking these men to be the straight staff bearers." Flat Dog nodded at a man carrying a straight staff, also wrapped in otter skins and about three feet long.

Since one of the two was a Naughty One, Sam could hear what was said. The older man spun the pipe in a full circle and offered it to the young man.

Instead of taking the pipe, the young man looked the older full in the face and said, "Please do not bring me this responsibility. I'm afraid I'm weak. I might flee."

"The bearer of a straight staff," whispered Flat Dog, "is expected to plant it in the ground at the first sight of an enemy. Then, no matter what happens, he must make a stand there and not run away. If a fleeing friend pulls the staff up for him, then he may run. Otherwise he has to stay and fight."

The older bearer of the pipe then offered it to another young man.

This man also declined the honor. But the pipe bearer did not take no for answer easily. He presented the pipe again and was again refused.

Now a younger man began to harangue the honoree. "Smoke the pipe," he urged. "You're a brave man—smoke it."

"That's his brother," Flat Dog said softly.

A third time the pipe was presented, and a third time refused.

"You're the right age to die," the brother went on. "You're handsome. All your friends will cry. Your family will mourn, they will fast, they'll cut their hair. Everyone will remember your courage."

The pipe bearer offered the pipe the fourth time, holding the stem directly in front of the honoree's mouth.

"This is the last time they'll ask," Flat Dog said.

The honoree looked at the pipe but didn't take it.

"He's afraid to die," said Flat Dog.

Abruptly the brother reached out, pulled the young man's head down and forward by his hair, and forced his lips to the stem.

"Now he must smoke," Flat Dog said.

The young man smoked.

"He thinks that if we encounter enemies," Flat Dog said, "he is sure to die."

Another young man, one of the Little Foxes, had accepted the pipe and was smoking.

"Ten altogether. Two who go in front," said Flat Dog, "two straight staff bearers, two crooked staff bearers, two who come at the rear, and two who must be the bravest of all."

During the smoking, which took a lot of time, Flat Dog explained the duties of each of these club officers. The front and rear men weren't marked by any special insignia, and their jobs were simply to lead and bring up the rear. The straight staff men had to sink their staffs into the ground the moment they spotted the enemy and make a stand there, not retreating. The crooked staff bearers had the same duty, except that they were allowed to run back a little before making their stands. "Those who are the bravest of all," Flat Dog, "must throw their lives on the ground. Because of that, they get to pick their food first at any feast, and eat before others begin."

Sam knew that among the Crow, warriors got killed far less often than their stories suggested. Even one death was a cause for the whole village to mourn extravagantly. He itched to know the odds of survival of a season as a club leader, but dared not ask.

Suddenly the pipe was put in front of Flat Dog. He looked up into the face of the pipe bearer, then quickly across at his brother. Blue Horse nodded.

"I am a Kit Fox," Flat Dog said in a tone of sincere recitation. "I want to die. But I must say no to this pipe for this season. Blue Horse and I plan to go with the white men on the beaver hunt."

A murmur swept through the Naughty Ones.

The pipe was proffered a second time, a third, and a fourth. It seemed the bearer held no expectation of a positive answer. Each time Flat Dog said a quiet no.

The Naughty Ones buzzed with the news, and many of them looked at Flat Dog and Blue Horse with surprise or amusement, admiration or disapproval.

Flat Dog didn't look at Sam.

Sam didn't know what to think.

During the next couple of hours two or three young men did refuse the pipe successfully. As far as Sam could tell, this was no great shame.

At last all ten leaders were chosen. Each of the staff bearers now carried a bare stick as a symbol of his leadership to come. The straight staffs were peeled poles of pine tapered to a point. The hooked staffs had the same body, with willow limbs tied to the top and curved.

Finished choosing their leaders, all the Kit Foxes marched out of the lodge. First came the two who go in front, then the straight staff bearers, then the drummers. The rank and file, including Sam and Flat Dog, came next, then the most brave of all, the crooked staff bearers, and the rear ones.

They paraded through the camp, singing several Kit Fox songs. People came out of their tipis to watch. The families of those chosen darted back into their tipis to fetch otter skins, or offered their neighbors something in trade for the skins.

Flat Dog told Sam, "We can't quit dancing until they come up with one whole skin to cover each staff."

After many songs had been sung, they sang the one Kit Fox song Sam knew—

"You dear Foxes, I want to die, so I say."

He joined in enthusiastically, sending the words up to the sky over and over. He wasn't sure what they meant, but he swooned into them, and in a certain way meant them.

Then everyone went to their lodges. Blue Horse fell in with Sam and Flat Dog. "The men honored with staffs, at their parents' lodges a man will come who has carried that staff in the past. He will sew the otter skin on. Then they will all come back out dressed in their best clothes. Kit Foxes who have done well with the staffs in the past, they'll come up to these young bearers. Maybe they'll take the staff and smoke with it. Then they'll say something like, 'When I carried this staff, I killed an enemy,' or 'When I carried this staff, I went straight through the line of the Head Cutters and they weren't able to touch me,' and wish the new bearer the same good fortune." "Head Cutters"—that was the Crow name for the Lakotas, the ones the white men called the Sioux.

At his lodge Sam invited Blue Horse and Flat Dog in to eat.

They helped themselves from the pot outside and sat by the fire inside.

"Let me understand this," Sam said. "You've fixed things so I have to take you with me on the beaver hunt. Right?"

The two brothers smiled at him. "Exactly right," said Flat Dog.

* * *

SAM WAS PONDERING things the next evening when he heard some scratching at the bottom of the lodge cover. The Crow young men played a game Sam thought was rude. They'd sneak up on the lodge of a girl they fancied at night, when she was sleeping. Then they'd worm a hand underneath the lodge cover and grope the girl, if possible in a private place. A touch meant victory. *No girls in this lodge,* thought Sam. And right now he regretted that.

A hand edged under the lodge cover. He started to whack it hard. Then he saw a feminine hand. A hand he knew.

He reached out and touched Meadowlark's fingers. She turned her hand over—yes, he knew this palm—and offered him a pouch. He picked it up. It was a medicine pouch, and beautifully beaded with the tiniest beads made. It was gorgeous.

He grasped the hand, but it slipped quickly back under the cover. He heard a giggle and quick footfalls.

He clutched the pouch to his chest. *She loves me.*

Also, he now had a pouch for medicine that would always remind him of his real name, Samalo, or Joins with Buffalo. He would tie up a swatch of matted hair from a buffalo head and keep it in the pouch.

Suddenly he was filled with good thoughts. Maybe this whole thing was going to work out. Meadowlark loved him— she would wait for him. Next summer, with Blue Horse and Flat Dog's help, he would come back to the village like a hero, eight horses in hand, or more.

Meadowlark's parents had thrown a glove on the ground.

Sam took up their challenge.

PART TWO

Stalking
Beaver

Chapter Twelve

Blank. Empty. Mountains well off to the west, mountains well off to the east. Big river in the middle, with desert scrub all around it.

No sign of the brigade.

Sam was sure his count was right, or close. It was April 14, or maybe a day or two later. The phases of the moon, full, half, and new, had made it easy to keep track of the weeks on his counting stick. Sixteen weeks and a day since they left Ashley on the Platte.

Sam looked around. Desolation in every direction, including his heart.

Memory: Last June he went ahead alone, with a promise to meet Diah and Fitz and the boys where the river got deep enough to float. He waited eleven days. They never showed up.

Then his imagination ran wild. They were all killed by Indians. They got lost and would never find their way home. In this vast, apparently endless landscape, desert horizoned by mountain followed by desert and again horizoned by mountain, a man could never find his way home. There was no such place as home, not anymore, not for the men who came out here to hunt beaver.

On the twelfth day he'd set out downstream for the settlements. He had only eleven lead balls left, and so would seldom be able to hunt. He wasn't sure whether this river was the Platte or the Arkansas, whether he would hit the Missouri four hundred miles above St. Louis or the Mississippi three hundred miles below it. In other words, he was good and lost.

He damn near starved to death. He got captured by Indians

who would have tortured and killed him, except for Third Wing. He got caught in a prairie fire and survived by hiding in a buffalo carcass with Coy. After more than two months of wandering, he stumbled into Fort Atkinson.

Maybe in the end, the reality had been wilder than his imaginings.

Here he was again, waiting for a brigade that didn't come. He looked around at his five friends, Gideon, Beckwourth, Third Wing, Blue Medicine Horse, and Flat Dog. Coy, too, panting there in front of Paladin. Sam felt a throb of gladness next to his pang of fear.

This time coming over the South Pass had been easy. Mid-April, mid-March, an entirely different story, new grass instead of deep snow and howling winds. They crested the continental divide, came onto the headwaters of the Sandy, a pathetic stand-in for a river, and followed it here to the Siskadee. All the way they looked for sign of Ashley's horses, nearly fifty of them. Not a hoofprint. At the junction of rivers they looked for the cairn Fitz said he would leave. Nothing. No sign of human beings, not even Indians.

This was Snake country. Crows and Snakes were longtime enemies. Snakes had run Sam's outfit's horses off this time last spring, not far from here. Not a place to be wandering around carelessly in a small party.

They settled in to wait.

COY SENSED THEM first. On the fourth day Sam was taking evening watch on top of a sandstone outcropping, stroking Coy's back. Suddenly the coyote pup jumped up and pointed ears, nose, and eyes up the Sandy. The wind was blowing down the little river.

Sam stood for long minutes before he saw anything. *But,* he thought, *twenty-two men and maybe forty horses make a lot of sound and smell.*

Finally, one rider skylined on a ridge. By the silhouette Sam recognized Fitzpatrick.

In seconds, it seemed, all six of them were hightailing it up the river.

Whoa. Here came the outfit. But it was in poor shape, most of the men walking and leading heavily laden horses.

Still, the welcome was warm.

"Look who's still above ground."

"This nigger thought them Crow women diddled you to death."

"Glad to see you, hoss."

"Look who's still got his hair!"

"'Bout missin' an ear, though."

These greetings from Ashley, Fitzpatrick, Clyman, Zacharias Ham, and all the others, every man looking hale and hearty.

Blue Horse and Flat Dog hung back, uncertain. Sam waved to them to come up and meet the general.

After the introductions Ashley said, "Looks like you came through well."

"You, too," answered Sam.

Ashley shook his head. "Lost seventeen of my best horses to the Crows. Recently." The general couldn't help throwing an odd glance at Blue Horse and Flat Dog.

"Wasn't our Crows," said Gideon. "All of us been layin' 'round camp lazy all winter."

Now Flat Dog showed off his English. "Some of our young men think, run horses off is most fun anything."

Zacharias Ham threw a woolly look at the two Crows. "We'll learn 'em what's fun."

"You men are welcome in camp," said Ashley.

"They want to trap with us," put in Sam.

"Welcome to that, too," said the general.

So it was settled. Sam had never known he was nervous.

Quickly the camp settled into fires against the evening chill, roasting meat, and stories.

First the Ashley men caught Sam and the fellows up on what had happened since they left. January the brigade spent toiling up the South Platte until, at last, they got within sight of the Rocky Mountains—that brought a cheer. February was given mostly to waiting in a cottonwood grove and looking at the spectacle of snow and ice ahead. At the end of the month they forced a crossing of the main range, a bitter three days struggling through snow. Then they emerged onto the Laramie Plains, a fine country along the North Platte, full of game. The next range, the Medicine Bow Mountains, turned them back. But it was March now. They slowed down and moved northward, trapping the creeks of the east side of the range. The next pass led to a paradise of game, the valley of the North Platte River.

April now, time to head for the Siskadee. The Wind River Mountains lined the western horizon. Fitzpatrick, though, told how the horses got run off, and how he led a party to get them back. They came on two animals so weak the Indians had abandoned them, but never caught up with the rest.

That's how the brigade came to the Siskadee half worn-out. Plenty of smiles, though. The horses were loaded with plews aplenty.

Sam, Gideon, Beckwourth, and Third Wing gave back their own stories. The favorite was about Paladin. Blue Horse told in good English how Sam trained her in the freezing river. He still chuckled about how cold Sam looked standing rib deep in that river.

"But his mind," said Gideon, "it always point to the day he ride her against ze buffalo. When he shoot a buffalo riding her, he get new name. Medicine man, he promise, new name."

Sam was embarrassed, so he took over the telling, and got as far as when the buffalo stampeded for the river. "I rode hard at those buffalo. I could hear bellowing as they went off that cliff ahead. And then . . ."

Abruptly, Beckwourth jumped in, "And then, he got the brightest of his bright ideas. I can shoot a cow right now. Riding hard, he takes aim, he gets her in his sights just perfect and . . ."

"Off the cliff goes!" hollered Gideon. "Cow, horse, and rider."

The beaver men applauded.

Sam retreated to petting Coy.

"Sam, mare, cow, all topsy turvy over ze cliff." Dramatic pause. "He lands in middle of the buffalo driven off ze cliff."

"They ain't all hurt," Beckwourth put in. "This one old bull, he lowered his horns and looked at Sam between 'em just like sights. He charged."

"And ze mare," interrupted Gideon, "she save his miserable life. She run at buffalo—boom—knock him off balance."

"The bull," Beckwourth burst in, "he gets his feet back under him and lowers that head."

"Then Blue Horse, Flat Dog, and ze medicine man, they shoot him a little bit wit' arrows. We shoot him a little bit with lead. Ze mare, now she run up to ze bull and . . ."—Gideon opened his arms wide to his audience—"she bite him on the snout!"

The men cheered.

"So the one that earns the new name," said Beckwourth, "is the mare. Paladin. But we oughta called her Save Your, short for Save Your Ass."

The men roared.

After a while, in the following silence, Sam said, "I got a new name, too."

"You did," Gideon allowed. "Ze medicine man gave him a name."

"What are you called now, Sam?"

"Joins with Buffalo," said Sam.

Men made faces. One farted loudly, causing a bubble of laughter.

Fitzpatrick went up to Sam and clapped him on the shoulder. Sam kept his hands on Coy.

"To your fellow mountain men, lad, to us you will always be known as *mi coyote*."

TIME TO GET serious about the spring hunt. Ashley divided them into four outfits. Fitzpatrick would take his south, to trap the mountains visible on the horizon. Zacharias Ham would lead men west to those mountains easy to see. James Clyman would lead his north along the Siskadee and trap its head-waters, right where they'd gone before.

Himself, Ashley would do a journey of exploration. He wanted to know whether this river was the Colorado, which flowed into the Gulf of Mexico, or the Multnomah, which emptied into the Columbia, or the Buenaventura, which emptied into the Pacific near Monterey, California. The men said nothing. Everyone knew that if this was the Buenaventura, the road was open to the Golden Clime—fur men would be the first to reach Alta California by land!

Sam quietly asked Clyman to choose him and his friends to make an outfit together. He knew Clyman wouldn't mind a multicolored brigade.

James just nodded.

THE TRAPPING FELT good to Sam. Up in the morning at first light, coffee, get mounted, move out. Ride with your partner up a creek coming down from the Wind River Mountains to the east. Watch for slides, dams, chewed cotton-woods, any beaver sign. Pick a likely spot to set a trap, especially one out from a slide. Move downstream, splash into the creek, which right now was snow run-off from some of the highest, coldest mountains in the nation. Wade up to the spot and set your trap. Put a big stick through the ring at the end of the chain, so the beaver can't swim off with it. Dip a small stick into your horn of castoreum and bait the trap with it. Attach a floating stick, in case the beaver, despite all, swims off with the trap. Move upstream to the next likely spot, keeping an eye out for Indians all the way.

Sam's partner was Blue Horse, which made "keeping an eye out for Indians" funny. Sam took Blue Horse, Gideon took Flat Dog, and Beckwourth took Third Wing, in each case an experienced hand showing the ways to a new man, what they called a pork-eater. Clyman kept the camp.

Later you would raise your traps and ride up the creek, or on to the next stream, depending. After you trapped the wily rodent and he drowned, you still had plenty of work to do. You skinned out your beaver, taking only the pelt and the tail. Back in camp you scraped the hide free of fat and stretched it on a hoop you made from willow branches. The tail you threw in the coals for eating, a delicacy. Your pack horse would bear your plews, or you'd cache them for retrieval later.

In this way the little Clyman outfit worked its way up the river they called the Siskadee. Sam knew that just across the mountains he was working, on the east side, was the winter camping place of the village led by Rides Twice, the village where lived his love, Meadowlark. By now, surely, the village had moved down the Wind River, made its big turn to the northeast, worked their way through the big canyon, and come to where it changed its name to the Big Horn. There they would do the spring buffalo hunt. There, sometime this summer, Sam would ride into the village leading eight horses and claim her hand.

For now, though, the creeks were running full, the pelts were prime, he had good comrades, and it was time to make a living.

SAM THOUGHT IT was the weirdest thing he ever saw.

They had worked their way north along the Siskadee to where she came out of the mountains, no longer a big, fat, slow snake of a river but a sprightly colt. He and Blue Horse trapped their way up a creek half the day and down it the second half. They were riding into camp an hour beyond sunset, in the very last of the light. And he distinctly saw three fires instead of the one there should have been. And the men around those fires, where Clyman and their friends should have been, were . . .

Indians!

He looked at Blue Horse guiltily.

"Snakes!" his friend hissed.

Sam dismounted. They tied the horses to a cedar and put Coy on a lead rope. Sam jerked his head to the left, and they eased up a sandstone outcropping.

When they got there, Sam chuckled. Beyond the Indian camp, clear enough to the eye, was the camp of the fur men. Sam counted five figures—everyone accounted for.

"We've got company," he said to Blue Horse.

Just in case, they rode a wide circuit around the Indian camp.

"Snakes," said Clyman.

"How many?"

"Fourteen."

"How many guns?" said Sam.

"Two that I saw."

"They're friendly," said Beckwourth.

"Say they are," corrected Clyman. "Want to trade."

"What can we trade them?" said Sam.

Everyone knew what was in their panniers—a few beads, a little jerked meat, some good twists of tobacco.

"We need horses," said Clyman. "We gotta try."

The entire brigade had been short of horses from the start.

"I will trade my pistol for a horse," said Gideon.

Clyman shrugged. "We'll try."

All the men looked at each other warily. From their expressions, Sam judged, the Crows trusted these Snakes even less than the mountain men did.

"We'll hobble the horses and make a rope corral too," Clyman said. "We'll also set a double guard."

"And tomorrow," said Beckwourth, "we'll do some old-fashioned horse-trading."

SAM CLAMPED HIS teeth together to keep them from chattering. He wiggled his toes, left foot, right foot, left foot, right foot—the toes were likely to freeze. Damn Rocky Mountains in the springtime.

The sky wasn't any lighter than a few minutes ago. In an

hour the world would be warmer, and his time on watch would be over.

One by one, he poked each gloved finger up and down, the left fingers on the barrel of The Celt, right fingers on the stock. He pulled the hood of his blanket capote tighter around his face. He wanted to stomp his feet, but didn't dare. Guards were supposed to be absolutely silent.

He reached down and patted Coy. While the others slept, Coy went with Sam on watch every time.

His eyes probed the darkness. The half moon let patches of light through, but the cottonwoods threw big blotches of blackness. Chances were better for hearing an enemy than seeing one.

Probably nothing will happen. Nothing had ever happened while Sam was on watch. Yet he took standing guard with complete seriousness. He would always take it seriously, and would always be scared.

Tonight he was also worried about Third Wing, the other guard. His friend . . . Sam didn't know. Maybe he thought Third Wing hadn't spent enough time at this duty. Maybe he thought Third Wing had too motherly a way about him to fight hard. Maybe . . .

Sam was worried.

Third Wing's job was to stay by the horses penned in the rope corral. Sam's was to stand in different spots around the camp, each one with a good vantage point. To keep his eyes and ears wide open, and if he saw or heard anything, to yell like hell.

The silence made Sam's ears ache.

Now the sky was a shade lighter. The half moon made only gray shadows. The world was no longer black but dark gray.

"Hunnh!"

Instantly, Sam yelled, "Indians! Indians! Indians!"

He shouldered his rifle—this light gray spot, that dark gray spot—seemed like he was pointing it in every direction at once. He saw no one.

"Indians!" he bellowed louder.

Damn! That "hunnh" sound, it was a human being getting hit hard by something, and it came from the horse pen.

I better get over there.

"Blam!"

Sam heard it and felt it at the same time. He grabbed the left side of his chest.

Godawmighty, I'm shot!

But it didn't hurt.

Why?

He looked around. Dark human shapes were darting around the horse pen.

Shouts came from his camp. "Indians! Indians!" Help was coming.

Get going!

He wiped his right hand on his face. Dry, not wet. No blood.

He ran lickety-split toward the horse pen.

The mounts were jostling around, but they weren't running. For sure the rope that made the corral was cut. *We fooled you! When you cut the corral, you thought you could run the horses off. But they're hobbled.*

He saw human arms, legs, heads here and there. He tried to sight on one, but knew he was more likely to hit a horse than a thief.

He almost stumbled over a moccasined foot sticking out of a gray shadow.

He bent over it—Third Wing, unconscious. He groped for the head. Both hands came away gooey with blood.

"Horse thieves! Horse thieves!" That was Gideon roaring. Sam recognized the blam! of Gideon's .58, largest of all the men's rifles.

Lots of footsteps coming toward the horses.

Sn-n-i-i-i-ck!

Flame seared his chest!

He felt his right ribs. Blood. An arrow, probably . . . *My blood!*

He went berserk. He ran crazy-legged into the shadows in the direction of the arrow.

"You bastards!"

I will die with your blood on my hands!

Movement. Maybe movement, going away from the horses. He slapped The Celt to his shoulder and fired in the direction of the flicker in the half light.

Damn! Stupid! Now his rifle was empty.

He dashed to the horse pen. The corral rope was on the ground. Paladin was still there, cross-hobbled. Gideon's horses too. Every man had his own way of not ending up afoot.

The beaver men ran around the horses, looking for horse thieves to shoot.

Sam reloaded. *I'm going to kill someone before I die.*

"The Indian camp! The Indian camp!" Clyman shouted.

Sam and Beckwourth sprinted out of the cottonwoods upstream toward the Snake camp.

Arrows flew around them like flocks of birds.

Sam dashed back into the trees. He gasped for breath. "All right!" He shouted to Beckwourth. "I'm all right."

He knew he wasn't, he had a mortal wound, but he hadn't been gored by the burst of arrows. "I dance past death!" he roared. It was unbelievable, like running through raindrops and not getting wet.

He realized Beckwourth was standing beside him.

They looked around the trees.

A red ridge blocked their view of the Indian camp upstream.

"Let's charge the bastards!" said Beckwourth.

"Yeah!" said Sam.

"No!" said Blue Medicine Horse in English, coming up.

"Let's get high and shoot down on them," said Flat Dog.

"We'll get up that ridge," Clyman said.

Every man stopped and looked at the leader, then nodded.

"Sam, you're hurt. Let me see."

Sam raised his right arm. A finger poked at his ribs painfully. Something bit the back of his arm.

"You're lucky. Arrow gouged your ribs, bounced off into your arm. You'll be all right."

Sam was hugely relieved, and maybe half-disappointed.

"Beckwourth, Blue Horse, Flat Dog, go with Sam," said Clyman. "I'll help Gideon watch the horses. And take care of Third Wing."

"Third Wing's near dead," said Beckwourth.

"Bad hurt," corrected Clyman. He fixed Sam with ice-gray eyes. "You can help him later. Remember, Sam, you're in charge."

Me?!

"Let's go kill Snakes," said Medicine Horse.

THE FUR MEN ran fast to the top of the little ridge. They crept up and looked over without showing themselves too much. "Down!" Sam ordered Coy. The pup circled and curled up.

From there the Snakes' dilemma was obvious. Their camp was on the south side of the creek. Across from it, in a finger between two low ridges, some boys held the Indian party's mounts ready. No doubt, as soon as the trappers' animals were loose, the Snakes had intended to stampede them off. Which had turned sour on them.

Now the Snakes were mostly pinned down in the cottonwoods where they'd camped or in the brush along the creek. If they tried to ride off, they'd have to bring the horses out from that finger of land between the two ridges. Then the trappers would have clear shots, and this ridge made a nice shooting angle.

The mountain men looked at each other, faces set hard. Third Wing's blood cried out for vengeance.

"How many do you see?" asked Sam.

Everyone saw two or three boys, probably, holding the Shoshone horses far to the back. Out of range.

Blue Medicine Horse said he saw two men hidden behind the trunks of cottonwoods. Within a couple of minutes the other trappers saw a hand or a bow or a flap of clothing stick out. Two men in the trees.

The brush stirred here and there. Nothing visible to shoot at.

Sam got a chill. He looked around. No, this was the highest point for about a quarter mile. No one could shoot down at him.

"We could work around and take the boys and steal the horses," said Beckwourth.

Everyone said "Yeah" before they thought. Getting even, that sounded good.

"We don't know where all the men are," said Sam. "Half of them could be laying a trap to get us if we go for the horses."

And what if they come up behind us, or from the side? Maybe every man had the same thought at the same time. All four of them looked around warily.

Sam said, "Blue Horse, back down off this edge a little. Keep a lookout," said Sam. "All the time. Make sure no one comes up on our backs."

Blue Horse nodded and went.

"We'll take turns at that."

Coy mewled, like he was agreeing.

Sam turned back to the Indian camp. He, Flat Dog, and Beckwourth laid flat on their bellies, peered over the lip of the hill, and looked sharp. "A bunch of them is down in that brush somewhere," said Beckwourth.

Flat Dog said in a heavy accent, "Or somewhere else."

Rocks exploded in front of Sam's face.

"Boom!" spoke a rifle.

A big puff of black smoke fizzed up from the brush.

Sam rolled several feet down the hill, brushing at his face.

Beckwourth fired beneath the smoke. Just then they saw a figure with a rifle scurry into another bunch of willows.

"Waste of DuPont and Galena," said Beckwourth. Trapper talk for powder and lead.

Looking across at Sam, Flat Dog said, "You got some little flecks of red war paint."

Sam brushed at the bleeding scratches. Coy licked at them.

"We better stay here and not go looking for trouble," said Sam. "And we have to make damn sure of our targets," said Sam. His blood was singing revenge in his ears.

No one had DuPont and Galena to waste. Blue Horse and Flat Dog carried maybe a dozen arrows each. Sam had the bow and arrows he wasn't so good with.

Sam grabbed pieces of sandstone in each hand and shoved them up in front of Beckwourth and Flat Dog. "Build something for us to hide behind."

In ten minutes it was done, a low wall with gaps between the rocks to look through, and to stick the muzzle of a rifle through. Sam, Beckwourth, and Flat Dog stretched out behind and watched. Coy curled up at Sam's feet.

They settled in.

"What I think," said Jim, "is that it's going to be one hell of a long day."

NOT ONLY LONG, it turned out, but hot and thirsty. They were exposed on an outcropping, in full sun without a hint of shade, a swig of water, or a breath of wind. The Rocky Mountains proved once again they would freeze you all night and broil you all day. Coy whimpered. The pup didn't like it when they stayed far from water.

Sometimes the trappers saw movement in the brush. Occasionally Beckwourth shot at the movement, and once he thought, from an outcry, that he killed a Snake.

About midday Flat Dog, standing watch, said, "Here comes Gideon."

The big French-Canadian ran a zigzag pattern from cover to cover, carrying a small, flat keg. Then he looked around, shrugged, and walked up the open hillside. "Sorry," he said when he reached them, "Clyman and me, we not think until now, you no got water."

Every man drank his fill, and Sam cupped hands for Coy to drink.

"You go down now," Gideon said to Sam. "I take over here. You go see Third Wing."

IS HE DEAD? He wasn't moving. His skull was broken open, probably by a stone axe or a tomahawk. Streams of blood made cracks down his face, like a stone broken by a sledge hammer. Blood tangled his black hair, and red stained the big hanks of Sam's white hair tied into it.

Brought low.

Coy uttered a whine and laid down between Third Wing's feet.

Sam sat next to his friend, wet a forefinger, and held it in front of Third Wing's nostrils. Air cooled the finger.

"He won't last," said Clyman.

"Hugh Glass lasted," said Sam.

Sam stepped over to the creek. Coy followed and lapped. Sam drew air in big and let it out big. He felt as though, in all that vast Western sky, his lungs couldn't catch breath. When he was calm, he fished in his shot pouch and brought out a rag, a piece of cloth he used for tearing patches for his rifle. He wet the rag in the cold running water, walked back, and sat down by his friend. He squeezed drops of water from the rag into Third Wing's open mouth.

The parched lips made no movement. The dry tongue gave no sign. Sam saw the eyelids flutter, though, and that gave him hope. He put his hand to the medicine pouch around his neck.

Clyman moved around, rifle in the crook of his left arm. He was padding from tree to tree in the cottonwood grove. From every station he studied the plain for sign of enemies. Luckily, the campsite offered no good cover for sneaking up.

Sam put his mind deliberately on Hugh Glass. Everyone knew Glass was dying. Major Henry left two men to bury him while the brigade rode on. They abandoned Glass. The old fellow came to and started crawling back to the fort where they started, a couple of hundred miles away. He made it.

Third Wing was going to make it.

COY HEARD CLYMAN'S footsteps before Sam did. Sam refused to look up. "Don't kid yourself," said Jim, "Third Wing's luck has run out."

Sam said nothing. He reached down and took Third Wing's hand. Maybe his friend would take comfort from that. Coy licked the joined hands.

"Why don't you take a snooze?" said Clyman. "You look tired. It's going to be a long night, and I'll need you for two watches." He padded away on his rounds.

Sam certainly wasn't going to nap while his friend struggled for life. He took his patch cloth, wet it from a keg, and dribbled water into Third Wing's open mouth. No response except for ragged breathing.

He leaned back against a cottonwood and took Third Wing's hand again. It was a fine afternoon. The sun felt good on his face, the little breeze felt good, and he liked the small rustling of the cottonwood leaves. A good day. Death danced "Skip to My Lou" around the edges.

HE WOKE WITH a start. How long had he slept? *Why is my hand cold?*

Oh. He shook his hand free.

It was Third Wing's hand that was cold.

Coy crooned out a moan.

Sam just sat. Death had wiped his mind clean.

When he heard footsteps, Sam said softly, "James."

Clyman came up, looked from Sam to Third Wing and back. "You want to do the burying?"

"That would be hard."

"Me and Beckwourth will do it. Go relieve him."

* * *

NOTHING WAS A whit different on the ridge. Not a shot had been fired since Sam left. "Them Snakes moved around a little," said Jim, "but too quick. They're waiting for dark."

"And then what?"

Beckwourth shrugged.

Gideon was asleep on his back, wheezing like a bellows.

Blue Horse and Flat Dog lay behind the low rock wall, eyes on the Snake camp.

"Go down to Clyman," Sam told Jim. "Tell him I'll take care of Third Wing."

Beckwourth rose, whacked the red dust off his leggings, and headed down the hill.

"Down, Coy," said Sam. Last thing he wanted was the pup to skyline himself and get shot. He looked at the sun. Mid-afternoon, maybe five hours until dark. Too damn long.

Sam took Beckwourth's place as lookout.

A couple of hours later he thought time was moving the way dust particles blew off this hill. Tiny bits moved, and they didn't go far. The sun would go down about the time the hill changed shape one half of a smidgeon.

He saw a willow wiggle. *Clumsy bastard you are,* he thought, *to bump a tree that hard. You deserve to die.*

He stuck The Celt's muzzle through a slot in the rock wall and drew sight on the willow. Then he thought how dumb this was. His chance of hitting anyone was small, his chance of killing almost nothing. He might end up wishing he had this lead ball later, and the powder to shoot it. He might end up out of ammunition, just like he did last summer.

To hell with it, he'd lost a friend and he was angry. He held his sights low down on the bush and pulled the trigger. Boom!

The branches and leaves wiggled. *My Indian name should be Slayer of Green Leaves,* he mocked himself.

Beckwourth came back up the hill and sent the two Crows down. "You need a break," he said, "sit in the shade."

"We don't need a break," said Blue Horse. He and Flat Dog were still watching the Snake camp with infinite patience.

"Get gone," said Beckwourth.

They did.

Sam took their place behind the rock wall. "What's going to happen tonight?"

Jim shrugged. "They'll attack us or they'll clear out."

Both men thought on this.

"I'm sorry about Third Wing."

"He saved my life," said Sam. "I liked him. I'll miss him."

A raven swooped close overhead. *"Cra-a-w-wk."* Maybe the raven thought this was too many people in his backyard.

"Know what else?" said Beckwourth.

Sam looked at him curiously.

"You ever think, ninety of you went up the Missouri last spring, fifteen got killed by the Arickarees? Seven of us come up here trapping, one got killed so far." Jim paused. "You ever think . . . ?"

Silence.

At length Sam said, "The next one is gonna be me?"

"No, me," said Beckwourth.

They looked at each other, wordless.

ALL NIGHT FOUR trappers slept and two stood guard. Clyman gave Sam the first and last watches. The night was perfectly quiet, eerily quiet.

At first light Blue Horse and Flat Dog were already on the ridge overlooking the Snake camp. They'd gone up in the darkness to avoid being spotted.

After a look they stood up in plain sight and walked down.

"They're gone," said Blue Horse. Which everyone had figured.

A search of the camp, the brush, and the horse pen showed they'd left nothing, certainly not a dead man to even up for Third Wing. Sam did get to learn the print of a Snake moccasin and set it down firmly in his mind.

They sipped coffee and ate jerked meat.

"What you boys thinking?" asked Clyman.

"Time to move," said Beckwourth. "Six is not enough in Indian country." Jim didn't look guiltily at the Crows when he said this, but Sam did.

"Right," said Clyman. "Let's go find Fitzpatrick and trap with him."

Sam said only, "Third Wing."

"I want to say some words for him," said Clyman.

Sam felt the pang again. When he learned to read, he would have words for important occasions.

Blue Horse and Flat Dog didn't want Third Wing planted in the ground. The others agreed. No one had to add—"He's not a white man." There were no trees in sight, except here along the stream.

"I think," said Sam, "Blue Horse and Flat Dog should have his horses."

"One horse, each of the three of you," Clyman said. "The rest of us, we'll divide his weapons."

Silence was assent.

So Third Wing's grave turned out to be a cottonwood tree indistinguishable from any other, in a cottonwood grove barely distinguishable from any other.

They hoisted him up, the two Crows below and Sam on the lowest branch. It was an embarrassingly awkward and intimate piece of work. Sam could hardly believe how, well . . . It didn't seem decent that something so *bodily* could be the remains of his friend. Didn't seem decent that what animated Third Wing could be so completely gone, gone, gone.

He got Third Wing propped across two branches. Poor, but the best he could do. He looked long at the face. Then he reached out, grasped the hanks of his own white hair one by one in Third Wing's, untied them, and put them into Third Wing's hands.

Blue Horse handed up the robes, and Sam tied them around Third Wing, head to toe. They would keep the birds off, for a while.

"Words," he said to Clyman.

"In the midst of life we are in death. Earth to earth, ashes to ashes, dust to dust; in sure and certain hope of the Resurrection unto eternal life."

"I have some words," Gideon put in. The bear man hesitated. "This is a prayer of my father's people, the Hebrews. We call it the Kaddish, and it is a prayer for those who mourn the dead. It exalts the name of God and asks that His kingdom be established on earth in our lifetimes."

Gideon began to recite. The words themselves meant nothing to Sam, but he found himself swept up in their rhythms. Meaning surrendered to incantation, thought to feeling. For those long moments Sam swam in sounds of memory, longing, grief, love. For those moments death seemed less hideous.

When Gideon finished, no man broke the silence, and they rode on.

PART THREE

Rendezvous

Chapter Thirteen

S am could hardly believe this business of finding someone in a wilderness a thousand miles high and two thousand across, but it worked. They picked up the trail of the Fitzpatrick outfit easily, a dozen or so horses following the Siskadee. They even found Fitz's camping spots. Soon the two groups joined up and trapped the Uinta Mountains (the men had named them after the Indians who seemed to be called Uintas, or Utahs, or Utes).

Ashley was still gone down Green River with an exploring party, Fitz said.

"What the devil's Green River?" asked Sam.

"What the general calls the Siskadee, *mi coyote*. That's its official name now, the map name."

"What's wrong with Siskadee?" said Sam.

"It's not the white man name," Fitz said. It was the Crow word for the river, and meant sage hen.

It was time to make a living. Sam liked roaming the country and getting to know Indians better than he liked trapping. When you came back the trap you'd set in the cold creek, if you were lucky, a beaver had inspected the stick to see if a rival was coming into its territory. CLAMP! No matter how it struggled, if you'd done your work right, the beaver would drown. Now the work began. You skinned it out. Back in camp you scraped the fat off the hide and stretched it on a hoop made of willows. The results of your labor were two: you stunk of blood and fat, and you had something to trade to General Ashley for supplies you needed to survive another year in the mountains.

In mid-June they set out for the place General Ashley had appointed for a midsummer rendezvous of all his mountain men.

Ashley told his three captains, Fitz, Clyman, and Zacharias Ham, that on his way down the Green River, he would mark a meeting place in a certain way. Fitz had written it down. After going at least forty or fifty miles downstream, he would cache all his trade goods and unneeded baggage at some conspicuous point. If a river entered on the west, that would be the place. If there was no river, it would be some place above the mountains the river seemed to pass through. Here Fitz had down Ashley's instructions exactly, including spelling. "Trees will be pealed standing the most conspicuous near the Junction of the rivers or above the mountains as the case may be—. Should such point be without timber I will raise a mound of Earth five feet high or set up rocks the top of which will be made red with vermilion thirty feet distant from the same—and one foot below the surface of the earth a northwest direction will be deposited a letter communicating to the party any thing that I may deem necessary."

Fitzpatrick commented that the general would never be celebrated for his literary style. Sam wasn't sure what that meant.

What Sam couldn't believe was, it worked. Here they were, all the American trapping outfits from all over the west side of the mountains—Pacific drainage, all of this, maybe the wildest country left on the continent. By a mark simple as a mound of rocks they came together on a broad flat on this stream they were calling Henry's Fork, above the general's Green River.

They came in one outfit at a time, and greeted friends. Ashley's men had been in the mountains only three years, but the friendships felt strong and deep.

"This child is glad you're still wearing your hair."

"Glad to see you, old coon, I heered you'd gone under on the Salt River."

"Good to see you above ground, hoss."

Sam observed quietly that a lot of them, sun-darkened

white men for sure, called themselves "this nigger" and others "you nigger," without any implication of race at all. *Strange,* he thought. But then races here were a jumble: American whites, French-Canadians, Mexicans from Taos and Santa Fe, blacks, and Indians.

The man Sam most looked forward to seeing was Jedediah Smith—Cap'n Smith to some of the men, Diah to those, like Sam and Gideon, who'd known him before he became a captain. Diah acted glad to see Sam, too, almost effusive for this restrained Yankee. He said he'd spent the winter going clear to some place called Flathead Post on some river named Clark's Fork of the Columbia, far to the northwest.

Bill Sublette was also in, after wintering on Bear River with Captain Weber, and young Jim Bridger with them. Sam wasn't clear how well he wanted to get to know Bridger.

A party of men under Johnson Gardner had fallen in with Weber—free trappers they called themselves, not employed by Ashley or anyone else. Sam wondered what that was like, operating without the protection of a big outfit like the Ashley men, having no one to issue you horses or supplies, trapping wherever you wanted to, and owning a hundred percent of your fur at the end. He wondered if those free trappers would make more money than he did.

And the Weber-Johnson outfit brought a surprise—twenty-nine French-Canadians who used to work for the Hudson's Bay Company in the far Northwest. Gardner had offered them $3.50 a pound for their beaver, and prices for supplies far lower than the John Bulls offered. Immediately they'd come over to the American side. They were old hands from their look, men like Gabriel, in the beaver country a long time. Most of them had Indian wives, Indian children, and Indian ways. Sam watched them carefully, and enviously.

Eight horses for Meadowlark.

THE TRAPPERS SPREAD their camp under the cottonwoods on a flat alongside Henry's Fork of the Green River. There

wasn't much need for shelter, for here the country was more
desert than mountain. Bedrolls and some tents, brush shel-
ters, and tipis were scatted near mess fires. The talk over
morning coffee was about where the Ashley party might
be—every other brigade was into rendezvous. The general
had set out to find out where Green River went.

"Maybe it went to hell," someone offered.

"Maybe the general got lost," Gideon said.

"Maybe he got seduced by the maidens of California," said
Beckwourth.

Blue Horse gave Sam a look like, "Explain this to me
later." Sam knew Blue Horse spent time explaining things
to Flat Dog, too; but the younger brother's English was improving.

Sam said nothing in answer to the maidens of California
remark, but wondered whether so small a party, eight men,
might have been stalked and killed by Indians. "Killed by
Indians" was a phrase that sang wickedly through his mind
more and more, and through his dreams.

"I hear you got to be a hero," boomed a voice behind him.

Sam wheeled. Micajah.

Sam jumped to his feet and shook Micajah's paw, careful
to keep the clasp light and quick.

Micajah and his brother Elijah were the biggest men Sam
had ever seen. They weren't big like trees, tall and limb-
shaped, but like kegs. Their thighs were keg-sized, their upper arms similar, and their enormous chests and bellies were
full-sized barrels. Maybe they were signs that the Bible
stories about giants were true.

Way back on the Ohio, Micajah and Elijah had been working crew on the keelboat that brought Sam to the West. Captain Sly Stuart took on one passenger, a sassy madam named
Abby. In Evansville, Indiana, Micajah and Elijah attacked
Abby, Sam, and his friend Grumble, intending to steal the
gold coins sewn into the stays of Abby's corset. In the big
men's view, their proposed victims were a boy, a whore, and
a gambler. The boy, whore, and gambler turned out to be

more dangerous than expected, especially the whore. Micajah ended up fleeing, and Elijah ended up dead.

"I don't know what you mean," Sam mustered. He didn't like being called a hero.

When Sam ran into Micajah months later by surprise, Micajah was blaming him for Elijah's death. But when Micajah got sober—there wasn't enough liquor in the wilderness to keep him drunk—they made up.

"They tell a big story about you," Micajah went on, "walking the whole Platte River by yourself, starving, coming out to Atkinson all right." There was sneer in the tone.

"The hero's Hugh Glass," said Sam. "I just did what I had to to survive."

Coy sat next to Sam's legs and stared fixedly at Micajah. Sam marked it down as strange behavior, but kept his attention on the big man.

"Wal, hoss, you're my hero," Micajah said, and exposed his big, yellow teeth in what was supposed to be a smile. "What's this?" He pointed at Coy.

"My pup," said Sam. He didn't want to say "coyote."

"Looks like a damn prairie wolf to me, Hero." It meant the same as "coyote," but Sam disliked both terms equally. Coy was Coy. "You want a prairie wolf for a pet?"

"Saved my life on that long walk," Sam said. "Maybe we ought to call him Hero."

Micajah gave out a roar of a laugh. "Maybe we oughta. A prairie wolf hero, ain't that the cat that caught the cradle?" He clapped Sam hard on the shoulder. Sam stumbled sideways, tripped over Coy, and went ass over teacups into the dirt. Coy skittered off making little yelps.

"Come on, Hero, get up, we're gonna have some fun over by the river. Men competing." Micajah grabbed Sam's hand and yanked him to his feet.

"See you over there," Sam said, and turned his back.

Blue Horse gave him a look like, "You have funny friends."

* * *

THE NEXT MORNING Micajah interrupted their morning coffee. "Sam," he said, paused dramatically, and squatted. "You and me, we oughta do something. Show each other we're friends. I know you'll play the comrade to me—that's the kinda man you are. And I am your friend, but you don't seem sure of that."

Micajah waited, one eyebrow cocked.

"What do you have in mind?"

"A little shooting show," he said, tapping the butt of the pistol stuck in his belt.

"Not pistol," Sam said. Sam didn't have one. And a pistol might be a sensitive matter. At the Crow village, winter of '24, Micajah and Gideon fought best two of three falls, and Gideon won Micajah's pistol.

"Naw, not pistol. For this you'll want it accurate as it can get." His face looked full of good humor.

"What?"

"We shoot the tin cup off each other's heads." It was an old and favorite trick of the alligator horses of the big rivers, the keelboat men. It was used to show how strong a friendship was, or that one had been patched up.

"Hell, no," said Sam. That was something he'd never do, not with anyone. Even if he had perfect confidence in the other fellow, it was too risky. Hell, what about the wind? It was a game for drunks and wild men.

"It's safe. You've caught me sober."

Sam shook his head.

"I challenge you, as a matter of honor." That was supposed to be the invitation that couldn't be refused.

Sam didn't want to play. "Not a chance," he repeated.

"You don't, I'll take it unkindly," said Micajah.

Gideon threw words in fast. "I'll do it. Sam's not that sure of himself. I'll stand in for him."

In the strange world of river honor, this was allowed, and Micajah couldn't refuse it.

"Let's get at it," said Micajah, and stood up.

They picked an open spot within view of most of the mess fires. Fifty paces apart they stood, and they weren't long paces.

Micajah was genial and kept it light. "You take the first shot," he told Gideon. "Since we have no whiskey to make our pledges," he mock-complained, "we'll do it with the best drink in the world, Rocky Mountain creek water."

He downed a cup, and so did Gideon. Then Micajah took Gideon's hand and said, "In this way, I pledge everlasting friendship between you, me, and Sam."

Gideon said the same words in a light-hearted tone.

Sam felt damn weird, but he had no intention, ever, of playing this game, especially with Micajah.

They took their positions. Micajah looked sassy as he waited, hips cocked. Just as Gideon's flintlocker came level, no hesitation, BLAM!

The tin cup flew. Micajah danced a jig.

Micajah's shot was just as quick and accurate.

Dozens of men grinned at each other.

Gideon and Micajah joined arms at the elbows and danced around.

WAITING FOR ASHLEY, the trappers held competitions—foot races, horse races, wrestling, and whatever else they could dream up. They played euchre endlessly with the few decks of playing cards in their possible sacks. They made bets on contests of knife-throwing and tomahawk-throwing—take seven steps back and throw at a piece of cloth pinned on a tree. Sam watched and decided he had something else to practice during the long winters, learning to throw a knife or tomahawk accurately enough, and hard enough, to stop an attacker. He was damn impressed with the realization that this was a dangerous country.

Some men also hunted. Some fished. But mostly they did what all their successors would do during the long evenings while the twilight glowed and the sun rimmed a western range on the horizon with gold. In a country without newspapers, and almost no books, they talked.

Every kind of talk. Shop talk—where such and such a creek heads up and what river it flows into. Where you can cross a certain mountain, and where it peters out into plains. What spring might save your critters and your own hide on a long, dry crossing, if you know where it is. What berries are good to eat, and when; which ones taste all right in a stew, if not by themselves. What roots are nourishing, and which ones might make a poultice, or a remedy for headache or looseness of the bowels.

Endless talk of animals, too. What the habits of Old Ephraim, the most dangerous animal of the country, seem to be; how prairie wolves act different from wolves. How you catch up with an ermine or a river otter and what their hides are worth in trade to Indians, or worth in dollars back in the markets of the States. Where elk can be found in spring, summer, autumn, winter. How, if you hang your shirt or hat from your ramrod, you might get an antelope to walk right up to you. How antelope hide makes a fine shirt for dress up in front of squaws, but deer hide is better for leggings, moose hide for winter moccasins, buffalo to wear like a blanket in winter.

Talk of weather, too, a rain so hard it opens a gully right in front of you. Lightning that dances on the horns of the buffalo. A dust storm that will choke you if you stay out in it. A night's blizzard deep to a mule's muzzle. A flash flood that swept away our horses, beaver packs, possibles—everything.

Indians: What tribes were usually friendly, meaning the Crows and to Sam's surprise, the Snakes, which some of the men called the Shoshones. Those "friendly" Indians still might kill your friend and steal your horses. Which tribes were never friendly, meaning the Blackfeet. Which made the most durable moccasins, which tanned hides the finest, which did the best beadwork, and which had squaws most eager to go to the willows, and were most fun when they got there.

The news got handed around. Sam thought the most dramatic was Jedediah Smith's story. Trapping to the north and west of the Green, he and his half-dozen men had come on a bedraggled party of Hudson's Bay fur men led by a fellow who called himself Old Pierre. These men were from Flathead Post, on Clark's Fork of the Columbia, far to the north and west. They hailed originally from the region of the St. Lawrence River, all the way beyond Montreal, they said, but some of them had been on western waters for more than a decade. Bearing names like Godin, Godair, and Geaudreau, they were French-Canadians—half-breeds—and the American fur men called them by the tribe they said they came from, Iroquois.

These trappers, separated from their main outfit, had been harassed by Snakes, and the Indians were aroused because a chief had been killed. Would Captain Smith, they asked, in exchange for the hundred and five furs they had, escort them to the camp of their leader, Alexander Ross?

Jedediah Smith knew an opportunity when he saw one. The combined party would be safer than either outfit alone, and he would be guided through country he didn't know and get paid for it. And then he could follow the main outfit in safety all the way to their home post, mapping out beaver country all the way.

Now he was back, with knowledge of lands with plews aplenty. But his tale, along with Johnson Gardner's, meant bad news as well as good: The British were trapping the prime Snake River country to the northwest. Here on the west of the mountains, the territory was disputed. Both the U.S. and Britain claimed it. Whoever got the beaver first would carry the day, and neither side would do the other any favors.

Now a realization began to dawn on Sam and everyone else. This rendezvous wasn't a one-time thing. It was *the* way for all the men who roamed the mountains to get together. Summer, like winter, was a time you couldn't be out making a living—the beaver pelts were too thin to be worth taking. So why not rendezvous? See your friends, and note which ones you wouldn't see anymore. Get the stories of what happened to everyone, and be warned, or know where you would likely have a welcome. Rendezvous would be like a giant bulletin board, keeping all men up to date on doings in the fur country.

Now they were impatient for Ashley to show up, so they could trade their year's catch for all the things they needed, powder and lead, maybe a pistol or another trap, coffee, sugar, tobacco, and blankets, cloth, beads, bells, vermilion, all the foorfuraw that gave you entrée in a village because the squaws wanted it.

Some of the men saw that they were accomplishing something else, too. At this first rendezvous in the summer of 1825, they started to build their community's body of knowledge. Hard-won detailed facts about a land of daunting vastness and astonishing topographical complexity, creek and plain, mountain and badlands, and all the creatures who inhabited it, four-legged, winged, rooted, crawlers, and most important, two-legged. As carpenters knew about different woods and about tools, the mountain men needed to know about a country that was equal parts inviting and hazardous to your health.

Also, during these long evenings, they told stories. Some of them were simple. How Antoine got drowned in the Milk River. How Manuel and Ezekiel rode up the Mariah and never came back. How Joe and John got surprised by Injuns but outran them and warned the camp.

Some of these stories Sam knew. How he and Clyman and Sublette survived a bitter night on South Pass. How old Glass found the grit to survive after being left for dead. (No one told this one in front of Bridger, and mostly they didn't name young Jim as one of the men who abandoned Glass—Sam wondered why.) How Sam, and then Fitzpatrick and Gideon with others, got put afoot and walked down the whole length of the Platte, seven hundred miles, near-starving all the way. Several men clapped Sam on the back after this one was told.

And here, finally, Sam heard the story of John Colter and

his escape from the Blackfeet told properly. Some of the American hands here had been in the mountains for fifteen years before the Ashley men came. Some of the French-Canadians had been here for several generations. Auguste, a graybeard with two Mandan wives, told the tale:

"Colter," Auguste began, "he was *some*. He come out wit' Lewis and Clark and stay, he *stay*—ze only man who don' go back to ze settlements but by God *live* in ze mountains. When old Manuel Lisa, ze Spanyard, he come upriver, here is Colter to show him ze ways and ze creeks and passes. With Colter's help, Lisa get on wit' ze Crows good. When ze Crows get into a big tussle wit' ze Blackfeet, though, Colter, he fight on Crow side and ze Blackfeet spot him—enemy.

"Soon not long Colter and a trapper name Potts go trapping in Blackfoot country, keeping zeir eyeballs skinned.

"One morning zey work a creek near Jefferson Fork in canoe when, all of ze sudden, zey see Blackfeet on both banks. Not just men, women and children too, which is a good, means is no war party. An Injun, he motion for zem to come ashore. Right quick Colter head in—no other place to go. He hope maybe zey just get rob and let go.

"Colter, he step out canoe and sign he come in peace. When Potts start get out, an Injun jerk his rifle out of his hands. Colter snatch ze rifle back an' hand to Potts, who push ze canoe to midstream. 'Put in,' Colter says to Potts, 'right now. Ain't no place to run. Let 'em see you ain't afeered of 'em.'

" 'You crazy?' says Potts. 'You can see zey going kill us. Torture us first.' Blackfeet, they be bad Injuns for torture.

"An arrow hits into Potts' thigh. He ups rifle and shoots Injun as grab his rifle. Right quick Potts is pin cushion for arrows.

"The women, now they send up grieving cries the way zey do, the men start whoop and yell for revenge. Colter, he know what comes. Hands grab him and he no resist. They take everything he own and rip off his clothes, but he don' fight it. Warriors come at him shaking zeir tomahawks, and he act like he don' notice. He means to stay calm, no matter what.

"The Blackfeet, zey sit in a council. Not so long a chief comes to Colter and ask if he is fast runner. Colter, he consider his answer—you don' hurry talk wit' Injuns. Looks like maybe a chance here, poor as a gopher agin a griz, but a chance. 'No,' says he, 'I'm a poor runner. The ozzer Long Knives, zey think I'm fast, but I am no.'

"The Injuns chew on this. Soon ze chief takes Colter out onto a little flat. 'Walk out past that big boulder,' he signs— 'zen run and try to save yourself.'

"Colter sees ze young men is stripping down for race. So he walk. He keeps walking past ze boulder, knowing zey start when he set to running. Finally zey whoop and he take off.

"He head for Jefferson Fork, about five, six miles off. Don' make much sense, but nothing make sense. He no outlast 'em on land, Blackfeet be good trackers. Maybe he can get in river and wipe out his track and. . . .

"At least he give zem a run for it.

"He just run. Eyes see, legs run, that's all—run. Way that child figure, while you run, you live.

"He no look back, not for long time. When he take ze chance, he sees Injuns spread out all over ze peraira, 'cept one. That one is mebbe one hundred yards behind, and carry spear.

"Right here, this is when Colter begin to t'ink mebbe he have chance. He gives thought to Jefferson Fork, probably two, three miles ahead more. He pick up pace a leetle. The mountain air come in and out of his lungs big and good.

"He feels dizzy sometimes, and sick to his meat bag sometimes, but that Colter, he keeps runnin'. After a while his back, it starts prickle, like it is expecting ze point of that spear. He no help himself, he must look back.

"The Injun is only twenty yards behind and ze spear, it is cocked.

"That does it. Colter turn to Injun, spread his arms, and holler out in ze Crow language, 'Spare my life!'

"That Injun, maybe he is took by surprise. Anyhow, when he tries stop and throw ze spear all at once, he stumble and fall on his face. The spear sticks in ground and breaks off in his hand.

"Old Colter, he pounce. The Injun holler for mercy. Colter grab that busted spear and drive it right into his gut.

"Then Colter, he take a big look around. No sign of Injun anywhere. Shinin' times. Off he runs wit' a spring in his step, head for ze river.

"Not so long he hear whoops, which mean ze Blackfeet find zeir dead comrade. He just run harder.

"When he finally see Jefferson Fork, he spot an island down a little wit' a pile of driftwood at ze top. He has idea. Right quick he dive in—damn, that river so cold!—and goes wit' ze current down to ze driftwood.

"Now he dive down like beaver and come up in ze pile. Thick logs sticking every which way, blue sky up above, O *sacre bleu*! If Injuns get too close, he can duck down in ze water.

"Those Blackfeet splash all around and whoop and holler to *le bon dieu* in heaven, but not one sees Colter. They disappear downstream and come back, so zey probably know his trail no come out of ze river. After a while zey quit.

"Old Colter, he wait until far after dark. Then he ease out and swim wizout no splash down ze river, float down a long way, in case zey check for his track agin.

"What is ahead, that is a job for a mountain man. Walk two hundred miles naked. No rifle, pistol, nor knife. Nothing but roots and bark to eat. Sun and wind burning and drying ze skin.

"Finally he come to Fort Lisa, and ze gate guard not know him—he is so gaunted and sunburned, all scratched and bloody. After they hear his story, all men say, 'Colter, zat hoss have hair of a bear in him.'"

ASHLEY CAME IN late on the last day of June, and brought some surprises with him. Leading the Ashley men to rendezvous was a brigade out of Taos. Reports of trappers working from Mexico echoed through the mountains, but this was the first outfit Sam had seen. Etienne Provost was the leader.

Sam watched them unload and set up camp. They spoke three languages, Spanish, French, and English. They were Frenchmen from Canada (not French-Canadians but white Frenchmen) and dark Spanyards; that's what the men called them, though Mexico had gotten her independence four years ago. These trappers were different, and their outfits were different, these men from Taos. Some of them carried ponchos instead of capotes, and they lifted odd-looking saddles from the backs of the horses, the saddle horns as flat and big as saucers. Sam reflected that a fellow could sit around the fire tonight and trade stories in a handful of languages—there were Americans, an Irishman for a different accent, Frenchmen, about thirty Iroquois, French-Canadians who spoke Cree, two Crows, a couple of dozen Mexicans. Coy sat close by Sam and glared at the strangers and growled.

Then Sam heard a voice in English that seemed familiar. Coy jumped up and trotted forward, dodging horses, and jumped up on . . .

Sam sprinted forward and gave the man a bear hug so hard it was almost a tackle.

"Hannibal McKye," he stuttered out.

"Sam. I knew you were close when I saw Coy."

"Glad to see you above ground."

"Hail, friend," said Hannibal. His speech was always a little strange. What could you expect of the son of a Dartmouth Classics professor and one of his students, a Delaware girl?

Coy squirmed around Hannibal's legs until the Delaware petted him.

"Have you turned into a mountain man?"

"No," said Hannibal. "After I saw you at Atkinson"—Hannibal had found Sam on the trail near the fort, passed out from starvation—"I went back to St. Louis to get outfitted again." Hannibal's profession, or one of them, was trading with the Indians. Oddly, he did it alone, apparently not afraid of having his scalp taken or his horses or trade goods stolen. "Had a good winter, partly because of some friends of yours, Abby and Grumble."

Abby the madam and Grumble the con man, two of the finest people in the world. Sam couldn't stay in the mountains all the time, if only because he had to see Abby and Grumble once in a while.

"What is this?" Sam had never seen a horse the color of the one Hannibal's saddle came off of. It was a stallion, slate blue, with dark stockings and tail, and a dark stripe on the back.

"The Mexicans call it a *grulla*," said Hannibal. "His name is Ellie."

"Ellie?" A girl's name for a stallion? Also, it was Sam's mother's name.

"Short for elephant. Hannibal was a general from Carthage. He marched against the Romans on elephants."

"Oh, well, Ellie is some good-looking," said Sam.

"And an athlete," said Hannibal.

Again, Hannibal seemed to have the finest in horse flesh.

Sam grinned into the eyes of his friend. "My fire's over by that cottonwood, just this side. When you're ready, come and sit and tell your story."

A while later (time in the mountains was never measured in minutes) Hannibal staked the *grulla* nearby, keeping the horse in sight. He helped himself from the coffee pot on the fire and sat.

Sam began with, "I never thanked you properly for what you did."

Hannibal cocked an eyebrow at him.

"That Christmas Day," Sam said.

Hannibal nodded and smiled.

Christmas Day, 1822, Sam often thought, was the most important day of his life. It seemed to be the worst and turned out the best. The day before, Christmas Eve, was just the opposite.

On Christmas Eve, his birthday, he'd gone to his special place in the forest near his home, which he called Eden, to remember his father. Lew Morgan died in Eden that day in 1821.

In the middle of his reminiscing, Katherine turned up. She was his neighbor and the girl he secretly fancied. As a birthday present, she'd brought him a picnic and, as it turned out, the first act of love of his life.

The next day, Christmas, was emotional acrobatics. At Christmas dinner Katherine and Sam's big brother, Owen, announced their betrothal. Sam wanted an explanation from Katherine, but got none. He fled—and ran into Hannibal.

Across a fire, with the aid of some food, Hannibal helped him come to terms, partly, with what had happened. And helped him, gently, see into his own heart. What Sam wanted most in life was to go to the West, adventuring.

Incredibly, nudged imperceptibly by Hannibal, he went that very night, straight from the campfire. He followed his heart's compass to the Ohio River, down it to the Mississippi, up to St. Louis, and signed on to go to the Rocky Mountains as a mountain man.

Madness. Divine madness.

"You said something that night," Sam said across the flames. "I didn't really get it. Something about a wild hair. What was that?"

Hannibal grinned. "I've said it several times, mostly to my-self. 'Everything worthwhile is crazy, and everyone on the planet who's not following his wild-hair, middle-of-the-night notions should lay down his burden right now, in the middle of the row he's hoeing, and follow the direction his wild hair points.'"

Coy squealed and looked at Sam pathetically. The two men sat with the embarrassment of too many words about things that are hard to talk about.

"I'm crazy, you know," said Hannibal.

Coy barked.

"The pup agrees," Hannibal said.

Sam raised his eyes over rim of his coffee cup and said,

"You were going to tell me about Taos, and how you ended up here."

Hannibal shrugged. "There was an outfit heading for Santa Fe to trade. I went, I traded, I made a few dollars. Up in Taos, where I went for the devil of it, I met Etienne Provost's partner LeClerc. He was bringing supplies up to Provost in the Ute country, and I thought I'd like to see it. When I met Provost, I liked him and wanted to get to know the Utes, so I stayed . . ."

They both laughed. The narrative of bouncing around in one direction after the other . . .

"Hell," Hannibal, "I never know what I'm going to do next."

"I guess you live without planning."

"I guess."

They were both laughing too much. Coy made simpering noises.

When they looked up, Blue Medicine Horse and Flat Dog were standing next to them, waiting.

Sam introduced the two Crows to Hannibal, who offered them coffee.

After the Indians sat carefully—Sam noticed how mannerly they always were—Blue Horse said, "Everyone wants to know about that horse."

That brought on a discussion about Hannibal's *grulla* that only horsemen could appreciate. Though he was interested, Sam felt half left out. He did, however, learn how good Flat Dog's English was getting.

"Your horse looks excellent, too," said Hannibal. The three had stepped over to inspect Paladin. This brought Sam's mind back to the discussion.

"She's a good horse," said Sam.

"And she saved your ass," said Blue Horse. He and Flat Dog had learned that "ass" was a slightly vulgar word, and got a kick out of using it in English, which they would not have done in Crow.

Sam told Hannibal the story of how Paladin saved him from the buffalo bull. He finished with, "She is a good horse, but how can you tell?"

"Horses are athletes, or not, just like people. This animal doesn't look strong, but she has fine grace and balance."

Sam twisted his mouth in a pretense that he understood.

"In a race, for instance," Hannibal went on, "a clumsy horse will lose distance. A well-balanced horse covers the ground more efficiently, and therefore faster."

Sam could see that "efficiently" and "therefore" were too much for Blue Horse and Flat Dog, so he explained.

"So how about a race?" asked Blue Horse.

Coy barked in apparent approval, and they laughed.

"Several men want to run against you," said Flat Dog, a good English sentence for him.

"Including us," said Blue Horse.

Flat Dog began, "And some want to . . ."

"Bet." Blue Horse supplied the word.

"You got a race," said Hannibal.

BEFORE THE RACES the next day, most men got their business done with General Ashley. The general, typically, wanted to get his trading done in one day and start back to civilization.

This very first rendezvous made Ashley a believer. Summer was the best time to get a trade caravan to the mountains and back. The men had to have supplies. For survival, they needed fire steels, powder, lead, and flints; for their sanity, tobacco, coffee and sugar, plus an occasional trap, rifle, pistol, knife, tomahawk, or coat, and all the items they traded to the Indians. If Ashley brought these goods to the mountains, the men wouldn't have to spend months going all the way to St. Louis, or at least to Taos, to outfit themselves.

Ashley saw that and more. He realized that bringing trade goods to an annual rendezvous would be less risky and more profitable than running fur brigades. So he sat down with

Jedediah Smith, the young captain who had impressed everybody in the mountains, and offered Smith a partnership—Ashley to supply from the city, Smith to lead in the mountains.

Diah said yes. He didn't tell his partner that his ambition ran far beyond profit. He said nothing of his desire to see what was over the next hill, every hill in the West. Nothing of his yearning to be the first man to cross the continent to California. Nothing of his desire to use his compass and his eye to make pencilled maps, rendering the entire West for cartographers. He just agreed to a business proposition.

For Ashley this day's agenda was trading. He kept a careful record of what he traded to everyone. He gave the free trappers three dollars a pound for their beaver pelts, these plews weighing on average two pounds. He sold them tobacco at $1.25 per pound, coffee and sugar at $1.50, cloth at six to eight dollars a yard, two yards of ribbon (something to make an Indian woman smile) for a dollar; he exchanged a dozen fish hooks for two dollars, a dozen flints for a dollar; he sold butcher knives at $2.50 each, wool strouding at five dollars a yard, earrings, bells. The old types of muskets, *fusils,* went for $20 each—these were for trading to the Indians, since mountain men demanded the newer, more accurate guns, with rifling in the barrels.

One outfit, Johnson Gardner's, actually bought razors, scissors, and combs. The other mountain men chuckled at the idea that Johnson intended to have his men groom themselves.

The general settled up with his hired trappers at reduced rates for their beaver, because they were being paid wages as well.

Sam waited his turn. This was the moment, the occasion for which he'd stood in cold creeks until his knees and scraped hides until he smelled worse than a dead rodent. But like every other man, he needed DuPont and Galena. He needed trade items for the Indians. And much of what else was in Ashley's packs. He bought more than his pelts would pay for, and ended up in debt to the company.

Some of the men grumbled at the prices, which were five and ten times what Ashley had paid for the goods at St. Louis. The brigade leaders, though, defended Ashley. The cost of transporting goods to the mountains was huge in time, effort, and dollars, and was sometimes paid in blood as well.

Ashley kept one fact to himself. In the first three years his fur trade operation had lost money. Now he was heading to St. Louis with plews worth nearly fifty thousand dollars. He was becoming a rich man, and back in Missouri an important man.

The fur men of the Rocky Mountains were miffed about one big gap in all this trading. Ashley had no alcohol. Nothing to drink now, when they were in the mood for a party, to celebrate surviving the year; and nothing all year long, when they were working hard; and most important from a practical viewpoint, no liquor to trade the Indians. Booze made the trading much better.

Dozens of men groused at Ashley as they walked away, "Next year bring whiskey."

THE FUN DIDN'T stop, though, for Ashley's trading. The men set up a race course that circled the tents and tipis. It wasn't the smooth sort of course set up in towns and cities. In fact, a dry wash running toward Henry's Fork cut through it twice, the second time only fifty yards from the finish line.

There were a couple of hundred saddle horses in camp, and a score that the men wanted to watch run, or that their owners believed fast enough to race.

Not that others weren't valuable. Buffalo horses, for instance, needed a lot of bottom. A buffalo would outsprint a horse for a quarter mile, and might hold the lead for a mile, but eventually a horse with endurance would bring the hunter alongside for a shot. The strength of these animals wasn't a burst of speed around the camp.

Trail horses had their own value. They needed to be calm

and sure-footed for some of the steep, narrow mountain tracks.

These were excellent horses, but not race horses.

The men worked it out. Every competitor put up a pound of tobacco as an entry fee. The horses would run in pairs. If you lost a race to any other horse, you were out. Everyone could bet, and you could make side bets on your horse. But the big prize was winner-take-all. You had to win every race to win all the tobacco.

"Enter," Hannibal said to Sam. "Paladin is fast."

"I've never done this."

"So learn."

"Do I have a chance?"

"Against every rider but me."

Down at the mouth, sure he'd lose, Sam put his tobacco on the pile. James Clyman, running things, acknowledged his entry with a nod.

Tom Fitzpatrick walked up with tobacco, too. He was leading his fine sorrel Morgan.

Blue Horse entered his paint mare.

Flat Dog said tobacco was too valuable to throw away.

Coy slunk behind Sam, as though he was ashamed of Flat Dog.

Godin, one of the Iroquois, came forward on a small horse the men called a "cayuse," a term Sam hadn't heard. "Pony bred by them Cayuse Indians up to the Columbia River," someone said. "Sure-footed little things."

Two other Iroquois brought up Indian ponies. Everyone distinguished between Indian ponies and what they called American horses, which were brought out from the States, and larger.

Several men led forward horses that looked nondescript to Sam.

"They don't look like any racers," said Sam.

"They aren't," agreed Hannibal.

The eighteenth and last entry was Micajah, with a grin that

said he was sure of winning. He rode up on a big, powerful-looking bay. The horse looked every bit of eighteen hands high, a horse truly big enough for Micajah's immense bulk. He handed down his tobacco from high in the saddle. "Meet Monster," he said, "the hoss of the mountains."

"Is Monster the one to beat?" Sam asked Hannibal.

The Delaware shook his head. "Micajah's a clumsy rider who tries to jerk his horse around."

Sam didn't really understand that.

"That man mean as he looks?" said Hannibal.

"He is when he's drinking," said Gideon. He and Beckwourth had just walked up.

Hannibal appraised Micajah and said, "Good thing we don't have any liquor."

Coy made a loud yawning sound.

"Maybe pup's a booze hound," said Hannibal.

The riders loped around the course, checking footing and obstacles here and there. When they came to the dry wash each time, they picked places to cross. Most of them ran their mounts back and forth to get them used to diving into the wash and clambering out without losing much speed. The two crossings would be tricky moments of the race.

After most of the men headed back to the starting line, Hannibal was still repeating the jump into the wash. Sam took his cue and did the same until James Clyman hollered for them.

Beckwourth provided Clyman with a deck of playing cards. James shuffled just the hearts and spades, deuces through tens, and tossed them in a hat for the men to draw. Sam drew the deuce of spades, which meant he raced the fellow who drew the deuce of hearts, Art Smith, on one of the nondescript horses.

"I'm lucky," said Sam.

"Your whole time in the mountains," said Hannibal, "you've been walking in luck."

"Except with women," Gideon joked.

The first race was intriguing. Blue Horse was to run his

paint against Micajah and Monster. The riders minced their horses up to the starting line. Blue Horse's mare was fidgety, but Monster kept so still he might have been bored.

"David and Goliath," Hannibal said.

Clyman stood off and threw his hat in the air. When it hit the ground, the racers were off.

Blue Horse whacked the paint's hindquarters with his quirt. The bay got off half a step behind, and Micajah seemed in no great hurry.

Flat Dog cut loose a Crow war cry. *"Hi-yi-yi-yi, Hi-yi-yi-yay."*

Blue Horse whipped the paint again. "Looks like he means to get in front and stay there," said Hannibal.

The horses approached the dry wash, Blue Horse about two horse lengths ahead. The mare shifted her gait to go into the wash just right. At that moment Micajah whipped the bay and roared like a boulder crashing down the mountain. The bay charged hard and bumped the mare as she got her footing for the leap down, right in the hindquarters.

Blue Horse and the mare went a-tumble.

Micajah roared again, and Monster powered across the wash and up the other side. The big man was putting the whip to the bay now, and Monster showed his speed.

"Good horse," said Hannibal.

Coy yipped a protest.

Amazingly, Blue Horse was on his feet, back on the mare, and sprinting after Micajah.

"Never will he make it," said Gideon.

"We'll see," said Hannibal.

On the far side they only caught glimpses of the racers in between tents and tipis. Sam could make out that Blue Horse was riding like a fury and catching up.

As Monster came to the edge of the wash, Micajah's balance seemed uncertain, and the bay hesitated.

Blue Horse closed fast. Sam thought maybe Blue Horse intended to bump the bay. No, Sam saw, that was just his jump-off into the wash.

As the paint neared the edge, Micajah slid to the right and blocked the way.

The paint pulled up and pranced off. The edge crumbled. Horse and rider rolled into the wash.

Coy sent up a mournful howl.

Blue Horse was on his feet instantly. Sam was relieved—he thought the mare had rolled on Blue Horse.

The rider grabbed for the reins, but the mare threw her head, and the reins whipped out of reach.

Blue Horse lunged and caught them. Up the opposite side of the wash they bolted.

Micajah had a big lead now, though, at least half a dozen horse lengths with about a hundred yards to run.

Blue Horse came on hard, positioned high toward the horse's neck and whipping her hard.

"Look at that," said Hannibal. "Blue Horse is perfectly balanced and Micajah chugs along like a keg tied to the saddle."

Micajah won by two lengths.

Sam turned to Clyman. "He cheated. Micajah cheated. He bumped Blue Horse and made the paint fall."

Clyman looked at him with long-nosed amusement. "We didn't set any rules, as far as I can recollect."

"That's an educational remark," murmured Hannibal.

Gideon and Beckwourth grinned at each other.

Blue Horse caught Sam's eye and shook his head no. "I didn't know how whites do it," he said. "Next time I will."

Sam couldn't believe he wasn't mad, but Blue Horse seemed calm and easy.

They watched two races between indifferent horses. Sam knew he could get Paladin to run better than that.

"What did you mean about Blue Horse being high and Micajah chugging?" Sam asked Hannibal.

Hannibal and Blue Horse smiled at each other.

"Blue Horse had a good position in the saddle," Hannibal said. "High, balanced, sending the horse messages only with the reins and the whip."

"And speaking in her ear," said Blue Horse.

"Micajah had his big weight bouncing up and down hard on the horse, which works against the 'run fast' message and, worse, throws the horse off balance."

"What should I do?" asked Sam.

"You're a good rider. Shorten those stirrups, 'cause you're going to gallop or sprint all the way. Rise out of the saddle and really move with the horse."

Some of the races were interesting, some weren't. Sam noticed that the Iroquois on those cayuses won their races against the American horses.

Fitzpatrick ran against Godin. It was a terrific race until Fitz swung wide as they headed for the finish line. Suddenly Sam heard a loud crack! Horse and rider went ass over teacups.

The horse didn't try to get up. Fitz looked at it, checked out the ground where it went down, came back and got his pistol.

"Prairie dog hole," said Hannibal.

Bang! Black smoke roiled up from the pistol. The horse made one convulsive movement and went rigid.

"Bad luck," said Sam.

"Bad luck and poor observation," said Hannibal.

And, for an average trapper, half a year's earnings lost.

But it was time for Hannibal, who'd drawn the seven of hearts, to race. His opponent was the leader of the Iroquois, a fellow known to all, apparently, as Old Pierre, and he was riding a cayuse.

Sam felt nervous at the start. He had no doubt Pierre was wily, and was dying to know how Hannibal would run the race.

At the starting line Hannibal rose up close to the *grulla's* left ear and spoke softly. Clyman's hat sailed into the air. When it hit, Hannibal angled Ellie to the outside, well away from Old Pierre. He didn't use the whip, but the stallion ran beautifully.

At the crossing Ellie bounded into the wash in one leap, and out in another—no clawing up and down for this horse.

Pierre started yelling in French. Gideon said, "*Mon dieu,* he is angry."

On the far side Hannibal and Ellie had several lengths on Old Pierre, and their lead was growing. Ellie Elephant leaped into and out of the wash the second time in the same way. "That horse won't be beat," Blue Horse said.

"Unless he's out-tricked," said Sam.

Hannibal let the *grulla* run home, fast but comfortable. He never raised the whip in his right hand.

"My God, what a horse," said Beckwourth.

"And rider," said Gideon.

Sam's race was the last of the first round. "Take your position on the outside. I'd try to get right ahead and stay ahead," said Hannibal. "When you get to the wash, veer away from the other horse, so he can't play any tricks."

"Sam Morgan," said Sam to the other rider. He looked like a Kentuck man. He didn't take Sam's offered hand, but muttered, "Asa."

The race was pure fun. Paladin showed plenty of speed at the start and got a lead. Sam took Hannibal's advice and kept well away from the other horse when crossing the wash. By the time he came to the second wash, Sam had enough lead on Asa not to worry about where he was.

Paladin made the sprint to the finish in fine form.

Asa led his mount away grumbling, without a word to Sam.

"That man's just not having any fun," said Hannibal.

"I want to quit," Asa told Clyman loudly, "and I want my tobacco back. My horse is acting lame."

Coy stood up and bristled at the man. Everyone else stared at him. They were all gathered near Clyman, holding their mounts by the reins. No one had seen any sign of lameness during the race.

"Seems the fellow doesn't like losing," said Hannibal softly.

"Dammit, I said I want to quit. And I want my tobacco back."

"Well, hell, Asa, you already bet."

"Shut up, Cam," said Asa. "I'll whip you all unless I get my tobacco back."

Hannibal whispered to Sam, "Looks like some of the men have liquor."

"Quit your damned whispering. I say I want my tobacco back. What do you say?"

"More power to you, my friend," said Hannibal.

Clyman intervened. "We do have nine riders left, which is unhandy. If we had eight, an even number, it would work out better."

"Quit mouthin' and give me my tobacco back."

"My friend, I'll make you an offer," said Hannibal. "If I win, I'll return your pound of tobacco."

"Not good enough. Do you all say the same?"

"I do," said Sam.

Godin did too. One by one, each winner agreed, until they got to Micajah.

Micajah grinned fiercely and said, "To hell with you."

"Then I'll whip you and take it."

Micajah laughed nastily and said, "That's a deal."

"Is it settled, then?" said Clyman. "The winner will give Asa his tobacco back, unless Micajah wins."

"Which I will," said Micajah.

"I'll enjoy kicking your ass," said Johnny.

"All right," Clyman went on, "four races this round, two next round, and then the final."

Everyone nodded. Coy barked like a town crier making an announcement.

Sam's next opponent was Godin. His cayuse was a wiry thing, hard-muscled, looking like it had been through a lot of battles, and the losers of those battles were dead. Godin himself looked at Sam with a glint of amusement.

"He has a thousand tricks," said Gideon.

"You can't be ready for all of them," Hannibal said. "He saw you steer clear of Asa, so he'll be expecting that. If I were him, I'd jump out hard and all the way inside, get a lead. Then, if you catch up, he'll probably whip Paladin's face. That means you'll have to go far outside to pass him, and run a longer distance."

Sam's heart sank. "So what would you do if you were me?"

Hannibal told him. Sam didn't like it.

"He's right," Gideon said. Beckwourth nodded.

"Let's get going, Sam," said Clyman.

Sam swung up into the saddle. He looked hard at Hannibal, who was smiling big.

"Just do it," said Hannibal.

Sam decided he would.

Sam gave Godin the inside position. The riders smiled at each other like predators. Both horses pranced, ready to run, about to fight the reins.

Up went the hat.

When it knocked up a puff of dust, Sam turned Paladin right into Godin's cayuse and whipped her hard. Her front shoulder banged into the cayuse's hind quarters.

After a moment, the horse and rider caught their balance. The cayuse wheeled and snapped at Paladin.

Sam and the horse, though, were already a step in the clear, taking the far outside.

The cayuse came after Paladin like a rocket, neck stretched out, head lowered, teeth bared. One length, three, five, the cayuse attacked ferociously. Paladin fled like mad.

The cayuse was getting close. Sam shifted his weight to the inside and reined Paladin sharply that way. As they turned, the cayuse nipped Paladin's left hip with his teeth. Paladin bounded forward with a speed Sam didn't know she had.

Instantly, they were hard on the wash. Sam nudged Paladin to a crossing spot that was difficult but possible. This time she leaped, took two jumps in the wash, and hurled herself up the other side.

Sam didn't need to give her whip again. She could probably hear the cayuse on her outside and coming up. She ran like hell.

The cayuse shrieked. That horse was never going to quit.

For a little while Sam thought Paladin might just outrun the cayuse. In the far turn, though, opposite the starting line, the critter managed to get close.

Sam put the whip to Paladin, but was careful to give no sign until he executed his plan. When the cayuse's head came alongside Paladin's rump, he slashed the animal in the face, hard.

The cayuse veered sideways, screamed, and pulled up. Then he collected himself, urged by Godin's shouts, and set out in pursuit that was hotter yet.

Too late. Paladin had more speed anyway, and now she was running beautifully. The cayuse had shown the moxie to put on a burst and catch up once, but not twice.

Sam took a safe, quick route across the wash and kicked her home.

The biggest grin on the field belonged to Hannibal.

Sam jumped off the mare before she was fully stopped, threw his arms in the air, and yelled *"Yi-ay-ay-ay, Yi-ay-oh!"*

Coy made the best imitation of that cry he could manage.

Godin was full of dark looks. He had to rein the cayuse away hard. That horse still wanted to fight.

"Don't mind him," said Hannibal. "You give him a chance, he does the same to you."

Suddenly Paladin began to limp on her front right foot. Hannibal went to her quickly and lifted the foot. He poked at it and flipped something out. "A pebble in the frog," he said. "She should be all right."

Sam checked Paladin's left hindquarter. The hair was rubbed all wrong, the skin scraped but not broken.

"I'm sorry," Sam told her.

The mare took a step on the front right foot, a little gingerly, as though to say, "This is where the hurt is."

Blue Horse and Flat Dog walked up. They'd borrowed buckets and brought water from the river. "Let's rub her down," said Blue Horse.

All three of them did. Sam also gave her a drink from the crown of his hat, just a little. Coy insisted on getting a drink from the hat too. When Sam slapped the wet hat back on his head, it felt great.

Paladin still put that foot down as though it was tender. "Walk her around," said Hannibal. "Let her work it out."

Sam hardly saw the next two races. He was too busy with Paladin, and too concerned about her. Hannibal won easily. Micajah won.

While two Iroquois on cayuses got ready, Hannibal said, "Come out here."

Sam led Paladin alongside Hannibal to the second wash crossing. "Micajah's the spade four, so you're gonna get him. He'll pull every dirty trick there is. You've got to stay away from him."

Hannibal led the way up the wash a little. "Not bad," he said. This place to cross was not too steep and had fair footing. Coy dashed back and forth as though to demonstrate. Hannibal stomped the edge, knocking dirt down and making it smoother. Then he surveyed the area, the distance back to the inside along the tents, and how far it was to the finish line.

"All right, stay to the outside, let him lead, and stay on his tail. Halfway through the race, on the back side, start moving up. When she begins to really run, take her well outside. Angle straight for this spot." He surveyed the distances again. "You'll be running four or five lengths further than Micajah. But Paladin has the speed, and the way Micajah rides slows Monster down. I think you can do it."

"Long way," said Sam, eyeballing the same distances.

"If you get close to him, he'll pull something on you."

Clyman hollered for the winners to gather round.

"Just a minute," called Sam.

"Now!" ordered Clyman.

Coy headed for the starting line. Sam and Hannibal followed.

Hannibal and Jacques rode first. It was no contest. Hannibal led by a wide margin all the way. Horse and rider finished looking casual. The Iroquois whipped his horse to the finish cussing, man and mount drenched in sweat and crusted with dust.

While they ran, Sam stewed.

When his time came, Sam asked Blue Horse to hold Coy away, on an improvised leash. Sam lined up well to the outside. Micajah came right with him. Sam reined Paladin around to the inside. Micajah crowded in on him. As Sam tried to get back outside, Clyman got tired of waiting and sailed the hat into the air.

When it hit, Sam threw caution to the wind and slapped Paladin for a quick burst of speed. He got a lead and decided he would go hell for leather and keep it.

At the first crossing of the wash Paladin altered her pace a little to get ready for the plunge downward.

Wham!

A huge collision—the world lurched upside down. Paladin was above him. Where was Earth? . . .

Whumpf! They hit on the slant of the cutback. Paladin tilted over him, and Sam felt the saddle horn gore deep into his stomach. Darkness, darkness. Sam accepted death.

Death was strange, dizzy, slowly spinning around. What death was, was . . . No air, a place without air. You waited a little, and then you died—no air at all, no air . . .

His chest heaved, and air gushed in. He lay there, accepting its sweetness. When he had drunk his fill, he opened his eyes.

Coy licked his face. Paladin stood looking down. Her reins tickled his ears. "Hello, friend," he said.

Then he thought, *My champion was almost a killer. My killer.* This struck him as funny beyond anything that had ever been funny. Laughter shook him, he was like a leaf shaken on the frothing water of laughter.

Someone . . . His shoulders.

Suddenly he was sitting upright, held by Hannibal and

Blue Horse. "I'm all right." It came out as a squeak, so he said it again in a shadow of a voice. "I'm all right. I think. Maybe."

"She rolled right over you," said Hannibal.

Blue Horse lifted Sam's shirt up to his heart. A round spot just below his ribs dotted his flesh crimson and white. "The saddle horn got him right there," Blue Horse.

"It's going to get purple," said Hannibal.

"Let's get you on your feet," said Blue Horse.

They did. Sam felt shaky as a one-year-old taking his first steps.

They boosted him out of the wash. His first sight back toward the starting line was Micajah finishing the race on Monster and waving his hat triumphantly.

Some of the trappers actually booed. Others cackled.

Sam toddled back, supported on both sides. Coy whined. Paladin followed calmly.

When they got back to the starting line and walked in front of the mounted Micajah, almost touching Monster's muzzle, Sam told Hannibal, "Get even for me."

Micajah snickered.

WHEN HANNIBAL CAME to the starting line, Ellie's saddle was gone. Hannibal would ride bareback, with just a rope of braided buffalo hide around Ellie, in front of where the saddle should sit.

He didn't look at anyone, not Sam, not Clyman, not Micajah. It was as though he were waiting alone.

Right off, Micajah started crowding Hannibal the same way he'd done to Sam. Looked like he was getting away with it too, staying with Hannibal wherever he went. When James Clyman cocked back the hand with the hat, they were far to the inside, Micajah bumping against Hannibal.

When the hat reached its zenith, Hannibal abruptly pivoted Ellie straight around and kicked. They passed so close the riders bumped stirrups as Ellie dashed to the outside.

The hat saucered to the ground. Hannibal reined Ellie to the left and charged for the first crossing.

Micajah chugged along behind, not taking the inside but straight at Hannibal.

Coy whined, and Sam caught his breath in fear of what would happen at the wash. At the edge Ellie suddenly wheeled to face Micajah, reared, and flailed his legs at Monster's face.

Monster reared and kicked.

Ellie, his feet back under him, made a quick move to the left, a quick one to the right, and crashed into Monster.

Horse and rider went tumbling. The lip of the wash gave way and they rolled down, six legs kicking the air.

Hannibal turned Ellie and bounded across the wash. Then Ellie began to run as only a splendid horse can run, smoothly, powerfully, freely.

At first Monster skittered away from Micajah. Finally the big man got hold of Monster's reins and heaved himself into the saddle. He stared at Hannibal and Ellie, already halfway around the course. He turned and walked Monster back to the starting line. Jeers greeted him. Coy howled triumphantly, and everyone laughed.

Hannibal approached the finish line. Some trappers began to cheer. Gradually Ellie slowed to a lope, and Hannibal stood on his back. It was beautiful, a man erect on horse's back, both moving together.

Now everyone cheered.

When Hannibal crossed the finish line, he jumped to the earth on Ellie's left side, holding the hide rope with his right hand. From the ground, he bounded cleanly over the horse, landed on the other side, and bounded back across.

After three or four jumps he sat on his back again and took the reins. He brought Ellie back to the starting and finishing place and grinned hugely at his admirers.

Chapter Fourteen

Where in the hell," said Sam, "did you learn that?"

Blue Horse, Flat Dog, Gideon, and Beckwourth were crowding as close as Sam, and as avid.

"I didn't tell you what I did when I ran off from Dartmouth," said Hannibal. He led Ellie away with a grin. "I was very tired of studying Greek and learning about this war or that under Caesar. I wanted some fun. So I got a job at the circus."

After a pause Blue Horse said, "What's a circus?"

"I'm not sure," said Sam.

Hannibal set his victory tobacco on the bank and led Ellie into the river. He drank. "I worked for the John Bill Ricketts circus, the big one in Philadelphia."

Everyone waited impatiently.

"In a circus a horse runs circles in a ring and the rider does tricks on his back."

"Like we just saw," said Sam.

"Yeah, and lots more. Jumping through a paper hoop, for instance. Someone holds up a big hoop, you ride toward it, dive through, and do a flip back onto the horse."

The three innocents stared at each other.

"Make a hoop with your fingers," Hannibal told Sam. He did. Hannibal made a horse and rider with his fingers, and showed how the rider did a somersault through the hoop.

Six eyes got as big as eyes get.

"How do you control the horses without reins?" said Blue Horse.

"They're trained to respond to your voice. We call them 'liberty horses,' horses that run free without reins or saddles and do what you tell them."

"You did this riding yourself?"

"I started taking care of the horses, though I didn't know a thing about horses. If you're an Indian, they think you're a horse man. Then I became a trainer, and finally got to do the riding. It was fun."

"And you quit doing this?" said Sam.

"Everything wears out its welcome."

Sam took several deep breaths. "Will you show me how?"

Hannibal smiled at him.

"Me too," said Flat Dog.

"We've got time now," said Blue Horse.

Hannibal regarded them all. "Sure, why not?"

GIDEON JOINED IN and they made a ring from ropes and stakes. "A ring," Hannibal repeated. "Round pen training. Forty-two feet across, exactly forty-two." No one knew why, but they built it.

Then Hannibal demonstrated a lot of tricks that could be done—not only standup bareback riding and jumping from one side of the horse to the other and back to a mounted position, but also doing somersaults to and from the back of the horse, and doing a handstand on its back. He also showed them how to make a horse do maneuvers by itself, guided by verbal commands or hand signals.

The three young horsemen watched mouths agape. Gideon gave them a smile and sat down to watch from the sidelines.

"What do you want to learn?" said Hannibal.

They hesitated.

"Come to think," Hannibal went on, "let's figure that out after lunch."

While they ate the buffalo stew that always simmered over the fire, and threw bits to Coy, the three students talked it over. None of them saw much advantage in knowing how to jump from one side of a horse to the other. Not much advantage in riding a horse standing up either, but they all wanted to learn it. "I'd love to parade through the village, the three of us," said Blue Horse, "standing up on our horses."

The main thing, they all agreed, was learning to command a horse when you weren't on its back. They didn't know exactly what they could use that for, but it looked very handy. They would also teach Paladin to come to Sam's whistle, which they knew was handy. "We'll be horse kings," Sam cried.

They started that afternoon and spent the next week training their horses, then another week. And, as Hannibal said, training the riders. Coy, unfortunately, had to be tied off to one side.

First they taught the horses to respond to commands of voice and command. This was done in the round pen. The owner of the horse acted as trainer, giving the commands from the center. Gideon on the outside used a whip lightly to get the horse to go in the right direction. When the horse did the right thing, the trainer rewarded it with a handful of sugar.

Sam, Blue Horse, and Flat Dog took turns as trainer.

"We're not gonna have sugar for our coffee for a whole year," said Sam in mock complaint.

They couldn't get any more because the general had packed up his caravan and headed for St. Louis. Jedediah Smith, his new partner, had gone with him, saying he'd be back in the mountains by winter. Jim Beckwourth had gone along.

Third Wing dead, Beckwourth gone. Sam missed them. He wouldn't see most of the other trappers until next year's rendezvous, set for the same time on Bear River, north and east of the Salt Lake.

Outfit by outfit, most of the trappers drifted toward wherever they planned to trap that autumn. They didn't hurry. There was plenty of time.

Sam, Hannibal, Gideon, and the two Crows stayed. Their training days ran long into the summer evenings. One night over a late supper Gideon asked, "What we gonna do this autumn?"

Sam looked around at his current outfit, three friends, himself, and Coy. Not a brigade you could take on a big trapping expedition.

He raised a questioning eyebrow at Hannibal. "I'll be going back to Taos."

"Still maybe fifty men here," said Gideon "We could hook up with someone."

Sam shook his head. "I'm getting married. Soon."

Gideon chewed on that. He knew it meant a raid on some tribe for that eight-horse bride price, and a return to Rides Twice's village.

"This child will go along. I guess we are free trappers, then."

Sam smiled. His outfit for the raid and going back to the village would be Gideon, the two Crows, and himself. A small party, maybe not a safe one. But Sam felt daring.

"What's a free trapper?" asked Flat Dog. He was more forward than his brother.

"We aren't working for anybody," said Sam.

"What's working for anybody?"

"Doing a job someone else wants us to do, and getting money in return."

Flat Dog and Blue Horse gave each other odd smiles. "No Crow would do that," Flat Dog said. His expression said it would be demeaning.

"What it means is, we're on our own," said Gideon.

"For better or for worse," put in Hannibal.

"Like us," said Flat Dog, grinning.

"If we work our tails off," said Sam, "we could go back to rendezvous with a lot of plews and be rich."

Everyone mulled on that. Finally Blue Horse spoke up. "You want to be rich?"

"I want to get married. And stay in the village all fall and winter with my new wife."

"We gonna trap in the spring?" said Gideon.

"I thought we'd trap the Wind Rivers, you and me, and Blue Horse and Flat Dog if they want. Fall and spring. We ought to do all right."

Gideon nodded. It was his judgment, unspoken, that there was no point in speaking up against young love. "Free trapper," he said. "An equal shot at being rich, broke, or dead."

Everybody chuckled, but not much and not long.

* * *

THAT EVENING HANNIBAL suggested that he and Sam take a walk along the river. They stopped on the edge of the Henry's Fork, Coy at Sam's heels. Sam found a flat stone and skipped it across the slow-moving water, one, two, three skips.

"This has been a good time," said Hannibal.

Sam nodded yes. The sun was nearly down now, near the rim of the western hills. The evening cool would be a relief. He hoped Hannibal wasn't going to wax philosophical.

"I want to show you a trick," Hannibal said. They stood near some willows. It was a plant Sam had learned to love, the red branch with green, finger-shaped leaves. It grew along water courses in the West, and so was always a good sign for a man with a dry throat.

"Stand by that willow." Sam did. "Now take out your knife and hold it at me. Pretend you've disarmed me and are holding me."

Sam slipped his butcher knife out of his belt and it held it on the Delaware.

"Watch carefully." Hannibal held out his hands to show that they were empty. Then he raised them and put them behind his head. "Remember, Indians will mostly accept this gesture. They've learned that it's the way white men surrender." He grinned. "They like that."

Hannibal's right hand slashed out near Sam's face.

A thin willow branch tilted. The top turned end over end as it tumbled to the ground."

"What . . . ?"

"That could have been your face."

Hannibal did something with his hands and opened a palm to Sam.

There lay a piece of polished walnut, about four inches long and thick as a finger. On each end four rings were carved, and painted red, yellow, black, and white, the colors of the four directions. A hair ornament, Indian style.

"Take it."

It was light, smooth, well-oiled.

"Open it."

Now he saw the thinnest of lines in one of the rings. He pulled on the two ends, and the ornament came apart. One end was a wood sheath, the other a gleaming, wood-handled, double-edged blade an inch or two long.

"Feel it," said Hannibal.

Very, very sharp.

"A knife I had a gunsmith make for me. I have two of them." He rummaged in the pouch until he found a second one. "I'll give you that one."

Sam was mesmerized by the little weapon.

"Keep it really sharp. That's what makes it work."

Sam slid it apart and put it back together. It pleased him, and reminded him of Abby's hidden knife. Hers was the size of an emery board and looked like part of the hem of her dress.

"Here's what I do with it." Hannibal turned his back to Sam. He slid his piece of wood into his thick, black braid, and adjusted it just so. It looked good as a hair ornament.

Now he slipped it out. Only the knife part came, the blade catching the light in the last of the sun. Hannibal made a pretend slash, and another willow stick flew off. "It makes a hell of a cut, lots of blood. But it's the shock of getting sliced right across the face, maybe the eyes, that makes it nasty."

"I love it," said Sam.

So they sat on some rocks and Hannibal let Sam learn to braid hair. He undid and then rebraided Hannibal's black thatch several times.

Coy got impatient and jumped into the river to play.

As Sam worked, Hannibal said, "Do us both a favor. Don't show any of your friends this knife trick. Or else these knives will be all over the mountains, and the Indians will learn the trick. And the whites and French-Canadians and Spaniards."

"Not a word."

After three learning sessions on Hannibal, Sam braided his

own white hair. He inserted the walnut hair ornament and practiced sliding the blade out easily.

Finally he nodded several times. "It works," Sam said.

"Keep it sharp," said Hannibal.

"I guess I'll be braiding my hair every morning."

Hannibal smiled, knowing what Sam was thinking. "Or find a woman to do it for you."

THE NEXT MORNING Sam spent teaching Coy to ride Paladin.

It was frustrating. Oh, the little coyote caught on quick enough. It was something else. When they stopped for lunch, Sam munched until he'd figured out what. He went and found Gideon, Blue Medicine Horse, and Flat Dog and told them all the same thing. "Let's go."

By midafternoon, they set out for Powder River country. They had a pledge to steal those eight horses.

PART FOUR

Gaining
the Prize

Chapter Fifteen

I t's the right setup," said Gideon.

Nobody used a word like "perfect." Too many things could go wrong.

From a timbered ridge they looked down on the small village tucked into a curve of Crazy Bear Creek, soon after the stream dropped from the mountains to the plains. It was a dozen lodges.

Scouting, they had found a much bigger village of Sioux—Head Cutters, in the Crow language—further down Powder River. But they wanted a small one. The best way, Blue Horse said, was to find the horses held in one place, so you could drive them all off. That way they couldn't come after you, or at least you could get a big advantage. "Many lodges, many horses, more pursuit," he said.

Here there were maybe forty horses, about a quarter mile upstream from the village on some good grass.

"They'll still have their buffalo horses," Sam said. These were staked by the lodges.

"No pursuit, no fun," said Flat Dog.

They put camp by a little rivulet well off the ridge. A small fire would be safe here because the aspen would burn smokeless. They couldn't relax for a moment, not in Head Cutter country.

"Let's stake the mules up the trail," Gideon said. "Five miles maybe."

While the two brothers watched the village, Sam went with Gideon. They found some water and good grass and hobbled and rope-corralled the mules and Blue Horse's and Flat Dog's mounts. "Be embarrassing," Gideon said, "to go to steal someone's horses and have them steal yours."

Not just the horses, either. Saddles, traps, extra powder and lead, blankets, coffee, goods to trade to the Indians—all their possibles, everything that made life in the mountains more than a desperate scrape-by.

"Is this far enough?" said Sam. He was picturing stopping for the animals while pursuing Head Cutters filled the air with arrows.

"We don't leave 'em behind in five miles," said Gideon, "we got bigger troubles than losing our horses."

When they got back to the little camp, Blue Horse was staring into the fire. Sam knew he was worried. He'd been hinting.

Sam helped himself to coffee and jerked meat.

Blue Horse said, "To go to war, a man must see something."

The four eyed each other across the little fire.

Flat Dog nodded his agreement with his brother.

Sam and Gideon knew what Blue Horse meant. Crows went to war because of medicine. One man had a dream of success, or in a vision saw enemies falling, or many horses. If he had a history of strong medicine, if his war parties had succeeded before, other men would agree to join in. Or some would consult their medicine and see that this was not the time for them to go to war.

No one in this outfit had proper medicine for war.

Lying in front of his knees, Coy looked up at Sam pathetically.

Sam pondered. Then he said, "I think maybe I have seen something." He waited. "I've dreamed about this constantly. Not running the horses off. Driving them into the village, everybody looking at us, Meadowlark being proud."

He sipped his sugarless coffee. Actually, he hadn't dreamed it. More like daydreamed it. "Is that medicine?"

After a little bit Blue Horse shrugged. "White men are different," he said. "Maybe that's how your medicine comes."

Nobody spoke for a moment. "You with me?" Sam said.

Blue Horse smiled and nodded. "You are my friend."

Sam looked quizzically at Flat Dog.

"I'm always good for a fight."

"Wagh!" exclaimed Gideon.

Now they were looking down on what seemed like a good situation. "This timber's good cover," said Sam. "Let's make a plan and move in the morning."

"Not too much plan," said Flat Dog. "Action."

Coy yipped. Sam let him yip. Anywhere in the West there was nothing suspicious about a coyote yipping.

SAM WATCHED BLUE Horse and Flat Dog get up, gather their weapons, and wrap their blankets around their shoulders. The Big Dipper said halfway between midnight and dawn, and the night was chill.

He shook himself. He wouldn't be able to sleep while they were getting started. The rest of the night was going to feel long. He sat up. Coy looked up with accusation in his eyes, 'What are you doing?'

The brothers looked across the remains of the fire at Sam. Their smiles were plain in the light of the three-quarters moon. "It is a good day to die," said Blue Horse in Crow.

"Die or fly." That was Flat Dog, always the wise-ass.

With that they were off.

Sam held a hand close to the ashes. Warmth, therefore coals. He could get fire easily. He added small twigs, blew, and soon had flame.

He rummaged in his goods and found the sack of roasted coffee beans. He put them on a flat rock and ground them carefully with another rock, taking his time, mashing them all the way to powder. As he did it, he was full of big thoughts.

"Coffee would feel about right," said Gideon from his blankets.

The usual rejoinder was, "I'll bring you breakfast in bed, too." But Sam said, "'A good day to die,' what does that mean?"

"Don't know," said Gideon.

Sam added the fresh ground coffee to the grounds of several previous days in the pot. Then he poured water in and set the pot on the fire.

"What do you figure?"

"Something like, 'Let's go live so grand, so extra grand, it would be good to die like this.'"

"Mmmm."

The smell of coffee wafted on the night air.

He wished he had some sugar left.

Coy whined like he did too.

SAM COULD HARDLY stand it. The sky was getting light, but he couldn't see.

Early morning fog smeared itself over the creek. Somewhere below, Blue Horse and Flat Dog were slipping toward the horse herd, and toward the sentry. The one sentry, they thought. But they would check carefully for a second.

"We Crows," Flat Dog had said, "like to count coup on Head Cutters."

Sam looked across at Gideon. He was behind a boulder too. It would be good cover when the time came. Between them was a well-used pony drag trail running up the creek. Soon it would turn south, parallel to the mountains. In half a day they'd turn west up a creek and cross the mountains to the basin where the Big Horn River ran, and where Rides Twice's village would be. It wasn't a subtle escape route, but it would be wide open and fast. If Sam and Gideon did their work well, being quick was what they needed. Four men, more than forty horses, and one coyote racing across the mountains.

Rumble!

At first he wasn't sure he heard it. Yes, *rumble!*

Sam grinned at Gideon. The horses were on the move. No outcry from the sentry. Blue Horse and Flat Dog had done it perfectly.

"Yi-ay, Yi-ay!" they would be yelling to make those ponies run. They would snap their blankets at the horses too, but Sam wasn't close enough to hear.

The Sioux, who preferred to be called Lakotas, would hear the racket. Asleep or not, they'd jump up and come hard after the herd.

He grinned. The few with horses to ride would come hard.

He thought he saw movement at the edge of the fog. Yes, ponies going headlong for the timber, right up the trail.

He checked The Celt's priming. Everything ready. He had to make the first shot count.

Soon the ponies roared past, manes and tails flying, hooves throwing clods of dirt and clumps of pine needles into the air. Right behind them came Blue Horse and Flat Dog on stolen mounts, riding bareback, running the herd hard.

We did it!

Sam watched the edge of open ground between the fog and the timber. One Lakota rider. After a long moment, two more.

Another long moment, two more. Now every horse staked in the camp was in the action.

The first rider galloped furiously up the trail, whipping his mount.

Sam took a deep breath and sighted on the horse. *No horse, no pursuit.* He relaxed, and as he let the breath out pulled the trigger.

Blam!

For a moment he couldn't see through his own black smoke. Then he saw—horse gimping around, rider running into the trees. *All right!*

He started reloading fast.

The next two riders came around the bend.

Sam was just beginning to ram the ball home. He wouldn't be ready for a while.

Gideon let them get close. Sam knew he intended to create the impression of two shooters on that side of the trail.

Blam!

One rider pitched off the horse backward. The horse skittered off into the woods.

"Way to go!" yelled Sam, still ramming.

Blam! This was Gideon's pistol.

The horse reared, and when it came down fell onto one side.

Off jumped the rider, down behind the animal.

The horse struggled back to its feet, unable to use one front leg. Sam thought, *Shot in the shoulder.*

Coy sprinted toward the horse and rider, barking furiously. "Coy!" shouted Sam, half in a panic. "Come! Come, Coy!"

The coyote turned, looked at Sam, hesitated, and started trotting back. Sam breathed again.

Two more riders came around the bend.

Sam rammed furiously. He wasn't ready, and both of Gideon's guns were empty.

The riders stopped. Seeing the lame horse and the rider behind it, plus the downed rider, they figured out what was going on. Off into the woods they sprinted.

"Let's go!" shouted Sam.

He sprinted toward Paladin, Gideon right behind him.

In a flash Sam was in the saddle and whipping Paladin up the trail. He could hear Gideon coming too.

He dropped the reins—he could depend on Paladin now—and rammed that ball home. They were going to need it.

Sam felt Paladin's speed under his butt. Nothing could feel better right now.

He turned to look at Gideon. Dammit, Gideon's horse was falling back a little. They had some time—the woods would slow the Lakotas down—but not much.

Coy was dropping back too. But no one would bother a coyote, and he would come along.

Sam kicked Paladin and hollered to her for speed. He was thinking hard.

He kept looking back. Gideon wasn't too damn far behind, but . . .

On the third or fourth look he saw the Lakotas well

behind Gideon, smack in the middle of the trail, coming as fast as they could.

About a quarter mile on he whirled Paladin off the trail and dropped her reins. He gave thanks now that she would respond to his hand signals or whistle. He dashed behind a tree.

When Gideon passed, Sam hollered, "Go like hell!" Coy ducked behind Paladin.

Within seconds the Lakotas were in sight.

Sam leveled The Celt. He didn't want to let them get too close. Finally he took a long shot.

The Lakotas bolted in opposite directions, into the trees.

He'd missed, but Sam was satisfied.

They wouldn't charge forward now. They'd circle and come up on the place where his smoke hung in the air. And Sam would be long gone.

SAM AND GIDEON picked up the brothers' mounts and the pack mules, no problem. Before long they caught up with Blue Horse, Flat Dog, and the stolen ponies. The four grinned at each other—*we did it*.

Still, just in case, they ran the horses hard for three or four hours. It was fun, the herd like one huge galumphing animal, bodies, necks, legs, manes, tails, everything flying along, cavorting through the air, and the rumble of more than 150 hooves, noisy as a waterfall. The August day would be hot by noon, so this was the time to move along. They figured safety lay in getting the hell out of there.

Sam and Coy dropped back every so often to wait and put fear into the pursuers. The trail was crossing plains here, and the visibility was good. The first three times, he just scared the two Lakotas at long range. Finally he let them get close, almost too close, and shot one of the mounts square in the chest. "One horse left," Sam said to himself, and ran like the devil with his empty rifle.

He jumped into the saddle. An arrow ripped open his shirt

sleeve and his forearm. He put the whip to Paladin but good. Two more arrows flew just out in front of him. Finally, Paladin's speed took them out of range.

He caught up at a creek where they were letting the horses drink a little. There Gideon poulticed Sam's arm with a concoction he swore by.

Now Gideon waited and laid the ambush. He didn't catch up for a long time. "Nobody comes anymore," he said.

"We can't take that for granted," said Sam.

"Let's give the horses a breather," said Blue Horse. There was some good grass, so they did.

Sam took thought. This break would be short. Blue Horse and Flat Dog had been up and moving since maybe 3:00 A.M. There was good visibility from the rise behind them. "I'll watch for a few minutes," he said.

But Sam saw no rider. *One man won't try to take us. If there is one left.* He stretched and worked the muscles in his bloodied arm.

After half an hour they hit the road.

TWO MEN TO drive the herd, a lookout well to the front, another to the rear. That's how they ran it, the two Crows front and back, the white man and French-Canadian with the herd.

The trail wound down toward another drainage, a nice little creek edged by leafy cottonwoods. Here they would leave the main pony trail and head up the creek into the mountains.

When they rode into the shade of the cottonwoods, Sam took a deep breath of the air, cooler here along the creek. Coy dashed into the water, lapped some up, and pranced around in it.

Then Sam saw Blue Horse come riding slowly back toward them. He tensed. *What the hell is wrong?*

Warriors stepped from behind almost every cottonwood. Lakotas. Their bows were drawn, their few rifles cocked.

Blue Horse kicked his pony a little and came back closer to Sam. A terrible smile scrawled itself across his face.

A voice sounded in a strange language. Blue Horse turned to the right toward it, looked into the trees.

An arrow rammed through Blue Horse's chest. Sam saw the point come out below his shoulder blade.

Slowly, Blue Horse teetered out of the saddle backward. He hit the earth head first. His neck bent at a terrible angle, and his body crumpled.

Several warriors kicked their ponies up to Blue Horse to touch his body first, or second, third, or fourth, so they could claim the honor, the coup. First was an arrogant-looking man with a two-horned buffalo headdress, second a pock-marked man. At ceremonies they would brag about this deed.

From the creek Coy whined plaintively.

Gideon whipped his horse straight into the trees and bellowed like a madman. Arrows whipped through the air. One must have hit the horse, for the beast screamed. Another sank into Gideon's hip, and he bellowed louder.

Sam wheeled Paladin and dashed straight back along the trail.

No one shot an arrow, fired a ball. *Maybe they really want Paladin.* Fire rose up Sam's gullet. *Maybe they'll try to catch me, we can outrun . . .*

Two sentries walked their mounts into the trail ahead of him.

Sam wheeled Paladin to the left, just beyond the cottonwood grove.

A half-dozen riders trotted out in front of him.

A half-dozen more flocked behind him.

Live for an hour and you may live until tomorrow.

He dropped the reins. He set his rifle butt on the ground and held the muzzle lightly. He made his mind blank and very clear. *They don't know Paladin will respond to my voice.*

Riders from behind came up close.

Two arms ripped Sam backward out of the saddle and slammed him to the ground. The arrogant-looking, two-horned Lakota smiled down at him. *Strong man,* Sam realized through his dizziness. The pock-marked warrior threw a loop around Paladin's neck. Two Horns seized Sam's rifle.

Other Lakotas seized Sam and hauled him to his feet. A loop settled around his neck and pulled half-taut. The pock-marked warrior held the rope and grinned sardonically at Sam.

Blue Horse dead.

Gideon hurt bad, likely dead.

Sam hoped Flat Dog wouldn't ride blindly into this disaster.

Paladin stolen. Coy stolen. The Celt stolen. All our possibles stolen.

I messed up.

I'm dead.

WARRIORS WALKED UP to Sam, their faces lit with satisfaction. One took his shot pouch. Others grabbed his butchering knife, his hat. Someone stripped off his cloth shirt and belt. His breechcloth fell into the dust. His moccasins went—since they were Crow made, they would be saved and worn, or traded for value. Someone snatched his *gage d'amour,* his emblem of Meadowlark's affection, and ripped it off. Last, someone took his medicine pouch, with the buffalo hair. Joins with Buffalo had lost his buffalo medicine.

He stood totally naked. He showed no emotion. It would not do to show anything.

They waited. No one said or signed a word to Sam. He felt like trail dust.

Coy trotted over to him. Sam petted the little coyote, then decided to put him through some tricks. By turns, Coy laid down, rolled over, and jumped up to touch Sam's held-out hand with his muzzle.

Some of the Lakotas watched curiously. But the bastard who took Sam's rifle, Two Horns, growled something and they looked away.

In a few minutes an entire village of Lakota came up, all their belongings trailing behind pack horses on pony drags. Big Bellies, women, old people, children, and a phalanx of warriors.

Now Sam understood what had happened. They had ridden headlong into an entire village of Lakotas on the move. He feared something worse. The way these people were headed, they might even be joining the village whose horse herd Sam had stolen. *Good Godawmighty.*

Bad luck. "No, mountain luck," said Hannibal's voice in his head, "which runs just as bad as good."

The Head Cutters . . . Sam reminded himself that they wanted to be called Lakotas. They had young men from the warrior societies out in front as scouts. Instead of Blue Medicine Horse spotting them, they had somehow spotted him. No one would ever know how that happened. Warriors sign their mistakes in blood.

It is a good day to die.

The entire village moved up the trail. Sam walked behind the pock-marked warrior, tethered like a mule. Paladin and the pack mules walked nearby, tethered to pony drags. Coy minced along behind Sam, whimpering.

Where is Gideon? Sam hadn't seen him since he charged off into the cottonwoods, an arrow jacking up and down in his hip. Probably his friend ended up fifty yards down the grove, a hundred at most, arrows sticking out of his back like needles from the branch of a pine tree.

Again, Sam hoped like hell Flat Dog wouldn't come riding into this mess. If Sam knew a god to pray to, he would ask now that Flat Dog see the advance scouts, or the village itself, and get the hell gone. But Sam wasn't sure the God of his childhood held sway out here.

He walked. He paid attention. He cleared his mind, so he could see any opportunity for escape. All day, no opportunity. Before the sun dropped behind the Big Horn Mountains on the west, the parade rode right into the village Sam feared.

His heart went rigid. *Damn well no mercy from these people.*

He stood, rope around his neck, while the women put up the tipis and unpacked their belongings. The pock-marked warrior who held the other end of the rope watched Sam idly. Carefully, Sam showed no particular interest in anything he saw.

Two Horns, now holding The Celt, faced Sam. 'The people will talk about you in council,' the fellow signed, with an indolent smile. Sam knew how that would come out. Tomorrow he'd be turned over to the Lakota women, well bound. They would begin the delicious torture, making his death come as slowly and painfully as possible, giving him every chance to be immensely brave as he died in stoic silence.

"Tonight we will hold you in a small tipi," said Two Horns. "Don't try to get away. Two men will stand guard. Outside, where you can't get at them. If you come out, they will kill you."

IT WAS A small tipi, maybe a travel lodge. Sam was bound, and had to lie on his back the whole time.

The first problem was getting untied. He'd give a lot now to be able to get his hands on the hair ornament knife in his braid. *A weapon.* The thought stirred his heart foolishly. *A weapon.*

There was nothing at all inside, so nothing Sam could use. No stones encircled a fire pit. No fire pit. No wood to build a fire with. No flint and steel for making a fire. Nothing but the poles, the lodge skin, and the rope that held the tipi down against strong winds.

Sam snorted. They didn't want the little lodge to blow over and let him escape. Hannibal's voice said in his head, "Even the wind can be your friend."

He laughed.

Sam snorted. They didn't want the little lodge to blow over and let him escape. Hannibal's voice said in his head, "Even the wind can be your friend."

He laughed.

He rolled over. Rolled over a couple of times the other way. Found out that was the limit on his freedom, rolling over.

He thought. He didn't feel afraid to die, not especially. He looked around the tipi in the dwindling light, and on the panels of stretched hide between the poles he saw parts of his life, like pictures hung on the walls of a home. Himself and his father, wandering the woods, Sam learning. The feeling the night he untied the painter on the boat there at the family landing, and let go into the current and into the wide world, one of the best feelings he'd ever had. The piercing loneliness of the week and a half he'd waited for Diah and Fitz and the fellows and they didn't come. His dream of melting into the buffalo, so he and the beast were one. The village crier circling through the lodges, declaring that a young man had earned a name, Joins with Buffalo, or in his language, Samalo.

These experiences were his life. If it was time to quit living . . .

He felt it like a gut burn. No. Because they didn't include sharing love with Meadowlark. No.

He snorted, and felt a spasm of stubbornness. When he breathed back in, his breath smelled like buffalo breath. He gave a crazy chuckle.

"Buffalo is your medicine." That's what Bell Rock told him. "Watch the buffalo and see what they do. Notice that when the bulls fight, they are not quick, they're big and heavy, but they never flee. A bull will fight until he wins, or he will fight until he is defeated. But one thing he won't do—run away."

Sam thought of his medicine pouch, with his swatch of buffalo hair. Gone. But he didn't think he needed it. He thought of the bulls and what Bell Rock said about them. They fight until they win or die, but they never run away. He wondered how . . .

And finally he had a thought. The center rope was anchored to a gnarled piece of limb driven into the ground as a big stake. *I could, maybe I could . . . scrape the ropes of braided rawhide on the head of the stake, and scrape them and scrape them, and maybe they'll slip down.*

He inch-wormed to the stake. He lifted his legs and after a couple of tries caught the bottom strand of rope on its head. Then came the job. He jerked. And pulled. And jerked. And wriggled. And jerked and pulled and jerked and wriggled again. *I don't know or care how long it will take.*

At last the bottom strand slipped over his heels.

He heard a peg being pulled out of the door opening.

What if they see?

He rolled quietly away from the center stake and lay still, facing the door. He pointed his feet inconspicuously the other way.

The last peg slipped away, and Pock-Marked ducked in. They looked at each other in the last of the twilight that seeped down from the center hole at the top of the poles.

"Are you afraid?" signed Pock-Marked. "I suggest you spend the night wrapped in the blanket of your fear. In the morning, when you ask, I will save you all that pain with a quick cut of your throat."

He laughed. "We permit men to be cowards." He disappeared.

From the inside the door appeared to reassemble itself.

Now that the bottom strand had slipped over his heels, Sam got the rest off easily.

He stood up. It felt good.

In the new darkness he knelt, backed up to the center stake and started working his hands against it hard.

He didn't know how long it took him. It was the most frustrating task of his life. Catch—pull—nothing. Catch—pull—nothing. Catch—pull—nothing.

When he finally found a way, it took a lot of skin off his thumbs. He stuck the sore digits in his mouth and tasted warm, salty blood.

He stood now, moved around silently, swung his arms, and

stretched his cramped wrists and fingers. He tied the rope around his waist. Might come in handy. He took out the hair ornament knife and ran his fingers along the sharp edge. Plenty sharp to cut a throat.

Then he stood on his tiptoes and looked up at the center hole. No sign of the moon, Big Dipper out of sight, no idea how much night was left.

Half the night, he guessed.

How do I get out of here?

Pull the stake and use it as a club.

He no more had the thought than he rejected it. If he began to pull out the pegs that held the door together, that would take a lot of seconds, and both guards would be standing there laughing when he stuck his head out.

He wanted to pace but didn't dare. Sometimes he looked up in the hope of a glimpse of the moon. Finally he sat down cross-legged. He remembered not to think. That's what Hannibal taught him. If you keep your mind still, you get ideas.

Where is Flat Dog?

It didn't matter. Since Blue Horse died—since Sam got Blue Horse killed with his horse-stealing scheme—Flat Dog probably wouldn't try a rescue. Sam couldn't blame him for that. Regardless, Sam could not wait to be rescued. Tomorrow morning death would open the tipi door.

When the idea came, at last, it came as a picture.

Without any special thought, he acted. He grabbed hold of the center rope and began to shinny up. Half way to the top his arms started screaming at him. He had to rest—he almost let himself drop to the ground. Then he realized. One chance. Arms never fresher than now. One chance. Reality: Do it or die.

At the top he stuck a foot way out. He squirmed and pushed and nearly fell before he got a toe in behind the lodge pole. A little more squirming and it was wedged between the pole and the lodge skin.

He seized the pole with his exhausted left hand. He took a deep breath, then another. At last he let go of the rope with his right hand and swung free.

Reprieve!

Now, though, his muscles were getting used up fast in a different way. *Time running out.*

The lodge skin split under the blade of the hair ornament knife. He gushed out relief.

Quick!

He made the split longer and stuck a leg through. Silently, he slipped his head and shoulders through.

He was in the world again. In the light of the moon he could even see. His own moon shadow angled down the lodge cover.

This position was damned awkward. He . . .

Sam slid to the ground and went tumbling.

On your feet! Now!

Running footsteps.

He rolled behind a sagebrush.

Pock-Marked ran up, knife ready. In the moonlight he looked up and saw the gaping hole in the top of the lodge.

And saw nothing more, ever.

Blood gushed all over Sam's knife arm. He held the limp body for a moment. Then he let it fall and looked briefly at the bloody neck. *You offered to cut my throat.*

A raised tomahawk caught the moonlight as it swung down.

Sam dodged and rolled.

He looked up and saw the dark figure raise the tomahawk again. Sam ducked inside its arc and rammed his head into the man's chest. As they went down, he tried to slash the man's back with his hair ornament knife, but couldn't tell if he got deer hide or human flesh.

Tangled arm and leg, the dark figure and Sam slashed at each other.

SLAM!

Someone else whammed into them. All three men rolled

in the dust and darkness. Sam spilled away onto his back. His mind hollered, *Run!* The new man lifted a tomahawk.

Sam's arm was caught. He looked up into the tomahawk and swallowed his own scream before he died.

The blade swung down and crashed into the Lakota's skull.

"Let's go!"

It was a loud whisper—in the Crow language!

Sam followed the figure into the sagebrush. It paused and turned, and in the moonlight Sam saw Flat Dog's face. He motioned into the darkness, and Sam followed him at a run.

SHOUTS SOUNDED BEHIND them. Quickly the Lakotas would discover their dead comrades, and the escape.

They ran.

Suddenly there was Paladin, staked. Coy danced toward Sam.

Flat Dog jumped onto his mount. "Let's get out of here."

Sam jumped onto Paladin. No saddle, and Paladin would be fine without a bridle.

"Let's slip off quietly," Flat Dog said. "They can't track us in the dark."

After a hundred yards Sam said, "I gotta get my rifle."

"Forget it!"

Sam realized he didn't know where it was anyway. *The Celt is gone.* His one legacy from his father.

"I got Paladin for you, and Coy with him," Flat Dog said, as though to say, "And that's enough."

They came out onto the trail downstream of the village. "This trail, they won't be able to see any tracks. With luck they'll look for us the other direction," Flat Dog said.

They walked the horses all night. Sam half froze. Even August nights are cold when you're stark naked.

When the sun came up, they concealed themselves in a willow thicket and slept.

Late in the afternoon they gathered juneberries and ate

them. "I'll hunt tomorrow," Flat Dog said. The only hunting weapon they had left was his bow.

"Where are we going?"

"We'll follow the mountains north. There's another pass up that way, and we'll cross to the Big Horn."

They rode all night, and Sam froze again. Being naked had its disadvantages. He thought glumly that when they started riding during the day, he'd sunburned all over. Then he grinned at himself. All over except for the small strip where the ropes belted his belly, a funny sight.

Flat Dog killed a doe. They ate all they could that night and the next morning carried the hind quarters and left the rest. "Gotta get out of Head Cutter country," said Flat Dog.

Sam pondered his situation. He'd lost everything he owned except his horse, dog, and hair-ornament knife. Rifle gone, knife gone, clothes gone. No more powder and lead, no more pemmican, no more coffee. No traps to get beaver with. No bow and arrows. Nothing to trade to the Indians.

He'd lost his friends.

Ghastly.

A clear, rotten thought clanged into his mind. *Instead of getting eight horses to win Meadowlark, I killed her brother.*

He spent the rest of the day getting sunblistered and swimming in remorse.

That night and morning they gorged themselves on the hindquarters and ended up picking the last flesh off the bones. Amazing how much you could eat when you knew no more food was available. Coy looked back at the bones as they rode off. "Better to go hungry than get scalped," Sam told him.

Up came a mental picture of Coy scalped. Sam started laughing and couldn't stop. Paladin turned her head and gave Sam a queer look. Flat Dog looked at Sam. He laughed the way a spring bubbles out of the ground, and he didn't know whether the water of his laughter was sweet or alkaline.

* * *

FROM THIS CAMP they could see where the Big Horn River flowed, and where it cut through some mountains to the north. According to Flat Dog, the village now would be where the Stinking Water River flowed into the Big Horn. Later the big buffalo hunt, with several villages gathered together, would be held near the Pryors.

Sam was learning where the mountains lifted up and how the rivers ran, all a big picture in his mind. He wished he could write it all down, like Jedediah did, and make a map. Which was a damn funny thought for a man who didn't read or write, and didn't own even a scrap of paper.

But on this warm evening in August, in a pleasant camp on a nameless creek, that wasn't on his mind.

"I'm sorry I got Blue Medicine Horse killed."

"Don't use his name," said Flat Dog.

"I'm sorry."

"You didn't do it. The one who isn't here, he made a mistake."

Silence. As if that was enough.

"I feel terrible about it."

This drew a flicker of sharpness in Flat Dog's eyes. "Warriors pay for their mistakes."

Silence.

"I found all the signs," Flat Dog went on. "I could tell a lot of what happened. The one who isn't here, it was his job to see anyone we were riding into. He didn't."

"He was my friend." Then Sam thought that Blue Horse was Flat Dog's brother, and felt ashamed of himself.

"I took care of him. Wrapped him in his blanket and put him in the fork of a tree. After one or two winters I'll go back and put his bones in a rocky crevice."

Sam started to ask if Blue Horse was scalped, but he already knew the answer to that.

He tried to find something good about their situation. Well, on the trip home he would learn to ride bareback, since his saddle was gone. And he would train himself and Paladin always to turn with pressure of the knees instead of the reins.

He wished they had coffee. He wished they had food. He wished he didn't have to ride into the village tomorrow dead poor and stark naked.

Now that he thought of it, literally naked was too much of a problem. "Big favor," said Sam.

Flat Dog looked up at him.

"I need a breechcloth. Don't see anything to use but your shirt."

Flat Dog looked down at his chest. It was a perfectly good deerskin shirt but nothing special. He stripped it off. "You owe me a shirt."

Sam started cutting a breechcloth from the tail of the shirt. The very sharp hair ornament knife worked well. "This is going to be one very short breechcloth," he said.

"Cut two. We'll find someone to sew them together."

Sam looked at the material. "I'll have enough for a couple of pairs of moccasins, too." Barefoot could get painful.

He took off a sleeve and sliced part of it into a belt for the breechcloth, the rest into strips to braid into another rope.

"You owe me a shirt," Flat Dog repeated, laughing a little.

"I owe you everything."

PART FIVE

Passage
Through
Darkness

Chapter Sixteen

Miles from the village, Sam felt his flesh redden. In his imagination he saw that, sunburned as he was, his skin would glow redder yet when they entered the village. Red Roan would watch him and smile. Gray Hawk and Needle, seeing they had lost a son, would turn their backs on Sam and refuse to look at him. Meadowlark would run into her lodge and weep.

He lived in this moment of humiliation all afternoon, running it over and over through his mind. He told himself that the real moment only had to be lived once, but he couldn't help rolling it through his mind again and again.

They spotted the village across an open plain, on the south bank of the Stinking Water. The moment was coming. Sam steeled himself.

Then, for some reason, no more than two hundred yards away, Flat Dog had said, "We have to go up on that hill."

When they got there, Flat Dog's words surprised him again. "You have to sit here." Sam dismounted and plopped his breechclothed bottom down. Coy joined him and looked up at Sam anxiously.

The hillock overlooked the camp. Flat Dog dismounted, walked the few steps to the crest, and waved his blanket in a big circle. "I have to get the people's attention," he said.

This seemed odd—the sentries surely had told the camp that a small party was coming in.

"Now they know someone has been killed," he said.

He waved his blanket toward the Big Horn Mountains. "That tells them what direction we're coming from," he said.

He flung one end of the blanket to the ground at his side, once. "Now they know we've lost one."

One? Six men rode out of this camp, and two were returning. Beckwourth was just gone somewhere else. Third Wing, Gideon, and Blue Medicine Horse were dead. Dead.

Flat Dog walked over and sat down by Sam. "Since they've seen me," he said sadly, "they know which one."

Sam pondered what that meant.

In a few minutes Red Roan and two other young Kit Foxes showed up. Coy stood up, bristled, and growled. Sam calmed him down.

The three sat and asked questions of Flat Dog, disregarding Sam. Flat Dog answered very factually and very fully. It seemed to Sam that he recounted every little thing they did after they left rendezvous to steal horses from the Head Cutters. The session seemed to last for hours.

Sam noticed nothing in particular that reflected on him except one story. Flat Dog told how Blue Medicine Horse had worried that no one in the party had medicine to go to war. At that point Sam told about his daydreams. Blue Horse and Flat Dog thought maybe that was how white men got their medicine and decided to go against the Head Cutters the next morning.

Not one of the interviewers looked directly at Sam, but he had never felt more thoroughly condemned.

At last Red Roan and others rose and walked down the hill to camp.

"We stay here," said Flat Dog.

That evening the wives of Kit Foxes brought them food and water. For some reason they weren't allowed to touch the cups that held the water. The women put water to their mouths like they were small children. No longer having a hat, Sam had to ask them to bring a small bowl for Coy to drink out of.

One woman brought a buffalo robe. Without looking at Sam, she dropped it on the ground and said, "For Joins with Buffalo," and walked away.

When they were alone, Sam went to Paladin, then turned

and looked at Flat Dog expectantly. Flat Dog shook his head no. "We stay here," he said, "until the village finishes mourning."

He sat on a silvered cedar log and took an arrow from his quiver. He gazed off toward the Big Horns for a minute or two. Then, suddenly, Flat Dog stabbed himself in the left shoulder with the arrow point. Then he stabbed himself about a dozen times on the left arm, each cut making a trickle of blood.

He began to weep. At first he cried softly, moaning a little. The moans grew in volume. They grew in intensity. They swooped up and down. They squeezed soft and bellowed loud.

As he moaned, he changed hands and stabbed himself on the right arm. Over and over, seemingly without counting, he inflicted small wounds on himself.

His moaning grew extravagant. It was as though he was trying to gauge the depth and breadth of his grief for his lost brother. He pitched on an ocean of sorrow, rode a swell of fierce pain upward and dropped down into a trough of anguish. Then the next pain lifted him high into the bleak vista of his heartache.

With the arrow he wounded himself about half a dozen times on each cheek.

At last he sat rigid, frozen by the prospect of a loss as wide and deep as any ocean.

Sam heard the drums beating in the village, and the voices joined together in a great song of woe. Now what he had seen in two winters of living with the Crow people came home to him. He had seen men and women with wounds like those Flat Dog just scarified himself with. Men and women with joints missing from a finger, where they had expressed violently their sorrow, and their anger at their loss. Women who lost a close relative chopped their hair almost to the roots, and mourned until it grew to its original length. Families gave away most of their belongings, and grieved formally for two moons, or sometimes an entire year.

When a relative was killed by an enemy, Sam remembered, the family mourned until a member of the offending tribe was killed in vengeance. It hit him hard—until a member of the offending tribe was killed in vengeance.

Flat Dog emerged from his seeming trance and once more began to give voice to his sorrow. Long into the night rose the beat of the drums and the village songs of mourning. Long into the night rose Flat Dog's wail.

The next day Sam realized that they were in a kind of exile. All day they sat on top of that little hill, and then another day and another. Sam lost track after three. Every day they sat on the hilltop, all day. Flat Dog sat looking mournful, or far away. Sam waited. Or thought about his dead friends. Mostly waited.

Coy looked at them peculiarly, and jumped onto his food and water gratefully when it came.

It was the second night that Sam began to grieve. He started with a kind of madness. He began to moan along with Flat Dog—he didn't know why, just had the impulse to make a kind of duet. Flat Dog sang high and loud, Sam soft and low.

Tears came.

True, hot tears.

Thoughts of Blue Medicine Horse swam through his head. How hard he worked, so exactly, to learn English. How he opened his heart to Sam because of that rabid coyote. How he helped Sam train Paladin, and helped save Sam's life during the buffalo hunt. How he counseled Sam wisely on how to behave in a way acceptable to the Crows. This man's duty was to protect his family, but he brought the stranger into their circle of acquaintance, tragically.

Most of all, Sam couldn't help thinking of Blue Medicine Horse as the man who risked his life to help Sam get eight horses to win Meadowlark's hand. And lost his life.

Sam's mourning lifted him high into anguish, low into despair.

He thought of the brother who could not help to assure the

safety of his younger brothers and sisters. Who could no longer help feed his family. Who would be unavailable to defend the tribe against enemies. Who would never delight a young woman with his love. Who would never add to the life of the tribe through his issue.

A human being lost.

A new wave lifted Sam, and he knew how far his sorrows reached beyond the death of Blue Horse. He had lost Gideon, his first real friend in the mountains. He'd failed to protect Third Wing, the Pawnee who saved his life out of pure generosity.

He lifted his lament to the night sky.

The memory of his father, Lew Morgan, washed over him, tumbled him head over heels in a flash flood of sadness. It had no words, only pictures of his father's kind face, or his compact body doing work, lifting a deer onto his shoulder, carrying a ham in each hand, walking behind the mule and forcing the plow blade into the soft, spring earth.

He wailed and wailed.

Worse, Sam himself had become a killer. He had killed the Pawnee sentry Two Stones. He had slain Pock-Marked, his Lakota captor. Altogether he had walked the halls of the drama of life and death as one who sheds blood. He recognized, with the heaviest of hearts, that he walked the earth with bloody hands.

In this fullness of recognition, he knew that the earth was, forever, the cradle of birth. It was equally, and also forever, the cold arms of death. He knew himself as the bearer of both life and death, and knew that he bore in his blood his own death.

He wailed long into the night.

Chapter Seventeen

L ow estate.

That was Hannibal's phrase. Hannibal was always using words no one else knew. When Sam asked him what it meant, Hannibal said, "Down and out."

When he and Flat Dog finally went into the village, Sam found out what it meant, really, to be in low estate.

He had sewn the two pieces of breechcloth together, so his nether end was more or less covered. He had no shirt or hat, and, worse, no shoes. No shelter. The buffalo robe was his on loan. He had no food and no weapons to hunt with.

It stung, also, that he had lost his *gage d'amour* and his medicine pouch. They were the only gifts he'd ever gotten from Meadowlark. And the medicine pouch held the matted hair that was his buffalo medicine.

The Celt was gone. The Celt . . . His bow was gone.

What did he have in place of all his possibles, everything he owned?

Guilt.

Flat Dog got them shelter. They moved into a brush hut with two other Kit Foxes, Naughty Ones like themselves, he said. These turned out to be Stripe and Straight Arm, who inflicted the name No Arrows on Sam.

Bell Rock invited them to supper at his lodge that evening. He didn't have to say it was to fend off starvation.

Around the brush hut Stripe and Straight Arm hardly spoke to him at all. Sam was glad.

The next day Flat Dog left to join his family in mourning. They would live out somewhere alone for some weeks, Sam knew. At least he didn't have to face Gray Hawk and Needle, not yet. He also wouldn't get to see Flat Dog. Or Meadowlark.

He felt defeated.

The first job, he made himself decide, was to get food. He

used his single weapon, the hair ornament knife, to cut finger-thick willow shafts along the river. He peeled them and laid them out to dry. They would make arrows. He'd learned from Blue Medicine Horse—the memory twisted his heart—to use thick ones. The small ones would get too thin when they were scraped straight.

Owning almost nothing, he dried extras to trade for arrowheads and sinew to lash the points on.

While they dried, he rode out with Paladin and Coy to gather serviceberries. Since he had nothing to carry them in, he picked double handfuls, devoured them, and rode to the Stinking Water to drink. He liked the taste of the red and purple fruit, and the cool river water. Though the river got its name from hot springs upstream, the sulfurous taste was long gone here. Coy and Paladin liked it, too. Sam would have napped in the sun by the river, but he was afraid of what he might dream.

Gathering berries was women's work, but Sam refused to care. Tonight he would put serviceberries into the stew Stripe and Straight Arm would have. Though he was sure they wouldn't let him starve, he wanted to make a contribution. Tomorrow he would find a good root-digging stick and dig up some Jerusalem artichokes.

He was mostly worried about getting through the night.

The next day, doing that, he made a discovery. Life was simple. Necessity: Find enough food for today. There were no other necessities.

He made another discovery. He liked life this simple. It had clarity. Find food or starve. The finding wasn't so hard. He liked life this way.

He started to wonder why anyone ever made it harder.

The answer came quickly. Winter.

He knew he deserved to be poor.

Winter would come.

When Sam brought his contributions to the supper pot, Stripe and Straight Arm nodded their approval but still didn't say much to him.

Sam understood. The way the village saw things, he had taken a party on a raid, come away empty-handed, and gotten a man killed. In fact, that was exactly what did happen. He would have shunned himself.

Stripe and Straight Arm, though, frowned at Sam when he fed Coy meat from the pot. Almost as if he understood, the little coyote started hunting chipmunks and squirrels. Sam's sense of justice was offended.

In the dark of the night, whether he slept or waked, his sense of justice also condemned him.

After several days Sam borrowed a deer shoulder blade with a hole drilled in the middle. Slowly and carefully, he used the bone to scrape the willow shafts to a single diameter. When he returned the shoulder blade, he gave the owner several straightened shafts and borrowed a piece of basalt with a groove worn in it. With this tool he took the knots off and rubbed the remaining shafts smooth.

The next part tested his patience. He heated the shafts over the fire and rubbed oil on them until they were supple. Then, borrowing a bone with a hole in it from Straight Arm, he used that as a lever to straighten the shafts slowly.

Last came the most trying part. He held each shaft a long time while it cooled.

He had no skill at lashing the points on. So he begged for help from Bell Rock. It was one of Bell Rock's sons, Weasel, who showed Sam how to get tight lashing. Sam gave the young man two finished arrows for his help.

Bell Rock chuckled at that and said, "Do you think you could accept a dinner for nothing?"

Sam didn't think he deserved it, but he accepted.

He had three finished arrows. At the end of dinner he had to ask for the loan of one of Bell Rock's bows.

Bell Rock reached behind him and unwrapped an object Sam had paid no attention to. It was a bow fashioned from the thick, heavy horns of big horn sheep. He handed it to Sam.

"It's yours. A gift."

Sam turned it over and over. It was a stiff, powerful bow, and would take a strong draw.

"Let it make you strong," Bell Rock said.

Sam pulled on the bowstring. He needed all his arm power to get the string back to shooting position.

"I want you to have that," Bell Rock said. "I believe in you. You're a good young man."

Sam felt a gush of relief. Then he reminded himself, *I got Blue Medicine Horse killed.*

He practiced all the next day, shooting his arrows at a circle drawn into the soft earth of a hillside. When he went to bed, his right arm ached. When he slept, his dream tormented him.

The next morning the arm was screaming at him. At dawn and dusk he watched for deer, observing the paths they took to the water. Midday he spent gathering gooseberries and wild onions.

The following day he got up before first light, excited. He left Coy tied to a tree near Paladin. A coyote might scare the deer off.

In half an hour, big bow in one hand and three arrows in the other, he stood utterly still beside a boulder alongside the Stinking Water. He'd picked this spot out when he watched two does and their fawns drinking last evening. The abundance of heart-shaped tracks said they came here a lot, and others too.

He hoped he looked like part of the boulder.

He wished he could hunt bucks instead of does. It was his father who taught him to take the bucks. "The does will bear the young," Lew Morgan said. But Sam would take whatever came.

Now his days of hunting in Eden came back to him strongly. It hadn't been a real Eden, just a spot he and his father liked. They named it that because Lew Morgan had once told his younger son, when Sam wasn't old enough to hold a Pennsylvania rifle steady, that he could play Adam and give names to all the animals and plants. The names were original. Deer were mooshmen. Trees were starks. Wild roses were garbies. A bear was a woze.

That was a good day. Sam remembered lots of good days with his father. He didn't think about the lousy days after Lew Morgan died, and Sam's brother Owen took over as head of the family.

It was Lew Morgan who taught Sam how to become absolutely still in the woods, how to make yourself part of things, so that after a while even the birds would forget about your presence and return to their songs. Then all the animals would relax—and the deer would come.

I had a rifle then.

He hadn't let himself think about the rifle his father willed him since it got stolen. What did it mean to him? He'd had the gunsmith Hawken engrave CeLᴛ on a brass plate on the stock and circle the name with Celtic love knots. That said it all.

What would Sam do? Some Lakota—Sam was tempted by the hand-slap name the Crows used, Head Cutter—was walking around with his father's rifle. That couldn't be, simply couldn't be, allowed.

There's nothing I can do about it now.

He felt a tingle.

Doe. One fawn. Picking their way through the cottonwood grove, noses up and alert.

They would get no scent of Sam. The wind was upcanyon, and he'd picked his spot upwind of the tracks.

Slowly they came. When they stepped out of the trees and onto the bank of the river, he might get a shot.

The doe changed directions, heading a little left.

Damn. That would make the shot longer.

Frustrating. If he had The Celt, a hundred yards or so would not be an issue. But this big-horn bow was another story. He couldn't brace it against a tree trunk, and he couldn't hold it steady for long. He wouldn't be able to take his time on his aim.

He considered trying to slip closer, and rejected that. Even when she had her head down to drink, the doe would be too alert for a significant move. He would wait and hope.

The two deer came half out of the trees. The doe sniffed the air carefully. She looked upstream and down.

They emerged and walked steadily to the river. Into the stream. Drinking.

Sam couldn't stand it. The bow had plenty of power for this distance. It was up to him to make a good hold.

Check of wind, arrow nocked, now drawn. His forearms and biceps screeched. Steady . . .

The arrow flew a couple of feet over the doe's back.

She bolted, and the fawn behind her. They ran in their upright, prancing way until Sam could barely catch an occasional glimpse of a white tail flicking through the cottonwoods.

The arrow could be found later. He might get another shot. Carefully, he lined up the boulder he stood by and a tall cottonwood across the river. The arrow would be on that line, maybe in the water.

When he did get another shot, it was even longer. This time a doe and two fawns. The arrow sailed behind the doe, and a little above. A gust of wind, maybe.

She just stood.

Quickly, Sam nocked his last arrow and drew. *Steady!* he shouted at himself inside his mind.

A clean miss.

The doe ignored anything she might have heard or felt, drank a little more, and then trotted daintily back into the cover of the trees.

Sam wanted to stomp the bow.

He didn't.

He spent an hour hunting the arrows. One was in the soft sand of the opposite bank. One was in front of a head-sized rock in a riffle, the shaft broken. The third he never found. Maybe it landed in a deep spot and floated away. But he didn't find it washed up downstream either.

One morning's hunting, no meat, one arrow left.

Dejected, he went and got Coy. They walked along the river to cut more willow shafts to dry.

SAM WATCHED THE evening shadows lengthen. They were closing in on him, the gentlest of traps. He felt as though he could almost hear them whisper. He wished he could make out the words. But he knew the message was mockery.

No meat for you.

He sniffed. He'd waited since sundown, no deer. Still no deer. Not a one had come to water, or not this water.

He stroked his single arrow, felt the smoothness of the shaft. He ran his finger along the serrated edge of the flint. Sharp enough.

Come, deer, come.

A shadow stirred.

No, he'd imagined it.

The shadow edged forward.

Deer.

Yes, a doe and a spotted fawn.

They ghosted forward one step at a time, as though they knew better.

Now the wind came downcanyon, and Sam was downstream of the deer. They stopped twenty feet from the edge of the trees, suspicious, feeling the predator they couldn't smell.

The doe turned straight toward Sam. The fawn echoed her stance.

He stilled himself, maybe even his heartbeat. *This is a chance.*

The doe faced straight toward him. She lifted her muzzle and sniffed.

Wrong sense.

She turned back the way she'd come, and stopped. The fawn imitated her.

Sam held his breath. He didn't have a decent shot. A

sapling blocked the doe's middle. The fawn stood in front of her. Small target.

They're going to run.

Sam hefted the bow and instantly let the arrow fly.

A hit! A sort of hit. Sam thought the arrow had actually ricocheted off the back of the fawn and into the doe behind the shoulder blade.

For an instant the doe stood quivering.

Deciding whether to die?

Then she bolted.

Sam dropped the bow and ran like a maniac.

She hadn't been hit hard. The arrow worked up and down in her ribs like a pump handle. But maybe she wouldn't go far, couldn't go far.

When he cleared the trees, the doe and fawn were standing on the prairie, looking around. They saw Sam and ran upstream, their bottoms bouncing in the last of the light.

Am I going to lose her?

Sam ran like hell and shrieked like a banshee.

Out of pain, or shock at the sound, the doe stopped.

Sam ran and roared.

When he was a dozen steps away, she ran directly away from the river.

He veered that way. He would have hollered but was out of breath.

The doe stopped and pivoted.

She's crazy with pain or fear.

The doe dashed straight at him.

They collided. Shoulder bounced off shoulder. For a split-second Sam thought the arrow would actually stick in him.

The doe went down.

Sam pitched to the ground, rolled, and found his feet.

The fawn skittered a few steps, stopped, and looked back, quivering.

The doe clambered up and started to run.

Before she got three steps, Sam jumped on her back.

She bolted upward, like trying to jump onto the moon.

Sam held on.

He jerked the ornament knife out of his braid, reached around the doe, and slit her throat.

She crashed down. Sam went tumbling through the grass. He sat up. She wasn't moving. His right forearm was covered with blood.

Sam looked at the fawn. It danced lightly away.

Sam did as his father taught him, and said, "Godspeed."

Then he bellowed, "Hallelujah."

Chapter Eighteen

It was a comedy. He'd broken his last arrow, probably when he banged the deer's shoulder. He gutted her out with his ornament blade, which was the length of a finger joint. Butchering required a butcher knife. Still, he got it done.

He staggered into camp, exhausted by her weight. Sam dunked himself in the river to get the dust caked with blood off. Straight Arm and Stripe gladly helped finish the butchering. Sam took the heart and liver, his by right, and broiled them on a stick over the flames. He thought that was the best meat he'd ever tasted.

As the others finished the butchering, he wondered if his dreams would be haunted again. Or did action, maybe, chase away the phantoms?

He thought of tomorrow. He would spend the day on women's work—cutting the meat into strips and slowly drying it over low flames.

Now they fed on the back straps, share and share alike. He gorged himself.

He broke ribs off and gave them to Coy, as many as the little coyote wanted.

Tomorrow he would also set about making new arrows. He'd trade the deer hide for a pair of moccasins. Which would still leave him poor. He had no rifle. He had no traps to take beaver to earn money for a rifle. Or powder and lead, or a butcher knife, or coffee and sugar, or anything else that would make him a white man.

He was so belly-heavy he could barely move. He crawled to his buffalo robe.

I have meat against the winter.

And guilt enough to last a lifetime.

IN THE MIDDLE of the night Coy mewled and woke Sam up. He wondered if the little coyote was hungry again. He reached down and petted Coy's head. Suddenly, he had one clear thought: *That meat, actually, won't last the week.*

He also thought that being poor wasn't all right. It didn't shine, as Beckwourth would say.

Sam was in a big hole.

He needed to trade for things. Material goods. White man stuff.

He took stock. He owned Paladin, as much as any man could own her. But he would never trade her. The tricks she could do, they dazzled his mind and lifted his spirits. And no one else could get her to do them.

He didn't own Coy, who was no good in trade anyway. He gave the coyote's ears a good rub and lay back down.

He had his legs, arms, and brain. And heart. What would that get him?

He could shoot some beaver, probably, with arrows. That was the hard way, compared to setting a trap and coming back later. If the beaver swam for its lodge, what would he do? Swim into the lodge? With maybe several beaver there, that idea didn't shine.

A few of the Crows had traps the fur men had traded them for almost nothing, in the hope that the Indians would learn to be fur hunters. They weren't, not to amount to anything. Sam could take deer and trade hides and meat for traps. Yes, that's what he'd do.

Then he'd spend part of the fall and winter getting enough plews to trade for . . .

Just a minute. Was he going to *trade* for a rifle?

He couldn't do that. Had to get The Celt back, some way. Had to get The Celt back.

He shoved that out of his mind. He heard the inside of his mind whisper, "Too damn dangerous."

He had to work hard, work like hell. He had to get stuff, had to prove himself.

Because Meadowlark would never marry a poor man, a disgraced man.

He turned over in the buffalo robe. He looked at the blackness of the sky through the leaves and branches of the hut. He wished it was light, so he could get going.

MEADOWLARK AVOIDED HIM. Everyone in the Gray Hawk family avoided Sam, even Flat Dog.

At midday they'd returned and set up their tipi in the lodge circle. They said little to anyone, and few approached them. Maybe that was a way of honoring their grief.

The family shunned Sam. They refused even to look in his direction.

He rode Paladin upriver, Coy following, to a willow patch to cut more shafts for arrows. By God, he was going to become an arrow manufacturer. The only way he could rise in the world, now, was to make arrows. Trade them or take deer with them. No other way.

In the evening Sam waited in the cottonwoods and watched the other young women come to the river to get water. Meadowlark didn't come. Needle made the trip, surely to keep Meadowlark away from Sam.

When Sam got back to his brush hut, though, Flat Dog sat there talking to Stripe and Straight Arm. He shared a deer hindquarter with the three of them. Sam had hung it up, thinking the cold September night and cool day wouldn't spoil it, not in one day. Sam showed Flat Dog the gift bow from Bell Rock, and described his deer hunt for comical effect. Flat Dog said very little in return.

When they were finished, he said to Sam, "Let's build a brush hut."

Sam smiled big. "First thing in the morning." At least two Crows were treating him decently.

"First thing," said Flat Dog, "we hunt. I'll lend you some arrows. Then we build the brush hut."

TWO WEEKS LATER the village moved. Everyone marched down the Big Horn to the Pryor Mountains. Along with the other Kit Foxes, Sam rode as a policeman. He felt good to be doing the job along with Flat Dog, Bell Rock, and Red Roan. They kept order in the long line of pony drags, and watched out for the enemy. The trip was uneventful. Sam was glad the Kit Foxes still treated him as one of them.

Other villages met them near the foot of the Pryors. Together they made one great camp, a series of lodge circles up and down the river. Sam was, sort of, one of over a thousand of Crow people.

He was still a poor man, but not desperately poor. He owned a dozen arrows and an otter skin quiver, two pairs of moccasins, a shirt, and two buffalo robes. The robes were rubbed half hairless by wear, and wouldn't get him through the winter.

In another way he was desperate. Meadowlark avoided him completely. She didn't stand outside her lodge in the evenings to meet any suitors at all, not even Red Roan. She didn't sit outside in the afternoon sun, sewing with her friends. She didn't mingle with the people of the other villages to trade news of what had happened since the spring hunt. She seemed never to come out of the tipi. The entire Gray Hawk family, except Flat Dog, was keeping to themselves. And they were keeping Meadowlark away from Sam.

Flat Dog confirmed it. "My mother and father haven't forgiven you for leading that raid. May never."

The raid where "the one who isn't here" died. Flat Dog never used Blue Medicine Horse's name. No one did.

Sam didn't use it. But he dreamed about Blue Medicine Horse.

He tried to keep his voice casual. "Not Meadowlark either?"

Flat Dog seemed to ponder while he chewed a slice of blackstrap. "I don't know."

They were broiling the backstrap on sticks over open flames. They ate fresh deer meat most evenings now, and Sam was killing his share. His arms and shoulders were getting noticeably bigger, the muscles more defined.

Sam looked at Flat Dog straight in the eyes. "I dream about him."

Flat Dog looked at Sam questioningly.

"The one who isn't here."

Flat Dog lowered his head.

"Maybe it's me that can't forgive."

Flat Dog snapped his head up.

"Forgive myself."

"It wasn't your fault. It . . ." Flat Dog sounded frustrated.

Sam said slowly and clearly, "Forgive myself."

Flat Dog thought for a long moment. "Tomorrow we better go see Bell Rock."

SAM, FLAT DOG, and Bell Rock were sitting naked outside the sweat lodge, sweat pouring down their bodies. The evening was cool, soon to be cold, and Sam was glad for it.

Sam looked at his friends. He had told Bell Rock, simply and truthfully, that the death of the one who was not here was disturbing him, even disturbing his dreams.

Bell Rock said they would sweat.

Between rounds they smoked the pipe. After offering the smoke to the four directions, the sky, and the earth, Bell Rock asked for wisdom for each of them, to know how Sam might be healed.

At the end of the sweat, Bell Rock said in his usual way,

acting offhand about what was important, "You should think about holding a sun dance."

Sun dance. Sam knew vaguely about it. A ceremony where men put skewers through their chests and hung by ropes from lodge poles. When he thought there wasn't so much difference between him and Indians—began to think maybe he could be Indian—he thought of the sun dance, shuddered, and knew he was white, white, white.

"Maybe you should ask for all the buffalo tongues to be saved."

To another Crow, Bell Rock would have said those words without mention of a sun dance. Characteristic Crow indirection, Sam knew that much, but he didn't know what tongues had to do with it. He decided to keep his mouth shut and his stupidity hidden.

He did know the autumn buffalo hunt, the big one where they joined with other villages and got meat for the entire winter, was coming in the next few days. Men were making medicine to bring buffalo to the people. Scouts were out looking for the great, shaggy creatures.

"Save the tongues from the hunt that's coming up?" he asked.

They were all embarrassed that Sam didn't know. But they all understood it was because he was new to being a Crow. His friends were good about taking the time and trouble to explain. And then, after one explanation, expected him always to know.

"We hold a sun dance sometimes," Bell Rock began, "when one of us has been killed by an enemy, and someone has a great thirst for revenge."

"That would usually be a relative," said Flat Dog. After hesitating, he added, "It might be a close friend."

"The man who asks for the dance, he's called the whistler."

"He doesn't ask for the dance directly," said Flat Dog. "He tells someone we should save all the buffalo tongues, and that someone tells the chief, and the chief tells the herald to spread the word."

"Why buffalo tongues?"

"During the ceremony, which takes a number of days," said Bell Rock, "the whistler must give buffalo tongues to the principal families, and to all those who help him."

Sam nodded.

Bell Rock and Flat Dog looked at each other a long moment.

"All right," said Bell Rock, "for now we will answer your questions about the ceremony. Then you will ask your heart, and ask the grandfathers and grandmothers, and the four directions, and all the powers, whether you should do this."

"Why does the whistler do the ceremony?"

"He seeks a vision," said Bell Rock.

"He is hoping for a vision of revenge," said Flat Dog. "He blows the eagle-bone whistle and asks to see an enemy killed. Then he rides against the enemy and fulfills the vision."

"Whose help is needed for the ceremony?"

"The effigy owner, mainly," said Bell Rock.

"Some men own effigies that have the sun dance medicine."

"The owner, we call him the father. The whistler is the son."

"The sun dance is not just for one man," said Flat Dog.

"Other young men will sacrifice their blood for a vision."

Yes, the ones who skewer themselves, Sam thought. It gave him the willies.

"The sun dance is for all the people. They join in with all their hearts, and share in the blessings."

Sam took a long moment to think. "I don't know how to decide such big stuff."

Bell Rock said, "First, ask your heart, not your head."

"And," said Flat Dog, "I have something that may help you." He reached for a bundle wrapped in a deer hide and handed it to Sam. "A gift."

First Sam found a hide bag made from sheepskin. It was a very simple bag, rectangular, with a thong fringe but no bead or quill decoration.

Inside was a pipe stem and a bowl of red stone. The stone

was carved into the shape of a T, with four rings around the part that held the tobacco. These, Sam knew, represented the four directions.

He also knew that a big moment had arrived. Flat Dog and Bell Rock were inviting him to become a carrier of the sacred pipe, as every Crow man was.

Sam looked at Flat Dog. He knew the hours required to shape the stem and the bowl, and the expense of getting a woman to sew the bag. He also knew that a quiet statement was being made. This was not an elaborate pipe; it was barely decorated at all, and it was short. Not the pipe of a man of consequence, but of a beginner.

"Thank you," he said to Flat Dog. Breath in, breath out. "I accept."

"Then," said Bell Rock, "we will dedicate your pipe by smoking it."

"From now on when you can't decide something, or you need special strength," said Flat Dog, "you'll ask your pipe."

ON THE NEXT evening Sam came back to Bell Rock. The medicine man asked if he wanted to smoke.

"Not tonight," said Sam. "I just want information."

Bell Rock waited.

"Will the people save the buffalo tongues if a white man asks?"

"They will if I support it."

Sam nodded. "Will an effigy owner consent to be my father?"

"I will."

Now a long pause. "Will the people join in with all their hearts, if a white man is the whistler?"

"Most will, some won't."

Sam grimaced and thought. "This will make it all right, what happened?"

"He will never be here, and you will always miss him. But it will be all right."

"Anything else you want me to think on?"

Bell Rock smiled. "Maybe you should think of yourself more as a man, not just a white man."

THE NEXT EVENING scouts came into the camp with news. On the other side of Pryor Gap, on Lodge Creek, they had found buffalo, many thousands of buffalo.

That night the heralds walked around the camps crying out the news: "There will be a big buffalo hunt."

The next morning experienced men rode out to see the herd and the country around it. Maybe they would set up a jump, where the buffalo could be driven off a cliff. Or maybe no jump would be handy, and they'd decide on tactics for a surround. For a thousand mouths and a long winter, they needed a lot of buffalo.

That evening Sam Morgan, a pipe carrier and no longer just a white man, spoke a few words to Bell Rock.

Bell Rock sent Flat Dog to the chief, Rides Twice.

Though Rides Twice may have been surprised, he merely nodded. Even a chief did not ask questions when Spirit spoke.

Within an hour the camp herald made their rounds of the lodge circles, crying, "Save all the tongues. Do not let the children have any. Save all the tongues."

To say it more directly—"A man is going to hold a sun dance. His name is Samalo, and he comes from Rides Twice's village"—that would have been entirely improper.

Since a sun dance was a rare event, the people asked each other who had pledged to make this ceremony, who the whistler would be.

At first it seemed that no one knew. Then the news was traced to the village led by Rides Twice, and the name Samalo came forth.

Samalo? It was a name no one recognized.

Some said that it meant Joins with Buffalo in the whiteman language.

"White man?" people whispered to each other.

"Samalo?"

Many people were skeptical. Why would a white man seek to become a whistler? Why would he seek a vision of revenge? What relative of his died at the hands of the enemy?

The answers were vague and contradictory. Sometimes the words "son of Gray Hawk" were spoken, but no one was sure.

Many asked, "Should we join in a ceremony where a white man is the whistler?"

Some answered, "If the Effigy Owner brings the medicine, we must."

Young men said to themselves, "Should I shed my blood in a lodge where a white man is the whistler? Seek a vision?"

Some answered, "The medicine of the effigy is not often with us. I must seek a vision."

More answered, "This is very strange."

Fortunately, there were buffalo to hunt. Thousands of buffalo.

Chapter Nineteen

The herd spread itself out over thousands of acres, over plain, through ravine, in the creek, up the hill, hard against the canyon walls. Vast as a forest, it covered the earth to the end of sight in three directions. Unlike a forest, it could get up and haul tail. When it did, it would be the biggest, wildest, stompingest beast . . . Sam couldn't even imagine it.

He grinned sideways at Flat Dog, and his head did a little dipsy-doo. Meat for the winter. Also, a chance to prove Paladin was a fine buffalo runner.

They were lying on a low cedar ridge on the southeast edge of the herd, overlooking it all. Lodge Creek, meandering through the middle, was visible only because its cottonwoods stood tall and yellow-leaved above the dark brown mass.

Most of the Kit Foxes of Rides Twice's village were near Sam and Flat Dog, some on the ridge, some a hundred strides back holding the horses. Those were the orders.

Red Roan's sister held Coy well back from the action. Red Roan gave a strict order, unwilling for the coyote to come anywhere near the herd.

That was the other part Sam could hardly believe. Of all human beings he'd been around, the Crows were the least likely to give anyone orders, or take them. Even in a battle, each man fought individually, according to his own lights. They didn't seek victory as a group, but honors as individuals. In anything you did, if you said your medicine was that you should act in such-and-such a way, no one would bother you about it.

Apparently, the buffalo hunt was run just the other way.

The hunters divided themselves into their soldier clubs, Kit Foxes, Knobby Sticks, and Muddy Hands. Each club in each village was assigned a position and a strategy.

Those buffalo in that draw? Cut them off from the others and shoot them from above.

That bunch of cows? Disguise yourself in wolf skins, or as bushes, creep as close as you can, and shoot silently.

Slip around into those trees, ease up close, and get as many as you can without stirring them up.

Most important: No one was to show himself on a ridge top on horseback. No one was to shout or wave a blanket. If anyone had a gun, he was not to fire it too soon. No one was to make a ruckus.

Inevitably, at some time, the herd would get agitated. They would chuff and stomp. They would mill about. They would run.

A herd of several thousand head at a full run, hooves flying, tails waving, heads bobbing, horns waving menacingly. Sam wanted to see that, and he was scared as hell of being in the middle of it.

His Naughty Ones were assigned to wait and watch. The quiet killing would be done by the most experienced hunters among the Little Foxes. When the stampede began, so would the chase.

Sam could see Little Foxes from his village sneaking toward an edge of the herd. They held big pieces of sagebrush in front of them as they crawled over a low ridge. In the coulee, out of the sight of the buffalo, they ran swiftly. On the next ridge they became sagebrush again, and wormed forward slowly.

Others were wolves, padding forward on all fours, their faces hidden behind wolf muzzles.

After a long while Sam began to see arrows whizzing through the air. Cows faltered. Some fell. If the opportunity was right, every hunter would shoot at cows—bull meat was tough and stringy.

In eerie silence the hunters tried to strike mortal blows, but not to finish the buffalo now. Plenty of time for that later.

When a cow would fall, the animals near her would mill around her body, poke her with their horns, and kick at her. They clustered around any fallen one, sniffed, bawled out plaints of loss.

Twice some bulls acted wild, like the smell of blood from their kind drove them mad. They ran forward and licked the wounds. Once two of them lifted a dead cow off the ground with their horns. Tongues thick with blood, eyes aglow, the bulls were an awful spectacle.

But they didn't run off. Everything but that. Sam remembered that the trappers sometimes called slow-minded people "buffler-witted." Now he knew why.

Finally, one bull pawed the ground and let out a terrible roar, deep and wild. He ran out toward the hunters, threw his rump in the air as he pivoted on his big front legs, and dashed back to the herd.

A few more arrows . . .

The herd fidgeted. Cows ran around directionless. Two bulls charged each other and banged heads fiercely. Sam felt like he should hear collision, but it was too far away.

Suddenly Red Roan jumped onto his horse. He yelled, *"Yi-ay-ii-ay,"* and galloped toward the herd.

The Kit Foxes flung themselves on their mounts and charged. Everyone yelled and waved blankets.

The herd hesitated, quivered, and ran.

In headlong panic beasts sprinted in every direction. They crashed into each other. They attacked the horses bearing down on them. With wonderful agility the mounts evaded the slashing horns, and the riders maneuvered into position alongside for a bow shot, or the thrust of a spear or lance.

Far to the left, far to the right, all around this end of the herd, Sam heard the hunters shouting as they attacked. Clots of buffalo here and there began to run, like arms and legs of a single great beast.

Suddenly, as though a gong sounded in the brain of every buffalo, they all ran north along the creek.

Sam heard something he'd never heard before. He felt it in his skin—it vibrated in his bones. Ten thousand buffalo hooves pounded the earth in a fury. It seemed as though the earth itself, under the great tramp, trembled.

Suddenly, a bull pivoted at full speed and charged a rider in front of Sam. The horse hesitated, or perhaps stumbled. A horn caught a hindquarter. A terrible whinny squealed out against death. The rider was down and out of sight, perhaps trampled, perhaps running for his life.

Paladin sprinted headlong at a speed Sam didn't know she had. He used no reins, but she responded perfectly to his knees. As though by instinct, without guidance, she drew alongside a good cow.

Sam drew the big horn bow far back and whizzed an arrow into the cow.

Hit! And well hit! She staggered.

Now he could see only about a hundred buffalo, a dozen riders. The air grew rank with the smell of dust and dung, blood and urine. Sam drew, aimed, shot, drew, aimed, shot. His veins sang an exultant and terrible song of slaughter.

Abruptly, the trap was sprung. A score of buffalo closed

in on him. Pretending only to stampede, they crowded Paladin, penned her in, bumped her. Was she going down?

Sam got a flash of his brain being trampled by hooves.

Paladin eased her stride and slid out to the right.

Clear! Safe!

The trap again! Buffalo thick about him, so close a hand couldn't pass between them, jostling, screaming, and always pounding forward in headlong panic.

Crash!

Sam pitched off.

Insanely, he sprawled over the back of a buffalo and bounced. He kicked wildly, slammed onto the back of another one. He roared with crazy laughter. *Maybe I'll walk on buffalo to the edge of the herd.*

Whumpf!

He hit the ground ferociously. His breath was knocked away. Before he could pass out, his mind screamed at him to get on his feet.

A cow nearly ran right over him. His dodge was slow, and her shoulder knocked him headlong.

On your feet!

He charged against the stream of buffalo, waving his bow. Dashing about, he stuck two fingers in his mouth and pierced the air with his shrill whistle.

Could it be heard? In this tumult nothing else . . .

Suddenly Paladin was alongside him.

He made the highest, cleanest leap of his life onto her back.

They got the hell out of there.

Two cows sprinted away from the herd at a tangent.

Sam galloped after and whanged an arrow into one.

But a fever seized him. He had to be part of the great, running, weaving beast of madness again.

He steered Paladin into the herd. He rode, he shot, he rode, he shot, addicted to the pell-mell of blood and death.

Until he ran out of arrows.

Then he arced out of the herd. Slowly, drained, he looked around. Black carcasses dotted the earth behind him. Women and children flocked around them like birds drawn to carrion. He rode slowly among them. The women slit the great animals from throat to genitals. The guts spilled out into the dust. Huge flaps of skin, pulled onto the prairies like tables, held heart and liver, glistening.

He looked for his arrows. Some laid on the ground, but most stuck out of buffalo flesh, usually several in one animal. He found three of the great masses of meat he had felled. He didn't have to think about the meat. He'd asked Flat Dog to give all but one to his family.

Flat Dog brought back this reply: The family wanted no meat from Joins with Buffalo, but their women would butcher it and give it to the elderly.

He watched the women butcher out tens of thousands of pounds of meat. They would load it on pack horses to haul back to camp, and everyone would feast.

He retrieved his arrows. Most would be fine to use again.

A woman he recognized from Rides Twice's village walked up to him and held out something bloody. A huge, raw piece of liver. He took it with both hands. It wanted to slither away and plop into the dust, but he sank his fingers in. Blood and juices ran over his hands and down his arms. He lifted the liver to his mouth, sank his teeth in, and swallowed a big piece raw. Something primal thrummed in him.

Chapter Twenty

The people stayed in one big camp to dry the meat on head-high racks over low flames. Also, with mixed feelings, they stayed to prepare for the great ceremony, and be part of it.

True, they did save the tongues, but some talked against it. "This isn't right," they whispered. "One man, Bell Rock, has no authority to decide for the whole tribe. Joins with Buffalo isn't a Crow." That was all, but it was plenty.

They also told and retold the story of what happened on that ill-fated raid, how Sam led a good young man to his death. "A man who would go to war against the Head Cutters without medicine. What is he, crazy?" People snorted and spat in disgust.

The meat on the racks drove Coy wild. Sam found him scraps. When Coy did a good job of riding on Paladin's back, he got rewarded.

Bell Rock brought it up to Sam directly. "This talk is no accident," he said. They were broiling hump ribs over the supper fire. It seemed to Sam that all he did now was work on arrows between huge bouts of meat consumption. He threw Coy a half-eaten rib and looked questioningly at Bell Rock.

"Two people, Yellow Horn and his wife Owl Woman, they started all this talk, and they're spreading it."

Yellow Horn and Owl Woman. Sam knew vaguely who they were. They lived in Rides Twice's village. Sounded like he should find out why they were causing trouble. He said, "Maybe I should talk to them."

Bell Rock shook his head. "After the dance." He gnawed. "Or after the raid."

After the raid. Bell Rock spoke like his confidence was perfect. But Sam's wasn't. Maybe in the ceremony he'd get a vision of revenge, maybe he wouldn't. If he didn't, he damn well wasn't leading any raid of revenge. He'd learned that lesson. He rubbed Coy's head.

Bell Rock said, "I have a lot to do to get ready for the dance."

So Sam spent time learning how to make pemmican from Bell Rock's wife, Coming-from-the-Water. Her daughters smiled at Sam learning women's work, but he figured he'd better learn how to do everything he could. He was living on a thin edge.

What the Crow people made from the buffalo was astounding. It was nearly their entire diet, roasted, boiled, jerked, or stored as pemmican. The organ meat was treasured, the liver often eaten raw, the gall drunk as spice. The bones were cracked for marrow. The intestines were kept to make boudins, a sausage some white men thought the finest of all Indian delicacies. They saved the tallow as butter, and sun-dried strips of back fat for a gourmet treat.

The list of what they made other than edibles seemed endless. Men used the thick skin of the head for shields, or turned the horns and head into a hat. A horn might become a container for powder. A good hide, beautifully tanned by a woman, became a calendar. Men recorded each year's happenings as pictures on these robes.

Beyond that, it was women's work. Winter hides, finely tanned with the hair on, became blankets to sleep under, or wraps to wear, thick moccasins against the cold, or surfaces for the geometrical paintings made by women. Summer hides, with the hair removed, turned into lodge covers. After they'd served their purpose as lodge covers, they became parfleches, handsomely decorated boxes where family belongings were kept. Or summer moccasins. Or leggings. Or they could be put to all the uses of rawhide, even making dolls for children.

The hide was just the beginning. The sinew became thread, and splitting it for thickness was a valued skill. The hooves became rattles, or were boiled to make glue.

It was all more than Sam could remember.

The business at hand, though, was making sure of enough pemmican. First he dried the meat thoroughly, which took several days. Coy and the camp dogs went around with their muzzles up during the drying—the smell of the meat drove them wild. But it was spread in strips on racks as high as a tall man's head.

Then Sam pounded the dried meat into small shreds. For some reason, Coy thought this was funny, and made playful runs at the meat while Sam whacked it on a flat stone. Meanwhile, he had fat melting in a pot. While the fat was getting runny, he and Coy gathered chokecherries and serviceberries. Then, still under instruction, Sam dumped in handfuls of the berries into the fat and mixed that concoction with the meat, equal parts by weight. Last, he stuffed the whole tightly into a skin sack and sewed it shut.

The result was kind of like a sausage made by the Pennsylvania Dutch, Sam thought. "It will last for months, even years," said Coming-from-the-Water. "Especially if you don't feed it to the coyote."

When Sam showed Bell Rock a sack of pemmican he'd made, Bell Rock said a little gruffly, "It's past time for everything but your journey to the lodge of the sun. Sit down and we'll smoke a little."

Sam patted the ground behind him and instructed Coy to sit. The little coyote had gotten good at keeping still for long periods.

They smoked Bell Rock's pipe this time, observing all the small rituals that were proper. Then Bell Rock went into his lodge and came back bearing something wrapped in deer hide. With an air of respect he set it between them.

"The sun dance effigies," he began, "they came to the people in the following way. Dances Four Times was fasting on a mountain when he saw, to the west, seven men standing on another mountain."

Sam knew that "fasting on a mountain" was an oblique way of saying, seeking a vision. Lots of what the Crow people talked about, if it was important, they spoke of at a slant.

"Before them a woman stood, holding an effigy in front of her face. The men beat drums with skunks painted on them and sang songs. Dances Four Times memorized the songs.

"He looked away for a moment, and when he looked back, they were standing on a closer hill. When he looked away and then looked back again, they were walking across a nearby bluff. When he looked away the fourth time, he heard a noise where he was, and there they were sitting beside him.

"The Moon—for the woman was the Moon—stood with the effigy wrapped in buckskin in her hands. Again the men began to sing. At the close of the first song, without any movement from Moon, the effigy's head popped out of the wrapping. At the end of the second song, Moon shook the bundle and stepped back. The effigy revealed its arms. When the third song was finished, it exposed itself to the waist. At the conclusion of the fourth song, the effigy appeared wholly, in the form of a screech owl."

Sam stared at the bundle in front of him, curious about what the effigy looked like.

"The owl perched on Moon's head, and then on the chest of the one who lay fasting.

"One of the visiting men suddenly drew a bow and nocked an arrow. 'Screech owl,' said the woman, 'this man will shoot you. You better make your medicine.' It rose up and flapped its wings.

"The man shot at the bird. Instantly the bird flew into his chest and started hooting from inside."

Coy mewled. Sam patted his head, and the coyote quieted.

"Then Dances Four Times saw a sun dance lodge. Moon and the seven men walked toward the lodge. Four times they stopped and sang a song, and then went into the lodge. In the lodge, on the north, was a cedar tree with an effigy tied to it. At the foot of the tree lay a whistler.

"Once again the seven men sang four songs. With each song Moon lifted up the whistler a little and then laid him back down. At the end of the fourth song she pulled him all the way up. She gave the whistler the effigy. He put it back on the cedar tree. Then they sang and danced to the effigy.

"The effigy represents the Moon, and the lodge is the Sun.

"Now, when anyone wants a sun dance, he asks an effigy owner to direct it." Bell Rock gestured to the bundle in front of him. "You have asked me.

"You and I and our helpers have many tasks. First we must, with guidance, choose the place for the dance. Then, in four movements, the people go to this site. We must perform ceremonies in the whistler's lodge. We must choose the proper trees for the Sun's lodge, fell them, and then with many ceremonies build it.

"Finally, we will enter the lodge.

"Joins with Buffalo, you seek a vision of revenge. For that

vision you will go without eating from the day we begin with ceremonies in the whistler's lodge. Then, when we enter the sun lodge, you will neither eat nor drink until the vision comes."

Sam's stomach flip-flopped. "How long?"

"No food for several days before we go into the sun lodge. After that, no food or water for however many days are needed until your vision comes. Maybe it will come the first night, maybe the fourth or fifth."

Sam thought maybe he couldn't go four days without water. Or a week without food.

"We will call on the spirits, and they will give you strength."

Coy crept over against Sam's thigh.

"Why are you doing this for me?"

"You have a good heart."

ON A BRIGHT mountain morning Sam walked toward a small tipi with Bell Rock and Coming-from-the-Water. He wore nothing but a breechcloth, so the cold air dimpled his skin.

This was his tipi during the ceremony. Nearby women were putting up a lodge for the buffalo tongues.

They walked without speaking, for this was an occasion of high seriousness.

Coy was tied up for the ceremony, taken care of by Flat Dog and other Foxes. "I don't want him there to remind you of who you are, or think you are."

Inside Coming-from-the-Water, in her formal role as the wife of the effigy owner, dressed Sam in a deerskin kilt and moccasins. The kilt had been sewn by a virtuous woman, a wife completely faithful to her husband. When asked to make this kilt, a woman might decline by saying, "No, I have a hole in my moccasin." If she didn't speak up, yet had been unfaithful, her lover would shame her publicly.

Coming-from-the-Water slipped moccasins blackened with

charcoal onto Sam's feet. They had been sewn by the wife of a man who killed and scalped an enemy. Black, which would be everywhere during the ceremony, represented revenge.

These two women, and almost everyone who helped with the ceremony, would receive a buffalo tongue. So would many warriors of distinction.

Bell Rock spoke solemnly. "On purpose I have told you very little about the actual dance. It may be difficult for you. Listen to me very carefully.

"This ceremony . . ." He seemed to take thought. "This ceremony has many, many songs, many, many deeds, many, many parts. They won't make sense to you."

He looked Sam hard in the eyes. "So I'm asking you, for a while, to give up sense, or what you think is sense. I ask you join in without question."

He let that sit. "More, I ask you to do everything I say with the greatest attention and caring. When it seems trivial, do it anyway, and exactly as asked. Exactly as asked.

"Nothing is going to be terrible. You will not be cut, wounded, anything like that. I believe strongly that a great blessing waits for you in this ceremony. A great blessing. If you give yourself up to it.

"Do you agree?"

Sam felt committed. "Yes."

"From now on you will eat nothing."

Coming-from-the-Water took a skunk skin, slit it, and draped it around Sam's shoulders and chest.

"Come," called Bell Rock.

A half-dozen men came in, some carrying drums. Immediately, they started a song.

"Attention," said Bell Rock.

Sam sank his mind into the music.

From within the music, he only half-noticed what was done. Bell Rock painted all of him, head to toe, with white clay. He drew something on Sam's chest and back, and something below his eyes, and performed other rituals. Sam would remember the plaintive music perfectly.

After all this, the fourth song ended. Coming-from-the-Water handed Sam a small mirror. He looked at his own face and saw a stranger. His entire body was as white as his hair. On his chest were crosses, which he knew represented the morning star. Beneath his eyes flashed lightning bolts.

Sam felt like a stranger had stepped from within him, and was him.

The whistler's tipi was taken down, and the tipi holding the tongues. All the people rode and walked a couple of miles to a clearing Sam hadn't seen before. The dance site.

Bell Rock instructed two skilled hunters to go out and bring back one buffalo bull each. The bulls must be killed with only one arrow, he cautioned. If the arrow went clear through the buffalo, making two holes in the skin, the hunter was to leave the carcass and hunt another animal.

Bell Rock sent scouts out to look for enemies. Women busied themselves putting up the two ceremonial lodges. When the scouts came back, the people mock-treated them as enemies. Young men took their weapons and counted coup on them.

Then Bell Rock tied the effigy to a willow hoop, gave it to Sam, and said, "Walk alongside me."

Carrying the effigy, Sam led all the people to a cottonwood that had been chosen, for reasons he didn't know.

Again a woman who had no hole in her moccasin came forward. "This is a big gesture for her," Bell Rock said softly. "After she acts as our tree-notcher, if her husband dies, she cannot marry again."

The woman touched the cottonwood four times with the tip of an elk antler. A man painted a black ring around the three. Another one cut it down.

Suddenly, everyone rushed forward gleefully. They hit the tree with their hands, with sticks, with lances, and proudly counted coup. The tree represented the enemy.

The young men found twenty lodgepoles and dragged them to the dance site. Then, if they were among the first, they ran away, or pretended to run. But the Kit Foxes, acting as policemen for the dance, rode after them and brought them back.

Carefully instructed, Sam now painted the faces of the first four and brushed them all over with the effigy. By consenting to this ritual, these men accepted a great honor and responsibility—never to retreat from an enemy. The herald announced their commitments of courage to all the people, and the women trilled their acclaim.

Bell Rock chose a spot to erect the sun dance lodge. There he planted a small cedar tree and tied the effigy to it.

Before Sam lay down in the whistler's lodge for the night, he asked Coming-from-the-Water for a drink. She gave it, adding, "Drink as little as you can. The more you sacrifice, the more quickly your vision will come."

The next morning they built the sun dance lodge, which was huge. Bell Rock blackened his face. He and Sam wore cedar headdresses. Sam kept feeling more and more odd, like he wasn't himself.

The women cut willows. This lodge would be enclosed not with hides but limbs, and a head-high space would be left open so the people could watch.

First, though, a half-dozen group of men came one at a time. "War parties," said Bell Rock quietly. They marched into the lodge and pantomimed fighting. "They hope the effigy's medicine will give them a vision of a dead enemy," said Bell Rock.

Sam watched. He tried to give his undivided attention to the mock war, and to everything. He wanted to see, listen, smell, take in everything that happened, know completely what his sun dance ceremony was.

But his mind kept wandering. Sometimes he felt sleepy. As one group left and another entered, Sam smacked himself in the head with his own hand. He blinked his eyes several times and shook his head.

"Hard, isn't it?" Bell Rock gave him a half smile.

The worst was that his mind kept nagging at him. *Why are you doing this? This is absurd. You aren't an Indian. This is all superstition. Worse, it's savagery. What the devil are you thinking?*

"What you want," said Bell Rock, "is not to think. Just lose yourself in observing." He paused. "Some of the difficulty, though, is that you're weak from not eating. Tomorrow or the next day, that will get better."

Sam wondered why, as he got further and further from his last bite of food, his weakness would ease off.

THE NEXT DAY, it turned out, was the first of the great days. That's what Sam called them to himself. True, he didn't know why they were great, or even have a clear sense that they would be. He simply made up his mind to call them that, purely as an act of faith.

Dressed ceremonially in his kilt, skunk hide, and black moccasins, Sam left the whistler's tipi and, stopping four times, carried the effigy to the sun dance lodge. There Bell Rock met him and tied the effigy to the cedar tree at the height of Sam's eyes.

"From now on you will drink nothing until your vision comes," he said.

Coming-from-the-Water (no other woman was permitted to be near Sam) built a center fire, hung pots, and put buffalo tongues in them to cook.

Warriors entered the lodge one at a time and reenacted their fights against enemies.

At last Flat Dog appeared, carrying two hide ropes. Sam hadn't seen him since the ceremony began. Dressed only in a kilt, he came to be first to make the sacrifice of his blood.

Altogether seven young men came bearing hide ropes. They tied their rigging high on lodge poles, painted themselves white all over, and lay down on buffalo robes. Bell Rock went to Flat Dog, and afterward each man in turn. He handed Flat Dog an eagle-wing fan. Flat Dog put the hide handle in his mouth and bit down on it, Sam supposed to keep from crying out.

Between the nipple and the collar bone on each side, Bell Rock made two shallow, parallel cuts. Then he slipped a wooden skewer beneath the skin, so that it stuck out from behind the flesh of the chest on both sides. Finally he tied the ends of the ropes, which were fashioned into a Y, onto each skewer.

One young man, a tall fellow with a piratical scar on his face, sat calmly while Bell Rock made cuts on his back, above his shoulder blades. Bell Rock fixed the ropes from these skewers to buffalo skulls, and the young man danced out of the lodge, dragging the skulls behind him. He would dance until the skulls broke the skin and pulled free.

The drum began, and the day's first song swirled through Sam's mind. The young blood sacrificers danced. Sometimes they leaned back on the ropes and stretched their skin away from their chests. But always they danced. They would dance, Sam understood, as long as the musicians played, to the end of the day. Blood rivuleted down their chests and into their kilts.

Warriors came into the lodge, and went with the skull-dragger, to help. They recited their own brave deeds in the face of the enemy and added beseechingly, "May this man do likewise."

Now Sam came to it. He didn't understand, and he had to act. He faced the sun dance effigy tied to the cedar. He stared at it. And slowly, to the beat of the drum, he began to dance. He did a simple toe-heel step, repetitive, monotonous, soon automatic and forgotten. He blew the eagle-bone whistle, sending an eerie piping above the music of the singers.

At the beginning he repeated in his mind Bell Rock's words: "The people have been wounded. With or without fault, you brought that wound. Now you can gain the strength to heal it."

Soon, though, he lost track of all words, and of language itself. His mind drifted into a state . . . He could not have described it. The drum pounded, the songs rose, the men's blood ran down their chests, and Sam's mind ran headlong into the effigy.

The lower body of the effigy was wrapped in buffalo hide, hair turned in. The face had eyes and mouth roughly drawn in black. The hair was parted in the woman's way, and sprouted feathers in every direction. And the whole was littered with morning star crosses. Sam stared into the crude, blank eyes of the effigy. "Give me whatever power you have for me," he said silently. He danced. He stared. He danced. He danced until he forgot he was dancing, and why. Dancing was all.

Songs were repeated over and over. Men came to recite their deeds and went. The seven making the sacrifice of their blood danced. Sam stared into the blankness, or mystery, of the sun dance effigy, and he danced.

Sometimes he failed, or thought he was failing. He got distracted. He remembered the day his brother Owen's fiancée made love to him, or the day he slugged Owen. He remembered cowering inside the buffalo carcass during the prairie fire. He remembered the massive Gideon's gentle wit, and missed him.

Suddenly, he would snap back to it. *Attention. What I must do is pay complete attention to dancing and to the effigy.* And his mind would flow again into the song and the motion.

At some point he imagined, or dreamed, or envisioned himself as a sac being filled with the voices of the singers and the beat of the drums. Like an ambrosial liquid it flowed into him, sweet and satisfying. The sac of himself swelled with the liquid of . . . he didn't know what and he didn't care. He swam on the sea of music, he floated into the air like one of Benjamin Franklin's balloons he'd heard about, he drifted, joyous, fulfilled.

Suddenly—or it seemed sudden—the singers and drummers stopped. In his fantasy the sac that was Sam Morgan began to lose . . . whatever was him. The singers left. Fluid kept trickling out of Sam's sac. The tears leaked from his eyes. All his bodily fluids seeped away. Even his blood ran onto the ground, and he was a dry husk.

Those making the blood sacrifice leaned back against their ropes hard and broke free. Bell Rock removed their skewers. One by one, they departed.

Sam felt utterly deflated, drained of all energy, even of self.

Bell Rock helped him onto a bed of cedar leaves. He felt barely able to stagger, even with support. In his private world he had become a nothing.

Coming-from-the-Water put cedar on the burning charcoal at the foot of his bed, so the purifying smoke would drift through the lodge. And they left him, they thought to sleep, but in truth, as Sam felt things, to lie there empty.

It was the strangest feeling of his life, utter emptiness, everything gone that made up Sam Morgan, his memories, his feelings for people and places and things, his convictions, his skills, everything he had fashioned into a self. Yet in a way, it was pleasant.

He put his left hand out idly and felt something that shouldn't have been there. He picked it up. A pouch, a . . . A *gage d'amour*! Despite all, Meadowlark had managed to send him a message, one of love. Flat Dog must have left it here.

Now he decided to enumerate the things he was, things he could be glad of and grateful for. He was alive. He hadn't begged for water. Young men, though not as many as Bell Rock hoped, had used this sun dance to seek visions. The gods hadn't sent lightning bolts or an earthquake to punish him for presuming to dance like a Crow.

Then he switched moods. He railed at himself. He had no vision yet. He didn't even have a glimpse of what corner a vision might be hiding behind. Was he going to humiliate himself by failing to see anything? Was he going to thirst and starve and dance until he died, blind?

Now he had shaken the feeling of emptiness, but he was full of a mental business that was uncomfortable. He told his mind to gentle down, treating it like a skittish horse. After a while, it got out of the way, and after another while he slept.

* * *

EVERYTHING MAY HAVE been the same on the second day, but Sam felt changed, so everything was different.

He made up his mind not to think about whether he was empty or full or in any other state, simply to do the ceremony. Quietly, he let Coming-from-the-Water dress him as before, and Bell Rock painted him the same way.

As they walked ritually to the sun dance lodge, Bell Rock said softly, "Remember, whenever there is singing, you must dance. Later in the day that will get hard, very hard, but you must dance."

The first song rose up, Sam fixed his eyes on the effigy, and his feet moved.

Time passed, measured only in drum beats. The sun's shadow moved from northwest to north in the lodge, but Sam didn't notice. Seven pairs of feet, plus Sam's, were drawn to the earth as the stick was drawn to the drum.

Men came into the lodge and spoke words retelling their brave deeds. The people watched, and they hoped.

The music stopped. All the songs had been sung and repeated several times. The dancers rested. In a few minutes the endless motion began again.

During one break in the music Bell Rock cut a root Sam didn't recognize and held it to his nose. It felt like an elixir, and his spirits rose.

Music. Dance. Music. Dance.

The sun's shadow slid from the north side of the lodge to the northeast. Sam didn't notice. He danced and saw nothing but the effigy and heard nothing but the words, the melodies, and the thump of the drum. He swayed with the words, he undulated with them, he circled with them. He was the words and melody.

Sometimes pictures floated into his mind, every odd kind of picture, things not seen before on earth or in heaven, things he was seeing or dreaming or imagining now. Often he reminded himself to put his mind on the effigy and in the music. What worked best was to dance more vigorously. He lifted his knees high, bent his body double, threw his arms high, tried to dance himself to exhaustion.

Except that he was already exhausted. In his emptiness he didn't know where his strength came from. He asked the effigy for more strength, and felt it flow into his arms and legs. He felt it animate him. But the energy was the effigy's, or the music's, and he only borrowed it, as a wing borrows lift from the wind.

One more time the drum stopped. Four times they will stop, Bell Rock had said, and after the fourth you will sleep. Unless you have seen something.

Shadows rose on the brushy walls of the lodge—the wintering sun was falling.

The musicians rolled into a cadence that promised the last repetition of the last song. The day's dancing slid toward an end.

But the women would not let it end. They trilled their tongues, they cried out, they themselves danced—they forced the singers and drummer to go on.

And on they went, louder, stronger, firmer of beat, more passionate of voice. Sam swam into the lyrics. He heard no sentences but some words were Sun, Eagle, courage, blood, Grandfather.

When the singers rolled into the fourth repetition, normally the last one, the women again would not let them stop. In Sam's mind their trills turned into commands. "Dance, dance, fly, fly."

Harder and harder he danced, wilder and wilder, he knew not why.

Again and again the women insisted. Again and again the musicians roused themselves for one more time. Again and again Sam somehow, barely, found energy where there was none, and he danced, and danced . . .

He collapsed.

"Do not touch him!" the women cried.

Bell Rock sat quietly beside the fallen dancer.

* * *

SAM FELL FREELY. He saw nothing, heard nothing, couldn't know that he was falling, except for the sense within that he was . . .

Sam was within the earth. He grasped the tail of a snake. *My oldest enemy.*

The snake looked back at Sam and smiled, a smile impossible to interpret, maybe inviting, maybe mocking.

It writhed forward, dragging Sam behind. *Unconquerable enemy.*

Sam scraped against nothing, felt no resistance—being dragged felt almost like floating.

They slid through a kind of tunnel.

Sam accepted whatever was happening to him, and accepted the snake as his guide. Within him all was acceptance.

They came to a widening, a kind of chamber. The snake turned. Gradually, it coiled itself—not round and round, as snakes do, but stacking itself upward, lining itself against the wall.

Instantly, the snake's face was hideous, eyes flashing evil. The tongue lashed out into Sam's face. Scornful laughter flash-flooded through the labyrinth of his mind.

Sam shuddered. He wanted to duck backward, but there was nowhere to go.

He thrust his face toward the snake. Abruptly, within the storm, he felt calm. Yes, calm. Confidently, he reached around the slavering tongue and grasped the body of the snake with both hands.

So quickly and deftly even he didn't know what he was doing, he tied the snake into knots.

He drew back and looked at his handiwork. He had tied his mortal enemy into Celtic love knots.

Sam laughed immensely, laughed at himself, laughed at his fear, laughed at life . . .

And woke gently into ordinary reality.

*　*　*

BELL ROCK WAS looking down at him in a kindly way.

"I have seen something," murmured Sam.

Bell Rock cupped a hand at his ear.

Sam realized he hadn't spoken out loud.

"I have seen something."

He was aware that Bell Rock was hoping for the traditional words, "I think things will be all right." But Sam wasn't sure what he'd seen.

Bell Rock gave Sam a drink of water. He felt some Jordan had been crossed, and drank of it.

"Now let's smoke and you tell me about it," said Bell Rock.

A FEW MINUTES, or millennia, later Bell Rock repeated slowly, "And Snake is your oldest enemy."

"Yes, the oldest enemy of all my people." Sam felt utterly weak. At the same time, if Bell Rock had challenged him to climb a mountain, he would have set out confidently.

Bell Rock nodded several times. "You have asked to see a small victory over an enemy," he said, "and have seen a great one."

He stood up and walked outside the lodge. Through the branches, across the twilight, Sam heard him call to the people, "He thinks things will be all right."

A tumult of trills and cheers lifted Sam. He swooped up on the wave of sound, and slid down the far side, and slept.

PART SIX

Coming
Back

Chapter Twenty-one

L et's get close," said Sam.

"Big risk." Flat Dog eyeballed him. But Flat Dog wouldn't fight it. Since the sun dance, Sam's medicine had been too good for that.

The Head Cutter village spread out along the Buffalo Tongue River where it came out of the Big Horn Mountains. The evening fires defined the circle of lodges. They'd found the right village straight off because Sam trusted his instinct. It was the very first village they came to. They knew because Blue Medicine Horse's pony grazed with the horse herd. Flat Dog was impressed. Sam told himself to keep trusting his instincts.

Since the sun dance, Sam's prestige had been high. When he said there would be no large war party against the Head Cutters, just two men, the Crows hid their disappointment and accepted that. Flat Dog accepted it. People would have done whatever he said. Sam got everything he hoped for except a chance to talk to Meadowlark.

Now he fingered his *gage d'amour*. "Let's go."

Coy slunk along with them. The coyote knew the silence of the hunter.

The early darkness on this November night was halved by a gibbous moon. Sam wanted to stick to the shadows.

He had big problems. What Flat Dog wanted was only to take a Head Cutter scalp. What Sam wanted was to get his father's rifle back. The Celt belonged to Sam. So he had to find it. He hoped the man with the two-horned buffalo head-dress still had it. He had no idea how he would set about getting it, none. Maybe he'd set fire to the tipi and take advantage of whatever happened. No, that might do harm to The Celt.

Since the dance, actually, Sam had the sense that if he kept things simple, whatever he tried would work. He just needed to go straight toward whatever goal he had, and act without question, and things would go slick. That's what he was doing now.

They knew where the sentries were. They'd watched last night and the night before. The village wasn't on high alert, not during a winter camp. Winter was a poor time for raiding, unless your medicine was particular in telling you otherwise.

Very, very slowly, they worked their way close. In the trees behind the circle, not twenty steps from the lodges, they stopped. In his usual way, Coy moved with them and stopped with them. Sam could hear his own breathing, and made it slow and quiet. For a long time he and Flat Dog stood perfectly still, their blankets helping them endure the cold. They watched. Sam felt the danger in his nostrils, and he liked it.

The evening was mild. People walked back and forth across the circle, ducking in and out of tipis.

After an incredibly long time Sam began to wonder if he'd lost his mind.

Just then Flat Dog nodded slightly to the south of the circle.

The figure moving—Two Horns. Was it really him? Sam recognized the body shape, but the moonlight didn't catch the face. Had he come out of the tipi with the two sleeping dogs in front?

He crossed to one of the two tipis at the circle's entrance. Someone important. He scratched the flap and slipped in. Almost immediately, he came out and crossed the circle back to the tipi next to the one he came out of. This time he just stuck his head in. Then he went back past the sleeping dogs and into his lodge.

Sam and Flat Dog nodded at each other. His lodge, probably.

A girl came out.

Sam was intrigued. The girl, a teenager by her looks, just stood in front of the tipi. Soon he saw girls standing singly in front of two other lodges, and young men beginning to move around. One young fellow came up to the pair in front of Two Horns' lodge and folded the girl into his blanket. Courting.

Sam sat through an hour or so of courtship, warming himself with thoughts of Meadowlark.

Suddenly he whispered to Flat Dog, "Hold Coy. I'm going to get closer."

Flat Dog shot him a *you're crazy* look.

Sam smiled and repeated, "Closer."

He had an idea. Now he needed to make sure he could recognize the face of Two Horns' daughter.

He stole carefully through the shadows of the cottonwoods. He planned to get the lodge between him and the two young lovers and then slip out onto the moon-shadowed side for a look.

On full alert, he stepped out of the trees. Nothing. He padded to the back of the lodge. He could hear the chatter of women's or girls' voices inside. Suddenly, a man's voice rose over the others, and the female voices went silent.

Sam inched around the lodge and ducked under the right smoke pole. He decided he'd better get low. He crawled out far enough to see.

Damn. The girl's back was to him. Her boyfriend's face was clear in the moonlight, but . . .

Two Horns' voice again, louder but further away.

Two Horns stepped out of the lodge and said something firm to his daughter. She turned, and her face caught the light perfectly, a round face with an impish smile.

She looked directly at him.

Sam wanted to turn into dry grass, or a slinking dog, or a buffalo dropping. He was caught. He brought his legs up under him, ready to run.

But the girl chirped something merrily, threw a final glance at her boyfriend, and ducked into the lodge. The boyfriend called something to her. Sam wished he spoke Lakota. Now he would probably know her name.

Two Horns looked straight at Sam. For a long moment he studied the shadow.

Attack! Sam's mind screamed at him. *This is your chance! Attack!*

His legs tightened but didn't propel him forward. *Where was The Celt?*

Two Horns ducked back into the lodge.

SAM HID NEAR the path that the women used to get water the next morning, waiting for Imp. He couldn't keep calling her Two Horns' daughter in his mind. To him, her name was Imp.

She walked by with an empty pail, back with a full one.

Sam waited and watched carefully, his hand on Coy. Then they slipped away.

He talked about it with his friend. Flat Dog looked full of unspoken words, and Sam knew what they were. "Dammit, you're taking too many chances."

But Sam also had his instincts, and he felt sure of when to take chances and when not. "The water path is not a good place," he said.

Sam saw his friend's face struggle. Flat Dog always wanted to pitch in, not hold things back. Since he couldn't go against medicine, though, he said nothing.

"Let's just watch today," Sam said.

Just watching almost cost them their chance.

The Head Cutter men stayed in camp, talking or working on weapons. A dozen women went out into a field a mile away and dug at the earth with root sticks. A creek separated the field from a wooded hill. Sam and Flat Dog watched from the timber.

"Prairie turnips," said Flat Dog.

At midday Imp and an older woman came. "Two Horns' wife?"

Flat Dog shrugged. Lying down, Coy panted and looked curiously from face to face.

They could only watch—too many women around.

About midafternoon the women all left at once. As they were walking away, though, Imp suddenly turned and trotted toward the creek. Her mother waited, then walked after the daughter. Imp started plucking something off the wild rose bushes, probably rose hips.

Suddenly Sam knew. This was their chance.

The mother was still walking toward Imp. The other women were a hundred yards ahead. The way to the village led through some trees. *Keep picking.* Sam looked at Flat Dog, jerked his head sideways, and the three of them slipped down the hill.

Edge of the timber. Women still picking. Wait.

Now take a chance. Cross the creek. If they look, rush them.

He motioned to Flat Dog.

As Coy skittered across and Sam and Flat Dog waded unsteadily ankle deep, the two women dropped to their knees and started pulling something out of the creek. Watercress, Sam saw. They wanted watercress.

Sam reached the bank and walked steadily toward the women's backs.

They kept their faces to the creek.

Closer, closer. Sam scarcely dared to breathe. He wanted to laugh out loud at his luck.

Two steps away he slipped the blanket off his shoulders. Flat Dog did the same. Sam pounced and wrapped Imp in his blanket. She shrieked, but he held her tight.

Flat Dog had the mother, kicking and screaming furiously.

"Let's get out of here."

Coy howled, maybe in triumph.

* * *

"GO GET THE horses!" Sam half-whispered.

Flat Dog left at a trot. Coy stood guard over the two women.

The mounts were staked in high willows on the back side of the hill. Sam hoped Flat Dog got back before Two Horns came looking. He told himself Two Horns probably wouldn't show up until twilight. That was probably.

Sam looked at the women. He'd kept them in the blankets and bound one with his breechcloth, the other with the belt that held it up. He felt odd standing around buck naked below the waist, and chill from standing around without his blanket.

The women were quiet. They'd given up on crying out.

All three of them, and Coy, were hidden behind huge boulders on the field side of the creek. Sam peered around the end of one boulder toward the village trail.

When Flat Dog got back, Sam used his bridle rope to tie the women and put his breechcloth back on. Then he had a quick talk with Flat Dog, speaking Crow. The women probably didn't speak English, surely not Crow.

"We won't hurt the women," Sam said.

Flat Dog's eyes lit up. One of the great coups, an honor you could boast about for a lifetime, was to kill an enemy's woman right in front of him. Wife and daughter both—this was an incredible opportunity.

Sam could see that Flat Dog was thinking wildly. "Is this your medicine? Or just your peculiar white-man ways?" The first Flat Dog would respect. The second he'd jump right over.

Finally, Sam said, "You will kill Two Horns."

Flat Dog nodded. Coy gave a little yip.

TWO HORNS CAME out of the trees. Yes, he was carrying The Celt. Sam let out a big breath. It was working.

Two Horns was riding a pinto, probably on the off chance that there was trouble.

The Celt. Sam could feel the heft of the half stock in his

left hand, the smooth pull of the trigger under his right index finger.

Two Horns walked the pinto forward slowly. Though he was armed and mounted, his guard wasn't really up.

Wife and daughter. For a moment Sam lost track of his hatred. Then he thought of how the man counted coup on Blue Medicine Horse's body so thirstily, and got it back.

Two Horns was still a couple of hundred steps off. Sam thought he'd better act before he got within hearing distance.

He held Coy, because the coyote liked to play with Paladin. "Forward," he said in a tone the mare would recognize.

She walked out into the meadow and took a few steps.

"Circle left," Sam said, not too loud.

Paladin loped in a clockwise circle fourteen steps across.

Sam and Flat Dog looked hard at Two Horns, trying to guess what the man was thinking. Though he may have recognized Paladin, the horse was loose. Sam would bet Two Horns' mind was shouting, "Get that good-looking horse."

"Circle right," said Sam.

Paladin reversed course and loped out toward Two Horns and then arced back toward Sam.

Now Two Horns turned and rode away. Sam's heart lurched.

At the trees he stopped, dismounted, and tied his mount. He came walking forward carrying a short lead rope, in no hurry. He knew better than to rush toward the strange horse and scare her off.

When Paladin got nearest to them in her circle, Sam said, "Stand."

Paladin did. Sam would say no more, afraid of being heard.

Two Horns now approached gently.

Flat Dog drew his bow string far back.

Two Horns uncoiled the lead rope and held it out in both hands.

The arrow struck deep into his belly.

* * *

WHILE FLAT DOG took the scalp, Sam reclaimed The Celt. He put his rifle to his shoulder and felt its balance. A very good feeling.

"Touch him," said Flat Dog. Sam hesitated, then realized. Flat Dog had already made the first formal touch, coup, and the second belonged to Sam. He performed it seriously.

Then he had to get his shooting pouch off the dying man's shoulder. Two Horns was glaring fiercely at Sam, or trying to glare fiercely. The force was slipping away. Sam worked the pouch off. He looked into Two Horns' eyes. It took a long time to die from a gut wound.

Coy sniffed at Two Horns' blood on his belly, and Sam told him no.

Sam took Two Horns' knife too. Then, calmly, he cut the man's throat.

When he stood up, he asked himself if he did it out of compassion. The answer was, Yes, mostly.

He walked across the meadow, untied Two Horns' pinto mare, and led her back. A horse was good booty.

Then he untied the women, took the blankets off, and re-tied them, avoiding their eyes. This time he made the bonds only half tight.

One look into the field and they knew what had happened. Though they said nothing, he felt the daggers from their eyes.

Five minutes to get loose, thought Sam, *and ten minutes to run to the village. It will be dark by then. Time enough.*

Flat Dog came up with the bloody scalp dangling from one hand and dripping blood onto the tawny winter grass. He and the women looked at each other darkly. Sam didn't like seeing their faces.

"Come," Sam called to Paladin. "Let's go," he told Flat Dog.

"Fast," said Flat Dog.

Sam mounted Paladin, the new horse on lead.

Two Horns' widow said clearly in the Crow language, "I will remember you with hatred."

Chapter Twenty-two

They caught up with the village at the big bend in the Wind River, just above where it changed its name to the Big Horn. The people were moving to their usual winter camping place in a long line of pony drags, policed by the Foxes.

It had been surprisingly easy. Sam and Flat Dog loped their horses all that first night on the wide Indian trail in front of the Big Horns, switching mounts to let one always run unburdened. They went so long and hard, Sam had to let Coy ride behind him on Paladin. The coyote had learned to balance very well.

At dawn they rested for a couple of hours. Then they loped the horses for hours more, walked them, and loped them a last time. With the head start they got, Sam figured no Head Cutter would catch them.

They turned west along the Owl Creek Mountains and made tracks for the river. In summer water might have been scarce, but not in late autumn. On the way Sam discovered that the pinto was a good riding horse, with plenty of bottom. He'd call her Pinto and make her his traveling mount. Now he had one for traveling and Paladin for running buffalo. For a man who'd been practically naked in August, he was getting outfitted.

Sam could hardly believe the way they were welcomed into camp. First Flat Dog went near the camp, leaving Sam behind, and found the sentries. "Tell the women to get charcoal ready." That was all he had to say.

Soon Bell Rock came to Sam and Flat Dog with charcoal. They blackened their faces with it. This was what everyone longed to see, the sign that they had killed an enemy.

At the end of the day they rode into camp. Sam felt like The Celt gleamed, Paladin gleamed, and he gleamed with what he had done.

All the people formed a circle. In the center Bell Rock told Sam what was to happen. First he and Flat Dog were to perform the long dance.

They did. The people were perfectly attentive, poised to hear great things.

Then, at Bell Rock's instruction, first Flat Dog and then Sam told the story of the war party. When Flat Dog told how he shot the arrow and it sank far into the enemy's belly, the women trilled. When he described making the first touch, the trilling rose to the clamor of a thousand ecstatic birds.

Sam thought it was the most exciting sound he had ever heard, and felt a pang of envy.

Flat Dog pointed out over and over, though, how Sam's medicine and wisdom had led them. By Sam, they were led directly to the right village. By his plan, they captured the Head Cutter's women and drew him out to search for them. By his plan and the medicine of his wonderful horse, they brought the Head Cutter within range of Flat Dog's bow. He spoke of Sam making the second touch, and again the women trilled.

Then Sam told his story. His account of the same event was different, as all tellings must be, and Sam thought the women sounded just as enthusiastic. When he finished with his version of making the second touch on the fallen enemy, his voice betrayed a sense of anticlimax. The women sang out with their tongues, but there was a sense of waiting, waiting for . . .

Bell Rock, as the "father" of the expedition, cried out. "Flat Dog has made the first touch of an enemy with his hand."

Enthusiastic clamoring.

"Joins with Buffalo has made the second touch, and has led a successful war party."

Exultant clamoring. Sam felt like it lifted him off the ground.

"Two young men have achieved some of the highest of the four great coups."

Now Sam realized. Four coups to become a war leader—to touch an enemy with your hand, to wrest a weapon away from him, to steal a horse picketed in the camp, and to lead a successful party.

Not quite twenty-one years old, Sam had performed two of them.

He felt giddy.

Now a clansman of Bell Rock came forward and sang praises of Sam and Flat Dog. The songs were beautiful and extravagant.

Bell Rock said quietly to Sam, "Normally, your clansmen would make him gifts for his singing. Since you have no clan, my clansmen will do that."

Though the songs ended the festivities for the night, they jumped to a new start the next morning. The herald circled the camp, crying out news of the start of the dance. All that day and the next were filled with drumming, singing, and dancing. Only killing an enemy was enough to make the women dance, Bell Rock told Sam—stealing horses was not enough.

At the end of two days even Sam felt glutted with glory.

THE NEXT MORNING, when Sam and Flat Dog were still sitting in their blankets and breaking their fast with some jerked meat, Bell Rock appeared. He said, "Come smoke with me and Gray Hawk tonight."

After months, that's how it ended, the shunning by the Gray Hawk family. Meadowlark's face, and memories of touching her, exploded in Sam's mind.

When Flat Dog walked off with Bell Rock, Sam asked Coy, "Now Gray Hawk will talk to me?" Coy offered, as comment, only warm eyes. Sam had seen Meadowlark dancing exuberantly during the last three days. His repute among the Crows, he hardly dared form the words in his mind . . . "I guess I'm too big to ignore," he told Coy. He allowed himself hope. His heart danced.

Sam had work to do. Two Horns had used up most of The Celt's powder and lead, maybe on the fall buffalo hunt, or maybe just trying the rifle out. Aside from horses and coyote, Sam was a pauper. He lacked flint and steel for making fire, and nothing could be more basic. A pot to cook in. Plenty of moccasins. A capote. A couple more buffalo hides to sleep on and under. A tipi. A saddle, and a calf hide for a saddle pad. Ropes to hold packs on the horses, and to picket them. A tomahawk to make firewood with. A pistol, the best complement to The Celt. Coffee and sugar. Tobacco. Most of all, maybe, goods to trade to the Indians. He was tired of living in poverty.

So he needed to spend his winter days setting his two traps and getting a few beaver. Very few, for beaver were inactive in the winter. Then he needed to have a spring hunt, even if he did it alone. Since he'd missed the fall hunt, he didn't know where his outfit was. When he thought of it, he supposed that Diah, Fitz, and the boys had given him up, thinking he'd gone under.

He spent this day making arrows, a necessity that seemed never to end. He listened for gossip about Gray Hawk and his family. He learned absolutely nothing before he, Flat Dog, and Coy arrived at Bell Rock's lodge that evening. At the door flap Sam told Coy to sit and stay.

Bell Rock sat in the center behind the fire, Gray Hawk on his left, as was proper. Sam and Flat Dog sat to the left of Gray Hawk.

In silence Bell Rock used a coal to light his pipe. He offered the smoke to the four directions, Father Sky, Mother Earth. Turning the pipe once in a full circle, he handed it to Gray Hawk, bowl in the left hand, stem in the right. Gray Hawk took it just that way and smoked. Sam and Flat Dog followed suit.

When the pipe was empty, Gray Hawk spoke without preamble. "My daughter's brothers told you to bring eight horses and ask for her. I ask you not to do that."

Slammed down. Defeated. Crushed.

Sam made his mind focus on what counted: Meadowlark was lost.

He got out one word. "Why?"

"You may think it is because of Blue Medicine Horse."

It was permitted, for reasons Sam didn't understand, to speak the name of a dead person when you were smoking the pipe. He felt the name like a stab. He knew that Gray Hawk felt it more deeply, and always would.

"That's not it," Gray Hawk went on. "You have made it possible for us to end our mourning for our son. Thank you."

Now the older man waited for a long time.

"A wise person," he finally said, "tells us Crows to have nothing to do with white men. White men will bring death to the people, it is said."

Sam gawked. Of all the tribes in the mountains and on the plains, the Crows were the friendliest to whites. This was a bad turn.

"Who?"

"A wise person," Gray Hawk repeated.

Bell Rock lit the pipe, and they smoked in silence. After a while Meadowlark's father started to stand up. On one knee, he glanced sideways at Sam, put his gaze back in the fire, and said quietly, "You are a good young man."

Then he left.

The moment Gray Hawk replaced the door flap, Bell Rock said, "Owl Woman."

Sam searched his mind. He associated the name vaguely with a heavy-set, middle-aged woman full of dark looks . . . Now he remembered that two people had started the talk against his sun dance. Owl Woman and her husband, Yellow Horn.

"A woman who sees things," Bell Rock said.

Sam translated this in his mind, making allowance for the Crow customs of indirection and understatement. A woman who had strong dreams, or visions, ones people paid attention to.

"I will invite her and her husband to smoke with you and me soon."

Flat Dog wanted to talk more, but Sam wanted to be alone.

Outside he clucked at Coy, and they walked across the lodge circle. At the brush hut he pulled the head end of his blankets outside. He rolled in and looked up at the stars. Coy settled himself on the blankets at Sam's feet. So many stars, so far apart, such emptiness in between.

"Boy," he said, "the stars are working against us."

Chapter Twenty-three

When the long train of pony drags wound into the winter camping place, all eyes—those of the Fox policemen, the old men, the women and children—were on one spot. There where the outfit led by Diah had camped two winters ago, a solitary line of smoke rose to the sky.

Sam and Flat Dog looked at each other. The scouts knew who was there, or they would have warned the people. But who? White men?

Sam touched his heels to Paladin, and the mare flashed that way with her wonderful speed. He could hear Flat Dog coming hard behind him.

Three horses picketed—Sam recognized none of them.

A lean-to backed against a boulder. White men, for sure.

Sam reined up in front of it. Buffalo robes and blankets within, a fire in front.

Click! The dry click of a rifle hammer?

Sam looked up. Twenty feet above him a figure rose, silhouetted against the sun and hard to make out.

"Sam Morgan, you done lost your top knot."

He knew the soft, kindly voice of the Virginian—it was James Clyman.

Sam laughed out loud.

Next to him another figure, familiar but against the sun . . .

"This child is glad to see Joins with Buffalo hasn't joined with the buffalo grass."

Gideon!

WINTER CAMP. A good fire, old friends, plenty of meat, the first sugar and coffee Sam had tasted in months, and a good story. Mountain man heaven.

Sam and Flat Dog would hear of nothing except for Gideon to tell the story of his escape and survival at full length. "Last time I saw you," Sam said with a rush of feeling, "you were hightailing it south with arrows in you and your horse and Head Cutters flying thick as mosquitoes around your head."

"One arrow in me," corrected Gideon. "Here." He tapped his right hip. From the look of the way he walked, that wound was still bothering him. Maybe it always would.

"I can't believe you didn't get hit but once," said Sam.

Gideon made a snaky motion with his right hand. "We Frenchmen, we fly between dangers, whether they be arrows or bullets or angry husbands."

"You think you could tell this story"—Flat Dog searched for words—"in a true way?"

Sam was proud of his friend for learning to josh American-style.

Gideon sucked on his lower lip. "I get hit by two other arrows. One rakes across my back, leaves long scar, you will see. The other, it digs at my scalp, knocks my hat off, makes more blood than trouble."

He gave them all a wily look.

"What really happened?" Sam reminded him.

"Most ze Indians, they go toward you, Blue Horse, ze pack horses. Four devils, they comed after me . . ."

GIDEON POOR BOY whipped his horse like hell. He knew damn well he had no chance, so he meant to go under in high style.

When he cleared the cottonwood grove stuck bad in only one place, he roared. He wheeled his horse and raised his pistol. Four Head Cutters were on his ass. He aimed and dropped the front one clean. That would slow the buggers down. They knew he still had a loaded rifle. He kicked his drag-ass horse and worked at reloading the pistol.

A gravelly hill came up on his right. He rounded a curve and spurred the horse up it. He was possessed by an idea.

He turned hard to the right again—this horse wasn't going to be able to go for long. He galloped twenty yards back and hurled his mount and himself off the lip of the hill.

They careened straight into the three men after them. Gideon spurred the horse into the flank of the lead horse, and it knocked it ass over teacups. He ducked under the war club of the second rider, sped at the third man, knocked his lance aside, and buried his knife in the man's chest.

Without looking back, he spurred sideways and the second rider clipped his mount's hindquarters. Horse and rider went down. Gideon rolled and came up with his rifle raised. He fired almost point blank into the rider's gut, and the Indian flew toward heaven backwards.

Gideon lunged for the man's bridle. His hip stabbed him, and he screamed, but he got the rope. Unable to mount normally, he threw himself belly down across the pony's back, turned its head up the creek, and whacked its hind end hard.

When Gideon got into a sitting position, he looked back. Five or six more Indians coming, including the one he unhorsed, but well back.

His mind whirred. He laughed. A chance! This was even bigger fun!

GIDEON ONLY LISTENED. He dared not watch.

Knowing he couldn't outrun a half-dozen Head Cutters, not hurt as he was, he veered off into the first coulee he came to.

After a quarter mile it turned, and sandstone crags pushed in from both sides. That gave him an idea.

He pulled the horse up, slid off, and smacked its hindquarters as hard as he could. The pony started and then fled up the coulee.

Now the bad part. Gideon had to get into the rocks. The damned hip would fight him all the way.

Later he told himself, bragging, that it was like climbing out from the ninth circle of hell. But pain, what does pain matter to a man?

Half-dragging that leg, he hoisted himself up the sandstone, step by agonizing step, and around it into a little cleft.

He listened to the beat of the hooves. Probably they would gallop by, looking for the pony and rider. When they found the pony, they would hunt for the rider. Hunt up at the top of the coulee, if he was lucky. Eventually, very eventually, they would look hard at all the tracks in the coulee and trace him to these rocks. Then, well, a game of cat and mouse until dark, and another game of cat and mouse the next day . . .

Or one of them might have a superb eye. He would see the grass broken in a clump, and tracks more than a straight-running pony would leave. Then Gideon would be a mouse in a sandstone trap.

The hooves thundered by.

When they were halfway out of hearing, he grabbed the arrow with both hands, bellowed, and wrenched it out of his hip. His outcry would never be heard above the hooves.

He gazed morosely at the hip. "Heal, damn you." His uncle had dragged around a bad leg, and that always gave Gideon the willies. Nothing, to him, could be worse than being a cripple.

Up, up, he had to get out onto the ridge. Damn, why had he chosen the one thing he couldn't do, walk? He forced himself to chuckle through the pain. *Because they think I can't do it.*

Across the ridge into the next crinkle in the landscape, which turned out to have a tiny tributary to the creek. He slid down the hill on his bottom, his left bottom, the one that wasn't killing him. When he got to the creek, he lay flat in the shallow water and drank. Drink, drink. Maybe no other drink for hours, for a day . . .

He walked up the creek, his feet carefully in the water.

He hoped it was the opposite of what they would expect. He was going up into a sweep of grassy, treeless hills, where a man might be seen for miles around. He was going away from water, for this rivulet would soon be . . .

A marsh. In a quarter mile it was a little marsh where a spring rose. He looked at the muddy ground. He studied the sparse growth of cattails. No cover, not a bit. No cover on the hillsides either. What had he gotten himself into?

Hellfire. He started up the hill, practically clomping on his bad leg. *Hurt, you bastard, hurt as bad as you can.* Up he chuffed, and up and . . .

Time to crawl over the ridge top. He needed to be exquisitely tiny. Across the top, he inched and looked down the other side.

Hope.

Not much, but hope. An outcropping of sandstone, with a split. Maybe not big enough for a man of his girth. No, maybe not. But the only hope.

He scooted down the hill on his left butt. He crawled out onto the sandstone, dropped his legs into the crack, and lowered himself.

It wouldn't work. Damn every pound of buffalo meat he'd eaten in the last year. Damn his father for having the build of a bear. Damn all his ancestors.

He heaved himself up.

Out of luck. He was stuck. And, due to gravity, getting more stuck every minute he stayed there.

He heaved mightily with both his immense arms.

Stuck.

He got an idea.

He rotated himself. He walked his feet up the crack, tilting his upper body down toward it. He braced himself with his elbows. He pushed with his left foot. That hip slipped upward a little. He repeated the motion, and slipped back a little, sideways into the crack.

Have to lift both sides out at once, the way I'm widest.

He used the right foot, gaining one excruciating inch. He braced the foot and knee on opposite sides, twisted his body level, and pushed up with both elbows.

Out he popped.

He crawled off the sandstone and down the hill. Below the sandstone he looked back to curse his personal Golgotha. And saw it. The cave of his resurrection. He crawled up.

It was just a bigger split, no cave. He could actually crawl into it maybe three steps before it narrowed.

When it did narrow, it squeezed together only at the middle and top. On the bottom was still a decent hole. He got down on his belly and slithered forward.

Behind the squeeze, a cozy little room crook-necked to the right. He sat down, back against the far wall, legs on the sand. Straight up the split slithered down to a hand span, and it curved. He could stand, but he couldn't see sky above. And no one above could see him.

It was cool. The sun wouldn't broil him. He had nothing to eat. Nothing to drink. He couldn't move around.

He touched his ear and his hand came away sticky.

Syrupy blood.

He felt of his head. Bloody, matted hair. He remembered the slash of pain from the arrow that furrowed him. Well, the bleeding was stopped.

He studied the hip. Couldn't tell a thing about it. *Mon dieu,* he said to himself, *don't let me be a cripple.*

He slept.

The morning sun woke him and brought riders. He listened, but the language of the hooves was babble to his ears. He stood up and pulled his throwing knife. He was pretty good with it. If someone crawled into his hideaway, the fellow probably wouldn't crawl back out.

The next day, more riders from time to time, close and distant. Waiting.

He'd wondered how Indians went for days without water on their vision quests. Mostly a trick of the mind . . .

So. He hadn't bled to death from his scalp or his hip. He'd stood the thirst for two full days. He would leave tonight. He would be afoot, wounded, half-crippled, and alone.

He grinned. Not bad fixings for a mountain man.

"AFTER ZEM TWO days," Gideon went on, "I take thought. You and Blue Medicine Horse are dead. Flat Dog, I don' know—hightailing over the mountains, if he have good sense. I think where the Crow village might be. On the Big Horn somewhere, upper end maybe. Ze Crows, will zey help me? Don' know.

"One more chance. Ze general and Diah, they take the furs down the Big Horn to the mouth, float them down the Yellowstone. Then many trappers, they come back up the Big Horn, go toward pass to cross to Siskadee. Maybe can find zese trappers.

"So I crawl. No can walk, hip is worse, all stiff. Crawl. In two days reach timber, get big stick, stand up and walk leaning on stick. Walk up creek, through pass, down mountain, across plains toward river. Walk maybe a hundred miles, maybe fifteen sleeps.

"Eat? It is August. Lucky. I eat berries. Sometimes wild onions. Rose hips. You ever have serviceberries and wild onions in mouth at one time? Pretty funny.

"I hungry, maybe starving, but not starving to death.

"Get near river, sleep, one morning zis *fou,* zis madman, he stand over me." He nodded at Clyman.

"The Frenchy was sleeping on the sand within ten feet of the Big Horn. I wanted to throw him back, but Fitz said he was big enough to keep."

Gideon went on. "After fall hunt, I t'ink, Sam Morgan, if he is still alive . . . Maybe I shouldn't hope. If still alive, he goes with village of Rides Twice this winter. I go there. I give him cussing he never forget. Lead me into ambush, get arrow in hip, lose horses and all possibles, ever' damn t'ing make me a man, not a beast." He put on his worst mock-angry face. "I cuss you," he roared. "Now, what you do since August?"

"On account of he led us into an ambush," said Flat Dog, "he has given a sun dance."

That changed the expressions on the faces of Gideon and Clyman. They knew what it meant.

The story took the rest of the night.

Chapter Twenty-four

Owl Woman looked straight into Sam's eyes. He saw then and there that she intended to tell him the truth, her truth.

Bell Rock, the host, waited with a neutral face. Yellow Horn, Owl Woman's husband, kept his gaze in the center fire, like he wanted nothing to do with this.

"Because Bell Rock asks me to," she began in the Crow language, "I will tell you what I saw, exactly what I saw.

"It does not have to do with you personally. I believe you are a man with a good heart."

She took a deep breath and let it out. Then she seemed to go into a trance and report from there. "I had a dream. I was lost. I looked around in every direction, my head turning this way, turning that way, and I didn't know where the people were. Yellow Horn, our children, our grandchildren, the village, all the people of Absaroka, I couldn't find anyone.

"I was by a small, pretty lake in the region of the stinking, bubbling springs. I knew it was said to be a special place. From there waters flow from one end of the lake into the great water-everywhere to the west, on the other end into the great water-everywhere to the east. It seemed a good place of green grass and thick stands of lodgepole pines, except that I was alone.

"I didn't know which way to go, what direction to start

looking for the people. Soon, though, I heard something. It was hard to make out. Moans, maybe, deep, low sounds uttered by human voices, or voices that had once been human. I walked in the direction of those sounds.

"But before long, even the moans were lost. Instead I saw white people, lots of faceless white people, marching through the country on horses. They rode, they rode, they rode. They didn't see me. They didn't look at me or anything, they just rode with their blank faces pointed toward some horizon, somewhere far off.

"When I went in a different direction, I heard the human utterances again. I ran toward them. I lost them. I panicked. I heard them again and ran in another direction. I saw more faceless white people, riding, riding.

"Suddenly I was on a path alongside a pond, among the white people, marching, marching. They didn't see me, and I was alone. I could hear the moaning voices, soft, but close.

"On the pond were lily pads. Except that the lily pads were faces, the faces of the Absaroka people under a film of water. The faces were dead, the people were dead. In rows many, many of them, they lay dead. Their countenances were ghastly white, their eyes frozen open, their lips vermilion.

"I stood by the side of the pond and looked at the faces of all my people, dead. The white people marched by on their horses, not noticing. Forever they went on, forever and forever. And the people's death went on forever."

She emerged from the trance and looked at Sam. "I understood this to mean that the white people will come into our country and go past and keep coming and going past and keep coming endlessly, and because of them the people will die.

"I want our people to live. So it is very simple for me. I tell anyone who is willing to listen to have nothing to do with white men, nothing at all."

She sighed. "They do not listen, most of them. They want *things,* the many things you bring to trade. Needles, cooking pots, tomahawks, guns, cloth, blankets—all of these they want. Our women want them even more than our men. It will not stop. I cannot change everyone.

"But anyone who will listen, I tell them, 'Do not set your feet on this path. It is the path of death. And some listen. Gray Hawk and Needle, they listen. And they choose. Life, not death."

She heaved breath in and out once, as though she had run a mile. "Life."

Again she raised her eyes straight into Sam's. "Meadowlark's family respects you. I respect you. We know you mean no harm. But they see you, and I see you, the way we regard the first flake of snow in a pleasant autumn. The first sign of a long and terrible winter."

AFTER A FEW days Sam asked to speak with Owl Woman again. Yellow Horn sat with them, and once more Sam had the sense that the door of Owl Woman's heart and mind was in some way open, Yellow Horn's closed.

He felt like he had to deal with that first. To Owl Woman he said, "My heart is good toward you, and I sense that yours is good toward me. But Yellow Horn, I sense that your attitude is different. I ask why."

Yellow Horn scowled and worked his mouth but stopped himself from saying anything.

Owl Woman volunteered, "He has seen you work your power over the coyote and over the horse, so that they do your will. He believes that this power shows you possess a bad medicine. He thinks he, and all of us, should oppose this medicine."

She let Sam take that in. "I do not agree with him," she added, "and that is not what you have come to talk about."

Sam looked from Owl Woman to Yellow Horn and back to the woman. He accepted. He would pass by Yellow Horn's attitude.

He had thought and thought about what to say about Owl Woman's dream, and all his thoughts came to nothing. He ventured forth in ignorance.

"What you fear, I understand it," he began in the Crow language. "But it is a fear only, not a prophecy. Many dreams come to make us afraid, or give voice to our fears. They are not gifts of the spirits. They do not foretell the future. They are a child's fantasy only. On one breath of the wind of what is real, they blow away.

"Most white people will never come to this country. Never. It is not the kind of country they like. They want to plow the earth, plant, grow their crops, and harvest. They want to feed their cows, have calves, and eat the meat that grows inside their fences. They have no desire to follow the buffalo. That seems idle to them, worse than idle. And they would not like the earth here. It is dry. There is little rain. Never would they be able to till the soil and grow their food, as they like to do.

"This desire to grow things, to live in one place, to eat meat from animals they own—these wants live deep within them."

Owl Woman raised an eyebrow, and Sam knew she was reacting to the extraordinary idea that people could own animals. He pressed on.

"We white men who come here are rare exceptions. We like the life they hate. They hate the life we love.

"They have land in their own country, as much as they will ever want. Abundant land, waiting only for the axe to clear away the trees and the plow to cut the earth. They will never turn these arid plains into farms, or the high mountains into pastures."

Sam thought a moment. He was only saying what every mountain man knew. "As evidence I give you one fact. A few young white men come here. The women stay home. Home, a man's center, the place he belongs. Where his woman is, there is a man's home. No white women come here, or will.

"Some few of us beaver hunters will join with your women. Then the place where we live, where our hearts sing, it will become home to us as well. You will not become white. We will become red."

She nodded. It was an acceptance that Sam, at least, had become a Crow.

"Other beaver men, you will see, they will go home to their women and not come back. Already many have done that. Young men will have their sport, their great days of wandering and hunting. Then they will go home. You will see."

Owl Woman waited, gave Sam time to think whether he had anything more to say. He decided he didn't.

Finally she answered, "You speak with the voice of mind, I with the voice of dream. You tell what the two eyes of the head see. What I tell, that is seen only with the single eye that lives in the heart."

Chapter Twenty-five

What Owl Woman said about the eye of the heart disturbed Sam. He didn't know what to make of it. He spent that night telling himself that he and Meadowlark were finished. He spent the second night promising himself that he accepted this fate. *She isn't mine. She isn't mine. She isn't mine.* Maybe a little bit of him believed it, and grieved.

The next morning he ordered himself to stop maundering and get on with his life.

Regardless of what the future might bring, Sam had a present to get straight. He and Flat Dog, having nothing to trade for a lodge, cut poles and built a lean-to that shared one wall with James and Gideon's. That was shelter for the winter. Pemmican from the fall hunt, and the elk they would hunt in the snow, that made enough food.

Then the future. Sam didn't know what Flat Dog wanted, but he and Gideon needed plews to trade at rendezvous. He felt half-desperate to get a decent outfit again.

By comparison Gideon was lucky. When he escaped from the Lakotas, he wasn't stark naked. Aside from clothes, he had the gear he wore on his person, his rifle, pistol, shot pouch with powder, a few lead balls, and a vial of beaver medicine, throwing knife, butcher knife, patch knife, flint and steel, even the pipe and tobacco in his *gage d'amour*. Right pert fixin's, some of the beaver men would have said.

Sam needed all that and much more.

Luckily, Clyman was willing to let the two of them use his traps. Unless a man was desperate, the few winter beaver weren't worth the effort.

Sam and Gideon laid plans to work the nearby creeks in pairs. Up one creek, down another, back to the village.

So imagine when, in the twilight of their second day of work, they came into camp to find Needle and Meadowlark sitting at the mountain men's fire, talking to Flat Dog and Clyman.

Sam sat down and, keeping his eyes down, helped himself to the meat in the pot.

It was proper, in a way. Proper for a mother and sister to come talk to Flat Dog. Proper for a young maiden to talk to friends of her brother's, if she treated them like other brothers, and there was no prospect of courtship.

There is no courtship, is there?

Half an hour later, when the women got up to leave, Sam got up with them. He walked them back to their lodge. Needle had promised him three pairs of moccasins for an elk hide. Now she was going to draw around his foot with charcoal on deer skin to get his size.

When Needle came back out with the charcoal, Meadowlark came with her. While Needle was bent over Sam's foot sketching, Meadowlark mouthed three words to Sam. They were in English, a language she had never spoken a word of. But she had heard Sam say these English words many times to her: "I love you."

He looked into her face, and she opened it to him. He saw nothing there but sadness, and in her eyes infinite sadness.

Having let him see, she tucked her head away, turned, and slipped back into the tipi.

SAM USED FLAT Dog. That made him feel guilty, but he could see no other way to do it. The message was simply, "Meet me under the overhang at midday."

He stood half crouched, though there was no reason to crouch. His blood thrummed with anxiety. Would she come?

This was a place the river had undercut the bank in the spring, when it was high. A fir tree stood on the point, and some of its roots were exposed below, where Sam stood. In another spring or two the river would cut too much dirt away, and the fir would pitch into the melt-swollen waters.

Now the river had backed away, winter-thin. The overhang was cold. The sun, low in the late-winter sky, never reached this cave. Sam shivered. He looked along the sandy strip upstream, back toward the village.

The corner of his eye caught the fall of a shadow, and he jerked his head the other way. Meadowlark, with Flat Dog. She reached for Sam's hand, as she knew he liked, but she wasn't smiling.

"Better to be alone?" he said in the Crow language.

Flat Dog's face stayed impassive.

"It's better if my brother's here."

"I love you," Sam said in English.

"I love you," she answered, and maybe her lips did start to smile.

In Crow he went on, "Let's go away together. I have traded Muskrat Woman for her travel tipi." It was a ragged affair, and they both knew it. "Spring is coming, and warm weather." He paused, unable to think of what to say.

"I love you," she began, then proceeded in Crow. "Joins with Buffalo, I cannot go outside the will of my family, my people. I will live my life in the circle of a Crow village. In that circle are safety, caring, warmth, companionship, everything that matters. I will raise my children here.

"Many people believe Owl Woman's dream. Especially my mother and father believe it."

Sam wanted to rage that this was impossible. The beaver hunters were a couple of hundred men, the Indians ten of thousands. But he knew better than to argue.

"Unless you can change their minds . . ."

She turned away slowly. For a moment he thought she would turn back and say something more, something different. But she set her shoulders back the way she came, and in an instant was out of sight.

Sam looked into Flat Dog's eyes. There he saw compassion. In that moment he was sure that he and Flat Dog would always be friends.

"I'm sorry," said Flat Dog. "For both of you."

WEEKS PASSED, FOR Sam, in a fever. He and Gideon trapped. Sam and Flat Dog hunted elk. Sam made arrows to trade for small items. Around their nighttime fires, the beaver men told stories, sometimes stories of the frontier back in the States, a land of fable kinged by alligator horses who could whup ten panthers at once and eat their whelp for breakfast. More often now they told stories of their own kind, the men variously called mountain men, mountaineers, and beaver hunters, men of the white, black, brown, and red tribes, men who had done things that would be remembered, that people would look back and tell stories about, tales with heroes worthy of big stories. John Colter's run from the Blackfeet. Hugh Glass's crawl across the plains. Diah Smith and the griz that bit his head. And they knew, wordlessly, that they themselves were doing deeds worth remembering and telling stories about. Sam wondered if he was a hero.

He barely heard these stories, though. His mind was in a roil about what to do about Meadowlark. He saw her often, but never alone. He looked at her when he thought no one would notice. Sometimes she looked at him, and he saw in her eyes that she grew sadder and more hopeless by the day.

He had no idea what to do, until he asked himself what would happen in one of these big stories.

He had never been so frustrated in his life. Three straight days. Normally Meadowlark came to the river for water in the time between sunset and darkness. One woman from each lodge did. The first evening, though, she came with another girl, both talking gaily, so Sam did nothing. The next evening Needle came instead. The next evening, the same. Sam knew very well that Meadowlark usually made this trip, not Needle. He asked himself over and over if they had figured what he was up to. But they couldn't possibly. He had been very careful.

It wasn't happening. He was ready, and beyond ready.

This evening no one had come. Full darkness was gathering, and no one had collected water for the Gray Hawk household tonight. An impossibility, yet it was true.

Squatting out of sight, he fidgeted.

A shadow. It glided along the path, flickering between trees. He couldn't see who it was. In the near darkness, it grew close and passed. The figure seemed to be running. He never did see who it was. Unbelievable. It was the right size and shape for Meadowlark, but most young women in the village were about that size and shape.

What to do?

He hurried to the path and from there walked openly toward the river. If it was Meadowlark, well and good. If not, he would give a casual greeting and keep going like nothing was . . .

Meadowlark, almost in his face. In the last of the light he saw several emotions on her face, pleasure in meeting him, sadness, pain, and more.

He smiled at her and stepped aside to let her pass.

She squelched a smile and walked forward.

He acted swiftly. From behind he flung the deer hide around her mouth and between her teeth, threw a quick knot, and pulled her back tight against him.

Her body felt so good along his. It had been so long . . .
She flailed.

Go!

He seized her behind the knees and shoulders, lifted her, and trotted through the cottonwood trees. Paladin and Pinto were tied about a hundred yards away, and he could carry her that far on the run.

He lifted her and seated her on Pinto. The pony was tied on a lead to Paladin, in case she might try to bolt.

He took both her hands, looked directly into her eyes, and said, "I'm kidnapping you. I want you for my wife."

Coy mewled in a way that sounded like, "Ple-e-e-ease," and Sam couldn't help smiling.

He tied Meadowlark's hands behind her. "Are you going to scream?"

Hesitation. Wild eyes. Thought. At last she shook her head no.

Good. Safer this way. He took the deer hide off her mouth. A sentry would pay no attention to two Crows riding on a trail in the darkness. No one would miss Meadowlark for a while, and then it would be too late.

He mounted Paladin and started off at a walk. A quarter mile on, he kicked the horses up to a lope. The trail was easy going, and Coy kept up comfortably.

Before too long, they left trail and turned up Black Creek. Riding at night was slow, but they were headed for a good place. The best place, he thought—a wide, well-watered valley on Black Creek within sight of the great Absaroka peaks to the north. The mountains would be snowy, but the valley floor, mostly free of snow, would be full of elk. In a week or two the grass would come green. When he and Flat Dog had first come here, they watched a hawk hunting in the open meadows. As they watched, the sun set, and the hawk's broad wings caught its evening colors gloriously. They named it Ruby Hawk Valley.

The travel lodge was already set up there, and it would do for a while. He had chopped, split, and broken up plenty of firewood. He had brought pemmican enough for a couple of weeks. He had traded for a blanket to sleep under, in addition to the buffalo and elk robes. He had made a household, one of poverty, but his. Theirs.

AT THEIR CAMP he gritted his teeth until his molars ached.

She didn't say a word. She hadn't spoken since he abducted her, and she didn't speak while she got water from the creek and watched him build the fire. He spread their bed robes near the flames so they could sit a while. Coy snuggled up next to her leg, but she ignored him.

Sam didn't know what she might need to say, or hear. What he needed to say, he'd said by bringing her here.

She looked at him funny. It was odd, in the Crow way of things, for a man to be arranging the inside of the lodge. He assumed they would get used to each other, if . . . A big if.

He sat behind the fire, took his white clay pipe from the *gage d'amour* she had given him, packed it, and lit it. This gesture, at least, she would be familiar with. Now she petted Coy's head, and he accepted that.

She looked at Sam, just looked. He couldn't tell what was in her face. Nothing, it seemed. Or maybe it was everything, held very still.

He looked back at her. And smoked. And looked.

His bowl of tobacco was gone, burned. He tapped the ashes onto the edge of the fire. He looked around the lodge. The glow of the fire made the lodge skins rise. In the light Meadowlark's face glowed.

He reached for his woman, put his arms around her, and kissed her. He kissed her passionately, and in a moment both of them were kissing passionately. Their embrace lifted him up, and time spun away.

After a while he stroked and caressed her in various places. Later still he slipped her moccasins off, and then her dress, gently. He looked at her, all of her, and noticed that she enjoyed his look.

He took off his own clothes, lay down beside her, and folded her into his arms.

They began as in a slow waltz. First they explored one possibility, then another. Hour revolved upon hour, embrace upon embrace, body upon body. Through the night they did everything they wanted to do. Coy slept like nothing was happening. An hour or so after sunrise, they dozed off and slept until midday.

Then Meadowlark pounced on Sam.

THEIR FIRST FULL day was different, what was left of it. When they woke, Meadowlark went to the creek for water, and Sam built a low fire in the lodge. They nibbled on pemmican, and fed Coy more than they ate. They made love. This time they played melodies like yesterday's, and the harmony was the same, but the tempo was slow, relaxed, indolent. The feel shifted from fiery to languid, from stormy to sweet. Again, toward dawn, they slept.

When they woke, they stood, somehow, on a shore where they had never been.

They took care of tasks without speaking or looking at each other—water, fire, food.

When they finished, now stretched out naked on their robes and close to the flames, they looked long, each at the other, and saw the same friend, lover, spouse. The eye-holding looks grew longer. Though they couldn't have said what these looks meant exactly, they held something new, something more than lust, more than play, more than laughter, more even than love.

Light drained out of the tipi. In the smoke hole, the sky turned the color of a dove's breast. The air they breathed was melancholy.

Sam breached it. "The one who is not here?"

Meadowlark nodded. "My brother, Blue Medicine Horse." In the use of his name, somehow, coiled defiance.

"I miss him."

"And I miss him."

"Feels like he's here." Sam felt the risk in his words, sharp as razors.

"He is as real to me as the warmth of the fire."

"I'll never stop missing him."

She just nodded.

Sam felt the guilt seep into his heart like chill water into a cellar. "I'll never stop feeling . . ."

She saw it and put a finger to his lips. "You were not to blame. Flat Dog said . . ."

"Flat Dog forgave me. I don't know if your parents did." Then he said the hard part. "I don't know about you."

She cocked her head like a doe, half-startled.

He made himself speak directly into her eyes. "I brought agony into your life." Nothing abject in the words, only honesty and pain.

She shifted into a sitting position and looked down into his face. After a few moments, she asked him to put his head in her lap. He did.

"Did you ever have a big grief before?"

He looked like she'd slapped him. "I did. When I was a kid, my brother died. His name was Coy."

She smiled in recognition of the name. She stroked his hair. "Tell me about Coy."

As though misunderstanding, Coy the coyote slid up onto his haunches and began to howl softly. His cry took the shape of the word "ho-o-o-wl."

Sam spoke as though content with the coyote's accompaniment. He remembered ramblings in the Pennsylvania forest. Turtles found and brought home. Rides on the family mule. Swims in the river. Fights. Watching the stars and giving them names, special names, names to be held only between two brothers. His words sounded childish as he spoke them, commonplaces, things all siblings shared, pennies without polish. But it felt good to say them.

Sam stopped. The coyote renewed his call, louder, more echoing. Sam pictured the sounds wandering in all the lonely places of the planet. Then, for whatever reason, the song ended.

"When he died, what did you . . . do with him?"

"We put him in the ground." He thought that probably sounded barbarous to her. It felt barbarous to him.

"Did you sing?"

"Yes, hymns." He took thought and added, "Songs to wish him well, songs to say good-bye. Dad got a preacher man—medicine man—out from Pittsburgh, first preacher I ever met, to say some words. Big words about the big things, living and dying."

She stroked his face. "Do you remember any of the words?"

"Bible words, words from our . . . sacred stories. I wish I could bring them back clear. Maybe some day I'll learn to read and find them."

She bent down and kissed his face lightly. Her long hair caressed him.

He flinched at the sudden memory. " 'Beauty for ashes'—that's what the preacher said. He said he'd come to comfort those of us that grieved, to give us beauty for ashes, and the oil of joy for our mourning."

He looked up between her small breasts into her face. There he witnessed, in the soft light of the fire, a radiance that was beyond all eloquence. He saw love. He saw the gift that passes understanding, peace.

Her fingers stroked his forehead and cheeks. "Sam," she said, "the man known as Joins with Buffalo, my husband. For this death I forgive you. Accept my forgiveness. Beyond that, I offer you my heart. Find in my love beauty for the ashes of your grief, and the oil of joy for the pain in your heart."

During that long night, their loving explored a universe far from the previous night's. Where there was play, now came tenderness. Where eagerness, deliberation. Where excitement, unity and completeness. Near dawn they slept as on a boat upon the great and mothering sea. They were lifted, eased, lifted, eased, and infinitely at rest.

* * *

SAM LAY BACK on his robes, beneath his blanket, Meadowlark sleeping next to him. Usually, when he was single, he woke up at first light, well before the sun rose. Maybe she liked to sleep in. Coy nestled by her head, choosing her way, not Sam's, which tickled him.

He knew damned well he'd never felt this good.

Three days, living in a new world. A life of discoveries ahead.

And a life of lovemaking ahead. He didn't want even to think any of those other words, not about what he and Meadowlark did. He'd had some experience of sex before, and for him it always had a flicker of aggression in it, sometimes of anger.

With Meadowlark it was . . . Even if he could read books, and quote Shakespeare like James Clyman, even then he wouldn't have the words for it.

For once he'd done the right thing. Finding the woman for his life and attaching her to him, that was the most momentous thing a man could accomplish. Doing the right thing, when you've done a lot of wrong ones, felt incredible.

Meadowlark was open about not being so sure they were doing the right thing. Maybe Rides Twice's village still wouldn't accept them. Maybe they'd have to live in another Crow village. Her mother's original village wintered well to the east, on the edge of the Wolf Mountains. Needle only saw her parents and brothers and sisters once a year, at the big fall hunt.

Or maybe, Sam said, we'll spend some of our time with a fur brigade, hunting.

"Maybe," Meadowlark said.

What each of them knew was simple and clear. They would always be together, as close as back and belly when they slept, as close as mingled breath when they made love.

He cricked his neck and rolled his shoulders. He always felt energetic first thing in the morning. Two of the three days he'd made the morning trip to the creek to get water. Meadowlark protested sweetly—he mustn't do women's work, that was unseemly. He thought she'd get used to it.

He slipped from under the robes, looked at his sleeping wife, and at the pup asleep by her head. They loved each other, which was damn good. Sam looked at the fire, long since out. He would start it when he got back from the creek. Right now he was thirsty.

He slipped the pegs out of the lodge door, bent, and duck-walked outside. This time of year, near the equinox, the sun rose straight to the east, and lodge doors always faced that way. Just as he looked, the red-orange sun gathered itself from a sheet of light along the ridge top into a bright ball. It blinded Sam a little, and he laughed with pleasure at the light and warmth.

Yi-ii-ay!

Sam got slammed hard to the ground on his side, a body on top of him and pinning his arms to his ribs.

He screwed his head back and saw . . .

Flat Dog's face.

"What the hell are you doing?" Sam yelled nose to nose with his friend.

"Saving your life," said Flat Dog mildly.

Half a dozen men stepped up, led by Red Roan. Several had arrows pulled back and pointed at Sam. Two had war clubs raised. Yellow Horn was holding a lance and growling.

"If you raped Meadowlark," Red Roan told Sam, "I'll kill you." Anger coiled in his voice like a rattler.

Meadowlark rose out of the doorway, protecting her modesty with their blanket. She bristled at Red Roan, and her eyes turned to fire. "Everything that was done, we did together. I wanted what he wanted."

Red Roan slowly, very slowly, turned his eyes back to Sam. "What you've done is wrong," the chief's son said, "and you will pay."

SAM RODE INTO the village as he'd led Meadowlark away, his horse on a lead tied to another man's mount, hands lashed behind his back. He felt like Coy, who was slinking instead of trotting.

As Sam rode, he pondered something. Back there in Ruby Hawk Valley, he threw a lot of anger in Flat Dog's face. And his friend answered gently, as though he didn't notice the anger, or it flew by his face and didn't touch him.

Sam wanted to learn to do that.

On the ride back he found out what happened. They let him talk to Flat Dog, but not to Meadowlark, who was forced to ride in front next to Red Roan.

Flat Dog said they'd checked on one likely spot the first day, another the second, and on the late afternoon of the third, they saw the travel lodge in Ruby Hawk Valley. Flat Dog had told them places that were probable, areas he and Sam had hunted and Sam liked. Actually, this wide spot on Black Creek had been his first guess, but he misled them. They crept close in the middle of the night. Coy had gone into a barking fit, Sam remembered, but he assumed whatever noises the coyote heard were animals.

"I didn't lead the party there first because I hoped to give you enough time to be gone."

"Why did you come at all?" Sam knew the answer, but he wanted to hear it.

"I thought they'd kill you if I wasn't there."

Sam had never thought that warriors might come after him and Meadowlark. She hadn't either. He asked Flat Dog why they came.

"It's unusual," Flat Dog admitted.

"Who got it started? Never mind, I know. Was Yellow Horn or Red Roan the loudest?"

"Yellow Horn," said Flat Dog. "I think Red Roan would have let it go."

"What happens now?"

"She'll be Red Roan's wife."

Sam felt as though a lightning bolt cleaved him top to bottom. He'd meant, "What happens to me now?" But Flat Dog's answer told him that, too.

PART SEVEN

Lost

Chapter Twenty-six

Gideon had the only sensible suggestion. "Let's find the brigade."

The four men looked at each other, Sam and Clyman the white men, Gideon the French-Canadian (which in his case meant Cree and Jew), and Flat Dog the Crow.

"Crazy," was Sam's immediate response.

"You no talk about crazy," said Gideon, "considering."

It was the very evening Sam had been brought back in shame and separated forever from Meadowlark. They were sitting around their fire.

"I don't think it's crazy," said Clyman. "We sure got cause to get with 'em."

The reason was that Clyman had six traps, and no other man had any. You couldn't make a spring hunt without traps. Also, four men might make a risky hunt, even if they stuck to the creeks here in Crow country. Being with a brigade would be safer, in any country.

Sam didn't feel a bit like talking about what they were going to do. His mind was strictly on how he'd been brought down. *What an idiot I was, thinking I'd "finally" done the right thing. I made the biggest mess of my messy life.*

Gray Hawk had made that absolutely clear. First he and Needle went to Meadowlark and talked quietly with her. Then Needle led Meadowlark away. Gray Hawk walked up to Sam as he was leading his horses back to the lean-to, his head hanging. In a soft, lashing voice Gray Hawk said, "Get out of here. Get out of this village. I will never let you near my daughter again."

Now Gideon and Clyman worked out how they would get a fall hunt. Probably the brigade would be along the Siskadee somewhere. "The sign, she will be easy to pick up," said Gideon.

"If they're not on the Siskadee," said Clyman, "we know where else they hunt."

The conversation batted back and forth considerably. Flat Dog paid sharp attention, Sam none.

The conclusion was that Gideon and Clyman intended to look for the brigade. "I have no possibles," said Gideon. "I need a fine spring hunt."

"What you gonna do when you can't find the brigade?" challenged Sam.

"Meet up with all the coons at rendezvous," said Clyman.

It was set for the Bear River this summer, north of Salt Lake.

"At ze worst," Gideon said, "we will come together wit' zem at rendezvous."

"Can't miss rendezvous—see everybody, trade. Ashley will bring lots of whiskey, he promised."

"Diah and Fitzpatrick, they're inviting lots of Indians. Come and trade, they'll tell the Indians." The bear man gave a huge grin. "Whiskey and Indian women . . ."

"Count me out," said Sam.

"I want to go," said Flat Dog.

Gideon and Clyman jerked their heads toward each other, taken by surprise. Then they nodded. "Welcome," said Clyman.

"I don't give a damn what any of you do," said Sam.

THE THREE HUNTERS spent the next morning packing up. They asked if they could trade Sam something for his travel lodge. He said he didn't care what they took.

Coy trotted from the departing group to Sam, and back, and back and forth, confused about what was going on.

In late morning they were packed and ready. The three looked at Sam.

"You sure you don't want something for this travel lodge?"

He didn't answer. He didn't want one thing on earth but what he couldn't have.

"You sure you want to stay here?"

No answer.

"You coming to rendezvous?"

No answer.

Flat Dog handed his reins to Clyman and walked over and sat down by Sam. He blew out a couple of big breaths. "You want me to talk to Meadowlark?"

Sam snapped his head toward Flat Dog.

"You want me to ask what she wants you to do?"

"I . . ." Sam stopped his foolish answer.

"I'll tell you exactly what she says, whatever it is."

Sam thought. He had a feeling like a fish jumping in his heart. "Yes."

Flat Dog stood up and spoke to Gideon and Clyman. "You mind waiting a while?"

"We're easy," said Clyman.

Flat Dog disappeared for half an hour. He came back pursing his lips.

"Meadowlark says to tell you this. 'I love you.' She said it in English. 'If you stay here, you're throwing your life away. Someone will kill you. Then I couldn't live. Go, please go. I love you. Go.' "

Flat Dog stood up. The three swung up onto their horses, and Clyman took the pack horse lead.

Coy looked from Sam to the mounted men, back to Sam and back to the three, and gave one loud bark. He barked again.

"Go ahead," said Sam. He took hold of Coy.

They went.

Before they rounded the first bend in the river, Flat Dog turned in the saddle and looked back. He could see the boulder where Sam sat and the trees behind. He wished he could see a rider coming their way.

Sam and Coy didn't catch up with them until they were ten miles downstream.

Chapter Twenty-seven

Sam woke up when Paladin flabbered her lips. It wasn't just the sound, but the spray that came with it. When it was a fine night and he slept outside, she woke him like this. The other horses, including Pinto, were moved out of camp at first light and put on grass until the company was ready to get going. Not Paladin, though. Sam kept her staked right by his bedroll, wherever it was. She woke him because she got jealous of the other horses, or she wanted her treat, Sam didn't know which.

Coy raised his head and shook it. He'd caught the spray too.

Sam reached beneath his buffalo robe and got some bark of the sweet cottonwood, which he kept close at hand for these occasions. Paladin gulped it down greedily and flabbered her lips again.

Sam sat up and found Gideon sitting up too. "Time, I guess," said the big man.

Sam looked around the camp. It was sizable, about thirty men. He, Gideon, Flat Dog, and Clyman had found this outfit easily. They came over the Southern Pass and trapped south along the Siskadee and then up Ham's Fork. They met these trappers, led by David Jackson, working their way down Ham's Fork after wintering in Cache Valley of the Bear River.

And with them, a friend. Jim Beckwourth, the strapping mulatto, was in the outfit. He'd gone clear to St. Louis with Jedediah Smith, and come back with Jedediah too. He was full of stories. As usual, Sam cut them down by half before he believed them.

Jackson, though, seemed like a man who considered the facts before he spoke. He spoke of one place so sweetly that Sam made up his mind he had to go see it.

"There's glorious country," Jackson told Sam, "north of the Siskadee. At the top, where it bends back, you go on over the divide and come on the Hoback River, the one the Astorians followed. Go down that to where it joins the Lewis Fork and up that river, you come to the finest hole you'll ever see. Mountains on all four sides, on the west high ones that are always snowy. Creeks full of beaver rolling down from all four sides. Too high to winter, and needs a sharp eye when you're getting in and out, but a heaven of a place to trap." He added with a reluctant smile, for David Jackson was a shy man, "The boys call it Jackson's Hole."

Jackson's Hole. And the good news was, Jackson was headed back there right now.

Sam and his companions went up the Siskadee with the Jackson brigade. Tonight they'd camped on the river bank, right where it started a shepherd's-crook turn back into the Wind River Mountains. As usual with a big party, they made a square camp right on the river, divided into four messes. At night they staked the horses about ten steps apart, between their bedrolls and the river. Every morning the horse guard close-herded them out onto some grass.

Now Sam could see horses grazing on the top of a nearby hill, further away than usual.

The mess's fire was dead out.

"I have to put Paladin out to graze," said Sam unnecessarily.

"I'll start the coffee," said Gideon.

The other men of the mess, including Flat Dog and Beckwourth, were beginning to stir.

Sam restaked Paladin no more than twenty or thirty steps from camp. He didn't want her loose, and he didn't want her clear up on that hill. Some of the men thought he was peculiar, keeping a horse and a coyote right next to him at night, but they didn't know how special this horse and coyote were.

He wanted to check Pinto's hooves. Sam thought she was walking a little gingerly when they came into camp last night.

Sam started up the long hill, Coy at his heels. A dozen steps away they stopped. Sam realized he wasn't carrying The Celt. "It's all right," he told Coy. The horses were guarded, and not far off.

He was huffing and puffing when he came up to Pinto. Coy ran ahead to the little mare. She was pulling up grass at the left edge of the herd, highest on the summit ridge. She had a way of snatching bunch grass hard out of the ground, throwing her head a little, like a kid taking a toy from a sibling.

Pinto grazed right where the ridge rose into its summit and the timber of the north slope bunched nearly to the crest. Sam walked right up to Pinto and dropped the halter on her head. Pinto didn't have a lot of virtues, in Sam's opinion, but one was that she let herself be caught easily.

Coy barked at something.

Sam knelt to check the left front hoof.

As his head dipped downward, an arrow furrowed his scalp.

Sam took a split second to breathe. He held tight to the reins and jumped toward Pinto's back.

Pinto crow-hopped and Sam missed. Coy yapped like hell.

The guard, where the hell is the guard?

He tried again to get on, but now Pinto was shying in every direction, way out of control. An arrow waved jauntily from her left hip.

Keeping Pinto between him and the timber, Sam ran.

"Yi-ii-yii!" An Indian hollered, and charged toward them.

Damn. Sam couldn't run flat out leading Pinto, especially not with her acting up. He dived behind a bush.

Coy charged the Indian, and got kicked away for his trouble. Coy huddled behind the bush with Sam and Pinto.

The Indian started walking—sauntering, actually—and stopped about twenty steps away. He was grinning arrogantly.

Yeah, you caught me without a gun. Sam felt of his scalp. Lots of blood. He stuck his long white hair to the bleeding spot.

The Indian squatted and eyed Sam like an animal he'd trapped.

Sam looked desperately toward the camp. Men were stirring. He yelled at the top of his lungs, "HE-E-ELP!"

No reaction. Too far.

The Indian made some signs. He looked Blackfeet, from his clothes. That language Sam didn't know a word of. 'Give yourself up,' he signed, 'and I won't hurt you.'

Sam's answer was to get out his belt knife, a good weapon, but not against arrows. Blackfeet were the worst.

'I won't even eat your dog,' the Blackfeet signed.

The Indian waited. After a while he signed, 'If you lay down your knife, I will lay down my bow and arrow. Then we can meet and talk and be friends.'

Sam tucked the reins under his arm and signed, 'How many of you?'

The guards must be dead. Just like the Blackfeet not to stop at stealing the horses, but to want to kill some people too. Maybe all the people, and steal the furs, utensils, guns, the whole kit and caboodle.

The Blackfeet took a few steps closer. 'Notice,' he signed, 'I have already laid down my bow and arrow. Come out.'

The bastard sure wasn't aware of the way he walked or stood, like he was ready to pounce and drink blood.

Sam ran his brain hard to figure the situation. His summary was—worse than desperate. He couldn't run and expose his back. He couldn't attack. Eventually, the Blackfeet would tire of this game or his friends would come up.

On the hill the horses were gone, no doubt gathered up by Blackfeet.

Sam's knife hand felt wet and sticky. His blood had run all the way down the arm of his shirt. Thinking he ought to stanch that bleeding with a rifle patch, he reached for his hunting pouch.

Whack! An arrow broke a limb in front of Sam's face and glanced off.

Coy yipped and ran at the Blackfeet.

Instinctively, Sam jumped and ran after Coy.

The damn Indian got another arrow nocked and shot just as Sam came onto him bellowing.

Pain! Sam's ribs screamed.

Sam screamed louder and drowned out the pain.

He embraced the Blackfeet. The man swung a tomahawk, and Sam felt its bite on his back.

Once Sam knifed the Blackfeet—twice!—and got solid flesh.

Cries rose from the hilltop like angry calls of a thousand geese.

Blackfeet charged down the hill, and a musket cracked the dawn silence.

Sam ignored Pinto and ran downhill pell-mell.

Maybe catching Pinto will distract them.

Pinto gave a loud whinny of protest. Sam pictured her kicking Blackfeet, fighting for her freedom, and maybe saving Sam's life.

Sam ran like a blue whistle.

Arrows shimmered through the air.

Sam nearly stepped on Coy, and almost lost his balance avoiding the coyote.

No more musket blasts. They must have had only one.

Sam sprinted across a spot that was nearly level and plunged onto steeper ground. It was tricky, getting sure footing on such a steep slope. Sam bounded, trying to make each foot placement exact, but . . .

He tumbled headlong and rolled, and rolled, and rolled . . .

Snap to! He wondered if he'd lost consciousness for a moment. The Blackfeet were too damn close.

Musket shots! A bunch!

No, rifle shots!

Gideon was charging up the hill on Paladin, Beckwourth

and three or four men running hard behind him. Several others had stopped to reload.

The Blackfeet flocked back up the hill, two men helping their wounded comrade.

"Here's a chance at a fair fight, you bastards!" screamed Sam.

As though that was all the energy he had, his mind whirled and grayed out.

"THIS IS GONNA hurt."

It did. Sam's ribs barked at him again.

Flat Dog held up an arrow. "In your ribs. It was just hanging in the skin, almost clear of the ribs."

Coy sniffed the arrow, wanting the blood. Flat Dog grinned and pushed him away.

"Almost . . . ," said Sam through gritted teeth. *Why couldn't the damn arrow have* almost *hit me?*

"You've lost a lot of blood. I'll help you onto Paladin. We'll go back to camp, but we're taking it slow."

Sam pigeon-toed his way down the hill to his horse. He felt a gush of relief at seeing her unhurt.

Then he saw Gideon rolling around on the ground behind her. He was cussing and fooling with his foot. Suddenly, he held up an arrow triumphantly. "I got the devil, zis child did." The arrow was bloody.

Beckwourth and another trapper helped Gideon to his feet.

"We gotta get back before they decide to attack," said Beckwourth. But he walked and led Paladin. The two men supported Gideon, one-footing it slowly behind.

THEY BUILT A breastwork. Brush, limbs, saddles, pack saddles, furs, kegs, blankets and other trade goods—everything went into their fort. It was three-sided, the river forming the fourth side. "If they want to charge across the Siskadee," said Jackson, "they're welcome to it."

The river was running full in spring flood.

All the men, nearly thirty, fit inside. What normally would have been seventy horses was one—Paladin. The Blackfeet had all the others.

Flat Dog said he was going to scout. Before Sam could say, "Hey, that's risky!" he disappeared.

Clyman poulticed Sam's scalp, back, and ribs as best he could. Sam lay resting on his bedroll, under orders to stay put. Coy crouched like a stone lion beside Sam's head. The back wounds were shallow cuts. The arrow didn't get inside the ribs, hadn't done any internal damage.

James seemed more concerned about Gideon's foot. "Lots of little bones in a foot," he said. "You may not walk so good again."

His hip had healed, only to give way to a bad foot.

Gideon rasped, "Next time I get hit in the leg. Then, if hits big artery, I die fast. If miss artery, am fine. But not a cripple." He sighed. "Not a cripple."

"My guess is," Jackson said to the men's unspoken question, "they're a horse-stealing outfit meaning to go against the Snakes. Them Snakes have good horseflesh. If I'm right, there might be twenty or twenty-five Blackfeet."

"I *seen* that many," someone said.

"Flat Dog will tell us how many there are," said Sam.

A voice came from behind where Sam lay—"If he don't sit down and eat breakfast with 'em."

Sam was glad he couldn't see who said that.

"They won't want to attack us beavers with rifles behind a breastwork," said Jackson.

"Not a chance," someone chipped in, reassuring himself.

"Besides," said Gideon, pain coppering his voice, "now they got our horses."

The men laughed uneasily.

There was nothing to do but wait.

* * *

FLAT DOG SAID they were gone. "Cleared out."

"Skedaddled," a Kentuck said from behind Sam.

All the men gathered close. Sam and Gideon lay on their bedrolls at the front. Coy curled around Sam's feet.

"Got our horseflesh instead of the Snakes'," Jackson said.

"They stuck us good," Beckwourth said.

"I want to go after them." This was Flat Dog.

"What you gonna go after 'em with?" said Jackson sharply.

"I run," said Flat Dog soberly. "I run and catch up with them."

From the rear came laughs and raspberries.

Flat Dog's expression never changed.

"It ain't funny," said Beckwourth loudly. "A man can run down a horse if he's good and has a lot of stick-to-it."

Flat Dog gave Jim a look like, "You understand."

Jim said, "Maybe I'll just go along with Flat Dog."

"It ain't safe," said Jackson. Seemed like he wanted more to measure them than keep them back.

"I'm going," said Beckwourth.

Flat Dog gave him a small nod.

Silence. Coy snuggled closer to Sam's feet.

Jackson squatted down by Sam. Coy gave him a suspicious look, but Davey ignored it. "Morgan, I'm going to ask you for something. It's big, real big to you." He looked Sam hard in the eyes. "Let them take Paladin."

Beckwourth spoke up. "We don't need the horse. Sam loves that horse."

Flat Dog watched Sam curiously.

"You're a member of my outfit. We take care of our own when they're hurt. I could order you. The safety of the whole outfit depends on them horses. But I'm asking you."

"Flat Dog?" asked Sam.

"Would help. We take turns riding and walking, stay fresher."

"Jim?"

For once speechless, Beckwourth shrugged.

Flat Dog squatted and spoke softly to Sam. "I won't kid you, she may not come back. But if I come back, Paladin will."

Sam knew a solemn pledge when he heard it.

It was a matter of how you treat a friend. He took a deep breath and let it out. "All right," he said. He struggled to his feet, minced over to where Paladin was staked, and rubbed her muzzle. Coy whined.

Flat Dog and Beckwourth had a quick conversation with Jackson about where to meet. They were gone in hardly more time than it took to reload a rifle. Flat Dog rode, and didn't look back at Sam. Trails get cold fast.

THE BRIGADE DUG a big cache for their belongings—plews (packs and packs of these), saddles, trade goods, kegs for water, kegs of whiskey—everything except their rifles and what they carried around their necks, over their shoulders, stuck in their belts, and the like.

They worked in silence, not speaking of the hopes that remained. The best hope, they believed, was that they would run into some friendly Snakes. The Snakes had apparently decided that having fur men in their country was a benefit. If the Snakes believed their story, they might come back to the cache with the whites. Then Jackson would barter his Indian trade goods for enough horses to carry the men and their furs to rendezvous.

Another hope, fainter: That Flat Dog and Beckwourth would steal the horses back, or enough horses to carry the belongings, even if the men had to walk. Catching up on foot, or the same as on foot, as Beckwourth and Flat Dog were attempting to do, then getting those horses back—most men thought it was ridiculous.

What they didn't want to think about was walking the whole way to rendezvous, having no furs to trade, and being forced to come back later to raise the cache. Rendezvous this summer was on the Bear River. A long walk—you went back down the Siskadee, cut over to Ham's Fork, crossed a divide over the Salt River Range, descended to Bear River, and followed that around its big bend to Cache Valley, several days' ride above the big Salt Lake. Nobody wanted to walk a couple of hundred miles, but they would if they had to.

That day, for sure, they couldn't start walking. Gideon's foot gave him too much pain, and Sam was half dizzy.

The next day Sam was much better, but Gideon's pain was sharp. "Why so much hurt in such a little hole?" complained the bear-sized man.

Jackson had the men construct a litter from poles and a blanket. They dragged Gideon along, with the big man grousing loudly.

That night the puncture wound looked red, and Clyman thought it might be infected. Puncture wounds, they knew, were the most likely to fester. The next day it was red, oozed puss, and was even more painful. "Infected," James said soberly.

Now every man was thinking of gangrene. Gideon squeezed his eyes closed and said nothing.

One morning Gideon sang canoeing songs as he bumped along. During the afternoon he acted tired, but he told occasional cripple jokes. The brigade walked quietly downriver, trying not to jounce him too much.

One night the swelling and redness seemed no better. The next, the wound looked green around the edges. Clyman sniffed. "It's beginning to stink."

Except for Sam and Clyman, men stopped talking to Gideon. No one wanted to cozy up to mortality.

The next day Gideon sang songs again. And either he forgot his English or his mind was weakening. He didn't speak, and sang only in French.

Sam slunk along beside the litter all day, and Coy slunk behind Sam.

Late one afternoon they made camp along the river with a

good grove of cottonwoods at their backs. Clyman checked the foot. The green around the wound had turned to black. Red streaks ran up the calf. "Blood poisoning," said James loud, like an announcement.

The men looked at each other. Everyone knew.

Suddenly, they heard a kind of a roar. *What is that? Horses!*

Men ran for the best cover available, trees, bushes, boulders. They primed their muzzleloaders.

Horses for sure. The roar was becoming *rat-a-tat-tats*.

They couldn't see beyond the cottonwoods. Friends? Enemies? They squirmed. They looked along their sights.

"Some niggers, coming on us in the broad open," whined a nasal voice near Sam.

A voice came through the trees, or voices.

Men heaved big breaths in and out. Hammers snapped back. Powder was poured into pans, ready for the flint spark.

The voice made melody.

Sam lowered The Celt. "It's Beckwourth," he said happily.

"How does you know?" whined the voice.

"He's singing, 'My Lord, What a Morning.'"

"Yi-ii-ay!" So it was Flat Dog too. And Paladin. Sam grinned big. He gave the long, loud whistle he used to call Paladin to him.

About a score of horses *rat-a-tat-tatted* into the grove on the trot. Sam saw his big white mare come galloping around them, looking for the source of the whistle.

Sam laughed. Flat Dog slid off the mare and the friends grinned at each other.

Sam set to stroking Paladin's fine head, sliding up onto her bare back (which made his injured side hurt), checking out her hooves, and the like. Beckwourth and Flat Dog headed for fires and meat fresher than the jerked stuff they'd been eating. The men gathered around, curious.

In the end it was left to Beckwourth to tell the story of how they got the horses back. Well, some horses—twenty-one to be exact.

Jim was big with the story. The tale of their trek over the

pass to the north and down the Hoback River was epic. The episode of sneaking up on the Blackfeet camp was nerve-tingling. The attack on the guards was hair-raising and bloody, and Jim himself was as mighty as Joshua at the walls of Jericho. Someone said he seemed to have killed, by his own hand, more Blackfeet than there were in the party. When he got to the part about running the horses off—*all* the horses—someone called out, "Jim, if you run off all the horses, where's the other forty-nine?" Guffaws all around.

Jackson asked some hard questions. Were the Indians on their tails? Was the camp in danger of attack right now?

"I don't think so," said Jim. "They had all the lead they'll be wanting."

Flat Dog confirmed that he had doubled back at first light this morning and found no one on their back trail.

Jackson pulled at his chin and allowed that the Blackfeet might be satisfied with getting away with fifty horses, particularly if they lost a couple of men. Blackfeet took dead comrades hard. Their idea of winning was strictly to go home unscratched.

Jim and Flat Dog felt damn lucky, Jim said, to find the outfit not many sleeps from where they left it.

That brought out some grousing noises.

"But any coon can see why, that's sure," said Jim. He kept himself from looking at Gideon.

"Matter of fact, we're acting like we don't know the true business of this evening," said Clyman.

Men peered at him like they didn't know what he was talking about.

Clyman asked softly, "What do you say, Gideon?"

"Do it," Gideon roared in English. Everyone recoiled from the violence of his tone. "For sake of *le bon dieu,* do it."

He shook himself wildly on the litter. "I am coward. A man, *vraiment,* he choose death over cripple. I am no longer such big man. I am afraid to die. Do it."

Chapter Twenty-eight

S am knew that he and Clyman were somehow elected.
Jackson broke out whiskey, enough for Gideon only.
Gideon got drunk enough to pass in and out of consciousness.
Sam, Clyman, and several other men whetted their knives as
sharp as they could. Sharp blades would make it easier. They
thought of themselves. In Gideon's place, they would insist
on sharp blades.

Flat Dog looked at his friend's wound and ran his eyes
from it to Sam to Clyman to Jackson and back to the wound.
He couldn't feature what on earth they were about to do.

"I've never done anything like this," said Clyman. It
sounded like a statement of fact, not an excuse.

"Me neither," said Sam.

The long May evening would give a lot of light, probably
enough. A fire was built within reach of the surgeon. They
put a log under Gideon's knee.

Flat Dog sat down bewildered, but no one noticed.

Though no man there had performed an amputation, or
even seen one done, frontier people had heard about how such
things were performed. "At the knee," Clyman. "We don't
have a saw to cut through the shin bones, and they say the
joint is best anyhow."

Jackson tied a tourniquet around the thigh and cranked it
tight, using a stick for a lever. Sam felt sheepish that he hadn't
thought of the tourniquet. *What other ghastly mistake are we
making? Are we doctors or killers?*

A half-dozen knives gleamed on a slab of sandstone next
to Gideon.

"I'll hold his leg," said Sam.

Gideon lifted his head for a moment. "I want Sam to do
the job," he said.

Everybody stared. They thought he was gone. Jackson

poured more whiskey down his throat. "Sam," Gideon choked out. "He's my man."

Clyman looked at Sam and nodded. James went to the foot, squatted, and clamped the foot between his knees.

"I want Flat Dog hold leg," said Gideon harshly. "You watch careful," he said to Clyman.

Flat Dog took the leg. His mind was whirling. *Surely these white men weren't about to . . .*

Clyman regarded Flat Dog carefully, then duck-waddled up beside the knee.

Sam picked up his own butcher knife, held the blade in flames for several moments and studied the knee carefully.

After consideration he made his first cut.

Gideon screamed.

IT TURNED OUT that Clyman thought of things Sam didn't. For instance, you leave skin a couple of inches below the joint, so you'll have enough to fold back over the wound.

Sam worked in a sort of trance. Gideon bellowed sometimes—loud, wordless, howling roars with no apparent relationship to what Sam was doing. Sam heard, but they were remote and unreal to him. Even Gideon himself was remote, in a way. Sam saw only the flesh, the ligaments, the tendons, the cartilage, the bones. And the blood, too much blood. Part of his mind wondered whether Gideon would survive the blood loss. Most of Sam's mind was focused, with a dreamlike intensity, on the joint itself.

Every frontiersman, every rural cook, had seen lots of joints of animals, and had some basic idea of how they worked. Sam went forward with this knowledge and common sense—that was all he had, and hard necessity.

He switched knives often. Other men whetted them again.

Flat Dog held on grimly, his face pale, his mind numb.

No one spoke, except that Clyman occasionally pointed and said, "There," or "Like that."

Gideon's hollering occurred in another world.

Then Sam was to the bones. He had to go between the knobby bone ends and pull the leg apart, not cut it apart.

Soon the joint no longer joined anything. Sam let out a big breath of relief. From here he more or less knew his way.

After another eternity, or passage through a surreal world, Clyman eased Gideon's lower leg away. It was done. For better or worse, done. Forever done.

Flat Dog dropped the half leg. Then he flopped onto the ground on his back.

Clyman handed Sam an axe whose head glowed lurid red. Sam nodded to himself. He understood. He pushed the flat side of the head firmly against Gideon's stump. Sizzle, steam, stink.

Gideon, unconscious, uttered no sound.

Sam looked at his work, turned the axe head over, and applied the other side to another part of the stump.

Gideon writhed and uttered soft, mewling sounds.

Flat Dog sat up and stared at what was happening. He didn't know human beings did such . . .

Jackson handed Sam needle and thread. Sam took the flaps of flesh that had once covered the upper part of Gideon's calf and folded them over each other. The bloody wound was completely covered. Patiently, with a coppery feeling of revulsion in his mouth, Sam sewed the pieces of flap together.

He sat back on his heels. He put down needle and thread. He let his head drop. Done.

"Well done," said Clyman.

"Damn well done," said Jackson.

Flat Dog couldn't decide whether it was well done, or insane.

Sam felt . . . He could not have said, so many strange, winding, blowing feelings, wisps of gauze in a breeze of consciousness.

The men, who had watched with rapt attention, began to drift away. Time for coffee, time for a bite to eat.

Jackson said, "I think we ought to loose that tourniquet, see how bad it bleeds, and tighten it again. Keep doing that until the bleeding stops."

The brigade leader looked inquiringly at Sam, as though he now had some authority.

Clyman set the calf and foot in Sam's lap. "Seems like you oughta be the one decides what to do with this." Then he took over at the tourniquet.

Sam cradled the severed leg in silence and wept gently.

He sat by himself for half an hour or so, rubbing Coy's head.

In the very last of the evening light, he carried Gideon's leg upstream into the densest part of the cottonwoods. A melancholy memory walked with him—how he had done the same for Third Wing in this same valley. He climbed into the biggest cottonwood he could find and carefully set the half leg in a fork. Then he took thought, pulled the tail of his shirt out of his trousers, and cut a long, wide strip of hide off the bottom. He wrapped the leg in that. It seemed respectful.

He slid down the tree and stumbled back to camp, wanting and not wanting to see his maimed friend.

Gideon was sleeping. Not sleeping forever, from what Sam could see.

Clyman had taken the tourniquet off.

As far as Sam could tell by the firelight, the wound wasn't bleeding.

He took Gideon's hand, held it for a moment, squeezed, and put it on the bear-man's belly.

Though he stretched out near Flat Dog, he didn't sleep all night. He scratched Coy's ears and watched the stars. They wheeled very, very slowly across the sky, dancers beyond the reach of time. Somewhere, somehow the world turned. Time tick-tocked, somewhere.

Sam looked but didn't think. In the first light he closed his eyes and eased off.

THE NEXT MORNING Flat Dog got breakfast for two and took one bowl to Sam, who was just waking up. Gideon lay nearby on his litter, half-conscious.

"Let's see if we can get Gideon to eat something," Flat Dog said.

Sam sat up, wiggled his eyebrows to wake up, and eye-balled Gideon. "Probably not," he said, and accepted his own bowl.

"If we can," said Flat Dog.

James Clyman joined them. The other men stayed at their mess fires. Flat Dog noticed how most of the men didn't want to associate with a badly injured man. Were they embarrassed by his wound? By his . . . half-human state? Or was it just an aversion to being so close to injury and death, like it might be catching?

A man without a leg. Flat Dog had seen dogs without legs, but never a man. A man *deliberately* made legless.

"Lot of sitting to be done today," said Clyman.

And for a few days, thought Flat Dog. *If we want him to live. If he wants to live with one leg.*

Sam's head was hanging. He looked exhausted from the ordeal.

Clyman seemed even-keeled. Not much excited Old James, as he called himself.

Flat Dog still felt like somebody'd whacked him in the head with something heavy and made him silly. He kept looking at Gideon's face, down at the missing leg, back at the face, and across at Sam, and then repeating the whole cycle.

Clyman spooned a little broth onto Gideon's closed lips. The lips opened and the tongue accepted. Clyman spooned more. The eyes opened, and the head lifted a little.

Coy went up to Gideon's leg, sniffing. The one-legged bear man cuffed at the coyote irritably, missing by a wide margin, but Coy skittered off. Gideon lay back down and closed his eyes. "I'll eat a little," he said softly. "Though, *le bon dieu,* maybe I should starve until I die."

Clyman spooned it to him.

"I'm going to hunt today," Flat Dog told Sam.

"I'm too tired," said Sam.

Flat Dog nodded, smiled with his eyes at his friend, and headed off.

White people had always been strange. The men traveled without their families. For years, amazingly, they went without their families. They earned lots of *things,* but seemed to have no reason for owning them, except to do more traveling without their families and get still more things. They liked adventure. Flat Dog now understood the adventure part, and enjoyed it himself.

But Gideon. Gideon, and what Sam had done to Gideon, that slapped Flat Dog in the face. It brought up questions that stunned him.

Flat Dog rode out to find elk or deer, but his mind was elsewhere. He was learning something tremendous, maybe, something that knocked his idea of the white man cockeyed. He hefted this new bit of understanding, rubbed it with his fingers, prodded it, checked it from every side to learn its true nature.

SAM AND FLAT Dog inspected the wound. Coy wanted to sniff it, but Sam pushed him away. Sam said the wound seemed to be healing fine. No bleeding. Jackson had already said the outfit would travel tomorrow, Gideon on a litter. They were in luck—now the litter would be pulled by horses, not men. But all this only half-mattered to Flat Dog.

When they had poured coffee from the pot on the mess fire, Flat Dog said, "I don't understand cutting off a man's leg. It's wrong. This is not life, a man should not be like this. It's . . . wrong."

Sam said a bunch of something.

Flat Dog heard the words but he didn't regard them. At the end he asked one question. "So Gideon will use a crutch for . . . however long he lives?"

"No, he'll wear a peg."

Flat Dog made a gesture of complete bewilderment. Sam got a piece of driftwood, held his own foot to his butt, and mimicked walking on a peg. "He'll strap it to his leg with a leather belt."

Flat Dog understood, but . . .

They drank coffee for a while. Coy lay with his head on his front paws and made pathetic eyes at them. Finally, Flat Dog said, "My uncle told me something. Life is a butterfly, delicate and beautiful. You cup it in your hand gently, but it is always ready to fly. Your life is an opportunity to dance with it. If you grab it, though, you'll kill it. When it wants to fly, you must watch it wing away and love its beauty."

Sam studied Flat Dog for a moment. "Say that another way."

Flat Dog shrugged. "It is a good day to die."

WHEN HE WOKE up the next morning, Sam realized he was wondering if Flat Dog was still there. Two or three times during the night he'd dreamed that he woke up and his friend was gone forever.

Flat Dog sat up in his blankets.

Sam grinned crookedly at him. Coy went to him to get his head petted.

Jackson called the men together. The stolen horses belonged, he said, most of them, to the Ashley-Smith company. The twenty-one that came back, fourteen belonged to the firm. Sam would get Paladin back, and because of his job on the surgery, a horse to replace Pinto. Beckwourth and Flat Dog would get back the two horses they started with, plus one each for their good work in recovering the mounts. The rest belonged to Ashley-Smith.

"Now you, Morgan, Beckwourth, Flat Dog, I have to ask you. We need all the horses for the moment, to carry the equipment."

"And carry Gideon," Sam put in.

Jackson acknowledged that with a nod.

Gideon still kept his head down, as though he didn't see or hear a thing.

"Is that all right?"

Sam spoke up. "I'm not easy with Paladin being used as a pack horse."

Jackson thought on that. Then he said, "How about if she's the one drags Gideon? With you beside her?"

Sam pondered, then nodded yes.

The rest of the day was given to sending men back to the cache, opening it, loading up the furs and as much other gear as the horses could carry, and getting back to the camp where they started. A lot of equipment got left in the cache, since they were short of horses.

The next morning they headed downriver toward rendezvous, slowly, like a one-legged bear. Sam thought, *Now we'll find out if Gideon can stand the travel, or withers away.*

WHERE THE BIG Sandy flowed into the Siskadee, below the Southern Pass, they came onto a huge and recent trail—two or three hundred horses, most of them shod. They knew it for what it was, Ashley's supply train, headed for rendezvous.

They camped that night at the river's mouth, where the general and his men had camped. The evening air was bright with possibility. A recent trail—maybe they could send ahead and get help from Ashley. They were worn out. Their moccasins were in tatters from walking. Catch the Ashley crew in two or three days maybe, and in five days have horses back here. A chance to ride. This country wasn't for walking, and mountain men were critters that belonged on horseback. Let's *ride* into rendezvous.

Within the hour, before the coffee pots were empty, Jackson called them together and said what every man hoped to hear. He and Clyman would leave the next morning, catch up with Ashley, and get whatever mounts they could. At the very least the brigade would get a rest for a few days, and the horses too. Men exclaimed "Wagh!" and "Hoorah!"

Late that evening Sam and James Clyman were walking Gideon. For three or four days they'd exercised the bear man morning and evening, supporting him on both sides while he clomped along one-legged. "That big body has to have some exercise," Clyman had said. Coy pounced at the bottom of a sagebrush, maybe at a small critter the men didn't see.

Flat Dog and Beckwourth walked up. "We got a present for you," Jim told Gideon. Flat Dog took one hand out from behind his back and stuck whatever it was toward Gideon. For a moment Sam didn't realize . . . A crutch.

Sam grinned. Gideon groaned.

"Maybe not today," Beckwourth said, "and maybe not tomorrow, but soon."

Gideon groaned again.

Beckwourth flashed his toothy grin at Sam. "You two are going to have to coach our friend through his healing."

Sam looked at them, puzzled.

"We're going to meet my village on the Big Horn," said Flat Dog.

"Him and this child both," said Beckwourth.

"Do the big buffalo hunt. See my family."

Sam felt betrayed.

"We'll be back for rendezvous."

"Late, maybe, but we'll be there," said Jim. "We got six weeks before it's supposed to start."

They smiled like they were keeping secrets. It pissed Sam off.

Noting the forlorn expression on Sam's face, Beckwourth said, "Six weeks isn't long."

When dark fell, Sam lay in his blankets rubbing Coy's belly and wondering if it was the amputation. For sure Flat Dog had a hard time with Sam's cutting off a limb, the idea of Gideon being a cripple.

Or maybe Flat Dog had just seen enough of white men.

The red man and the black man were gone the next morning before anyone else woke up.

PART EIGHT

Rendezvous

Chapter Twenty-nine

The first couple of days Sam wandered around the rendezvous site half-addled, missing Flat Dog, and brooding about his situation.

A year ago he'd left rendezvous to go on a raid to get the horses he needed to win his woman. Since then, he'd gotten the horses, and lost them. Gained the woman he loved, and lost her. He'd gotten his best friend killed, Blue Medicine Horse. He'd lost another friend, Third Wing. He'd lost everything he owned, even his clothes, every stitch and every single possession except the knife he kept hidden in his hair. He'd gone through a powerful ceremony, the sun dance, which at the time made him feel like a Crow forever. Now he was banished from the Crows.

"Pup, I'm still broke." The spring hunt he'd counted on had gone bust when the Blackfeet got the horses. He had very few plews to trade to Ashley-Smith here at rendezvous. If he wanted to trap on his own in the coming season, he'd need to use those plews to get powder and lead, and trade goods for the Indians. He couldn't afford a pack mule or two, a pistol, a capote, a keg to carry water, a tomahawk, a throwing knife . . . Hell, he couldn't even dream up a list of all the things he needed and couldn't afford.

"I don't want to hire back on with the company. Feels like a come-down." True, they provided you an outfit, and offered the safety of numbers. The price was, you trapped where they decided to trap, you took orders, you wintered where the brigade leader chose, and at the end of the year you paid Ashley half your catch for the privilege.

"But we need an outfit. It's safety. That sticks in my craw."

He rubbed Coy's ears and murmured again, "Safety." Sam was glad, sometimes, to think that if he lost his hair, Coy would still be fine.

"Here it is, even bigger. I'm not white and not Indian, not any longer." The beaver hunters he ran with, well, he fit in well enough with that motley crew. If you sat down to trade stories with a dozen of them, like as not four would be American backwoodsmen, three French-Canadians who were more than half Indian themselves, two Spanyards from Taos who were also half Indian, two Iroquois or Delawares, and maybe one mulatto. What man of any color could be left out of a rainbow battalion like that?

"I'm changed." Changed beyond the braid he wore his white hair in, his breechcloth, his moccasins. He had the Indian's soft way of walking now, the careless but proud stance, the ever-watchful, ever-moving eyes. He would feel more at home at a Crow dance than a Christian church. To him the sacred pipe wafting its smoke up to Father Sky had as much power as the Bible, or more. "And my heart belongs to a Crow woman."

He pulled on his chin. "I am a cast-out."

He jolted himself out of his mood. "Hey, we're here to relax."

The general had brought them into rendezvous a month early. In the mountains you never knew. Early, late—it depended on whether the plains decided to rain on you, or hail, or fill every gully with swift water and flood every river out of its banks, so you could find no ford and had to wait. It depended on whether the mountains decided to bring another snow or two, and block the passes. It depended on whether the Indians ran your horses off and left you no way to haul the treasured supplies to the men who craved them.

Since few mountain men were in camp, Sam decided to spend most of each day working with Paladin. He wanted to learn that trick Hannibal did, jump off one side of the horse, hit the ground, and bound up and over to the ground on the other side, then repeat until you wanted back into the saddle.

Now that might impress some Indians, who were the best horsemen in the world.

He also set his mind on teaching the mare a little circle dance. He would have her go forward in a curvet, a leap where the hind legs left the ground just before the forelegs hit; then she would sidle sideways, curtsey, rear, turn, and prance back to him, flashing her forelegs high. She would go sun-wise, what white folks called clockwise, because that was the way everything should go. He could awe Indians with this trick, he thought. The Medicine Horse dance, he would call it, in honor of his friend.

He also decided to try to teach Coy a somersault. If Coy learned that, he might be able to learn to do it on Paladin's back. Hey, a fellow had to have some fun.

Sam talked Gideon into crutching over to the training ring with him. As Sam circled Paladin around the ring, Gideon yelled out encouragement, orders, or curses, depending on his mood. Coy watched, envious of the attention. Which meant he would give good attention to learning his own tricks.

After about a week Sam, Gideon, and Paladin wearied of the training, and Cache Valley began to fill with friends.

Two long hunting seasons since the 1825 rendezvous, two long hunts on the remote creeks with only a few companions and the wily beaver for company. These fur hunters were hungry for human faces and lots of talk. Rendezvous meant gossip, stories, and news. It meant a chance to hand over plews for needed supplies. It meant the raw taste of whiskey (Ashley had kept his promise), the sharp-sweet taste of coffee with sugar (lusted after almost as much). It meant a chance to buy new flints, powder, and lead. It meant tobacco, for chewing, smoking, and trading to the Indians. It meant everything else a coon needed to make himself welcome in an Indian village, especially the foofuraw the squaws loved.

This second rendezvous also offered something new, two circles of lodges of Snake Indians, or Shoshones, as they called themselves. Sam shook his head. Twice he'd had trouble with these Indians, and he'd lost a friend to them, Third

Wing. But other trappers had made peace with them, and the Snakes had apparently decided to be friends. So be it.

Sam recognized a trapper sitting on a big slab of sandstone. This man was carrying on activity seldom seen among the mountain men, writing.

Sam clapped him on the shoulder and sat down. Coy tried to lick the man's paper, and he jerked it away.

"Potts. Glad to see you've got your hair." They'd spent a winter together in Rides Twice's village, the winter of '24, Sam in Jedediah's camp, Potts with Captain Weber's outfit.

Daniel Potts looked Sam in the face. "I've heard you lost yours a couple of times."

Sam laughed. The story of his walking seven hundred miles down the Platte River, and other stories, weren't going to get smaller over time. The added story of Third Wing demanding Sam's white hair in turn for releasing him—that tickled the men.

He eyed the pen, ink, and paper enviously. "You write down stories like that?"

"I'm writing my brother Robert," said Potts. "I make the life out here sound good."

"It is good," said Sam.

"A mite more dangerous than I make out," said Potts, and they shared a chuckle. "I can get poetic. Listen to this. I'm telling about Cache Valley:

"This valley has been our chief place of rendezvous and wintering ground. Numerous streams fall in through this valley, which, like the others, is surrounded by stupendous mountains, which are unrivalled for beauty and serenity of scenery."

Sam couldn't resist. "Well, here at the first of June, it is full of waters. Come August, that will be a different story." They laughed. Every man had seen the sere grasses that covered most of the plains and valleys of the West during the summer and fall. Each plop of a horse's foot threw dust up to where you had to breathe it.

Potts gave Sam a merry eye and read on: "You here have a view of all the varieties, plenty of ripe fruit, an abundance of grass just springing up, and buds beginning to shoot, while the higher parts of the mountains are covered with snow, all within 12 or 15 miles of this valley."

This time Potts corrected himself, grinning. "That fruit, well, the berries will be ripe in August. The grass is coming on strong, that's the truth, and the snow will last on the mountains another couple of weeks yet."

He read. "The river passes through a small range of mountains and enters the valley that borders on the Great Salt Lake."

He raised both eyebrows comically at Sam. "Which is a lake so salty that nothing grows in it or around it, you couldn't irrigate with it, and it will kill you if you drink it."

Sam had heard all about the Salt Lake—everybody had— from Jim Bridger and Etienne Provost at the last rendezvous. Dared to go down the Bear River, Bridger went alone and found a body of water that tasted like pure salt. Everybody decided lucky Jim had come on the Pacific Ocean. Only when Provost saw the far shore, later, did the word spread of a huge, salt, inland lake.

"You been there?"

Sam shook his head no. Coy whined at the very thought.

"It's one crazy piece of lake, hoss. You can roll yourself up in a ball and bob up and down in the waves like a cork. You stand up and hold out your arms like Jesus on the Cross, and the water props you up. You can make any design with your body and hold it—you'll never sink."

"Jedediah said he wants to circle in a boat and find the outlet."

"Yeah, the outlet, that's the thing. That river probably leads right to California. That's what the maps say—Ashley calls it the Buenaventura. How'd you like that, coon?"

Something flickered in Sam's mind. California . . . Coy squealed, *Mmnn, mmnn, mmnn.*

Sam regarded Potts. "So how come, when you write your brother, you just don't tell him the way this place is?"

"Don't you see, hoss? This ain't like no other place. It's bigger, uglier, more beautiful, higher, drier, more dangerous,

more of a kick in the ass . . . Wagh! We got grizzly bears bigger and meaner than ten of their panthers back home. We got
mountains make theirs look like pillows. We got deserts even
the A-rabs can't imagine. And you know what? The books say
Californy's got trees a thousand years old, as tall as the clouds,
and wide enough at the bottom to build a whole town in.

"Not to mention we got boiling springs where the Old Gentleman hisself lives just under the surface, and hot water
fountains that shoot two hundred feet high.

"Hell, you can't tell the plain truth about this place—no
one would believe it."

SMALL PARTIES OF men continued to wander in, about
half of them Ashley men, half free trappers. The date set for
rendezvous was July 1, but most men arrived early.

Sam and Gideon spent the days catching up with friends.
Sam accompanied Gideon wherever the big man was willing to walk on his crutch. Mostly they walked from mess fire
to mess fire, and there were plenty. Ashley and Jedediah had
combined their outward-bound parties, about a hundred of
them and twice as many horses and mules carrying thousands
of dollars worth of goods—$30,000 Ashley claimed, as much
as half a dozen ordinary office clerks, for instance, would
earn in a lifetime.

Of the fur hunters, fifty were into rendezvous already, both
Ashley men and free trappers. Ashley said half of his men
were still out, and was willing to bet a cup of whiskey they'd
end up with a hundred trappers and two or three times that
many Indians. As he spoke, his eyes turned into gold coins.

Hundreds of animals, both American horses and Snake ponies, meant the camps were well spread out along the river,
and the horses and mules herded even further out.

As Gideon hobbled from mess fire to mess fire, Sam and
Coy kept him company. The big man ate and ate and ate—
buffalo was plenty. With good food and old friends he seemed
to be regaining his zest for life.

The trouble was, Sam was losing his. He didn't know why. Rendezvous wasn't fun. Or not yet.

Catching up with the news was the good part. Who had gone where, discovered what river flowing which direction, who'd come on Indians and fought 'em and made 'em come. Who'd lost his hair, who'd rode up a cold, winding creek and was never seen again. Who took a squaw. Who got a squaw, bought her all the foorfuraw she could wear, and had her run off. Who'd got how many packs of beaver, and where.

Beyond the news and the tales of what happened where, a new kind of story reared its head, the yarn, what some might call stretchers. Though these yarns might not be strictly accurate, they were something bigger and handsomer and more captivating—they went beyond the facts to truth.

Jim Bridger seemed to be the best storyteller. In fact, Sam saw the young Jim, who bore a bad reputation after the Hugh Glass incident, had developed considerable regard among his fellow trappers. Sam liked the fellow himself. He had a slow way of walking and a slow way of talking, an easy geniality, a serious face that hid a love of fun, and a world of pull-your-leg humor.

Bridger told one story, for instance, about a place he called Echo Canyon. Big canyon it was, so it had a big echo. Why, it took eight hours for a shout on this side to make the trip across and bounce back. So the booshway used the canyon as an alarm clock. At night when the men rolled up in their blankets, he walked the edge and hollered, "Wake up! It's time! Time to get up!"

Eight hours later, sure enough, here come the echo back—"Wake up! It's time! Time to get up!" And the boys rolled out slick.

Everybody's favorite, though, was Bridger's grizzly bear tale. "One evenin' I come back into camp soaking wet, clothes scratched and torn, no pants nor breechclout on my hind end.

" 'What happened, Gabe?' the boys asked, worried there might be Indians around.

"I was down along the river, and maybe I got between a

sow and her cubs. Anyhow, all of a sudden, here comes a monster silvertip roarin' out of the willows right at me, a geyser of plenty pissed off.

"I dropped my rifle and scooted up a tree. But this old griz, she walks up, gives that tree a true *bear* hug, and tears 'er plumb out by the roots.

"Whooee. I got throwed and didn't know where I'd come to earth. Lucky, it was right in river. Quick I takes off downstream, swimming fast as a fish. That silvertip, though, she was *some*. She jumps in after me, and right quick, hell, I see she's catchin' up fast.

"Now I begin to hear a big roar—the falls is coming. I got to get out! Drop my pistol, off with my leggings, and splash hard toward the far bank. There I flop out on the shore and am catchin' my breath when what do I smell? Griz breath. She's clambering right up next to me.

"I dive back in. No hope but one, I decide, and that the same as none. It's either Old Ephraim's teeth and claws or—the falls!

"Swoosh! Out over the edge I sail, all mixed up in water and sky at once, and breathin' both.

"Smack! I hit that pool at the bottom, and underwater I go, held down on slimy rocks in the pounding falls by a current that's stronger'n any bear in this world. How I got up to the surface I'll never know, and when I did, I still couldn't breathe. The smack skedaddled my breath far, far away.

"Then finally comes one breath, and while this child is just a gulpin' air, he looks up and sees, and sees . . . I couldn't believe my eyes. There was Madam Silvertip soaring over the edge of them falls, heading straight down on top of me.

"I made lickety-split for the bank. Things was looking bad, though. If that griz wanted me bad enough to come over them falls . . ."

He shook his head in hopelessness.

"On the bank I decided to make my stand once and for all. I took out my butcher knife" (here he set himself in a knifefighting stance) "and faced my tormentor.

"Straight at me she comes, fast and fierce. Boys, I . . ."

He shook his head and shivered, like the memory still haunted him.

"What happened, Jim?" some eager soul would usually say. "What happened?"

"That bear, she killed me and et me."

NEW OUTFITS CAME in, led by Provost, Weber, Sublette, and Fitzpatrick. Sam greeted old friends, and one man who seemed to be both friend and foe: Micajah. Sam shook his hand with a wary smile. Micajah pretended like he was about to use the grip to throw Sam over, but then he laughed and walked away.

As everyone got into camp, times got better. Ashley took the bungs out of more whiskey kegs. Trading got furious. Snake women got friendly. And the games got riotous. Every kind of physical competition, running, jumping, racing, wrestling, target shooting, and several kinds of card games. Anything one man could best another in and win a dollar.

Gideon started having fun at the shooting competitions. He couldn't hold a rifle—one hand was required for his crutch—but he was a first-rate shot with a pistol. Several times he challenged men with rifles to one-on-one shoots and beat them. Though Sam was worried that Gideon didn't have enough plews to get much more powder, he said nothing. These shoots were the first spark of life in his friend.

The evenings grew spirited, too. Fiddles came out, including Gideon's. Every kind of tune sashayed through the long twilights, and mountain men and Indian women stepped lively to the tunes. They drank many a toast to lift the merriment, and often as not headed for the willows to top it off with a little sport.

Sam noticed uneasily that Micajah got drunk every night. The giant knew that he was steady when sober, crazy when drunk. But he took a notion: In the mountains, he said, there wasn't enough whiskey for a man to be a drunk, so when the chance came, he might as well indulge freely. Twirling a slight Snake girl, Micajah saw Sam staring at him. "Oh, take it back to the States, Morgan," he shouted. "You're worse'n a preacher."

Later, spinning another girl, Micajah called, "Come on, Sam, kick up your heels. Get out here and have some fun." He even brought the girl over and joined her hand to Sam's. But Sam felt a spasm of self-disgust. The hand wasn't Meadowlark's.

Sam wasn't ready for fun. He was stuck in what he couldn't forget. Sometimes he mulled on Blue Medicine Horse's death. Sometimes Third Wing's. Sometimes he couldn't help staring at Gideon, crippled, a fiddler who would never dance again. Every night, in the wee hours when the dark world hovered near, he thought bitterly of Meadowlark.

Meadowlark, wife of Red Roan.

He recalled, deliberately, movement by movement, what he and Meadowlark had done during their honeymoon in his tipi. Then he recounted the same movements, postures, caresses, smiles, joinings, and in place of himself he inserted the form of Red Roan.

He didn't like himself for that.

As he often did when he didn't like himself, he took Coy for a walk. Sometimes they talked, too. This time Sam didn't feel the need to say anything. By the brittle moonlight they walked up a hill overlooking the camp. The hill was steep and the climb a breath-stealer—somehow it felt right to do something hard.

From the top Sam looked out over rendezvous. The dark blobs were people, or bushes, depending on size, or trees. The shiny threads were creeks. The red-gold glows were campfires, probably with men sitting around them, sipping coffee and trading stories. Off to the left rose the tipis of the Shoshone camp. The low fires inside made the lodge covers glow, cones of light in the wilderness. It seemed a grand sight.

Sam sat and rubbed Coy's head for a long time. Men, women, and children were in those tipis. Families.

THE TALK ACROSS the fires in the mornings was that General Ashley was leaving the business. He was selling out to a new firm, Smith, Jackson, and Sublette, made up of three top brigade leaders. In four years, Ashley had gone from deeply in debt to owner of a bonanza in furs, 12,000 pounds of peltries worth five dollars a pound, if he could get them safely to St. Louis. Now the General intended to spend some time in Missouri enjoying his wealth. He would bring supplies to rendezvous, but no more. Some men said he intended to run for governor. It was left to Jedediah Smith, David Jackson, and William Sublette to explore, trap, venture, struggle, and make or lose the next fortune in beaver pelts.

"Sam?" Gideon's voice. Sam was training Paladin, which took full concentration. "The cap'n requires your attention." Diah was standing there waiting. An anarchist in spirit, Gideon always spoke titles like they were silly.

Sam put the mare on a lead and walked over to talk to his friend. Jedediah was all business. "I'm going out to the southwest, to look for beaver. You want to come?"

Sam considered his poverty. *But damn it, I like to be on my own.* Since he had only half an outfit, though, he might have to sign on with the new firm.

"We'll be a score of men. You're a good trapper." Jedediah didn't use phrases like, "You know what way the stick floats." He also didn't often say much that was personal, about himself or others. Sam supposed Diah's few words were a high compliment.

The offer had a lot behind it. Sam knew Jedediah had traveled northwest, clear to Flathead Post and back. He'd been straight west across the Snake River Plains, a starving country. Now southwest, searching for beaver, or maybe trying to fill in the blanks on his maps, or maybe just giving in to the urge to see new country, any new country, anywhere.

"I'll think on it."

Jedediah turned, accepting that as answer enough for right now.

"What about the cripple?" said Gideon. "You have any job, it's a very humdinger for a cripple?"

Jedediah looked at Gideon, perched on a block of sandstone. "Poor Boy, my prayers are that you'll be fine. You'll ride into the next rendezvous. Maybe you'll even be wading into cold creeks again."

"You Americans, you are sentimental," said Gideon. But his tone was soft.

Sam led Paladin back into the training ring, musing. Diah's invitation was a surprise. Sam would listen to the camp talk. What did Diah really have in mind? It really might be new territory for the new firm to trap. To the northwest, Oregon was jointly held with the British, and the Hudson's Bay Company was doing all it could to keep the American fur hunters out. To the southwest a few miles was Mexican territory, and few beaver men hunted there.

But, then, Jedediah might be thinking of California. If he was, he wouldn't say so.

The world had heard report of the golden clime from the British and American sailors who visited those shores. The tales were glowing. Flowers bloomed and crops grew twelve months a year. The Indian and Mexican women were alluring. The country was beautiful, the mountains magnificent, the rivers mighty. Maybe a young, disenchanted, lonely American could start fresh in California.

ON A DAY just beyond the solstice, it is long twilight of summer evening. The sun drops behind western mountains, but its light lingers in the world, gentle as a lover's fingers stroking long hair. Snake women ghost through the camp. Some of them wear the finery their husbands have traded for, or they themselves have accepted graciously from trappers for their love.

Sam sits on a rock braiding a quirt from deer hide thongs. Paladin wouldn't take to a quirt, but Sam can trade it to some trappers for something he needs, like a patch knife. A fetching young woman walks past, smiles at Sam with a hint of coquetry, and hesitates. It's modest enough behavior, but for a Shoshone woman provocative.

Coy eyes her suspiciously. Sam strokes his head and watches the young woman walk on toward the circle where the fiddler is tuning up for the evening's fun. She's young enough to be unmarried, but old enough to have a husband. He'll probably never know. Since she's all dolled up, though, he knows how the evening will end for her. Not with him. He's not interested. He wishes he were.

Her scent wafts back to him on the evening breeze, and makes him miss Meadowlark even more.

Paladin whickers. Maybe Paladin wants to mate. If her time comes while they're at rendezvous, Sam will pick out the best stallion he sees and breed her.

This is his family, a horse and a coyote, missing a woman. Missing *the* woman.

The evening air seems special. The world pauses in a moment of perfection and holds its breath, forgetful of tomorrow. A mouth harp lifts a tune into this lucent tranquility. A moment later a fiddle joins it. The men will soon abandon their meals or games for dancing.

Gideon's voice clamors loud and jangly over the music.

Sam stands up and looks. A hundred yards away Gideon is pivoting around on his crutch and yelling at some irritant. Sam peers hard, and sees who the irritant seems to be— Micajah.

Quickly, Sam leads Paladin that way. Gideon's half crazy these days, and . . . Yes, Gideon and Micajah swore eternal friendship at the last rendezvous, and they even included Sam—three-way eternal amity. Gideon and Micajah did it with the traditional rite of shooting the cups off each other's head. But Sam feels uneasy. Has Micajah really forgotten the fight at the Crow village, two falls out of three, when Gideon

outwitted him? Has Micajah really forgotten the time in
Evansville when he and his brother Elijah tried to rob Abby,
Grumble, and Sam, and Elijah ended up dead?

When Sam gets there, maybe the shouting is over. Sam
restakes Paladin. In front of a group of men, Micajah is circling Gideon, who pivots on his crutch. "You are right, I admit," says Gideon in a placating tone. He holds a pistol out to
Micajah. "You are right. You beat me."

Micajah stops, looking at Gideon. His eyes are . . . calming
down. He nods. He walks up and takes the offered pistol, then
sticks it in Gideon's belt. "You done an honest mistake," he
says, and offers his hand. Gideon shakes it.

"Besides," said Micajah, "I never forget." He steps to one
of the on-lookers and takes a whiskey jug. He takes a swig.
"You, me, and Morgan—we are friends forever. I drink to
it—the three of us, comrades." He takes another swig.

Then he strides over to Gideon and offers the jug. "Come
on out here, Sam," calls Micajah, "and drink with us."

Gideon swigs. Sam goes out, Coy following reluctantly.
Handed the jug, Sam swigs.

"Sir Samuel Morgan," Micajah cries, "it is time that you
made the pledge of friendship yourself. This time *you* will
shoot with me. Off my head you will shoot the cup of whiskey."

Sam can't tell if Micajah is half-drunk or just acting that
way. *Probably drunk by decision rather than inebriation,* he
thinks. He looks at Gideon and shakes his head no.

"No," shouts Gideon, "Sam is not that kind of man. Sir
Samuel does not stoop to vulgar games."

"Friendship," cries Micajah. "We must renew our pledges
of friendship."

"We will, pledges of friendship. You and I will shoot, and
Sam is included by . . . tradition." Gideon grins crookedly
at Sam. Sam thinks maybe he suspects trouble. But right
now maybe Gideon welcomes trouble. Will he accept, with
a Gallic shrug, a quick death?

"We will," exults Micajah. "Friendship."

Micajah struts off and takes a mock shooting position.

Sam mind screams at him, *You're only guessing.* Nevertheless, he says quietly to Gideon, "Don't do it."

"It is well," says the big Frenchy, and winks at him.

"Gideon . . ."

But Gideon walks away. *You crazy bastard . . .*

"I show my complete trust in you," cried Micajah, "by giving you the first shot. I insist that you, my friend, shoot first." He takes a tin cup from one man, a whiskey jug from another, and fills the cup. Delicately, he sets it on his head. "Shoot the cup," he says pointing. Then he puts his finger in the middle of his forehead and chuckles madly. "Not the flesh."

Coy trots to the group of men near Micajah. *That's odd,* thinks Sam, but he follows.

Gideon pours powder into his pan. With an extravagantly careless gesture, he brings his pistol level and fires, Wham! The sound slaps Sam in the face.

The cup flies off Micajah's head. He licks whiskey off his face with mock lust.

Now Gideon puts a cup on his own head and takes a jaunty pose.

"No," Sam mouths futilely.

Micajah wheels, plants his rifle butt between his feet, leans on the muzzle, and launches into oratory. "I first saw this feat performed," he says, "by the mountaineer's only competitor as the greatest frontiersman, the keelboaters of the Ohio. Half-horse, half-alligators they call themselves, and by God they are. Those men eat ten Injuns for breakfast and use their bones for toothpicks. They shoot the cup to bond together, a way of saying, 'We are brothers.'

"I first performed it with my older brother, Elijah." Micajah puts his head down, maybe remembering. Sam wonders . . . But all Micajah says is, "I miss him still. I have broken many of the commandments," he goes on, "but one commandment I hold sacred, the eleventh. A man shall be true to his friend. In that spirit I shoot."

Coy howls something to the skies.

Micajah primes his pan, lifts his rifle, and makes elaborate gestures of getting comfortable. At last, as he settles the barrel into position, Sam sees what he fears. A look of low cunning, peppered with blood lust, warps Micajah's face. It is unmistakable. Micajah cocks. His finger pressures the trigger.

Sam leaps forward. His hand knocks Micajah's barrel upwards.

At the same instant, Blam! The muzzle spits death.

Sam twists his neck toward Gideon, heart hollering that he has been too late.

The bear man stands, and the cup rests undisturbed on his head.

Slap! The open-handed blow knocks Sam to the ground.

Coy rushes Micajah, growling and barking. The big man kicks Coy in the belly, and the coyote goes tumbling.

Sam uses the moment to get to his feet. "I saw what you were going to do . . ."

"Bastard," shouts Micajah.

"You were going to . . ."

Gideon is crutching toward them. A dozen men crowd close. Micajah roars and lunges at Sam. A dozen hands restrain him.

Sam appeals to the crowd. "You all saw it, that look on Micajah's face. He was going to . . ."

"Reading a man's heart in his face, that's pretty tricky." The voice is a soft drawl, Jim Bridger's.

Sam appeals to Gideon. "Didn't you see it?"

Gideon shrugs.

"I am INSULTED!" Micajah roars to the skies.

Bridger looks around. "What do y'all think?"

Some say the insult was bad, damned bad. Others say young Morgan was sincere. No one says he saw what Micajah was about to do.

"Morgan," says Bridger, "maybe you ought to apologize."

"Never on this earth," says Sam. "He was about to kill my friend."

Micajah roars again, and then with words shouts, "I'll beat an apology out of you."

"Let 'em fight," someone says.

"Yeah, let 'em fight."

"May the honest man win."

One hand keeping Micajah back, Bridger holds Sam's eyes. "Maybe you should."

"It's not a fair fight," says Gideon. When he had two legs, Gideon was probably the only man in camp who might whip Micajah bare-handed.

"The man who's right will win," says a voice.

"True, that's the way of it," someone else says.

Bridger still looks at Sam. Sam nods.

"No weapons," says Bridger.

With preening movements, Micajah hands his rifle to another man, puts his pistol beside it, flings down his butcher knife, and sets down his hunting pouch, which probably has a patch knife in it.

"Morgan?"

"You see I have no weapons," says Sam, holding his arms out. That's almost true.

"There will be no killing here tonight," says Bridger. "This is a fight of honor, to see who is telling the truth. No gouging of eyes. Everything else goes. When one man can't go on, the fight is over."

Grunts and nods indicate that satisfies most onlookers.

"Break 'ees arm, ze interferer, zat will show him," cries someone.

Arm? Sam wonders if he'll escape with his life.

He gets onto the balls of his feet, ready. *Right now his mind, heart, feet, sinew—all of me must be a war.*

The last of the light has dwindled. A gibbous moon is enough to cast shadows. Blackness infiltrates everywhere, including men's minds.

* * *

FIRST COMES A bull charge. Sam waits until the last moment, sidesteps, and flicks a kick at Micajah's head. His foot feels bone, and he smiles.

Micajah gets up rubbing his shoulder. The charge wasn't serious, the kick maybe more than Micajah expected.

Micajah belts out a war cry, sprints at Sam, leaps into the air, and kicks with both feet.

Sam rolls sideways. One of the heavy boots clips his head. For a moment he's dizzy.

Micajah, having caught his fall with one arm, is on his feet and launches himself in a huge flop toward Sam. Sam rolls. One of his arms gets caught.

But Micajah bounces a little, and Sam snatches the arm away.

Quick as can be, Sam jumps on Micajah's back, gets a forearm on his neck, and cranks it tight with the other hand.

Micajah's neck muscles are so strong that Sam is not getting a choke. Micajah lumbers to his feet, pauses mightily, and hurls himself onto his back.

Sam barely pushes himself clear, rolls, and comes up on his feet.

Avoiding is not enough. Attack.

Voices cry encouragement, mostly to Micajah. Despite one voice, Gideon's, Sam feels the blood lust of the mob. Coy is howling piteously.

Sam decides to try something wildly unexpected. He charges Micajah, head lowered, intending to leap at the last moment and head-bash Micajah's face.

The giant lithely drops onto his back, raises his legs, catches Sam on his feet and hurls him straight the way he's going.

Sailing over, Sam thinks he sees Micajah's hand go to his boot, but he's not sure.

Sam rolls through the weeds, rages back, and launches a head kick.

Micajah's hand flicks, the kick is deflected, and Sam lands on his back. Oddly, Sam's calf is cut.

"A knife!" Gideon hollers. "He has a knife!"

"Don't see that," says Bridger.

Sam can't see one either.

Micajah hurls himself through the air at the prone Sam. In the moonlight something in Micajah's hand flashes.

Sam rolls. Something slashes his ribs.

Quickly, Sam rolls straight back into Micajah. *Inside the knife,* he screams at himself. *Stay inside the knife.*

He gets a wild idea.

Micajah rolls on top of Sam, and Sam lets it happen.

Sam blocks the knife arm with one hand. The bodies are too close. Micajah drops the knife and goes for the choke with both hands.

The choke is terrible. Sam will never get breath again. *Be quick or die.*

He jerks the small, sharp blade out of his hair ornament and stabs Micajah's throat.

The choke still holds.

Sam rams the blade deep into the throat and slams it home with the palm of his hand. It almost disappears, even the handle, into the thick flesh.

Micajah gouts blood into Sam's face.

Bridger and another man roll Micajah off Sam.

Sam breathes. He breathes again. The second time he inhales blood and blows it back out.

He rolls over and vomits into the dust. He breathes. He vomits, and does both again.

Bridger picks up the knife Micajah dropped and inspects it. He waits for Sam to come back to this world. Gideon squats beside them with the help of the crutch.

Sam looks up into their faces.

"I'm sorry. My fault," Bridger says. "You are *some.*"

Jim stands up. He calls to everyone, "Sam Morgan has won in a fair fight. Does any man say otherwise?"

Silence.

"Micajah drew the knife first. Everyone see it the same?"

Three or four yesses trot out.

"Then I say, by the rule of the mountains, Sam gets ever'thing Micajah owns. Rifle, pistol, horses, ever'thing."

Bridger walks off. The dancing has started, and the other men head for that. In the mountains, blood doesn't stop the fun.

Sam props up on his elbows and looks into Micajah's horrible face. He tells Gideon, "I'll bury him in the morning."

"Zat will be taken care of," says Gideon.

Sam sits up.

"We should get to the river," says Gideon.

Two half-wrecked men, one on a crutch, support each other in painful steps to the water. One coyote skitters along behind. Sam splashes into the shallows and lies face down. After a moment he looks into Gideon's face and says, "Who the hell am I?"

"A good man," says Gideon.

But Sam doesn't seem to hear. "Who the hell am I?"

Coy howls, maybe asking the same question.

Chapter Thirty

S am shook himself awake. He was lying face down, near his blankets but not on them. He sat up and brushed the dust off his face. He looked across at Gideon, lying tidily on his blankets, eyes taking Sam in. "I have blood and dust caked on my face?"

"Just dust."

"I better get to the water and wash off."

"I am been dreaming of last night."

"Me too." All night Sam had dreamt slivers and slashes of the fight. It gave him the chills.

He grimaced. Some sort of low, lower than Sam Morgan ever intended to get. A life where you fight with your fellow trapper, he tries to kill you, and you do kill him. Self-disgust flared up in Sam's belly like bile.

"Sam," came the voice. Horses' hooves thumped.

Sam realized now that this was what had woken him up, this thumping. He saw movement behind a nearby sagebrush. Several horses and . . .

Beckwourth came out from behind the bush. "Good to see you, hoss."

Sam stood slowly, looked gladly into the face of his black friend, and clapped him on the shoulders. He nearly felt teary. Beckwourth laughed.

"I got a present for Gideon."

He brought his hand out from behind his back.

It was a peg leg. A wooden peg a couple of feet long, glowing with oil. A wooden bowl on top of the peg. Attached to that, a thick rawhide strap about half a foot high, long enough to wrap around twice, and with thongs to tie it.

Gideon crawled toward it. "You made this?"

"We did," said Flat Dog, stepping out from behind the horses. "A man who can make an arrow shaft smooth and straight can make a peg smooth and straight."

Sam clapped Flat Dog on both shoulders, and Flat Dog clapped Sam back. He felt dizzy—dizzy with pleasure, with change, with the whirl of the world . . .

"I got a present for Sam," said Flat Dog, holding an arm out.

Out from behind the horses stepped Meadowlark, beaming.

SAM WANTED TO borrow a tent instantly. She insisted on walking with him to the river and cleaning him up. They didn't talk. Words wouldn't carry what needed to be said. Stories could fill in the gaps later.

She insisted on putting up the small lodge she'd brought.

Sam and Meadowlark disappeared into the lodge and stayed all day. They discovered themselves again as lovers. As friends. As husband and wife.

After an hour or two, words overflowed like streams in the spring. Every tale of every struggle over three months of separation got told, at least in part. Still, the silences said more than the talk. Then words would bubble forth again, froth and spray down the mountain of their feeling, and fall once more into deep, still pools.

She had one essential statement for him:

"I am your woman."

She saw the uncertainty in his face. "No man but you has ever touched me," she said.

He wept. They both wept. They held each other. They rolled all over the ground holding each other.

She also made sure that Sam understood that coming to rendezvous was her idea. "Flat Dog, he not so sure. I already decided, and was ready."

"I want to get married," said Sam.

Then he had to translate for her the white notion of marriage into the Crow language and the Crow way of seeing.

In the end she said, "A ceremony," and accepted gladly.

"A pledge to each other," said Sam.

They smiled deep into each other's eyes, both knowing that the real pledges had already been made. Sam's when he took Meadowlark to Ruby Hawk Valley. Meadowlark's when she fled her village to come to rendezvous.

Nevertheless, Meadowlark now said in English, "I will marry you."

Sam laughed. "Your English is way better."

In English she replied, "I live no with my family, live with Bell Rock two moons. He and Flat Dog teach me English."

Sam hugged her.

They didn't come out of the lodge until evening, and then they were famished.

Their last feast of that day was hump ribs and friends.

GENERAL ASHLEY CAME to Sam and Meadowlark's fire the next evening when he got word, and accepted coffee.

It was quickly done. Yes, the General would perform the marriage ceremony.

"Congratulations to you both," he said.

Gideon pitched in. "Congratulations!" The big man's spirits had bounced upward since he got his peg leg. He'd stuffed the bowl with padding, wore it constantly, and had leaned a little weight on it. His friends encouraged him to try a few steps, but Gideon said the pain was still too great.

Then Sam took a chance. "Diah," he began tentatively, "maybe be offended that we don't ask him to do it. With the Bible."

Ashley nodded. "You don't want the solemnization of your vows to be over-solemn."

Sam was tickled. General Ashley had a way of putting things. "We want it to be a party."

"Day after tomorrow will be July the Fourth, Independence Day. Jedediah has decided to spend the day going to the cache and raising it. He's taking two others who don't like drunkenness." The General looked at the couple benevolently. "And I've already announced that the whiskey will be free that day."

Sam grinned. "That will make a party." Then he frowned. "I've never been in church, but my two sisters were married by the traveling preacher when he came around. They gave him five dollars. I'm going to have to owe you that."

"Your good work has given it to me a dozen times over."

"Day after tomorrow's good with you?" Sam asked Meadowlark in the Crow language.

"What does Independence Day mean?"

Sam explained briefly why it was a huge ceremony day for Americans.

She risked speaking in English. "It is good. By this ceremony, I no more depend on my father, mother." She said directly to Sam, "You tell me *all* about this ceremony."

Sam agreed.

"And it is two days from now," Meadowlark continued in her English. "Good. I need time to look my best."

THE NEXT MORNING, long after the usual hour for breakfast, they had a surprise visitor. Jedediah squatted in front of the coals. "May I have some coffee?"

Sam's heart sank. *Now we're going to get a lecture about the Good Book and how to be united in holy matrimony.* But he reached for the coffee pot, poured a round for everyone, and waited.

Diah threw Sam for a loop by addressing himself to Meadowlark.

"I want to say something to you in the strictest confidence. Strict for all of you," he added quickly to Flat Dog and Gideon. Again he addressed himself especially to Meadowlark. "Have you ever seen the Pacific Ocean?" Flat Dog translated it as big-water-everywhere-to-the-west.

Sam felt a flicker of irritation. Diah knew the answer to that one.

But Meadowlark gasped. "No."

"Would you like to?"

"I'd love to."

Sam was drop-jawed.

Jedediah ran his eyes around the circle. "How about the rest of you?"

They all said they would, even Gideon.

Diah turned back to Sam. "Then I want you to come with my brigade. We're going to California. But we're not telling anyone that. Not *anyone*."

Meadowlark gushed out, "Yes." Then she gave her husband a look that meant, I'll explain later.

Sam chimed in with another yes.

Flat Dog started to speak and stopped.

"I want you, too," said Diah.

"Yes." Flat Dog grinned.

"What about Beckwourth?" Sam put in.

The captain shook his head. "Captain Sublette has asked him to go with an outfit toward Blackfeet country. They expect it to be lively."

Jedediah plunged on. "I don't know how long we'll be gone. We may not find beaver in the dry country to the southwest. I'm told we'll find plenty in California." Sam wondered if Diah had learned that from the Britishers when he went to Flathead Post. "We don't know whether the Mexicans will make us welcome."

Sam reflected that dangers always seem an enticement to Jedediah.

"It's settled then?"

Sam couldn't believe it. Marriage and an adventure to California. His head spun. "It is," he said.

Flat Dog nodded.

Gideon said, "I want to go."

Jedediah looked at his peg leg.

Gideon hopped up on it. He caught his balance carefully and took his first steps, straight to Jedediah.

The obvious pain made even Jedediah flinch.

"I'll be able to ride," he said, "and you know this child can shoot."

Jedediah looked at the French-Canadian with a face drenched in sympathy.

"Poor Boy," he said, "we leave in one moon. If you can ride a horse then, you're hired."

The moment they were alone, Sam asked, "What did you want to tell me about the ocean?"

Meadowlark hesitated. "I dream about the water-everywhere-to-the-west. Often. In the dreams I dip myself into it, and the descend far, far down. I see strange and wonderful creatures . . ."

Sam grinned to bring them back into the light of day. "I'm wanting to jump into that thing myself. But not descend."

GENERAL ASHLEY HOLDS Diah's worn Bible open at his waist.

Sam waits in front of the General, looking back through the aisle created by the trappers. Behind him in the first row of onlookers is Jedediah Smith. Diah has hurried back from the cache to attend the wedding of his friend Sam. Next to Sam is his best man, Jim Beckwourth, also looking back.

At the end of the aisle stands Flat Dog, and on Flat Dog's arm is the love of Sam's life. The brother and sister have been persuaded that marching arm in arm is really the proper thing to do.

She is radiant. Sure of what she wanted, she spent weeks preparing to look splendid when she came to her husband. Her dress is made of two deer hides tanned very white, ornamented with bright beadwork on the cape and down the arms. The bodice sports a four winds wheel in the colors of the directions, red for east, yellow for south, black for west, and white for north, plus green for the earth and blue for the sky. The hem is fringed with bells that tinkle when she walks and will jingle-jangle when she dances. Her waist is girded by a wide belt woven of bright-colored yarns, the kind brought out from Taos, a special gift from Bell Rock and his wife. Ermine tails are wrapped around her braids, velvety white against glossy black, and her part is defined with a streak of vermilion. She has rouged her lips scarlet, and she wears a perfume she made herself from grasses, herbs, flower petals, and wild mint.

Gideon sits on a cottonwood log, peg sticking out jauntily, fiddle and bow in hand. Now he begins the entrance music he has asked to play. It is a traditional song of the Jewish people, based on a scripture from the *Song of Songs* and taught to him by his father. He puts the bow to the strings and lifts it into the air.

Flat Dog leads Meadowlark toward his friend, her husband. They do not walk but dance in the stately Crow ceremonial step, toe-heel, toe-heel.

Only Gideon knows the words to his song, and he sings them in his head.

> *You have ravished my heart, my bride,*
> *Awake, north wind, and come, thou south!*
> *Blow upon my garden that the spices thereof may flow out,*
> *Let my beloved come into his garden and eat its pleasant*
>   *fruits.*

As he fiddles, he weeps.

Meadowlark arrives in front of the General. Jedediah nudges Sam and gives him a surprise, a small gold ring for her finger. "A gift from Ashley-Smith," he whispers.

Smiling tipsily, Ashley begins, "Dearly beloved, we are gazzered here together . . ."

Fitzpatrick and Clyman, standing close to this master of the ceremony, grin at each other and echo, "Gazzered."

Sam smiles merrily at Flat Dog.

Soon Ashley is saying something about "not by any to be entered into . . ."

"Entered into," says Fitz, "that's the thing."

". . . lightly, but reverently, discreetly, advisedly, soberly . . ."

"We're past that point," says Clyman.

"Wagh!" cry half a dozen drunken voices. "*Well* past."

The General cannot suppress a smile. ". . . Now speak or forever hold his peace . . ."

"I'll speak, by God. I want her for my own self." This is Beckwourth, the best man.

Ashley pushes forward, perhaps skipping sanctioned and esteemed passages. ". . . Forsaking all others, keep thee only unto her, so long as ye both shall live?"

Sam turns and looks fiercely into the eyes of his beloved. "I will," he roars.

Following Fitzpatrick's signal of a raised fist, fifty men holler, "Me, too!"

The General is blubbering with laughter.

Mercifully soon, he arrives at the point where he instructs Sam to say his crucial words.

First Sam holds up the ring for all to see. Then he shouts to the mountain tops, "With this ring I thee wed."

Meadowlark lets him put it on.

She says, "And I wed you."

Then she permits a kiss that is probably the most conspicuous public display of affection ever permitted by a Crow woman.

"What God hath joined together," announces Ashley, "let no man put asunder."

"Joins with Buffalo!" shouts Beckwourth. "Meadowlark!"

A dozen voices echo his cry. "Joins with Buffalo! Meadowlark!"

Gideon strikes up another tune. This time it's "Mairi's Wedding." The newlyweds lead out and the whole company, whites, Frenchies, Spanyards, Delawares, Iroquois, and even some watching Shoshones dance behind them. The whites and Frenchies do jigs. The newlyweds and Indians dance with restraint, toe-heel, toe-heel. Some of the white men sing.

> *Step we gaily one we go, heel for heel and toe for toe,*
> *Arm in arm and on we go, all for Mairi's wedding.*
> *Cheeks are bright as rowans are, brighter far than any*
> *   star,*
> *Fairest of them all by far is my darling Mairi.*

Around the fire they dance, across the buffalo grass, between the shrubs of sage, and on to Sam and Meadowlark's lodge.

Quick as a flash, the couple dashes in.

Beckwourth hollers, "I wonder what will happen in there."

He backs up, takes a run at the lodge, and scrambles right up the buffalo skins. Just as he starts slipping, he lunges and grabs a lodgepole sticking out of the smoke hole. He pulls himself up. He pretends to peer down inside, where the lodge fire is nearly out, and the fleshly fire is not yet lit.

He throws a mock leer at the crowd.

A hundred men laugh, propose toasts, stumble over bushes, and collapse onto the ground. Some head for the Shoshone tipis, seeking their own fun.

Inside, Sam and Meadowlark undress each other slowly. They look at each other with wonder. Sam takes her left hand, raises it to his lips, and kisses the gold ring. Then he tumbles her onto the buffalo robes.

AUTHOR'S NOTE

BEAUTY FOR ASHES is the second novel of the Rendezvous Series, which tells the story of the fur trade in the American West during its glory years, from the early 1820s to the
late 1830s. It is an adventure tale and a love story told against
a background that is scrupulously researched.

Most of the characters around Sam Morgan are historical.
William Ashley, Jedediah Smith, Jim Beckwourth, Tom Fitzpatrick, James Clyman, and many others are characterized
as the record shows them. Aside from Sam, the main fictional
characters are the Crow characters, Gideon, Third Wing, and
Micajah.

The fur trade, its conditions and circumstances, the landscape, the Indian peoples, and so on are also drawn carefully
from the record. The struggles and subsequent success of the
Ashley firm were just as suggested here. I have described
the first and second rendezvous from accounts of men who
were there. Ashley's instructions on how to find the meeting place (complete with "pealed trees"), for instance, is
as he wrote it; Daniel Potts's letter telling his brother about
the second rendezvous is what he actually penned.

My hope is to create, over the entire series, an authentic
picture of a particularly splendid time in America, even more
full of danger, conflict, wild possibility, villainy, cowardice,
heroism, tragedy, and joy than most eras in American history.

A final note: Money was very different in the 1820s. A
profit of $50,000 then may be the equivalent of a couple of

million dollars now. The $1.50 a trapper paid for a pound of coffee was wages for a day or two back in the States.

Most of the unfamiliar words the mountain men use here are defined in the glossary in the first novel in the series, *So Wild a Dream*.

ACKNOWLEDGMENTS

FOR THE MATERIAL on the Crow people, thanks to my friends among the Crows, especially the men of medicine, Larsen and Tyler Medicine Horse. I also relied on the bible about Crow culture, Robert Lowie's *The Crow Indians*. I have relied for the doings of the mountain men particularly on two fine books, Dale L. Morgan's *Jedediah Smith and the Opening of the West* and Fred R. Gowans's *Rocky Mountain Rendezvous*.

Thanks to Jan Blevins, Richard Hoyt, and others who provided crucial information.

My editor, Dale Walker, is a rock.

The Honorable Clyde Hall, man of medicine of the Shoshone people, has acted as my mentor for twenty years. Thank you, Clyde.

Heaven Is a
Long Way
Off

◆―⊃◯⊂―◆

To Meredith,
all my harem in one

ACKNOWLEDGMENTS

DENNIS COPELAND, ARCHIVIST of the Monterey Public Library, provided materials. New Mexico historian Stan Hordes saved me from errors. Three books about Nuevo Mexico were invaluable: Marc Simmons's *Coronado's Land,* L. R. Bailey's *Indian Slave Trade in the Southwest,* and Paul Horgan's *The Centuries of Santa Fe.*

I couldn't write without the help of friends and family. Heidi Schulman helped me along. Eric Stone guided me to an 1820s map of the Los Angeles area. Lana Latham was my point woman for interlibrary loan. Jan Blevins helped me with the French language. Dick James was my particular advisor about mountain men. As always, Dale Walker, Richard Wheeler, and Clyde Hall were my companions and consultants on the journey. My wife, Meredith, my agent, Nat Sobel, and Dale Walker read the manuscript and steered me toward the truth. I am grateful to all of them.

Rideo ergo sum.
(I laugh, therefore I am.)

—HANNIBAL MCKYE

A NOTE ABOUT HISTORY

THIS BOOK BEGINS by following the second journey of the Rocky Mountain fur traders to California, a major event in their history, and then swings into the further adventures of Sam Morgan, which are imaginary.

The events involving Jedediah Smith, especially the massacre and escape at the Mojave villages, are dramatized on the basis of the documentation we have. The quotations from his journal are what he wrote. The captain's troubles in California are depicted accurately; his epistle in Chapter Ten, while invented, is based on a letter he did write.

The picture of Nuevo Mexico in 1828 is drawn from history, including the sketch of the Indian slave trade, which was horrific, and continued under American rule and even beyond the Civil War.

Likewise my depictions of the fur trade at this time, and of the rendezvous of 1828, are intended seriously.

The heart and soul of this novel, and of all in the series, is the heart and soul of Sam Morgan.

INTRODUCTORY NOTE

OKAY, YOU'RE IN a spot. Here you hold the fourth novel in a series in your hands. (I hope they're eager hands.) You have no way to know what wild adventures you've missed in the first three volumes, what achievement and failures the Rocky Mountain fur trapper Sam Morgan has marched through. You don't know his friends or enemies, his loves or his dislikes, his heart, his soul.

Here are some notes to help you get started.

SYNOPSES OF THE FIRST THREE VOLUMES,
1822–1827

In *So Wild a Dream,* challenged by the half-breed Hannibal, Sam follows his heart west. After traveling to St. Louis with the con man Grumble and the madam Abby, he goes to the Rocky Mountains with a fur brigade and begins to learn the ways of the trappers and the Indians. At the end he is forced to walk seven hundred miles alone, lost and starving, to the nearest fort.

In *Beauty for Ashes,* Sam courts the Crow girl Meadowlark. Helping Sam in a daring feat to win her hand, one of her brothers is killed. Seeking peace, Sam goes through the rigors of a sun dance, and Meadowlark elopes with him. Her family takes her back by force and kicks Sam out of the village. But Meadowlark runs away to join Sam, and at the trapper rendezvous they are married.

Dancing with the Golden Bear launches Sam and Meadowlark to California with a fur brigade. After terrible hardships crossing the desert, they reach the Golden Clime and the ocean. But Meadowlark dies in childbirth. As he embarks on a harrowing journey across the Sierra Nevada and the deserts beyond, Sam passes through the dark night of the soul.

CAST OF CHARACTERS
of the
Three Preceding Books

SAM MORGAN, an eighteen-year-old Pennsylvanian who leaves home for the Rocky Mountains.

HANNIBAL MCKYE, a scholar and an Indian, born to a Dartmouth professor and a Delaware woman. He's also a former trainer of circus horses.

GRUMBLE, a con man of erudition and style.

ABBY, a beautiful and clever madam.

MEADOWLARK, a Crow girl who marries Sam.

BLUE MEDICINE HORSE and FLAT DOG, her brothers.

GRAY HAWK and NEEDLE, her parents.

RED ROAN, son of the Crow chief and rival for Meadowlark's hand.

GIDEON POORBOY, a bear of a French-Canadian, Sam's trapping partner.

SUMNER, a slave who claims his freedom and follows Grumble into the con life.

JULIA RUBIO, daughter of a California don, later Flat Dog's wife.

CESAR RUBIO, her father, owner of Rancho Malibu.

COY, Sam's pet coyote. In a huge prairie fire Coy led Sam to safety inside the carcass of a buffalo, and they've been inseparable since.

PALADIN, Sam's mare, trained in the skills of circus horses.

HISTORICAL CHARACTERS

JEDEDIAH SMITH, an educated and religious Yankee, one of the principal leaders of the mountain men, later co-owner of the main trapping firm.

WILLIAM ASHLEY, the entrepreneur who opens most of the West to beaver trapping.

JAMES CLYMAN, a trapper friend of Sam's who sometimes tells the stories of Shakespeare's plays.

JIM BECKWOURTH, a mulatto and a trapping companion of Sam's.

TOM FITZPATRICK, an Irishman who becomes a brigade leader.

JIM BRIDGER, trapper, brigade leader, and yarner extraordinaire.

BILL SUBLETTE, a trapper and partner of Jedediah Smith.

HARRISON ROGERS, ROBERT EVANS, SILAS GOBEL, and other trappers of the California brigades.

FATHER JOSÉ SANCHEZ, head of the mission at San Gabriel, California.

Chapter One

They were late arriving, and the last of the sunlight spread red-gold across the summits of the western mountains. A fresh, damp smell lifted up off the river, a promise of a blessing as evening came to the desert. A breeze stirred among the willow branches along the banks. The finger-shaped leaves caught the light of the sun and tossed it, red-gold-green, into the soft evening air.

Along the top ridges the cinnamon mountains turned the color of candied apples, and grew amethyst shadows on their lower slopes. The Colorado flexed and muttered on its journey from the mountains to the sea.

Sam Morgan looked around. Again he found the desert strange and alluring. He said to himself, *What the hell am I doing here?*

"On the adventure," said Hannibal. Sam's friend had an irritating habit of reading his thoughts.

Village leaders were riding out to meet them. It would be impolite to go closer to the village before courtesies were exchanged. Impolite even though these were the Mojave villages, where the fur brigade had spent a couple of weeks last autumn and knew the Indians were friendly. So Sam, Hannibal, and Captain Jedediah Smith sat their mounts in this place. Sam cursed. He squirmed in the saddle, itchy from his own sweat after the long ride. His pet coyote, Coy, sat in the shade of a creosote bush and panted.

"There's a sorry piece of the adventure."

Sam turned his head. A few paces into the brush three

Mojave boys had built a small fire and were torturing horny toads.

The biggest boy reached into a hide bag, plucked out a toad, flat and ugly and the size of a palm. The creature had daggerlike spikes all around its head, and it was fighting its captor.

The boy laughed and threw the toad onto the fire.

Coy barked.

The toad skittered out of the fire like a stone hopping across water.

The smallest boy snatched the toad up and held it close to his nose. The toad sprouted blood from its eyes—Sam had seen this trick before. The boy jumped and threw the toad into the air.

Another boy snatched the creature on the fly and tossed it onto the fire.

The small boy wiped blood off his nose and grinned.

The toad came lickety-split out of the flames and slithered under another boy's knee. The boy grabbed the toad coming out the back side.

Coy squealed, like a plea for mercy.

A picture floated into Sam's mind—damnedest thing, he couldn't imagine why. He saw his infant daughter suckling at the breast of Sam's . . .

Meadowlark. Dead.

He shook his head to make the picture go away. But it stayed right where it was.

The biggest boy took the toad from the younger one and dropped it into the flames.

This time it first blew itself up big, and then, amazingly, never moved again.

Coy growled.

Sam started to rein his horse toward the boys. Hannibal put his hand out—no. Sam stopped. "What made them like that?" whispered Sam.

"A bad one leading good ones," said Hannibal.

Sam's eyes asked for help. Sometimes Hannibal knew

things. Some of the men called him Mage, short for magician.

"Let's go," said Jedediah.

Sam handed Paladin's reins to the magician and fell in behind Captain Smith on foot. About fifty yards off several leaders of the tribe waited to meet the trappers, and beyond them on the willow flat Sam could see the brush huts and crop fields of the village.

Safety, he thought.

Sam took a last glance at the boys. They were still mesmerized by toads and fire. *Life goes topsy-turvy into death.*

He forced himself to turn and study the Mojave leaders. There was Red Shirt, front and foremost, smiling broadly, wearing the garment that gave him his name. As far as Sam knew, it was the only shirt among the Mojaves, and worn only on state occasions. The Mojave men wore only loincloths, and the women only short skirts of bark.

Sam was not glad to see Red Shirt, not after he stole Gideon's wife a year ago. But it was Sam's job as *segundo* to stay with Diah, see how he handled things, learn what to do. Diah wanted Sam to be a brigade leader soon. Also, Sam had a knack for communicating with Indians, in sign language or even gestures and grunts.

Alongside Red Shirt was Francisco, the Mojave who had been to the Spanish settlements near the ocean and knew some Spanish. Behind these two stood three other leaders.

"Buenas tardes," said Francisco. *"Bienvenido, Capitán! Bienvenido, White Hair!"*

Sam's hair had been straw-colored, almost white for all of his twenty-two and a half years. He said, *"Gracias. ¿Como esta ustedes?"*

Francisco extended his hand to Sam and then to the captain, showing that he remembered this white-man nicety. When they shook, Red Shirt grinned broadly. His entire face was elaborately tattooed with dots in vertical lines. When he grinned, the lines queered their way into strange curves. Sam didn't know if the dots were supposed to make a picture or pattern, but he knew the effect when the mouth curled the lines—it gave Sam the willies.

Francisco had a simpler tattoo.

Neither Sam nor Francisco spoke fluent Spanish, so they now resorted to gestures and single words to settle the rest. Sam laboriously asked permission for the brigade to trade and to rest its horses. Francisco translated into Mojave. Red Shirt said the people of the village were glad to give their hospitality to its friends, the men who hunted the beaver.

Now Red Shirt spoke what was probably his only word of Spanish. *"Bienvenido,"* he said, grinning. The grin made his tattoos squirm like snakes.

Captain Smith waved to the rest of the brigade to come forward.

"¿Bienvenido? Welcome to what?" said Sam in English.

"Maior risus, acrior ensis," said Hannibal. The Mage liked to say things in Latin.

"What does that mean?" asked Sam.

"The bigger the smile, the sharper the knife."

THE TWENTY-ONE TRAPPERS and two Indian women set up camp hastily on an open spot by the river they used for a campground last year. Just upstream of them was the circle of brush huts, several hundred of them, that made up the village. All around them were the vegetable fields of the Mojaves. The Indians planted close to the river, and rises in the Colorado irrigated the crops.

Last autumn, when they arrived in much poorer condition, the brigade stayed two weeks with the Mojaves to rest their horses and put some meat back on their ribs. On the men's ribs too—they traded for corn, beans, melons, pumpkins, everything the Mojaves had to eat. Then the trappers had known them as the Amuchabas. Now they thought of them as the Mojaves, the name for them in the Spanish settlements, and the name of the desert that faced all who would travel on to California, as this brigade intended to do.

The captain walked off to trade for corn, beans, and some of the bread the Mojaves made from the honey locust bean.

The other trappers rigged the camp. They unpacked and unsaddled the horses, led them to the river for water, and then penned them in a rope corral. They set up, laid out bedrolls, and put their possibles in the tents.

"Want to put a guard on the horses?" Hannibal asked Sam.

"Only at night." These Indians could be trusted. Sam and Hannibal, however, kept their personal mounts, Paladin and Ellie, staked by their tent.

Exhausted, as he seemed to be the whole trip, Sam propped himself against a cottonwood and napped. Coy curled up against his thigh.

"Garden sass!" said Hannibal, shaking Sam awake.

Sam got up and stepped to the low fire. Everyone gathered around and boiled and roasted the vegetables.

"Never thought I'd get tired of meat," Silas Gobel said, chomping down on an ear of corn. Though the Indians ground their corn dry, the trappers liked to boil it and then grouse that it didn't taste as good as sweet corn.

"That dried meat is *dry*," said Polette Labross. Everyone called him Polly. They'd had nothing else to eat from the Salt Lake all the way down through the redrock country to the banks of the Colorado River, dried meat and not enough water.

"Even my pecker is dry," said Gobel. He gave a sly smile. "But not for long around here."

"Sailors on the loose in port!" said Bos'n Brown.

Last year the Mojave women were as eager as the vagabond trappers. Sam thought, *I won't be partaking.*

"Bitterness bites the man who puts it on his tongue," said Hannibal.

Sam shot him a glance. *Reading my thoughts again. Are they scrawled across my face like words?*

He looked around the fire. Friends all, and he was damned glad to have them. When you rode the mountains and plains and deserts, your friends saved your life, and you saved theirs.

Coy looked at the boiled corn, boiled beans, and bread. He whapped his tail on the ground. He whined.

"He wants a blood sacrifice," said Hannibal.

Sam had gotten an education from following Hannibal's sayings. Maybe some day he'd get Hannibal to teach him to read and write. He fished in his possible sack and tossed Coy a little dried meat.

These five men gathered to eat and sleep together every evening, for no particular reason other than they liked each other. Sam was a Pennsylvania backwoodsman; Gobel, a king-sized blacksmith; Bos'n, a man who'd spent his life at sea; Polly, a grizzled mulatto; Hannibal, a man of mixed blood, white and Delaware Indian.

Trappers were always a jumble of races. Sam liked that. Among the Frenchies and their Indian wives you might hear French, Iroquois, Cree, Shoshone, and English oddly mixed in one or two sentences.

Captain Smith was odd himself. On the one hand he was a book-learned Yankee who carried a Bible and nearly wore it out with reading. On the other hand, most of the trappers thought he was the smartest, toughest man in the West. No leader was more respected. He'd been Sam's first brigade captain, and their bond was strong.

Sam thought the most intriguing man of the lot was Hannibal McKye. Since his father was a classics professor at Dartmouth College and his mother a Delaware, Hannibal grew up speaking two languages. He learned to read not only animal tracks but Greek and Latin. He could discuss Greek philosophy, Caesar's wars, and Shoshone beadwork. To top it all off, he worked in the circus and learned their horse tricks. It was partly his wizardry with horses that made the men call him the Mage.

Sam and Hannibal had crossed trails from time to time on the plains and in the mountains, but they'd never traveled together until now. Hannibal wanted to see California. Sam had a reason to go back, a reason that was very good and very bad.

"I need sleep," said Sam. He walked to the river, filled his hat with water, and took it to Paladin. The mare looked strong for this stage in the trip. She was a fine-looking Indian pony, white with a black cap around the ears, a black blaze on the chest, and black mane and tail. The Crows called this kind of pony a medicine hat.

When she'd lapped the crown of the hat dry, he led her out of the rope corral and staked and hobbled her on some good grass near his bedroll. Since she was specially trained, he kept her close every night.

He lay down on his blankets, looked at the stars, and then let his eyes blur. His bones sagged into the ground. Coy lay beside Sam's head, as always.

Maybe it's just the trip, he thought. *Maybe a few days' rest . . .*

This journey had been so much easier than last year's. Both times they left rendezvous in mid July. Last year they got to the Mojave villages in early November, this year in mid August. The difference was knowing the route and where they could find water. When they got here last year, half the horses were dead and the men were gaunt. This year the horses were gaunt but alive and the men were fine.

Except Sam. He thought about tomorrow's task, which he didn't look forward to. Then he let himself picture the reason he was going back to California.

Esperanza, my daughter.

"Spark!"

The woman looked up from weeding the pumpkins.

As Sam approached, a quirk twisted her face. No, she wasn't glad to see him.

"I'm glad to see you," he said, walking forward.

Francisco tagged along. It was like Sam had two pets, Coy and the Mojave interpreter.

"What you want, Sam?" she said with a gleam in her eyes.

So she was turning it into a flirtation. Spark was no one's

idea of a romantic figure. She looked a bride's well-used older sister. Her face was a little mashed, her bare breasts were narrow and pointy, and she now sported the Mojave look—a tattooed chin. Five parallel lines curved from her mouth to under her jawbone, with some sideways squiggles. The Shoshone woman had declared herself Mojave.

"Just to say hello." He squatted. So did Francisco and Coy, and after a moment Spark. She had decent English from her three months with the brigade last summer and fall.

He broke a slab of dried meat into three pieces length-wise, gave one each to Spark and Francisco, and ate. Meat of any kind was a treat for the Mojaves.

"Thought you might want news of Gideon."

She gave a flirty wiggle of her eyebrows.

He was tickled, thinking, *It's not going to work, lady.*

They looked at each other, munching, waiting. He decided to change the subject to her new man.

"How is Red Shirt?"

"He is good man. Big man." Sam wondered how many wives he had. With the Mojaves' fields of crops, at least Spark wouldn't go hungry.

Sam nodded to himself. Out with it. "You broke Gideon's heart."

"I am woman. Put man's moccasins outside lodge when I want."

Sam stared at her, thinking, *You barely let his moccasins inside.*

She'd been a slave in the Ute camp at Utah Lake when they found her. Jedediah bought her, and as the brigade journeyed south, she and Gideon fell in love. Or so everyone thought, and Gideon thought. They'd shared a lodge for a couple of weeks—married, in the fashion of the country.

Then, when the brigade started west across the Mojave Desert, she slipped off and joined Red Shirt's family.

First Gideon had nearly lost his life. Did lose his leg. And then the one-legged man lost his new wife. He dived into despair.

"He's doing well now," Sam said.

She concentrated on the meat, which took a lot of chewing.

"He became an artist in California." He realized she wouldn't know what "artist" meant, and probably didn't care either. "He makes very beautiful earrings and necklaces from gold and silver and turquoise and shells." That should impress her.

She looked at him proudly. "I make baby."

She didn't have a child on a blanket or a cradle on her back. Then Sam realized. The stiff bark of Mojave women's skirts always stuck out behind, a little comically. Spark's also stuck out in front. Her belly was bulging.

The name came like a pang. *Esperanza* . . .

Sam tried to remember. Was Spark with Gideon's child, or Red Shirt's? Did it matter?

She looked at him with huge satisfaction.

"You broke his heart," he said.

She waited a moment and said, "Thank you for the meat. Now I weed the pumpkins." She got up and walked away.

Sam and Francisco ambled back toward the trapper campground.

Francisco said in Spanish, "See Captain Smith?"

SAM THOUGHT FRANCISCO just wanted to cadge a present of some kind, but he had something else in mind. He sipped his hot coffee, grimaced, and said, *"¿No dulce?"*

Sam answered that the party had no sugar.

Between small sips of hot coffee Francisco slowly informed them that this past winter a band of Mexicans (Spaniards, he called them) and Americans had come from Nuevo Mexico down the Gila River and up the Colorado to these very villages.

Sam and Jedediah looked at each other. They had been first into this country, but not by much. Trapping brigades were heading west out of Taos and Santa Fe, they knew that, but they didn't know any had come this far.

"Find out if they crossed to California," Diah told Sam.

After more sips of coffee, Sam told the captain no.

"That's a relief." Jedediah wanted the California beaver country for his own company, Smith, Jackson & Sublette.

"Francisco says the trapping outfit took beaver from the Colorado and didn't want to pay for it. They quarreled and split up here. Some of them went up the Colorado River. He doesn't know where the others went."

Now Diah indulged one of his real passions. He got out the notebook where he wrote his journal and his maps. In the sand he drew the Colorado as it came down from the north to these villages. He got Francisco to draw it farther south, to the mouth of the Gila. The Yuma Indians lived around the mouth of the Gila, Francisco said, and Jedediah made a note. Then the interpreter drew the Gila coming in from the east, and where the Salt River flowed into it. But he didn't know where either river headed up. He said the Colorado emptied into the ocean several sleeps below the mouth of the Gila.

Jedediah copied the information from the map in the sand into his notebook and closed it with a smile.

THAT NIGHT THE men were boiling for a dance.

On the long trip south from rendezvous Sam had found a new musical partner—Polly Labross was a peach of a fiddler. A black man from Montreal and once a *voyageur,* Polly knew French-Canadian songs. Sam had learned to pipe the melodies on his tin whistle, and had even learned some lyrics in French.

The trappers moved up to some flat ground near the huts. When Polly started tuning the fiddle, Mojave women gathered to watch. Polly scraped out a verse of "Ah, Si Mon Moine Voulait Danser," and a dozen women crept close.

Sam played a second verse and chorus while Polly doublestopped harmony. Polly looked like a sly old dog, his hair mottled gray and his beard black, with a shape that seemed almost Chinese. His soft eyes hinted at a wisdom that embraced thousands of secrets he wouldn't tell.

"Let's go," hollered Bos'n Brown. He grabbed Gobel's arm and set out jigging. Gobel was Goliath, Bos'n a small and lithe David. Bos'n was a sassy fellow, quick with a quip. Now he took the woman's role—he hopped, he bounced, he swung his bottom like a girl's, he even jumped into the air. Gobel swung him 'round. They had a big time.

The Mojave women, remembering last year's affair, started dancing in place. The dance style of the fur men was nothing like their own, but they liked it.

Sam sang in a light, clear voice over Polly:

If my old top were a dancing man
A cap to fit I would give him then

chorus:
Dance old top, dance in
Oh, you don't care for dancing
Oh, you don't care for my mill la, la
Oh, you won't hear how my mill runs on

As Polly explained it to Sam, it was a tease. The dancers were asking a monk to join them. In every verse they tempted him with something different, a cap, a gown . . .

If my old top were a dancing man
A gown of serge I would give him then

In the next verse they tempted him with a Psalter, then a rosary, and so on, but the monk never danced, and they hooted at him.

No one gave a damn about this story, but the tune was lively.

Now Bos'n spun away from Gobel and held out his hand to one of the women. She grabbed hold, and around the circle they went, the woman . . .

It was Spark! She followed clumsily but eagerly.

Well, Sam reminded himself, he'd told Bos'n that she danced with several men last year, and went to the bushes with at least one, Red Shirt.

Polly jumped faster into the tune, and Sam took a break.

Other Mojave women joined in, and several men. Among them—surprise! Last year two teenagers had tried to steal Paladin, Skinny and Stout, Sam called them in his mind. He had gotten her back only by chasing them halfway across the river, and one nearly drowned under a cottonwood log beached on a sand bar. But Skinny and Stout were dancing now, and apparently having a good time.

A pretty woman held out her hand to Sam, smiling. She was smiling, and she said something in her language, probably asking him to dance.

He couldn't help looking lingeringly at her breasts. "No," he said.

She said whatever it was again, and reached out and fingered his hair. Women always seemed to like Sam's white hair.

"No," said Sam again, and took her hand away. He wished he wanted to touch a woman, hold a woman, lie down with a woman.

She turned to the next man without a hint of regret. It was Robiseau, one of the French-Canadians, and he whirled away with her. Sam thought of Robiseau as Merry One Tooth, for the number of dentures he had in the upper front, which he showed off in a perpetual lunatic grin.

When Merry One Tooth danced off, his wife glared after him. Then Red Shirt came up and motioned to her, and she danced off with the chief. Robiseau winked at her.

At least half the trappers now were bouncing along, and both trapper wives were dancing with Mojave men.

Polly changed the tune to a sea shanty, a slow capstan song that would give all the men a chance to ease the women close:

When Ham and Shem and Japhet, they walked the cap-
  stan 'round,
Upon the strangest vessel that was ever outward bound,
The music of their voices from wave to welkin rang,
As they sang the first sea shanty that sailors ever sang.

"Don't you want to dance?" said Hannibal.

"Think I'll turn in," said Sam. *Away from temptation,* he thought, *and with my memories.*

"Sure."

As Hannibal disappeared into the darkness, Sam wondered if his friend wanted a woman. Probably so. Even magicians liked sex.

He stretched out on his blankets, reached to where he knew Coy would be, and scratched the coyote's head. In the dark, when he couldn't see, the smell and sound of the river were stronger. He remembered the brute force of its current—pound and splash, spin and suck. Its whirlpools pulled him to its bottom and to sleep.

SAM LOOKED AT his arms, which were all scratched up. Sweat was running into the scratches—the August sun felt like coals in a woodstove. He frowned across at Hannibal, who grinned. Hannibal's arms were probably worse than Sam's.

They were standing ankle deep in the river cutting more cane for the two rafts. It took a lot of float power to carry twenty-three people and their cargo across the swift, turbulent Colorado. This gear included barrels for water, blacksmith tools, tomahawks, traps, kegs of gunpowder, and much more. There were the trade goods for Indians. And the trappers bore their own gear. A typical man had a rifle, a butcher knife, two horns for powder, a blanket, an extra pair of moccasins, and a pouch containing a bar of lead, a tool for making the lead into balls, a patch knife, a fire-striker, char cloth, and so on, altogether another ten percent of his body weight.

Sam and Hannibal shouldered the last loads of cane on both shoulders and labored upstream along the bank. When they got to where the other men were binding the cane into the rafts, they dumped their loads and sagged onto the ground.

Coy mewled. He often seemed to pity men doing hard labor.

The Mojaves were gathered around to see the trappers off. Red Shirt was there, Francisco, Skinny and Stout, Spark, seemingly most of the village, hundreds of men, women, and children. Partly, Sam supposed, they wanted to see how the trappers built a cane raft. With trappers working and calling to each other and Mojaves talking, everything was hubbub.

"Captain," called Sam. Smith looked around. Whenever Sam addressed Diah in an official way, he called him by title. "Hannibal and me, we'll swim over with the horses."

"You?" Jedediah asked at large, "Who's a strong swimmer?"

"Me!" said Hannibal and Virgin at once.

Tom Virgin was old, Sam guessed probably in his forties, but he was tough and strong. Sam liked him.

"Hannibal, Virgin, ride the river with the horses."

"Captain, I'm sticking with Paladin."

Smith looked at Sam and knew his *segundo* wouldn't be denied. "All right, three of you. Sam, hang on to that horse."

"Let's go," said Hannibal. All thirty-some-odd mounts, including Paladin and Ellie, were rope-corralled a hundred paces downstream.

"Hold on," said Diah. He was looking across the river. "You feel sure of hitting that sand bar?"

"It'll work," said Sam.

The trappers would set out in the rafts and pole across. The current would bear them downstream. Remembering last year, Jedediah and Sam figured they would float about as much down the river to the bar as across it. They allowed a good margin for error.

Now the first raft was loaded—eight trappers plus the captain and half their gear.

Sam, Hannibal, and Virgin started downstream to run the horses into the river. Coy tagged along.

"Wait!" said Sam. He ran to the raft that was still on the bank and lashed the rifle his father had left him, The Celt, to the bundle of rifles there. Most of the men had wrapped their rifles in canvas and tied them to this second raft. This rifle was important to Sam. It was the only memento he had of his father, Lew Morgan.

"Me too," Hannibal and Virgin said together. A man swimming the Colorado didn't want something as heavy as a rifle in his hands. Hannibal roped both rifles in.

Off the three hurried down to the river.

"Push off!" cried Jedediah.

Coy barked once in the direction of the raft and scooted after Sam and Hannibal.

The trappers on the raft shoved hard against the bank with their long poles, and the raft surged into the river. The current grabbed them hard. The raft spun in a full circle, making some of the men fall down. Everyone laughed. A big wave lifted the raft, and it dropped down the back side with a belly-sucking lurch. Men made whoopsy noises.

At that moment all the Mojave men yelled fiercely and attacked the ten men left on the bank.

The first blows whisked through the air. Two men got pincushioned, others were wounded here and there.

Spears were hurled. Polly Labross went down with a shaft through his chest, blood gouting from his mouth onto his gray beard.

Warriors rushed in and struck with spears and knives.

Silas Gobel was slashed by at least two knives but roared, picked a man up, and threw him at the other treacherous warriors.

Mojaves ran into nearby brush and came out brandishing war clubs.

Several trappers got off shots with their pistols—the rifles were lashed to the beached raft—but the Mojaves swarmed on them.

Jedediah and eight other men watched in horror from the river. It was like seeing ants rush onto a dying mouse.

The current yanked them relentlessly downstream. "Pole, damn it!" yelled Jedediah. He set an example.

The trappers had been gaping at the attack. Now they stuck their poles deep into the water, found the bottom, and shoved.

Two men pushed upstream.

"We can't go against the current," shouted Jedediah. "Pole for the other side!"

They did, hard.

From a hundred paces downstream Sam, Hannibal, and Virgin, armed with only their pistols and butcher knives, sprinted back to their comrades. Coy ran ahead of them, growling and yowling. Sam saw Bos'n Brown fall, and two Mojaves pounced on him. Robiseau staggered out of the melee, his back sprouting arrows.

Before they were halfway back, a score of armed Mojaves ran toward Sam, Hannibal, and Virgin.

Coy turned and dashed the other way.

Sam fired, and a man dropped.

Hannibal fired.

Suddenly everything was chaos.

A capricious wind whipped up a dust devil. Sand and smoke swirled around the trappers.

Warriors ran into the dark pall, screaming and swinging war clubs.

Virgin went down, his skull bloodied.

"Run!" yelled Hannibal.

Sam and Hannibal sprinted toward the horses, a dozen Mojaves after them.

Sam thought, *I'm dead*.

He ran like hell and caught Hannibal and got half a step on him. Coy fell in with them.

Suddenly, out of the brush downstream, the horses stampeded. Three or four Mojaves ran behind, driving them.

Salvation! thought Sam.

He put his fingers to his mouth and gave a loud, piercing whistle, rising low to high.

Hannibal did the same, looping from high to low and back twice.

Paladin and Ellie cut out of the herd and ran toward Sam and Hannibal.

Thank God! Sam's mind screamed.

The herd followed Paladin and Ellie. "Hallelujah!" shouted Sam.

When Paladin got close, Sam grabbed her mane and swung up bareback. Hannibal did the same on Ellie.

Sam saw Virgin staggering toward the river alone, holding his bleeding head in both hands. Coy ran toward the old man, then pivoted and came fast after Sam.

An arrow caught Paladin. She fell, and Sam pitched over her head.

Hooves rat-a-tat-tatted all around him. Dust and horse manure flew everywhere. Coy poised himself and yipped furiously at the horses pounding by.

A sharp edge slashed Sam's hip.

He whirled and swung his fist.

The Mojave jumped back, cocking his spear. It was Stout, who had the face of a snake.

Sam grabbed his butcher knife and thrust forward.

Stout slammed his spear into Sam's wrist.

The butcher knife went flying.

Stout grinned in triumph.

Sam grabbed his empty pistol and threw it at Stout's head. Stout ducked and the pistol sailed by. Stout laughed.

Yes, you bastard, I'm disarmed.

Sam fingered his trick belt buckle. Coy barked furiously at Stout.

Sam smiled. "Right. Hey," he told Stout out loud in English, "look what I'm doing." He jerked at the buckle, and his breechcloth dropped.

Stout's eyes darkened at the insult. He bounded forward.

Coy launched himself at the warrior's groin. Somehow Stout thrust the spear.

Sam spun.

The point nipped his ribs.

When Sam came full circle, he crowded inside the spear point. His belt buckle had turned into a steel blade in his hand, and he drove it into Stout's belly.

He jerked it out, looked at the blood, picked up his breechcloth, and wiped the blade.

Stout sat down hard and loose.

Sam looked with satisfaction at his glassy eyes.

Coy gave a last bark and snipped at Stout's face.

"Thanks, Gideon," he said.

His friend had smithed him a dagger with a belt buckle as a handle. Sam slid the blade back into his belt, deep, fastened the buckle, and put his breechcloth back on.

He walked over and picked up his pistol. Since The Celt was lost, the pistol was essential. He looked around. The herd had run off toward the hills, and the Mojaves were chasing them. *Thirty horses,* he thought. A huge triumph for them.

Where was Hannibal? Sam didn't know. If he could, Hannibal would have led the herd into the river. Where was Paladin? With the herd. Injured.

All right, no Mojave was close. A grove of cottonwoods marked the bank. Sam loped toward the water, Coy bounding alongside. He hit the top of the bank in stride and made a long, flat dive.

The river was a turmoil. Waves slapped him in the face. They rolled him over. Suck holes grabbed at his legs.

He flailed at the water with his arms, he kicked at it with his feet. He fought the goddamn water. He battered it. He punished it. The river laughed and tossed him up and caught him. It jerked him under and let him up.

Sam whacked at the river with arms and legs.

Long minutes later, minutes he couldn't remember, a mewling woke him up. Coy, he realized. Consciousness picked at his brain.

A hand touched him. He opened his eyes. Hannibal. They were on the far bank.

"I'm checking your wounds."

He prodded at the gash in Sam's hip and the slice along his ribs.

"You'll be fine."

"Where's Paladin?"

"Don't know."

"Where's Ellie?"

"Dead. Let's get up to the others."

"Dead!"

Hannibal pulled Sam to his feet. "The ass cut Ellie's throat. I cut his."

They stumbled upstream, splashing in the shallows, feet sinking into the sand bars. Pictures invaded Sam's mind, images of the handsome stallion lying on the sand, neck pumping out blood. Then he thought of Paladin and wondered how her hindquarter was. His blood prickled.

Around a couple of bends stood Captain Smith and eight other men. Diah was looking across the river with his field glass. The trappers looked at each other with the bright knowledge of mortality in their eyes.

Diah lowered his field glass. Sam could hardly hear his words. "They're all dead." Sam looked across the river. Hundreds of Mojaves milled around. From this distance he could make out no one in particular. He pictured Red Shirt's face, Francisco's face, Spark's. *What in hell* . . .

"Why?" said Diah.

No one answered. These Indians were friendly last autumn. Why?

They looked at each other, mute and afraid.

Now the captain's voice of command came back. "Let's get out of here."

Chapter Two

Though they'd lost half their equipment, without horses they couldn't carry even what was left. They stared bitterly at the gear. The captain put their food in his own possible sack, fifteen pounds of dried meat—that was all they had to eat. Then he filled his sack with trade goods for Indians, beads, ribbon, cloth, and tobacco. He grabbed several traps. His possible sack got heavy.

He told the other men that they had to walk a dozen sleeps in blazing heat. Considering that, they should take whatever they wanted. "This was company property. Now it's your property."

Sam looked at Diah's sack and considered. Eleven men, fifteen pounds of meat, twelve sleeps (if they were lucky), that didn't add up. And there was no game out there.

Five men still had their rifles. Sam grabbed the single tomahawk and held it high. He knew how to throw one. *My anger will make it a vicious weapon.*

He barely paid attention to what the others picked up. Knives seemed to go first, then traps, then bridles, in hopes of getting horseflesh. Last, they picked up more items for the Indians. These men had learned a hard practicality about that.

When each man had the load he wanted to carry across the Mojave Desert, Jedediah said, "Scatter the rest across the sand. Tempt them."

They did. The thought of savages boiling over this equipment fevered the brain of every man. There was no point in asking how soon they would be here.

"Drink your fill," said Jedediah. "We have only one kettle to carry water with."

The men flopped onto the sand and sucked up all the river they could. Coy did the same. Sam refused to think of what it meant, starting across the Mojave with no water casks and only one kettle.

They started walking west.

"They know where we're headed," said Jedediah. "We have to get to that first spring."

The men chewed on that. They looked around at the barren country. Desert scrub, desert scrub, desert scrub, and no place to hide.

Fragments of ugly reality spun through their heads. The screams of their dead friends. The flash of knife, the silhouette of arm-cocked spear. The mud made by blood in the dust. The thump of human bodies on the sand.

They tramped. They waded through grief. They looked slyly toward their own deaths, which lay ahead.

Only Coy kept his head perked up.

After a few minutes Hannibal said, "You know why older women are better in bed than young ones?"

Sam was stupefied.

Hannibal went on, "Ben Franklin wrote this. I'm going to quote it."

"Hannibal!" complained Sam.

"Go ahead, Mage," said two or three voices.

"'In your amours you should prefer old women to young ones. This you call a paradox, and demand my reasons. They are these: One—because they have more knowledge of the world, and their minds are better stored with observations; their conversation is more improving, and more lastingly agreeable.'"

"Conversation," someone mimicked.

"'Two—because when women cease to be handsome, they study to be good. To maintain their Influence over man, they supply the diminution of beauty by an augmentation of utility. They learn to do a thousand services, small and great, and are the most tender and useful of friends when you are sick. Thus they continue amiable. And hence there is hardly such a thing to be found as an old woman who is not a good woman.'"

"I've knowed some wasn't good," said Isaac Galbraith. He was a Herculean man with a strong Maine accent.

" 'Three,' " Hannibal barged forward. " 'Because there is no hazard of children, which irregularly produced may be attended with much inconvenience.' "

"Sacre bleu," said Toussaint Marechal, "can you no speak straight out?"

" 'Four,' " persisted Hannibal, " 'because through more experience they are more prudent and discreet in conducting an intrigue to prevent suspicion. The commerce with them is therefore safer with regard to your reputation, and regard to theirs; if the affair should happen to be known, considerate people might be inclined to excuse an old woman, who would kindly take care of a young man, form his manners by her good counsels, and prevent his ruining his health and fortune among mercenary prostitutes.' "

"Zis *hivernant* me," said Joseph LaPoint, "I take whatever come." *Hivernant* was Frenchy talk for an experienced wilderness hand. LaPoint was called Seph by everyone.

"Godawmighty, Hannibal!" said Sam.

"This is good," the captain said softly to Sam.

Sam shut up. He noticed, though, that Jedediah was keeping a very sharp eye out.

" 'Five,' " said Hannibal, " 'because in every animal that walks upright, the deficiency of the fluids that fill the muscles appears first in the highest part. The face first grows lank and wrinkled; then the neck; then the breast and arms; the lower parts continuing to the last as plump as ever . . .' "

"We're turning around," interrupted Jedediah.

He wheeled and headed back to the river at a trot. Every man followed him close. "The Mojaves are coming," Diah said quietly to Sam.

They would have a better chance in the cover of trees along the river.

WHEN THEY GOT to the river alive, they eyed each other as though sharing a secret joke. In a grove of cottonwoods they felled small trees, grumbling that they had to use knives, since Sam wielded the only tomahawk. They made a flimsy breastwork from these poles. Then, waiting, men began to lash their butcher knives to the ends of light poles, making lances.

No need to speak about the situation. Only five of them had rifles. Sam and Hannibal had pistols, useful only at short range. Since they got their powder horns soaked swimming the river and there wasn't time to dry it, the other men gave them powder. Three men had no weapons but the lances. The river protected the trappers' backs, but the Indians could attack from three directions. They would probably outnumber the trappers fifty to one. More than one trapper pictured the Indians' hands still dripping red with the blood of their comrades.

Sam said to himself several times, "Make them pay." That's all the defenders could get for their lives.

As he worked, he thought of other reasons to make them pay. The bastards had The Celt. They had Paladin. Probably Skinny would try to keep Paladin, but Red Shirt would claim her for himself, because of the wonderful tricks she could do, the routines Sam and the Mage had taught her. Sam grimaced. The chief wouldn't know how to signal Paladin to perform, and wouldn't understand why she didn't.

On the other hand, Paladin wouldn't get the fun of doing the circus routines again.

"Let me see those wounds," Hannibal said.

Sam turned his hip to his friend (this was the convenience of wearing just a breechclout), then raised his shirt to show the ribs.

Hannibal fingered both of them. "Tonight I'll put poultices on them."

Sam grinned at him. *Tonight—that's optimistic.*

"What's that blood on your belly?"

"A Mojave's." Sam whipped out the belt-buckle knife and mock-pointed it at Hannibal. "Gideon made this for me, said it was thanks for amputating his leg." The two friends held each other's eyes a moment.

Sam snapped the knife back into its belt buckle guise, and flashed it out again. "Easy to get out."

Hannibal inspected it. The blade was the sheathed part, fashioned in the double-edged style of a dagger and very sharp.

"So you have two secret blades," said Hannibal, fingering it. They each had a knife concealed as a hair ornament. "You ought to wash the blood off."

Sam thought about the stabbing, about Stout, and about his dead friends on the far bank. "No, I'll keep it for a while."

Coy barked. Head to tail he pointed toward the river behind them.

Five rifles trained on the brush in that direction.

"Hey!"

The voice came from the riverbank. Every man looked down his sights or held his lance in that direction.

"Hey!"

"That's English!" said Hannibal.

Thomas Virgin's half-bald head peeped out of the bushes. It was still bleeding.

Sam ran forward and supported the old man. His shiny head sported a lump nearly the size of a fist. The wound was still trickling blood. Sam remembered he'd been clubbed. A stone war club could do a lot of damage, often fatal damage.

Virgin was soaked, and he'd lost everything. His britches were gone (he preferred those to a breechcloth), his shot pouch was gone, his belt, his knife, and his belt pouch were gone. He lost his knife and pistol. The old man was nothing but flesh, moccasins, and a torn cloth shirt.

"I dropped ever'thing in the river, one by one," he said.

"You wouldn't have made it otherwise," said Hannibal. He and Sam helped Virgin up to the breastwork.

How had the old man made it? Sam wondered. The sight of him lifted his spirits. But it wouldn't for long.

Coy sniffed Virgin like he was something alien.

"Everyone keep watch," said the captain.

"The next voice won't be English," someone muttered.

The men eyed each other surreptitiously.

Five minutes ticked by. Ten. The men spent it by cutting brush and stuffing it into the breastwork. It wouldn't do much, but . . .

LaPoint said in a quavery voice, "Can we do it, Captain?"

Marechal snickered.

"Captain?" echoed someone else.

Sam grimaced. The men wouldn't ask if their blood wasn't running chill.

"We'll drive them off," said Jedediah.

His voice was calm, firm. Sam was amazed. He and the captain looked at each other, and Sam saw that Diah knew better. Knew for sure.

He and Diah had nearly died on the Missouri when the Rees fired down on them on an unprotected beach. Most of the men stayed on that beach forever. Diah and Sam and a few others escaped.

They almost died together just three months ago, crossing the salt waste from the California mountains to the Salt Lake. Bashed by heat and weakened by thirst, they actually buried themselves in the sand. But they rose from those graves and walked.

Sam said to himself, *Every man's luck runs out.*

Jedediah glassed an area south in the brush, then let the glass hang from the lanyard around his neck. Sam looked carefully and saw them even with the naked eye. Yes, the Indians were coming.

"Rifles, spread out across the breastwork."

Galbraith, Marechal, Swift, and Turner placed themselves where they could shoot in three directions.

"I'll call the fire," said Smith. "We'll always keep two rifles in reserve. I'll name two men, and those only fire."

The riflemen nodded. "Under no circumstances empty all rifles at once."

Coy stood stiff, facing south. He heard or smelled the enemy.

Sam's hands felt ridiculous without The Celt. Hannibal

looked as edgy as he felt. Sam wished he and Hannibal had Swift's and Turner's rifles. Ike Galbraith was a great shot—he could knock the heads off blackbirds at twenty paces. Marechal was a good hunter. But Sam wasn't sure of Swift and Turner. *Goddammit! I'm the one to defend my own life!*

Indians showed themselves now, defiantly standing in the open and then ducking back.

"Galbraith, Marechal, ready," said Jedediah.

The shooters trained their sights on whatever targets they could. It was a long shot, over a hundred paces, but there was no wind. Four Mojaves were visible.

"Fire!"

Two Mojaves dropped. A third grabbed himself, perhaps wounded, and started running away.

A dozen Mojaves ran away. A score. A hundred.

Several hundred Indians bolted from cover and streaked away from the trappers, scurrying around rocks, bounding up hillocks. Their hide loincloths flounced in the afternoon sun.

"Rabbits!" called Hannibal.

"Rabbits!" yelled the other men. "Rabbits!"

The trappers stood up and shook their fists in the air. They clapped each other on the back.

"Sum bitch!" yelled one.

"We done it!" yelled another.

"*Victoire!*"

"Zey are tinned cowards!" cried Marechal.

Diah and Hannibal looked at each other, and everyone at them. They shrugged and started laughing.

"Tinned?" said Hannibal, slapping his thighs.

"Tinned cowards!" hollered Sam, shaking his fist.

They all took up the cry. "Tinned cowards!" They stumbled around like they were drunk. They embraced each other.

Everyone celebrated but poor Tom Virgin, who was unconscious.

"All right!" said the captain loudly. "Get a drink from the river and get back here! This might not be over!"

But it was. The trappers waited, alert, until nearly dark.

Jedediah got Virgin awake and spoke soft words to him. Virgin struggled to his feet.

"Let's go," said the captain.

They marched through the night hungry and thirsty.

"Better than during the day," said Sam.

"Better than being dead," said Hannibal.

Sam kept an eye on Virgin. The wounded man weaved as he walked, but he managed to go slowly, steadily forward.

The trail was an old one, worn by long years of trading with people of the seashore. The Mojaves wanted the shells of the sea, and the coastal peoples wanted Mojave melons, pumpkins, corn, squash, and beans. The captain and Sam had ridden the stretch three times last fall, the first being a false start. It wasn't a hard trek, even in the dark.

Sam knew, though, that the sands blew, and blew, and signs of the trail would be wiped away in some places, perhaps for miles. Parties steered by landmarks of hills and mountains, which were murky and deceptive at night.

His spirits were low. As he tramped, he talked to himself.

We've got no way to carry water, said the nervous part of himself, and added mockingly, *one kettle.*

Gonna be parched all day, every day, said some other part. This part was more relaxed.

What if we miss a spring? said Nervous.

What if? said Relaxed.

We've got about one day's supply of food.

Shining times, answered Relaxed.

Ten- or fifteen-day trip, said Nervous, starving.

That's how I remember it too.

We've lost all our horses and nearly every damn thing.

Hallelujah!

Tom Virgin's going to slow us down.

Or he may die.

Why are you so easy about it?

Just crazy, I guess.

The outfit came to the spring before the sun got hot the next morning. They drank. They ate a little meat, very little. Because the August sun would get blistering hot, they stayed by the spring all day. Mostly they slept in the shade of bushes or rocks. For an hour in midafternoon Jedediah worked on his journal.

When he finished, Sam moved next to him. "What did you write?" As a brigade leader in training, Sam wanted to know.

"First, what happened when we pushed off into the river, and the names of the men who died." Diah looked at his own page. "'Silas Gobel.'" Sam and Diah looked at each other. Gobel was one of the companions buried in the blazing sands two months ago. He rose up from that death only to walk blind into another.

"'Henry "Boatswain" Brown,'" Jedediah read on, "'Polette Labross (a mulatto), William Campbell, David Cunningham, Francois Deromme, Gregory Ortago (a Spaniard), John Ratelle, John Relle (a Canadian), Robiseau (a Canadian half-breed).'"

A checklist of slaughter. Sam took a big breath in and out.

"Next, a list of the men still with me." Sam could see the ten men around him—aside from Sam and Hannibal, Galbraith, Marechal, Virgin, Turner, Swift, LaPoint, Daws, and Palmer.

"Then an account of how we drove them off at the riverbank."

"Read it to me."

"Here's part of it. 'We survivors with but five guns were awaiting behind a defense made of brush the charge of four or five hundred Indians . . . Some of the men asked me if we would be able to defend ourselves. I told them I thought we would. But that was not my opinion.'"

The captain and his *segundo* looked each other in the eye. Hannibal walked over and sat close. Coy lay down against Sam's thigh.

"A wise man learns his letters, my friend," the magician told Sam.

"Yeah."

"A brigade leader needs a record," Jedediah said.

"That's what a clerk is for," said Sam. He didn't add that he wasn't eager to be a brigade leader. Something about it bothered him.

The brigade's clerk, Harrison Rogers, was ahead in California. Meanwhile Jedediah kept the ledgers himself, company property sold or given away.

"Learn to read or not?" said Hannibal.

"Learn to read," said Sam, "some time." He turned to Diah. "So what are we going to do?"

"Go to the Californians."

"Damn." He looked at Hannibal. "Last year they practically jailed Jedediah because we didn't have passports. They told us we could go only if we hightailed it out the way we came and stayed gone."

Jedediah spoke up now. "We left coastal California by the same pass. Then we went to a desert the Spaniards haven't settled and north to some mountains they haven't approached. I don't think they have any honest claim to that country."

Hannibal nodded, understanding.

"We can't go straight to the brigade?" said Sam.

"We need horses, we need food, we need weapons, we need a lot of things. Father Joseph will help us."

"He's the head of San Gabriel Mission," Sam told Hannibal. He looked back at Diah. "And the governor may arrest your ass this time."

Jedediah gave a thin smile. "We'll be quick on our feet."

Sam frowned.

"Sam, I know you're anxious to get to Esperanza. We said we'd be there by September 20, and we will."

Sam walked off. He thought. He fretted. He looked down at Coy. He looked at Tom Virgin, who tumbled to the ground like a rag and slept every time they stopped.

Sam thought, *Life goes topsy-turvy into death.*

* * *

THAT NIGHT, WANDERING among the desert hills, Jedediah stopped the line of men. For a moment he looked around.

"You know where we are?"

"No," said Sam. They'd traveled this route only once, with guides, and in the daylight.

Everyone sat down. Some sprawled, and Virgin seemed to pass out. They'd trudged all night, zigzagging through creosote bushes, dipping down into dry washes and clambering up the other side, mounting hillocks and descending again onto flats that appeared infinite, but flexed irritatingly up and down. Now the captain doled out the liquid from their one kettle, a swallow at a time for each man except himself. "I'm used to going without," he said. He made Virgin sit up and take an extra swallow. That was the last drop.

"God, more water," said LaPoint.

"Balm of Gilead," said Hannibal.

"We're lost," said Jedediah.

That got their attention. The captain didn't know where the next spring was. Every man wondered if he would taste water again.

"Daybreak soon. Let's rest until then."

Coy whimpered. *He thinks this is ridiculous,* thought Sam. They stretched out. Some slept. Most couldn't.

At first light Jedediah said, "I'm going up that hill to spot the trail." There was the advantage of the field glass Diah carried.

A while after sunrise he was back. Sam could see the result in his face.

"I don't know. The trail goes on one side of that hill or the other, but I can't tell which."

The men were too tired to grouse.

"I want one man to go with me to look for water."

"I'll go," Sam and Hannibal said at the same time.

"No." He looked around. "Galbraith, come with me. That hill"—Jedediah pointed toward a much higher one—"that's the direction we need to go." It was the opposite direction of the rising sun. He pursed his lips, thinking. "If Galbraith and I don't come back, head that way. Sam, you're in charge. You'll recognize where the next spring is."

Sam let all this flap through his brain. *If Diah doesn't come back . . .* All right, the party had missed one spring and was hoping to hit the next one. If Sam could spot it.

"Understood."

Diah and Ike Galbraith walked off.

"I don't know if I've got any *move* left in me," said Hannibal.

"I'll carry you if you'll carry me."

They watched their friends disappear around a hill.

Sam studied Virgin, asleep, his mouth hanging open. The bulge in his skull looked terrible.

"All of us could easy die," said the Mage.

IN AN HOUR Galbraith was back, looking amazingly hearty.

"We found water. The captain's there sleeping."

"Zis man, my Ike, he has ze hair of ze bear inside him." This was Marechal.

"The water did it for me. Let's go. It's only gonna get hotter."

Sam roused Virgin and they tramped off.

The little spring was marked by a few bushes where fluid seeped from rocks at the bottom of a hill. Jedediah sat up as the outfit approached.

They were too dry to talk. Each man scooped a little water into his hands and slurped it up. The trickle was tiny, and they took a lot of time, one after another, filling their bellies with liquid. Waiting made them wild-cyed. Finally, they were lazing by the spring. They watered their stomachs over and over, and rubbed water onto their faces and arms and legs, and wadded their clothes up in the spring.

"We'll stay here today," said Jedediah. "Right now I'm going to climb that hill"—it was the highest in sight—"and look for the trail and the next spring."

Off he went.

"Hellacious almighty," said Galbraith, looking after the captain.

"We walk all night, no water," said Marechal.

Hannibal said, "We can't even piss."

"Jedediah walks up a hill and back by himself while we rest," said Sam, "and then he hikes off and finds water."

"Now," said Galbraith, "with me panting and desperate, he marches off to climb a big hill in the heat of the day."

"And he'll come back ready to walk tonight." Sam rolled onto his side to nap. "That's why he's the captain," he said.

THE CAPTAIN DID spot the trail in the glass, about five miles to the south, and he saw where the next spring was. That night he led the party straight across open desert, not bothering with the trail until they rejoined it at the spring. They rested there all day and all the next night. Jedediah rationed out a little dried meat, about a third of what a man needed for sustenance, every other day.

Sam was wondering if they could afford to rest, with food running out.

Marechal said under his breath to Sam, "Hardly no water, hardly no meat, no whiskey any, you *Americains* . . ."

The next day they trekked across the desert during the day. The heat was awful, but the risk of getting lost seemed worse. Jedediah remembered a shortcut pointed out by last year's guides, who thought it too stony for horses. Now they took it.

The sun hit them like a club. Every step was a struggle. They trudged, they wandered, they stumbled. Sam and Hannibal took Virgin by the elbows to steady him. All were too parched and too exhausted to utter one word of complaint.

Occasionally men got a little satisfaction by cutting off slices of cabbage pears and chewing on them. The juice was a blessing on the tongue, and when you chewed the fiber, you could pretend you were eating.

The men were disgruntled, discouraged, failing. Jedediah

boosted them continually with encouraging words. "It's not far now," he would say. Tramp, tramp, tramp on the sand. "There'll be a spring against the hill." Tramp, tramp, tramp. They stopped, and the captain glassed. "See the dark spot at the bottom of the hill there? Those are bushes, and bushes mean water."

Some men lifted their eyes and gazed blearily in the direction of the hill. Maybe someone saw the dark spot. No one mentioned the thousands of footsteps between here and the hill.

Late in the afternoon Virgin collapsed. Seph LaPoint plopped down beside him.

Smith bent over Virgin. "I'm done," he said. No more words came out.

"Me too," said LaPoint.

The captain studied them. Sam thought, *They don't have strength even for words . . .*

"Tom," said the captain, "you've soldiered this far. We all admire you." He looked back and forth from Virgin to LaPoint. "You've got grit. You'll both make it.

"Normally, I'd cover you with sand, keep you cooler, but we don't have any shovels." He thought. "Scoot into the shade of the greasewood here. When you can, dig in the sand with your hands. Make a shallow hole, get in it, and cover up."

LaPoint snickered.

"Seph, it's your job to dig for Tom and cover him."

LaPoint shrugged.

"Do it. Sam saved his own life this way."

"I will," rasped LaPoint. His voice sounded like a scrape on a washboard.

"I'll bring water."

They walked on. Sam's heart twisted at leaving, but he resisted looking back. The first time this happened, two months ago, he and Diah and Robert Evans left Silas Gobel behind. Gobel, who was now nothing but bones. The second time, Diah and Gobel had to go off and leave Sam and Evans. Both times Diah had found a spring, both times someone carried a kettle back, and both times the men were saved.

Sam checked the sky for buzzards. *I wonder if I'll have to see them circling over Virgin and LaPoint.*

Or these eight figures trudging across the Mojave Desert.

Just after sunset Diah led them to a spring.

"I'll go back," said Sam.

"Me too," said Hannibal.

Two men to carry one kettle, but Sam was glad of the company.

What a world, he thought, *where nightmares get to be routine.*

THAT NIGHT EVERYONE talked about the Inconstant River. Drank and talked and drank some more and talked about the Inconstant. Their thirst felt so wide and dry they didn't even miss food.

LaPoint wanted to know why it was called Inconstant.

Sam smiled and answered dryly, "Because the water disappears into the sands and then comes back up and disappears again."

"In lots of places you can dig for it," said Jedediah.

Sam held up his bare hands and looked at them. He said good-naturedly, "My hands are begging to dig."

The men chuckled. Anything for a chuckle, as downhearted as they felt.

"It flows out of the mountains to the west," Jedediah said. "One way or another, there's water steady enough up the river."

Sam added, "Last year there were Indians at the foot of the mountain. We traded with them."

"We can cross the mountain in two days," the captain said, "and we'll see deer."

Men slunk off to separate boulders and bushes to sleep. They didn't feel much like talking, didn't feel like company. Some were slipping off into a private place in their minds where they could die peacefully. Sam wondered whether Virgin would wake up in the morning.

He knew the men were bothered by a lot of things. They were starving. They were half-thirsting. Their bodies were wasting. If they traveled like this for long, they'd die, no question.

"I can tell you this," said Hannibal. "Death hath dominion here."

Sam shook off that thought. Something else was bothering him.

MOUNTAIN LUCK, THEY called it. Desert luck too, Sam supposed. Like mountain luck, it could be very good and very bad.

The river was drier than the year before. At first Sam was worried about water. But in the middle of that first day walking up the Inconstant, Hannibal spotted two horses.

The captain stopped the outfit and circled the mounts, looking for their owners. He found two lodges and eased up to them gently enough that the Indians didn't have a chance to run away. Paiutes, they said they were. He made them presents of some beads.

Then he brought the men up. The Paiutes trembled visibly, men, women, and children. Sam could see that every impulse was to run like hell, but they stayed. Slowly, Jedediah began to trade with them. He offered more beads, which pleased the women. He put out cloth, which thrilled them. He laid down a double handful of knives. In an hour or two he'd traded for both horses, some water pots, and big loaves of candy made from cane grass.

The brigade had this candy last fall. It was funny stuff, a loaf of sugar hard as a rock. You knocked off pieces with a tomahawk or your knife. Strange food, but the sweet tasted great and any nourishment helped.

The Paiutes told the trappers that the lodges of the Serranos were still at the foot of the mountain, where the river came out. All the beaver men were sitting in front of the Paiute lodges, sucking on chunks of candy.

"We'll be able to trade for food and horses there," Jedediah said with satisfaction. "The closer to the Spanish settlements, the easier to get horses."

Last year, Sam remembered, the Serranos made a rabbit drive through the desert, many hunters marching, and put on a feast for the trappers.

They loaded the horses, took their leave of the Paiutes, and resumed their march. The Serrano lodges were about three days ahead, and the horses, not the men, were the beasts of burden.

Sam looked carefully at the captain. Jedediah would never say it, but he was proud. His brigade had blundered into a disaster at the Mojave villages. Without water, without food, and without horses, he had brought them across the worst desert anyone had seen.

That night when they bedded down, they knew they were going to live.

First day up the Inconstant—the river was almost completely dry—but they had water in the pots. They found a standing pool to camp by. The men stripped and dunked their entire bodies in the liquid.

Second day, there was water enough in occasional places in the riverbed—they would have been fine even without the pots.

On the third day they walked into the cluster of lodges that made up the Serrano village. Their guides from last autumn weren't here, but the chiefs remembered the fur men well. Jedediah gave them presents, they gave the trappers dried rabbit meat.

The men fell on the meat like vultures. While the captain traded for two more horses, they gorged themselves. Then they napped and gorged themselves again. They lay down, slept, woke in the middle of the night, and filled their bellies once more. They acted ravenous and uproarious.

Sam ate as big as any man, and spent the night churning his mind about what he had to do. Every day this journey, going to California, bothered him. The only home he had, it wasn't here. And now things were about to get worse.

In the morning, while the captain was making sure of the hitches that held the gear and newfound food on the horses, Sam touched Jedediah on the shoulder. Smith turned to him.

"Diah, I have to go back."

"YOU WHAT?" THE captain's voice crackled.

Men were craning their necks to hear this conversation. Jedediah took Sam's elbow and moved off. Hannibal followed. Jedediah looked at him, hesitated, and then nodded.

"What are you talking about?"

"Paladin is back there. My father's rifle is back there. I can't walk away."

"You are second in command here. You have a responsibility."

Sam poked the dirt with a moccasin. "One to myself too."

"Sam, you can't do this."

"If I have to, I'll quit." He paused and added, "Sir," the first time he'd spoken that word to Jedediah in several years.

"It's too dangerous."

"It's risky."

"Water, food, you can't do it."

Sam just looked at him. They both knew the outfit had just done it.

"You giving up on Esperanza, Flat Dog, and Julia?"

Sam's daughter, Meadowlark's brother, and his wife. "Not a bit. I'll be along."

"Late."

"Yes."

Jedediah looked toward the horizon to the east, where they'd just walked, and said, "Let's sit."

They did. Sam barged ahead. "I'm going to trade my pistol." Sam pulled it out of his belt and put it in his lap. "The Serranos will give me what I need for it. I'll have more than we did coming across."

Jedediah huffed out a big breath. "You mean it."

"Yes."

So they worked it out. The captain and Sam would make the trade together, so the Serranos wouldn't know Sam was going off alone. Even friendly Indians could be tempted by the vulnerability of a lone man.

They got their choice of the herd for the pistol, several of Sam's .50-caliber balls, and a little powder. Hannibal picked out a brown gelding for Sam. "This is a hell of an animal," he said, "an athlete."

The men grinned at each other. The Serranos had owned horses, but probably not firearms. Not that one pistol would do much good. With these balls a man might learn to shoot, but he'd play the devil getting more ammunition.

Jedediah provided a couple of knives and some beads to get Sam a stack of dried meat. He gave Sam a pot to carry water.

"I mean to steal some vegetables from the Mojaves too," said Sam.

All three of them chuckled.

"You'll be two weeks behind," said Jedediah. They'd spent seven days crossing from the Mojave villages to here.

"Or less," said Sam.

"I'll have to go in to see the governor at Monterey," said Diah.

"If they don't arrest your ass at San Gabriel."

The Mexicans thought Americans were their enemies. Sam chuckled. What a laugh. Twenty fur men against the entire Mexican army.

"While I'm gone, I'll leave the brigade on the Appelaminy, right where they are."

"I'll catch up."

Jedediah twisted his straight, thin mouth and thought. Finally he said, "I'm going to lend you something." He slipped the lanyard over his head and handed Sam the field glass. "You'll need it more than me."

Sam's heart pinged a little. The glass was a big item to Jedediah, not only useful but a symbol of command. He thought of handing it back, but then thought of scouting the Mojaves. It would come in handy.

He said, "Thank you, Diah."

By midmorning the brigade was ready to go west, Sam itching to get started east. They parted ways well outside the village, so the Serranos wouldn't know.

There Hannibal sprang his surprise. "I'm going with you."

"No. No way. This is my job."

"Two are safer than one," said Hannibal.

"A lot safer," said Jedediah, who was known for his lone journeys in the wilderness.

"I want to go," said Hannibal.

"Nothing in it for you."

"You're my friend."

Sam slid up onto the unfamiliar brown gelding. "He was *my* father."

Off he rode, alone.

Chapter Three

At first light Sam lay in the shallows and dunked his face in the water. The Colorado. Hallelujah, praise be, the river. He drank when he felt like it. He craned his face back out of the water. He rolled over and wet his back side. He lolled and soaked himself.

Coy lapped at the edge and stayed back. Standing between man and coyote, the brown gelding slurped and slobbered and stamped and splashed all three of them. Sam had named the pony Brownie.

Sam had managed the return trip in five days, two less than coming over. Knowing the route and the springs, and having a waxing moon, he'd traveled long and hard every night. Resting during the day, neither he nor the horse sweated away so much water. Half the time he rode, and half he walked.

Sometimes he felt like loping alongside the horse, but he resisted. He needed all his strength, and the mount's. He thought he was a good plainsman, a good man in the mountains, and he was getting to be a good man in the desert.

He had about ten pounds of dried meat, and he ate a pound or so every day. Coy hunted mice and pack rats and devoured them. The grass near the springs was plenty for a single horse. The trip seemed easy, actually. Sam told himself it was easy because it was the right thing.

Now he had to get the job done.

For watering man and beasts, he'd carefully picked a spot blocked from the village by a river bend. Now he tied Brownie to a tree, crept through the willows, and glassed the collection of huts downstream. He sat and watched until the sun cleared the eastern horizon. He didn't want the sun to reflect off the lens and give him away. Keeping low, he walked back to his horse, scrunching up his mouth. He hadn't learned anything new.

Sam knew he could find the horses, which would be kept herded somewhere beside the river. He didn't know where The Celt was. That would take some scouting.

He pulled the horse's stake and walked upstream. Somewhere above and on this side he would sleep all morning. Later he would swim the river, drifting down with the current, and take a look around. He'd find the horses and scout the village. He'd look for Red Shirt too. Ten of Sam's friends had been murdered here, and Red Shirt was the chief.

SAM HAD TO laugh.

He lay on a ridge watching the horse herd. He was so close he didn't even need the glass. Today the horses were south of the village, between two hills that sloped to the river, where the critters could get to water. They were loose-herded now and would be close-herded at night. Every week or so they'd be moved because the desert grass was so scanty.

The Mojaves kept the horses well guarded because they

were enemies of the Yuma tribe, which lived downstream at the mouth of the Gila River.

Right now, Sam thought, *you boys got your eyes on the wrong enemy.*

He hadn't been worried about finding the horses, just his rifle. There were four or five hundred Mojave warriors. They'd stolen a baker's dozen rifles, but just one Celt. How would Sam ever find it?

Now he was grinning because the problem had just solved itself.

The Mojaves must be big on show.

Two guards were keeping an eye on the horses today, one tall and skinny like a reed, the other stocky, with a limp. And for no earthly reason those guards were carrying rifles. It made no sense. They wore no shot pouches, no powder horns. Which meant they couldn't actually fire the rifles. Probably they hadn't even figured out how yet. Still, they carried the weapons, probably proud of their symbols of thunder-striking.

Sam didn't recognize one rifle, might be anyone's. The other one was The Celt, and it was in the hands of the reedy fellow. That gave Sam a tingle.

He watched Paladin. Her white coat and black markings gleamed in the strong sunlight, black cap around the ears, black shield on the chest, and black mane and tail. "Hello, gorgeous," Sam whispered.

He watched her move around, grazing. She looked fit, her hip healed.

Suddenly he thought, *I hope she's carrying Ellie's foal.*

Sam and Hannibal had put Paladin together with the stallion, and had seen Ellie cover her.

Damn. If she wasn't in foal, she would be after a couple of weeks in this herd.

He decided he better check that The Celt hadn't been damaged. A man who didn't know how to fire a rifle wouldn't know how to take care of one.

He made sure the sun was behind him and trained the field glass on The Celt. The rifle looked fine. Hammer intact and not cocked, triggers still there, stock all right, butt looking normal. This glass was something. He felt like he could almost make out the name on the engraved butt plate, Τhe Celt. Celt was one of the few written words he knew. He inspected the rifle one more time. He'd have to make sure that Reed hadn't stood it on its muzzle instead of its butt and clogged the barrel with dirt. He'd also have to check that the ball, patch, and powder he kept in The Celt were still seated in the barrel. He wouldn't want to have a need, lift his rifle, and find out he was just pointing a stick at someone.

He smiled to himself. As things were, he could walk right up to Reed in broad daylight. Reed would aim The Celt at the intruder, intending to unleash lightning. The flint would go *click!* against the pan, and nothing would happen. While Reed was puzzling things out, Sam would drive a blade into his innards.

Sam considered that thought. Yes, he wanted to kill someone. These Mojaves murdered ten of his friends. And not in an honest fight—through treachery. No, he didn't mind his heat for revenge. But when it came to the actual killing, his stomach would churn.

It was midday. Probably the guards would be changed at dusk. Reed and Limp would go back to the village, and The Celt would go with them.

He could make his move now. Sam's way was to be daring, to act without planning everything out, to strike whenever opportunity seemed to open and ride out the storm. The edge always went to the bold.

Yes. He could take the guards out quietly one by one. He could grab The Celt and Paladin, swim the river, and ride hellaciously for California. He might also run the horse herd off. If he did that, the Mojaves would either have to take time to gather the horses or chase a well-mounted man on foot.

He'd be giving up the chance to get more rifles back, and to get even with Red Shirt, but . . .

He got to his hands and knees. He felt it rise in him. *I need to act.* He saw what to do. Guards had to drink, especially on a sun-blasted day like this one. He would wait by the river and take the first man in silence.

The second . . . ?

It took time to slip back into the ravine, circle the herd on the upstream side, and get into the cover of the brush alongside the Colorado. He dropped to his knees and drank deep.

Coy lapped gingerly. He never seemed to need much water.

Sam surveyed the ground, which would become a killing field. The other advantage here, he noted, was that the rush-rush of the current would cover the sounds of his movements.

He slipped back through the willows, searched for the guards, and got a nasty surprise.

Four guards stood together talking.

Sam waited and watched. They chatted. Reed and Limp waved, walked away toward the river.

Damn, they were changing the guards. In the middle of the day.

This thought gave Sam a chill. As he'd slipped down from the ridge to the river, he'd crossed paths with the arriving guards.

Reed and Limp strolled casually through the brush, worrying about nothing.

Sam put a hand on Coy and kept low in a clump of willows. Reed was carrying The Celt. Sam ached to jump out and grab his rifle. But it didn't feel right.

Reed and Limp drank from the river, looked around, laughed about something, and headed along the bank toward the village.

Sam followed on the sly.

HOURS LATER, BACK at his bivouac, Coy resting and Brownie grazing nearby, Sam added up his information. He knew the spread of the brush huts on the sand flat thoroughly. Now he'd seen that Reed's hut was on the northern end, and he had a pretty wife with a child on the way. The wife had a mole next to her left nipple, what among white women might be thought of as a beauty mark.

The Celt was tucked into the hut—not lying directly on the sand, Sam hoped. Reed sat on a cottonwood log with other men, all of them straightening arrow shafts. Beauty Mark puttered around the hut. Then she went to work the fields by the river with other women. Sam followed them, bush to bush. For a moment the hut was unattended. But Sam's white skin and white hair would be spotted.

He slipped back here to rest and wait for the cover of darkness. Surely The Celt would be in the hut tonight. He pictured the dome of brush. It was outlying; it faced east. A fire pit blackened the sand in front of the door, evidently where Beauty Mark did the cooking. A shovel leaned next to the entrance. That shovel irked Sam—Jedediah had traded shovels to the Mojaves just a couple of weeks ago.

It would be dicey to slip into the hut with the couple sleeping there, dark or not. And if he woke them, he'd have a hell of a long run to reach the herd and get Paladin.

Would the Mojaves guess the horses were a target? He thought so. Then they would boil around him like hornets. He couldn't take the chance.

On the other hand, he did have a trick that might let him get Paladin out of the herd . . .

He shook his head to clear it of doubt. Hell, maybe the Indians would have a get-together tonight, some sort of ceremony, and his rifle would be unwatched.

One comfort—the camp dogs wouldn't get excited about Sam or Coy. After the days spent around each other, the dogs were used to them.

Oh, didn't he miss his pistol now? He was thinking of how the Mojaves panicked at the firing of two rifles on the day of the slaughter. But he traded his pistol for Brownie, who was essential.

Well, he thought, *maybe I'll just have to do what I like to do, start the trouble and then improvise like crazy.*

On that note he took a cat nap.

* * *

THE NIGHT WAS chill. Lying on a boulder, Sam hugged himself. Coy was all eyes on the village, and Sam was riveted on a single hut, Reed and Beauty Mark's.

Curiously, the horse herd was more closely watched than the village. Looked like enemies in this country were more likely to steal horseflesh than to attack such a big camp.

Everyone was asleep, had been asleep for hours. Sam didn't see a good opportunity yet. *Damn, If I don't get a chance by first light, I guess I'll just go like a berserker.* That was a word he'd learned from Hannibal the magician.

Oh, cuss and to hell with it.

Sam stood up on the boulder. *Now.*

He looked at the moon, sagging down the western sky, full-bellied. Now was the time. Maybe the moonlight would be enough to find The Celt.

He slid off the rock, and Coy leapt down. Sam padded slowly, carefully toward the hut. He kept balanced. He avoided touching the limbs of bushes. He made sure of every foot placement. After every step he waited and listened.

He circled the hut and approached the back side. The moon shone bright here. The willow leaves, dry on the branches, let speckles of moonlight into the hut.

A dozen feet behind the hut Sam squatted. He could make out nothing in the interior but shadows. He couldn't even be sure where the sleeping figures were. If they were like Crows, Reed and Beauty Mark slept at the rear of the lodge.

He studied the area above where the couple's bed probably was. Crows, Sioux, most Indians of the plains and mountains hung their rifles from leather thongs at the rear, well off the ground. Maybe . . .

He thought about it.

He covered his face with his hands so his eyes would let in more of the faint light. He popped his hands away. Yes, he was pretty sure. Parallel to the earth, three or four feet off the ground, at the very back of the lodge he could see a long, rodlike shape.

The Celt.

He hardly dared think. Could he do it? Slip both hands silently through the branches? Yes. The branches bent to shape the lodge stood well apart. Hold The Celt with one hand and cut the thongs with the other? He probably could. Slip The Celt back out of the branches? That would be tricky. *But what a hoot, if I can get away with it.*

He cautioned himself. *When I get it, I can't fire it.* There was no telling whether the muzzle might be blocked with something.

He stood up again. Step by step he eased forward. Coy stood to one side, sniffed, and watched curiously. Every step closer, every step closer.

Now he could almost smell the sleeping couple, almost hear the deep, rhythmic breaths. He could hardly believe that The Celt was within reach.

He snaked his right hand through the lodge branches. Silence. Had he done it?

He grasped the rifle.

Except it wasn't The Celt. He had his hand on . . . a flint spearhead.

Sam smothered a laugh and almost peed on himself.

He was holding Reed's spear!

"Mmmm!"

Every hair on his body squiggled.

He jerked his hand out and leapt back.

Someone spoke.

Sam jumped. He breathed and calmed himself. A female voice. Sounded like "ark-fart," but he knew only about twenty words of Mojave.

He padded slowly backward, watching the hut.

Now the man's voice sounded.

The woman's.

He lost his poise—he turned and sprinted back behind the boulder. Coy trotted at his heels.

He crouched and listened.

Nothing. He seemed to have disturbed no one. No movement came from Reed and Beauty Mark's lodge, and no sounds loud enough to hear. He tried to melt into the rock.

Silence. Waiting. Breathing again.

Soon a surprise. Across the village he saw tinder flame up. An infant fire lit the face of a woman bending over it.

He watched and waited, every sense super-alert.

Beauty Mark came out of her hut, got down on her knees, and started making a fire. The way she was going about it, it looked like she would singe her bare nipples.

Around the village other fires spurted up, a dot of orange here, a flicker there.

Beauty Mark hung a metal pot over the flames on a tripod, a pot the fur men had traded to the tribe. She poured water from a clay jug into the pot. She dumped something else in.

Sam understood. He'd seen the women picking beans yesterday afternoon. Now they were boiling them. They probably did the cooking early so they wouldn't have to lean over fires during the heat of the day.

Sam noticed that night was lifting, the sky easing from black to gray. First light.

He made a very simple choice. Go berserk!

He gripped his tomahawk in one hand and his butcher knife in the other. He sprinted toward the hut pell-mell, bellowing as loud as he could.

Beauty Mark jumped back in alarm.

Sam ignored her and went for the lodge. He leapt with both feet onto where he thought Reed would be stretched out. His knee hit what felt like a raised head.

He jumped into the air and came down ass first on the center of the lodge. Branches splintered. Sam and the lodge dome banged to earth.

From inside Reed roared. Beauty Mark was shrieking.

The broken lodge branches rippled. Sam could see Reed crawling toward the entrance. He kicked and hit a butt. He looked sharp, kicked again, and seemed to catch a neck.

Beauty Mark jumped onto his back.

Sam roared and threw himself over backward onto the branches. He came down square on Beauty Mark's chest, and heard the breath *whumpf!* out of her.

Reed was crawling out of the smashed entrance.

Sam clubbed him with the flat side of the tomahawk.

Reed got to his feet but staggered sideways. Sam slammed the tomahawk blade at his shoulder.

Beauty Mark came at Sam clawing.

He put his hands on both of her breasts and shoved fiercely. She went flying backward.

The whole camp was aroused. People howled. Men ran toward him with weapons in hand.

Sam spotted The Celt's butt plate sticking out of a hide wrap on the dirt floor of the hut. He heaved the rifle out and ran like hell.

Two arrows whistled by his pumping arms. Coy dashed at the attackers, barking ferociously.

Sam whirled. The Mojaves slowed down or stopped. He raised and pointed The Celt. The warriors hurled themselves to the ground, behind bushes, or behind lodges.

Fooled you! The rifle wasn't even cocked.

Sam whooped and ran. In an instant Coy was alongside him. They dodged around bushes. For now the brush would save him. No one could get a clear shot.

Fifty yards into the brush Sam turned hard to the right to head for the herd. Paladin . . . He ran like a madman. *Paladin will save us.*

He jumped into a dry wash, bounded across, and scrambled up the other side. There he faced a grove of cottonwoods— and forty or fifty armed and angry Indians.

He stopped. *Oh, hell, I can't berserk my way out of this one.*

He jumped back into the wash and fled upstream.

A dozen, two dozen, three dozen Mojaves jumped in and called out their war cries. Others ran along the banks. They came at him like baying hounds.

Come on, feet, do it.

Sam sprinted for everything he was worth. *I can't slip out of this one . . .*

When he put one foot on a fist-sized rock, it turned and he went down hard. His shoulder plowed a groove in the gravel.

Rising to a knee, Sam saw a huge Mojave bearing down on him. The man cocked his spear.

Sam lifted The Celt.

A gun roared.

Blood squirted from the Mojave's chest, and he crashed to the ground like a felled tree.

What the devil? A gun? He almost checked The Celt's muzzle for smoke.

From the left bank, the direction Sam came from, a cloud of white mist floated over the wash.

All the Mojaves ran back toward the village.

A head rose over the bank.

Hannibal?

Another head appeared.

Hannibal on Brownie!

The Delaware jumped Brownie into the wash, galloped to Sam, and skidded to a stop in the gravel. Sam hopped up behind Hannibal.

The horse labored out of the wash and ran toward the herd. As they went, Hannibal reloaded his pistol.

"We've got them buffaloed," he yelled, grinning hugely. "You all right?"

"The horse sentries heard that shot."

"We'll take them."

Brownie and Coy topped the next to last ridge and plunged into the ravine.

A sentry loosed a flock of arrows at them.

Sam and Hannibal dived off the horse in opposite directions and scrambled behind bushes. They were too close, maybe twenty-five paces, and too exposed.

Pain lightninged up Sam's arm.

His left hand sprouted a shaft and feathers. He yelled, and his knife clattered to the ground.

A second sentry rose on the ridge, pointing a rifle at Sam and Hannibal.

Sam cackled loudly. "What do you mean to do," he hollered, "scare us to death?"

Hannibal stood up, leveled his pistol, and shot the arrow warrior square in the chest. His body lifted and dropped backward.

Instantly Sam and Hannibal charged the rifleman.

The fellow threw the rifle down and ran.

From the top of the ridge Sam threw his tomahawk at the man. It hit him handle-first on top of the head and bounced forward. The Indian hightailed it for the hills.

Hannibal grabbed the abandoned rifle.

Sam whistled piercingly, low-high.

Paladin tossed her head and cantered toward them.

Hannibal smiled. "Magic."

Sam touched her muzzle, jumped joyously onto her back, grabbed her mane, and rubbed her ears.

Brownie trotted up to join Paladin. Hannibal grabbed the rope bridle and vaulted on.

"Let's go!" Sam yelled, and kicked Paladin toward the river.

Hannibal said, "I'm going to get something for our trouble."

Quickly, they separated a group of seven horses from the main herd. Hannibal drove them toward the water. Sam dashed Paladin at the rest of the herd, shouting and waving his hat. They broke like a flock of sparrows and ran in all directions.

Sam put Paladin to a gallop after Hannibal and the seven stolen horses. From the bank he saw their heads bobbing up and down in the river. Without missing a step, Paladin leapt into the shallows and soaked Sam. In a few steps she was swimming. The cool of the river was a blessing.

Chapter Four

W hat the hell did you do?"

"Saved your ass. Let me see that hand."

Sam showed him the puncture wound. Back by the Colorado, Hannibal had pulled the arrow through. Coy tried to lick the hand, and Hannibal shoved his muzzle away.

"I'm going to poultice and bandage it now."

"You followed me?"

"No need. I knew where you were going. I came along far behind."

Hannibal made a paste with ground herbs from his belt pouch. He wrapped them in cloth, dunked them in a water jug, and applied them to the wound.

"This is damn likely to fester, but we'll do our best."

"Why did you follow me?" Sam would worry about his hand later.

"It's my fault you're in this country at all."

This was a kind of joke between them. On Christmas Day nearly five years ago Hannibal found Sam moping over a girl and dared him to do what he really wanted to do, go to the West.

"That's it for now."

They were stretched out in some rocks a hundred paces above the first spring. The nine horses were rope-corralled a quarter mile away, on poor grass.

Sam and Hannibal scooted onto their bellies and rested their barrels on rocks. They made sure priming was in the pans and that the rifles were on half cock. They made sure their cover was good and their sight lines were good.

The Mojaves, if they followed, had to use this spring. Then two good riflemen would have some fine targets. Hannibal didn't know the rifle he'd snatched from the sentry, but that made an extra firearm.

"I've still got those words written down."

"Too bad you can't read."

They both chuckled.

"They're getting hard to make out."

Sam opened his shot pouch, spread out a patch of rabbit fur, unrolled a piece of oiled cloth, and unfolded the piece of paper within. The hand was stiff and achy and the bandage felt cumbersome. He handed the paper to Hannibal.

"Illegible," said the Delaware. "Too many times wet, too dry, too much folding and unfolding."

" 'Everything worthwhile is crazy,' " quoted Sam, " 'and everyone on the planet who's not following his wild-hair, middle-of-the-night notions should lay down his burden, right now, in the middle of the row he's hoeing, and follow the direction his wild hair points.' "

"What bit me in the tail that night?"

"Maybe you'll write it down for me again."

"Sure. When we don't have enemies hot behind us."

Sam looked to the east and pointed with his bandaged hand.

From these rocks they had a fine panoramic view back toward the Colorado River.

"I see them too," said Hannibal. "We don't get to slip out of anything."

"I wouldn't have it any other way."

Waiting was the worst part. Watching your enemy. Mulling on his intent. Picturing blood and torn flesh. Hurting in your middle, because you know that the blood might be yours.

Sam flexed his hand. He hoped the damn thing didn't make it hard to shoot. But he had confidence—The Celt shot dead center.

They watched the Mojaves ride up to the spring at a lope. A half dozen of them carried useless rifles. Sam and Hannibal grinned at each other.

The Indians held their horses back from the water while two scouts inspected the tracks around the spring. Francisco was one of the scouts, and Red Shirt seemed to be the war leader. Handsome, friendly, slick Francisco. Treacherous Francisco. Quickly the interpreter found the tracks of the mounts moving along the foot of this rocky spur toward where they were corralled.

The Indians let the horses drink first. When the men dismounted and stepped toward the water, Hannibal fired.

Red Shirt thudded to the ground.

Sam saw no need to hold his fire. The Indians couldn't scramble up these rocks before he and Hannibal reloaded. He pulled the trigger and Francisco went down.

Sam thought grimly how easy this was, with the barrel resting on a big rock.

A few Mojaves jumped onto their horses. One man yelled at the enemy and waved a rifle.

Hannibal fired, and the yelling man got knocked under a horse and trampled.

The rest of the Mojaves jumped on their horses, and all skedaddled, taking three riderless mounts with them.

"What do you think?" said Hannibal, reloading fast.

"We'll be able to watch them halfway back to the river," said Sam.

While Hannibal made sure the Indians were riding away, Sam walked to the horses and brought them back to the water.

Hannibal dragged the three bodies in a pile away from the spring.

The two took turns all afternoon, sleeping and watching. The Mojaves stayed gone.

Being near the three dead men gave Sam the willies. He didn't want to get an angle where he could see Francisco's and Red Shirt's bodies. He imagined they stank already. He was mad at the buzzards circling overhead, eyeing the dead.

"What are you thinking about?" asked Hannibal.

"Esperanza," lied Sam.

Then, however, he did think about his daughter. Over and over he imagined holding her. And embracing Flat Dog, her uncle. And Julia, her aunt.

When dark fell, Sam and Hannibal rode toward the next spring.

"SISTER SUSIE PICKED a peck of peppers," said Hannibal to the plop of the horses' hoofs.

"A peck of peppers Sister Susie picked," answered Sam.

"Plenty of peckers," put in Hannibal, "Sister Susie plundered."

Jedediah grinned at him. "McKye," he said lightly, "you put a cloud into a fine day."

"Sister Susie deemed them dapper Daves."

The eighteenth day of September was in fact fine. Sunny and warm, views of what the Mexicans called the Sierra Nevada stretching for miles to the east, the river hard by, and miles of wheat-colored grasses in every direction.

Sam felt heady. In a few hours he would see Esperanza, and Flat Dog, and Julia. Jedediah, Sam knew, was happy. He'd told Rogers, the brigade's clerk, to hold the brigade in that camp on the Appelaminy until September 20. If the captain didn't appear by then with supplies and more men, Rogers was to consider him dead, take the remaining men in to the Russian fort at Bodega Bay for supplies, and make his way home however he could.

They would arrive this afternoon, two days before the deadline.

And Hannibal? He seemed to like the world every day, however it came. Sam looked at his friend's face. Sometimes it made him twist with envy, the way his friend seemed to enjoy everything. He had a saying for it. "Life is a whirling devil of trouble, thanks be to God."

Only a little while more.

* * *

ROGERS, ART BLACK, and Joe Laplant stood up, waved, and came running. "Good to see you, you old coons!"

Then they looked behind the captain at the other riders, and their faces changed.

Jedediah saw it. "We have nothing," he said. He'd promised to come with a pack train of supplies of every kind. Instead he brought ten riders, half of them without rifles, not a single pack animal, and no equipment.

"Hellfire," said Rogers.

The captain and his clerk looked at each other, speaking without words.

Art Black, though, was looking sheepishly at Sam.

Jedediah reached down to shake Black's hand, and Art didn't even notice.

"They're gone," he said.

Sam opened his mouth and nothing came out.

"Disappeared," Black said.

Rogers kept his eyes down and kicked at the dirt.

"Esperanza?" Sam squeaked.

Black nodded. His eyes ached the truth up to Sam.

"F-F-Flat Dog and Julia?"

"Gone. Probably kidnapped. No idea where they are."

"When?"

"About two months ago."

Gone. Sam almost fell off Paladin.

Rogers changed the subject. "The rest of the men are out hunting." He looked at the ten gaunt riders and their mounts. "We have plenty of meat but we're out of everything else. They'll be back before dark."

"I'm sorry," Black said to Sam.

Art Black was a decent man. Sam had never liked Rogers.

The two outfits greeted each other, one by one. They hadn't seen each other in over a year. The men from Salt Lake, intended to be rescuers, were the ones who needed rescuing.

Whatever they were saying, Sam could see their mouths move, but he couldn't hear the words. He got off Paladin and led her down to the Appelaminy.

The mare drank. Sam had the illusion, repeatedly, that he was tumbling head over heels into the river.

His infant daughter, gone.

One of his best friends, gone.

His best friend's wife, disappeared.

He sat down by the river for a long time. He rubbed Coy's head. He listened to the water and watched it turn and swirl. Paladin splashed in the shallows. When he was ready, Sam staked the mare on some grass and walked back to the fire. The hunters were back, and everyone was gathered around and feeding on elk.

"Give me the story," Sam told Rogers.

Head down, the clerk began. "The child was colicky all the time," he said in a tone that suggested it wasn't his concern. "Señora Julia wanted a *médico* or a *curandera*. She had a notion about some herbs or something." Sam didn't know whether the tone was contempt for Mexicans or the irritability one married woman can cause in a camp of rough men.

Rogers looked up from his food at Sam and smiled eerily. "Some Indians led them toward San Jose. They thought they'd come on a rancho, either mission or private, and get some help. Didn't figure they'd have to go all the way to San Jose.

"Indians come back, said the party stopped at a farmhouse a day's ride that direction." He indicated west with a vague wave. "Men took 'em at gunpoint. I rode over there with some of the boys. Farmer said, 'People in Monterey wanted them,' wouldn't say nothing else."

Sam glared at Rogers, thinking the clerk would have done more if it wasn't an Indian, a Mexican, and a half-breed child. He clenched and unclenched his fists.

Coy tensed, glaring at the clerk. Rogers gave the coyote a nasty look.

"Give me that liver," Hannibal said to Rogers.

Sam snapped his head toward his friend.

Rogers picked up the liver with the tip of his butcher knife and extended it to Hannibal.

"Hannibal, I . . ."

Hannibal interrupted. "Eat. Eat good. You're going to need it."

Sam got up and walked down to the river, Coy trotting along.

After he stared at the dark water for a while, Hannibal sat down next to him and tossed a hunk of meat to Coy. "Color prejudice shows in all sorts of ways," he said right off. "Even in people who say they don't have any."

Sam didn't answer.

"We'll find them."

"Yes." He turned a grim face to Hannibal. "That bastard at Monterey got them."

"I know the story. Let's get back."

The celebration that night was pathetic. The men left waiting here were down in the mouth about what the captain hadn't brought—everything a trapper needed, from goods to trade to the Indians to critical items like powder, lead, traps, knives, and coffee.

The men who came from the Salt Lake were miserable about their friends killed by the Mojaves, and having to tell the story.

Everyone grumbled in their food. They traded piece after piece of news, sometimes personal information, sometimes an item that bore on their mission to trap beaver, sometimes a story that was funny or nutty or unbelievable.

Jedediah caught up on the business news from Rogers. The men left behind had had an easy time, fine weather, lots of good hunting, Indians that were both peaceable and honest. Good beaver trapping, except in the summer.

The captain didn't say it, but he knew that Smith, Jackson & Sublette had paid wages both summers and the men hadn't had a chance to earn the firm a dime.

Sam sat in a deep pool of unbelief.

"The Spaniards," said Rogers, meaning the Mexicans, "sent some riders up here from San Jose. They wanted to know what we were doing in the territory. I told them hunting beaver."

"Did that satisfy them?"

"Seemed so." Rogers's eyes said, *But they're Spaniards, and you never know.*

Hannibal said quietly to Sam, "Let's get some rest. We leave in the morning."

SAM LOOKED OVER his breakfast coffee cup at the captain. "We're going to Monterey."

"Why don't we ride together?"

Sam mulled. He knew the captain had to go. He needed to ask for passports and for permission to trade for the equipment the outfit needed.

The governor would tell the captain he had no right to be in the country, and he was probably a spy. "Why," the governor would press, "did you come back after you promised to leave the country and never return?"

At least something was worth a smile this morning. Sam said, "You may end up in the *calabozo.*"

"With you. Listen—wait. I'll leave in two or three days. We'll stop in Saint Joseph, maybe you'll get news there, and I'm sure they'll make me go on to Monterey to see the governor."

Sam shook his head no. "I'm too worried."

Jedediah raised his eyes to Sam's. "I give you a lot of rope, you know."

This brought Sam up short.

"Sometimes you act like you don't work for Smith, Jackson & Sublette. As if you just hang around with us when it's handy."

Sam dropped his head. "I guess so."

"A brigade leader can't do that. The company comes ahead of the personal."

Sam nodded. He looked the captain straight in the eye. "Not with me."

Coy whimpered.

"Go on then," said Jedediah, his tone edgy.

Sam and Hannibal were gone within the hour.

Chapter Five

As they rode to Monterey, Sam thought, *I need to get my daughter to her country, Crow country.*

To the music of Paladin's hoofs he walked through the dark door of memory and looked at the unbearable past. Meadowlark died of childbed fever. Sam had a daughter and no wife. He buried her at the mission in Monterey. After the friars had said their words, he spaded the dirt back onto her coffin, thunk after thunk after thunk.

Then the handsome son of Don Joaquin Montalban arrived, asking for Señorita Julia Rubio. With a cunning smile, he extended his false invitation. Would she care to visit an old family friend at their rancho?

Julia understood what was going on. These old family friends were in league with her father, who had spread word that his runaway daughter was to be found and returned. So she answered firmly: "My husband and I will gladly receive the don this evening at the mission."

The young don looked contemptuously at the Indian who presumed to be the husband of the beautiful youngest daughter of the great Rubio family of Rancho Malibu. He looked at their rough fur trapper companion, Sam Morgan. "Not possible," he said. Then he gave his bodyguards orders to seize the señorita.

In the fight the young don died, two of his three bodyguards died, and his carriage driver fled.

Now Sam looked at Coy, trotting beside Paladin. He was envious. "You don't remember," he said to the coyote. *At least not in the haunting way that I do.*

Sam ran the pictures through his mind over and over—the surprise of the bodyguard when Sam's belt buckle turned into a knife. The slash of glinting blade, the kick of foot, the spout of blood, the fall and roll, the lifetime of events that spun themselves out across a minute or two.

The deaths.

His indifference, his utter indifference to everything.

And now Don Joaquin or other agents of Julia's father had kidnapped Julia. And her husband, Flat Dog. And Esperanza.

All Sam wanted to know was whether they were dead or alive.

He had advanced beyond indifference. Revenge bubbled in his throat like lava.

FROM THE SUMMIT of the Santa Lucia Mountains the Pacific stretched before them to a horizon where sea misted into sky. Sam's dad's voice sounded in his mind—*Forever.*

Monterey Bay itself was a small dollop of ocean cupped by pincers of land on the north and south. Near the southern pincer lay the presidio, the arm of the Mexican government, and farther south the mission, the arm of the church. The presidio was a stockade a couple of hundred yards long. Originally, all secular intruders into this Indian land had lived within the fort. Now buildings leaned against the outside of the stockade, and a town was springing up nearby, a few adobe homes forming a plaza, and other adobes and thatched huts on the hills above. Compared to the mission, all of it was rough and tumble, dirty, and crowded.

The mission where Meadowlark died, far from her home . . .

Where my daughter was born, far from home.

Sam jerked himself back to the present. He looked at Coy and touched his spurs to Paladin.

He had ridden for three and a half days chewing on one question: *Are they alive? Has Montalban killed them?* He didn't speak of it to Hannibal. They rode in silence. But he obsessed about it. Sometimes he told himself he knew: Flat Dog had been murdered, mother and baby spared.

Two brothers. Blue Medicine Horse went with me to the Sioux villages and got killed. Flat Dog went with me to California and got killed.

He did not let himself think consciously of Meadowlark. *The family will despise me.*

Walking Paladin down this slope, he felt a chill.

"No way to know what we're coming into," said Hannibal.

"Let's be careful," said Sam, "and head for the mission."

As they approached Mission San Carlos Borromeo de Carmelo, Sam felt its enchantment. The buildings were elegant adobe structures in a Moorish style, with arched walkways, red-tiled roofs, and a handsome central quadrangle with a fountain. These sun-struck adobes were an ideal of beauty to Sam. The church was even more impressive, built of dressed stones and adorned with bell towers.

They passed the barracks and Sam kicked Paladin to a trot. Soldiers made him edgy.

Sam's eyes roved the mission. He loved it and hated it.

"How many soldiers?" asked Hannibal.

"Not enough to control the Indians."

"So priests enslave their souls."

Sam and Hannibal put their horses in the corral.

Then, by unspoken consent, they walked to the small cemetery. Sam stood by the small, grassy mound, hat in hand, Hannibal behind him. Coy curled up in the grass at Meadowlark's feet.

Her grave was marked with a simple oblong of wood. MEADOWLARK MORGAN, it read, 1808–1827, REQUIESCAT IN PACE.

Sam hadn't seen the marker before. He and Flat Dog had been obliged to leave in a hurry, after the Montalban trouble.

He took thought now. "The Indian converts are buried here."

Hannibal looked at him questioningly. "This is consecrated ground. But she was not a Christian."

Sam just looked at the grave. He hadn't understood at the time. There was a lot he hadn't understood.

"This must be the kindness of the priest. Those Latin words, they mean, 'Rest in peace.' "

Then the feelings swelled in Sam like music, a sorrow inexpressible in words. He swam into the sounds, a depth and breadth of loss beyond comprehension. Tumbling feelings, pictures of Meadowlark, brushes of her flesh, hints of the smell of her skin. In exquisite pain he held her. She felt warm. He loved her. Then she felt cold, as on that day. He loved her. He hated living without her.

He forced himself to the surface of consciousness. He told himself once more, as he had many times—so commonplace, a fever after childbirth. So commonplace. Dead.

Coy yipped.

"I am sorry to interrupt," came a voice behind them. Sam turned and saw Padre Enrique, the brown-robed head of the Franciscan mission. In decent English he said, "Sorry, Sam. You have no idea what danger you are in. Come with me."

SAM FELT SURE he would never forget the picture before him. In the mission library at a table sat Flat Dog, reading a book.

Flat Dog jumped up and braced Sam by both shoulders and shook Hannibal's hand.

"Reading?"

"Father Enrique is teaching me." He gestured at the book-lined walls. "There are two thousand volumes here."

The priest set down a flagon of wine and four glasses. "I regret to interrupt, but we must make plans. Trouble will come." He sat at the big table and motioned for his guests to sit.

The padre poured. Sam didn't particularly favor wine, but out of politeness he drank.

Padre Enrique was a tall, thin priest with a huge, hooked nose and enormous brown eyes filled with intelligence and kindness. He moved jerkily, like a marionette. Sam had not been surprised, four months ago, to discover that the priest could lead a large enterprise successfully, hold hundreds of Indians in sway, run huge herds of cattle and sheep, and manage vineyards, orchards, and fields of beans and corn. He had been surprised by the kindness.

"I'm sure you have . . . apprehended what happened. Don Joaquin gave out word that anyone who found the so-called murderers of his son would be rewarded handsomely. The manager of the farmhouse where Flat Dog, Julia, and Esperanza went for help, he betrayed them for the gold."

Flat Dog put in, "Julia is with her father at Rancho Malibu." The deadness in his voice chilled Sam. "Esperanza too." Then his face changed somehow, streaks of hope and bitterness. "She's carrying our child."

"Child!" said Sam.

Flat Dog managed a sort of smile. "Yes, child."

"Let's go get her."

The priest said, "Flat Dog is here under arrest."

"Arrest!" said Sam.

"They let me out of jail during the day to study Christianity."

"Flat Dog is an excellent student," said the Franciscan.

"My marriage vows were to become a Christian."

Sam looked to see if Flat Dog's eyes were merry, but his friend kept his face blank.

"We are making the progress daily," said Father Enrique. "Literary and spiritual."

Sam couldn't believe it. *Flat Dog is learning to read before me. Is he really becoming a Christian?* Then Sam remembered that he himself had become a Crow for Meadowlark's sake.

"Why in jail?" said Hannibal.

"He is charged with the murder of Agustin Montalban y Romero, son of Don Joaquin Montalban y Alvarado."

"And two ruffians," said Sam.

"Yes."

"Why haven't they hanged him already?" asked Hannibal.

"Because I intervened. I told the governor that I saw the fight, and Flat Dog acted in self-defense. Also Montalban is not pushing for a quick trial."

"Why not?" asked Sam.

"Because he is using Flat Dog as . . . a bait to lure you here."

"You, amigo," mocked Flat Dog, "are the real killer. You snatched out your belt buckle and cut a man's throat. You sliced his faithful servant from his collarbone to his balls."

"So we have stepped in the dung," said Hannibal, "and good."

"Yes." The priest's eyes grew intense. "Sam, your white hair is a flag. The stable hands saw you, others saw you. Soon the whole mission will know, and soon, possibly this evening, certainly tomorrow, Montalban will know." It was already late afternoon.

"Then?"

The priest shrugged. "Perhaps I can protect you for now. I can arrest you and jail you. If that works, in eventuality, Montalban, he forces a trial."

The priest sipped his wine and considered. "Already I have spoken a falsehood. I said I saw what happened and that both of you acted in self-defense. In fact, I didn't see it, and cannot give that testimony officially. Therefore conviction and execution."

"You have kept Flat Dog alive . . . why?"

"Justice," said Father Enrique. "I believe in justice." The Franciscan smiled a little to himself. "And I want to save his soul."

Sam's spirit spun like a dervish.

"So Sam and Flat Dog will hang," Hannibal said.

"I doubt it. Why would Montalban wait for a trial?"

Sam and Hannibal studied each other.

"Do you . . . ?"

Father Enrique said, "Yes, I have suggestions. For the sake of justice I will help you."

HE OFFERED THESE suggestions over dinner. Huge, steaming platters of food were served, enough to fatten up men starved by the desert—three kinds of meat, beans, corn, squash, and huge loaves of bread, pudding, plenty of wine and water. Other brown-robed priests set to with a will. Sam couldn't imagine how Father Enrique stayed so skinny.

The father had permitted Coy into the dining room, and everyone tossed him scraps. Sam wondered how the padres treated the slaves who served the food. Indians, he noticed, and curiously one black. They padded about invisibly. *Slaves,* Sam thought to himself, a skeptical eye on Father Enrique.

"Why do you imagine Montalban will exempt you from his wrath, Señor Hannibal?" asked the padre.

"Haud facile me interficere."

"What?"

"You know Latin." He translated for Sam and Flat Dog. "I'm hard to kill."

"You look like an Indian," said the Franciscan.

"I am Indian. One who intends to stay in possession of his soul."

Avid curiosity flushed the padre's face, and Hannibal had to explain to him that his father was a professor of classics at Dartmouth College and his mother a Delaware, a student at the college. "I grew up speaking English and Delaware, and reading Greek and Latin."

"Amazing!"

Sam pitched in. "Don't get ideas about sailing him to Europe with a sign that says, 'WHAT CIVILIZATION CAN DO FOR THE RED MAN.'"

"Of course not," said the priest.

That's exactly what you were thinking. Sam covered the thought by turning away and feeding Coy.

"Padre, guide us," said Hannibal.

"I want to put you on El Camino Real at first light," said the priest.

"El Camino Real?"

"The trail that runs from mission to mission, called the King's Highway. You will go south, toward Rancho Malibu. Is that not what you wish?"

"Damn right," said Flat Dog.

"A long journey, more than a hundred leagues."

"More than three hundred miles," translated Hannibal.

"There are nine missions, counting the one nearest Malibu. I will give you a letter of safe passage for the heads of the missions. I am the ecclesiastical head of all the California missions—they will give you whatever you need."

"Sounds sweet and easy," said Sam. That wasn't what he was thinking. His mind was thrumming, *Another long journey in the wrong direction*. But he couldn't go home to Crow country until he had Esperanza.

The black slave slid a pudding in front of Sam with what seemed to be a flourish. He wore a pancho with a hood.

"It is not easy. It is a very long ride. You have enemies. And that hair of yours." The priest touched it. Coy mewled. Sam tossed his head, flicking the hand away.

"And your outfits. You would be easily identified as foreigners, even at a distance."

"What will we do?"

The priest leaned forward with a conspiratorial smile. "We'll dress you in disguise," he said. "And we'll take care of that hair."

"How?" said Sam.

An oratorical voice came from behind them. "With the help of a master of disguise and deceit."

Sam started. *Who the devil . . . ?*

A round priest approached the table and bent over Sam. Then he threw his cowl back.

"Grumble!" yelled Sam, and jumped up and hugged him.

An elegantly dressed woman stepped from the shadows next to them.

"Abby!" said Sam. He hugged her too.

Everyone else exchanged greetings. Coy wagged his tail and accepted head-patting.

"I agreed to your friend's little charade," said the priest.

Grumble swept on, "Our party would not be complete without . . ."

The black slave came around Abby, flipped his hood back, and stuck his head theatrically into Sam's face. "A black man, you white folk don't hardly notice him."

"Sumner!" Sam shouted.

THE WHITE-HAIRED TRAPPER and the eggplant-colored youth traded *abrazos*.

"We have business," said Grumble.

"Yeah, we got to save they white asses," said Sumner.

"My red ass begs your pardon," said Hannibal in a silly tone, pointing at his bottom. They introduced themselves.

"Don't call mine white neither," said Flat Dog. They clapped shoulders.

"Business!" said Grumble firmly.

An Indian slave dragged a trunk forward. Sam knew it well. He traveled with it on two steamboats from Pittsburgh to St. Louis. He was sure it was still full of costumes, decks of marked cards, jewelry both real and fake, and other accoutrements of a con man.

"How did you three get here?" said Sam. He could barely stand still. Grumble and Abby were the two oldest friends of his five years in the West. Sumner had come to California with the brigade last fall, as a slave.

"All that will wait," said Abby. She was a vision—hennaed hair, pale lime gown, and a sky-blue scarf.

"We're going to get you disguised," said Grumble. He studied Hannibal and Flat Dog. "In fact, Mr. McKye first. Padre, can you get the clothes of a mission Indian of his size? Those shirts of rough cloth you give them, hideous stuff, and loincloths. He's dark and black-haired, so . . ."

Abby said, "He's already wearing loincloth and moccasins."

Grumble regarded Hannibal. The breechcloth seemed to make him shudder. "Just a different shirt, much shabbier. I have something else for Flat Dog later. Meanwhile, will you show Sam, Abby, and me to a room where he can be dressed and made up in private? Sam is the trickiest."

* * *

FLAT DOG READ aloud in Spanish. He went slowly, some-times correcting himself, but he was having fun—showing off. Father Enrique translated the words into English for Hannibal and Sumner:

"I believe in one God, the Father, the Almighty, maker of heaven and earth, of all that is seen and unseen. I believe in one Lord, Jesus Christ, the only Son of God, eternally be-gotten of the Father, God from God, Light from Light, true God from true God, begotten, not made, one in Being with the Father . . ."

Hannibal chuckled. "The Nicene Creed. Let me get this straight. His native language is Crow, and he speaks good English, but he's learning to read in Spanish."

"It seems best to teach the Indians in a language that itself represents the height of civilization," said Father Enrique.

"You can always tell a height civilization," said Sumner. "They got slaves."

Hannibal and Flat Dog suppressed smiles. "It has been so many years . . ." Now Hannibal grinned and began as hesitantly as Flat Dog, *"Credo in unum Deum, Patrem om-nipotentem, factorem caeli et terrae, visibilium omnium et invisibilium."*

"Too many Christians around here," said Sumner.

"Not including yourself?" the priest asked.

"Got better sense. But I can read and write English."

Father Enrique nodded. "You are three exceptional . . . men," he said. They all wondered if he'd been thinking of saying "savages." "Nonetheless," he said to Flat Dog, "your soul is not yet made safe in the hands of God."

He looked at the ormolu hands of the ornate clock on the wall. The pendulum ticked like a nun correcting their ways. "It's getting late. I wanted to wait for our friends, but . . .

"Flat Dog, I will give you your freedom on one condition."

All three "exceptional men" tensed.

"Before you leave, you must be baptized, make your first confession, and take Holy Communion."

"Why?"

"I will save your body. God will save your soul. Are you willing?"

Flat Dog hesitated.

Sumner was grinning broadly.

"Remember your marriage vows. Father Sanchez consecrated your union with Julia on the condition that you become a Christian."

"I'll do it," said Flat Dog.

"Now," said the priest.

GRUMBLE AND ABBY sat Sam in a chair. They brought out a corked bottle of a brown liquid. One portly figure and one slender figure bent to the task. "Walnut juice," Grumble said.

Coy gave them a peculiar look.

They rubbed it firmly into the skin of Sam's face, even the corners of the nostrils, the lips, and the edges of the eyes. "The craft is demanding," Grumble said.

Abby smiled. "This is what women do every day."

It was what she did, Sam knew. As a provider of liquors, games of chance, and seductive women, she had to look splendid, and she always took pains.

Sam forbade himself to wonder exactly what was going on. Walnut juice?

"What are you two doing here?" He'd last seen them at the Los Angeles pueblo. They headed north on an American sailing ship, looking for a home for their chosen enterprise. Abby managed the booze and ladies, Grumble the gambling.

Grumble began painting the grottos of Sam's ears with a fine brush. "We disembarked here, looked around, and discovered the town was in its infancy, though the setting is very beautiful. We sailed on to San Francisco Bay and found even less of a town."

"I'm building a home here, an adobe, and then I'll open my usual sort of business." Abby gave an impish smile. "The mission is all holy men, but the presidio is all soldiers."

"I'll join her eventually, but the building period is boring. I want to go back to Los Angeles pueblo for a while. It's vulgar, but alive."

Abby said, "I like to sin in a beautiful place." She checked Sam's face. "Those white eyebrows will never do." With a tiny brush she dabbed something greasy and black onto them.

Grumble went back to the corked bottle. "Now your hands."

Sam stuck them out, and Grumble colored them. "Walnut juice?" whined Sam.

"Beautiful, isn't it? It's a little dark for most Californios. So handy. Too dark nips suspicion in the bud. The missions grow orchards and orchards of it." He smeared the juice up over the wrists. "You must not show your arms," he said.

Carefully, Abby covered Sam's neck with the brown liquid.

"Why were you ready with my disguise?"

"Didn't your captain say he'd return by September 20? Flat Dog said you'd show up here. You're a few days early."

Sam smiled to himself. *Flat Dog knew I would come.*

Abby said, "Now use this mirror." She handed an ornate one to Sam. "Look for white spots. The costume will be the coup de grace, but we mustn't have any of those nasty little white spots."

Costume?

Coy tapped his tail on the floor. Sam understood the wagging was anxiety, not delight.

Sam studied himself in the mirror. *I'm a darkie.*

Abby piled his white hair on top of his head. With Sam's wooden hair ornament and long pins such as she used in her own coiffure, she fastened it up, stood back, and surveyed her work.

"No white spots except the hair," said Sam.

"Excellent," said Grumble. "Now . . ."

He draped a black wig on Sam's head. The hair was shoulder length and gleaming. Grumble made careful adjustments.

"You're not making me into a woman!"

"Scarcely."

Abby circled to Sam's front and let the bundle in her arms drop full length. It was a brown Franciscan robe. "The cowl," said Grumble, "will even hide your face from prying eyes. Put it on over your clothes while I change." The con man disappeared behind a folding screen. "Be sure to replace the moccasins with sandals," he called.

Sam donned the robe. He tied it with the tasseled belt. Abby slipped the pectoral cross over his head and dropped it onto his chest. He fingered the rosary. He started laughing. They both laughed and laughed and couldn't stop.

Grumble popped out from behind the screen, arms wide in the declarative gesture of an actor. He wore an English gentleman's riding outfit, knee-high boots, leggings close-fitting on the calves and blousy around the thighs, a beaver hat in a serious business color. "Every inch a blue blood," he intoned in a plummy voice.

They hooted and clapped each other on the back.

Then Sam said, "You in costume? You're going with us?"

"Sumner and I," answered Grumble, "are your escort. You require our protection."

FLAT DOG STUDIED the water in the font.

"Holy water," said Hannibal.

"Wu-wu juice," said Sumner.

Flat Dog held these two odd thoughts, as though rubbing a stone between his fingers. "It's a relief to be in here," he said.

"Far away from the altar," said Hannibal.

"That thing done give me the willies," said Sumner.

None of them looked through the entryway down the length of the church at the huge, painted statue of the Christ, nailed to the cross and dying.

Now Father Enrique approached in white and gold robes. He looked into Flat Dog's eyes and spoke with gravity. "Do you understand that with these words you are embraced by the arms of the holy catholic and apostolic church of our Lord Jesus Christ?"

Flat Dog pictured Julia's beautiful face, her golden skin, her tawny hair. "Yes."

The padre put his hand into the shadowed water.

"Ego te baptismo in nomine Patris et Filii et Spiritus Sancti." As the priest spoke, he sprinkled holy water on Flat Dog's head three times—Father, Son, and Holy Spirit.

Flat Dog thought, *Now I am a Christian.* It gave him a chill. *I promised Julia.*

"Come to the confessional."

Flat Dog knelt in the small box and spoke of his many sins. He had killed people. He had fornicated. He had lied. He had taken the name of the Lord in vain. Since he was well prepared, he enumerated these sins quickly. The priest gave him a psalm to say as penance and absolved him.

Flat Dog shivered.

Father Enrique disappeared.

Flat Dog, Hannibal, and Sumner went into the nave and sat, as instructed, on the front pew, in front of the altar. Now the new Christian looked up at the God with the bleeding hands and feet. To him it was not credible or right that a father should sacrifice his son for the sake of strangers.

At the far end of the nave Grumble and Abby entered.

Father Enrique appeared in front of the altar with a flagon of wine and a gold plate that bore the bread.

"Christians are invited to the sacrament of the Eucharist," said Father Enrique.

Grumble and Abby genuflected before the altar and knelt at the table bearing the host.

The priest at the rear, oddly, slipped into a back pew.

Flat Dog came to his knees beside his roguish friends, who were apparently Catholics.

Father Enrique spoke words. Later Flat Dog remembered only "body and blood of Christ."

As the party treaded to the rear of the church, a brown robe came in and tossed back his cowl. It was Sam.

Flat Dog laughed and clapped him on the shoulder.

"You're a Christian now?" said Sam.

"Yes," said Flat Dog.

"Dumb slave religion," said Sumner.

"Christian and Crow," whispered Flat Dog. "Both."

Chapter Six

In the half-light before dawn they met by the corral. Shadows flitted across the dust and the rails. Horses stirred, restless.

Sam was bleary-eyed. Grumble, Flat Dog, and Sumner looked worse. Flat Dog dressed as an Indian slave.

"Black man don't need no outfit to make him look like a slave," said Sumner. But then he got an idea. Suddenly he spoke in an upper-class British voice. "I want to be a proper British servant," he said. "Once I am properly dressed, no one can deny me."

Grumble's chest provided the broadcloth of an English manservant, breeches buckled below the knee, stockings, and a dark coat. The wide-brimmed hat was a logical addition for a sun such as never shone in England.

Sumner looked down at himself, pirouetted proudly, and made a low bow to Grumble.

Coy barked vigorously at Sumner. Sam laughed out loud.

"You don't understand art," Sumner told the coyote.

"We clever gents," said Grumble, "now present the world with a British aristocrat and his attendants—a servant, a priest, and two mission Indians."

"The fair-skinned people of this continent are overfond of class distinctions," said Sumner.

"The don will be looking for three American fur trappers," said Padre Enrique. He sounded dubious.

Grumble surveyed them all. "All the actors are dressed for their roles," he said happily.

Coy barked at Flat Dog again. Then he dashed at the wagon wheels—it was more wagon than carriage—and pranced back, barking, eager to go.

Sam and Flat Dog got into their saddles. The rising sun was still behind the Santa Lucia Mountains. "Time to move," said Hannibal.

Abby gave Sam a good-bye peck on the cheek. When Sumner presented his face, she pinched his bottom.

The Delaware dressed as a mission Indian drove the wagon, Sumner beside him, Grumble seated behind and above the two of them, the gear in the box behind. The Franciscan priest had outfitted them generously—wagon, two draft horses, casks for water, dried meat, fruit, even a cask of wine. At Hannibal's request they also had a small keg of gunpowder, because their powder horns were half empty.

On the plank seat between Hannibal and Sumner perched the most visible weapon, a scattergun. Grumble had a pistol in his belt, which he might brandish foolishly at anyone who confronted them. The mountain-style rifles belonging to Sam, Hannibal, and Flat Dog were behind the passengers, laid loose under canvas, in case of emergency. No one knew what weapon Sumner might be carrying, or dared ask.

"Everyone clear on our story?" repeated Grumble. It was that the British blue blood, Grumble, was seeking contracts with the various missions for cow hides and tallow. The missions away from the coast were not yet involved in this commerce, very profitable for both sides.

"Go," he told Hannibal. The wagon lurched forward. "This cursed conveyance may bump us to death," Grumble said to no one in particular. In his pouch, to show anyone who asked, he carried the letter of safe passage from Padre Enrique to the heads of the nine missions where they would stop. Sam and Flat Dog had protested that the niceties of reception and hospitality at each mission would slow them down. Grumble insisted they'd need all the niceties they could get. Hannibal added that the party needed the safety missions offered.

As they rolled, Hannibal said, "You're a mystery."

Sumner smiled. "I done worked at it."

Hannibal laughed at the lapse back into slave English.

"And I assure you I can perform like a trouper." This was fancy talk again.

So they traded stories. Sumner said, "I was born near Santo Domingo, on a cane plantation. Since my mother worked in the big house, I grew up there, and played with the white kids. Our master was the second son of a viscount, or some such foolery. I grew up speaking the king's English. By serving meals, I even learned elegant table manners. I could pass myself off as, perhaps, the third son of a viscount."

Hannibal laughed.

Sumner shifted back to slave speech. "At night, though, down at our hut, we was with the other Niggers, including my father and his brothers and their wives, and they all spoke Spanish, nothing but Spanish. So I grew up talking both tongues."

"Two roles," said Hannibal.

"When I was sold to New Orleans, I done caught on to bow-and-shuffle English."

After Hannibal told about being born to a professor of classics and a Delaware student, raised speaking two languages and reading three, they agreed that they didn't know who had the stranger life.

SAM WAS NERVOUS about Grumble's little game. He didn't like not having The Celt in his hands. It made him feel naked. He'd concealed his other weapons. A butcher knife and his belt-buckle blade were covered by his robe. The hair

ornament blade was hidden in one sleeve. He wished he still
had the pistol he traded to the Serranos.

He fussed with the robe between his legs and Paladin's
saddle. He hated the damn thing—it made riding embarrassing. He glanced sideways at Sumner, and saw that the black
was tickled at the modest white boy. Inside Sam's robe was
folded Father Enrique's map of El Camino Real, its towns,
and its missions. Grumble carried another copy in his coat.

Now Sam spotted the first place marked on the map, Montalban's rancho. "Be watchful," Father Enrique had warned
him. "Don Joaquin is vengeful."

Actually, the rancho looked like nothing much.

The grounds were handsome, a fine lay of land on the far
side of the Salinas River. The don had planted fields, orchards, and a vineyard visible from the road. Probably herds
of horses, cattle, and sheep grazed the hills beyond. These
hills were brocaded with grasses that looked too rich and tall
to be real. They were bright as brass, thick as hair, and stood
as high as a horse's withers. Sam had never seen such grass.
But he was no herdsman.

The house, on the other hand, was unimpressive, an
ordinary-looking adobe of modest size, without a courtyard
or other beautification.

Coy drank out of the creek that ran through the property
as though nothing was amiss.

"Father Enrique told me," said Grumble, "that the don
complained greatly about having to build his house of mud.
But there's not enough timber around here."

"He's rich," said Sam irritably.

"But he doesn't enjoy it," said the cherub. "The old man
was a great landowner in Mexico. Montalban was one of the
younger sons. When his wife died and his daughters were
married off, he accepted exile to this miserable province to
make his son what he could never be, the master of a grand
estate." Grumble gave Sam and Flat Dog a look.

"The son of a bitch was trying to steal my wife," said Flat
Dog.

"The pistol was his, and it went off accidentally," said Sam.

"What a comfort that must be to Don Joaquin," said Grumble.

Sam couldn't see any sign of life around the place. There must be Indians working the fields, but he saw no one.

"Who are you and where are you going?"

From Paladin's saddle alongside the wagon, Sam had watched the four riders coming from the south, growing in his field of vision and on his nerves.

Immediately Sumner picked up the scattergun from the wagon seat. No one of either party misunderstood the threat. At that range it would be a devastating weapon.

Coy walked in front of Sam, growling, his spine hair sticking up.

Rising next to Hannibal, Sumner said in his fanciest English, "My master wishes to know who dares to ask such questions." When they just stared at him, he repeated it in good Spanish.

From behind, Grumble spoke in plummy tones, and Sumner translated. "Good sir, I present this letter of safe passage from Father Enrique Hidalgo, head of all the Franciscan missions of California."

He gave it to Sumner, who held it out. The lead rider had to dismount and look at it. Sumner kept the paper in his grip.

Sam knew damn well who this was, one of the ruffians from the time the young don tried to abduct Julia, the man Sam had slit from collarbone to balls. Too bad he'd lived. Sam kept his head down, his features hidden by his cowl.

Flat Dog recognized the fellow too. Sam could feel the anger radiating from Flat Dog's body. The two mounts minced nervously.

"I represent Don Joaquin Montalban y Alvarado. On the authority of the commandante of the Presidio of Monterey we are searching for two criminals who have escaped from Mission San Carlos Borromeo de Carmelo."

Sam got enough of the Spanish to be offended at this arrogant ass.

"We have every desire," Grumble said, Sumner still translating, "to cooperate with the authorities. I am Edward Muddleforth, second son of the Viscount of Piddleston."

Sam was surprised Sumner could translate this foolishness without a grin.

"These men comprise my retinue."

"Where are you going?" repeated Collarbone to Balls.

"We travel to Mission Nuestra Señora de la Soledad and other missions on business."

"I see." His disbelief curled his lips. But the sneer was probably a pose, Sam thought. Beneath it Collarbone to Balls seemed to be accepting the story.

"Have you seen other travelers on this road today?"

Coy barked once.

"None," Grumble answered truthfully.

"Three Americans dressed as hunters? Carrying long rifles?"

"No travelers."

Collarbone nodded slowly, thinking. "We ask you to be on watch. We will probably see you again as you travel south."

"Glad to be of service," said Grumble.

Collarbone pulled his reins to the side to ride around the wagon.

Sam breathed again.

Flat Dog reached to his hat. Sam saw his friend's face do funny things. Casually, he took the hat off, rubbed his hair back, and looked full face at the Mexicans.

Collarbone's face changed to a truly memorable look of recognition.

Then he looked at Sumner, who was holding the scattergun. The black man gazed at Collarbone without expression.

The sides of Collarbone's grin turned down. His mount edged backward. He squeezed words out. "We'll be on our way then."

As he rode around the wagon, Sumner turned to watch

him, the gun following his body. The other three riders trailed after Collarbone with mystified faces.

When they were out of sight, Sam growled at Flat Dog, "What the hell did you do that for?"

"That son of a bitch stole Julia. He stole Esperanza. He put me in jail. I want to kill him."

"That's good," said Hannibal, "because now he intends to kill you."

Grumble added softly, "And the rest of us."

Hannibal said, "What he intends will be different from what he gets."

SAM AND HANNIBAL chose the battleground that suited them, a grove of trees along the river. It looked like a normal campsite, had a place where they could rope-corral the horses on grass, and offered a jumble of boulders for cover.

Coy trotted around the campground sniffing, like an inspector.

Sam, Hannibal, and Sumner made what appeared to be a normal camp, put up tents, gathered wood for a fire.

Flat Dog walked down to the river and sat alone. No one criticized him, but there was a lot of edgy body language as they prepared.

Grumble laid out a tarpaulin and had a picnic, pretending nothing was happening. It made Sam's nerves worse. The cherub should know a shooting war wasn't amusing.

Coy cadged scraps of dried meat from Grumble. Grumble kept looking up into the cottonwood branches and smiling.

"How many men do you think Montalban will bring?" asked Sam.

"All he can get," said Hannibal. "But not many of his Indians ride or shoot."

Sumner squatted and talked to Grumble. They both looked up into the trees, pointed, and whispered.

Sam got the scattergun and handed it to his black friend. "You any good with this?"

"I'm a con artist, not a gunman."

Sam was sure he was a good con man too, since he'd accepted Grumble's tutelage.

"Look, it fires a lot of pellets, and they spread out as they go." Sam held his hands a foot or two apart. "You don't aim it, you point it." He showed Sumner how the trigger, flint, and pan worked.

"That's all good," said Sumner, "but Grumble and me, we got an idea. A little surprise for the bad boys."

Grumble and Sumner sketched out their plan for Sam and Hannibal. Heads nodded, and smiles flashed. Sam and Sumner climbed the trees and began the rigging. Sumner moved through the trees like an athlete. Sam, bulkier and more muscled, was sure a branch was going to break under him. But they got it done.

Sam took off his robe—he wanted to fight in a man's clothes. Then he walked down to the river to join Flat Dog. The Crow had his sacred pipe out of its hide bag and was lighting it. Sam took thought. He started to get his own pipe out, but then he sat and shared Flat Dog's. They offered the pipe to the four directions, they smoked, and rubbed the smoke on themselves. Sam contemplated his Crow name, Joins with Buffalo. He thought of how buffalo never run away, but stay and fight to the last of their strength—that's what it meant to be a buffalo bull. This was what the medicine man in Meadowlark's village, Bell Rock, told Sam. He asked the powers for the strength to live up to his name, and he prayed that no one in his party would be hurt tonight.

When they were finished and the pipe bowl and stem were separated, so that the pipe was no longer a living being, Sam said, "Do you miss it? Crow country?"

Flat Dog gave a dry laugh. "We've been in a lot of places where a Crow's dog wouldn't even drink the water."

Sam's mind roamed back there—the land of the Wind River, the Big Horn Mountains, the Yellowstone River, the hot springs, the forests. "I miss it too," he said. "It's home."

Flat Dog gave him a look. "It will be Esperanza's home."

"It's where we belong."

"We're going," said Flat Dog.

"Very roundabout," said Sam.

He walked back into camp and surveyed the rigging. He thought the trick would work.

How will the don come? he asked himself.

Sam himself would scout and move stealthily.

But he was no fiery don.

THEY WERE SET. The campfire was down to coals. Around the fire lay five blanketed figures. If a curious person had taken time to look at the hats, he would have seen those of the Englishman and his manservant beside two blankets together and three Californio hats and saddles beside other blankets. Had this observer been curious enough to touch the blankets, he would have felt the stones underneath.

Don Joaquin Montalban y Alvarado, however, was not a man to come creeping up on his enemy. Riders, horses, and men of foot stormed the campground as a fire rages before the wind.

They came so suddenly, so swiftly that Grumble was nearly late with his knife. The don's horses roared into the campground, the men yelling out war cries and firing at the sleeping figures.

Coy barked furiously, but Sam held him back.

Grumble sliced hard at the rope.

The keg of gunpowder dropped straight down from where it hung below a limb and directly onto the fire.

The explosion hit like lightning. Tree limbs sailed through the air like torches. Sparks flew into the sky like fiery birds.

Eight enemies on foot brandishing axes and knives crashed at random into trees, boulders, and the earth.

The five mounted enemies were mostly beyond the campground when the keg blew, turning their horses to charge back among their blanketed foes.

The horses were blown backward, sometimes landing on

the riders. As the attackers scrambled to their feet, Sam, Flat Dog, and Hannibal fired from behind boulders.

Well instructed, Sumner held the scattergun at the ready. Grumble held fire with his palm-sized gambler's pistol.

The firelight made sighting difficult, and only two out of three shots struck. Then the three mountain men charged the enemies still standing, or staggering, or trying to get to their feet. Two fired their pistols, and Sam swung his butcher knife.

Enemies died.

Coy hurled himself at enemies, snarling and biting.

Sam, Hannibal, and Flat Dog hacked wildly at the remnants of the enemy force with tomahawks and knives. They didn't know whom they cut, but they struck hard.

Eventually, the tornado blew itself out. All stood still, their eyes mad. Embers around the campground smoldered. Small clumps of grass smoked, crisped, and went out. Sam could smell the river air again.

Sam counted. Hannibal and Flat Dog stood near him. Coy rubbed against his leg. Grumble and Sumner came out from behind boulders. Grumble was holding his face. "He couldn't resist looking," Sumner said, "and he's a little burned."

Flat Dog knelt over a prostrate figure. Coy approached the figure's head, sniffing.

"Check to make sure they're dead," said Hannibal.

Sam had to swallow hard. *They came here to kill us.*

They were dead. Some of them were mangled, some dismembered.

Sam wanted to vomit.

Flat Dog walked to him holding a bloody scalp.

Sam raised an eyebrow at him.

"Montalban's," said Flat Dog.

Coy whined.

Montalban's. Sam didn't want to touch the thing. He hoped he could get rid of the memories.

* * *

DAYLIGHT CONFIRMED ELEVEN bodies. Grumble and Hannibal thought they'd seen thirteen attackers, which meant two escaped.

"I doubt that they'll be back," said Grumble, smiling. "Ouch!" His face shone from the grease he'd rubbed on his facial burns.

Five riders, two dead horses, two horses they were able to round up.

Four saddles. One was a gorgeous work of tooled leather and silver studs, probably Montalban's. On or near the bodies of the four riders they found four rifles and three pistols. From the riders and men on foot they took an assortment of knives and daggers. Each mountain man claimed a pistol. The rest of the booty they carried off in the wagon.

They got going as soon as they could. Even before the bodies ripened, death stood rank in their eyes and nostrils.

Chapter Seven

I don't like it," said Hannibal.

"I hate it," said Flat Dog, but he didn't mean the situation. He meant his fury about his wife.

Rancho Malibu stretched before them, wide plains on the inland side of ragged coastal mountains. Now, in October, golden grasses colored the flats along the creek and the steep slopes. Scrubby trees spotted the hills. The ranch house and buildings stretched along the creek. Planted fields, an orchard, a vineyard, and grazing lands spread away from the steep slopes of mountains.

Sam couldn't help thinking of what lay behind him, the vast Pacific Ocean. There he and Meadowlark camped on Topanga Beach, and their new friend Robber showed them the wonders of the tide pools. Meadowlark had been thrilled by the anemones and the sea horses.

A few days later Flat Dog and Julia eloped to that beach,

borrowed the tipi, and spent several days exploring each other. Until Julia's father barged in and snatched away his daughter. He also gave Flat Dog a thrashing with a knout, a Russian lash with bits of metal embedded in the rawhide. Flat Dog's back would be bumpy as a plowed field for the rest of his life.

"Watching isn't getting us anywhere," said Sam. He could feel the rage coming from his brother-in-law.

"Let's do something," said Flat Dog.

Sam tried not to think what it must be like for Flat Dog to know his wife was in one of those two houses, full of their child, but he couldn't see her, talk to her, touch her.

The three of them had watched the rancho from this ridge for two full days. Having found out how practical a field glass was, Sam traded a captured pistol for one in Santa Barbara. Passing through eight missions on the way south, they'd been welcomed everywhere and protected along El Camino Real by Padre Enrique's letter. Funny world, to Sam, where influence counted for more than skill or good sense.

Two days of watching told them that Mexican hands worked around the rancho's outbuildings and in the vineyards and orchard. Occasionally, herders could be seen in the distance. Don Cesar, the *patrón,* rode the property each afternoon with his son-in-law Alfredo, and they were out on horseback now. They stopped at the vineyard to talk with an old man, then dismounted to inspect something. Then they rode on.

"Sumner would love this," said Sam.

"A life where you do nothing but watch your 'inferiors' labor for you," said Hannibal.

Now father and son rode to the corral, dismounted, and let a stable hand take the horses. Each man then strode to his own house. The don's adobe, by the Pittsburgh and St. Louis standards Sam knew, was not particularly grand. He remembered its comfort, and its one strange room, which housed Don Cesar's collection of weapons, and the don's pride in his instruments of torture and destruction.

Two days and no sign at all of Julia.

Reina, her sister, took her two children outside every day for a couple of hours. She and Alfredo shared the modest adobe next to Don Cesar's.

"Do they ever go anywhere?" asked Sam.

"Julia won't be traveling now," said Flat Dog. "She's almost eight months."

"Californio women, meaning rich Californio women," said Hannibal, "aren't like Crow women. Toward the end they don't travel. They lie in."

"I just want to go kill the son of a bitch," said Flat Dog.

Sam saw that in his friend's face.

"Not a good idea to kill your wife's father," said Hannibal, "no matter how much she hates him."

Flat Dog made a rude sound.

"We don't want to hurt him," said Sam. "Just to get her. And Esperanza."

Flat Dog was silent.

"Let's go talk to Grumble," said Sam.

They'd let Grumble and Sumner ride into Mission San Fernando alone. The mission was only ten miles north of the rancho. No point in adding Grumble to the watch party. "Just one more face someone from the rancho might recognize," Sam had said.

"Going in, that's risky," said Hannibal.

"I've got an idea," said Sam.

"You? That's plain dangerous," said Hannibal.

THE THREE BUMPED along in the open carriage.

"My dear," said Grumble, "you've never looked lovelier."

"Nuns don't have to be pretty," said Sumner. He adjusted the wimple around his head. "I hate this brown. It's the color of shit. And they's nuns 'cause they ain't pretty."

"Some men might want to try a nun," said Hannibal.

"Pervert," said Sumner.

Grumble had told him to steal a monk's robe from the

laundry. In the dark Sumner had filched a nun's outfit. Which Grumble suddenly decided was even better.

"Let's get our minds on business," Grumble said. He was brown-robed as a priest, and all smiles at the disguise.

Hannibal drove the carriage. He'd never been to the rancho, so couldn't be recognized. He looked over one shoulder. Rubio and his son were in the vineyard and riding away from the house. He'd timed it right.

They'd gotten good information at the mission. Grumble and Sumner discovered that once a week a priest traveled to Rancho Malibu to accept confessions and administer the Eucharist, and a nun from the convent went along to tutor the boys in reading. Thus the plan.

Sam and Flat Dog were hiding along the road north to the mission, probably half mad with fear and doubt.

Hannibal reined in the carriage directly in front of Don Cesar's adobe. *Right in the lion's den,* he thought. His chest tightened. A stable hand appeared to help with the horses. A cigarillo jutted up into the air from his lips, unlit.

As Cigarillo carried the harness, Hannibal led the animals. He was outfitted as a poor Indian, so that no one would expect him to speak good Spanish and he would have no business near the main house. He looked back at his friends, making their way to the front door. Under his loose shirt Hannibal was armed with knife and pistol. *But I'll be at the corral, and damned little help from there.*

"I don't like this," said Sumner in a falsetto voice.

"You'll be amazed at how easily people accept a costume," Grumble said. "You can be a policeman, a sailor, anything you like. That's the charm of it."

Grumble rapped on the door and they were admitted. The maid seemed to accept the friar and nun as a matter of course. Since he and Sumner had met the don last winter, Grumble's face and hands were walnut-stained a deep brown, and from his trunk of tricks he'd put on a silver beard.

"I don't like this," Sumner repeated.

"Your falsetto is really very good."

To Grumble's relief it was Doña Reina who came to greet them. Two boys ran down the corridor behind her, playing at war.

As I am playing at war, thought the cherub.

"Permit me to introduce myself," he said in his uncertain Spanish. "I am Father Lorenzo come to pay my respects to the family. This is Sister Annunzio."

"Come in," said Reina. Her face showed signs of wear and worry, and no interest in her visitors.

As they followed Reina down the corridor and into a parlor, Grumble felt a familiar rise in his energy. *I like a frisson of danger.*

Sumner lifted his wimpled head to him, as though to say, *This is more than any damned frisson.*

When they sat, Reina said, "My father and husband are out in the fields, but I'll let my sister know you're here." Her voice was lifeless.

When they were alone, Grumble said softly, "I relish deceiving people."

Sumner said, "I can tell you're nervous. You babble."

Grumble chuckled. "And you?"

"The life of a thief is more honest."

Julia walked in, one child in her arms and another big in her belly. *My God,* thought Grumble, *she really is near her term.*

Julia was a beautiful woman, with comely features, tawny hair, and golden skin, and she was quick-minded. Her eyes were bright and alert and—and perhaps suspicious.

"My child," Grumble began immediately, "I am Father Lorenzo. I am new to the mission, and come to pay my respects to the family."

At the sound of Grumble's voice her face grew wild. *She knows,* Grumble thought. He pursed his lips. *She spent plenty of time with us.* Julia's eyes flashed from one face to other, and her face mottled with color. He rushed forward with words. "This is Sister Annunzio."

"Buenas tardes, Señora," said Sumner.

Julia opened her mouth but nothing came out. Disbelief? Joy? Alarm? Grumble wished he knew.

Reina came in bearing two glasses. "You'll want some wine," she said.

Grumble and Sumner accepted the wine and sipped. Reina disappeared.

"Are you well, my child?" said Grumble. "Physically?"

Julia clearly couldn't speak.

"I'd be glad to accept your confession, if you like."

She nodded.

Reina came in and handed Julia a glass. Julia downed the wine in a single gulp. She looked around wildly and handed the baby to Reina.

The four sat and stared at each other nervously.

"I'm pleased to meet the two of you," said Grumble, "and look forward to meeting Don Cesar and Don Alfredo."

"Why have you come?" asked Julia. Tension thrummed in her voice. After a moment she added, "Father."

Grumble pretended. "I was born in Padua. I've been serving at Mission San Carlos Borromeo de Carmelo, near Monterey, and am newly assigned to Mission San Fernando Rey de España."

Reina looked oddly at her sister, turned back to her guests, and said, "Is Sister Annunzio also a newcomer?"

"I have seen the boys when they've been at the mission," said Sumner, "but this is my first time at the rancho. It's beautiful."

Julia's hand was about to shatter the wineglass.

"My child, perhaps it's time for you to make your confession now."

"Of course, Father."

IN THE SMALL room Julia sat on the narrow bed, not pretending. Grumble drew a chair close. "Flat Dog is waiting for you," he said softly. "Sam is with him."

Julia gasped. She clutched her hands around her belly as though to hold the child in.

"We are going to take you out of here right now. If you want to go."

Julia looked like she was going to burst with emotions. She managed to nod yes.

Grumble put his arms around her and held her. Her head thrashed wildly. Quietly, he told her what she was to do. From time to time she whispered, "Yes." She seemed tongue-tied, but at the end she got out one thought. "Trust Reina. She's on our side." She leaned into him and wept, great, heaving sobs.

Eventually, after Julia had cried long enough to recite the sins of a highwayman, Grumble softly told her the rest of the plan. She nodded yes several times. He said with a sincerity that surprised even him, "God bless you, my child." He wished he could give her absolution.

When Julia left the room to get her sister, her face was marbled red, white, and gold. *Good,* he thought, *she will be convincing.*

Reina came in and knelt. She looked up at Grumble, looked down, and began the ritual words, "Forgive me, Father, for I have sinned."

Grumble interrupted. "Doña Reina," he said, "I am not a priest and Sister Annunzio is not a nun."

Horror floated through Reina's eyes.

Grumble couldn't help smiling as he said, "I am Grumble, she is Sumner."

Reina jumped. Grumble put a hand on her shoulder to keep her from running off.

Julia glided into the room. "Let us explain . . ."

HANNIBAL CURSED. DON Cesar and his son were walking their horses back. *Just when I thought we might get off clean.*

He jumped down from the corral fence, trotted into the

barn, and got the harness. Cigarillo gave him a peculiar look—like *Who told you to get the carriage ready?*—but the Mexican brought the two draft animals out of the corral. Together they started the harnessing.

Don Cesar threw Cigarillo an imperious look. The stable hand walked toward the dons, his shoulders swaying sassily, took the reins of both horses, and led them away for water and oats.

The front door of Don Cesar's adobe scraped open. Out came a horrendous moan, a ululating cry of pain.

Don't overdo it, Hannibal thought.

Two women came out, one of them Sumner in his nun's getup. The other must be Doña Reina. They held the ends of a heavy blanket, which emerged in bright colors from the shadowed corridor.

The moan soared upward again. It came from the shape half wrapped in the blanket, apparently Julia.

Grumble staggered out, struggling to support his end of the blanket.

"The baby!" exclaimed Doña Reina.

The don's face rearranged itself from arrogance to childlike horror.

Hannibal ran to help. He grabbed Julia and lifted her out of the blanket. Reina took Esperanza from Julia. Hannibal hurried toward the carriage, bearing the stricken woman.

"What the devil is going on?" demanded Don Cesar.

"Papa, it's a month early! The baby is coming a month early!"

"Then why are you moving Julia?"

Sumner minced forward in quick tiny steps and put his hand on the don's forearm. "She needs help. It's very dangerous. We must get her to the midwife."

"Who in hell are you?"

"Sister Annunzio," said Reina, sounding out of breath. "Papa, we've got to get her help."

Hannibal deposited Julia in the carriage.

Again she issued a horrifying moan.

Good woman, thought Hannibal. He climbed up and took the reins.

"I'll ride to the pueblo for the doctor."

"Not enough time," said Grumble. "Quicker to the mission and the midwife, far quicker."

"Who in the hell are you?" snapped Don Cesar.

"Father Lorenzo, who is trying to save your grandchild's life. And your daughter's."

Grumble hopped into the carriage behind Sumner, and Hannibal lashed the horses into motion.

Don Cesar's policy was, When uncertain, shout. "Alfredo, get the doctor! Bring him to the mission! Now!"

The don himself snapped at Cigarillo to bring his horse. Mounted, he trotted to the carriage and fell in behind. "What in hell . . . ?" he muttered. "What the devil . . . ?"

ABOUT A MILE along the dirt road the Indian driving the carriage stopped.

"What are you doing, you idiot? My daughter's life is at stake!"

"No," said the Indian, "yours is." He cocked the pistol and held it straight at the don's chest. "Dismount!"

The don did.

Two American beaver hunters ran out of the cluster of scrubby trees.

"Grumble, get the reins."

The priest did.

Grumble! The don recognized that name. He was beginning to understand . . .

Reina got down from the carriage with Esperanza in her arms. Julia stepped out next to her sister.

Don Cesar stared at Julia, uncomprehending.

Now the beaver hunters trained their rifles on the don's chest.

Don Cesar recognized them. Sam Morgan, the American clown with the Indian wife. Flat Dog, the Indian who usurped his daughter. And Sam's scraggly dog.

"Julia!" the don snapped.

The beaver hunters seized his arms.

She walked directly in front of him, glaring. She was perfectly well. His lips slipped into a snarl.

"Father," she said, "I disinherit you."

She cocked her open hand well back and slapped him.

The hands let him go, and he nearly fell.

Julia glared, challenging him.

Coy jumped forward and nipped at the don's leg. Rubio kicked at the animal. He looked rage at his daughters.

"Oh, Papa," said Reina, "you deserve it."

Flat Dog stepped up to Julia, embraced her, and kissed her, a huge kiss. Julia kissed him back with passion.

The don looked away.

Hannibal looked at Grumble, holding the reins, and nodded. Then he put his pistol in his belt, turned, plucked his rifle off the seat, and looked down its barrel at the don.

"Our friends will go on to . . . wherever they choose to go," said Flat Dog. "I, Julia's husband, the father of your grandchild, I will escort you home."

"And me," said Hannibal, prodding the don with his cocked rifle.

Flat Dog gave Julia one more kiss. He said softly, "I have to do this."

"I understand."

"Soon."

"Yes."

SAM MORGAN LOOKED into the carriage at Julia, Sumner, and Reina, who was holding his daughter. He reached for her and held her for the first time in half a year, almost her entire life. She yawned and closed her eyes. His mind went moony.

"She is a gentle baby," said Reina, "always peaceful."

Sam gawked at Esperanza.

DON CESAR CURSED Flat Dog and Hannibal all the way back to the rancho. He walked, led his horse, and cursed them.

Hannibal interrupted him. "You're impressive. Only a man of education has such magnificent imprecations."

The huge rowels on the don's spurs made his steps crooked and awkward. In a quarter mile his ankles were torturing him, and his creative energy waned.

However, his tongue was relentless. He denounced his captors. He denounced Julia and his grandchild. And he cursed the priest and nun who helped to perpetrate this atrocity. "I will make them pay," he said. "I am a loyal friend and supporter of that mission, and Father Antonio will stand by me. That priest and nun will pay."

Flat Dog and Hannibal smiled at each other and kept their guns on their prisoner.

Soon Don Cesar and the two riders came on an elderly Mexican in a big sombrero who was pruning a grapevine. The mountain men put their rifles across their laps, looking idle. Sombrero looked questioningly at the don. "It is all right, Miguel," the don said. "It is all right."

When they neared the house, Cigarillo came out of the barn, his unlit cigarillo an inch shorter but still jutting up to the sky. "It's all right," said the don. "I'm fine."

At the door of the adobe Flat Dog said, "Who is inside?"

"Two women, a maid and a cook," said the don.

"If there are only two," said Flat Dog, "fine. If there is a third or a fourth, you die." He glared at the don.

Don Cesar Rubio shrugged.

Flat Dog kicked the door open.

From the corral Cigarillo saw the American hunters pushing Don Cesar inside with their rifles. He decided that now would be a good time to relax somewhere else with a bottle of mescal.

The captors and the don stepped into the entry hall. "Call them," ordered Flat Dog.

"Lupe. Juanita."

Two women crept from separate rooms into the corridor.

"Is anyone else in the house?" said Hannibal.

The women shook their heads no. They looked terrified. "Lead me to the parlor. We will sit like guests. Have you ever been privileged to sit in that room?"

The women minced into the parlor, and Hannibal followed them.

"Down the hall," said Flat Dog, his rifle in the don's back.

He marched Don Cesar down the long corridor and into a special room at the end, where he kept his prized collection of weapons. The walls here were adorned with instruments of destruction—a conquistador's sword and breastplate; a match-lock rifle; two fine dueling pistols; a cutlass from a pirate vessel; a jeweled dirk belonging to a Spanish grandee; several styles of whips and lashes, including a cat-o'-nine-tails.

The don had displayed these marvels proudly to Flat Dog and Sam last winter. "The cat," he said, "is preferred by the British. And this is the choice of the Russians. The knout."

He took it down to show them its nastiness. "Wire is interwoven with the rawhide, you see." Then he tapped the handle into his hand with an air of satisfaction.

Now Flat Dog took down the knout. Its memories crawled up and down the flesh of his back.

The don's eyes bugged and swelled. He remembered perfectly. He saw the eruptions of Flat Dog's skin, the spewing blood. He heard once more the Indian's screams, and remembered how he relished them.

"Down on the floor," said Flat Dog.

Don Cesar went.

"All the way. Flat on your belly."

Don Cesar obeyed.

Flat Dog leaned his rifle in a corner. Then he tapped the handle of the knout in his hand.

Chapter Eight

The rains came.

That first night Sam, Grumble, Sumner, Julia, Reina, and the infant Esperanza drove to the pueblo of Los Angeles. They considered finding a place to stay there, but it would have been a hovel. As soon as they started on toward Mission San Gabriel Arcangel, rain started sluicing down. The road along Arroyo Seco turned to mud, and the dry creek bed trickled. Before Sam got the carriage to the mission, the horses were sliding around in the muck. Sam and Coy, in the open, were soaked and chattering.

Father Sanchez got out of bed to make them welcome. He even brewed hot coffee and poured them brandy to go with it. Sam silently wished blessings on the good Father José.

They all got into their beds quickly.

Sam insisted on keeping Esperanza with him. The child had been cheerful as long as the light lasted, and after dark slept. Men went to one room, women another. Sam slept slouched in a chair, his arms around his daughter.

The next morning rain still sluiced down.

At midmorning Hannibal and Flat Dog came in. They'd slept a few hours and then ridden through the rain. They accepted bread, butter, and coffee. Hannibal took his food to bed. Flat Dog put an arm around Julia, and they headed for another bedroom.

"He's awful tired," said Sam.

"She's eight months along," said Grumble.

"I wager they'll have some fun," said Sumner.

Rain and gray, rain and gray. They napped and rested all day.

At dinner Sam looked at the friars and asked his friends in English, "What are we going to do? Rubio will come for us."

"Not for a few days he won't," said Flat Dog. He told the

story of the knout-lashing. It came out flat and hard. He showed them all the knout, and the dried blood still on the rawhide and the metal studs.

"Father José is a good man," said Grumble.

"He married me and Julia."

"He knows what we've done, all of it," said Hannibal.

"But he can't protect us long," said the cherub.

"My father will pursue us wherever we go," said Julia. Reina nodded.

"Gentlemen," said Sumner, "the harbor. A ship."

They looked at each other. They nodded. "A ship," two or three of them said.

Not even a California don could attack an American or British sailing vessel on the high seas.

THE NEXT MORNING Sam and Hannibal had lunch in town. They'd left the mission while Flat Dog and Julia were still in bed, and before Grumble and Sumner got up.

A friend walked into the cantina.

"Ike Galbraith!"

Sam and Hannibal stood up at their table and shook hands with Galbraith.

"Sit and eat!" said Hannibal.

The big Mainer sat. Even seated, he was half a head taller than either of the two tall men. "Damn rain," he said. On this second morning it was still pouring.

"This un heard white men was at the mission." He did a second take on Hannibal. "Sorry, you know what I mean."

Under the table Coy whined.

"It's all right, Ike."

They poured Galbraith coffee and handed him tortillas.

"I hope everybody hasn't heard we're at the mission," said Sam.

"Damn silly hope," said Galbraith.

They told him how Flat Dog had gotten Julia back, and made Rubio pay.

"That shines," said Galbraith.

"He'll be coming after us," said Sam.

"After a few days," said Hannibal.

"Slow going in this rain anyway," said Galbraith.

"Hard even to ford the Los Angeles River," said Sam.

The road crossed the river just above the pueblo without benefit of bridge.

"That dinky thing, she's a-roaring," said the Mainer, chuckling. "What you beavers doing in town?"

"We sold some things," said Hannibal.

"One of the dons up near Monterey wanted to get me and Flat Dog hanged, or better yet bushwhacked," said Sam. "We sold most of his men's saddles, rifles, pistols, and knives."

Galbraith's eyes flashed his understanding. "Sounds more profitable than plews."

Sam and Hannibal smiled and nodded. Good to have something to smile about. Sam thought happily of the coins in his shooting pouch, a lot of them.

"We're alchemists," said Hannibal. "We turned our lead balls into gold."

"Think I'll come back to the mission with you," said Galbraith.

"We could use another hand," said Sam.

ON THE MORNING of the third day the rain fell in sheets.

They were putting their heads together, everyone at one big table. Father José had given them good news. "My American friends," he said in Spanish. "Good tidings. An American ship leaves San Pedro for San Diego on the tide tomorrow evening."

Sam fed Coy under the table. He'd discovered that the coyote would snap up a crust of bread if it was smeared thickly with butter.

"Right about now a ship would be a fine way to travel," said Grumble. He and Sumner had decided that Los Angeles wasn't safe for them either, not for a while.

"Safe to get there?" asked Sam. The harbor at San Pedro was a long, hard day's drive south.

"Two and a half days since Flat Dog whipped Rubio," said Hannibal.

"He's damn well not doing any riding yet," said Flat Dog.

Sumner said, "I want to take no chances."

"Let's do it," said Grumble.

Sam and Hannibal, Flat Dog and Julia—everyone looked at each other. They were agreed.

Julia squeezed Reina's hand.

"I'll be all right," she said. "Father rages, but he will never hurt me, and Alfredo would not let him."

A voice came from the outside. "Where are the Americans?"

Sam jumped up. He thought maybe he recognized that voice.

The heavy wooden door opened and Robert Dingley limped in.

Sam and Flat Dog said at once, "Robber!"

He looked like hell, face scratched and bruised, silver beard and hair matted and dirty, and one leg gimpy somehow.

Coy squealed.

"What happened to you?" said Sam.

"What's gonna happen to you, only worse. Rubio's men beat me up."

Introductions and explanations were urgently made. Robber was an American seaman who had abandoned ship to live the carefree life in California.

"What are you doing here?" said Sam.

"Looking for you. Getting away from Rubio's men. Either or both."

The story was that he had been enjoying life in his shack up Topanga Creek in his usual way yesterday morning. Rubio's men showed up suddenly, demanding to know where Sam and Flat Dog went. "I couldn't tell them nothing. Been nearly a year since I saw you."

Robber's eyes asked where Meadowlark was. Sam wasn't ready to talk about that.

"So they beat me up."

"Don't you love them Rubios?" said Flat Dog.

"I'm through with this place," Robber said. "It was only a matter of time before Rubio run me off anyway."

"Come with us," said Sam. "We'll go to San Pedro, get a ship, get the hell out of here."

"Sure," said Robber, "and you better get going. Those men were heading back to the ranch to pick Rubio up and charge straight here."

"Rubio can't ride," said Flat Dog.

"They thought he could. And maybe they'll come without him. Either way, they're coming."

"Anyone in the pueblo will tell them where we are," said Galbraith.

The table broke into babble about how to slip down to San Pedro without getting caught. Everybody had a different idea—they agreed only that it would be dangerous.

"Listen," said Robber, but no one heard him in the talk.

"Listen," he said loudly.

They fell silent.

"I know where Rubio will never look for us."

They waited.

"In a boat. On the Los Angeles River. Which ain't never a river except now."

"Yes!" said some.

"But if he sees us," others said, "we'll be sitting ducks."

"It's a good idea," said Grumble. "Devious."

In a whirlwind of talk they came up with a plan.

They would borrow a rowboat from the mission. Robber would row Sumner, Julia, Esperanza, and Grumble down Arroyo Seco to where it flowed into the Los Angeles River just above the pueblo, and on downriver to the sea. Sam, Hannibal, and Flat Dog would ride along the bank above the river, on the lookout for Rubio and his men.

"I'll come along too," said Galbraith.

Sam liked that. Galbraith was the best shot he knew.

"When do we leave?" said Flat Dog.

"Now," said Sam.

Everyone stood up to get ready.

"Sister," said Julia in Spanish, "will you come as far as the sailing ship with me?"

"Are you all right?" said Reina. Julia's face was drawn, strained.

"Flat Dog?"

Her husband went to her, took her hand.

"I think the baby, it begins now to come."

RIDERS IN THE rain. Sam's eyes searched for dark figures in a gray world. Rain drummed on his hat and dripped off like a curtain. Rain slashed across the hills, the gullies, the landscape. He had trouble seeing, and that was dangerous.

He looked southwest along the dirt track, where the riders would probably come from. He looked west toward the hills, where they might show up. He looked every direction but down toward the water. He, Flat Dog, Hannibal, and Galbraith had agreed to keep their eyes off the stream, for that would give away the secret. There the frail boat tossed on the swollen creek called Arroyo Seco, a boat bearing friends, bearing women, bearing his daughter, bearing a baby striving to enter the world.

When he and Paladin forded the creek above, the surge felt rough. It looked rough and sounded rough. What a joke— Sam hadn't even seen water in that gully before.

Coy skittered along in front of him. Fortunately, the coyote paid no attention to the boat.

Sam hoped Robber was good with those oars.

He checked to make sure his powder was dry. He chuckled cynically to himself. *If Rubio's men show up, with or without the don, there'll be no talking things over.*

He looked at Flat Dog. His friend's horse slipped around on the wet track, just like Sam's, Hannibal's, and Galbraith's, and the packhorse that bore their gear. Flat Dog's eyes probed at the rain, and shadows in the rain. But Sam suspected the landscape he surveyed was inside. His wife was in labor down below, in the boat. His child was being born, maybe, in the rocking, plunging craft. Being born into a world of gray rain and black murderers.

That was enough to turn any man's insides into a desert.

JULIA CURSED. SHE cursed in Spanish, for her pains seemed to have squeezed away her English. The pains came every several minutes. When they did, she blanched, her body went rigid, and her curses outroared the flooding waters.

Mainly, and most eloquently, she cursed Flat Dog, the cause of these terrible pains, the one true culprit. She cursed the current, normally a trickle, now trundling along like a horse with a rough gait. She cursed the bumps and lurches. She cursed the rain, which soaked her. She cursed her need to squat. With the boat bouncing, she felt like she would bounce off to the left, or bounce to the right, and plunk into the river. But when she lay down, or took a seat on one of the hard benches, the pains were worse.

Every few minutes the boat bottomed out on a place too shallow to float. Everyone but Julia got out into ankle-deep water, dragged the boat through, and jumped back in before the jumpy thing got away. She damned them all, the grinding stop, the rough passage, and the jouncing as her fellow passengers jumped back in. She damned the lot of them, loudly and creatively.

Grumble, who had spent his life in low dives among vile-tongued men, was impressed at her eloquence. Sumner was much amused.

Except for Julia's magnificent performance, Grumble would have been grumbling. He had chosen a life of art, the art of the con. He was not a fellow for physical heroics, nor flight in wretched weather from enemies bearing the lust to kill.

Manning the oars, Robber hollered at Grumble, Sumner, and Reina from time to time to bail water out of the bottom of the boat. He had given them each buckets for the purpose. Julia cursed the water, which sloshed around and soaked her back and her bottom and the place where the baby was worming its way into the world. She cursed the baby, she cursed the bailing, she cursed the splashes, and she cursed the stupid rain.

Reina and Sumner took turns holding Julia in her squatting position and holding Esperanza. This child was showing her usual good spirit, looking around at everything with an expression of wonder. She never uttered a complaint.

Julia made up for Esperanza's reticence. She amplified her cursing now. She damned all male animals—they had those stupid appendages they just had to, had to, had to indulge—*Those damn things are the authors of pain in the world*.

"This creek is feisty," said Robber. "When we flow into the Los Angeles River, it might turn into a monster."

"I've never seen the Los Angeles River aroused," said Grumble.

"You ain't seen it after this much rain."

Julia denounced the curse God put on women in the Garden of Eden, the pain of bearing children, never to end, never to end. She cursed God himself, who was just another male. And she cursed His Holy Mother—*I don't give a damn why, I'm just cursing her.* At the start of every labor pain, or when she couldn't think of anyone else to curse, she returned to execrating Flat Dog.

Grumble heard oaths that were new on the horizon of his personal experience.

"Here comes the river," said Robber, gesturing to the right. He rowed the boat toward that bank. Where the new current plunged in, the water roiled, the waves tossing into the air. It reminded Grumble of a horse herd stampeding, their manes flying—it was as loud and scary as a stampede.

Robber heaved the boat through the roiling where the two currents met. The new, big current seized the small craft and turned it backward.

Robber yelled at the river, pulled fiercely on the oars, pivoted, and got himself faced downstream again. The boat rocked and bounced on the bucking river.

Everyone got splashed head to toe, as though they weren't already wet enough.

Then the water eased off to mere jostling, and full speed ahead, lickety-split.

Reina and Sumner patted Julia, held her, arranged the wool blankets tight around her. "They can't keep you dry," said Sumner, "but they'll keep you warm."

Julia swore bitterly.

Soon Robber warned his passengers, "The Zanja Madre dam is coming up."

"Dam?" said Grumble, Sumner, and Reina in one voice.

Robber looked at them. "How do you think the fields get irrigated? This dam makes the ditch."

"What are we going to do?" cried Grumble.

"Pull the boat out and portage it around."

Julia spewed out imprecations.

Grumble said, "Just tell me what to do."

Robber nodded, as though to say, *Good man*.

He stood up at the oars and peered downstream. "I can't see it."

They all looked downstream. The rain thinned, and the sound of the river blocked out . . .

"Oh, shit," said Robber.

He dropped to his seat and rowed like hell for the left bank.

"We're not gonna make it!"

Julia shrieked.

Now they all saw the dam of mud and brush. In a sheen of light the river thrummed straight over it.

Robber stood up and stared frantically at the dam. Frantically, he maneuvered, remaneuvered, got them a stroke this way and a stroke that way. "I don't see the best spot to go over," he hollered. "We may flip!"

The bow jutted into space. The bottom scraped.

"Oh, God," yelled Robber.

"Madre de Dios!" bellowed Julia.

Sitting in the stern, Grumble felt the waters swamp that end of the boat. "We're sinking!" he shouted.

Robber heaved on the oars, and the bow tilted downward.

They teetered over the dam.

Julia screamed.

The bow dived into the river several feet below. The undertow grabbed it.

The stern swung around the bow.

Robber rowed furiously, trying to jerk the stern downstream. Current boiled over the dam and into the boat.

Robber roared as he made a mighty heave.

With a sucking sound the bow popped out of the undertow.

All of a sudden their craft was small, flooded, and low and wobbly in the water.

"Bail!" shouted Robber.

The passengers bucketed water from the boat to the river. Bucket by bucket the boat floated higher. Soon it was on the water and not in it.

Finally, Robber could row to shore. He jumped out and held the boat with the painter.

Julia cursed Robber.

After Grumble, Sumner, and Reina clambered out, Reina holding Esperanza, Robber lifted Julia from the boat and set her on the ground.

She didn't protest. She was silent for the moment, her face grim and fixed, her mind riding toward the agony to come, plunging on the wild and stampeding stallion of pain.

Robber turned the boat upside down, then righted it, and pushed it back into the river. They got in, helped Julia get balanced in her squat, and headed downstream.

Grumble muttered to himself, "Heaven is a very, very long way off, and hell is hounding our heels."

* * *

THE WIND PICKED up and the rain fell harder.

"Look sharp," said Sam.

In Indian country you knew where enemies might be. In the underbrush along the creek. In the timber. Behind the ridge. Here they could come from any direction.

They turned the horses away from the river, along the irrigation ditch, to avoid giving the boat away.

Here on the eastern edge of the pueblo he could see too many hiding places. Crooked tracks led away from the bank, and hovels dotted the byways. A few structures were adobes. Any wall, any pen, any bush could hide an enemy.

No call for an honest fight here. Ideal spot for an ambush.

He didn't know whether he was chill from the rain or from fear.

An old woman came out of a hovel hunched over, a multicolored blanket draped over her head. She looked at the four riders passing along the river. Her mouth dropped into a U and she hurried back inside.

Sam strained his eyes down every track, around the edges of every building and fence, behind every tree, and saw nothing or everything. In the rain—streaming down, whipped by the wind—in the rain everything moved. Or nothing.

Long after the pueblo was behind them, his skin prickled. Turning in his saddle, he could see only hints of the village, dark shadows in the rain.

THE RAIN WAS the backdrop, unnoticed. Grumble paid it no mind, and the other boaters stopped grousing about it.

Though Julia's protests were unrelenting, Grumble accepted them as he accepted the rain and cold. Reina said, "The pains are coming closer together."

Grumble was tired. He couldn't remember, ever, being so tired. "How far?" he asked.

Robber didn't answer.

"How long to the harbor?"

"I don't know. By road from the pueblo, twenty-five miles. By river, I don't know. Longer." He looked at the current. "The river's going godawmighty fast, but it's a long way."

For an hour or so, the ride had been fast and uneventful. Grumble thought wearily, *Just the way I want it.* He grimaced.

"Will we make it tonight?"

"If we do, it will be way, way after dark."

"Julia's not gonna wait that long," said Sumner.

The men looked at each other. In the rain and the mud it would be one miserable night.

And the baby? Grumble wondered. *Can the baby survive?*

"The other river's coming up," said Robber.

"Other river?"

Robber smiled slightly. "The Rio Hondo."

Robber was a man of the waters, Grumble knew. He understood swells and tides, storms and following seas. It was no surprise that hills and the rivulets they formed, rains and the currents they created, these would be within his ken. People who didn't understand such things, well, Robber probably thought them a little silly.

Grumble didn't mind.

Robber pointed out the Rio Hondo coming in from the left, another lift to a current that was already bounding. "I'm going to hug the left bank," said Robber. "We want to feather into this new force as silky as possible."

Grumble was collecting Robber's jargon of the waters.

"It won't feel like a feather, though," said Robber.

It felt like they hit a rock. The bow bumped up and sideways. Julia yelled, and followed that with a spew of Spanish babble.

The river jabbered louder, and nattered and gabbled, and gurgled. It whacked the gunwales and slashed its waves over and into the boat, drenching the occupants. It slapped and jiggled the boat, squirreled it sideways, and teeter-tottered it. Robber was furious with trying to keep it straight. After a jigger-jerky ride, they slid into water that wasn't quite as rough.

Robber spun the boat sideways, so he could see upstream and down. His eyes rounded, his lower lip trembled, and he said, "Oh, shit!"

Grumble looked up the little *rio*. Toward them roared a wall about two feet high, a wall of churning water.

"Flash flood!" cried Robber.

Every eye was fixed on the roaring wall. They gasped for the last breath they might take on this earth.

The waters fell like an avalanche on the stern of their boat. The bow tilted toward the sky. The undertow grabbed the back end and ripped it sideways. The boat corkscrewed, the bow shot upward, and everything and everyone in the boat pitched into the tumult.

Grumble thought of nothing but grabbing Julia. He seized her under the arms and kicked like hell. Water ripped them, it rocked them, it buried them, it threw them high—it pummeled them and somersaulted them—it flung them like dirt from an explosion.

Yet being flung aside and whirled around meant . . . Grumble lay on his back and kicked like hell. "Kick!" he hollered at Julia, and felt her motions down below. "Kick!" He thrashed on his back, sometimes with his head underwater, Julia on top of him, faceup.

The eddy grabbed his shoulders and jerked them upstream. He made his last cry sound epic: "Ki-i-ck!"

Waves tumbled and flummoxed him. He kicked. Then suddenly he was sure they were going upstream instead of down. He fought for his breath, for his sanity. They bobbed along like corks. By God, they *were* going upstream. The current blasted downstream like a train of runaway wagons, and this eddy mildly eased its way the other direction.

He turned them toward the bank. In a few minutes he could actually stand up. It seemed like a miracle.

He took inventory.

Ten paces above them was Sumner, on his hands and knees in the shallows.

Another twenty paces above Sumner stood Robber, hip

deep in water, his arms wrapped around Reina, her arms wrapped around Esperanza. They all had expressions of absolute stupefaction on their faces.

Reina fussed furiously with the blankets around Esperanza's face. The child sneezed, and everyone laughed.

Only the boat was missing.

THE ROAR OF wild waters, then the shouts—the four riders looked at each other, then whipped their horses down the grassy slope toward the river.

"Help!" Grumble yelled.

Flat Dog jumped off his horse on the fly, sprinted to the bank, and plowed through the water to Grumble and Julia. In a jiffy he had his wife on grass above the bank, resting.

"Blankets!"

"They're soaked," called Robber, who was holding Reina's hand and pulling her out of the river.

"Blankets anyway!"

Sumner staggered toward the bank.

Sam saw one dark shadow in the water. He jumped in and found the water was only waist deep. An arm's length beyond him it was raging. The shadow turned out to be a blanket, and he ran to Julia with it.

Ignored, Grumble crawled out of the water, crawled to Julia, and sagged to the ground.

Everyone hovered over Julia.

She said in Spanish, "The baby's coming now, the baby's going to come now, the baby's coming now."

THEY MADE CAMP right there. In a few minutes wet canvas was tented to make a sort of shelter, and Flat Dog had a small fire going.

Robber found the boat a quarter mile downstream, caught on some brush, and brought it back.

Sam and Hannibal staked the horses and went on foot to

scout. Rubio or not, the party had to stay right here. Though the air felt swollen with moisture, the rain had eased off. They topped the rise behind the camp and looked up their back trail. Mists hung low. Sam's eyes swept the grasses, bushes, and trees with his naked eyes. Then he lifted the field glass and swept them again. Coy cocked his head, as though listening.

Reina and Sumner made Julia comfortable near the fire. Grumble mumbled the prayers left from a Catholic boyhood in Baltimore.

In twenty minutes Flat Dog had coffee bubbling. Julia rejected it angrily, and glared and cursed her husband. The others were grateful for the tin cups of hot, steaming brew.

Grumble was warming his hands on the cup when Sam and Hannibal came treading softly into camp. Sam said, "They're here."

Chapter Nine

We can defend this spot," said Hannibal.

It was a low rise between the river and the creek, which here ran almost parallel. A hundred paces below, the creek crooked hard left into the river, just below the camp. *Just below our people.*

The banks of the river and of the creek had plenty of cover, trees and bushes. This rise had almost none.

Sam and Hannibal crowded behind the one low tree on the rise. Flat Dog squatted behind a boulder that barely hid him. Galbraith lay in some high grass, the best he could do.

Coy kept prancing out from behind the trees and sniffing the breeze.

"How many?" asked Flat Dog.

"At least a dozen," said Sam. He was holding the field glass on them. They were strung out, dipping up and down on the hillocks, and he couldn't see them all at once.

Galbraith kept silent.

"Rubio there?"

"Out in front."

"He is some sumbitch," Flat Dog said from his boulder.

"They're on our tracks," said Sam.

"Leading them right to this spot," said Hannibal.

"And if they get by us," said Flat Dog, "leading them straight to the boat."

Sam's fantasy called up a crying newborn, and the child's cry floated like a croon to the murderers.

Sam surveyed the area. "I hate to give up the high ground," he said, "but . . ."

"No choice," said Hannibal.

"A cross fire," said Sam. "Right here, a cross fire."

Galbraith nodded once. Quick to act and slow to speak, he crawled off the rise, bent low, and took cover on the slope. The other three looked at each other. Flat Dog started after Galbraith, probably to be closer to Julia.

"Flat Dog," called Sam. "Leave Rubio to us."

His friend looked back and nodded.

Sam and Hannibal ducked down toward the creek. The cover was poor all the way to the willows along the bank. "In those cottonwoods," said Hannibal, indicating the far bank.

The men were sloshing through the water when Coy stopped at its edge. His spine hair rose, his tail pointed, and he growled.

Sam saw it. "Cub!"

Hannibal looked sharp, but could see only wiggling leaves of bushes. "Black bear or griz?"

"Couldn't tell."

They both watched the shrubbery where the cub disappeared. "Berry patch," said Sam.

Where there was one cub, there were probably two. Where there were any cubs, there was a sow. It was the sow who would be dangerous, very dangerous if you got between her and one of the cubs.

"Griz," said Sam. "Just saw her hump." A grizzly had a shoulder that, compared to a black bear's, tented up.

Coy snarled and gave a short, sharp bark.

The silvertip rose on her hind legs. The cub rumpety-rumped past her. Mama pivoted and padded along behind the cub.

"Hightailing it," said Hannibal.

Sam watched the spot. "I hope so. Sure gives me the willies," he said.

They picked shooting stations behind cottonwoods. Their barrels rested on limbs. The shots were a reasonable distance, wide open, and there was no wind. But the mist, which thickened and cleared from moment to moment, could ruin visibility.

"I don't like these odds," Sam said. The fur men had four rifles, which would take a minute or so to reload after the first volley. Rubio's men had a dozen or more rifles. Both sides had pistols.

Sam watched the rise. Turning his back to the berry patch made his skin tingle. Coy kept looking that way.

"Any strategy?" said Sam.

"Yeah. Blow hell out of them."

No need for the field glass now. Tense, Sam and Hannibal chewed their lips, rubbed their fingers, and stamped their feet. They watched for death to approach above. They listened nervously for the first sound of life arriving below. *And the damn griz is behind me,* thought Sam.

The lead rider came into view. From glassing him earlier, Sam knew it was Rubio. He looked along his sights.

"Take Rubio down with the first shot," said Hannibal, "so Flat Dog won't have to."

"Right."

"I'll hold fire."

TWO WORLDS FOR Julia, one black and one gray. In the black world she was a mote of dust spinning in a whirlwind of agony. She saw the whirlwind in ultra-clarity, the riffles of wind wild and glittering. Compared to any in real life, it was monumental, gargantuan, as big as the reach of the Milky Way across the night sky. Within this cyclone of energy the dust mote known as Julia Rubio Flat Dog gyrated around and around in unbelievable fury. And on this terrible power she rose up and up and up and up . . .

Then, abruptly, it set her down into the gray world, here on the ground, in this day of mist, on this soggy ground, in these wet blankets, with these two good, pitying people, Reina and Sumner, holding her hands on each side.

Julia knew she would die. The next time the whirlwind snatched her up she would break open, she would fly apart, and the life would spray out of her in bloody droplets into the savage air.

The baby will live, she thought. She didn't understand that, but the baby would live. She was glad.

And she was glad to die. Eager to die. Anything except . . .

The black world took her again. In an instant she was screaming upward into the whirlwind.

SAM KEPT HIS eyes on the riders. Coy pointed like a bird dog toward the berry patch where the griz disappeared. *Damn, I hate this.* Rubio was enough to worry about.

The foremost horse and rider loped into range. Rubio was reading the sloppy tracks himself. His mount cantered forward steadily. The shot was still long.

Rubio slowed his mount to a walk. *Dammit.* If the don was good at reading sign, he'd see the tale soon enough—horses cutting suddenly downhill toward the river, without any sense—moccasin prints among the horse prints.

It was time. Sam told himself, *Mexicans can't outshoot mountain men, no way.*

He squeezed the trigger, thinking clearly, *Surprise better be the trump card.*

* * *

JULIA FLAT DOG, born Julia Rubio y Obregon, made the supreme effort of her eighteen years. She gathered all her thoughts, all her juices, all her muscles, all her force, everything she was and a lot more, and—Madre de Dios—pushed! Once! Twice! Reina and Sumner were exclaiming, cheering her on, but her fierce concentration made her deaf. Only the urge and the effort existed.

A third time! She teetered on the edge of success and fell back. Immediately, with a force she never dreamed she had, Julia made a huge fourth push and—*blessed virgin!*—she expelled the cursed, awful, alien thing from her body. It felt like excreting a melon.

"You did it!" cried Sumner.

Grumble, sitting at her head, applauded.

"Es en muchacho!" exclaimed Reina. It's a boy.

Robber joined in Grumble's applause.

Beaming, Sumner wiped and dried the baby.

Reina held Esperanza close to the new child. "This is your cousin," she said.

The new fellow roared out a protest at this strange world. He roared another one at the cold and the damp. Everyone chuckled.

Grumble cut the cord, and Reina put the baby to his mother's breast.

Julia was swimming back toward the surface of the ocean of awareness. She noticed a weight on her chest. She felt it with her fingers, and her mind rose toward the light. She held the weight where she could see it.

A baby. Her baby. A child, a human being. A living union of her and Flat Dog. A boy. He glowed with an angelic light. He was the most beautiful creature she'd ever seen.

Emotion lifted her on a huge wave, a swell of ecstasy. She clutched their creation to her bosom.

After a long while, she managed to say, "He is Azul Flat Dog. After Flat Dog's brother, Blue Medicine Horse, who died."

Happily, she unsnapped her blouse and put Azul's mouth on her nipple. As she felt the first suck at her milk, a rifle boomed.

CESAR RUBIO STOOD up in his stirrups to see the tracks. Then three waves crashed on him almost simultaneously— he felt an agony in his hip, he heard an explosion, and he crashed off his mount to the ground.

"Hell," said Sam, "he moved and it hit him low."

Two shots boomed from the direction of the river.

Rubio's men wheeled, looked, milled, raised their rifles, and saw nothing to shoot at.

One man was on the ground, another sagging and bleeding in his saddle.

A rider decided the creek was better than the river and charged down the short slope into bushes and trees.

All followed him.

Hannibal shot one man out of his saddle.

Hearing the blast and seeing the smoke, the line of riders angled upstream.

Rubio's mount came last in a jerky gait. The don's boot was caught in the stirrup, and his body dangled like an effigy, bouncing across grass, rocks, and mud.

Just as the riders disappeared into the cover, Sam shot again. The last rider flinched and grabbed but kept his seat.

"They're into the berry patch," he said, looking wild-eyed at Hannibal.

They both reloaded fast, fingers flying.

For long moments they heard nothing and saw nothing.

From the corner of his eye Sam saw Flat Dog and Galbraith crawl across the top of the rise, half-hidden in the grass, rifles ready.

The griz roared.

"If hell has church bells," said Hannibal, "they sound like that."

Eight or ten riders burst out of the thicket like a flock of ducks shotgunned by hunters.

Flat Dog and Galbraith fired from the high ground.

Sam heard an answering shot and saw the smoke, but the barrel seemed to be pointed straight up in the air.

More riders burst out of the berry patch. They wavered, gathered, and flew back north, the way they came, toward the pueblo, toward home. Anywhere gunfire and grizzlies might not tear hell out of them.

Rubio's horse came last, awkwardly, with Rubio's weight flopping along on one side. The don thrashed desperately to get his boot free. Suddenly, in a paroxysm of effort, he wrenched the foot loose and collapsed onto the muddy earth. His horse abandoned him at a gallop.

Sam looked at his enemy, now brought low.

Flat Dog started down the hill toward Rubio.

"Let him be," called Hannibal.

All four trappers waited. They watched. Coy grew rigid, pointed, and growled.

The sow griz approached the injured don with mincing steps. She was curious but wary. She stopped and looked. She sniffed the air, and the trappers felt glad to be downwind of her. She took several minutes getting to the crumpled figure.

She swatted it a couple of times, in a testing way.

Rubio flung an arm up in a half circle and back to the ground.

The griz roared and tore his shoulder with her teeth.

The two cubs crept close.

The griz roared louder. She whacked the body with her snout. She snuffled. She growled, bit, and waggled her head.

An arm came away in her mouth, hand up, accepting the rain.

Sam and Hannibal walked up the rise to join their friends. They looked at the bleeding bodies of the fallen. They looked at each other. They wanted to share their amazement, but there were no words.

They trotted away from the griz, toward camp. Not a man of them wanted to see more of what was happening with the griz and . . .

"Just before the first shot," said Galbraith, "I thought I heard a baby bawl."

Flat Dog ran toward Julia.

Chapter Ten

There on the bank of the river Hannibal took charge of telling the sisters. "Your father is dead."

"How?" said Julia, her voice shaking.

"It's strange," he said. "It's beyond strange. We fired at your father's party. They fled into a berry patch along the creek." He hesitated. "A grizzly bear attacked him and . . . It was almost beyond belief."

All of them looked at each other, wide-eyed.

"The others rode back where they came from. Fast."

Reina and Julia looked at each other. "Do you want me to go look?" said Reina.

Julia kissed Azul's head and then looked up at her sister. "No."

THE CAPTAIN OF the *Madison*, glad to have the gold coins for the passages, welcomed Sam's party to the harbor in San Pedro and his ship. "I was seeking you," he said, but did not yet explain.

The partings at San Pedro were brief and bittersweet. Reina wanted to return to her home, to rejoin her husband and children and see to the burial of her father.

All but Reina—Sam, Hannibal, Grumble, Flat Dog, Sumner, Galbraith, Robber, Julia, and the two infants—set forth on the evening tide on the *Madison* to San Diego.

Sam and Hannibal stood near the penned horses. The

night was windy and the seas high. Coy watched the poor animals, who could do nothing but try to maintain balance as the boat switched from tack to tack and rocked from wave to wave. Sam was worried about Paladin, and the captain required that some one of the party watch the horses continually.

Sam looked westward upon the dark waters. China, he supposed, was out there somewhere. "I set out to find a home," he said to Hannibal. "I found it—Crow country. And now I'm as far from it as I can get. Hell, I'm even off the continent."

"Think about it. These waters began in Crow country. They came down the mountains and across the desert and joined this ocean. On the water you're always home."

Now Captain Bledsoe emerged out of the darkness. "I bring you a letter from Captain Jedediah Smith." He handed it to Sam, who passed it to Hannibal.

"Will you read it to me?"

Hannibal did.

To Samuel Morgan—

Dear Sir, and your companions Mr. McKye and Flat Dog,

I write in strong hopes that your fortunes have been better than mine. Leaving two days after you, I rode to Saint Joseph Mission, where I found in charge one Father Duran, a melancholy and thoroughly disagreeable man. He would not hear my request to pass through to the governor's residence in Monterey, and thus I could not join you there. Instead he put me in the guardhouse and told me that an officer would come from San Francisco to try my case. During the intervening days he made no provision for feeding myself or my men, and we were obliged to throw ourselves on the kindness of the elderly overseer.

It proved that an Indian had accused me of claiming the country on the Peticutry River. When the commander arrived, however, one Lieut. Martinos, instead of punishing me in accordance with the wishes of Father Duran, he sentenced the Indian to an undeserved flogging.

After two weeks the governor finally wrote from Monterey, bidding me to come there under guard.

In Monterey Governor Echeandia proved as difficult as ever. He gave me the liberty of the town, but no satisfaction with my problem. The town I found quaint, but the inhabitants too free and careless in their ways. There I received word of your difficulties at the mission and your journey southward to rejoin Flat Dog's wife and your daughter. I hope that effort has proved successful.

Through many discussions here the governor maintained his position that I am an intruder in the country, and my status can only be resolved by a journey to Mexico City. After some inquiries I determined that he meant for me to pay for my own passage to Mexico, and expressed my outrage that a man should be expected to take himself to prison at his own expense.

The governor further insisted that my men come in. I suggested that they were closer to San Francisco and wrote Mr. Rogers to proceed there.

The captains of four ships in port then kindly vouched for me and promised to be responsible for my conduct. Upon that event Echeandia gave me three choices, to go to Mexico, wait for instructions to come from Mexico, or leave the country by the route by which I entered.

More than eager to rid myself of California, I chose the latter. The governor signed a passport which enables me to purchase provisions. I am soon, therefore, to travel to San Francisco on the *Franklin,* equip myself, and leave the country.

In these circumstances there appears to be no opportunity for you, Mr. McKye, and Flat Dog to take your places as employees of Smith, Jackson & Sublette. I have therefore discharged you as of the date you left our camp on the Appelaminy. I hope that we shall all greet each other gladly at the rendezvous next summer.

> Believe me
> your sincere friend,
> Jedediah S. Smith

Sam gazed out at the dark sea, stretching all the way to China. He turned and studied the wavy black line made by the coastal hills of California. He walked to the lee rail and looked at the country. Hannibal followed and stood beside him. Coy rubbed against the other leg. The men propped their hands on the rail and leaned out. Here you could hear the prow cutting through the water.

"A country of troubles," said Sam. "For me."

The memories were too fresh to be spoken. Meadowlark had died there. Sam had killed men there. "The authorities are probably looking for me too."

"Hell, the Mexican constabulary probably wants you, me, Flat Dog, Grumble, Sumner, Jedediah Smith, every American who's set foot in the province."

Sam felt the wind at his back, its scent strong with something . . .

Flat Dog walked up. "Time for my watch."

"I can stay longer," Sam said.

The Crow shook his head. "Look in on Julia, will you?"

Flat Dog's wife was facedown on the bunk in the small cabin, sobbing. Her sobs racked her whole body, and her cries drowned out the wind, the seas, and the noises of the rigging and sails.

Suddenly Julia twisted violently onto her back. She convulsed with sobs, over and over and over.

Hannibal gave Sam a look of warning.

She shouted, "I hated the *diablo*!" She slammed her fists against the bedclothes at her side. "I hated him!" She glared at Sam and Hannibal.

Coy yipped.

Esperanza woke up bawling.

Immediately Julia sat up. "Hand her to me."

Sam did.

Julia raised her blouse without hesitation, put Esperanza on one breast, and lay back down. "Stay with me," she said, "please stay."

Her chest began to heave again.

Sam and Hannibal sat down on the end of the bunk and looked at each other uncomfortably.

Sam glanced at Julia and for the first time admitted this thought clearly to his mind: *When I lost Meadowlark, I lost Esperanza.*

"It's true," said Hannibal.

Sam shot him a look. *Damn, get out of my head.*

"Sad but true."

Azul whimpered.

Julia held her arms out. Sam put her son in them. In a moment she had a child on each breast.

I lost her.

Soon the children were asleep. "Take them, please."

When Sam did, Julia began to bawl again, and then to wail.

Sam curled up on the floor and tried to sleep.

Hannibal sat in a corner, leaned back, and closed his eyes.

TWO HOURS LATER they were back on watch with the horses, peering into the darkness.

Coy growled.

"A change in the weather, gentlemen."

Captain Bledsoe, evidently wandering his ship at night. The odor of his pipe was as strong as the smell of the sea. "It's time. They don't have four seasons on this coast, just dry season and rainy season. The storms can blow hard. This sea is not pacific." With a quick smile at his pun the captain continued on his rounds.

Sam smiled to himself. Odd how many people in his life gave importance to words. Pacific not pacific. Grumble treasured words, so did Hannibal. Sam's father, Lewis Morgan, had had a tongue voluble and creative. A Welsh tradition, said his father. *I should learn to read.*

"We already had our California storms," said Hannibal.

"I want to go home," said Sam.

"California is beautiful and languid," said Hannibal.

Coy whined and thumped his tail.

"One day it will be American."

Sam looked at Hannibal in surprise, and then back at the dark continent off the port bow. His single thought was, *What on earth do I do now?*

Hannibal said, "Let's drive horses to the mountains and sell them."

IT TOOK THEM a week to arrange things in San Diego.

First they brain-stormed their plans. The men had gold in their pockets, from selling the saddles, firearms, and other weapons. Since they'd all played the roles of fighters and rescuers, they would divide the booty equally.

Robber and Galbraith weren't interested in taking horses anywhere. They liked the little town and the easy life in California. They would stay.

"Who else wants what?" asked Sam.

"I think it might be well to take leave of California for a time," said Grumble.

"I goes where my massa goes," said Sumner, the apprentice con man.

They laughed at the darkie accent. Coy gave one sharp yip at all of them.

"Where are we going to go exactly?" said Flat Dog. "Winter's coming on."

"Winter's the time to cross the desert," said Sam. He would never forget that terrible June crossing with Jedediah, Gobel, and Robert Evans.

"Let's go to Taos or Santa Fe," said Hannibal. "Spend the cold months there before we head for rendezvous."

They considered and one by one the men nodded. Julia just

listened. Since her one night of wild grief, she had seemed even-keeled. Flat Dog remarked to Sam that with two children to take care of, she showed less interest in men's doings.

"All right, we can probably buy horses from the mission," said Sam. Jedediah Smith had seen the huge herds when he was force-marched to San Diego last winter. The Californios had far, far more horses than they had any use for.

"What do you think we'll have to pay for them?" asked Sumner.

Grumble said, "At Mission San Carlos Borromeo de Carmelo we paid six dollars for a pair."

"And they were broke to harness," said Sam. "These will be unbroke."

Flat Dog said, "And at rendezvous we can sell them for . . . ?"

"Fifty to a hundred each," said Sam.

"That appeals to my larcenous heart," said Sumner.

"Can we get fifty animals?" said Flat Dog.

Hannibal shook his head. "We have to buy supplies."

"Say thirty," said Sam.

Grumble put in, "How many can we drive?"

Sam and Hannibal took thought. "Five men," said Flat Dog.

"Don't count me," said Grumble. The cherub hated riding, and hadn't forked a horse once on their entire journey. "I may walk the whole way."

"We could drive a hundred easily," said Hannibal.

"All right, here's a proposition," said Grumble. "I'll put my hand in my trunk and bring out enough coins to bring our horse count to a hundred."

"Grumble, you have that much gold?" said Sam.

The con man gave a dry smile. "For me money is a tool." He looked merrily at them. "This way we all get a handsome profit. Divided by five, up toward a thousand dollars each. But I get something in the bargain."

"Oh, no," said Sam.

"We'll winter in Santa Fe, yes?"

"Probably," said Hannibal. "Or Taos."

"Santa Fe is bigger, so let's head there. The deal is, one day or night a week each of you plays a little game with me."

"Chicanery," said Hannibal.

"Con games," said Sam.

"Exactly," said Grumble.

"Nothing that will get us arrested," said Sam.

"I am revolted by jails," said Grumble.

"It's a deal," said Hannibal.

One by one, they all agreed—Sam, Hannibal, Flat Dog, and Sumner. Coy gave another yip.

"Let's get mares," said Sam. "There'll be foals in the spring before we go to rendezvous."

"Good thought."

And on into the night they planned.

San Diego was a cinch. Aside from the mission and presidio, the town was only four adobes and about three dozen dark huts overlooking a fine bay. The letter of safe passage assured their hospitality at the mission. They avoided the presidio, where some officer might demand passports.

In a week they bought their hundred horses, got supplies, hired an Indian guide, and got started east across the Mojave Desert.

"Let's not go anywhere near the Mojave villages," Sam told the guide in Spanish. He was an older man, with a look of having seen everything.

"No," the man answered, "we go to the Yuma villages."

So they did.

For the first time since leaving rendezvous Sam thought, *I am headed home.* Roundabout, but home.

The desert was easy enough. Julia traveled almost as comfortably as a Crow woman, even with the two children. Sam felt like an old hand there now, and the guide knew where to find water. The crossing of the Colorado River wasn't bad—in November the river was low. Coy not only kept up with the herd but led the way—the little coyote didn't like swimming, so he did it fast.

At the Yuma villages they were welcomed as enemies of the Mojaves. They gave the Indians some presents, hired a new guide, and passed on rapidly. The route of the Gila River, said the Indians, had been used by other trappers, those from Taos.

Now they got the story of that trapping party and the Mojaves. The trappers worked their way up the Colorado, the Yumas said, to the Mojave villages. Red Shirt demanded payment for the beaver they'd taken out of the river. Incensed, for the Mojaves had no interest in the beaver, the trappers refused. In the ensuing fight several Mojaves were killed.

"And took it out on us," Sam said to Hannibal.

Up the valley of the Gila they went, clear to where the Salt River joined it, and above. Though the river was full of beaver, they didn't pause to trap. Their minds were on getting the livestock safe to Santa Fe. Coy stayed near Paladin's hoofs and helped control the herd.

The Apaches watched them closely all the way, but didn't seem to want to make trouble.

Flat Dog, Julia, and the small children spent every night in a tipi. She fed both of them at her breasts, and tended to all their needs.

Spending his days alongside the herd, watching for trouble, Sam realized that he felt more like Esperanza's uncle than her father. He reflected that Julia and Flat Dog were the real family, and would be the parents in the eyes of the Crow people.

I have no family, he thought often.

That night, as all of them sat around a warm, crackling fire, he felt like playing his tin whistle. He hadn't touched it in California. He played an old tune in a minor key. Coy joined in with a mournful howl. Sam spoke sharply to him, and he fell into a resentful silence.

After one time through the tune, Hannibal raised his husky bass voice with the words, and Julia hummed a high, floating harmony over it all:

I am a poor wayfarin' stranger
A-wanderin' through this world of woe
But there's no trouble, no toil or danger
In that bright land to which I go.

I'm going home to see my father
I'm going there no more to roam
I'm just a-goin' over Jordan
I'm just a-goin' over home.

Sam thought, *It's how much I miss my dad, that's why I played this song.*

After singing the second verse, Hannibal put in the other chorus—

I'm going there to meet my mother
She said she'd meet me when I come . . .

Sam wondered if his mother, that good, weak woman, was still alive. If so, she was under the thumb of brother Owen.

When Sam put away the tin whistle, he realized how much he'd missed playing it. He reached down and scratched Coy's head. The coyote felt like an old, old buddy.

The next night Sam played again for a few minutes. Then he did something totally spontaneous. He said to Grumble, "Teach me to read."

Grumble and Hannibal competed for the privilege of teaching Sam. Grumble wrote out a list of the twenty-six letters of the alphabet. Hannibal taught Sam how to recite them to "Baa, Baa, Black Sheep."

"Now you can sing the alphabet while you ride alongside the herd by yourself all day."

Near the headwaters of the Gila they saw the rough road that led up to the copper mines, and wagons coming down. They crossed the divide above, coasted down the mountains into the huge valley, and turned north along the Rio Grande.

As they drove their herd up the river toward the capital city, Sam picked out his first words from a copy of the King James Bible, one of several books that Hannibal carried. He found reading frustrating, maddening, and worse. The way English is spelled made no sense to him.

By the time they passed the hamlet of Albuquerque, he was understanding his first English sentences. Soon he learned to pick out sayings he'd heard all his life—"Eye for eye, tooth for tooth, hand for hand, foot for foot."

"Not enough for me," said Sumner. "You take my eye, I take both yours."

Coy squealed.

"I abhor violence," said Grumble.

Sam sounded out the next one Hannibal had marked for him slowly. "Thou shalt love thy neighbor as thyself."

"The world chooses not to live by that admonition," said Grumble. No one disputed with him.

"Why can't they use plain talk?" said Sumner. " 'Thou,' 'thy'—it's dumb."

"He that is without sin among you, let him first cast a stone at her."

"I'd recommend that one," Grumble said.

"You're just afraid of getting stoned," said Sam.

"You white folks," said Sumner. Everyone looked at him. "Bible words," said Sumner, "made me dump that whole religion down the outhouse."

They all looked at each other around the fire.

Finally Hannibal shrugged. "Sam, if you want to know some gods, read up on the Greeks. Sex, murder, revenge, incest, the whole kit and caboodle."

Sam looked at Flat Dog. "What do you say about this? Give us a story about Crow gods."

"They're not really gods," said Flat Dog, "more like heroes."

Julia cleared her throat. Flat Dog looked at his wife. Her face gave warning. He smiled at Sam and shrugged.

"All right," said Sam. He turned to Julia. "What about you?"

"I am a Catholic. Religion is something I do, not something I analyze."

Coy whined and looked at Sam for attention. He cocked his ears forward and then backward. Sam scratched his head.

"So what do you want to *do*?" asked Hannibal.

"Go to mass on Christmas Day. Get me to Santa Fe in time to go to mass."

They rode into the city on Christmas Eve and close-herded their horses on good grass on the Santa Fe River above town. Flat Dog went with Julia to the Church of Our Lady of Guadalupe the next morning to celebrate the anniversary of the birth of Christ.

And Julia had more to do. The next day the priest baptized their son Azul into the Christian faith. At her request, which felt like a command, Sam Morgan stood as the infant's godfather.

Father and godfather, he thought. He didn't know what it all meant.

Chapter Eleven

The priest, Father Herrera, took them visiting. "This is the casa of the Otero family." Sam, Coy, Hannibal, and Flat Dog trundled along beside the priest. "Señora Luna, the sister of Señora Otero, is likely to help you, I think. Since it is the day of the birth of our Lord, she is in town."

Sam liked Santa Fe. It was perched on a high plateau below snowy mountains. The low buildings were all adobe, and columns of smoke rose straight up into a golden light that shimmered. The town was built along the river, and the streets wound out from the plaza unpredictably, twisting like roots of a tree. He had no idea where this winding lane would lead them, but the town was striking, even beautiful.

He hadn't seen so many people in several years, several thousand of them. The men of means wore huge-brimmed hats, the rowels of their spurs were enormous, almost comical, and they threw a blanket over one shoulder in a dashing style. Their horses were the same wiry Spanish ponies he'd seen in California.

"Señora Luna owns Rancho de las Palomas," the priest had said. "It is a splendid ranch of great size. The wagon trains, on El Camino Real from Santa Fe on the way to Chihuahua, they stop and trade there. The señora does an exemplary job running the enterprise." Sam's Spanish really wasn't up to words like "exemplary," but he got the point.

Hannibal raised an eyebrow at the priest.

"A widow," the padre said, "and an accomplished woman."

"Paloma?" said Sam as the three of them ambled lazily along. "That's a new one on me."

"It means 'dove,'" said the padre. "There is a fine Spanish novel called *Linda Paloma*. Beautiful dove."

"Here we are," said the priest, opening a gate into a courtyard.

The casa was handsome in the Santa Fe way, *vigas* jutting out above walls of plastered adobe. But they weren't going inside. Father Herrera led them into a courtyard and introduced them to two sisters, Señora Paloma Luna y Salazar and Señora Rosa Otero y Salazar.

"Excuse me a moment," said Señora Luna, finishing some sort of work with her hands. Sam was stunned. He'd expected a woman well along in years. The señora was in her early thirties, he guessed, and possessed of a grave beauty.

Señora Otero acknowledged the introductions, excused herself, and stepped into the house. The priest went with her.

Señora Luna came forward, holding a long string of red chiles. She hung it from a *viga,* retreated, and looked at it and the entire row of them along the house. *"Ristras,"* she said. "I find beautiful things irresistible."

Sam thought, *She is beauty.*

She made sure of each of their names, gave Coy a pat on the head, and invited them to sit. The winter afternoon was mild and the sun strong. "It's pleasant out here," she said. "Very well. Padre says you have a business proposition for me."

They explained. If Señora Luna would permit them to turn their horse herd out on her grass, Sam and Flat Dog would train her horses as saddle mounts. "One horse each," Flat Dog offered. Sam couldn't have squeezed a word out.

He and Señora Luna gazed at each other.

"Also," said Hannibal, "you will get new blood for your mares."

Coy made a squealing yawn, perhaps in approval.

The señora snapped back into the conversation.

"Do you train with the *jaquima*?" she said.

"Sure," said Flat Dog. Since Indians didn't use bits at all, he and Sam were used to training riding horses with the piece of equipment called in English the hackamore.

"Sam is something special," said Hannibal.

Sam flushed red, which he always hated because his white hair made him look redder. The señora couldn't resist a smile of amusement.

"May we show you tomorrow?" said Hannibal.

"Yes, of course," she said. "I'm sure we can work something out." She gave them instructions on how to get to her rancho, which was down the Santa Fe River.

"I remember the place," said Sam. He was half proud that he'd found words and gotten them out.

Señora Luna rose. "Tomorrow, then, with your herd."

"Yes," said Hannibal.

"When will you take the horses to head for your fur hunters' summer rendezvous?"

"Early May," Hannibal said.

She thought. "Four and a half months." She turned to Sam. "I think we can form a profitable relationship."

Sam nodded.

"I'll expect you in the afternoon."

She stood. So did they, Sam tardily.

"You must call me Doña Paloma," she said. "We'll all be friends." But she was looking at Sam.

Walking back through the narrow streets, they talked about Doña Paloma. Sam had nothing to say. Flat Dog and Hannibal were full of admiration for her beauty, her low, husky voice, her intelligence, her business sense.

"Sounds like the girl for you," Sam said to Hannibal, and heard the foolishness in his own voice.

"Me?" the Delaware said, chuckling.

Flat Dog pointed to his eyes. "Sam, he has a pair of these, but he doesn't see."

"It's you she's interested in," Hannibal said to Sam.

Sam shivered, but could think of nothing to say to that.

SAM'S NERVES WERE tingling like a teenager's, and that was making Paladin skittish. She pricked up her ears and turned them constantly, as though she might be able to hear what was wrong with her rider. Her hoofs slipped in the soft surface of the river road—this afternoon was warm and a winter thaw was on. She swished her tail edgily. Once she even stopped and turned her head, maybe wanting to go back. But she had horses to lead, and she knew the job. Sam rode in front of the herd, Coy beside him. Flat Dog and Sumner rode flank and Hannibal came along behind. They were accustomed to this work—they'd trekked a thousand miles with the loss of only one animal.

Now Sam shook the memories of that long trail out of his head and came back to his job. He turned Paladin sideways in the road and waved at the horses, turning them into the road onto the north side of the señora's property. Hannibal pushed them from the far side, and Flat Dog herded them from behind.

Paloma Luna came out on a good-looking sorrel mare and helped herd the new horses back toward her band. She wore a skirt that was split for riding and big spurs. Across her shoulders, with artless grace, were tossed two colorful blankets.

Sam's first thought was, *She's much too old.*

And then he felt a flush of shame for what he'd been thinking.

Coy started a howl that came up short in a groan.

"Now. Would you like to take a tour of the rancho?"

They would.

It sat in a pleasant valley along the Santa Fe River. On broken land along the north side she grazed sheep, cattle, and goats and bred horses—"Trying to improve the line," she said, "my personal effort." On the south side of the stream she raised pigs, and chickens, grew fruit, and planted crops; she irrigated these fields out of the river via a *madre acequia,* mother ditch.

"We put this vineyard in," she said. "In two more years we will have some grapes, and soon enough to produce wine, which we will make ourselves."

A middle-aged man walked up, probably to see the strangers. "This is Antonio, my foreman." She introduced everyone, which surprised Sam. "Antonio will produce the wine. He is proud of the vineyard, his project."

Sam felt dazed—maybe it was the beautiful woman and her fine seat on her mare, or maybe the dazzling sun. Though he liked her elegant Spanish (she offered no English), he didn't seem to understand half of what she said. He gathered that this ranch had come down through her family, and now that her husband was dead, she ran it, with the help of half a dozen Mexican-Indian families who lived in the *casitas primitivas,* rough houses, on the property.

"I will establish a blacksmith here," she said, "and a wheel-wright there. Along the creek we will build a mill. While my husband lived, the rancho did not progress. He was not interested in it. I love this land," she said, "and I am a serious woman of business."

As they rode back toward the main casa, the señora said, "What is this special thing that you want to show me?"

Hannibal grinned. "Watch. It takes a few minutes to set up."

Quickly they cut willow branches along the river and improvised a ring. Then Sam took the saddle and bridle off

Paladin. He stood in the center of the ring. "Señora," Hannibal said, "if you will join Sam." She did.

Sam whistled. Paladin came to him immediately. With
hand signals he set her to cantering around the ring clockwise. At another signal she reversed direction. He called
to her and she stopped and faced him. At another call she
pranced sideways, and then back to where she started. When
he motioned down with both hands and stepped behind the
señora, Paladin walked to the lady and bowed.

The señora laughed and applauded, delighted as a girl.

Then Sam whistled, Coy jumped onto Paladin's back, and
around the ring the mare loped, the coyote standing up on
her back.

"You are a magician!" said the señora. "Is Señor Flat Dog
equally talented?"

"You bet," said Sam.

"Then please train any of my horses, train all of them.
They will bring fine prices, so I will pay you well. Hand-
somely." She thought, hand in her chin. "Here is a proposal.
Señor Flat Dog, you have a wife, two children."

"One child his, one mine," said Sam.

"Then you may live in one of my casitas. It is not occupied
in the winter. You will be comfortable and close to your work."

Sam and Flat agreed with their eyes. "Sounds fine," said
Flat Dog.

"The horses of mine you train, we will sell them just before you leave. Untrained, they are worth about two hundred
fifty pesos. I will give you half of every peso above that
amount."

Sam shot a look of gratitude at his teacher. Hannibal
winked at him.

They went into the courtyard, which enclosed a well and an
horno, an outdoor oven. They sat, and a servant girl brought
them hot chocolate and *pan dulces,* sugared breads.

Sam felt like an idiot. As they chatted, the widow looked
at him constantly. "Your white hair," she said, "on so young a
man, it's charming." For a moment he thought she was going

to reach out and touch it. Instead she turned away to the wall, looked over and said, "This is my flower garden and herb garden. It looks so sad in the middle of winter. But perhaps you will see it in the spring. I have transplanted the wildflowers of the region. They make rainbows of color."

She hesitated. "Señor Morgan, Señor Flat Dog, may I show you your new home?"

It was thirty paces away and indistinguishable from the other casitas. "Perfectly fine," Flat Dog said. "I will bring my family tomorrow."

Sam looked at Flat Dog edgily. He often spoke as though Esperanza were his own daughter.

"Señor Morgan, Señor Hannibal said you are learning to read. My father owned some English books. He spoke the language, and he loved literature. Perhaps you would like to see them."

Coy let out a squeal.

Sam nodded that he would like to see the books.

"You will find them in the *cuarto de recibo*. You may use them this afternoon," she said, "and stay to supper with us if you like."

Her gaze made it clear that Sam alone was the focus of the invitation.

"Thank you," Sam mumbled.

A stable hand took Paladin.

"Good day, gentlemen."

Paloma Luna turned toward the house, and Sam and Coy walked beside her.

Hannibal said to Flat Dog and Sumner said in English, "See what learning to read will get you?"

Sam thought he saw the señora suppress a smile—maybe she did speak English. Coy followed the two of them into the courtyard and the casa.

AT SUPPER PALOMA Luna smiled seldom. Sam wondered if she felt the sadness he felt, an undercurrent of melancholy that sounded in the heart of everyone who lost a spouse, and would never go away. He felt sure she did.

A gray-haired Mexican woman dished up the food and an attractive young woman served them. The señora introduced Sam to her servants—the cook was Juanita, the young woman Rosalita. Remembering his manners, Sam rose and said he was pleased to meet them. He caught a hint of a smile from the señora. "I don't like it when people treat their helpers like they're not people," said Sam.

"Then you'll be interested in Rosalita's story," said the señora. "You Americans are informal. May I call you Sam?"

He nodded yes.

"Will you call me Paloma?"

He nodded again.

Dinner was shredded pork in a green chile sauce on corn tortillas, with beans on the side, and boiled carrots diced with onions, and goat cheese. "I'm sorry we don't have fresh greens," said the señora. "This country is so high and cold. But I love it. I love the starkness of the earth here, the way the rock sticks out like bones. I love the red earth. Especially I love the quality of the sunlight—this light, it's like a diamond. When I was a child, my father took me to Chihuahua so that I could experience a real city. I saw light like this nowhere else, absolutely nowhere."

Sam looked at her in silence. He wanted to feed Coy pork by hand but didn't dare.

"My grandfather founded this rancho and named it after my grandmother, Paloma. In each generation the first daughter is named Paloma."

Except that you are childless, Sam thought. The melancholy throbbed within him. He thought of Esperanza, who would spend the winter here with himself, Flat Dog, Julia, and her cousin Azul. He tried to take comfort in that.

"I said you would be interested in Rosalita's story," said Paloma. She glanced toward the kitchen. Rosalita and Juanita ate the same food at a small table, just through a wide entrance from the dining room.

"Do you know about the big trade caravans?"

"No."

"We are a very remote province. The word 'provincial' barely begins to describe how far away we are and how little the government in Mexico cares about us. Everything we buy comes in big caravans all the way from Chihuahua, six hundred miles to the south, and is very expensive. My father and I traveled with one of the caravans. The road, El Camino Real, is the one that passes before my front gate.

"Chihuahua itself gets traders who come up from Ciudad Mexico through the mountains of central Mexico, where the mines are. The mines get vegetables, cattle, sheep, jerked meat—everything to eat, plus manufactured goods. Mining towns," she said with a grimace. "The men think of nothing but digging fortunes out of the ground. They don't even produce enough for themselves to eat.

"The traders do much business in Chihuahua, and a few come on to this small and insignificant place. They bring all the fine things we do not make for ourselves, delicate fabrics, shoes and boots, iron tools, copperware, pottery—all items manufactured, and some nice things, chocolate, sugar, tobacco, liquor, ink and paper.

"They take back what we have to offer—sheep, wool, salt, jerked meat, piñon nuts, Indian blankets, and the skins of beaver, buffalo, bear, and deer."

"Piñon nuts?" said Sam, grinning.

"Yes, any kind of food. It is a poor arrangement for us. Our traders are always in debt because of it." She sighed and looked toward the kitchen. The two women were cleaning pots and pans noisily and jabbering. "There is another, bigger item of trade. Slaves."

"Slaves?" Sam thought of Sumner.

"Yes. The traders bring to us Mexican women and children taken by Indians from their villages in Sonora and Chihuahua. Our wealthy families buy them."

Sam knew nothing of this.

"In return," Paloma said bitterly, "we steal Indian women

and children from the villages and *rancherias* of our Indios and send them to Mexico. Families are destroyed both here and there. It is the most profitable part of the trade on the Chihuahua Trail—by far the most. Raid a village, kill some of the men, take all the women and children you can get." She breathed in and out. "Send Chihuahuans to this remote province, send Indians to Chihuahua."

Sam felt slapped in the face. His father, Lew Morgan, had always said slavery was a curse.

"In former times the big caravans came only once every two years. Now, because the traffic is so rewarding, the slave traders come several times each year."

"My friend Sumner was a slave," said Sam.

She nodded.

"I hate that. I helped him get free."

"It is barbaric," Paloma agreed. "The blankets you see all over my house—beautiful, aren't they? We call them slave blankets. Our wealthy families keep some of the Navajo women as slaves here, and they weave these blankets. I love them, but it makes me feel odd to buy them. I don't know whether my purchase encourages slavery or whether it makes the lives of the woman here better."

"I wouldn't know what to do either."

"Rosalita is a slave."

Sam just stared at Paloma.

"I set her free. I bought her two years ago and told her she was welcome to stay here on the rancho and work for a wage, or to go anywhere she wanted."

Suddenly Rosalita appeared at the table and put a small bowl in front of each of them. Sam looked carefully at her face, and she threw him a good smile. She didn't look oppressed.

"This is flan," Paloma said, "an egg custard with a sweet topping, sugar and butter melted together and burned a little. I am very fond of it."

Sam tasted it and said, "Terrific."

"With Rosalita this is not a fair arrangement. But it is the best I can do. As I have money to set more slaves free, I will."

Feeling like the words soiled his tongue, Sam said, "How much does a slave cost?"

"For Rosalita I paid one thousand pesos in trade goods—blankets, corn, and wool. She is attractive, so she cost a little more than a usual twelve-year-old." It was three or four months' wages for an ordinary working St. Louis man. "Her cousin, a girl cousin, was sold for two horses and six bushels of corn. I will buy her when I can afford her, so they can be together."

Sam tried to equate horses and corn to a human being. "Why doesn't Rosalita leave?"

"She would want to go back to her village, her family. But how can she get there? With one of the caravans that brought her here? They would sell her as a slave. Walk alone for six hundred miles? A girl?"

"I don't understand slavery at all."

Paloma looked at him for a long time before speaking. "You have a certain innocence. It is one of your charms. May I show you the rest of the house?"

The kitchen had what she called a shepherd's bed fireplace, something new to Sam. He'd sat in the *cuarto de recibo,* which seemed to mean the room where you receive guests, but hadn't noticed the pen and ink sketch of the casa made by her grandmother. He also hadn't noticed the multitude of blankets, large ones on the floor, smaller ones on the sofas and chairs.

"Yes, slave blankets," said Paloma.

"Thank you for letting me look at the books," he said. She nodded. He'd looked at some verses in a collection of English poetry. Though they'd been too difficult for him, he liked to parse them out. He liked the sounds.

"Notice the stencils of birds on the walls," Paloma said. The walls were plastered, white-washed adobe. "Palomas," murmured the señora. "The technique is called *tierra amarilla.* I love it."

He was enchanted. Her spirit was so intense, but she was utterly without guile, always direct.

"Now something special," she said, *"mi alcoba de dormir."* They went down a short hall and into a bedroom. A fire was burning in the small fireplace—Rosalita must have laid it. The room held a bureau, a vanity, a full-length mirror, and her high four-poster bed. She lit wall-mounted candles on each side of the bed, and two more candles on the vanity. The room took on a beautiful glow.

"Look at yourself in the mirror," she said, smiling. It was a full-length mirror with an ornately carved frame. He picked Coy up, but the coyote showed no interest in his reflection. Paloma stood close to them, and they all smiled. Paloma stroked Coy's head, and he nuzzled it into her hand. "You are handsome," Paloma said.

Sam was lost for words.

The señora took Coy out of Sam's arms and set him down. Then she turned back to Sam and kissed him fully on the mouth.

She took a step back, holding his gaze and her eyes holding the warm candlelight, and began to take off her dress.

THE NEXT DAY about noon, when they finally got out of bed, Coy whined desperately to be let out. They sat in the kitchen and drank coffee and ate sweet breads. Juanita worked at grinding corn, which Sam imagined was a never-ending job, and Rosalita cleaned the dining room. Sam felt a little uneasy, but the two servants acted like nothing was unusual.

Paloma saw the question in his face and said, "You are the first man to touch me since my husband died. I have been . . . in reserve for five years."

They went outside and to the casita to check on Flat Dog and Julia. "You are settling in well?"

"Fine," said Julia. It was one big room. Sam's guess was that she was relieved to be in a house instead of a tipi.

Paloma looked around the part of the room used for cooking. "Let me know if there's anything you need."

Sam picked up Esperanza and Azul and twirled around with them in his arms. The infants cackled.

Paloma came and looked closely at Esperanza's face. "She will be handsome, like her father. It would be perhaps better if she were beautiful." They all smiled broadly, and Sam and Paloma walked back to the kitchen of the main casa.

"Juanita, I will cook supper. Take the afternoon with your family. Rosalita, go do whatever you like."

Both women murmured *"Gracias"* and left immediately.

When they were alone, Paloma said, "Rosalita is being courted by one of the young men who works for me." She stood, came to Sam, and cupped his face with one hand and kissed him lightly. "You are a beautiful man. The crook where your nose must have been broken, it only makes your face interesting." She kissed him again. "Now I will start supper."

Sam sat in the kitchen with her and watched. First she cut the kernels off an ear of dried Indian corn. *"Chicos,* we call these." She covered them with water, and set them on the cooking stove to simmer. The fire in the stove was strong, and the *cocina* felt good, a warm radiance in a cold house in January.

Now she took meat from a box cooled by ice in the bottom and began to dice it. "Mutton," she said. "This is a dish of the conquistadores."

She worked in firm strokes. Now she paused and looked directly at him. "I have a passion for you," she said. "For the time you are in Santa Fe, will you live at Rancho de las Palomas and be my lover?"

She waited.

She poured a little oil in a heavy skillet, put it on the stove, and began browning the meat. "I do not care about appearances," she said. "I care nothing for what the families on the rancho think, nothing about what my neighbors may think. I do not even care what the priest thinks." She looked up at him. "As for the sin, I will confess it." She shrugged.

Now she took three red chiles out of a canister, washed and cleaned them, and put them on the counter. She chopped the red pods and began to mash them in a heavy bowl with water. She looked at him. "This passion," she said, "I want to dive into it, to lose myself in it. Is your wish the same?"

"Yes."

She lowered her eyes to the chiles and ground hard. He noticed how strong her hands were.

"You may tell your friends who stay in town whatever you like about us, without flaunting it. They will understand."

"Sure."

She put the mashed chiles and water into a sauce pan, and put the pot on the rear of the cookstove. "It will make a sauce," she said.

She wiped her hands on a cloth, sat on a chair next to him, and took both his hands in hers.

"We both must understand, then, that it will end. Spring will come, the grass will turn green, you will go to your rendezvous of beaver hunters, and I will set this passion aside. We two are"—she hesitated—"not suitable. You are beautiful. Perhaps we even make an attractive couple. But we are not in the long term appropriate." She used the Spanish word *apropriado*.

Sam's mind tilted a little. What they'd just done in bed felt very damned appropriate to him.

She rose and poured water into the pot with mutton. "It is best when it simmers all afternoon," she said.

Sam shook his head. After five years in the mountains, taking care over cooking seemed foreign to him.

She dipped her finger in the red chile sauce and put it to his mouth. "Taste it."

He sucked the good taste off her finger. He'd liked chiles from the first taste, green more than red, not the heat but the flavor. He cleaned the finger well, smiling at her mischievously.

"I'll pour us some wine. You want to go to bed?"

He did.

* * *

THE NEXT DAY they rode the ranch, and she began to tell him about her life. Specifically, her husband. Coy trotted along with his ears perked, like he was listening.

"I was a silly young girl, seventeen years old. Miguel came for me like a whirlwind. He was a handsome man with a flair for the romantic gesture. Gestures, I later found out, he had practiced widely throughout Nuevo Mexico. We married when I was eighteen and he was thirty. My father warned me about him." Sam knew her mother had died giving birth to her sister.

"For a year, perhaps, I kept my illusions.

"He was good to me in front of others. He made love to me eagerly. In front of our ranch families he treated me like a queen, and to our friends in Santa Fe he showed me off as a great catch. I began to get impatient when he was gone on what he called the business of his family, which was actually to pursue other women and play at horsemanship games with his rich young comrades. His family, it turned out, had scarcely any enterprises left to run.

"It was not until we stood beside my father's grave that I realized, from Miguel's new imperial manner, that he had married me only to get Rancho de las Palomas."

They turned the horses along the *madre acequia*.

"The next years were very difficult. I hate to talk about them. The worst was that I miscarried twice. Now I am unable to bear children."

She grew thoughtful, and her voice changed. "Then, one morning, they brought the news. As he and his friends did their daredevil riding, his horse suddenly shied. Miguel landed headfirst against a boulder and was quickly dead."

She stopped, and Sam reined Paladin up beside her. Coy raised his head to Paloma. Her gaze roamed the grapes she had planted, but Sam knew they were not what she was seeing.

"You cannot imagine. In my anger I had thought I wanted to deliver a fatal blow myself. But when it happened, I was desolate. I stayed in bed, without even a candle, for days. I drank wine, all my stomach could keep down. I crawled deep into the cave of loneliness and self-pity.

"And I didn't come back to the world for months. Months."

She touched her heels to her mount, and they glided on.

"Finally, our foreman pointed out to me that the rancho was deteriorating. My people were willing to work hard, he said, but only if they knew I cared. Since I didn't seem to care, inevitably, the rancho would die. 'Dust, weeds, and wind, nothing else,' he said."

Coy made a sympathetic noise.

"So Rancho de las Palomas saved me. It saved my grandmother, the first Paloma. She dug the gardens with her own hands, she planted the cottonwoods by the house, she helped lay the stones of the walk from the well to the *cocina*. She nursed the land as she nursed her son and daughter. It gave to her as she gave to it.

"Women are not made to be alone, Sam. We can be in connection to a man, to children, to our whole family, we can even be mother and child to the earth herself. But we are not meant to be alone. My gardens, my orchards, my vineyard, my livestock, my workers—they saved me. Saved me for this moment, this passion that makes me alive." She looked at him for a long moment and finally tried to shrug lightly.

He wondered exactly what she was thinking at that moment. He would have bet it was, *For a short time I have this young man, this naïve foreigner. What comes afterward, what else my life may be, I will seize this.*

"Let's ride." She kicked her sorrel mare to a lope down the dirt track, across the road, and onto the north side of her land. They galloped across tablelands, through broken gullies, up steep hills. Coy scampered alongside them eagerly—he liked to run. Finally, when they came up into the timber, she eased her mount to a walk and came gently to the ridge. In front of them, far down the mountain, lay a lovely lake among pine trees, like a drop of dew on a green leaf. They sat for long moments and gazed. It was like drinking the cold lake with their eyes.

The winter day was mild, and they sat on the rocks of the ridge and looked at the water and talked, or for long periods didn't talk. Sam knew he was enraptured.

Finally, Paloma said, "Tell me about Meadowlark."

Sam did. He spoke slowly and considered his words, but the words came and came. How he met her in the Crow village, left on a trapping expedition saying he'd come back, and failed to keep his promise—"I got separated from the outfit, got my horse stolen, had hardly any lead for bullets. Ended up walking seven hundred miles to the nearest fort."

"Seven hundred? Alone?"

"Yes."

He thought for a moment. The story about the prairie fire would hold for later, and how he crawled into the buffalo carcass and got his Crow name, Joins with Buffalo.

"I went back to the village, and her parents said to bring eight horses for her. Getting the horses . . ." Here he paused, because this part of the story was still hard. "Getting the horses I got her brother killed, Blue Medicine Horse. Then her parents kept her away from me. But we ran off together."

He took big breaths in and out. "After a few days they came and took her back. I thought I'd lost her for good. I left, went to rendezvous." He waited for a beat. "She showed up there with her brother, ready to get married."

They let that sit for a minute.

"She wanted to see the Pacific Ocean, so we joined up with a brigade going to California. First that ever did that crossing." He stopped for a moment, and memories moved through him like hymns.

He shrugged. "She gave birth and it killed her."

Paloma considered that. Sam looked at her and thought of her childlessness.

Suddenly she said, "Let's go!" and jumped onto her horse.

She loped back the way they came, and then it turned into a race. They shouted at the horses in glee and spurred them—down grassy hillsides, across rivulets, through arroyos. Coy sprinted alongside and sometimes barked vigorously. Paloma laughed at him.

At first Paladin fell behind Paloma and her mare, but Sam could feel that she was just biding her time. Few horses ran as often or as long as Paladin, and few had as much bottom. Still, the sorrel mare had sprinting speed, and Sam wasn't sure. His thought was, *Paloma wants me to beat her, but will do her damnedest to beat me.*

They roared onto the grasslands where the horses were grazing, the trappers' hundred with Paloma's, and the whole herd kicked up its heels and followed them. What a noise—Sam loved it, and it made him homesick for the buffalo plains, and the thunder of a buffalo stampede.

Suddenly Paloma turned her mare up a short, steep hill and through the underbrush into another small canyon. The herd didn't follow. *Too much work!* Sam thought happily. They crashed down a little creek, splashing themselves and whooping and hollering.

When El Camino Real came into sight, and the house beyond it, Sam slapped Paladin with his hat, and she charged. They passed Paloma the way a plummeting apple passes a drifting leaf. Sam wheeled Paladin to a skidding stop in front of the casa. When Paloma jumped from the saddle, she landed in Sam's arms. A stable hand took the reins, and Sam carried Paloma pell-mell to bed.

"WHAT IS GOING on inside my lover?" said Paloma softly. They were lying twisted in her sheets, naked, worn out by love. "I don't want your mind wandering. For this time we are together let it be with me."

He looked at the coals in the fireplace and answered truthfully, "Guilt."

Coy seconded the motion with a whimper.

She smiled warmly at him. "It didn't arrive until the fourth day. Not bad."

"Don't you feel guilty?"

"I feel triumphant. And so should you."

They looked at each other. Neither knew what to say.

"But your wife has been gone only . . ."

"Nine months. April to January."

Her eyes smiled at him. "Then it's time for you to be reborn, Sam Morgan. Time to emerge back into this world of the living, the world of things that still stand in the sunlight and grow." She gave him mocking eyes. "Things that rise from the dead, things that rise in the sheets."

"I miss her."

"I missed my husband for perhaps two years. He was a *pendejo,* but I missed him. Sometimes I woke up in the morning and reached for him. After a while I made myself sleep on his side of the bed, facing the edge. That stopped the reaching. Though I despised him, I expected him to be around every corner, and was always disappointed when he was missing. Always missing."

"I loved Meadowlark."

"You still do, the memory of her. But she's dead, Sam."

"Are you jealous of her?"

"As well be jealous of a mote of dust floating in the air."

She rolled over, tangled her hands in his white hair, and kissed him teasingly. "Let a woman who has walked this earth for a decade longer than you tell you this much. Life is for the living." She kissed him again. "The living. That's us. Can you let go of death for a while?"

She rolled him over on top of her.

"Yes."

Chapter Twelve

The winter was a time of rest for the ranch, and the work was much less for everyone except Sam and Flat Dog. Every day they trained horses, and Paloma watched what was different about their technique, wanting to learn. They stood with the horse belly deep in the cold Santa Fe River until they got it to accept a saddle blanket, then a saddle, then a sitting horseman. "It is faster," she said immediately.

She sweetened the deal. "Please train as many of my horses as possible. Good saddle horses will bring me two hundred pesos more than wild ones. So I will pay you a hundred fifty pesos each."

They worked with a will.

Sam and Paloma, though, took some afternoons to ride her land. They camped one night by the northern lake. They rode downstream and explored the valley of the Rio Grande. They visited a pueblo of Indians down that river, and Paloma traded for some beautiful pots. "Do they steal slaves from this village?" asked Sam.

"No, these pueblo peoples, they accept the Holy Church. We Nuevos Mexicanos take slaves from the Navajos, who hold to their old religion, and the pueblo peoples help in the stealing."

They camped along the river on the way back, and since the next day was sunny, they lounged and stayed there all day.

They also established a life beyond the ranch and beyond their absorption in each other. Every Saturday morning they rode to Santa Fe. Paloma went to confession, spent the rest of Saturday with her sister and nieces, and on Sunday morning attended mass.

Sam spent Saturday afternoon at the lodgings of Hannibal, Grumble, and Sumner, working on his reading. He would recite the words out loud, and one of his mentors would offer corrections. Sam began to go from fumbling, word-by-word reading to making words into sentences that added up to something.

At first Sumner just listened with a half smile. Then he began to help Sam as well. Unlike Sam, the ex-slave had learned to read and write, and could do it very well.

Grumble always started with Sam on the Bible. Sam would sound out the sentences and Grumble would repeat them sonorously, in an actor's voice. Sam liked the big, rolling language. He also liked some of the stories of the Old Testament, but others seemed strange to him. "I don't know why I should like a story about Abraham putting his son on an altar and getting ready to drive a knife into his heart."

"A story about obedience," said Grumble.

"I don't think much of that either," said Sam.

"No mountain man would," said Grumble. "Nor any con man."

On another Saturday Sam read about how the pharaoh's daughter found Moses in a basket in the bulrushes and saved the child. "Some stories are more like children's fantasies," said Sam.

"You're becoming a wise man," said Grumble.

"And I hate this thing about Samson. He's strong—he can pull a whole building down. So how can a woman make him weak by cutting his hair?"

"Maybe it's not the hair, it's the larger situation, involvement with a woman. Submission to a woman."

Sam shrugged. "Meadowlark didn't do that to me." Neither of them said anything about Paloma.

When Grumble read the Psalms to him, Sam just floated along on the language. He liked the way words turned into a sort of music.

Another Saturday Sam told Grumble, "I don't get it about Jesus of Nazareth."

Grumble arched an eyebrow at him. "No?"

"He strikes me as a sort of pale, holy kind of guy who doesn't know how to enjoy life."

"I'm glad to see you enjoying life again."

"Sometimes Jesus reminds me of one part of Jedediah, all serious and no fun." Sam threw Grumble a grin. "Without the part of Jedediah who can go longer and harder than the toughest, who can lead men anywhere."

"Your Captain Smith is a remarkable man." Sam had the impression that "remarkable" carried two or three meanings. Maybe one of them was that Jedediah, yes, was tough, and maybe a little crazy.

The cherub smiled now and said, "Think about it, though. What could require more toughness than the Cross? And it's a great idea, that a God would suffer what mortals do, death, in order to give us what is immortal."

Sam held the thought for a moment and shrugged.

With Hannibal Sam read aloud verses of Lord Byron's that Hannibal had marked:

> *Maid of Athens, ere we part,*
> *Give, oh give me back my heart!*

"You could smoke the pipe and ask Meadowlark for your heart back."

Sam chuckled.

"Or does Paloma have it now?"

Sam gave his friend the evil eye.

Hannibal took the volume and read,

> *I live not in myself, but I become*
> *Portion of that around me: and to me*
> *High mountains are a feeling, but the hum*
> *Of human cities torture.*

"'Become portion of that around me,'" Sam said. "I felt something like that once."

Hannibal nodded.

"When Coy and I hid inside the buffalo cow and she saved us from the fire. Felt it strong."

"You are Joins with Buffalo," Hannibal said. He handed the book back to Sam.

I stood
Among them, but not of them; in a shroud
Of thoughts which were not their thoughts.

"You feel like that?" said Sam.
"All the time," said Hannibal.
"Me too."

There is a pleasure in the pathless woods,
There is a rapture on the lonely shore,
There is society, where none intrudes,
By the deep sea, and music in its roar:
I love not man the less, but Nature more.

Sam took a breath and let it out. Coy squealed at him. "I felt that from the start. That's what I felt every time Dad and I went into Eden."

Hannibal made a sympathetic noise.

"The ocean, though, to me that means Meadowlark dying. She wanted to see it, she loved it, and it killed her. That's how it feels to me."

"Life is lived holding hands with death," said Hannibal.

"Is that a quotation of somebody famous?"

"Probably," said Hannibal.

Sam thought awhile, or sat in a place beyond thought, and went back to reading:

What men call gallantry, and gods adultery,
Is much more common where the climate's sultry.

"We need some sultriness," said Hannibal, "here in the Santa Fe winter."

"I got some." Sam grinned.

Let us have wine and women, mirth and laughter,
Sermons and soda water the day after.

Sam laughed. "My mom used to give my dad soda water when he got into the whiskey."

Man, being reasonable, must get drunk;
The best of life is but intoxication.

"Now that," Sam said, "is a verse the fellows would like."

"We don't need whiskey to be intoxicated," said Hannibal.

Hannibal also promised to get Sam some more books, so he could read on his own. That thought made Sam sad, because it reminded him that he and Hannibal wouldn't always be partners. Hannibal liked too well to go his own way.

ON HIS SATURDAY nights in town Sam kept his promise to Grumble and earned his share of the horses Grumble paid for—he helped with the cherub's deceptions. Here in Santa Fe, where Grumble wanted to stay for a while, that meant nothing more elaborate than card games. Certainly, though, no one could call what Grumble did either playing or gambling.

Every day Sumner worked on his card skills under Grumble's tutelage, practicing dealing off the bottom of the deck for hour upon hour. "Look here," he said, when Sam walked into their lodgings one Saturday afternoon. He put the two black aces on top of the deck and the two red aces on the bottom. Then he dealt Sam a four-card hand—all aces. Sumner did it several times. Sam and Hannibal watched intently, but neither of them could ever see that Sumner was dealing from the bottom.

Coy barked sharply, whether in applause or protest none of them knew. Sumner chuckled. "He wants to play. That coyote be a gamblin' man."

"Next step," said Grumble. He told Sam to put the four aces

together, split the deck, and tuck them directly into the mid-dle. Sam did. Grumble dealt a three-card hand to each man, three cards being the right number for the most popular card game in Santa Fe, called brag.

Each man got an ace.

"You gotta be a witch to deal out of the middle," said Sumner.

None of them had imagined such a thing could be done. They watched as Grumble did it again, and again. None could spot it.

"All right, teach me," said Sumner.

Sam could hear lust in his voice.

"When these greenhorns aren't here," said Grumble. "We con men want to keep some secrets within the fraternity."

"I'll never play cards for money again," said Hannibal.

"Best not," said Grumble with a sly smile.

Grumble said nothing about his biggest card secret. Abby had a Baltimore manufacturer make her decks of cards from her own design. Though the swirls and whorls on the back of each card looked the same, they were not. When Abby saw the backs, she knew what every card was.

Grumble possessed one of the decks, an advantage in card games that could not be beaten.

"Now, this last is what you might call an honest trick. In some games it's a big advantage to know which cards have been dealt and which are still in the deck, especially the face cards."

He handed the deck to Sam. "Sam, pick any thirteen cards, any thirteen, and lay them face up."

Sam did.

Grumble studied them for a few seconds. "Now pick them up. Hold them so Hannibal and Sumner can see them and I can't."

Sam and Sumner split the cards and fanned them.

"King, two queens, ten, three eights, seven, six, a pair of fours, trey, deuce," recited Grumble.

He was exactly right.

"Now I can memorize the face value of thirteen quickly. One day I'll be able to memorize the value and the suit."

No one had a word to say.

"Of course, as Sam knows, winning at gambling is child's play. What's fun is what you might call the more elaborate cons. Deceptions that become works of art."

"And we won't do those here, not while we plan to stay here," Sam said.

"As you wish." Grumble smiled. "Merely winning is a little dull, but we've managed to attract some monied gentlemen who see losing as a challenge to rise to. I look forward to tonight. Along about seven, as we say in Nuevo Mexico."

"DON GILBERTO, WELCOME!" Grumble called. A Mexican gentleman bounced up to their table, fat and dressed like a fop. This man's style was to think everything in the world was funny, including losing a hand. Which was a good thing, because he lost lots of them.

"Don't you ever take the game seriously?" said the American who sat across from the Mexican. This man, whose name was Charles, or Don Carlos to the other dons, played with a fierce American competitiveness and lost almost as often as Don Gilberto, and with a good spirit. Sam thought his gravy-dripping accent was comical. The man hailed from New Orleans.

Sam had discovered he didn't much like cards or smoky cantinas. But he got a kick out of seeing Grumble play the pigeons for all they were worth.

The pigeons tonight were Don Carlos and Don Gilberto. Grumble said the men of the upper class were all disenfranchised *hidalgos,* sent to this most remote of Spanish outposts as punishment, and so treated life as a bitter joke.

Sam couldn't remember Charles's last name. A Creole and a Catholic, he had come from St. Louis with a trading outfit on the Santa Fe Trail, taken Mexican citizenship, and set up a trading company. According to Paloma, all the traders dealt in slaves.

Two pigeons tonight, then, plus Grumble and cappers, "what we in the con game call our helpers." Grumble liked to put on the air of an elegant, wealthy alcoholic, always sloshed, and win only an occasional hand himself.

On one night Flat Dog and Hannibal would leave with full pockets, another night Sam and Sumner. And most nights one Santa Fe local would break even or win a little, and two would lose big. Which just made them more avid to come back another night and get even.

Brag was a simple game. Grumble predicted that within a decade a more complicated version called poker would dominate. Every player put a coin in the pot for ante and got three cards. Then, clockwise, the players bet—you got no more cards, and you either had to bet or fold. Sam didn't make his own decisions—he waited for a signal from Grumble. Around and around went the bets, and when only two were left, they showed their hands. The best possible hand was a pair royal, or "prial," three of a kind.

By Grumble's minute signals—he was reading the backs of the cards—he told his cappers when to fold, when to match the bet, and when to raise.

Though Sam was bored by the cards, he was intrigued by the men.

Now Grumble dealt, and on his left Gilberto made no one wait. "I play blind," he said. This meant he would bet without looking at his cards. "*Dos* pesos." The fat man liked to take big chances and laugh a lot. He'd probably lost fifty pesos so far tonight, a modest amount by his standards.

Don Carlos played cards the way he carried himself, tightly and stiffly. At the table or on the street, he always seemed to have a suspicious set of mouth and an eye eager for an edge. He caught up with the bet and added five pesos.

Sam and Flat Dog watched Grumble's small signals and built up the pot. When Sumner's turn came, he made a show of it. "Ah likes this," he said in his slave English, "Ah likes it fine, just fine. I see . . . how many to me, Mr. Grumble?"

"Thirteen," mouthed the cherub. His lips pursed. He thought these displays of Sumner's too ostentatious, but half of him enjoyed them.

"Thirteen to me. Thirteen pesos, that is, oh, don't I wish it was thirteen dollars. I don't hold with these no-account pesos."

"Suh," said Don Carlos. He disliked Sumner, and these antics only made it worse. "In front of that man," Sumner had confessed to Sam privately, "Ah loves to play the Nigger."

Now Sumner stood up, beaming, taking his moment in the sun. "Do NOT interrupt me. Do NOT get in my way. I am a man came to play and I will PL-A-A-A-Y." He made the word into a whinny.

Coy gave a short bark at him.

Slurring his speech, Grumble said, "Place your bet, sir." Sam never knew what Grumble did with the brandy— winners bought rounds constantly—but he knew very well that Grumble was sober and sharp.

"Thirteen, I say," and Sumner put those down, "I say thirteen"—he picked up his pile of coins—"and I raise, I raise . . . *ten*."

Ten was the agreed limit.

Grumble pushed out his coins crookedly, as though even his hand couldn't help weaving. He gave the table a cupid smile.

Around and around the table the bet went. After another round, Gilberto folded, still not having looked at his cards. "I must see what's going on in the kitchen," he said. "It smells delicious."

At his turn Sumner stood up again. He preened. He took a breath and held it. His eyes grew huge. It appeared that he would explode if he held his words inside any longer.

Carlos looked so irritated that Sam thought he needed watching.

"I FO-O-O-LD," said Sumner grandly, and sat down.

Coy whined.

Grumble, whose head now seemed to sag toward his belly, said, "You can't beat this company for bonhomie." He winked at Sam, because it was a word he'd taught Sam just today. The cherub pushed his coins out, and the betting went on.

When only Flat Dog and Don Carlos were left, they raised each other over and over. Finally the Louisianan lost his nerve and called.

Flat Dog smiled and slowly plunked his cards down on the table, one by one—three jacks. It was a hand to bet big on, for sure, but now the Crow waited. Not only could a prial of queens, kings, or aces beat him—by rule the best possible hand was three treys.

Carlos spilled his hand onto the table faceup. Three nines.

Everyone laughed and congratulated Flat Dog loudly. The pot he collected was two months' wages, and he was the big winner for the night.

Sumner got up and clapped both his shoulders from behind. "What a man! What a man!"

Don Carlos gave the black a sour look.

Sam was tickled. If Grumble enjoyed gulling anyone the most, it was Carlos. Aside from being arrogant, Grumble said, "The man is infected with racial hatred."

Whenever Sumner won, which was seldom, he scooted all the coins into his hat, stood up, did a dance, held the hat over his head, jingle-jangled the coins, and sang, "This child done won! This child done won!"

Sam said to him outside the cantina one night, as they walked home, "Don't you worry about going too far?"

"Black man can't go too far playing the fool. White folks nod their heads and say, 'Look at that Nigger. What a fool he be.' Believe anything, them white folks."

Grumble nodded in agreement.

Now it was late and Sam was weary of cards, weary of the brandy, weary of the smoky room. "Just one more hand," he said.

"Give this child of God that deck," said Sumner. It was his

turn to deal. Though he was under strict instruction from Grumble not to try dealing seconds or bottoms yet, Sumner always grabbed the deck with great enthusiasm, as though he could make something special happen. "I have a very good card here for my friend Don Gilberto." He snapped a card facedown in front of the don, who was almost too drunk to keep his eyes open.

"And equally good cards for"—he clicked them down in front of each man—"my friends Sam, Carlos, Flat Dog, the stodgy old Grumble, and my humble self." He stroked his own card as though it were a pet, and made a cooing sound.

"Now!" he said, pausing dramatically. "That first card is a beauty. Any one could be a winner. The question is the second. Here's for you, Don Carlos. What do you say, is it good?"

Carlos didn't touch his facedown cards.

"Our Louisiana friend has nothing to say."

Sumner dealt the other cards and paraded out questions for every man. Gilberto was loud in his confidence. Sam said, honestly, that he was too tired to care. When he peeked at his cards and saw two queens, he still didn't care.

Grumble said, "The dealer should not be a performer."

Sumner laughed and dealt himself the last card. "A card of genius, I assure you all. Without looking, I can tell you I have a pair."

Grumble's face didn't change, but Sam saw a glint in his eyes.

Sam slid his third card off the table, saw the third queen, and put it back down. He looked words at Sumner. *You're dealing off the bottom, you devil.*

Coy gave a short, muffled bark.

Sumner grinned at Sam. Was he proud of the three queens? Or did he know Sam's thought? *This is dangerous.*

Carlos went for a raise of five pesos whenever it was his turn to bet. Sam raised quietly, one or two pesos, without emphasis. Grumble had taught him to keep the suckers in the pot.

Sam was getting uneasy. Sumner wasn't just pretending to have fun. There was something here he really liked.

Coy shifted from lying at Sam's feet to sitting up. He also smelled trouble coming.

Round and round the bets went. Finally, three players were left, Sam, Don Carlos, and Sumner. The pot was huge, probably eight hundred pesos.

Suddenly Don Carlos dropped words into the air like individual stones plopped into a pond. His voice curdled with something that gave Sam a chill.

"I think the Nigger is cheating."

Quick as a snake, Sumner's hand dived inside his coat.

Just as fast, Grumble locked his forearm in a fierce grip. "Let us all remember our manners," the cherub said casually.

Everyone at the table tensed, ready to dive for cover or grab a weapon. Coy growled, and Sam thought that if he snapped out a bark, everyone at the table would attack everyone else.

"My dear sir," said Grumble to Don Carlos, "I think you know better. This child of nature has neither the guile nor the intellect to commit such chicanery."

Carlos's face was boiling red. Everyone waited, poised.

"I will prove it," said Grumble. "Sam, show us your cards." His voice was as smooth as a hand stroking a cat.

Sam turned over three queens.

It seemed like the whole table gasped. A prial, and a high one.

"Don Carlos, my esteemed friend, now your cards."

Carlos hesitated. Then, one by one, a sneer on his face, he turned them over.

King of diamonds.

King of hearts.

King of spades.

Now the gasp was louder. A higher prial.

"And last let us see what the good Sumner's cards are." Grumble reached out and turned them over himself.

Ace of spades.

Ace of hearts.

Ten of clubs.

Everyone laughed uproariously. No one had seen anything

so funny in his life. Don Gilberto, not Don Carlos, seemed to enjoy it the most. He guffawed, tried to drink his brandy at the same time, and spilled the brandy all down his front.

Everyone hee-hawed louder. Two of them were laughing out of relief—Sam and Flat Dog knew damned well that Grumble had palmed that third ace and dropped the ten in its place.

"Take your pot, sir," said Grumble to Don Carlos.

Carlos raked the coins toward himself.

"The finest pot of the night, it appears," said the cherub. "And I believe this will make an evening for me. Good night, gentlemen."

Carlos scooped the whole pot into his hat, stood up, held the hat over his head, jingle-jangled the gold and silver loudly, and did a mocking dance. All the while he fixed his eyes fiercely on Sumner.

Sam wanted desperately to go, but Grumble's rule was that they leave one by one, to put off suspicion of collaboration. Still, after two more hands Sam was on the street in the cold night air, breathing freely.

As they all crawled into their blankets later, Grumble said nothing to Sumner about the event except, "It would be well if you don't attend the games for a week or so."

So WENT THE winter for Sam. He spent five days a week with Paloma at the rancho, training her horses, teaching her his training methods, getting to know her in every way. Every weekday he had lunch with Flat Dog and Julia so he could be around Esperanza. One day while he was dandling her on his knee, Julia said, "Do you realize you are never quite comfortable with Esperanza?"

"I'm fine with her," said Sam.

Julia shrugged. "It doesn't seem so. Do you resent her for causing Meadowlark's death?"

"Sure not," Sam said quickly.

Julia cocked an eyebrow at him.

Sam picked up the child and turned away from Julia.

He spent weekends with his other amigos reading and gambling. At Rancho de las Palomas he earned some money, and at the gambling table he got hold of more. Though he spent some on cute baby clothes, his hunting pouch held a lot of coins, and he kept more in a pouch hung around his neck.

The best of the winter, though, was that he healed. Sam's body got its first rest, really, in a year and a half. He gained weight and fleshed out some hard edges on his body. Though Meadowlark's death still felt like a spike driven into his chest, he found a way to live with the pain. He knew that what healed him, mostly, was Paloma's love. Love in the physical sense and love, even if she never said so, in another and better sense. In her eyes he was a good man.

He improved his reading more and more, because he liked it and he worked at it. He even started picking out written Spanish words. When he and Paloma rode or walked the streets of Santa Fe, she would tell him the meanings of the signs in front of the shops. To help with pronunciation, she explained what sounds each of the letters made and had him speak the words after her.

One afternoon Sam and Paloma sat in the courtyard in the sun. Sam read one of her father's books in English. "English," she said, "what an ugly language, all full of sounds that grate on the tongue. And when you look at the words, you have no idea how to say them." Though Paloma's father did teach her some English, and she understood it, she disliked the language and declined to speak it.

"The only advantage of Spanish," he half mumbled, "is that the rules make it easy to figure out how to say the words."

"Spanish," she said, "is a lovely language of classic beauty. It flows as water runs smoothly over rocks. The Spanish language *is* beauty."

"I like English," he mumbled.

"Ha! I will show you."

She went into the house and brought back a book of

Spanish proverbs. "I will read to you of love," she said, "and we will make beauty into beast by translating it into English."

She read, " *'El hombre es fuego, la mujer estopa; llega el diablo y sopla.'* "

They wrangled out the English together: "Man is fire, woman dry grass. The devil dances by and blows."

"Do you hear?" said Paloma. "The Spanish is liquid— *'diablo y sopla.'* The English, it is bumpy."

"It has a nice punch, though." Sam couldn't help wanting to defend his native tongue.

"Another," she said. " *'Juramentos de amor y humo de chimenea, el viento se los lleva.'* Listen to that, how beautiful it is—*'el viento se los lleva.'* "

Again they wrestled it into English. "Promises of love, smoke from a chimney—the wind whisks both away."

"You are right a little bit," she said, "the English has nice muscles."

Sam kissed her lingeringly.

"Now I tell you one of my favorites," she said. "The way the sounds roll, it is beyond compare. *'Amor es en fuego escondido, una agradable llaga, un sabroso veneno, una dulce amargura, una delectable dolencia, un alegre tormento, una dulce y fiera herida, una blanda muerte.'* "

Sam replied by kissing her again, sensuously, and fondling her breasts. Her chest heaved deep and strong, and then suddenly the breaths came short and fast. She took Sam's hand, and led him fast into the casa, into the bedroom, and into love.

Afterward, they sorted out an English version of her proverb. "Love is a concealed fire," she said, her eyes aflame.

He bent and licked her nipple, murmuring, "And a lovely sore."

"A tasty poison," she whispered. She raised his lips to hers and teased his tongue with hers. "A sweet rue."

Sam put her hand where he wanted it. She smiled wickedly and squeezed. "A delectable suffering," she said. She squeezed harder and harder. "A happy torment, a delicious wound."

Sam rolled on top of her again. "And a soft death."

Much, much later she said, "English lacks music, but our bodies sing together beautifully."

They napped.

When they woke blearily, Sam gave her sweet kisses.

"Let me tell you one more proverb," she said.

"What?"

" 'Más fuerte era Sansón y le venció el amor.' "

"Which means?"

She enunciated clearly in English, "Samson had even more muscles than you, and love whipped his ass."

Chapter Thirteen

During Holy Week, which was in the second half of April, Sam didn't see Paloma for four days. They rode up the river road to town on Wednesday instead of Saturday. "Holy Thursday," she said. "We have the Eucharist in honor of the day Christ held the first one. Then Holy Friday, mass on the day he gave his life for all us mortal sinners. On Saturday the vigil, at dawn on Sunday the Resurrection and the mass to celebrate this great event."

"Vigil?"

Paloma laughed. "You are such a barbarian. The vigil is the blessing of the new fire, the lighting of the paschal candle, a service of lessons that we call the prophecies, the blessing of the font, and then the long sitting in the church, each person holding a candle, waiting for the great moment of the Resurrection. There, you see? I always go."

Not only went, it turned out, but spent the entire time with her sister and her family, and didn't see Sam at all.

The result for Sam was a lot of reading with Hannibal and Grumble, some wandering around Santa Fe with all his friends, and five nights of playing brag. The whole trip felt like a thorn whose tip had broken off in his hind end. The one good part was that he ended up with a lot more gold coins in his hunting pouch.

On Monday morning, as Sam and Paloma rode back down the river road together in the fine spring weather, he felt extra aware of the way she sat in her saddle, the way she turned to watch the river roaring downhill, leaping over rocks and making suck holes on the back side. She stopped and led her mare to the river. While both horses drank, Paloma watched the current surge. "I am enthralled by its power." Riding on, from time to time she pointed out the wildflowers in bloom on the side of the road, the orange cups of globe mallow, purple rags of locoweed, and the red bristles of Indian paintbrush. "They are getting ready to open, see?"

Coy pranced about wildly, as though the greening grass, the leafing trees had brought up the sap in him, and he couldn't just walk.

Farther along a sound came to Sam's ears that he could hardly believe. "Oh, Sam, this is . . . I can't describe it. Let's ride and find a good place to watch." She whipped her horse up onto a knoll, and he was right behind her. In a few minutes the caravan came. The racket was an assault. "That noise is the big wheels turning against the axles," said Paloma, almost shouting. "As you can tell, it is heard even a mile away. If they greased the axles, it would be diminished. But the muleteers say the sound is like music to them. They call them the singing carts."

In the forefront came horses and mules, hundreds of them. Behind this livestock trudged human beings, Indians, Mexicans, or mestizos, Sam couldn't tell which. Their hands and feet were shackled. "Slaves," said Paloma.

Paladin pulled on the reins, impatient. But Sam couldn't take his eyes off these people. There were three women, one perhaps in her thirties, one in her twenties, one a teenager but physically mature, and seven children who were probably between the ages of eight and twelve. All the women and children walked with the look of those who have been not only defeated and humiliated but beaten beyond despair into utter hopelessness, a state where life offers nothing but dreariness, darkness, and pain.

Sam felt a sharp burning in his heart.

The slaves trudged on and on. Nothing would ever change, and they knew it. They probably resented the bodies that enabled them to walk to their own debasement.

"It is hard to bear," said Paloma.

"Who will buy them?"

"Landowners like me. The only wealth in this province is land, which comes in grants from the government. Slaves work the land, or clean the houses, or do the labor of making crops ready for the table. Slaves do everything, if you are willing to have them, which I am not. From the look of these, most of them will also bear children who will also become slaves."

"Why don't they run screaming at their captors?" said Sam. "Why don't they break away? If you die, so what?"

"I asked Rosalita that. She said it is not possible at the time, not quite possible, to believe that death is better than where you are. But death would be better—that's what she said."

Now the slaves were out of sight, blocked by the carts and the mules and oxen that pulled them—hundreds of carts, it seemed to Sam. The screech was now almost unbearable. The wheels were huge rounds of cottonwood in one big piece.

"What do they have to trade?"

"Whatever we cannot produce, household utensils, candles, tallow, nice textiles, coffee, sugar, liquor—oh, it's such pleasure to see all the fine things and buy them."

They watched the carts wobble and creak on their way, and the dirty, dusty drovers pushing them along.

"How long have they been on the road?"

"It's about six weeks from Chihuahua. These traders are daring—they must have started as soon as the weather warmed up a little. This is the first caravan of the year."

She looked at him with girlish glee in her eyes. "Sam, let's ride back to town tonight. First the afternoon in bed and then back to town. It will be so much fun, you cannot imagine. The whole town will come to the *baile*."

"Sure." He was thinking that the bed sounded better than the *baile,* but . . .

"We will even stay in town. We will be wicked and take a room for the night. We'll have such fun."

Sam looked far up along the train of carts, but he couldn't see the slaves.

"Tomorrow we will go to one of the great ranchos and see something you'll never forget. You'll hate it, but you'll never forget it."

LOLLING TOO LONG in bed, they got to town long after the grand entry. "It is a wonderful sight," Paloma said. "The caravan men drive the carts along the river straight to the plaza. When they get there, they circle the plaza as fast as they can go, cracking their whips. From the uproar you would think it is a war. The children get very excited.

"As the caravan hurtles through the streets, the people hear the carts squealing and pour out. They run after the caravan on the way to the plaza, singing and shouting. From all directions everyone rushes to the plaza. We are all excited to see the fine things, to be able to trade for a pot of copper for the kitchen, to get new shoes for the family, to get a beautiful piece of silk that will make a skirt that may catch the eye of a certain man . . . And the merchants, after the first burst of trading, they stock their stores with the rest."

Now the *baile* was in full swing. The high-born, the merchants and tradesmen, the peasants—everyone thronged all over the plaza. Cantinas poured El Paso brandy and Taos whiskey liberally. Two groups of musicians competed to see who could play the loudest, with the most style, and attract the most listeners. Actually, the most dancers.

Hannibal waved at Sam and Paloma, and they crowded into the table with him, Grumble, and Sumner. Grumble ordered more brandy, and they all drank fast. Sam was feeling wild.

"Get ready," said Hannibal. *"Nemo enim fere saltat sobrius, nisi forte insanit."*

"What does that mean?"

"Only crazy people dance sober."

"Have you had enough to drink? Do you know the fandango?" said Paloma, a dark, sexy look in her eyes.

"I'm woozy," Sam said, "but for you I'll pretend."

"You will do much better than that. You will *dance.*" She took one of his hands and led him out among the couples in the plaza. "These are *fandanguillos,* more festive versions of the fandango. They are dances of . . . courtship would be the polite word. You direct Americans would say seduction. They are exuberant, unrefined, born of the desire of all creatures for fertility. It is not for talking but for doing."

Without warning she began and Sam followed, feeling like he was in a whirlwind. She tapped out a rhythm with her feet and snapped her fingers. He couldn't copy her steps, but he matched her attitude. She rose and, stepping high, they pranced past each other, shoulders almost touching, and faced each other once more. She teased and challenged. He pursued, she slipped away. He held her eyes piercingly. With her hands, shoulders thrown back, she shook her skirt in a taunt.

The music accelerated, its rhythm accented by castanets. Paloma clapped her hands and stomped her feet. Sam followed as though in a trance. The music itself seemed to tell him what to do. Now the music swirled faster and faster, like a waltz in three beats, but free of all drawing rooms, free of civility, as primal as a roll of thunder.

Stop. A total halt to the music. Paloma and Sam and all the other dancers froze. Tension throbbed.

Music again! Animated by the notes, the dancers grew wild. Passion surged through their poses. Arms and faces teased. Eyes, torsos, and hips challenged. Back and forth they soared, faster and faster, ever more passionate, ever more daring, and yet again faster.

When the orchestra stopped, silence clapped the ears. The dancers froze—sexual electricity charged the air.

Again the music charged forward, and Sam charged with it. He whirled, he grabbed Paloma, he slung her to the length of both their arms, he brought her back, she clung to him. Gently, gradually, she arched backward in his arms. The music came to a climax and was over.

Sam was dazzled with what he had done, and limp.

Paloma embraced him and whispered, "I want you to be like that inside me tonight."

His groin throbbed.

They went back to the table, drank more brandy, ate tortillas with pork and green chile sauce, and drank more brandy. Grumble paid for everything, and everyone had a great celebration.

Sam noticed that, as at the Los Angeles pueblo, dancers often went slinking down side streets, wrapped in a single serape. Paloma whispered in his ear, "How many children do you think will be conceived tonight?"

A gentleman in the garb of the Mexican elite, and with the arrogance, came toward them.

"*Buenas noches, señora.*"

"*Buenas noches, Gobernador.* Won't you join us?" Paloma made the introductions. "Gobernador Armijo is our former governor."

"Oh, señora," said Armijo, "must you call me a ruler in front of these democratic Americans?"

"My American friends are traders," said Paloma. "They have brought a herd of horses from California. Governor or not," Paloma told her friends, "Don Miguel is a great man in Nuevo Mexico. We have five preeminent families, and he is the head of one of them."

"The head of a donkey still brays like a jackass," said Armijo. Everyone laughed at this self-mockery, Armijo the loudest. He had two more bottles of brandy brought to the table, and proposed several rousing toasts. He sported a conspiratorial smile hinting that they were all devils together.

He made the company laugh several times more before saying, "Señora, shall we dance?"

Paloma gave Sam a smile, slightly nervous, he thought, and walked into the plaza on Armijo's arm.

Sam watched Armijo do the fandango with fascination.

"He barely moves," said Hannibal, "but his whole body bristles lust."

Sam watched his thick, high-arched eyebrows and drooping eyelids. He and Paloma, facing each other, moved sensuously, suggestively. Sam felt a stab of jealousy.

"That's a man who would come to power by any means necessary," said Sumner.

"And assume that anyone else would do the same, if they have ambition and daring," added Hannibal.

"He's like a child, swept up in his own desires," said Grumble.

The fandango ended, and Armijo led Paloma back to the table. "I must be off," he said to the group.

"I wish you well in your conquests," said Paloma, with a smile, "of every kind."

The ex-governor beamed and strode away, leering.

"It is Armijo's rancho we will go to tomorrow," said Paloma. "You are all invited."

"To what, señora," asked Grumble.

"A slave auction," said Paloma.

Sumner's eyes flashed, and his nostrils flared.

"Do you care to come?" she asked in a light tone.

Hannibal and Grumble hesitated and murmured, "Yes."

Sumner said, "Damn right."

Chapter Fourteen

Sam and Paloma dismounted in front of Armijo's casa. "Last year, when he was governor," she said, "Armijo would not have dared to host an auction on his own property. The government supports slavery, very much so, but the policy is not discussed." Sam tied Paladin and Paloma's sorrel to the hitch rail.

Now Grumble, Hannibal, and Sumner got down from their carriage. The cherub and the black man had ridden inside in style while Hannibal drove—that tickled them. Grumble liked to travel in the style of a gentleman. Actually, he enjoyed mocking and employing pretensions of gentility at the same time.

Paloma led them through a gate into a large courtyard. It was not a place of utility, like Paloma's, but a scene of beauty, with a central fountain and beds of wildflowers. About a dozen men were gathered there. One or two gave Paloma odd looks. They walked over and greeted Don Carlos and Don Gilberto, the American trader and the pumpkin-shaped Mexican, their gambling friends. A couple of the other Mexican men stared at Sumner. He affected not to notice.

Coy wanted to sniff out the people he didn't know, but Sam told him to sit.

Don Carlos introduced his American friends to the other dons. Most of them seemed indifferent to making new acquaintances. One gave Sam a truly sour look and whispered something to his companion about *"cabello blanco,"* white hair.

"Yes, Don Emilio," said Paloma, "isn't it beautiful?" She touched Sam's hair and flashed Emilio a smile that left no doubt that she was in possession of this splendid young man.

Don Emilio, a cadaverous-looking man with a sallow complexion, scowled at her.

Paloma and the Americans took themselves a few steps off.

"Like my outfit?" asked Sumner.

He was dressed the fanciest Sam had ever seen him, in a fine coat of dove-gray broadcloth and a cravat of gold silk with an edge of lace.

"Why, suh," Sam faked a genteel Louisiana accent, "you must be . . . Perhaps you are a planter from Santo Domingo."

They laughed together. In Santo Domingo Sumner had been a slave, not the planter.

"You and Grumble have been rummaging in Grumble's trunk of costumes, I can tell."

"I am a self-made man," said Sumner. "Whatever I want to be."

Sam thought, *I envy him just for saying that.*

They stood around and drank Armijo's brandy and chatted for a few minutes. Nothing seemed to be happening. Sam was so nervous his breathing was shallow. Then a man he recognized as a lead rider in the caravan came in through the back gate. A Spaniard, not an Indio, the way the Mexicans figured things. He was light-skinned, and his jaw outlined by a red-brown beard.

"Evil men should not be handsome," said Paloma.

Sam didn't think the fellow was a bit handsome, not with that harsh flash in his eyes.

An assistant oiled his way through the gate. By one hand he led a teenage girl by a chain between the shackles on her wrists. In the other he carried a whip. He looked at the girl and ran his tongue across his lower lip.

Something in Sam's stomach lurched upward.

Armijo walked to the center of the courtyard and addressed everyone. "Gentlemen and Señora Luna, this is the trader José Cerritos, of Chihuahua."

Coy growled

"Buenas dias," said the red-bearded man. "We have business to conduct." His words were lightly ironic, and his manner said, *We are men together. Let us revel in the pleasures of men.*

He gestured toward the girl with one hand, an invitation

to the eye. "This lovely creature is one part of our business. Maria comes all the way from the province of Chihuahua for your . . . consideration."

Paloma spoke softly. "Apaches probably stole her from her village and sold her in El Paso. It would have been months ago."

"She is healthy," continued Cerritos, "and she has learned to be submissive. With discipline you can teach her willingness to work." He seemed to put thoughts of pleasure into the word "discipline." "But she is not good enough for any of you, not yet." He looked at his audience with a bizarre mixture of contempt and something Sam couldn't decipher. "Maria is a virgin."

"Madre de Dios," said Paloma. "I have heard of this, but . . . Madre de Dios."

Cerritos turned and pulled her toward him by the chain. With a large key he undid her shackles, feet and hands.

The assistant fiddled with his whip, lust in his eyes. *Lust for sex or for blood?* Sam couldn't tell. Maria fixed her eyes, huge and black, straight ahead. Sam was sure her mind was on nothing but the whip.

"Not a chance of virginity, not after these two or three months," said Paloma. "In front of me. I can't believe this."

Cerritos untied at the collarbone the shirt of rough cloth the girl wore. With an absurdly delicate gesture, as though handling silk, he slipped it over her head.

Sam looked at Maria's fine, small breasts. *Stop it,* he told himself.

Cerritos pulled apart the strings of the bow tie at her waist, and with a gesture like a bullfighter handling a cape, he snapped her full skirt away. The girl stood naked. She stared at nothing. Though she struggled to keep her face still, tics rampaged across it.

Sam burned with shame.

Cerritos took her elbows and lowered her to the ground. Maria collapsed like sticks and lay flat, knees up, without protest.

Coy barked.

Sam looked at her closed eyes, her pursed lips, and her fingers clawing silently at the ground.

She hates it. Her rage boomed through him.

Cerritos knelt between her legs and dropped his trousers. He fondled her breasts and pinched her nipples hard. When she grimaced, he leered sideways at his audience. Then he leaned forward onto his elbows and stuck his stiff cock at her.

At the last instant her hips jerked sideways, as though to avoid him.

Cerritos laughed, reared his hips back, and thrust hard into her.

For a minute, two minutes, three, Cerritos rammed himself into Maria over and over. Sam could not look away, but he was glad that the rapist's arms blocked his view of her face. Mostly he saw Cerritos's body thrashing and the girl's knees rocking, like a boat being rowed.

"No," Paloma told him quietly, and held him back with a hand on his arm.

Cerritos finished, lingered an instant, and sat back on his heels.

Maria lay perfectly still, a corn-shuck doll.

Cerritos stood up, raised and belted his trousers, faced his audience with a hard face, and suddenly, strangely threw them a grin. "There," he said. "Now she's good enough for you."

Suddenly the tableau of watchers was released—an odd energy animated them. They moved about, touched each other on the arm, leaned over and whispered to each other.

Coy howled, drawing looks of displeasure from some of the Mexican men.

Armijo walked forward and stood next to Cerritos, staring at Maria. She knelt in the dust, put her clothes back on, and rose to face her audience. She put on a face that was blank as dried mud. It hurt Sam's heart.

He could not look at Paloma. Or Grumble, Sumner, or Hannibal. He felt deeply ashamed.

Why are some of us like this?

"The worst is past," Paloma said.

Armijo looked at the men, and one woman, he had invited to this event. His face sparkled with power. His thick lips gleamed with desire. His body said, *I am a man with the audacity to seize the good things in life. Are you?*

"He is voracious as a baby," said Paloma, "but not a bit innocent."

"Is he getting a share of the money?" Sam whispered.

"Of course."

An impulse ran through Sam. *Armijo needs killing.*

"I would suggest a starting bid of a thousand pesos for this fine specimen," said Armijo.

"Seven hundred," said Don Emilio.

Sam give the cadaverous don the evil eye. "Buy her," he told Paloma.

She shook her head. "I have pledged what money I have to buy Rosalita's sister."

Sam's mind roiled in anger. Armijo bid, Don Gilberto bid. The American trader abstained. Sam could not, did not, follow the bidding for Maria.

Suddenly Paloma left his side. She exchanged whispers with Don Emilio, several exchanges. It nettled Sam to see their faces so close together. But when she returned, Paloma wore a smile on her face.

"If he wins the bid," she said, "I will pay him a thousand pesos, and he will give me Rosalita's sister Lupe."

"He's probably tired of her in his bed," said Sam.

Paloma gave him a sympathetic look but said nothing.

Now Sam kept a keen ear on the bidding. The final price was *mil*-something pesos, over a thousand, but the numbers flipped by too fast for Sam's Spanish. The voice was Don Emilio's. He stepped forward, grasped the chain between Maria's wrists, and led her out of the courtyard. She hung her head and followed docilely.

Coy squealed.

"We will pick up Lupe on the way home today," said Paloma.

Sam's breaths came freer. He turned and told his friends what was happening. Hannibal and Grumble murmured their approval, but Sumner said nothing. His eyes were on fire. Sam couldn't look him in the face.

Next came a group of slaves, the oldest woman and her three children, girls who appeared to be about eight and ten and a boy who looked about eleven. "They would bring a higher price if the oldest was a girl," said Paloma.

More alkali in Sam's mouth.

The bidding barely passed a thousand pesos and stopped. Gobernador Armijo waddled forward to take possession of the four people.

Sam didn't think he could stay in this place. "Why are we still here?"

"Because leaving would offend Don Miguel," said Paloma.

Next came the woman in her twenties and two children. Sam couldn't bear to listen to the bidding, or watch the faces of any of the bidders, or of Armijo or Cerritos, or the so-called slaves. He didn't hear the price these people sold for.

"Last we have two boys, unfortunately without mothers," said Cerritos.

"If their mothers were captured, they probably died on the way," said Paloma. "Lots of them die. And when the women and children are stolen, the fathers are killed."

The boys were about ten and twelve, and they didn't look like brothers. Ragged, dirty, miserably dressed, one looking listless, the other rebellious. Looking at this boy's body, his rigidity, Sam realized he was all rage.

"What is offered for these fine young men?" said Cerritos. "They will grow into excellent workers in the fields. Also, they can be trained for any skill, blacksmith, wheelwright, whatever is needed. Very valuable. I ask five hundred for the pair."

"Two hundred," said Sumner.

Sam looked aghast at his friend. Was an ex-slave now going to own slaves?

Armijo glared at Sumner.

Cerritos said smoothly, "Two hundred, the man says. That

is . . . silly." He gestured with his hands, a motion that said, *Come to me with other bids.*

"Two fifty," called Don Gilberto.

"Two seventy-five," said Sumner.

"What are you doing?" Sam stage-whispered.

"Spending my money the way I want to."

"Three hundred," someone rasped.

"Are you going to free them?" asked Sam.

Sumner said, "Three and a quarter." He threw an irate glance at Sam. "I want to cut the head off slavery. I'm sure not going to support it."

Don Gilberto bid again.

Sam could hardly believe what came out of his mouth. "I'll split it with you," he said.

Sumner gave the biggest grin Sam had ever seen for him. He called out some bid—Sam didn't register what it was.

Someone topped Sumner's bid.

Sam stood shakily, dizzy with his own behavior.

"Let me take over," said Grumble, and he called out a number.

Sam weaved on his feet, stupefied, as voices called back and forth, spending his money—exchanging human beings for bits of stamped metal.

In the end Grumble won the bidding and walked forward to take charge of the boys. Fat Don Gilberto didn't look angry. There was courtesy between people who bought and sold human beings.

Now they all walked to the carriage, and Grumble brought the boys behind. Sam took the key from him, knelt down, and unlocked their hands and feet. Then he looked into their faces. "You'll be all right," he said gently. He tousled their hair with one hand. "You won't be slaves. We'll set you free. You'll be all right." He stood up.

Don Emilio walked by, saw Sam on his knees with the boys, and arranged his face into disapproval.

Grumble told the boys, "Get in the carriage."

Meekly, they did. The older one moved like a marionette.

Grumble said to Sam, "We'll settle up later. Your half is twenty-five dollars."

Sam could hardly believe it. For twenty-five dollars he had bought a human being, with bones, blood, mind, heart, and spirit.

Chapter Fifteen

They rode by Don Emilio's rancho to pick up Rosalita's sister Lupe. When they unloaded and dismounted in front of Paloma's casa, Sam thought, *We're overrun with people.*

Inside the scene ran to chaos. Everyone crowded around Paloma's dining table, and Juanita the cook set big pots to steaming—a big supper for all, maybe followed by full beds and bedrolls all over the casa.

Sam realized he felt invaded, and smiled wryly at himself for thinking of himself as the papa of Paloma's house. Coy trotted to the kitchen and begged, accustomed to getting treats from Juanita's pots.

Rosalita and Lupe ran to each other, embraced, swung each other at arm's length, and launched into a jabber of ultra-fast Spanish. "The kitchen," suggested Paloma. The two of them sat at the small table there, arms stretched across, hands clasped, words leapfrogging over one another.

"They have not seen each other in more than a year," said Paloma.

Flat Dog and Julia came in from their casita, with the children. Sam reached to pick Esperanza up, but she toddled away. She had been walking for about a month and had a mind of her own.

Paloma turned to Grumble. "Excuse us." He made room for her and Sam to sit next to the boys who were recently slaves.

She looked at them very directly. "I am Paloma Luna. You may call me Doña Paloma. This is my ranch, and you may stay here for a while until we decide what you will do."

One looked at her with a baby face and puppy eyes. The other, older, taller, and more muscular, was all eyes that blazed with anger. They both had dark skin and blue-black hair. *Indios,* thought Sam, *not Spanish, in the dumb way Spaniards arrange reality.*

"You are not slaves, do you understand that? Some bad men captured you, but we have freed you. Isn't that right?"

Sam, Sumner, Hannibal, and Grumble all said it was. Flat Dog and Julia watched curiously from the far end of the table. Julia was breast-feeding Azul.

"Juanita, please, bring *atole.* These boys look hungry."

Rosalita set big bowls of the gruel in the middle of the table for all. Lupe poured everyone drinks from two pitchers of aromatic hot chocolate.

"What are your names?"

"Pedro," said the one who looked perpetually frightened. He sipped gingerly at the chocolate.

"Tomás," said the bigger one. He drank directly out of his bowl, looking around like a wolf, half ready to fight for its food, half ready to run off.

"Pedro, Tomás, you are only boys, not ready to be on your own. We won't turn you out into the world by yourselves, do you understand?"

Pedro nodded that he did. Words seemed hard for him.

"We don't give a damn about that," said Tomás.

Sam bit his tongue. Who did this kid think he was?

Paloma ignored the rudeness. "For now this is your home, Rancho de las Palomas. If you are ever away from here and someone asks you, you live at Rancho de las Palomas." She looked at them hard. "You understand? Say it, Rancho de las Palomas."

Pedro mumbled the words. Tomás pronounced them loudly and sarcastically.

Both boys began to eat eagerly. Sam noticed that they didn't look at each other. Whatever else had happened on the Chihuahua Trail, these two didn't seem to have formed a bond.

"*Bueno*. Now you must meet your new friends. This is Sam Morgan, who paid a lot of money, enough to free one of you. This is Sumner, who also paid a lot of money for you. Say thank you."

"*Gracias*," each boy said. Tomás seemed to think it was nastily funny.

"Tomás, where do you come from?"

He named a village no one had ever heard of.

"Pedro, do you come from the same village?"

The boy shook his head no.

"Where is your village, Tomás?"

"In the Sierra Madre."

"Like saying in the Rocky Mountains," she told Sam. "The province of Chihuahua then?"

"Yes."

"Pedro, is your village also in the Sierra Mountains?"

"No, near the Rio Grande."

So they hadn't been around each other long.

Paloma went on. "I must tell you. The one thing I cannot offer is to send you home. If I gave you to a caravan going south, they would sell you to the first buyer who wanted you, just as happened here. You would be slaves again. So that cannot be. Do you understand?"

Both of them nodded yes.

"But hear me. You are free to go wherever you like. You are free, free as a bird to fly from tree to mountain, be sure of that."

She waited for them to mumble yes.

"If you choose to stay at my rancho, and that seems to be a good idea, I will make sure you have plenty to eat, clothes to wear, and a warm place to sleep. You understand?"

Mouths full, they nodded again.

"If you stay here, you must also know that there will be certain rules to follow, and chores to do. Just like for Rosalita, Lupe, me, everyone. And just like at home, no?"

Sam saw no particular reaction to the word "home." He guessed they'd given up on home. Maybe they'd seen their parents killed, their family houses burned to the ground, the entire village destroyed.

Juanita spoke to Rosalita and Lupe, and the two teenage girls began to bring platters of food to the dining table.

"*Bueno,*" said Paloma. "Now we eat, then we sleep, and tomorrow maybe we have some fun. How does that sound?"

"*Bueno,*" said both boys, their eyes on the food. It was the most positive sound Sam had heard from them.

The boys stayed up until everyone went to bed, Grumble and Sumner in the guest bedroom, the boys on pallets in the warm kitchen.

"Stay with us tonight," Flat Dog said to Hannibal.

"Sure."

Sam and Paloma walked to the casita with Flat Dog, Julia, and Hannibal. Sam offered to hold Esperanza's hand for the steps through the darkness, but she said "Papá!" and ran to give her finger to Flat Dog. Her other word, Sam had noticed, was "mamá."

She spoke no Crow or English at all. *Not yet,* Sam told himself.

At the door of the casita Sam picked Esperanza up and kissed her on the cheek. "I love you," he said, and handed her to Julia.

As Sam and Paloma strolled back toward the main house, she said, "That's the first time I've heard you say those words to her."

Sam looked up at the millions of stars—so many were visible at this altitude—and thought how far apart they were, how much empty space stretched between them. "It's been coming to me more and more," he said, "that she's the one way Meadowlark is alive."

"Good thinking," Paloma said.

"Now there's more to think on," Sam said. He walked a few steps. Even in April the night air was cold. "I've taken on responsibility for the lives of the two boys. What the hell am I going to do now?"

He smiled ruefully. She chuckled.

Though Paloma mostly preferred not to be touched while she slept, that night they spooned close to each other. Sam slept fitfully, and was grateful for her warmth.

His last thought was the memory of the Mojave boys who tortured the toads. *Why?*

THE NEXT MORNING Tomás was gone.

"Señora," said Juanita, "only one boy was here when I came in."

Sam knew that Juanita got to the kitchen well before dawn to start the day's tortillas.

"This other one, he was rolled right up against the legs of the stove, sucking his thumb. I couldn't work until I made him move."

Pedro was still rolled up in his blankets, against an interior wall now, looking at them all with wide, dark eyes, too frightened to be reached by Juanita's disapproval.

Paloma went to hunt for Tomás all over the house, though she had no hope that the boy was here. She asked all her guests if they'd heard anything. Sam went outside to search for the boy, or sign of him.

They met in the kitchen again with the same word, "Nothing."

"Rosalita," said Paloma, "go to the casita. Tell Don Flat Dog what has happened, and that I ask him to help Don Sam with the search."

Now Juanita was feeding Pedro hot chocolate and *atole*. Rosalita and Lupe were serving everyone else at the dining table. Grumble and Sumner were glum. Hannibal was rushing through his breakfast so they could get going. When Flat Dog came in, he and Sam ate on their feet.

"Unfortunately," Paloma told everyone, "I have no idea about this."

"Maybe one of the slave owners stole him," said Sumner.

"Impossible. It is a club, and I am a member. If they catch him, they will return him."

"Worse for the wear," said Sumner.

"Beaten," said Paloma.

"If he has headed down the Chihuahua Trail," said Hannibal, "someone will put shackles back on him."

"Absolutely. And if he goes to a pueblo, the same." Paloma added, "Though it is a soft kind of slavery there."

"If he's hiding somewhere?" asked Sam.

"In this rough country," said Hannibal, "he can't hold out long."

"He'll come back hungry. That's probably our best hope," said Paloma. She shooed the three of them out through the kitchen. "Go. Find Tomás. Tell him I will help him."

Sumner looked at Pedro, who was now squatting against a wall near the kitchen stove. The boy's hands were shaking.

Grumble handed Sumner a deck of playing cards.

Sumner grinned. "Hey, Pedro," he said. "Come here. I got something to show you. It's fun."

The boy edged as near as the archway.

Sumner waterfalled the cards. "Look here, see these pictures." He held them up to Pedro. The boy came close enough to see.

"See this card in my hand? It's called the king. Whoops! It isn't there. Look, both my hands are empty." Sumner showed the boy his hands, palms up. Then he reached up to Pedro's ear. "Look, here it is."

Pedro gaped his mouth open.

"Now it's gone. Where did it go?"

"¿Donde?" said Pedro, the first word they'd heard him say this morning.

Sumner reached into the waistband of the boy's pants and drew out the king.

Pedro giggled.

Paloma nodded at Sumner and Grumble in gratitude.

"Pedro is ruined for life," said Grumble.

* * *

NO ONE HAD seen Tomás. No horse gear was missing from the stable. Flat Dog, the best tracker, could find no signs along the riverbank. "There's no sense in looking for sign on that road," said Hannibal.

"Not with the traffic on it," Sam agreed. Coy mewled.

With Paloma they inventoried the house. The blankets the boy slept in were missing. Juanita said a bowl of *atole* was eaten and the bowl left on the counter, some leftover tortillas taken. That was all. She opened a couple of drawers, looked, and closed them. "Looks like he took my cleaver too."

"He's on foot," said Hannibal, "he has something to keep him warm at night. He took a little food, not much. Maybe he wanted the cleaver for self-defense."

"But why?" said Sam. "Why would he leave, with nowhere to go?"

They interrupted Sumner's card tricks to quiz Pedro. "Did he say anything about going anywhere?"

The boy shrugged, eyes on the floor. "No, señor."

Sam, Hannibal, Flat Dog, and Paloma looked at each other in frustration.

"So up the road or down the road?" said Sam.

"Up," said Hannibal. "He's damn well not planning to walk all the way to Chihuahua."

The miles upriver to Santa Fe revealed nothing. The town itself revealed nothing. They asked a dozen people along the main road—hell, they asked a score of people—but who would remember one Indian-looking boy out of so many? And it was impossible to ask everyone in a town of six thousand people.

Sam, Hannibal, and Flat Dog wandered around Santa Fe. They checked with the priest at each of the churches. They had lunch outdoors on the plaza where they could see. They rode up and down streets at random. They looped back on themselves, and circled back where they came from. When Coy looked at them quizzically, they ignored him.

Just before dark they trundled into Rancho de las Palomas discouraged.

Paloma stood in the doorway, blocking it. "Suppose you'd been captured and your parents killed and been hauled six hundred miles to be sold as a slave. Suppose you could get away for a day or two. What would be on your mind?"

"Kill Cerritos," said Sam.

"Then he's gone to Armijo's place," said Paloma.

She handed Sam a bundle of warm tortillas wrapped in cloth.

They ran for their horses.

Chapter Sixteen

Tomás Guerrero, a boy from an insignificant village on an unimportant stream flowing east from the Sierre Madre Occidental, had one strength. He knew absolutely what he had to do.

His father had taught him the meaning of the name Guerrero, warrior. Now the men of this family grew corn, beans, and chiles in their fine irrigated fields, and the children looked after their few goats. It was a good place, and the men of this village had for generations defended their families and their village against many enemies. With bow and arrow, with spear, with club they had acted when necessary as men, as *guerreros,* warriors. That was the blood that coursed through the body of Tomás, and through his mind and will. At this moment he bore a warrior's courage, a warrior's determination, and a warrior's fierceness.

He was waiting only for complete darkness. He had walked most of the day. He followed El Camino Real for a mile or two so that his tracks would be indistinguishable from others, and then walked through the sagebrush, through the trees, across rock, wherever he would be hard to track. He didn't know who was more likely to come after him, the men who would make him a slave again, or the foolish woman who would make him into a household servant or a farmboy. He was determined to elude everyone until he fulfilled his purpose. He kept the cleaver stuck down the back of his pants, covered by his loose shirt. He didn't want anyone to know he was bringing trouble.

At midmorning he made a wide circle around the city of Santa Fe. No city was important. What mattered was carrying himself as a man.

Once this afternoon he stopped to ask directions. He found himself uncertain which road led along the plateau to the rancho of the don, the man who arrogated to himself the power to own other human beings, to subordinate their desires to his own, to use them as his playthings.

A simple man who was cleaning an irrigation ditch told Tomás, "The road is there, beyond those fields and across the creek." The way to the rancho of the powerful man Tomás despised.

Later, when he got to the top of the rise and looked down at the rancho, he saw that it would be hard. First Tomás observed, noting everything and memorizing the arrangement of buildings, tracks, and gates. Then he crawled to the creek, concealed himself in the willows, and waited. When he saw a clear chance, he sprinted to the back side of a building. Then he crept behind a wagon. He slipped into a corral with some horses. At last he got into the barn and up into the loft, where he could see into the casa. These movements took him all afternoon, but he was very, very patient. His father had taught him that the first strength of a warrior, as for a hunter, is patience.

He was frustrated. From the loft he could see into the courtyard and through windows into the kitchen, the dining room, and even the room where rich people sat prettily and received their guests. He had seen two such houses in his lifetime, yesterday and today, but he was smart and able to put the layout firmly in his mind. He would be able to find his way around this one in the dark. His stomach was sour with contempt for the rich who lived in high style while others plowed their fields, planted, and did all the other labor that supported the *ricos*.

He was burning with two questions: Where was this particular *rico* now? And where was the human being he intended to make his slave?

In the rooms Tomás could see from this perch, he got no hint of an answer to either question. And now that the sun was down, the sky fully dark, and the house lit only by candles, he could see less.

On the other hand, the darkness would make it possible for a warrior to approach undetected, and to enter in stealth.

He climbed down the ladder and padded softly between the stalls. He inhaled the musty smells of straw, dung, and hay, and looked at the dark shadows of the necks and heads of the horses sticking over the stall doors, peering at the intruder.

The night was brighter than the barn, even though the moon was dipping toward the western hills. He moved quietly and told himself he had the confidence of a warrior. No one would be stirring now, unless the cook came outside. The don was probably at his meal in the dining room—with *her,* Tomás supposed. Even wicked men liked the company of a pretty woman.

Otherwise, probably, the don was alone. The children must be grown and gone. All afternoon he'd seen no family members at all, only the cook and a serving woman near the house, and elsewhere just field hands. He wondered if they were slaves. He hadn't seen the don, or her. It drove him mad to picture how they were probably spending the hours.

Already he had decided how to make his approach. The house was two long wings that made an L, and the two walls of the courtyard completed the square. He ignored the front door, far to the front left. He tiptoed past the gate into the courtyard, which gave access to the door that led to the kitchen. He treaded quietly along the wall outside the

courtyard, where he had seen ovens, a well, and at the far end
a fountain and ornamental plantings of cholla and chamisa.
Facing the courtyard where the two wings met were several
windows. He wondered what that room was—where the master slept, with a view of his garden? He circled around the back
of the house to the far corner and tiptoed all the way to the back
corner, where the two wings joined. He was only guessing,
but . . .

Yes, there was a small door here.

He slipped the cleaver out of his waistband and held it
high. From now on he must be totally alert and completely
ready. If he came on an enemy unexpectedly, he knew what
to do. His father told him over and over.

"When I was a boy, or barely a man, fourteen," his father
said, "we fought the Apaches. They came to steal our families, many of them. They rode into the village in the middle
of the day, when the men were working in the fields. They
rushed into our houses and seized our women and children.
If the men ran in from the fields in time, they killed them.
Even the boys my age, if we tried to fight, they killed us.

"My older brother, not yet married, he had walked into the
village to get food for the men. When the Apaches came, he
was stepping out of the door of our house. He threw down
the food and fought with his knife. I grabbed a cleaver from
the kitchen and rushed to fight beside him. He screamed like
a madman and swung his blade in every direction. I did the
same, I became a *loco*. By that fighting, I learned a great
lesson. The Apaches shot their arrows at us and threw their
spears, but we stood untouched, warriors. As a result they
did not go into our house. We were too much trouble. They
stole children from the neighbors instead. So if ever you
must fight, Tomás, do it like a *loco*. In his madness, a *loco*,
he is protected by the saints."

Tomás took off his sandals and set them down. Barefooted
would be quieter. He squeezed the handle of the cleaver and
gently opened the rear door. He stood outside a moment,
listening. Nothing.

He eased his head in the opening and peered down the corridor straight ahead. Nothing that he could detect, but the corridor was dark. He slipped through the doorway and stood very still, looking down the other corridor. There warm candlelight flowed through two open doors, making the hall a checkerboard of darkness and light.

Good, thought Tomás, *probably I will find them in the dining room.* He breathed deep. *Like thunder and lightning I will fall upon him, and I will bless her like a warm rain.*

He glided along the inside wall, his back to it. When he came to the first door, he stopped, waited, and quieted his heart. Slowly, he craned his neck into the entryway. To the left his vision was blocked by the door, which stood half open. In the middle of the room there was a long table, apparently for dining. Against the wall at the far end stood a high cabinet with glass doors and full of plates, bowls, cups, and glassware. Tomás felt a spurt of disgust for people who owned many sets of dishes, while a family like his had to eat from cheap bowls of clay.

Suddenly, the kitchen door swung open and a serving girl walked briskly through, carrying a covered dish. Tomás jerked his head back. He didn't know whether she'd spotted him, and his heart pounded.

By her footsteps he could tell she walked to the left end of the table, the one hidden from view. Words were spoken—"Here you are, sir" in a female voice, and in a man's, *"Gracias."* He let out a huge sigh. Evidently, the girl hadn't seen him. The footsteps tick-ticked again, her figure appeared with her back to him, and she disappeared into the kitchen. From there an older woman's voice said something sharply, and the younger woman's gave a clipped answer.

I am within a few steps of her now. He pictured her sitting meekly next to the old man, answering meekly when spoken to, obeying when instructed. She had been obeying since they were stolen from their home, which drove him mad.

Yet at the same time he loved her.

Can I do it?

He crossed to the outer wall. Then, facing the dining room, he crabbed sideways across, visible to anyone who might raise their eyes in his direction.

No one was there to look. He couldn't even see the don and his sister at their places at the table.

He slid swiftly to the far door to the dining room. This door also stood ajar. And he found a blessing—he could peer through the crack between the door and the facing.

At the head of the table sat the don, alone. *Where is she?*

He slumped in his chair, picking at his food without interest, staring at the dark windows that bordered the courtyard garden. His sallow complexion looked even more yellow in the candlelight.

Diablo, where is she?

He scoured his memory of the other long hall, the one on the left.

He half ran back down the hall—foolish speed, he knew. He sped by the other dining door without hesitation. Not before the corner at the end of the hall did he slow down.

He glanced down the hall and jerked his head back. Nothing but gloom. The first door stood partly open, and moonlight pooled on the floor. The far end of the corridor was inky.

He walked silently to the open door and peered in. The window facing the courtyard let in enough light to see. A small, plain bed, a table, a wardrobe, nothing more. Pole rafters held a flat ceiling. Candles stood in their wall holders, but he had nothing to light them with.

He slipped on to the next door, closed. Slowly, quietly, he pushed down on the flat handle. When it stopped at the bottom of its turn, he waited. The mechanism had been silent.

He eased the door open, waited. No one shouted, no one rushed at him.

He poked his head in. The room was identical to the other. Neither appeared to be in use. He closed the door and went on. Maybe the don lived alone in this big house.

He stepped quietly to the last door on this hall. He'd guessed that this was the large bedroom, for the master and his . . . woman. He reminded himself that he didn't know.

He palmed the handle, turned it, and held it down. After a deep breath in and out he opened the door and stepped in.

And glimpsed a figure. In front of the big window on the opposite side, aglow in the moonlight, hung the nude body of a woman.

Tomás weaved the few steps forward. He looked up at the head, and the cord that suspended her from the rafter. He reached out and touched the hand. Cold.

That cold coursed through him, pumped by his own heart.

"¿Maria?"

A voice in the corridor!

"My dear?"

The horror.

Tomás jerked his head around and saw the glow of candlelight. He froze.

Two candles came into view, each held by one hand. Behind them in the soft aura of light was the face of Don Emilio.

Aghast, Tomás turned back to his nude sister. Her head was crooked forward and her small feet dangling above the floor. The breeze from the window made her black hair stir against her limp forearm.

"Maria!" screamed Tomás.

As he screamed, he whirled to Don Emilio. Two faces, stunned, glared at each other.

"Murderer!" bellowed Tomás.

All of his rage at life raised the cleaver straight over his head and with both hands Tomás swung savagely down onto the don's skull.

Chapter Seventeen

He simply materialized in the doorway. One moment Sam saw an empty rectangle, the next a space filled with the dirty, skinny, bloody form of Tomás.

Paloma rushed to him and embraced him. Then she threw a look at the dining table that quelled everyone there: Do not ask this child any questions, not yet. Quickly she pushed Tomás through the dining room into the kitchen. "Scrub this boy in hot, soapy water," she told Juanita the cook, "and bring him right back to the table. He's probably starved."

Tomás gave Rosalita and Lupe, the serving girls, a funny look. They giggled, probably at the idea of him being stripped down and washed vigorously. Juanita, with her grandmotherly age and sergeant style, would be perfect for that.

In a few minutes Paloma got things arranged. She dispatched Flat Dog, Julia, and the infants to their casita. Pedro tagged after them. She reheated the stew of pork and green chiles herself and popped the tortillas into the warming oven.

Tomás sat, clean and in a robe of Paloma's. Juanita took his clothes, dirty and speckled with blood. His eyes darted from Paloma to Sam to Hannibal. Sam was sure the boy felt outnumbered. Which was good.

"All right, Tomás," said Paloma, "what has happened?"

Sam watched Tomás decide how to play it. He decided on defiance. "I killed the *diablo*." His lips curled as he said the words.

Rosalita put food in front of Tomás, and he pitched in.

"Killed who?" said Hannibal. They had ridden to Armijo's rancho, had talked to Cerritos, and knew the slave trader was in disgustingly good health.

"The one you call Don Emilio."

The adults flashed their eyes at each other. Why Emilio?

Tomás ate enthusiastically and gave them a weird, quivery grin.

Sam looked at Tomás and thought, *This attitude isn't going to last long.*

"I killed him with the cleaver." Tomás picked up the big knife and threw it flat onto the dining table, where it clattered, quivered, and grew still. The blade was caked with dried blood.

The boy looked at them with what he intended as pride.

Sam put a hand on his arm. "Why?" he asked.

"Why?" Tomás looked down at his plate. He dropped his spoon into his bowl of stew. He stared at it. Then he dumped the whole bowl in his lap. He stood up, food dribbling down the robe. Maybe he tried to scream the next words, but they came out as a series of hiccups. "Because the *hijo de puta* killed Ma-ma-ria."

Then the tears burst forth. Tomás wept, he sobbed, he shook convulsively.

Paloma put her arms around him. Sam patted his shoulder. Hannibal watched Tomás's face closely, tenderly. Then, slowly and patiently, the three adults drew the story out of the child and put it together:

The girl that Cerritos raped in front of everyone, the one "not good enough for you yet," she was Maria Guerrero, the older sister of Tomás. And all the other men had raped her, as often as they wanted, at least one every night, since . . .

"Maria, she . . ."

The first time they raped her, Tomás threw himself on her attacker. They laughed, beat him, and then did everything they wanted to do with her loudly, mocking him and laughing. When he threw himself on the rapist again the next night, they held him fast, brought him close, made him watch, and then beat him senseless. After that they separated the two completely. They were not permitted to walk together, to talk, even to sleep near each other.

Tomás did not know what would happen when they finally got to Santa Fe. He was hoping they would be sold to the same family and could escape together.

"But Cerritos, he made a point of it. When he sold her, he did not want anyone to know I am her brother, know she had any family nearby. Cerritos, he said these words, 'A tasty morsel, unprotected . . .'"

Hannibal and Sam looked at each other and reached an understanding. To help this boy they needed to know . . .

"You walked to Don Emilio's rancho?"

"Yes." They realized he'd seen it when they went to get Lupe.

"Then what did you do?"

Tomás had honest pride in the next part of the tale. He told how he watched, figured things out, approached, sneaked through the casa until he found the don at his table, explored the rest of the house in the dark, and discovered . . .

"She was in his bedroom. Naked. He came down the hall calling her '*Querida*.'"

A term of endearment—Sam felt it like a sting.

"I knew he soiled her all day long."

Sam sensed something wrong. "She was still in his bed?"

"No, she . . . No, she . . ." And he wailed and sobbed again. Some minutes and much soothing were needed to get the next part of the story.

"She was hanging in the moonlight, naked, by a cord from one of the rafters. *Muerto*."

For long moments no one could speak. Tomás looked from face to face. There were no words.

"You said he came down the hall?" This was Hannibal.

"Yes, just after I found her. Perhaps he heard me and thought it was her. He came carrying a candle in each hand. They showed me my target, they framed his head for me. I took that cleaver and . . ." He pointed to the big knife, raised his hands over his head in a double fist, and swung them viciously down. The blow rattled the dining table, and the equilibrium of his listeners.

"Are you sure she is dead?"

"I touched her."

"Sure he is dead?"

"I split his brain in two." The words danced to dark music in Tomás's eyes.

Sam, Paloma, and Hannibal looked at each other, understanding.

"My child," said Paloma, "you must rest." She put an arm around his shoulders and guided him toward the doorway. "We will talk about everything tomorrow."

SAM AND HANNIBAL spent the next day in Santa Fe and came back with a different story. "We didn't have to ask anyone," said Sam. "It's the talk of the town."

Paloma brought cups of coffee. As she started to sit, she said, "Wait, I'll get Tomás. He's done nothing but sleep all day."

"Maybe that's not such a good idea," said Sam.

"It is," said Paloma. "If he's old enough to kill a man, he's old enough to hear what comes of it."

When Tomás was across the table from them and fully alert, Sam started to give him the news.

Tomás held up a flat hand. "I don't care about the *cabrón*. Tell me about my sister."

Sam said gently, "We brought her body in the wagon. We stopped at the Church of the Virgin of Guadalupe, and the priest said the proper words over her."

To Sam the words felt like thrown stones.

Tomás's face was naked.

Paloma said, "Tomorrow, if you want, we will bury her outside the chapel here."

"Good." Tomás looked lost for a moment. Then he said with a twisted smile, "Now tell me about the *viejo hediondo*."

"Don Emilio is barely alive," said Sam. "No one knows whether he will live or die. He mumbles but says nothing that makes any sense. The doctor says maybe he has a fractured skull, or maybe he's only missing a big piece of scalp on the left side of his head. Either way, he's weak from loss of blood, and he has a high fever. No one will know anything for several days."

"Unless I get at him," said Tomás.

"Stop that," Sam said. He gave the boy a hard look.

"I will kill him," said Tomás bitterly.

"You won't," said Sam.

Tomás lashed out. "He might get well. He might remember me."

"You don't know what it is to kill a human being." Sam wished he didn't.

"He might send the *policia*."

"We'll plan for that."

Paloma held Tomás's hands and looked deep into his eyes. "We will protect you."

Sam added, "No more killing."

He watched Tomás's face carefully, and later he thought the boy's expression was relief.

Chapter Eighteen

Don Emilio did not cooperate. He neither lived nor died—he lingered. Though his servants listened carefully and the police asked often, nothing came from his delirium but babblings. Sam knew, because Grumble had a friend in the *comisaria de policia* and kept close touch. The police, naturally, were properly concerned about an outrageous attack on a prominent citizen. Such behavior could not go unpunished. But they had no suspects, not even a hint of who the culprit was. Nothing had been stolen, though the house was full of valuables, especially the chapel. Don Emilio was a widower, he lived alone with his herds and crops—why would anyone want to kill such a man?

After a week, Sam decided he had to speak up to Paloma. "We need to get started."

They were getting undressed for bed.

She looked at him, and he couldn't name all he saw in her eyes. Recognition, sadness, a sense of rightness.

She slipped into bed in her nightgown and patted the pillow next to her. "I know today is the first of May," she said. "Leave the candles on."

Sam slid in next to her naked. He didn't own enough clothes to have nightwear.

"How soon?" she said.

"A week maybe."

"All right. Today is Thursday. We have our horse sale next Monday. I will send a man to let everyone know. It's going to be quite a show, and you, sir, will make some money. Then you will be able to buy supplies to take to your important rendezvous and make a good profit."

That much was true, but it wasn't what Sam wanted to talk about. "It's going to be hard to say good-bye."

He saw warmth in her eyes as well. Maybe she felt comfortable with good-bye—he didn't. "What do you want me to say, Sam? That you must sell your horses to the other beaver men and make your bonanza? That you need to get back to the business of hunting beaver? That you must take your daughter to her grandparents, to the Crow village where she belongs?" She waited. They both knew all that.

Finally, Sam said, "I want you to tell me why we're inappropriate."

She just looked at him. "I've thought and thought about that. When I said it, my big thought was, I'm ten years older. Or it's because I'm Mexican and you're American. Or because we are from different class backgrounds, different education. I was raised to love things cultivated for beauty, you to love nature in the raw. And all of that is true."

She hesitated.

"But . . ."

"You tell me why we should be appropriate."

He tapped his chest with his fist. "I have a fire in here for you."

She just looked at him.

"When I look into your eyes, I see that you have fire for me."

She smiled. "That's just candlelight, sir."

"Talk true," he said.

After a long moment she said, "I think you've touched directly on it. Each of us has a fire in the heart. Mine is the fire of the hearth. I love my home, I love making a nest, I love creating a beautiful place to live.

"You, though, your fire is for adventure. It takes you hither and yon. You've been from the Atlantic to the Pacific. One day, when I see you again, I'll bet you've looked upon the Arctic Ocean."

Actually, Sam knew there was fur-trapping even up there—by the Russians.

She kissed him lightly on the lips. "You, *mi amante,* are a true adventurer, an explorer. You may dally with a nurturer like me. You even find peace and love at my hearth. But one day before long, your nature will require you to go wandering."

He was stuck for words.

"Husband? Not yet. Father? Maybe not yet either."

Now he was truly stuck.

She put both arms around him, buried her head in his chest, and said, "Don't go into that head of yours. Make love to me."

Chapter Nineteen

Getting ready for the sale was a furious time. Over the three days Sam, Flat Dog, and Hannibal put Paloma's horses through their paces again, getting them all sharp. Sam found only one he wouldn't want himself, a gelding that was a knothead. "One in every crowd," he told Flat Dog.

They also checked out the mounts of their own they'd trained for sale. Hannibal had made a list of Santa Fe prices of the most important supplies—powder, lead, coffee, blankets, traps, knives, foofaraw, brandy—and figured out they could turn a nice dollar on trade goods. If they could sell some of their horses at a good price here, they'd use others to pack goods to rendezvous and earn more money.

"I'm for it," said Sam.

"You're becoming a trader," Hannibal told him.

"Indians can't run off supplies like they can horses," said Flat Dog. Both Sam and Hannibal looked at him funny for saying "Indians."

Flat Dog chuckled. "Indians," he said, "means every tribe but Crows."

The good news about getting ready was that Tomás worked hard at helping. While Pedro went to town and stayed with Sumner and Grumble—"No doubt learning card tricks," said Sam—Tomás worked with the horses. He'd ridden his father's mule a lot, always bareback, because the family didn't own a saddle. As a result he had good balance on a horse. Sam told Flat Dog, "I think he's a natural rider."

"Natural athlete," said Hannibal.

Tomás would be able to demonstrate, during the sale, how well trained the mounts were, so gentle that even a boy could handle them. He also showed a willingness to work at learning English. When Sam and Hannibal spoke English among themselves, he asked what certain words meant, and they explained.

The fun was getting ready for the showy part. Sam, Hannibal, and Flat Dog knew that if they could get the buyers and watchers excited and inspired, the bidding would spiral higher and higher. So they rehearsed all their routines—Paladin and Brownie showed off their liberty training. Coy did his stuff. Sam and Hannibal did all their tricks on both of them. Flat Dog demonstrated a stunt he'd developed on his own. The riders could tell what an impression their show would make—Tomás and Paloma gasped and applauded.

At the end of the first day, over supper, Tomás said, "I don't want to stay here with Paloma. I want to go with you."

Everyone noticed that he said it to Sam, not to the three men, Julia, and the children. Sam thought, *Well, I paid for him.*

"You're in trouble. You may not have much choice about where you go," said Hannibal.

"But I want you to know you're welcome here," said Paloma.

"If the police aren't chasing your tail," said Flat Dog.

Everyone grinned, but no one thought it was funny.

"I want to go with you," Tomás repeated. "I want to be a mountain man."

Sam wondered what Tomás thought that meant—trick riding?—but he didn't answer.

All day Saturday and Sunday they worked on combining their various stunts with music. Antonio, one of the ranch's field hands, accompanied them on guitar, and Sam sang while he rode. In the evenings Sam and Hannibal taught Antonio the songs the horses knew. While Paloma went to Santa Fe on Sunday, to go to mass and remind everyone about the sale, they fine-tuned everything.

Tomás brought it up again that night—"I want to go with you."

"You're still a kid."

Tomás made a face.

From the size of the crowd that showed up Monday at noon, they knew that the word had spread far and wide: Something special was about to happen at Rancho de las Palomas. Gobernador Armijo came and announced that he was looking for fine stallions. Don Gilberto and Don Carlos presented themselves with eager faces. The other great families of the region—Chavez, Otero, Perea, and Yrizar—sent representatives to buy good breeding stock. Merchants of Santa Fe appeared, perhaps to buy well-trained saddle mounts, perhaps just to watch the show. It seemed that every Santa Fean who loved horses came out for the event. Paloma

sent Rosalita and Lupe through the crowd to pour brandy
liberally.

At last Grumble called for silence. He was splendidly
American in a plum morning coat and fawn beaver hat, which
Paloma had ornamented with a wide, sky-blue ribbon to mark
him as master of ceremonies. "Antonio," he declared, "give us
a fanfare."

To Antonio's music Sam and Hannibal dashed into the
improvised forty-two-foot ring, followed by Paladin and
Brownie. Coy pranced at their heels, excited. Paloma had fes-
tooned the horses' manes and tails with streamers of bright
cloth. The riders were beautifully decked out as well, in big
sombreros, short jackets, and beautifully quilled moccasins.
"Make the best show you can," Paloma had urged them.

Antonio quickly launched into a fast sea shanty, a jig the
horses knew. Grumble sang the words in English in a fine,
round basso:

When I was a little lad and so my mother told me
Way, haul away, we'll haul away, Joe
That if I did not kiss the girls, my lips would grow all moldy
Way, haul away, we'll haul away, Joe.

Hannibal and Sam signaled, and the horses faced each
other in the center of the circle, trembling with anticipation.
Hannibal lowered his hand in a wide sweep and called,
"Dance!"

Antonio strummed and Grumble sang.

King Louis was the king of France before the revolution
But then he got his head cut off, which spoiled his consti-
*   tution.*

On the first line the horses pranced sideways in the same
direction in rhythm to the music. On the second they stomped
and shook their heads.

Oh, once I had a German girl and she was fat and lazy
Then I got a French gal, she damn near drove me crazy.

At Sam's and Hannibal's hand signals, for the German girl
line they pranced the other direction. For the French girl's
craziness, they reared and pawed the air.

Now the audience cheered.

Way, haul away, I'll sing to you of Nancy
Way, haul away, she's just my cut and fancy.

To "cut and fancy" they made curvets forward, passed each
other, turned, and faced one another from the opposite sides.
Sam could almost hear the awe among the Nuevo Mexicans.

Way, haul away, we'll haul away the bowlin'
Way, haul away, we'll haul away, Joe.
Way, haul away, the packet is a rollin'.

Here the mounts reared again, and whinnied—

Way, haul away, we'll haul away together
Way, haul away, we'll haul for better weather.

And finally Paladin and Brownie bowed to one another.
Everyone burst into applause.

As Paladin's head was down, Coy sprinted toward Paladin
and jumped onto her back and stood on his hind legs. Paladin cantered around the ring, Coy's paws waving at the audience.

The clapping doubled.

Coy barked three times, as though celebrating himself, and
jumped down.

Flat Dog raced into the ring on his own horse for his moment of display. As the pony circled, Flat Dog swung down to
one side, reached under the horse, and shot an arrow into the

sky. When the crowd saw that the arrow displayed the Mexican flag, they whistled and stomped. Then Flat Dog passed all the way under the galloping legs and rose back into the saddle. Sam figured that was the first applause of the Crow's life.

Sam and Hannibal vaulted onto their mounts' backs and stood up. At first they just waved to the audience. Then, simultaneously, they somersaulted into the air and landed sitting down. Women in the crowd shrieked. Again and again they did it—stand, somersault, and land in riding position. When they did a leaping dismount together, the crowd went wild.

"That was fun," Hannibal said quietly to Sam.

Grumble now stepped forward with a showman's command of his audience. "And now," he said, "we begin the business of the day."

Tomás rode one of Paloma's geldings into the ring and did a figure eight, showing how nicely it reined. On command the gelding stopped and backed up.

"What are we offered," cried Grumble, "for this fine two-year-old? I call for five hundred pesos."

"Three hundred fifty," shouted Armijo.

Sam stopped listening and smiled to himself. Paloma's horses were going to sell for much more than she thought. He and Flat Dog would do well. And then they got to sell horses from their own herd. Flat Dog said softly, "We're gonna strike it rich today."

"Half rich," Sam agreed.

DINNER WAS A celebration. At Paloma's instruction Juanita cooked the most sumptuous meal she could manage, and the wine flowed freely. Everyone ate heartily and told jokes. Even Tomás, for the first time, seemed to relax and enjoy himself.

After dessert Paloma said, "Thank you all," she said, "today was so very good. Thank you, Mr. Grumble." Here she gave him the amount agreed on—"Plus," she said, "a bonus for cajoling my rich customers into such good prices."

Grumble looked at the coins and said, "Generous. Thank you."

She handed Sam and Flat Dog a stack of coins for their work on the seven saddle mounts she'd sold.

Flat Dog looked at the money and said, "We didn't even get starved or shot at."

"And for putting on such a grand display," she said, "something extra for each of you." Another stack of coins. The friends winked at each other.

"Last," she said, "something for Tomás, and a bit for Juanita, Rosalita, and Lupe for our fine meal, and one coin for Pedro so he can buy himself a treat."

Sam, Hannibal, and Flat Dog also shared a bit of their wealth with everyone. They looked at each other like conspirators. They couldn't get their minds off how much they would buy at the trading posts in town tomorrow.

Then Sumner walked in.

Everyone looked at the expression on his face.

"Don Emilio is awake and talking," he said. "In fact, shouting. He has told the police that the older of the two slave boys bought by me and Sam assaulted him. He demands justice. The police are on their way here now. I rode fast to get here first. They won't have any trouble picking you out, Tomás."

Everyone sat stunned.

Sam thought, *Damn, when we're all a little drunk.*

Grumble cocked his head, waited a moment, and said, "I have an idea."

"What?" said Paloma. This was her home.

"Better you don't know," said Grumble. "Sam, Tomás, let's confer."

Chapter Twenty

In the chapel Grumble gave Tomás a useful device the boy had never heard or dreamed of. Grumble quickly explained its normal use, which made Tomás look wildly at Sam and grin like a fool. Then Grumble explained how Tomás was to employ it in front of the police, which sobered the young man hugely. For a moment Sam thought Tomás was about to leap into fear and darkness, but then the boy seemed to make up his mind to see the thing through.

Grumble spoke to Sam briefly about the pistol kept in his belt. When Sam understood, he made certain adjustments to it.

"Act it out," said Grumble. "Both of you. An actor sells his reality to the audience."

Sam nodded. Tomás didn't. "It's the only way," Sam said.

Tomás pursed his lips. *"Bueno."*

Then the three of them knelt and prayed, or pretended to. Sam worried. He eased off on that when he thought how scared Tomás had to be.

They heard Paloma's voice down the hall. "Put your weapons away. Not in my house."

She appeared in the doorway. "The police have come for Tomás."

"Admit them," said Grumble.

That was unnecessary because the officers were already pushing past Paloma.

The candlelight in the chapel was dim, and the officers needed a moment for their eyes to adjust. Sam noticed that their pistols were in their belts.

"Tomás Guerrero," said the tall, fat officer, "you are under arrest for assaulting Señor Emilio Durán."

The three of them rose from their knees.

"The boy has confessed," said Grumble, "and is now ready

to yield his fate and his soul to God. He will go with you peaceably."

Sam scowled at Tomás, drew his pistol, and held it against his ribs, assisting the police.

Tomás looked crazily from the policemen to the pistol next to his heart.

"The devil!" he screamed, and swung wildly at Sam's face.

Sam's pistol boomed. The chapel filled with white smoke.

When the smoke cleared and Paloma brought a candle close, everyone saw this tableau: Tomás lay on the stone floor with a shirt bloodied over his heart. Sam stood over him, pistol in hand, with a nasty expression on his face.

Paloma gasped.

"I told you the kid was no good," Sam said in a snarl to Grumble.

Grumble knelt over the prostrate figure and started to pull the shirt away.

At that moment Tomás coughed violently, and blood gouted out of his mouth.

The two officers looked at Grumble. Everyone knew what that meant, a chest wound that made the victim cough up blood.

"Don Emilio is avenged," said Grumble.

"And I paid good money for that little bastard," said Sam.

Grumble felt for a pulse and then spoke to Paloma. "He's gone. We'll get the priest in the morning."

Paloma nodded.

The officers headed back to Santa Fe to give the good news to Don Emilio.

BACK IN THE dining room they had another dessert, more coffee, more wine, and by popular demand a repeat of the performance from Sam and Tomás, the actors, and from Grumble.

First Grumble, the stage director, showed everyone a

condom. "They are made from the intestines of lambs," he said.

"Mother Mary," said Paloma, "I heard of them, but . . ."

Then he showed them his vial of chicken blood. He poured some blood into the tip of the condom, knotted it off to the size of a finger joint, and clipped the remainder away.

Immediately, Tomás popped the balloon into his mouth and held it with his back teeth so everyone could see.

"When you clamp down," said Grumble . . .

Tomás did just that. Chicken blood squirted out, making everyone laugh.

"But the wound," said Flat Dog.

"Let me see that," said Paloma.

Tomás did. It was trivial. Still, Paloma clucked and put water on the stove to boil.

"Explain to them," Grumble said to Sam.

"I took the lead ball out of my pistol. All that was left was the powder and cotton patch." He showed them one of the patches normally used for firing a flintlock firearm, a disc the size of the tip of a finger. "When I pulled the trigger, the gun fired. Only the cotton blew out."

Grumble said, "Which hit Tomás hard enough to break the skin, but . . . I've done this before."

"Broke it quite a bit, I'd say," Paloma called from the kitchen.

Now Tomás leapt in eagerly. "I had the other condom in my hand"—he held his palm out—"and when Sam shot me, I clapped my hand hard against my chest."

They all pondered it.

"Lots of blood," said Tomás.

"The art of illusion," said Grumble.

"And now," said Sam, "what are we going to do with this little criminal?"

"I go with you." Then he repeated, for his first sentence in English, "I go with you."

Sam smiled. But then he thought, *I've already got a kid.*

No one spoke until Hannibal did. "Tomorrow we're going

to bury an empty box outside the chapel. Then we're going to buy supplies for rendezvous. And the next day we're going to head for rendezvous. Tomás will be riding with us."

Tomás grinned. *"Bueno,"* he said. *"Bueno.* I am a mountain man."

Chapter Twenty-one

What is it?" Hannibal asked Sam.

"Nothing."

Hannibal turned in his saddle and looked back at the casa. "She's standing under the covered entrance, watching us ride away. She's lovely, and the bushes leafing out on each side make her more lovely. The red *ristras* are swaying a little in the breeze."

"I feel like I've spent my whole life riding away."

"Is that it?"

It wasn't just Paloma. They'd said good-bye last night to Grumble and Sumner. The two gamblers intended to get back to California, Grumble said. Sam didn't know when he'd see them again.

He kept his eyes straight ahead. "I've got bigger things to worry about." He swept a hand to indicate all that was in front of him. There was a herd of ninety horses and about three dozen horse colts and fillies. A score of the horses bore packs of trade goods. Two riders led these packhorses on a string, Flat Dog and Gregorio, a hand Paloma had loaned to them. Out in front of the herd was a boy, Tomás. And beside Sam and Hannibal rode Julia, dragging a travois with the thirteen-month-old Esperanza and six-month-old Azul. They were heading down the Santa Fe River to where they would turn north along the Rio Grande, toward Taos.

"Look like enough?"

"Yes, but your mind is back there."

Sam still didn't turn his head. The last thing he wanted was to see Paloma standing in the sun on a fine May morning watching him go.

Sam forced his mind to practical things. "We can't push these horses now—too many haven't foaled yet."

"And when they have, we go easy to let the little ones keep up."

In fact, Paladin herself was one of the mares that hadn't foaled. Sam was riding a stallion he'd trained during the winter, the one that acted like a knothead and needed some kinks worked out.

"What else are you worried about?"

"It might be hard to hire good men in Taos."

All the Nuevo Mexicanos had assured the beaver-hunting Americans that Taos was full of men who had traveled up the Rio Grande and all the way to the Salt Lake to trap beaver, and knew the way well. These men, people assured them, were easy to hire at reasonable wages. Sam's thought was, *They damned well better be.*

"What else?"

"It's a long way to rendezvous with a lot of Indians along the way who'd like to run our horses off."

"And the rivers will be running full this time of year."

They both looked up at the high peaks of the Sangre de Cristo Mountains behind them. Only now was the snow beginning to melt. Soon it would make the rivers flood.

Sam breathed in and out big. "None of this is a big problem."

"We hope."

"Tomás."

They looked at each other.

It was a litany of trouble. Kidnapped, maybe witness to murder. Definitely a witness to rape and suicide. Then attempted murder of his own. Police attempting apprehension. A desperate trick that happened to work. A wound.

"He's got a lot to sort out," said Hannibal.

"Truth is, we don't know what the hell he might do."

"That's right."

Sam looked across at his friend.

"So you worry too."

"Sometimes. But I have a motto I live by."

What's that?"

"Rideo, ergo sum."

Sam shook his head. Whenever Hannibal quoted Latin, it felt like he was a wizard out of a kid's story, with secret knowledge no one else had. "Meaning?"

"I laugh, therefore I am."

Sam laughed. "And if I took up that motto of yours right now, I could stop worrying?"

"Also you could ride back and kiss that beautiful woman good-bye. I saw the way you two parted. Uneasy."

They poked along for a few steps in silence. The last words Paloma Luna had said to Sam were, "Don't come back for a few years. I need the time."

Maybe she was still outside watching. He looked back, but the covered entrance to the house was in shadows. "Rideo whatever," he said to Hannibal.

Sam wheeled the knothead and galloped back to the gate and to the casa. Coy sprinted at his heels.

Still standing on the porch, Paloma smiled and cocked her head at his appearance. "I'm back," he said. He gave her a rip-roaring kiss, and she returned it lustily. She laughed, and he galloped away.

When Sam caught up, Hannibal said, "All right to be going?"

Sam thought and said, "For the first time in two years I'm heading the right direction. Home."

"IT'S TWO TOWNS," said Sam.

"One Indian, one Mexican," said Hannibal.

The herd was grazing on good grass downstream, not far above the Rio Grande, watched by Flat Dog and Gregorio.

"The pueblo is beautiful." Tomás seemed mesmerized by it.

It was a ramble of multistory buildings, adobe the color of the reddish tan sand and windows and doors painted the light blue of the robes of the Franciscans who had ministered there for two centuries. The Mission San Geronimo stood firmly in the foreground, topped by three crosses. The buildings beyond were a jumble, yet at the same time came together in an attractive way, like boulders rising on a mountain ridge. Ladders jutted out of the kivas, the chambers where the men gathered and the ceremonies began.

"Crosses on a background of kivas," said Hannibal.

"How do they do it?" said Sam. "Take the old religion, scramble it together with Catholicism, and make sense of it?"

"Let's get to it," said Hannibal.

Below the pueblo stretched the Mexican town, a knot where business got done, strings of adobes thrown here and there, and cultivated fields beyond.

In the knot they found the place easily enough, Young and Wolfskill's store. Ewing Young was a Tennessean who had made good money trading between Missouri and Santa Fe and now proposed to make more money by leading parties of trappers throughout the mountains of the Southwest. His store and home were the nerve center of the beaver trade in Taos. Since this country was under the sovereignty of Mexico, however, he had no standing. Governor Armijo took every opportunity to oppose him. So Young had recently gotten Mexican citizenship. Or such was the scuttlebutt Sam and Hannibal had picked up in Santa Fe. Everyone told them that if they wanted experienced guides or trappers, Ewing Young was the man to talk to.

Mr. Young, however, was not in the store. The clerk was a small, sandy-haired teenager. Since he didn't offer his name when Sam and Hannibal introduced themselves and Tomás, Sam asked.

"Kit," the boy said softly.

In answers to questions he was polite but not forthcoming. No, he didn't know when Mr. Young would be back. Yes, he allowed that the town had some men who had trapped the country north on the Rio Grande and west toward the Colorado River, maybe quite a few.

Sam thought the youngster was partly stuck between being a kid and being a man. "Kit," he said, "may I buy you a cup of coffee?" Sam had noticed the potbellied stove and the pot on it.

Kit apologized for his lack of hospitality and poured three cups, no charge. Sam, Hannibal, and Kit sat around the stove like friends. Sam noticed that none was poured for Tomás, who now roamed the room.

"Call me Sam and him Hannibal. Have you done some trapping yourself?"

It turned out that the young man had a good deal of experience trapping. As he spoke, slowly, spending words like hard-earned coins, he admitted he'd been over much of the country to the south and west. Mr. Young was a strong leader and determined as a man could be. He'd taken brigades all the way to the Colorado out at the Yuma villages, all up and down the Gila and Salt Rivers, up on the San Juan . . .

Sam revised his estimate of the boy's age from sixteen to eighteen, a small but sturdy eighteen. "You like that life."

The boy nodded. His eyes never sat still on the men he was talking to, but skittered about the store restlessly.

"How about you?" asked Sam. "You've been on the San Juan yourself?"

Kit nodded.

"You know the country—why don't you come with us?"

"My time is promised. I'm going to Chihuahua."

A trading caravan then. Sam supposed it would take slaves. He wondered if Kit cared.

Hannibal was interested. "Is Mr. Young sending a caravan to Chihuahua?"

Kit shook his head no. "Another outfit."

"Will you give us some names then? Men you can recommend?"

"Yes, there's . . ."

Kit pounced and landed right on top of Tomás.

Quick as an eel, Tomás slipped away and shoved his assailant forward.

Kit half banged into a counter, wheeled, ducked under a punch, and tackled Tomás. They crashed to the floor and skidded across it.

Sam and Hannibal got to them at the same time and pulled them apart. Kit was almost more than Sam could handle, though Sam was stronger and half a foot taller.

"Look in his pouch," snarled Kit. "He's a damn thief."

Hannibal held out a demanding hand.

Tomás hesitated, then slipped the pouch off and slammed it into Hannibal's hand.

Hannibal let him go, and Tomás stalked off into a corner.

"He's got a fire steel in there," said Kit.

Hannibal fished inside and held up the steel.

"Come here to rob me, did you, boy?" The voice was a knife blade.

Tomás just glared at Kit.

"Tomás asked me if he could buy a steel," said Sam smoothly. "I've been teaching him to start fires with mine." The second part, at least, was true. "We'll be buying that and some other gear."

Kit looked Sam straight in the face, and the eyes said Sam was fooling with the truth. He set the fire steel next to a pad on the counter.

Kit sat and seemed to calm down. He said, "All right, I'd say Antonio Romero is a good man. He lives over at . . ."

Sam copied down the name and instructions.

"Then there's Esteban . . ."

As Sam wrote, he grinned sideways at Hannibal. He was proud—this was the first practical use for his winter's learning.

In ten minutes they were totaled out and on their way out the door.

Sam turned back. "Kit, I'm sorry for what happened here."

The youngster nodded.

"Why don't you come to rendezvous sometime?"

Kit waited, maybe deciding. "I might do that, Sam."

"What's your last name?"

"Carson."

Before they got to the Romero house, Sam and Hannibal spoke sharply to Tomás about stealing. "Besides," Hannibal said, "didn't you see what that young fellow is like? He'd be a wildcat to fight."

"I said I'm sorry," repeated Tomás.

That night Sam and Hannibal tossed words back and forth about Tomás. He was off kilter. No telling what he might do. They looked at each other helplessly.

THE NEW HANDS were Esteban—a Mexican in his thirties, an old man by mountain man standards—and Plácido, his teenage son. By the time they led the party across from the Rio Grande to the San Juan River and on west, Sam knew the older man was as good a pilot as people in Taos said. He knew the rivers and mountains, knew how to travel in Indian country, and altogether made a good hand. He was worth the fifty dollars he was getting. Plácido? Sam would rather have had another grown man. Both father and son planned to hire on as trappers for the fall season with other outfits when they got to rendezvous.

It was a good time for Sam. He rode behind the herd every day, balancing Esperanza on his lap for as long as she was willing to stay each session. His daughter was learning to talk. She called Julia Mamá. She addressed both Sam and Flat Dog as Papá, which stung.

Good times, though, were to be enjoyed. Spring was gentle and graceful on the land. Since they didn't go over any high passes, the snow was melted into life-giving fluid. Wildflowers sprouted everywhere. The days were warm, the nights crisp. The creeks were running full in a country that otherwise could put a lot of distance between drinks of water. Some days were windy, and they kept an eye out for sandstorms. But they moved along lazily, not rushing the newborn horses. They had no Indian trouble. They thought about the profit they would make at rendezvous. Life had a savory taste.

One evening Sam walked down along the river with Esperanza holding onto his finger. Soon she saw a prairie chicken and ran at it. The damned chicken didn't fly, but just ran around a log and froze. That wouldn't stop Esperanza. Around the log she scampered, knees pumping.

Now the chicken flew—about six feet, back over the log. It went into its disguise as a rock or a clump of dirt. Here came Esperanza back the other way. Sam didn't know whether she wanted to hug it or whack it.

They played this way for half a dozen rounds. Sam had never seen such a crazy prairie chicken, though they were well known to be dumb. Esperanza would have kept on all day, but finally the chicken flew up to the lowest limb of the fir.

Esperanza immediately began to crawl onto the tree. Unfortunately, this was half possible. The trunk was tilted sharply out over the river and barely clung to the bank. Sam grabbed his daughter, sat her down on the log, and took guard position at the base of the fir. She stood up, pointed at the bird, and started talking to it, not words but sounds—squeals, hums, coos, every kind of sound but a word.

Funny that fir—the current had undercut the bank, and some of its roots were exposed. By next spring it would join the river, float downstream, and end up on a sand bar when the flood waters dropped back. He watched the waters froth by. They went on forever. The Crows said only the rocks live forever, but that wasn't true—the waters lived forever, charging down from the mountain peaks, marching out over the plains, joining together with other rivers drumming their way to the sea. There they got picked up, carried back to the peaks, and started the forever circle again.

He watched Esperanza, who was still carrying on a big conversation with the prairie chicken, and the bird was sitting on the limb paying respectful attention. Esperanza would live—this was everyone's plan—in the village where

Flat Dog grew up, on the Wind River in winter and in the Big Horn Basin in the summer. Her grandparents, Needle and Gray Hawk, would certainly spoil her rotten. The two pivot points of her life would be the big buffalo hunt in the spring and the huge hunt in the fall, which brought lots of villages together. And the only language she would hear, except sometimes from her two fathers and one mother, would be Crow. She would play entirely with Crow children. She would learn to put up a tipi, dry buffalo meat on a rack, and quill moccasins. She would be raised with the Crow stories, in the Crow religion, and the Crow way of seeing the world.

Sam accepted all this. It was a good road to walk. He hadn't forgotten that he himself carried the sacred pipe and had given a sun dance.

"See," said Hannibal, "she already speaks foreign languages." He was walking toward them, Coy on one side and Plácido on the other.

Now Esperanza, maybe because she had a new audience, started in on her list of words. She had a fair number—"want," "milk," and a baby fistful of other useful words—and she babbled right through them. Then she stood up, stuck her hands out, and said, "Water. *Agua*. Water. *Agua*."

Tickled, Plácido gave her a drink from his canteen.

"Bilingual," Hannibal said, grinning. Sam had learned a lot of out-of-the-way words, hanging around with Hannibal. "She's getting three languages, right in the tipi."

Suddenly Esperanza dropped the canteen to the ground and held her arms up to Hannibal. He picked her up. From her higher stance she pointed at the prairie chicken and launched into a tirade of her sounds that weren't words. She gave that bird a good talking to.

Plácido hooted. Laughing, Hannibal staggered around in a circle, keeping a tight hold on Esperanza.

Sam told Hannibal, "I'm going to take her to rendezvous most years."

"Besides picking up a lot more English, some Spanish, some French, Iroquois, Delaware, she'll be able to talk to all the birds in their own tongues, prairie chicken, raven, hawk, osprey, eagle . . ."

Esperanza reached a climax in her prairie chicken lecture.

Coy yipped, and the bird flew off in search of peace and quiet.

"Down," said Esperanza. Hannibal set her on the ground.

She was good at this word. Every day, riding along with her dad, she got tired of being held and said firmly, "Down." When he dismounted and set her on the ground, she toddled over to the pony drag and crawled onto it. Sam lashed her in. There she could play with her cousin Azul or nap. At the age of six months Azul didn't interest her much yet, but that would come.

Though Julia and Flat Dog had cradleboards, keeping them on the drag was easier.

"Mamá," said Esperanza.

Sam and Hannibal started walking back with her slowly. She didn't want to be carried, but toddled along on her own. Then she forgot her need for mama and stopped to inspect everything interesting along the way.

The next morning, as they were finishing eating, Sam found himself alone by the fire with Tomás. He decided to speak up.

"You know what happened to Maria, none of it . . ."

"You say nothing about my sister."

Sam looked at the kid. Hannibal ambled over with his empty coffee cup.

"Tomás, you have to know your sister didn't deserve . . ."

Tomás stood up and hurled his butcher knife into a nearby aspen. He stalked off. The handle on the knife quivered.

Hannibal walked over to the aspen, studied the knife, and pulled it out. "This far in," he said, holding thumb and forefinger about two inches apart.

Hannibal filled his cup.

Sam looked after Tomás and wondered.

They decided the best way to help Tomás along, whatever

his emotional storms were, was to help him learn something. In the evenings either Sam or Esteban rode up whatever creek or river was handy, taking the two teenage boys and setting traps. They showed Tomás and Plácido how to spot beaver signs: the gnawed trees, the slides, the dams. Taught them how to ease into the water well upstream of where they wanted to set the trap. What depth of water to put it in, so the beaver could stand up to smell the bait. How to bait the small stick with medicine out of the stoppered horn. How to set a trap pole stout enough that the big rodent couldn't swim off with it. How to skin the drowned creature.

When they brought beaver back to camp, Julia took over, for she had learned well during her months in the Sierra Nevada. She showed both boys how to scrape the inner side of the hide clean and then stretch it on a willow hoop, so it could be put into a pack and transported on the back of a horse.

The boys got to keep the pelts they brought in, share and share alike. Tomás gradually got outfitted. A pony for five pelts, New Mexico price. A patch knife, a hunting pouch, two horns (small and large) to hold the two kinds of powder, a bar of lead, and a tool to make the lead into balls.

"You catch on quick," Sam told him.

Tomás gave a sly smile. "I am smart," he said.

"Yes," said Sam.

Finally—this was a proud day—he traded Tomás one of the outfit's mountain rifles for two plews.

Being a little older, Plácido already had a rifle and other gear.

The outfit took a nooner every day. The horses did well with a break in the middle of the day, a chance to water and graze. The foals particularly needed time to nurse or do nothing for two or three hours. During times like this Sam taught Tomás to shoot that rifle. How to make a round ball from a bar of lead. How much powder to pour down the barrel, and how to patch that with cloth. How to seat the ball on the patch. How to use the double triggers. Which powder to pour into the pan, and how to make the hammer whack the flint in the pan and create the spark that made the whole thing go *ka-boom!*

The first time Tomás fired the rifle Sam had to giggle at the expression on his face. Between the roar and the cloud of white smoke the boy was bamboozled.

"He's doing all right," Sam told Hannibal that evening.

"Would be good if he made friends with Plácido," Hannibal said. "That kid has a nice calm about him."

"Tomás is only surly about half the time," said Sam.

"He's damn near able to tolerate the man who saved his ass," said Hannibal.

Sam laughed. The truth was, they were both relieved at how the kid no longer seemed about to go twisty at any second.

During the next couple of days Tomás practiced shooting at trees, then at marks on trees. Sam supervised him carefully, instructed him about where to place his left hand on the stock, how to use the sights, how to get steady, and just how to pull the triggers.

Then Sam scraped the bark away from a spot on a cottonwood, and Tomás and Plácido competed shooting at it.

First round: Plácido hit the mark. Tomás missed the tree clean.

Second round: Plácido hit the mark. Tomás missed the tree clean.

Third round: Same result.

Sam could see that Tomás was trembling with rage.

"Enough for today," he said. "Tomás, don't worry about it. That barrel's too heavy for you right now, and you're wobbly. You'll get stronger . . ."

Tomás rammed Plácido in the chest with his head. They went down hard and came up fighting like cats.

"Pendejo!" yelled Plácido.

"Hijo de puta!" retaliated Tomás.

Sam tackled them both and knocked them to the ground. With a big effort he pushed them apart and got a kick in the *cojones* for his trouble.

"O-o-o-w!" Sam hollered. He kept holding the boys apart and glared at each of them in turn. "Anybody wants to fight, he fights me."

Tomás looked ready to charge. Plácido said, "Looks like maybe this is a good time to fight you, señor."

Sam grinned.

Tomás turned and walked away, mumbling something.

"Don't ask him what he said," Sam instructed Plácido.

SOON THEY WERE herding the horses down El Rio de Nuestra Señora de las Dolores, as Esteban called it.

"River of Our Lady of Sorrows," said Hannibal.

"The name would half keep me away," said Sam.

But it was a lovely stream, a mountain creek, meandering through meadows or bouncing downhill fast. "She comes to the desert," said Esteban. "To the Grand River, above where it flows in and makes the Colorado."

Sam was in no hurry to get back to a desert.

Early one morning just as the sun rose, when the morning smelled truly fresh, Tomás squatted by Sam's blankets. He was coming back from the last watch of the night. "Sam," he said, "your mare, she has her colt."

Sam sat up and saw the dewy-eyed look on the boy's face. "Let's go have a look." Hannibal sat up and went with them.

The colt had Paladin's markings exactly, the dramatic combination of white all over with black around the ears like a hat, black blaze on the chest, and black mane and tail.

"Beauty," said Hannibal.

Paladin was standing, and the foal, a horse colt, was nursing. The mare gave the three human beings a wise, satisfied look.

"Do you think he's Ellie's?"

Tomás knew about the stallion—Hannibal had talked about him a lot when they were putting the horses through their routines for the sale. The boy also knew how much Hannibal missed Ellie.

"The colt is big," said Hannibal. Ellie had been an American horse, not a Spanish pony. "One way you can tell is by counting the vertebrae. Be an extra one. So it's Ellie's."

They watched, wondering, smiling.

Perhaps enchanted, Tomás said, "I want him."

"What?" said Sam.

"I want him for my horse."

"Then you'll have to earn him," said Hannibal.

"Four plews," said Sam. Sam had been thinking of this foal for himself.

Tomás pursed his mouth. "I earn him." Again this was in English. And a little defiant, judged Sam.

ESTEBAN RODE AHEAD with Sam and Hannibal to the Grand River. The sight made Sam suck in his breath hard.

"Damn full," he said. They'd crossed to the north side of the Dolores to get above the confluence.

"Daunting," said Hannibal.

"What you call a beetch," said Esteban in his home-grown English.

It was early June, and the spring runoff was in full swing. The three of them watched the monster slosh against its banks, and out of them, and wondered.

Esteban said, "I know a better place. We must march one day to the north. There two other rivers come in, one on each side. Above that there is a . . . *paso*."

"Ford," said Hannibal.

Then on north over a divide to the Siskadee, Esteban explained, and up that river to the Uinta Mountains, and into Bear Lake by a route they all knew. A lot of desert ahead. Sam wanted mountains, like the ones in Crow country.

The morning of the crossing dawned fine and clear.

"Going to be hot," said Sam. He rolled out.

He and Hannibal had gotten in the habit of taking the time of predawn light to talk, a good time to be alone.

As soon as Esperanza woke up, she would burst out of the

tent and pitter-patter toward Sam's blankets. "Papá," she would call. And Sam would toss her up in the air and catch her.

He was satisfied that the kids would be safe on the crossing. Flat Dog and Julia would carry them in the cradleboards. Sam had ridden Paladin across the ford and back, and the horses could keep their feet the whole way. Still, they'd taken an extra day in camp, to rest the animals and the people.

Everyone knew his job. They made sure of the hitches on the pack animals. Then Sam, Hannibal, Flat Dog, and Esteban moved the loose horses toward the bank. The two boys kept the packhorses well back, and Julia stayed with them. The plan was to take the loose horses across, then the pack animals. Sam was glad to have Paladin between his legs for this job. He trusted her.

He and Hannibal looked across the horses at each other and nodded. Time. They signaled to Esteban and Flat Dog at the rear.

"Hi-iy-iy!" Sam yelled, and snapped a blanket at the horses. All four men yelled and waved hats and blankets. The herd bolted.

Sam and Hannibal galloped past the leaders and charged into the river. The herd plunged into the water. The river was a melee—horses whinnying, manes and tails flying, water splashing up in barrelfuls—it was crazy. Sam loved it.

Coy ripped along behind, in a rush.

The crossing was over almost before Sam knew it. He was soaked head to toe. *Easy. Hot damn. Let's do it again.*

They got the animals to circle, slowed them down, and took a few minutes to get them settled. The riders grinned at each other. Back across the river. Coy stayed where he was—he didn't like this back and forth stuff.

"Why don't you and Julia go now?" Sam said to Flat Dog. "There's some good shade right over there."

The Crow and his wife got the children in the cradleboards and the cradleboards on their backs. They pussy-footed their mounts down the bank and into the shallow water. "Stay here," said Flat Dog. "We'll be fine."

And they were.

Coy barked across the waters at Sam—what's going on?

The score of packhorses was trickier. A heavily laden animal was more likely to lose its balance in the swift current, and one might bang into another, and several could go down in a tangle.

While Julia sat with the children, the other riders worked the pack animals gently to the bank. Sam and Hannibal put two of the most reliable on lead lines and started them across. Flat Dog and Esteban pushed all the rest from behind. One by one, two by two, the horses stilted into the water. Once there, they looked more comfortable. The two teenage boys, as instructed, rode upstream of the middle of the herd.

Sam turned in his saddle, looking back.

Then he saw it.

A huge fir tree rampaged down the middle of the current, evergreen leaves dead and brown, roots pointed straight toward men and horses.

"Get out!" Sam yelled, pointing. "Get out!"

Everyone saw the menace. The roots looked like a madwoman's hair violently shaken. The whole tree raised and dived in the waves—it bobbed and sawed back and forth, an immense ramrod gone wild.

There was not one damn thing Sam could do to stop it.

He and Hannibal threw the lead lines away and slapped their packhorses on.

Luckily, some other horses followed. If they had seen the tree, panicked, tried to turn around, milled, done anything but charge straight ahead . . .

Sam turned Paladin and whipped her toward Tomás and Plácido. He shouted, "Go! Go!" Then he remembered. *"Vamonos! Vamonos!"*

Beside him, Hannibal spun Brownie around, but the horse got his feet tangled and fell. Hannibal pitched into the water.

From behind the herd Sam saw Esteban spurring his horse right where Sam was headed.

Tomás whacked his mount with his hat. The pony leapt and cleared the root ball by a whisker.

The roots hit Plácido and his horse dead on.

The horse went down, the boy went up.

Tomás wheeled his mount, but the animal refused to go back.

Tomás dived off the saddle toward the tree.

Plácido landed right where the trunk met the root ball. He grabbed roots with both arms and stuck his legs in among them. He was riding the damn thing!

The root ball clubbed the line of pack animals. Horses screamed. Ropes snapped. Gear ripped in every direction— kegs broke and sprayed their gunpowder, a bundle of wrapped rifles split like twigs, packs of plews got dunked, boxes of beads, bells, awls, and kettles careened into the turbulence. Right below the ford the river narrowed a little, picked up speed, and emptied into a hole.

Tomás grabbed the upstream end of the roots and started heaving himself out of the river.

Sam hollered, "Get out of there! Get out of there!"

He whipped Paladin again with his hat. "Go!" he shouted at her. The tree was no more than twenty feet away and zinging along.

Paladin reared and whinnied. The current hit her or the bottom betrayed her, and she fell on her back.

Sam let go—he dropped The Celt. Paladin ripped her reins away. As he got his footing, a wave knocked him down. He righted himself and launched his body, swimming and wading, toward the fir.

Just before he got to the tree, one edge of the root ball nudged the sand where the river channeled.

The top of the tree swung straight at Sam.

He grabbed branches and pulled himself up. Arms, face, and neck got scratched, but he got on. He looked wildly toward the boys. They were on top, together, and holding on tight. Ride the damn thing—yeehaw!

Then the tree rotated slowly and majestically in the water, and they all rolled to the bottom.

Beneath was madness. Sand and gravel scraped Sam's head and back below. The branches poked and scratched his front. In this universe there was blackness, wetness, insanity, and no air at all. A whole tree, an immense, dead tree beat him down, away from life.

On the surface the tree's tip held, and the fir turned all the way, top downstream and roots upstream.

Hannibal managed, desperately, to get onto the tree. He saw Esteban on it too, nearer the roots. But the human beings were underneath . . .

The tip swung all the way until it hit a gravelly bar and hung up. Now the roots turned inevitably downstream. Serenely, the tree made its complete circle. Then it plunged through the rest of the channel and flumed into the deep hole below.

Hannibal felt it begin another grand spin, once more to . . .

He dived upstream.

From beneath the water, roots, branches, needles, and three people sailed back into the sunlight and air.

Sam's lungs sucked in a world of air.

The tree bobbed gently.

Sam started to claw his way through the branches toward the boys. Were they both alive? He couldn't get down there. Maybe he saw two figures. Oh, hell, Plácido's chest was bloody.

"Jump!" he hollered, and he did.

He came up between two other figures splashing around in the hole—Hannibal and Esteban.

Being in the hole with a dead fir tree about fifty feet long and a dozen kicking horses was like being in a closet with a buffalo herd. Sam got kicked in a dozen places and got clobbered in one calf. Hollering, he swam madly, one-legged, for the near bank. Then he remembered, got to his feet, fell down from the pain, and went back to swimming toward the bank with one leg.

He turned onto his back, craned his head up far enough to see the boys. Tomás and Esteban were pulling Plácido under the arms toward shallow water.

Sam crawled toward the bank, his face sometimes underwater. Coy dashed into the river toward Sam and then leapt back, over and over.

Horses were thrashing and whinnying insanely. Some were probably hurt. Equipment was scattered through the hole like leaves picked up by a dust devil and flung hither and yon.

All Sam wanted was to find out whether Plácido was bad hurt, and hug the hell out of Tomás.

Chapter Twenty-two

Flat Dog took over. He dragged both boys onto dry land and started rescuing gear from the river, both what floated and what didn't.

Sam crawled to Tomás and embraced him. "You did great."

Tomás was more interested in Plácido's wound. He watched while Hannibal felt it. The gash lay just under the ribs on the left side. "Can't tell anything about it," Hannibal said.

"Bet he got punctured by a limb stub," said Sam. He'd gotten jabbed by a lot of them himself. His arms and face were scratched and gouged, and his shirt was torn.

Plácido was only half-conscious. They didn't know if he had water in his lungs, if he was hurt in the vitals, or if the pain had a grip on him. Hannibal looked into Esteban's eyes. "Nothing to do but wait and see."

Hannibal examined Sam's leg. Sam looked at Hannibal all over while his friend probed the leg. Hannibal was as scratched and bleeding as any of them. Sam didn't want to remember what it had been like, pinned by the tree on the bottom of the river, but didn't think he could ever forget— his dreams would be haunted.

"Not broken," Hannibal said.

Sam tried to put weight on it and fell down immediately. "Broke or not, there's no walking on it."

While he was down, Coy licked him in the face.

Paladin stood nearby, and Sam gave her the hand signal to come to him. She did, and he rubbed her muzzle.

Flat Dog came up and handed Sam The Celt.

He had to resist hugging the rifle. "Thank you, thank you," he said. He hadn't thought he'd ever see his father's flinter again.

For once Sam got the privilege of lying on the bank and watching the others work. He looked sideways at Plácido regularly. The boy wiggle-waggled his head from time to time. Sam didn't think his wound was mortal. Maybe he got thunked on the head by a rock when they were on the bottom.

Julia brought the infants up next to Sam. She nursed Azul while Esperanza played. Over and over the girl crawled across Sam's body, back and forth. Once she sat square on his belly, looked at him, and said, "Papá."

Most of the gear came back out of the river. Some of the powder kegs had busted, and the powder was gone. Other kegs were hauled out and the powder spread to dry. Big twists of tobacco and bundles of blankets were laid out in the sun. Some strings of beads were lost, others recovered. Some bundles of butcher knives came out, some kettles, some awls, and so on. Somehow all the barrels of *aguardiente* survived.

"We can't shoot back," said Hannibal, "but we can die happy."

"We won't know what we've lost until we compare what we have to the master list," said Sam.

"You going to do that?" asked Flat Dog.

"Probably not," said Sam.

"It is what it is," said Hannibal.

Two of the packhorses had broken legs. They struggled into shallow water and stood, heads down.

Flat Dog shot them. Coy howled.

Julia left the kids with Sam and set up two racks. Together she and Flat Dog butchered out the horses—women's work, but not in Julia's world—this was a new style, groping toward a new way to live for all of them, white American, Indian, and Mexican. She built a squaw fire, and they laid the strips of meat out to dry in the sun and wind.

Coy licked Sam's face. Evidently, everyone was reasonably glad to see Sam come out of the river. He was more than reasonably glad to be alive.

Tomás wandered by to look at Plácido. "What you did," said Sam, "you were incredible."

The boy beamed.

"I didn't think you liked Plácido."

Tomás shrugged and walked off.

Sam could never quite figure the boy out.

Later that afternoon Sam swung up onto Paladin and found that the pain of weight on the stirrup was bad.

When he limped back to his lazing place, Plácido had started moving around. Tomás was sitting with him, talking. They actually acted like friends. Sam smiled to himself and plopped down.

Esteban sat on his heels next to them. "Tomás," he said, "you saved Plácido's life. I thank you." Now both boys were looking seriously at Esteban. Sam thought maybe Tomás was beginning to understand: When you travel with a man, he sides you and you side him. No matter how hard it gets.

"Tomás," he said, "I want to give you something to show my gratitude. Something big. You think about it and tell me what you want."

Man and boy looked at each other.

Sam was proud of Tomás.

As Esteban started to get up, Tomás said nicely, "I don't have to think. I know."

"Just tell me," said Esteban, and he squatted back down.

"I want Paladin's colt."

When they headed north two days later, Tomás had the colt on a line, teaching him to lead. Esteban had surrendered some dollars of his wages for the colt. Sam also gave Tomás the pony he was riding, as a reward for what he did in the river.

Tomás grinned at him and spoke in English. He chose English whenever he wanted to be sure he was understood, or restate his point, as when he said from time to time, "I'm smart."

Now he said, "I teach him like Paladin, come when I whistle. Later I teach you, come when I whistle."

Chapter Twenty-three

R endezvous 1828 felt to Sam like the doldrums.
Part of it was outside things. There was no main supply train that year. Smith, Jackson & Sublette didn't bring one—Bill Sublette had gone to St. Louis with last summer's furs and come straight back with supplies, which arrived in November and got distributed throughout the winter. Normally, when the train arrived, so did enough whiskey for a hundred and more trappers and several hundred Indians. That usually turned rendezvous into a carnival.

Also, Jedediah Smith didn't show up. Nor did any word arrive from him. Diah had left the door open—he might or might not get to rendezvous, since he was heading north out of California—but it worried Sam.

He thought back over his years with Diah and wondered what had happened. Fifteen men under his leadership got killed on the sand bar below the Arikara villages. Another ten lost their lives on the bank of the Colorado. In both cases, Diah escaped by the skinny-skin-skin. Sam had seen both fights, which were more like slaughters. He wondered if Jedediah's luck had finally run out.

Sam felt maybe the doldrums came from inside, though, and he didn't know why.

Everybody was fine, his own leg no longer sore, Plácido's chest healed. Mountain luck, when you thought of what happened to them crossing that river.

Business was good for the Morgan outfit, as the men called

it. His tent and another small one run by Joshua Pilcher, the old Missouri Fur Company partisan, were the only ones open for trading. Sam, Hannibal, and Flat Dog sold most of the horses in their herd—the animals had walked for four months to get here—at good prices. The trade goods they'd picked up in Santa Fe sold quickly too, what was left after the river took its bite. What booze they and Pilcher had was quickly gone, and no trapper cared what he paid for it.

The talk of the trade blankets was what the Britishers were doing, or rather how the Hudson's Bay Company was poaching on American territory. The Oregon country, as everybody knew, was a joint occupation with the British—the whole Columbia River area, rich in furs. The Americans wanted to push that way. Those damned Britishers were trapping all the Snake River territory thin, so going west didn't shine for the Americans. Damn Britishers, they claimed everything by prior right, saying they'd been there first. When Americans saw HBC stamped on their property, they took to calling the company Here Before Christ.

When Sam and Hannibal closed the trade blanket for the day and were on their knees putting strings of beads back in their boxes, Hannibal said, "Smith, Jackson & Sublette are going to Flathead country. I want to go with them."

Sam looked up at him quick. Coy lay down and squirmed into the grass, looking from one to the other.

"I want to see Flathead Post, the lake, maybe even work with HBC for a while."

"Here Before Christ. O wise one," Sam said, keeping his voice as light as he could, "You want to see everything."

"That's true," said Hannibal. "One day I'm going to take a trade caravan down the Chihuahua Trail, see the city and the copper mines down below, maybe even Mexico City."

"You go, go, go."

"Vidi, vici, cepi iucunditas."

Sam knew *veni, vidi, vici*—I came, I saw, I conquered—but this was a new one. "What does that mean?"

"I came, I saw, I had fun."

Sam chuckled, but he was pretending.

"So," Hannibal went on, "I'll go to Crow country with you and then on to Flathead country."

Sam nodded.

"Now I better check on Brownie and Paladin."

With that he was off. Coy thumped his tail, looked after Hannibal, started to get up and go, but stayed. His eyes rose to Sam, uncertain.

"You're the only one who has been on all of it with me," Sam said.

When everything was put away in the tent, he just sat and petted Coy. "I am down in spirits," he told the coyote. He mulled. Everything changed all the time. He'd lost Meadowlark and Blue Medicine Horse to death, Third Wing too. Gideon Poorboy had lost his leg below the knee and decided to stay in California. Just this season Sam had started to California with a score of men and left half of them on the riverbank at the Mojave villages. He'd fallen in with Grumble, Sumner, and Abby, but they were off in different directions now. Sam and Hannibal had picked up Flat Dog, Julia, Esperanza, and Azul, but Robber and Galbraith came and then dropped out. Jedediah had taken his entire brigade to kingdom come, or maybe north to the Britishers, whichever he found first.

Sam was glad he had Flat Dog, Julia, Esperanza, and Azul, damned glad, but he was losing people, one after another . . .

He made himself get up and walk around, Coy at his heels.

The good part of rendezvous was seeing old friends, and Sam felt good greeting Tom Fitzpatrick, Jim Beckwourth, Jim Bridger, and a bunch of others. He and Fitz were mates from the first year, when they were in Diah's first brigade. Beckwourth spent a winter in the Crow camp with Sam, the winter he courted Meadowlark, still hard to think about. Bridger, well, Bridger got himself a bad name his first season in the mountains—went off and left Hugh Glass to die, even took his rifle and his possibles. But since that time Jim had proved to be a man who knew what way the stick floated, as they said, and had a reputation as the best storyteller of them all.

Hannibal fell in beside Sam and Coy, Tomás trailing him by a step. "Let's show this boy how much fun rendezvous is tonight," he said to Sam.

"I am not a boy," said Tomás. Since they got to rendezvous, he'd been speaking English all the time. "I am smart."

"Let's find him some company," said Sam.

The Delaware got a lascivious gleam in his eye. "Provide him some beads and vermilion, for the ladies?"

Tomás cackled. He'd heard about Indian women in the willows.

Sam blushed, and knew it. Blushing always made him self-conscious about his white hair. "No, tonight the boys will be telling stories, singing songs."

"Dancing," said Hannibal.

Tomás cackled again.

"Get your mind off that," said Sam. "Or at least Tomás's mind."

They squeezed in around a fire next to Jim Beckwourth. The big mulatto said, "You hear about our scrape with the Blackfeet just coming into camp here?"

"No," said Sam.

"Them Blackfeet," said someone. Everyone was sick and tired of the Blackfeet. Those Indians had been hostile since John Colter fought with them twenty years ago. The American beaver men had made friends with almost all the Indians except the Blackfeet, and were free to trap any country except Blackfoot.

"You want me to tell it?" said Robert Campbell. "I'll tell it straight." Campbell was an Irishman and a brigade leader, capable and serious about his business.

"Straight ain't no way to tell a story," said Beckwourth, and he launched in. "Just a few days ago we was camped maybe eighteen miles above the lake. Cap'n here, he finds the cook facedown and growing Blackfoot arrows out of his back, so he gets us fast up to a place where there's a spring and some rocks we can crouch behind. Me, I don't like hiding in any rocks, I like to go at my enemy out front and hard, but . . . We got to fighting, them shooting at us, us shooting at them. In the long run, though, it was no good, they being five or six hundred—"

"—maybe half that," put in Campbell—

"—and us being maybe thirty. After about half a day I saw someone had to do something."

"*You* did?" said Campbell.

"Cap'n, I'm just giving you a preview of how my grand-children will receive this story, except maybe the grandchil-dren that are Blackfoot." He threw a lascivious look around the circle. "I mean to top at least one chief's daughter in ev-ery tribe."

Tomás giggled.

"The only thing to do, as I was saying, was ride like the hounds of hell to the main camp here and get help. So, me and Calhoun—"

"—it was Ortega and myself," said Campbell—

"—we took two of the fastest horses and whipped them like banshee devils through the line of Blackfeet. Arrows and lead balls flew thick as hail—the angels themselves must have protected us—and in an hour or so we was here to the lake and roused the men, trapper and Injun alike, and back we rode like a gathering thunderstorm.

"When them Blackfeet saw us, they skedaddled."

"Actually," said Campbell drily, "they'd already left."

"How many men were killed?" said Tomás, his voice throbbing.

Sam couldn't believe the kid had put words out in this crowd, English words.

"One of ours," said Campbell, "and three wounded, and half a dozen horses dead."

"About a score of theirs dead," said Beckwourth with a grin.

"Three or four," said Campbell, "and the same wounded."

"Them Blackfeet," Tomás pressed on, "are they bad Injuns?"

A handful of men said at the same time, "The worst."

"Let me have a small . . . mouth of that," Tomás said to Sam.

"Sip," said Sam. "Or mouthful."

"Thanks."

He handed Tomás the whiskey cup, and the boy drank. "Thanks for the sip," he said.

Tomás was serious about learning English, and he *was* smart.

"Give us a yarn, Gabe." That was what they called Jim Bridger now.

Sam was glad Tomás had a chance to hear one of these stories.

Bridger began in an easy voice, "Me and some un the boys come up Henry's Fork one spring night, time it was nigh getting dark. I knowed the Yellowstone country some, but I got turned around and didn't rightly know where we was. So we stopped along a little crick and made camp in the dark.

"Come mornin', I woke up and saw as fine a place as ever stroked the eye. A big hole, with thick grass reaching off to timbered hills, and the prettiest little stream runnin' through her. Best of all, I seen a bull elk grazin' not a hundred steps off.

"'Meat,' says I, and rises and throws up Betsy. I shot—and that elk didn't even notice, just kept grazin'. Now Betsy, she shoots center, sure, and I couldn't piece things together in my mind. I crept gentlelike mebbe fifty steps closer, lines up Betsy, and lets fly agin. Same result.

"'Mebbe that elk is wearing armor,' says I. 'It is sure enough deaf.'

"Riled up, I walks straight over to the elk, raises Betsy like a war club, and swings the barrel right onto the critter's head.

"Old Betsy bounces off harmless.

"Well, I'll be.

"I grabbed the damned elk by the antlers and was about to twist when I realized—these antlers is stone. I kicked the elk and like to broke my toes. Whole damn elk is stone.

"Then I recollects—Black Harris and his story of the putrefied forest. He took a piece of downed tree to Fort Atkinson, and a Dutchman scientist there told him it was putrefied, done turned to stone.

"Now I looks around and sees that our horses are nibblin' at the grass, but their knees are shakin'. I reach down and feels of the grass, and the blades are putrefied. I reach up and feel the leaves of a aspen, and the leaves are putrefied.

"Suddenly, I notice. There ain't no birds making music. I can see birds, but I can't hear 'em.

"I lifts old Betsy again and knocks the nearest jay right off the branch. When I go over and pick up the pieces, I find out even the birds is putrefied. And I can't hear 'em 'cause their songs is putrefied!

"'Boys!' I holler out. 'Get up! Let's go! This place don't shine!'

"Shortly we is packed up and headed out, afore the horses starve to death and us with 'em.

"But this country, it has ahold of us. We ride north and find the big canyon of the Yellerstone in our way. East, big canyon of the Yellerstone in our path. South, same canyon. West, same thing. We are surrounded by the wide, deep canyon of the Yellowstone River, and no way out.

"Then I gets an idea. Seems good, but I figure I better give 'er a try first, this idea being on the wild side. I backs my horse up a hundred paces, gives her a good kick, and when we get to the canyon edge, I lets out a war cry and reins her up to jump. She does, and pretty as a wildflower in June, we just floats over the whole canyon of that Yellerstone and sets down on the other side soft as cottonwood fluff drifting to the ground.

"Now all the boys get the idea. They back up, stampede the packhorses, and come riding behind 'em hell for leather. At the canyon rim they all sail into the air—horses like wingspread eagles, you shoulda seen it!—and they all light right beside me on the far rim.

"They was all happy to be out'n the trap of that putrefied forest, but they was a mite amazed. 'Gabe,' they says, 'that was right smart, but how did you figure it out?'

"Says I, 'Well, everything in that place was putrefied, animals, grass, leaves, birds, and even the birds' song, so I realized—the law of gravity must be putrefied too!'"

The whole circle broke into appreciative chuckles.

Sam got up and wandered, Coy at his heels. Off somewhere he could hear fiddling, which meant dancing. He had no desire to dance, no desire for a woman, not when he felt Paloma so near behind him and Meadowlark's parents so close in front. But he wanted music, and he had his tin whistle in his hand.

Fiddlin' Red waved Sam over to the log where he was perched. "This old hand," Red announced to the assembly, "last year this time he was starting to shine on that whistle. Give us a tune, Sam, what will it be?"

Sam said, "The Never-Ending Song of Jedediah Smith."

This was the song Robert Evans and Sam and Sumner and all the men of the first California brigade had written together in tribute to their captain. It was a lively affair in 6/8 time, good to dance to, and Sam took it fast.

Lots of men sashayed Indian women around, but no one sang.

Sam said, "Don't you remember the words?"

He let Fiddlin' Red take the tune this time, and he sang the words himself.

We set out from Salt Lake, not knowing the track
Whites, Spanyards and Injuns, and even a black
Our captain was Diah, a man of great vision
Our dream Californy, and beaver our mission.

"Now comes the chorus," he cried. "Join in." Coy yipped twice.

Captain Smith was a wayfarin' man
A wanderin' man was he
He led us 'cross the desert sands
And on to the sweet blue sea.

No voice lifted up with Sam's. He plunged onward.

We rode through the deserts, our throats were so dry
If we didn't find water, we surely would die
The captain saw a river, our hearts came down thud
The river was dry, and we got to drink mud.

After this verse, though, he got discouraged. Not a single voice joined in. Didn't they remember the captain, and admire him and the outfit that was the first to go to California? He gave them one more verse with the whistle alone and abandoned music for the night. He felt unaccountably sad, and lonely.

He stopped behind one circle. The boys were playing old sledge, and for a moment Sam thought Tomás was playing. Then he saw that Tomás didn't have a hand and was only watching over one man's shoulder.

A heart was led, and Tomás's player followed with a lower heart.

"Why didn't you trump it?" whispered Tomás.

All four players shushed him.

Sam didn't like this sight. The boy had been fascinated by Grumble's skill with cards.

Tomás said something softly to the player, and the man handed him his whiskey cup. Tomás sipped.

Coy eased up and sat next to Tomás. He gave Sam a begging look.

"Tomás," said Sam, "bedtime."

The boy threw Sam an angry look and then shook his head slowly. "I'm having fun."

Sam walked off and Coy followed. "It's none of my business," he told the coyote.

Coy whimpered.

In the wee hours somewhere Tomás crept into the tent and stretched out on his blankets between Sam and Hannibal. As soon as he lay down, he vomited where he lay.

"God help us," said Sam. He marched the boy to the lake and cleaned him up. Except that Tomás vomited again. They moved knee deep into the lake and Sam held an arm around his waist. Tomás vomited again. And then one more time that seemed to be the last.

Coy stood on the bank, pranced, and squealed.

Sam decided no words were necessary and held the wobbly Tomás on the way back to the tent. Hannibal had moved all three sets of blankets outside—the night was clear.

The boy passed out like a match in a gust of wind.

"Not grown-up yet," said Hannibal.

"Too near and yet too far."

SAM WOKE UP with his mind a muddle. He'd felt out of sorts the entire rendezvous. He could still smell Tomás's throw-up. Everything was askew, and nothing felt right.

He sat up to look around and saw Bell Rock standing a few steps away, gazing at him.

Bell Rock! And behind him four other members of the Kit Foxes.

Sam stood up. Suddenly everything was changed. He must enter a world of Crow customs, Crow manners. This was a time to do things right.

He introduced Hannibal and Tomás briefly and said, "I will take you to Flat Dog's lodge." Your kinsman, the man you are looking for.

He could see the questions in their eyes, but it was not his place to speak. In the Crow way Meadowlark was a member of Flat Dog's family, and Bell Rock's. Her husband wasn't her relative, and a relative must bring the news.

They walked to Julia and Flat Dog's tipi, Tomás and Coy trailing. Sam felt an irrational flicker of anger at Tomás.

Flat Dog and Julia were sitting around the outside fire, eating deer meat. The two children played busily. Flat Dog stood up immediately, strip of tenderloin in hand. He looked at his relative and the other Foxes. Sam knew what he was thinking: *This isn't how things are supposed to be done, and now there's no way to do them right.*

Flat Dog motioned for the visitors to sit down, and they did, Tomás next to Sam.

He addressed the five Crow visitors with a thick tongue, "My sister is no longer living."

The Crows were struck silent with the knowledge: *A member of my family is dead—a woman of my village is dead.*

They thought of their responsibilities, how they would inform her parents and all the people of the village, and the grieving that must ensue.

Sam thought, *This is my life. For better and right now damn well for worse.* He reminded himself of correctness.

Azul squalled, and Julia gave him one of her breasts. Esperanza played outside the circle of grown-ups, picking up ants, chewing stems of grass, and letting out the occasional war cry.

At last Flat Dog said to the visitors, "She died giving birth. This is her daughter, Esperanza."

Here was the intolerable contradiction. A life taken, a life given.

Sam knew he must make a gift of horses for the life taken. He wondered how the new life would be received—*My daughter.* Except that Esperanza was not his daughter, not as the Crows saw it—she belonged to Meadowlark's family. Already, in a practical way, she belonged to Flat Dog and Julia. Sam didn't count. His heart twisted like a rag being wrung out.

Flat Dog said, "This is my wife Julia."

Crow eyes took in the woman and the knowledge.

"This is our son Azul."

Eyes smiled at the gift of a new life.

Everyone sat without speaking further. The obligations,

mourning and rejoicing—the responsibilities, the grief to come—all was overwhelming.

Sam was swamped with memories. Bell Rock had befriended him, and was his guide to the Crow way of understanding the world. This medicine man introduced him to the sweat lodge, made his pipe, and dedicated it. Most of all, Bell Rock sponsored the sun dance that Sam gave after the death of Blue Medicine Horse. Bell Rock was Sam's spiritual father.

Bell Rock did not have to tell Sam why he and his companions had come to rendezvous. Two years ago Sam had run off with Meadowlark against her parents' will. Red Roan, son of the chief, and her relatives came to Sam and Meadowlark's lodge, where they had spent a few idyllic days absorbed in each other, and took her back by force. After a few days she told Sam that she loved him, but he had to leave the village.

He got out, surrendering Meadowlark in his heart.

At rendezvous a couple of months later, here came Flat Dog escorting Meadowlark. She had run away, and her brother supported her gesture of the heart. Incredible. She and Sam got married in a mountain man ceremony. They were deliriously happy. They went to California so she could see the ocean. And then . . .

An interminable time passed in silence. Finally, Flat Dog asked if the visitors would accept food, and Bell Rock said they would.

When they had eaten, Sam said, "I will go with you to the village, present their granddaughter to Gray Hawk and Needle, and make a gift of horses." In other words, *I will face up to what I have done like a man.*

Bell Rock looked at him for a long moment. Then he said, with sorrow in his voice, "Red Roan has already made a pledge. If you come back to the camp, he will kill you."

Sam tried not to let his surprise show.

"He didn't even know . . ."

Bell Rock held Sam's eyes. "No one will stop him." Meaning, *I cannot help you.*

Everyone stared at these awful facts.

Sam looked at Flat Dog. The Crow raised his eyes. "I am your friend." He took a deep breath and let it go. "I offer to fight Red Roan for you."

They all knew why. The white man would never win that kind of fight.

Sam said only one word. "No."

He reached to one side and rubbed Coy's ears. He stared into space. *The village is against me. Even Flat Dog and Bell Rock cannot defend me. I am finished there.*

SAM AND HANNIBAL prepared for the fight.

They talked first, but that was short.

Hannibal—"Why go there at all?"

Sam—"I have to face up to what I did."

They looked at each other. Going to the village and refusing to fight would never work. Sam would be branded a coward. Then any man in the village might attack him from behind any tree at any time. An arrow would whiz and . . .

"Tell me about Red Roan."

"Most Crow men are tall and rangy. He's taller and rangier. He's a war leader—*the* war leader in that village—and has lots of coups. He's cocky as hell. Arrogant."

"And what does he think about you?"

"He thinks I'm an ignorant white man who got his cousin killed. And stole his girl."

Hannibal pondered. "What are his advantages?"

"Experience with hand weapons." This would be fought lance, war club, knife, or shield, no firearms, no ability to kill at a remote distance. A face-to-face confrontation, and a true battle of honor. "And he's mostly had the upper hand with me."

"Tell."

Sam was embarrassed to recount the stories. Red Roan courted Meadowlark while Sam skulked in the shadows and watched. Red Roan set up Sam to be humiliated in an

arrow-shooting contest with his nephews. And when Sam and
Meadowlark ran away for their honeymoon, Red Roan came,
snatched Meadowlark away, and marched Sam back to camp
as a prisoner.

"He's got mind domination on you," Hannibal said. "He's
made you think he's stronger than you."

Sam started to protest, thought, and fell silent. "What do I
do about that?"

"Awe him," said Hannibal. "Awe everyone."

So they set out to do what was necessary. First, they traded
for a lance, a war club, and a shield made from the thick skin
of a buffalo bull's head. Among the Shoshones Sam found a
lance and stone war club that felt good. He started carrying
them everywhere he went, to get used to the heft and balance.
He also practiced all afternoon each day. Throwing a lance
at trees didn't seem particularly odd, but bashing them with
the war club was very strange. He knew his new skills with
his weapon would count for little against the experienced Red
Roan.

Second, in the mornings they made some special preparations that might make all the difference. Very special. Before
long they were ready, and told Flat Dog so.

Flat Dog had finished the business for the three of them.
He sold the last trade goods they wanted to let go of, keeping
some back for gifts to Meadowlark's family and for trade to
the other Crows. He dealt with Tom Fitzpatrick and got company credit for their share of the beaver they'd traded for.
This credit would last Flat Dog, Sam, and Hannibal a good
while.

And they got a surprise. Jim Beckwourth asked if he could
go along with them. "I like the Crows," he said. Sam remembered that during the winter he spent in Rides Twice's village,
the mulatto had had an active social life. They agreed—
another hand going to Crow country would be good.

The last evening Sam, Hannibal, and Flat Dog decided to
divide up the rest of the horseflesh, twenty animals. When
the three got to the herd, Tomás tagging along, Paladin came

trotting over to Sam, her colt behind her. Sam spoke one word, and Coy jumped up on Paladin's back and stood up on his hind legs. Tomás burst into laughter—he always loved that trick.

When each man had picked out stallions, mares, colts, and fillies, they started back toward their tents. Sam had picked out four to give to Meadowlark's parents, the obligatory gift. "We're well arranged," Hannibal said.

That did it for Sam. He turned to Tomás. "What are you planning to do, go with Esteban and Plácido?"

The Taoseños had signed on with a group of free trappers intending to trap South Park, the country around Pikes Peak. Then they'd winter in Taos.

The boy shook his head no.

Sam indicated Hannibal. "Go to Flathead country with him?"

Same shake of head.

"Well?"

"I want to be with you."

Sam was flabbergasted. Flat Dog and Hannibal seemed kind of tickled.

Sam waited until they sat at the fire in front of Julia's lodge. He began with, "In two weeks I may not be alive. Probably won't be."

Tomás looked the other way, but Sam thought his eyes were teary.

"Talk real with me," Sam said. "I probably won't be alive."

Tomás turned to face Sam with a hard expression. "So? I don't have nobody now, I won't have nobody then."

The men looked at each other and at Tomás.

The talk took all evening, with Sam, Tomás, Hannibal, Flat Dog, and Julia. Esperanza toddled around and played in the dirt. Azul crawled around and sometimes ate dirt. The adults talked. Tomás didn't get to say much, and his sullen look didn't help his cause.

In the end it all came down to—well, why not?

"All right, you can hang around. If Red Roan doesn't kill me."

Hannibal said, "If Sam's dead, I'll be glad to have you along."

But Sam had to ask Tomás straight. "Why do you want to be with me?"

"Too soon to separate a colt from its mother," Tomás said with a crinkly smile.

This was a little fraud. Paladin's colt could suckle any of eight or ten mares.

Sam frowned. "Look, I'm a Crow." This was half true. "My daughter is a Crow. I'm a member of the Kit Foxes. I speak the language. I carry the sacred pipe. Don't be fooled by my skin."

"Or your hair?" Tomás asked with a sly smile.

Sam tugged at his white locks. He thought about it. He realized what Tomás's fantasy was. "I think you don't understand. If I survive, I'm not going to be a trapper and roam the country. I'll live in another Crow village. I'll be a warrior like the other young men, and a buffalo hunter."

"*¿Verdad?*" When Tomás got surprised, he slipped back into Spanish sometimes.

"Yes, true. I want to see my daughter. If I live with another village, I will. Pretty often. Maybe I'll make another family. I like the way the Crows live."

Flat Dog said, "Tomás, I think you like the trapping life. You have no idea if you'll like the Crow life."

Tomás glared at him.

Sam reached out and picked up Esperanza. Coy tapped his tail—maybe he was jealous. "I left Pennsylvania," Sam said, "and found a new home. I made a new family. Now the only family I have is Esperanza." He could hardly believe he was saying this, barely even knew he thought it. "But she's my family, not yours. Why would you want to be around my one little kid?"

Tomás jumped up and ran off. Sam couldn't tell, because he was so quick, whether he was in tears or in a rage.

Nobody spoke for a while. Sam looked at them guiltily.

Flat Dog said, "You have almost no family."

"And she's an infant," Julia said.

"But Tomás," Flat Dog said, "he doesn't have any."

Sam didn't see the boy again until he woke up the next morning. Tomás lay right there, between Hannibal and Sam, looking at Sam.

"I want to go with you," he said. "I bet I can get a Crow girlfriend."

Sam nodded. "Glad to have you."

Tomás grinned.

Coy growled. Sam wondered what the devil that meant.

Chapter Twenty-four

Across the mountain to the Siskadee, over South Pass, down Wind River and through Wind River Canyon. Now they had to do some guesswork. August. Flat Dog, Bell Rock, and the Foxes thought the village would still be up against the mountains. Not until the next moon would they go downriver to join the other villages for the big autumn buffalo hunt.

So the party went up Owl Creek and over the divide to Goose Creek. Sam was saying these names to himself like a litany. Though he barely knew them, really, he had camped on them with Rides Twice's village, he had courted Meadowlark on them, he had given a sun dance on one of them, and for him they were legendary.

He was nervous. At the evening camp on Goose Creek, Flat Dog shot a deer. He was at home now, a man in his own country, and he acted like it. He was expansive and at ease. All the Crows were.

At breakfast, while they roasted fresh deer meat on sticks, Flat Dog said, "What's wrong?"

Sam didn't answer. Julia kept her head down. The two children whined.

"Everybody's on edge," said Beckwourth. "Julia, she meets her new in-laws. She finds out what it's like to live where there ain't no one to empty the chamber pots, not even any chamber pots."

"I gave that up long ago," said Julia. "I wipe dirty baby bottoms all day every day."

"Wouldn't be right if you weren't uneasy." Beckwourth tossed a big grin at Tomás, and handed the boy a strip of tenderloin. Tomás took it and stuffed it into his mouth.

"This boy, he's got a big story, hardly anybody treat him right. What he's gone through . . ."

Sam was about to give Jim a warning look, but the mulatto stopped himself. "Remember, boy, you need someone to side you, I will.

"Now Sam, he's another case. He's just plain afraid. He . . ."

"Jim, that's enough," said Sam.

Beckwourth opened his mouth again.

"I said enough."

Hannibal smiled at Sam.

When they got packed and started for the Gray Bull River, no one's mood was good except Jim's and Hannibal's.

THE VILLAGE WAS right where the Crows expected, where the Gray Bull River came out of the mountain and plunged across the plain toward the Big Horn. They camped on top of the last hill above the camp, and Flat Dog waved his blanket as a signal to the camp. Now people knew the party came bearing news of a death. Sam could think of nothing but the time he and Flat Dog had done this before, reporting the loss of Blue Medicine Horse. It was unbearable.

In due time three Foxes came out. Flat Dog told them the news very factually. Though they were curious about why

Meadowlark had gone far west to the big-water-everywhere, they did not ask questions about the death itself. Everyone knew death in childbirth. Soon they and the other Foxes carried the report to the village.

Needle would grieve wildly and cut her hair off, Sam knew, and her mourning would not end until her hair was back to normal length. Gray Hawk might cut a joint off his little finger. But mourning for a passing in the normal course of life—that would not be like mourning for the killing of a young person by an enemy. And the family would carry the grieving, not the entire village.

Sam's task was not to grieve for Meadowlark, not any longer. He and Robert Evans dug themselves graves in the sand of the great desert west of Salt Lake on a blistering afternoon, and he left the blackness of his heart in that hole.

Bell Rock walked back up the hill. With a grave face he said to Sam, "Gray Hawk refuses your gift of horses."

Fine. No surprise. Done.

Sam had one job now—to make himself ready for Red Roan.

THE EVENING FELT never-ending. All through the lingering twilight Red Roan circled the camp, chanting out his plaint like the village crier. "The white-haired man is a coward. The man with white hair is a ghost." This was a great insult. "The white-haired man has brought us only grief. The white man has brought death into our lodge. I challenge him to a fight tomorrow. I challenge him to meet me, the son of the chief of the village of Rides Twice. I challenge the barbarian to come against a war leader of the Absaroka nation and fight until one of us is dead."

He beat out these words over and over, like music to march to. A funeral march.

Hannibal said, "Let's get out of here."

Though Sam couldn't make out the words from here, he knew what was being said. His mind flitted to Gray Hawk and Needle. Like a raven perched high on their lodge poles, he tried to hear what was being said in their lodge, imagine what was going on in their hearts and minds. Nothing good, he knew. Twice now he had brought them death, and they would return to him only death.

A few people in the entire village, perhaps, bore him good-will. Julia and Flat Dog, Bell Rock and his wife. All other hearts, he knew, were set hard against him.

"Let's get going," Hannibal said again.

Sam got up, The Celt in hand, ready to follow. So did Tomás and Coy.

Hannibal led the way to the river. The three of them sat in the shallows, naked. Coy watched them from the bank and whined. Sam didn't know why Tomás wanted to be with him tonight, but he didn't care.

In the distance Red Roan's caterwauling stopped. Sam smiled at Hannibal. "Flat Dog has done it." Sam asked his friend to go to Red Roan, after his foe had sounded off suf-ficiently, and tell him that Sam would meet him at dawn.

Sam and Hannibal talked about that easily, comfortably. Then they talked about other things. The two men told stories of their youth, memories of particular pleasure. Hannibal talked about gathering berries with his mother. Sam spoke of wrestling with his younger brother Coy. Hannibal told of his father reading Ovid to him aloud, translating the thoughts into awkward English, and then reading the Latin again, so-norously. Sam recalled his mother's apple pies spiced with cinnamon, left in the warming oven so he could go back for a second piece before bed. On and on they talked, remem-bering only joys, or transforming sorrows into a kind of joy through the alchemy of understanding.

Sam noticed that Tomás sat fixed on them, completely ab-sorbed, but saying nothing. Sam didn't know why Tomás cared about these stories—he didn't know what stories Tomás himself might have to tell—but tonight he didn't care. He was simply enjoying his own life.

Eventually, they got very tired, arose, wrapped themselves

in blankets, and slept on the bank of the Gray Bull River, the water shur-shurring by.

Sam rose with the first hint of light. He and Hannibal made a few preparations. Tomás watched, and Sam could not read the boy's face.

Eventually, the people assembled, a great circle in front of the lodges, every man, woman, and child come to see what might happen.

With his friends Sam walked to the circle with a blanket wrapped over his head, as many of the women came. Hannibal carried his weapons.

Red Roan rode his warhorse into the center of this circle, stripped to a breechcloth, lance in one hand, war club in the other, the shield on the forearm above the club. Again he began to call out the words of challenge.

Sam was ready, and he didn't want to indulge his foe.

He dropped the blanket and reached for the weapons.

"Everything is a roll of the dice," said Hannibal. "Go for it whole hog."

Sam chuckled. He looked into the eyes of his friend. He set the club and shield on the ground and stuck the lance into the earth. Then he turned and stepped into the circle, excited.

Exclamations burst out of the crowd. The white-haired man had come without his mount and without his weapons. People couldn't believe it. An unarmed man on foot stood no chance. Red Roan would ride him down and stomp him under his warhorse's feet.

Sam walked around the circle in the direction the sun went, his eyes on Red Roan. When he started to see impatience on his enemy's face, he whistled.

Paladin galloped into the arena and toward Sam. Hubbub ran through the crowd. The mare was naked of saddle, naked of bridle. Did the white-haired man intend to ride her like this?

As she neared him, Sam whirled one arm from the shoulder and Paladin galloped past him and around the entire arena. Children exclaimed and pointed at the beautiful animal.

This time she stopped beside Sam, and he vaulted onto her back. Paladin went into her show-ring canter, gentle and rhythmic. Sam felt a rush of elation at being on her again. He thought, *By God this is the way to go out!*

Immediately, he was on his feet, riding bareback and standing. He began to sing to Paladin the song that helped them feel the motion together, the lope of horse and—now!—the somersaults of the man. Singing at the top of his voice, Sam leapt into the air, somersaulted, landed with both feet on Paladin's rump, and somersaulted again. Round and round he went, rump to air to rump, bawling out his ecstasy.

The children shouted with glee, and the women covered their gasps with their hands.

Sam could have bounded forever.

Red Roan ended the display with his war cry. Screeching, he spurred his horse directly at Paladin.

Sam dropped into a forked seat and cried to Paladin for speed. Red Roan had speed, but not enough to catch Paladin quickly, or perhaps at all. As Sam rode by his lance, he yanked it out of the ground, turned Paladin hard into the center of the ring, and faced his enemy.

Startled, Red Roan stopped. Sam laughed and hollered in English, "No way can you ever have seen anything like this. What on heaven and earth am I going to do next?"

He charged.

Lance level, eyes on Red Roan's breast, he goaded Paladin forward at full speed.

Red Roan reacted late, but he reacted. He raised his war club and spurred his mount. He would teach the foolish, unshielded white man. He would get even for the white man's stupid antics, for the way he got the people—Crows of Red Roan's own village—to admire him. He would flick the lance aside and smash the white man to a pulp.

At the last moment Sam kneed Paladin, and she swerved in front of the warhorse.

Red Roan found his club on the wrong side! He tried to

screw his body around for a swing across his mount, but was too late.

Sam whirled Paladin hard left and rammed her straight into horse and rider.

For a moment Sam's world was topsy-turvy.

Red Roan's horse went down screaming, the warrior under it.

Paladin regained her balance. Sam wheeled her in a desperate turn and bellowed for speed.

Red Roan got to his feet, limping, bewildered.

Sam thundered down on him, lance poised.

At the last instant Red Roan dodged to Sam's left. Sam hurled the lance, but Paladin's neck kept him from changing his aim fully. The lance missed and sank into the earth, its butt quivering.

Sam ran Paladin straight over Red Roan, human and equine limbs flying.

Quickly, Sam brought Paladin full circle and sprinted down on Red Roan again.

Red Roan tried to gain his feet enough for a swing. Sam edged Paladin to the off side, then brought her back and bumped Paladin's shoulder into the warrior hard. He went head over heels, and the war club went flying.

Now Sam circled Paladin wide, watching the stumbling figure. He jumped to his feet on Paladin's back and spoke to her. She sprinted toward Red Roan, who stood gape-mouthed. Just before Paladin ran over him, Red Roan slid sideways.

Sam leapt and kicked Red Roan full in the chest with both feet.

Each man landed on his back, but Sam was up like a flash.

Red Roan barely stirred.

Sam pounced on him and sat on his belly.

They looked at each other, wide-eyed.

Red Roan squeezed out a gargly laugh. "You lost your weapon, white man. What are you going to do, scratch my eyes out?"

Sam reached for the belt around his waist, the one that seemed to hold up his breechcloth, and popped the buckle. In front of Red Roan's face he held as sharp and fine a knife as had ever been smithed.

Darkness entered Red Roan's eyes. He gazed at Sam. Finally, he said, "Kill me, white man."

Sam saw moccasins and looked up. Hannibal stood there. So did Gray Hawk. So did Rides Twice, his face grave.

Hannibal nodded yes. So did Gray Hawk.

Red Roan said to his father, "I want to die."

Rides Twice turned away.

Straight and hard Sam drove the blade deep into Red Roan's throat. Blood bubbled around the handle. Sam drew the blade out, and blood welled.

A long rasp of death eased from Red Roan's mouth.

Sam put the buckle back, looked around, and heard.

Dozens of Crow women were trilling for him.

Scores were silent, glaring.

He walked off. He bent down and petted Coy. He looked into the eyes of Tomás. He felt . . . amazed, incredulous—words couldn't get near it.

Hannibal touched him on the shoulder.

Sam stood back up.

"You were astounding," said Hannibal.

Sam just nodded.

"We'd better get out of here."

"I've got something to do," said Sam.

"I'll get your back," said Hannibal.

Sam walked around the circle of villagers, sunwise. He weaved a little as he went. About a third of the way around he saw Flat Dog and Julia. He padded up to them.

"Thank you, brother," he said to Flat Dog.

"You are welcome, brother."

Sam reached to Julia and took Esperanza. He held her at arm's length and looked at her. The little girl wiggle-waggled her head.

"Hi, Papa," he said in English.

"Hi, Papa," she said, and chuckled.

"Come along too, please," he said to Flat Dog and Julia.

Sam held her close, and the five of them made their way on around the circle. Sam looked at the faces of people he knew. His friend Bell Rock and his wife. Owl Woman, his enemy but a good woman. Her husband Yellow Horn, his enemy and a dangerous man. The boys he competed with once, when they won all his arrows.

At last he came to Gray Hawk and Needle. Gray Hawk stood rigid, his face fixed. Needle held her blanket wrapped over her head against the morning chill.

He looked into their eyes, wanting to be sure he didn't miss anything. Gray Hawk's were dark, impenetrable. Needle's . . . he wasn't sure. Perhaps he saw a hint of warmth there.

He held Esperanza out at arm's length. "I love you," he said. "What I'm about to do, it hurts, but it's for you."

He held her now to Needle. "This is your granddaughter," he said, "Esperanza. I am alone, and a child needs a mother. I give her to her uncle Flat Dog, to her aunt Julia, to you, her grandparents, and to all the people of this village to raise in a good way."

Needle took the child and clutched her close.

Esperanza turned in her arms. "Papa?" she said and reached toward Sam.

He quelled the pain and turned away.

Sam and Hannibal walked the rest of the way around the circle. Sam looked at the faces. When he got back to his blankets and to Tomás, he said, "Now we can go."

Chapter Twenty-five

They rode toward the Yellowstone country. Hannibal had heard about the hot springs and wanted to sit in them. Beckwourth told wild stories about how there were devils just barely under the ground, and they made it tremble, and shot geysers of boiling water into the air. Tomás looked around wild-eyed, uncertain what to believe.

"You'll see the geysers in a few days," Sam told him. "They're crazy, but fun."

They reached the first of the hot springs that very afternoon. "Colter's hell," Beckwourth called it. They sank themselves into the hot water and munched on jerked meat Julia had sent with them. They lounged. They lolled. The water felt very, very good.

"What are you thinking?" Tomás asked Sam. They could see what he meant was, *You won, why aren't you jumping up and down?*

"About Esperanza," Sam told him softly.

Tomás took that in. Then he gave Sam a fine smile. The boy had been beaming all day. "It's all right, Dad," he said. "One day we'll go back and get her."